Textbook written according to revised syllabus of S.Y.B.Com.
prescribed by University of Pune from 2014-2015.
Also useful for other universities in Maharashtra.

CORPORATE ACCOUNTING

Prin. Dr. Kishor N. Jagtap

Dr. Sunil D. Zagade

Dr. Sunil S. Shete

Dr. Hanumant M. Jare

Prof. Suresh Bhirud

Prof. Bhaskar Naphade

Diamond Publications

CORPORATE ACCOUNTING

Prin. Dr. Kishor N. Jagtap, Dr. Sunil D. Zagade,
Dr. Sunil S. Shete, Dr. Hanumant M. Jare
Prof. Suresh Bhirud, Prof. Bhaskar Naphade

First Edition : June 2014

ISBN : 978-81-8483-572-4

© Diamond Publications

Type Setting :
Aksharwel, Pune - 411 030

Cover Page :
Sham Bhalekar

Published by :
Diamond Publications
264/3 Shaniwar Peth, 302 Anugrah Apartment
Near Omkareshwar Temple, Pune - 411 030
☎ 020-24452387, 24466642

info@diamondbookspune.com
www.diamondbookspune.com

Sale Distributor :
Diamond Book Depot
661 Narayan Peth
Appa Balwant Chowk
Pune 411 030
Tel. - 24480677, 66020282

PREFACE

It is a matter of great pleasure for us to present this book to our esteemed readers and students. This book has been designed as standard text on 'Corporate Accounting' for Second Year B. Com.

This book comprehensively covers the entire syllabus of S. Y. B. Com. Course of University of Pune w. e. f. June-2014. It has been written to meet the requirement of students. The special features of the book are :

- Full coverage of the revised syllabus.
- Chapter outline at the beginning of each chapter to give a bird's eye view of the topics covered in the chapter.
- Point wise explanation of each topic in the chapter.
- Topics are logically arranged in numbered paragraphs exactly according to the modified syllabus.
- Proposed questions at the end of each chapter.
- Extensive use of diagrams, tables and various forms to give visual view of key concepts and techniques.
- Conversional, lucid and simple language.

Every effort has been made to provide the readers with most up-to-date and authentic material on the subject.

We are very grateful to our publisher Mr. Dattatray Pashte of Diamond Publication, Pune who have rendered all possible assistance in bringing out this book. We wish to acknowledge our deep gratitude to staff who have assisted and helped us in preparing this book.

We will consider our efforts amply rewarded in case the book proves useful to the students and Faculty Members of the subject.

Suggestions of readers are welcome and shall be acknowledged with gratitude.

With best wishes.

Prin. Dr. Kishor N. Jagtap
Dr. Sunil D. Zagade
Dr. Sunil S. Shete
Dr. Hanumant M. Jare
Prof. Suresh Bhirud
Prof. Bhaskar Naphade

Contents

CHAPTER 1

Accounting Standards

1.1 **Introduction**
1.2 **Nature**
1.3 **Scope**
1.4 **Purposes**
1.5 **AS - 5 : Net Profit or Loss for the Period, Prior Period Items and Changes in Accounting Policies [Effective Date: 1st April, 1996]**
1.6 **AS - 6 : Depreciation Accounting (Revised) [Effective Date : 1st April, 1995]**
1.7 **AS - 10 : Accounting for Fixed Assets [Effective Date: 1st April, 1991]**
1.8 **AS - 14 : Accounting for Amalgamation [Effective Date: 1st April, 1995]**
1.9 **AS - 21 : Consolidated Financial Statement**

1.1 Introduction

Accounting standards are accounting rules and procedures relating to measurement, valuation and disclosure issued by the Council of The Institute of Chartered Accountants of India. Accounting standards are stated to be the norms of accounting policies and practices by way of guidelines that should be followed while preparing accounts and disclosed in the annual financial statements. The accounting standards are intended to apply only to items which are material.

Since accounting standards are the rules to be followed in the preparation of financial statements, these are regarded as a *mechanism* for resolving the conflicts of interest among various preparers and users of accounting information. Accounting standards are generally appropriate to the normal conduct of business and are in conformity with local conditions. Accounting standards serve public interest and are based on a conceptual framework of accounting. Necessarily, the utility of accounting standards results in a consequential improvement in the quality of preparation of financial statements.

1.2 Nature

Accounting standards are *mandatory* in nature. They are mainly applicable to the published accounts of limited companies. However, in case of sole proprietorships or partnerships, accounting standards mandatorily apply when the financial statements are statutorily required to be audited.

The accounting standards apply to the preparation of general purpose financial statements, i.e., Balance Sheet, Profit and Loss Account, and other statements and statutory notes which form part of the financial statements. It is necessary to examine whether the mandatory accounting standards are complied with in the preparation of financial statements. If there is any deviation, adequate disclosure should be made so that the users of financial statements become aware of such deviations.

Accounting policies have a *direct effect* on the working results and the financial position of a business concern. Accounting policies are the specific accounting bases adopted and constantly followed by a business unit in the preparation of its financial statements. Owing to varying circumstances, different accounting policies are adopted by different business enterprises. Accounting standards, therefore, require that all significant policies adopted in the preparation and presentation of financial statements should be disclosed and should form part of the financial statements. Any change in the accounting policies which has a material effect, and the amount by which any item in the financial statement is affected by such a change should be disclosed. Lastly, if a fundamental *accounting assumption* is not followed, the fact should be disclosed.

Accounting standards could be national, international or both. Every national institute frames its own accounting standards, which generally are in keeping with the international norms. In effect, the development of accounting standards in India has been contemporaneous with that of the International Accounting Standards, which are formulated by global organisations of accounting bodies. As such, there is not much difference among the parameters of these standards.

1.3 Scope

1. Accounting Standards are to be issued in conformity with the provisions of the applicable laws, customs, usages and business environment of our country. If there is any conflict between the accounting standards and laws (because of subsequent amendments in the law), the provisions of the said law will prevail and financial statements should be prepared in conformity with such law.
2. Accounting Standards can not override the local regulations.
3. Accounting Standards are intended to apply only to items which are material.
4. The Institute will use its best endeavours to persuade the government, appropriate authorities, industrial and business community to adopt these standards in order to achieve uniformity in the preparation of financial statements.
5. In carrying out the task of formulation of Accounting Standards, the intention would be to concentrate on basic matters.

1.4 Purposes

The concepts of accounting have permitted a variety of practices to follow and, in effect, different results can be drawn from the same set of data. Consequently, the lack of uniformity of such practices has made it difficult for users of accounting information to compare the results of different enterprises. The overall direction of the accountant should be towards *uniformity,* so that accounting information may become comparable, leading to better analysis and comparison of performances.

The need for accounting standards is based on the necessity of harmonising the diverse policies and practices adopted by different business firms. When accounting standards are followed, accounting information become transparent and, in effect, it helps towards meaningful comparison and study. It also ensures consistency in the accounting statements of a business enterprise from year to year. In effect, it facilitates a more meaningful comparison among accounting statements of different enterprises. As a result, the users of accounting information can understand and make proper use of accounting statements for decision-making.

The need for the *uses* of accounting standards are as follows :

(1) Accounting standards promote better understanding of accounting statements, the disclosure of significant accounting policies and the manner in which accounting policies are disclosed in the statements.

(2) Accounting information is more useful if it is published on a comparable basis, and *comparability* is not possible without accounting standards.

(3) Accounting standards provide a generally accepted language for financial statements that renders them more comprehensible to the users of accounting information.

(4) Accounting standards may be regarded as a means to establish that the collective wisdom and experience rather than the viewpoint of individual accountant may prevail in the matter.

Status of the Accounting Standards issued by the Institute of Chartered Accountants of India

Number of the Accounting Standard (AS)	Title of the Accounting Standard	Date from which mandatory (accounting periods commencing on or after)	Entity to which applicable
AS-1	Disclosure of Accounting Policies	1-4-1993	All
AS-2	Valuation of Inventories	1-4-1999	All
AS-3	Cash Flow Statement	1-4-2001	Level - I and Non - SMC
AS-4	Contingencies and Events Occurring after the Balance Sheet Date	1-4-1998	All

Number of the Accounting Standard (AS)	Title of the Accounting Standard	Date from which mandatory (accounting periods commencing on or after)	Entity to which applicable
AS-5	Net Profit or Loss for the Period, Prior Period Items and Changes in Accounting Policies	1-4-1996	All
AS-6	Depreciation Accounting	1-4-1995	All
AS-7(Revised)	Construction Contracts	1-4-2002	All
AS-8	Withdrawn and included in AS-26	-	-
AS-9	Revenue Recognition	1-4-1993	All
AS- 10	Accounting for Fixed Assets	1-4-1993	All
AS- 11 (Revised-2003)	The Effects of Changes in Foreign Exchange Rates	1-4-2004	All
AS- 12	Accounting for Govt. Grants	1-4-1994	All
AS- 13	Accounting for Investments	1-4-1995	All
AS- 14	Accounting for Amalgamations	1-4-1995	All
AS- 1 5 (Revised-2005)	Employees benefit	1-4-2006	All
AS- 16	Borrowing Costs	1-4-2000	All
AS- 17	Segment Reporting	1-4-2001	Level - I and Non - SMC
AS- 18	Related Party Disclosures	1-4-2001	Level - I, II and all companies
AS- 19	Leases	1-4-2001	All
AS-20	Earning Per Shares	1-4-2001	All
AS-21	Consolidated Financial Statements	1-4-2001	See Note- 1
AS-22	Accounting for Taxes on Income	1-4-2001	-For Listed Companies

Number of the Accounting Standard (AS)	Title of the Accounting Standard	Date from which mandatory (accounting periods commencing on or after)	Entity to which applicable
		1-4-2002	- Companies other than listed
		1-4-2006	- All
AS-23	Accounting for Investment in Associates in Consolidated Financial Statements	1-4-2002	See Note - I
AS-24	Discontinuing operations	1-4-2004	Level - I, II and all companies
AS-25	Interim Financial Reporting	1-4-2002	Note-2
AS-26	Intangible Assets	1-4-2003	All
AS-27	Financial Reporting of Interests in Joint Ventures	1-4-2002	See Note-I
AS-28	Impairment of Assets	1-4-2004 1-4-2006 1-4-2008	- Level-I - Level-II } and all companies - Level-III
AS-29	Provisions, Contingent liabilities and Contingent Assets	1-4-2004	All
AS-30	Financial Instruments - Recognition and Measurement	To be announced	Non-SME
AS-31	Financial Instruments -Presentation	To be announced	Non-SME
AS-32	Financial Instruments -Disclosures	To be announced	Non-SME

Note 1 : AS-21, AS-23 and AS-27 (relating to consolidated financial statements) are required to be complied with by an entity if the entity, pursuant to the requirements of a statute/regulator or voluntarily, prepares and presents consolidated financial statements.

Note 2: If an entity is required or elect to prepare and present an interim financial report, it should comply with this standard.

1.5 AS - 5 : Net Profit or Loss for the Period, Prior Period Items and Changes in Accounting Policies [Effective Date: 1st April, 1996]

Introduction

The Profit and Loss Account for any accounting period should be prepared in such a manner that it is comparable with those of the other years and with the financial statements of other enterprises. This standard is intended to enhance the relevance and reliability of the financial statements of the enterprise.

Though the financial information provided by the Profit and Loss Account about the financial performance of an enterprise is historical in nature, yet users use this information to evaluate the enterprise's future performance.

Objective

The objective of this statement is to prescribe the classification and disclosure of certain items in the statement of profit and loss so that all enterprises prepare and present such a statement on a uniform basis.

This statement requires the classification and disclosure of extraordinary and prior period items, and disclosure of certain items within profit or loss from ordinary activities.

It also specifies the accounting treatment for changes in accounting estimates and the disclosures to be made in the financial statements regarding changes in accounting policies.

Scope

1. This Statement should be applied by an enterprise *in presenting profit or loss* from ordinary activities, extraordinary items and prior period items in the statement of profit and loss, in accounting for changes in accounting estimates, and in disclosure of changes in accounting policies.
2. This Statement deals with, among other matters, the disclosure of certain items of net profit or loss for the period. These disclosures are made in addition to any other disclosures required by other Accounting Standards.
3. This Statement *does not deal* with the tax implications of extraordinary items, prior period items, changes in accounting estimates, and changes in accounting policies for which appropriate adjustments will have to be made depending on the circumstances.

Definitions

Ordinary Activities

Ordinary activities are any activities which are undertaken by an enterprise as part of its business and such related activities in which the enterprise engages in furtherance of, incidental to, or arising from, these activities.

Example : X Ltd, is a software development company operating from Kolkata. Recently they have started a training institute for future software developers. All activities relating to training institute will be treated as ordinary activities.

Extraordinary Items

Extraordinary items are income or expenses that arise from events or transactions that are clearly distinct from the ordinary activities of the enterprise and, therefore, are not expected to recur frequently or regularly.

Example : Sale of old machinery and furniture at a profit / loss is an ordinary activity but sale of excess land adjacent to existing factory should be treated as an extraordinary item. Similarly, loss due to earthquake shall be treated as an extraordinary item.

Prior Period Items

Prior period items are income or expenses which arise in the current period as a result of errors or omissions in the preparation of the financial statements of one or more prior periods.

Example : Inventory had been overstated in 2006 but it was detected only in 2007. It is a prior period item.

Accounting Policies

Accounting policies are the specific accounting principles and the methods of applying those principles adopted by an enterprise in the preparation and presentation of financial statements.

Net Profit or Loss for the Period

All items of income and expense which are recognised in a period should be included in the determination of net profit or loss for the period unless an Accounting Standard requires or permits otherwise.

The net profit or loss for the period comprises the following components, each of which should be disclosed on the face of the statement of profit and loss:

a. profit or loss from ordinary activities; and
b. extraordinary items.

Profit or Loss from Ordinary Activities

Any item of income and expense within profit or loss from ordinary activities are of such size, nature or incidence that their disclosure is relevant to explain the performance of the enterprise for the period, the nature and the amount of such items should be disclosed separately. This disclosure will enhance the transparency in

Example : Sale of old furniture is an ordinary transaction, the profit or loss from such sale should be disclosed separately because it is not related to operation of the business.

reporting income and expenses.

A separate disclosure of items of income and expense is necessary in the following cases.

a. the write-down of inventories to net realisable value as well as the reversal of such write-downs;
b. a restructuring of the activities of an enterprise and the reversal of any provisions for the costs of restructuring;
c. disposals of items of fixed assets;
d. disposals of long-term investments;
e. legislative changes having retrospective application;
f. litigation settlements; and
g. other reversals of provisions.

Components of net profit

Net profit or loss for the period consists of two components :
- Profit or loss from ordinary activities
- Extraordinary items.

These components should be disclosed on the face of statement of profit and loss account.

Ordinary activities are defined as any activities, which are undertaken by an enterprise as part of its business and incidental to main business.

Profit/Loss from ordinary activities - Normally all items of income and expenses which are recognized in a period are included in the determination of the net profit or loss for the period. This includes extraordinary items and change in accounting estimates.

When items of income and expenditure from ordinary activities are of such size and nature that their disclosure is relevant to explain the performance of the enterprises for the period. The nature and amount of such items should be separately disclosed. Although these items are not "extraordinary items", examples of such items are :-
- The write down of inventories to net realisable value or reversal of such write down
- Restructuring cost or reversal of provision of restructuring cost
- Profit or loss on disposal of fixed assets
- Profit or loss on disposal of long term investment
- Litigation settlements
- Reversal of provisions
- Legislative charges having long term retrospective application.

Exiraordinary items: Extraordinary items are income of expense that arise from transactions that are clearly distinct from ordinary activities. They are not expected to recur frequently or regularly. The nature and amount of extraordinary items should be separately disclosed in Profit and Loss Account so that its impact on current profit or loss can be perceived. Example - Attachment of property of the enterprises or loss due to earthquake.

Examples of extraordinary items

- Loss due to earthquakes
- Attachment of property
- Government grants becoming refundable
- Government grants for giving immediate financial support with no further cost
- Governments grant receivable as compensation lor expenses or losses incurred in previous accounting period.

Prior Period item

Period items are income or expenses, which arise, in current period as a result of error or omission in the preparation of financial statement of one or more prior periods.

Example : Mr. Amit an employee of Induga Ltd. went on leave with pay for 9 months on 1-1-2010 upto 30-9-2010. His monthly pay was Rs. 15,000 while 'preparing the financial statement on 30-6-20 1 0 for the year ended 3 1-3-2010, the expense of salary of Mr. Amit for 3 months (1-1-2010 to 31-3-2010) was not provided due to omission. When Mr. Amit joined on 1-10-2010 the whole salary for 9 month (1-1-2010 to 30-9-2010) was paid to him.

In this case three months salary (1-1-2010 to 3 1-3-2010) of Rs. 45,000 is prior period expense and following entry should be passed :

Salary A/ c	Dr.	90,000
(15,000 × 6)		
Prior period expense	Dr.	45,000
(Salary)		
To Bank A/c		1,35,000

Suppose in above example Mr. Amit was terminated from service on 1-1-2010 and was re- instated in service by the Court on 30-9-2010 with all back salary. On 1-10-20 10 as per Court order. Company paid the nine months salary to Mr. Amit, as the company accepted the Court verdict. Then there is no prior period expense and the following entry to be passed :

Salary A/c	Dr.	1,35,000
To BankA/c		1,35,000

In this case there is no error or omission while preparing the Financial statement for the earlier year ie. for the year ended 31-3-20 10. As the company intentionally did not make the provision for salary for 3 months of Mr. Amit because company terminated his service.

Disclosure of prior period items : The nature and amount of prior period items should he separately disclosed in the statement of profit and loss in a manner that their impact on current proftt or loss can be perceived.

- Error in calculation in providing expenditure or income.
- Omission to account for income or expenditure.
- Non-provision of travelling expenses for travel already undertaken.
- Non-provision for salary already due in earlier year.
- Applying incorrect rate of depreciation.
- Treating operating lease as finance lease.
- Capitalisation of borrowing cost on working capital.

Change in Accounting Estimate

It means that estimate is revised due to change in the circumstances/ conditions on which the estimates was based. For example:

- Estimation of provision of Sundry Debtors
- Estimation of provision for any liabilities.
- Computing income-tax provision
- Estimating the useful life of fixed assets.

Effect of Change in Accounting Estimate - The effect of a change in accounting estimate should be classified in following cases:

- If an estimate pertains to ordinary activities, then change in accounting estimate should be classified as ordinary activities.
- If estimates pertain to extraordinary item, then change in accounting estimates should be classified as extraordinary.

Disclosure of Accounting Estimate

- The affect of a change in accounting estimate disclosed in net profit or loss
- The period of change, if the change affects the period only
  Example: Estimation oF provision of sundry debtor
- The period ol change and future periods, if the change affects both
  Example: Estimation of the useful life of the fixed assets.

Examples of change of Accounting Estimates

- Re-estimating the residual value of fixed assets.
- Change in useful life of fixed assets.
- Actual bad debts turning out to be more or less than provisions.

Changes in Accounting Policies

In the following circumstances changes in accounting policies are made :

- For the compliance of accounting standard + For the compliance of the statute or law
- For better and appropriate presentation of the financial statement.

Disclosure of change in Accounting Policies

- Material effect should be shown in financial statement to reflect the effect of such change
- This effect should be disclosed in the year of change
- If the effect of change is not ascertainable, the fact should be disclosed
- If the effect of change is not material for current period, but it is material effect for the later period, then fact should be disclosed in the period of change.

Examples of change in accounting policies :

- Change of depreciation method from WDV to Straight-line method and *vice versa,*
- Change in cost formula in measuring the cost of inventories.

Change in accounting policy v. Change in accounting estimate

Problem : ABC Ltd. was making provision for non-moving stock based on no issue for the last 12 months upto 31 -3-2010, The company wants to provide during the year ending 31-3-2011 based on technical evaluation:

Total value of Stock	Rs. 1 crore
Provision required based on 12 months issue	Rs. 3,50,000
Provision required based on technical evaluation	Rs. 2,50,000

Does this amount to change in accounting policy? Can the company change the method of provision?

Solution : The change does not amount to change in accounting policy. The method is only a guideline and the better way of estimating the provision for non-moving stock. Further the amount of difference is also not material. Hence, it is not a change in accounting policy.

The accounting policy for valuation of inventories is lower of cost and net realisable value. Within this broad policy, some estimates are inherent, for example, in the making of provision for slow moving stocks. As a result of the uncertainties inherent in business activities, any financial statement items cannot be measured with precision but can only be estimated. The estimation process involves judgments based on the latest information available. Estimates may be required, for example, of bad debts, inventory obsolescence or the useful lives of depreciable assets. The use of reasonable estimates is an essential part of the preparation of financial statement's and doet not undermine their reliability . An estimate may have to be revised if changes occur regarding the circumstances on which the estimate was based, or as a result of new information, more experience or subsequent developments.

In the given case the change is a change in an accounting estimate and not change in an accounting policy. Further the company should be able to demonstrate satisfactorily that having regard to circumstances provision made on the basis of technical evaluation, provides more satisfactory results than provision based on 12 months issue. If that be the case, the company can change the method of provision.

Limited revisions to AS-5 due lo adoption of new accounting standards -

A change in accounting policy consequent upon the adoption of an Accounting Standard should be accounted for in accordance with the specific transitional provisions, if any, contained in that Accounting Standard. However, disclosures required by paragraph 32 of AS-5 should be made unless the transitional provisions of any other Accounting Standard require alternative disclosures in this regard.

Significant difference among AS-5, IFRS/IAS and US GAAP

Prior Period Items - IFRS/IAS-8 prescribes that subject to the practicability, an entity shall correct material prior period errors retrospectively in the first set of financial statements authorized for issue after they are discovered by :
 (a) Restating the comparative amounts for the prior period(s) presented in which the error occurred; or
 (b) If the error occurred before the earliest prior period presented, restating the opening balances of assets, liabilities and equity for the earliest prior period presented.

A prior period error shall be corrected by retrospective restatement except to the extent that it is impracticable to determine either the period specific effects or the cumulative effect of the error.

IFRS/IAS-1 prohibits any items to be disclosed as extraordinary items whereas AS-5 specifically requires disclosure of certain items as extra-ordinary items,

Change in Accounting Policies - IFRS/IAS-8 requires that an entity shall account for a change in accounting policy resulting from the initial application of a standard or an Interpretation in accordance with specific transitional provisions, it any, in that Standard or interpretation; and when an entity changes an accounting policy upon initial application of a Standard or Interpretation that does not include specific transitional provisions applying to that change or changes on accounting policy voluntarily, it shall apply the change retrospectively.

Subject to the impracticability when a change in accounting policy is applied retrospectively, the entity shall adjust the opening balance of each affected component of equity for the earliest prior period presented and the other comparative amounts disclosed for each prior period presented as if the new accounting policy had always been applied.

Under US GAAP, SFAS-154, the accounting treatment of change in accounting policy and correction of errors is the same as in IAS-8.

Accounting Policy - The principles laid down for change in estimates are almost same in Indian GAAP, IfRS and US GAAP.

PROBLEMS

Problem No. 1 : At December 31, 2010, Matson Inc. was holding long-lived assets, which it intended to sell. The company appropriately recognized a loss in 2010 related to these assets. On Matson Inc.'s income statement for the year ended December 3 1, 2010 this loss should be reported as an

(a) Extraordinary item.

(b) Component of income from continuing operations before income-taxes.

(c) Separate component of selling or general and administrative expenses, disclosed net of tax benefit.

(d) Component of the gain (loss) from sale of discontinued operations, disclosed net of income-taxes.

Solution :

As per AS-5 (refer point 6.2-1) losses associated with long-lived assets, which arc to be disposed of, are to be reported as a component of income from continuing operations before income-taxes (or entities preparing income statements. Therefore, answer *(b)* is correct. Answer *(a)* is incorrect because losses on long-lived assets to be disposed of are neither unusual nor infrequent occurrences. Answer *(c)* is incorrect because these losses are not part of selling or general and administrative expenses and they are not disclosed net of tax, answer *(d)* is incorrect, because discontinued operations result from disposal of a business, not the disposal of long-lived assets held for resale.

Problem No. 2 : The company has to pay delayed cotton clearing charges over and above the negotiated price for taking delayed delivery of cotton from the Supplier's Godown. Upto 2008-09, the company has regularly included such charges in the valuation of closing stock. This being in the nature of interest the company has decided to exclude it from closing stock valuation for the year 2009-10. This would result into decrease in profit by Rs. 7.60 lakhs. Comment.

Solution :

AS-5 (refer point 6.5) states that a change in an accounting policy should be made only if the adoption of a different accounting policy is required by statute or for compliance with an accounting standard or if it is considered that the change would result in a more appropriate preparation or presentation of the financial statements of an enterprise. Therefore, the change in the method of stork valuation is justified in view of the fact that the change is in line with the recommendations of AS-2 and would result in more appropriate preparation of the financial statements. As per AS-2, this accounting policy adopted for valuation of inventories including the cost formulae used should be disclosed in the financial statements.

Also, appropriate disclosure of the change and the amount by which any item in the financial statements is affected by such change is necessary as per AS-1, AS-2 and AS-5.

Therefore, the undermentioned note should be given in the Annual Accounts.

"In compliance with the Accounting Standard issued by the ICAI, delayed cotton clearing charges which are in the nature of interest have been excluded from the valuation of closing stock unlike preceding years. Had the company continued the accounting practice followed earlier, the value of closing stock as well as profit before tax tor the year would have been higher by Rs. 7.60 lakhs".

Problem No. 3 : Fuel surcharge is billed by the State Electricity Board at provisional rate. Final bill for fuel surcharges of Rs. 5.30 lakhs for the period October, 2005 to September, 2009 has been received and paid in February, 2010. How this should be dealt in accounts for year 2009-10.

Solution :

It seems as a result of errors or omission in the preparation of financial statements of prior period if. 2005 to 2009. This material charge has arisen in the current period i.e. year ended 31st March, 2010, therefore it should be treated as prior period item as per para 16 of AS-5 and as such should be separately disclosed as per para 15 of AS-5 so that impact of this item on current profit can be known. It should be further noted that the item is not an extraordinary item as per para 10 of AS-5 as fuel surcharge expense arises from ordinary course of business.

Problem No. 4 : U.P. Rajya Setu Nigam Ltd. was awarded a contract of construction of a bridge for Rs. 100 crores on 1 -6-2006. Total contract cost estimated was Rs. 80 crores. The position of the contract on 31-3-2009 and 31-3-2010 was under:

	As ib 31-3-2009	As on 31-3-2010
Contract Price	100	100
Contract Cost incurred up to date	25	95 (100% complete)
Estimate contract cost of completion	60	NIL

While closing books of account on 31-3-2010, the chief accountant treated excess cost of Rs. 10 crores incurred as against estimated of R.s. (25 + 60) = 85 crores as on 31 -3-2009 as mistakes in estimation of cost, hence categorized Rs. 10 crores (95-85) as prior period expenses. Comment.

Solution :

Cost originally estimated by U.P. Rujya Setu Nigam Ltd.	Rs. 85 crores
Excess Cost incurred	Rs. 10 crores
Treatment given by the company	Prior period item

Hence, the treatment given by the company is incorrect.

Problem No. 5 : State how you will deal with the following matter in the accounts of U Ltd. for the year ended 31st March, 2010 with reference to Accounting Standard :

"The company finds that the stock sheets of 31-3-2009 did not include two pages containing details of inventory worth Rs. 14.5 Lakhs.

Solution :

As per AS-5 an item of expenses or income arises in current period as a result of omission or commission in the preparation of financial statements of one or more prior period is prior period item.

In this case stock sheet of 31-3-2009 (prior year) did not include two pages containing details of inventory worth Rs. 14.5 lakhs which is the omission, and this omission was detected in current period i.e. 31-3-2010. Therefore, it is a prior period item. Entry to be passed is as under :

Opening inventory A/c Dr.   Rs. 14.5 lakhs
     To Prior Period Income   Rs. 14.5 lakhs

Simple Problems

1) Whether the following items are (a) prior period items (b) change in accounting estimate (c) extraordinary items

- Arrears of salaries and wages of Rs. 10 lakhs for the previous year will be paid during the current year as per court judgment delivered in the current year. At the end of previous year, the company assessed that arrears of salaries and wages would not be required to be paid. So no provision was made at the end of previous year.
  [**Ans. :** None of these]
- Expenses of Rs. 50,000 of the previous year, which were omitted from books of account of the previous year due to an oversight.
  [**Ans. :** Prior period item]
- The amount of provision for doubtful debts as at the end of the previous year was Rs. 5,00,000, of these debts of Rs. 3,00,000 were realized during the year.
  [**Ans. :** Change in Accounting estimate]
- Sale of a significant part of the plot of land on which the footing is situated.
  [**Ans. :** Extraordinary items]
- Write off a huge debt of a major customer due for more than a year.
  [**Ans. :** None of these]

  2) Discuss the accounting principle as having relevance to the auditors relating to
- Prior-period items
- Extraordinary items
- Change in accounting estimates

3) Distinguish between "changes in accounting policies" and "changes in accounting estimates". How change in accounting estimates is accounted for in the books of an enterprise?

4) The Company found in 2009-10 that stock sheet as on 31-3-2007 had included twice an item ot Rs. 2,00,000.

[**Ans.** : Prior period item to be shown separately in profit and loss account for 2009-10]

5) A claim was lodged with a transport company for loss of goods of Rs. 3 lakhs during 2008-09, the payment of which was received in 2009-10. No entry had been passed in accounts when claim was lodged.

[**Ans.:** Amount to be credited to profit and loss account in 2009-10, if entry was not passed in 2008-09 due to uncertainty of ultimate receipt of claim (refer AS-9) otherwise prior period item]

6) During the year 2009-10, a medium size manufacturing company wrote down its inventories to net realisable value by Rs. 5,00,000. Is a separate disclosure necessary?

[**Ans.** : Yes, considering the nature and amount of such item]

7) A company signed an agreement with the Employees Union on 1-9-2008 for revision of wages with retrospective effect from 30-9-2007. This would cost the company an additional liability of Rs. 5,00,000 per annum. Is a disclosure necessary for the amount paid in 2008-09?

[**Ans.** : Yes, considering nature and amount of the item]

Advanced Problems

8) During the financial year 2009-10 of NDA Ltd. goods costing Rs. 1 crore were sent to consignee at the sale value of Rs. 1.50 crores. Consignee sold all the goods during the financial year 2009-10. But sent the sale invoice and statement of sales of Rs. 75 lakhs only.

During the financial year 2009-10, NDA Ltd- booked the sale of Rs. 75 lakhs only and balance Rs. 75 lakhs was shown as stock with consignee at cost price.

During the financial year 201 0-1 1, NDA Ltd. received the sale invoice and statement of sale of Rs- 75 lakhs which pertains to the financial year 2009-10.

NDA Ltd. booked sale of Rs. 75 lakhs as prior period item during the financial year 2010-1 1. Comment whether the accounting treatment done by NDA Ltd. is correct.

[**Ans.** : Yes, but corresponding opening stock to be adjusted with prior period item]

9) X Ltd. estimated 1% bad debts while preparing financial statement, for 2009-10. Provision for doubtful debts was created accordingly. However, it appears that in 2009-10 some debts are still uncollected. The management feels that an additional provision of 40%

is necessary on such debts. Should such change in estimate be treated extraordinary items or is it prior period items? Discuss briefly.

[**Ans.** : Change in estimate, separate disclosure]

10) A large textile company during financial year 2009-10 has written down its inventories to net realisable value by Rs. 8,00,000. State with reason whether separate disclosure is required in accounts for the year 2009-10.

[**Ans.** : Yes, if amount is material, otherwise not]

11) A limited company has been including interest in the valuation of closing stock. In 2009-10, the management of the company decided to follow AS-2 and accordingly interest has been excluded from the valuation of closing stock. This has resulted in a decrease in profits by Rs. 3,00,000. Is a disclosure necessary? If so, draft the same.

[**Ans.** : Yes, considering the nature and amount of the item, effect on profit to be stated by way of note]

1.6 AS - 6 : Depreciation Accounting (Revised) [Effective Date : 1st April, 1995]

Introduction

Different fixed assets, for example, buildings, machinery and furnitures are used by an enterprise for different purposes like production, administration, sales and service, etc. Expenditure is made early in the life of the assets for acquiring the assets but benefits are derived throughout their useful life.

When a fixed asset is acquired, it is recorded in the books of account at its acquisition cost and it is capitalised. In each accounting period, a portion of acquisition cost is charged to the Profit and Loss Account as expense. This accounting process of gradually converting the acquisition cost of fixed asset into expense over a series of accounting periods is called *depreciation*.

Objectives

Depreciation has a significant effect in the preparation of the financial statements of an enterprise. It will influence the profit / loss and value of assets of the enterprise. Different enterprises adopt different accounting policies for depreciation.

The main objective of this accounting standard is to prescribe the *guidelines for charging depreciation* for different assets.

Scope

This statement deals with depreciation accounting and applies to all depreciable assets, except the following items to which special considerations apply -

   (i) forests, plantations and similar regenerative natural resources;

  (ii) wasting assets including expenditure on the exploration for and extraction of minerals, oils, natural gas and similar non-regenerative resources;

 (iii) expenditure on research and development;

 (iv) goodwill;

  (v) live stock.

This statement also does not apply to land unless it has a limited useful life for the enterprise.

Definitions : Depreciation

Depreciation is a measure of the wearing out, consumption or other loss of value of a depreciable asset arising from use, effluxion of time or obsolescence through technology and market changes, Depreciation is allocated so as to charge a fair proportion of the depreciable amount in each accounting period during the expected useful life of the asset. Depreciation includes amortisation of assets whose useful life is predetermined.

Depreciable Assets

Depreciable assets are assets which

  (i) are expected to be used during more than one accounting period; and

 (ii) have a limited useful life; and

(iii) are held by an enterprise for use in the production or supply of goods and services, for rental purpose, or for administrative purposes and not for the purpose of sale in the ordinary course of business.

Useful Life

Useful life is either :

  (i) the period over which a depreciable asset is expected to be used by the enterprise; or

 (ii) the number of production or similar units expected to be obtained from the use of the asset by the enterprise.

Depreciable Amount

Depreciable amount of a depreciable asset is its historical cost, or other amount substituted for historical cost in the financial statements, less the estimated residual value.

Factors in the Measurement of Depreciation

The amount of depreciation to be charged for a particular fixed asset will depend upon the following three factors :

  (i) Cost of the asset

 (ii) Useful life of the asset

(iii) Residual value of the asset

Cost of the Asset

The cost of an asset is the basis for calculation of depreciation. For the purpose of determination of cost of an asset, the following points are important as stated in AS-10 "Accounting for Fixed Assets":

(a) Where an asset is purchased from a supplier : The cost of a fixed asset should comprise its purchase price and any attributable cost of bringing the asset to its working condition for its intended use.

Examples of directly attributable costs are :

  (i) site preparation;

 (ii) initial delivery and handling costs;

(iii) installation cost, such as special foundations for plant; and

(iv) professional fees, for example, fees of architects and engineers.

(b) Where an asset is self-constructed : The cost of a self-constructed fixed asset should comprise those costs that relate directly to the specific asset and those that are attributable to the construction activity in general and can be allocated to the specific asset.

(c) Where a fixed asset is acquired either in exchange or in part exchange for another asset : The asset acquired should be recorded either:

  (i) at its fair value; or

 (ii) the net book value of the asset given up, adjusted for any balancing payment or receipt of cash or other consideration.

Useful Life of the Asset

The useful life of an asset is its service life which can be defined as the number of accounting periods during which it will be useful to the business. The physical life of an asset may be considered longer than its economic life. When the operating cost of an asset is considered to be more than the revenue which it generates, it has exceeded its economic life and should not be kept in use. Since there is no way to measure correctly how long an asset will be useful, the asset's useful economic life is always estimated.

The useful life of a depreciable asset should be estimated after considering the following factors :-

  (i) expected physical wear and tear;

 (ii) obsolescence;

(iii) legal or other limits on the use of the asset, e.g., safety limitation or the expiry dates of assets taken on lease.

Estimation of useful life of the asset is very difficult. It is a matter of judgment and depending on the experience of the enterprise with similar assets. Depreciation will vary directly with the useful life of the asset. If the estimated life is too long, each year's depreciation charge will be less and profits in the periods before disposal will be inflated.

Depreciation is loss of value of an asset

It is a measure of wearing out, consumption or other loss of value of a depreciable asset arising from use and passage of time. Depreciation is nothing but distribution of total cost of assets over its useful life.

Depreciable assets
Those assets which -

- Are expected to be used for more than one accounting period.
- Have a limited useful life.
- Are held for use in production of goods and services (*i.e.* not for the purpose of sale in ordinary course of business).

Applicability of Accounting Standard

The accounting standard is applicable to all depreciable assets except, the following :

- Forests, Plantations
- Wasting Assets, Minerals and Natural Gas
- Expenditure on research and development Goodwill
- Live stock - Cattle, Animal Husbandry.

Calculation of Depreciation

- The amount of depreciation is calculated as under :
- Historical cost or other amount in place of historical cost like revalued amount
- Estimated useful life of depreciable assets
- Estimated residual / scrap value of depreciable assets

$$\text{Depreciation} = \frac{\text{Cost - (Scrap value at the end of useful life)}}{\text{Estimated useful life in No. of years}}$$

If straight line method of Depreciation is followed.

What is cost of depreciable assets? - It is total cost spent in connection with its acquisition; installation and commissioning as well as for additional item or improvement of the depreciable assets. The historical cost may change due to following factors :-

- Increase / decrease in long term liability on account of exchange fluctuation if option under amended AS- 11 is exercised.
- Price adjustment
- Changes in duties
- Revaluation of depreciable assets
- Other similar reason.

Estimated useful life of depreciable assets - It is period over which it is expected to be used by the enterprise. Generally useful life is shorter than the physical life. The useful life depends upon the following factors :

- Pre-determined by legal or contractual limits

    Example - Asset given on lease, the estimated life is period of lease.
- Depends upon the number of shifts for which the asset is to be used
- Repair and Maintenance policy of enterprise
- Technological obsolescences
- Innovation / improvements in the production method
- Change in demand of output Legal or other restrictions.

Estimated residual/scrap value of depreciable assets - It is estimated value of depreciable assets at the end of its useful life. It is generally difficult to determine the residual value. It is estimated at the time of acquisition, installation and at the time of revaluation of the assets.

Depreciable amount

It means historical cost or other amount substituted for historical cost less estimated residual value. Depreciable amount is allocated over the estimated useful life of depreciable assets.

Method of Depreciation

There are two methods of depreciation. These are : -
- Straight Line Method (SLM)
- Written Down Value Method (WDVM)

Selection of Appropriate Method - It depends upon the following factors :-
- Type of Asset.
- Nature of the use of such asset.
- Circumstances prevailing in the business.

Note : A combination of more than one method may be used.

Accounting Treatment - Selected depreciation method should be applied consistently from period to period.

Changes in Depreciation Method

Change in depreciation method is done in following conditions :
- For compliance of statute.
- For compliance of accounting standards.
- For more appropriate presentation of the financial statement.

Procedure to be followed in case of change in method -

- Depreciation should be recomputed applying the new method from the date of its acquisition / installation, till the date of change of method.
- Difference between the total depreciation under the new method and accumulated depreciation under the old method till the date of change may be surplus/deficiency.
- Such resultant surplus is credited to profit & loss account under the head "Depreciation written back".
- Such resultant deficiency is charged to profit & loss account.
- Such change of depreciation method should be treated as change in accounting policy and its effect should be quantified and disclosed.

Change in estimated useful life

When there is change in estimated useful life of assets, outstanding depreciable amount on the date of change in estimated useful life of asset should be allocated over the revised remaining useful life of assets.

Example : Plant has useful life of 10 years. Depreciable amount is Rs. 39 lakhs. The company has charged SLM depreciation. At the end of 6th year, the balance useful life was re-estimated at 8 years. The depreciation will be charged from 7th year.

$$= \frac{39-39/10\times6}{8} = 1.95$$

Change in historical cost due to exchange variation on long-term foreign liability, price adjustment and change in duties etc.

- Increase/decrease in amount of historical cost is added/deducted from the outstanding written down value on the date of change.
- Depreciation on the revised WDV will be provided prospectively over the remaining useful life of the asset.

Change in historical cost due to revaluation - Depreciation should be charged on the basis of revalued amount and on the estimate of the remaining useful life of such assets.

'Depreciation charge on addition/extension to an existing asset

- Additional / extension is an integral part of existing asset,
  It is depreciated over the remaining useful life of the existing asset.
- Addition/extension is not an integral part of existing asset.
  It is depreciated over the estimated useful life of additional assets.

When the depreciable asset is disposed of, discarded, demolished or destroyed

Net surplus or deficiency (i.e. sale proceeds less written down value) is credited/ charged to profit and loss accounts.

Disclosure

- Total cost of each class of assets - historical cost or revalued cost.
- Total depreciation for the period of each class of assets.
- Accumulated depreciation of each class of assets.
- Depreciation method.
- Depreciation rates or the useful life of the asset, if they are different than the rates specified in governing statute.
- A change in method of depreciation is treated as a change in accounting policy and is disclosed separately.
- Effect of the revaluation of the fixed asset on the amount of depreciation.

Significant differences among AS-6, IFRS/IAS and US GAAP

- AS-6 allows the depreciation on revalued value of the assets as the AS-10 on fixed assets allows the revaluation of assets. However US GAAP prohibits revaluation. IAS-16 allows fair value accounting (upwards) for fixed assets as an alternative treatment.
- A change in depreciation method under AS-6 is treated as a change in an accounting policy; whereas under TAS-16, and US GAAP, it is treated as a change in estimate, which affects the results of current and future periods. Under IAS-16, a retrospective application of this change with a cumulative adjustment of the surplus/deficiency against the current period income statement is not required.

PROBLEMS

Problem No. : 1 - A Plant was depreciated under two different methods as under -

	Straight Line Method	Written Down Value
1st year	3.90	10.69
2nd year	3.90	7.90
3rd year	3.90	5.84
4th year	3.90	4.32
	15.60	28.75
5th year	3.90	3.19

Required :

(a) It the company followed WDV for first four years and decides to switch over to SLM, what would be the amount of resultant surplus/deficiency ?

(b) If the company followed SLM for first four years and decides to switch over to WDV what would be amount of resultant surplus/deficiency?

Solution :

As per para 21 of AS-6 (refer points 7.7 & 7.7-1) when a change in the method of depreciation is made, depreciation should be recalculated in accordance with the new method from the date of the asset coming into use. The deficiency or surplus arising from retrospective recomputation of depreciation in accordance with the new method should he adjusted in the accounts in the year in which the method of depreciation changed. In case I lie change the change in the method results in deficiency in depreciation in respect of past years, the deficiency should be charged in the statement to profit and loss. In case the change in the method results in surplus, the surplus should be credited to statement of profit and loss.

(a) Surplus of Rs. 13.15 will be written back to profit and loss account.

(b) Deficiency of Rs. 13.15 should be charged to profit and loss account.

Such a change should be treated as a change in accounting policy and its effect should be quantified and disclosed.

Problem No. : 2 - The Company's plant and machinery was Rs. 3,000 lakhs as on 1 - 4-2009. It provided depreciation at 15% per annum under WDV method. However it noticed that about Rs. 500 lakhs worth of imported asset, which is component of above plant and machinery acquired on 1-4-2009, would be obsolete in 2 years. Company wants to write off this asset over 2 years. Can Company do so? Give comments.

Solution :

As per para 34 of AS-6 (refer point 7.10), where an addition or extension retains a separate identity and is capable of being used after the existing asset is disposed of depreciation should be provided independently on the basis of an estimate of its own useful life.

As it appears that imported asset of Rs. 500 lakhs, which is component of plant and machinery, is having independent useful life. Therefore, the company's policy to write off over two years is correct.

Problem No. : 3 - Gammon (India) Ltd. Uses horses to transport material from one place to another place on hilly area where construction activity is going on. It purchases horses worth Rs. 80,000 for transporting material on 1-4-2009. Useful life of horses was estimated 5 years, therefore company decided to write off depreciation on horses as per SLM over 5 years. Comment.

Solution :

The treatment followed by the company is not correct as per AS-6 Para l(v) (refer point 7.3) Depreciation Accounting is not applicable to Live Stock.

Problem No. : 4 - NDA Ltd. purchased certain plant and machinery for Rs. 40 lakhs. 20% of the cost net of CENVAT credit is the subsidy component to be realised from a State Government for establishing industry in a backward district. Cost Rs. 40 lakhs include excise Rs. 5 lakhs against which CENVAT credit can bed claimed. Compute Depreciable amount.

Solution:

In this case, it is first necessary to determine the historical cost of the plant and machinery. This is shown as Follows:

(Rs. in lakhs)

Purchase price	40
Less : Specified duty against which CENVAT credit is available	5
Originally cost of plant and machinery for accounting purposes	35
Less : Subsidy	7
Depreciable Amount	28

Alternatively, the original cost of the plant and machinery can be taken at Rs. 35 lakhs and a sum ol Rs. 7 lakhs can be transferred to deferred income account by way of a "subsidy reserve". While CENVAT credit can be presently availed of only in two annual installments of 50% each, that portion of unavailed CENVAT credit is also required to be reduced from cost.

Depreciable amount would be as under :
(a) Where the entire subsidy is adjusted against cost   Rs. 28 lakhs
(b) Where the subsidy is held as deferred income   Rs. 35 lakhs

PROBLEMS

1) An item of plant was purchased on 1-4-2008 for Rs. 2,00,000. The WDV depreciation rate applicable to the plant was 15%. The written down value of the plant as on 31-3-2010 was Rs. 1,44,500. On 1-4-2010, the enterprise decided to change the method From written down value to straight line. The enterprise decided to write off the book value of Rs. 1,44,500 over the remaining useful life of plant i.e. 15 years (Out of the total useful life of 17 years. 2 years have already elapsed)

Comment whether the accounting treatment is correct. If not, give the correct accounting treatment with reasons.

Ans. : No, recalculate depreciation and surplus credited to Profit and Loss A/c of Rs. 31,970 (cr.)

2) A company has acquired a Plant and Machinery at 6.5 lakhs on installments basis from a dealer (The cash down price is Rs. 6 lakhs). During the year, company paid Rs. 50,000 as down payment and Rs. 1.5 lakhs as the installment for the year. The company provided the depreciation @ 15% on Rs. 2 lakhs. Comment, whether the depreciation on Rs. 2 lakhs is correct with reasons.

Ans. : No.

Advanced Problems

3) How would you deal with the following situation?

(a) The cnterprischas adopted the straight line method for charging depreciation on new machine in factory, while continuing to charge depreciation on the old machinery of the factory on the written down value method.

(b) The enterprise has adopted the written down value method of charging depreciation on its plant and machinery in factory A and the straightline method for charging depreciation on identical plant and machinery in factory B.

Ans. : (a) permissible; (b) permissible

4) The managing director of a company asked you whether in the profit and loss account, depreciation on computer can be charged at the rate specified in the Income-tax Rules. Give your advice.

Ans. : Prima facie - No

5) The management of a company does not want to provide for depreciation on the assets in a particular year because the company has not used the assets at all during the year. Give your comment.

Ans. : Not correct

6) On January 1,2000, Bray Company purchased for Rs. 2,40,000 a machine with a useful life of 10 years and no salvage value. The machine was depreciated by the diminishing balance method and the carrying amount of the. machine was Rs. 1,53,600 on December 31, 2001. Bray changed to the straight-line method on January I. 2002. Bray can justify the change. What should be depreciation expenses on this machine for the year ended December 31, 2002.

(a) Rs. 15,360   (b) Rs. 19,200   (c) Rs. 24,000   (d) Rs. 30,720

Ans. : (c) Besides surplus of Rs. 38,400 to be credited in profit and loss account

1.7 AS - 10 : Accounting for Fixed Assets [Effective Date: 1st April, 1991]

Introduction

Fixed assets represent a significant portion of the total assets of an enterprise. In some industries like iron and steel oil refinery etc., fixed assets consist of 70% to 80% of the total assets. Therefore, fixed assets are very important in the presentation and preparation of financial statements. Furthermore, the operating profits of an enterprise will depend upon whether an expenditure represents an asset or an expense.

This statement deals with accounting for fixed assets. Generally, fixed assets are grouped into various categories e.g., land, building, plant and machinery, furniture and fixtures, vehicles, patents, trade marks, etc,

Objectives

The main objectives of this statement are:

(a) the recognition of the fixed assets; and

(b) determining their carrying amounts.

Scope

1) This statement does not deal with accounting for the following items to which special considerations apply:

(a) forests, plantations and similar regenerative natural resources;

(b) wasting assets including mineral rights, expenditure on the exploration for and extraction of minerals, oil, natural gas and similar non-generative resources;

(c) expenditure on real estate development; and

(d) livestock.

Expenditure on individual items of fixed assests used to develop or maintain the activities covered in (a) to (d) above, but separable from those activities, are to be accounted for in accordance with this statement.

Example : Irrigation equipments used for plantation are to be accounted for in accordance with this outside the scope of this statement.

2) This statement does not deal with the accounting for depreciation of the fixed assets.

3) This statement does not deal with the treatment of government grants and subsidies and assets under **leasing rights**.

Definitions
Fixed Assets

Fixed asset is an asset held with the intention of being used for the purpose of producing or providing goods or services and is not held for sale in the normal course of business.

Fair Market Value

Fair market value is the price that would be agreed in an open and unrestricted market between knowledgeable and willing parties dealing at arm's length who are fully informed and are not under any compulsion to transact.

Gross Book Value

Gross book value of a fixed asset is its historical cost or other amount substituted for historical cost in the books of account or financial statements. When this amount is shown net of accumulated depreciation, it is termed as net book value.

Identification of Fixed Assets

An asset wilt be accounted for as a **fixed asset** if the following conditions are satisfied :

(a) It is held with the intention of being used for the purpose of producing or providing goods and services; and

(b) It is not held for sale in the normal course of business.

In some cases, an enterprise may treat an item as expense though it would otherwise be classified as fixed asset, It is done because the amount of the expenditure is not material.

Example : Saraswati Printers (P) Ltd purchased a punching machine for Rs 500. Life of the punching machine is 5 years. As the amount of expenditure is small, it can be treated as an expense instead of recording it as a fixed asset.

It should be noted that the Standard permits the aggregation of individually insignificant items, such as tools, modules and dies, as one fixed asset.

Stand-by Equipment and Servicing Equipment

Stand-by equipment and servicing equipment are accounted for as fixed assets.

Example : Factory washing machine and stanri-hy generator are fixed assets.

Spare Parts

Regularly used spare parts are usually carried as inventory. It is merged to Profit and Loss Account when consumed.

However, if spare parts can only be used in connection with an item of fixed asset and their use is expected to be irregular, they are accounted for as fixed assets. They are depreciated on a systematic basis over the useful life of the principal fixed asset.

Component Accounting

In certain circumstances, the accounting for an item of fixed asset should be done on the basis of its *separable components*, if
  (a) they are in practice separable
  (b) their useful lives are different.

Example : Instead of treating an aircraft and its engines as one unit, it will be better to treat engines and aircraft as separate units. The useful life of engines are usually shorter than that of the aircraft. It should be noted that separate recognition will lead to better estimation of depreciation.

Components of Cost

The cost of an item of fixed assets comprises its purchase price, including import duties and other non-refundable taxes of levies and any directly attributable cost of bringing the asset to its working condition for its intended use; any trade discounts and rebates are deducted in arriving at the purchase price.

Examples of directly attributable costs are :
  (i) site preparation;
 (ii) initial delivery and handling costs;
(iii) installation cost, such as special foundations for plant; and
 (iv) professional fees, for example fees of architects and engineers.

The cost of a fixed asset may undergo changes subsequent to its acquisition or construction on account of exchange fluctuations, price adjustments, changes in duties or similar factors.

Fixed Assets

It is an asset, which is :

- Held with intention of being used for the purpose of producing or providing goods or services.
- Not held for sale in the normal course of business.
- Expected to be used, tor more than one accounting period.

Examples of fixed assets are :

- Land
- Building - Freehold
- Leasehold - Building
- Plant & Machinery
- Furniture & Fitting etc.

Applicability

- This accounting standard is not applicable to the following items.
- Forests, plantations and similar regenerative natural resource.
- Wasting assets like minerals, oil, and natural gas.
- Expenditure on real estate development.
- Live stock.

Fixed assets in- financial-statement

Fixed assets shall be shown in financial statement either at historical cost or revalued price.

What is Historical cost - The historical cost of acquired fixed assets consists of the following : -

- Purchase price
- Import duties and other non-refundable taxes
- Any directly attributable cost of bringing the asset to the working condition for its intended use like: -
  - Site preparation
  - Delivery and handling cost
  - Installation cost
  - Professional fees (i.e. Fees of engineers and architects).
  - Expenditure incurred on start up and commission of the project including the expenditure on test runs less income by sale of products.

- Administrative and other general overheads are specifically attributable for construction/acquisition/installation of the fixed assets.
- Amount of Govt. grants received/receivable against fixed asset should be deducted from the cost of fixed asset.
- Loss/gain on deferred payment on foreign currency liability if option under AS-11 is exercised.
- Price adjustment, changes in duties or similar factors.

Historical cost of self-constructed fixed assets - Such fixed asset, which was constructed by in-house efforts, is called self-constructed fixed asset. Cost of self-constructed fixed assets; includes the following : -

- All costs which are directly related to the specific asset.
- All costs that are attributable to the construction activity should be allocated to the specific assets.
- Any internal profit included in the cost should be eliminated.

Example : X Ltd. is constructing a fixed asset. The cost ol project is given below :

Materials	Rs. 7,00,000	
Direct Expenses	Rs. 1,00,000	
Total Wages of the company during the year	Rs. 1,20,000	1/12 is chargeable to Project
Total Administrative Exp. of the company during the year	Rs. 8,00,000	5% is chargeable to Project
Depreciation on asset used for the project	Rs. 12,000	

Calculate the cost of fixed assets

Answer :

Cost of Fixed Assets	R.f.
Material	7,00,000
Direct Expenses	1,00,000
Wages	10,000
Administration Overhead	40,000
Depreciation	12,000
Total:	8,62,000

Cost of asset acquired in exchange of existing assets: (i.e. consideration paid is non-monetary) - The cost of acquisition of fixed assets is determined under the different situations differently as under : -

- **Fixed Assets exchanged not similar -** Assets acquired should be recorded either at fair market value of asset given up or fair market value of asset acquired, if this is more clearly evident.
- **Fixed Assets exchanged are similar -** Fixed assets acquired is recorded at fair market value of asset given up or Fair market value of asset acquired, if this is more clearly evident or Net Book value of the asset given up
- **Fixed Assets acquired in exchange of share or other securities -** (when payment of fixed assets is made in shares or securities) Assets should be recorded at - either fair market value of asset purchased or Fair market value of share or securities, whichever is more clearly available.

Revalued price

When the fixed assets are revalued, these assets are shown at revalued price in financial statement. Generally, competent valuer does revaluation, through appraisal. Revaluations may be done using price index appropriate to the concerned fixed assets.

When a fixed asset is revalued, an entire class of assets should be revalued or the selection of assets for revaluation should be made on a systematic basis. That basis must be disclosed.

Method of presentation of revalued asset in financial statement - There are two methods for showing the revalued amount in the financial statement. These are: -
- By re-stating the gross book value and accumulated depreciation.
- By re-stating net book value adding there in the net increase on account of revaluation.

Maximum amount of revaluation - Revaluation of fixed assets should be restricted to the net recoverable amount of fixed asset.

Accounting treatment of revaluation - Treatment in accounting unuer different situations is as under: -
- **First time revaluation (upward)**
  - Increase in net book value is credited to owner's interest under the head 'Revaluation Reserve'.
- **First time revaluation (Downward)**
  - Decrease in net book value is charged to the profit & loss account.
- **First revaluation (downward) subsequent revaluation (upward)**
  - Decrease in net book value is charged to the Profit & Loss Account in the year in which downward revaluation was done.
  - Amount of revaluation that can be credited to Profit & Loss Account is restricted to the amount of devaluation earlier written off. Balance amount of revaluation should be credited to revaluation reserve.

- **First revaluation (upward) subsequent revaluation (downward)**
  - Increase in the net book value is credited to owner's interest under the head 'Revaluation Reserve'.
  - Amount of devaluation can be charged to revaluation reverse to the extent the revaluation reserve earlier credited is unutilized, the balance amount of devaluation is charged to profit and loss account.

Valuation of fixed assets in special cases

- **Assets acquired on hire purchase terms :** Such assets arc recorded at their cash price. However, the recording will be done as per AS-19.
- **Cost of jointly held assets :** Either the original cost, accumulated depreciation, and written down value should be stated in the balance sheet in the proportion in which the entity has right to utilize the asset. **OR**

  Pro rata cost of such jointly owned assets is grouped together with similar fully owned assets.
- **Fixed assets acquired at consolidated price :** Cost of each fixed asset should be determined on a fair basis as per valuation by competent valuers.

Improvements and Repair

There are two accounting treatments of cost of improvement and repairs. These accounting treatments depend upon the following conditions : -

- After the improvements and repairs, expected future benefits from fixed assets do not change. The expenses of improvements and repairs are charged to profit & loss account.
- After the improvement and repairs, expected future benefits from fixed asset will increase beyond the previously assessed standard performance. These expenses on improvements and repairs are included in the gross book value of fixed asset.

Addition or extension of capital nature to an existing asset

- **If integral part** of existing asset- it is generally added to gross book value of existing assets.
- **If separate identity** and capable to be used after the disposal of existing asset - it is accounted for separately.

Retirement and disposals

- Fixed assets are deleted from the financial statement either on disposal or on expected economic benefit is over.
- Gains or losses arising on disposal are generally recognized in profit & loss account.

Fixed assets are retired from active use and held for disposal

- Such asset is stated at the lower of net book value and net realisable value in the financial statement.

- Any expected loss is recognized immediately in the profit & loss statement.
- It should be separately shown in financial statement **i.e.**, balance sheet.

Disposal of previously revalued fixed assets -If there is profit, then it is credited to profit & loss account.

If there is loss, then it can be adjusted against the balance of revaluation reserve (arising out of revaluation of the same asset). If any.

Disclosure

- Gross and net book values of fixed assets at the beginning and at the end of accounting period showing additions, disposal, acquisition and other movements.
- Expenditure incurred on account of fixed assets in the course of construction or acquisition.
- Revalued amount substituted for historical cost of fixed assets, the method adopted to compute the revalued amount, and whether an external valuer has valued the fixed assets, in case where fixed assets arc stated at revalued amount.

Capitalisation of exchange differences incurred on fixed asset related borrowing

Instructions contain in Part I of Schedule VI of the Companies Act, 1956 regarding adjustment of exchange difference in the carrying amount of the fixed assets due to change in the rate of exchange of fixed assets linked liability denominated in foreign exchange has been super seded by issue of Companies (Accounting Standards) Rules, 2006. Therefore, AS- 11 (Revised 2003) will apply and such exchange difference shall be recognised in profit and loss account and will not be capitalised with the cost of fixed assets. However it is subject to option exercised by the entity as per amendments in AS-11 on 31-3-2009.

Treatment of CENVAT credit on capital goods (fixed assets)

Para 9.1 of AS-10 on "Accounting for Fixed Assets", requires that only non-refundable taxes and duties in respect of the fixed asset should be included in the cost of that fixed asset.

Cenvatable excise duty can be considered as a refundable tax. There-fore, CENVAT credit of such duty should be reduced from the purchase cost of capital goods concerned and recognised as a separate asset if the following conditions are satisfied: (i) The enterprise is entitled to the CENVAT credit as per the Rules, and (ii) there is a reasonable certainty that the CENVAT credit would be utilized and (iii) enterprise intends to avail the CENVAT credit.

The CENVAT credit in respect of capital goods is allowed for an amount not exceeding 50% of the duty paid on such capital goods in the financial year in which the goods are received in factory and the balance will be allowed in the subsequent year(s). If the conditions specified above are met and the enterprise decides to take CENVAT credit, the entire amount of CENVAT credit should be deducted from the cost of capital goods. The amount of CENVAT credit taken in the financial year, in which goods are received, should be debited to an appropriate account, say, "CENVAT Receivable (Capital goods) Account" and balance may be debited in another appropriate account say "CENVAT credit Deferred Account". In the subsequent financial year(s), when the balance CENVAT credit is availed of, the appropriate adjustment for the same should be made, i.e., amount of "CENVAT credit Deferred Account" with a corresponding debit to "CENVAT Credit Receivable (Capital Goods) Account". On actual utilization, the account will be adjusted against excise duty on the final products. Accordingly, the purchase cost of the capital goods would be net of the specified duty on capital goods. The unadjusted balance standing in the MODVAT Credit Receivable (Capital goods) Account, if any, should be shown on the asset side under the head "Advances".

In following cases excise duty, even though Cenvatable should be included in the cost of fixed assets

   (i) the enterprise does not intended to avail it; or

   (ii) the recognition criteria is not satisfied.

Review of balance in CENVAT credit receivable accounts - Balance in CENVAT Credit Receivable Accounts, pertaining to capital goods, should be reviewed at the end of the year, if it is found that the balance of the CENVAT credit are not likely to be used in the normal course of business within a reasonable time, then, notwithstanding the right to carry forward such excess credit in the Excise Rules, the non-usable credit should be adjusted in the accounts. As a result, the balance of the CENVAT credit receivable accounts in the financial account may be lower than the credit available as per CENVAT credit registers. In such a case, a reconciliation statement would have to be prepared indicating the amounts adjusted so that a track is kept for the difference between the balance and the difference between financial accounts and the credit available as per the excise registers can be explained in subsequent years also.

The adjustment of excess credit related to capital goods should be made to the concerned Capital Goods Account. The excess CENVAT credit, which is not utilizable in future within reasonable time, either availed or deferred, which related to fixed assets acquired, should be added to the cost of the relevant fixed asset. For accounting purpose, depreciation on the revised unamortized depreciation amount should be provided prospectively over the residual useful life of the asset. In case the fixed asset no longer exists, the relevant amount should be written off in the profit and loss account. To facilitate aforesaid treatment, CENVAT credit record should be maintained fixed asset-wise in the relevant R.G. Register.

Significant difference among AS-10 and IAS/IFRS-16 and US GAAP

Main difference is regarding revaluation of fixed asset. AS-10 allows revaluation, IAS-16 also allow revaluation. If revaluation model is followed but with detailed guidelines. US GAAP does not allow revaluation. Difference in exchange arising out of payment or translation of foreign exchange liability on account of fixed asset shall not be added to or subtracted from the cost of fixed assets as per AS-11 (Revised), which is in accordance with IFRS/IAS-21 and US GAAP. However AS-11 has been amended with option to capitalise such difference. However, this option has expired on 31.3.201 1.Now the exchange difference will not be capitalized as per AS-11. But this option has further been extended upto 31-03-2012 by the Ministry of Corporate Affair on Nth May 2011.

PROBLEMS

Problem No. 1 : On 1-4-2010 Induga Ltd. had sold some of its fixed assets for Rs. 100 lakhs written down value Rs. 250 lakhs, these assets were revalued earlier. As on 1-4-2010 the revaluation reserve corresponding to these assets stood at Rs. 200 lakhs. The profit on sale of property Rs. 200 lakhs shown in the profit and loss statement represented the transfer of this amount. Loss on sale of asset was included in the cost of goods sold. Comment.

Solution :

As per Para 32 of AS-10 (refer point 10.8-2), on accounting for fixed assets. On disposal of a previously revalued item of fixed assets, the difference between net disposal proceeds and the net book value is normally charged or credited to the profit and loss statement except that to the extent such a loss is related to an increase which was previously recorded as a credit to revaluation reserve and which has not been subsequently reversed or utilized, it is charged directly to that account. The amount standing in revaluation reserve following the retirement or disposal of an asset, which relates to (that asset, may be transferred to general reserve. Accordingly, the following journal entries are to be passed

(Rs. In lakhs)

Profit on sale of property	Dr.	200	
To Cost of goods sold			150
To General Reserve			50

Problem No. 2 : AD Softex (India) Ltd. expects that a plant has become useless which is appearing in the books at Rs. 10 lakhs gross value. The company charges SLM depreciation on a period of 10 years estimated life and estimated scrap value of 3%. At the end of 7th year the plant has been assessed as useless. Its estimated net realisable value is Rs. 3,10,000. Determine the loss /gain on retirement of the fixed assets.

Solution :

Cost of the plant	Rs. 10,00,000
Estimated realisable value	Rs. 30,000
Depreciable amount	Rs. 9,70,000
Depreciation per year	Rs. 97,000
Written down value at me end of 7th Year	
= 10,00,000-(97000X7) =	Rs. 3,21,000

As per Para 14.2 of AS-10 (refer point 10.8), items of fixed assets that have been retired from active use and are held for disposal are stated at the lower of their net hook value and net realisable value and are shown separately in the financial statements. Any expected less is recognized immediately in the profit and loss statement. Accordingly, the loss of Rs. 21,000 (321000-310000) to be shown in the profit and loss account and asset of Rs. 3,10,000 to be shown in the balance sheet separately.

Problem No. 3 : A company has purchased plant and machinery in the year 2006-07 for Rs. 45 lakhs. A balance of Rs. 5 lakhs is still payable to the suppliers for the same. The supplier waived off the balance amount during the financial year 2009-10. The company treated it as income and credited to profit and loss account during 2009-10.

Whether accounting treatment of the company is correct. If not, state with reasons.

Solution :

As per Para 9.1 of AS-10 (refer point 10.3) the cost of fixed assets may undergo changes subsequent to its acquisition or construction on account of exchange fluctuation, price adjustments, changes in duties or similar factors considering Para 9.1 the treatment done by the company is not correct. Rs. 5 lakhs should be deducted from the cost of fixed assets.

Problem No. 4 : NDA Co. purchased a machine costing Rs. 1,25,000 for its manufacturing operations and paid shipping costs of Rs. 20,000. NDA spent an additional amount of Rs. 10,000 for testing and preparing the machine for use. What amount should NDA record as the cost of the machine?

Solution :

As per Para 20 of AS-10, (refer point 10.3), the cost of fixed asset should comprise its purchase price and any attributable cost of bringing the asset to its working condition for its intended use. In this case the cost of machinery includes all expenditures incurred in acquiring the asset and preparing it for use. Cost includes the purchase price, freight and handling charges, insurance cost on the machine while in transit, cost of special foundations, and costs of assembling, installation and testing. Therefore the cost to be recorded is Rs. 1,55,000 (Rs. 1,25,000 + Rs. 20.000 + Rs. 10,000)

Problem No. 5 : On December 1, 2009, Induga Co. purchased Rs. 4,00,000 worth of land for a factory site. Induga razed an old building on the property and sold the materials it salvaged from the demolition. Induga incurred additional costs and realized salvage proceeds during December 2009 as follows :

Demolition of old building	Rs. 50,000
Legal fees for purchase contract and recording ownership	Rs. 10,000
Title guarantee insurance	Rs, 12,000
Proceeds from sale of salvaged materials	Rs. 8,000

In its December 31, 2009 Balance Sheet, Induga Co. should report a balance in the land account.

Solution :

As per Para 20 of AS-10, (refer point 10.3). the cost of land should include all expenditure incurred preparing it for its ultimate use (such as factory size) is considered part of the cost of land. Before the land can be used as a building site, it must be purchased (involving costs such as purchase price, legal fees, and title insurance) and the old building must be razed (cost of demolition less proceeds from sale of scrap). The total balance in the land account should be Rs. 4,64,000.

Purchase price	Rs. 400,000
Legal Fees	Rs. 10,000
Title Insurance	Rs. 12,000
Net cost of demolition (Rs. 50,000 - Rs. 8,000)	Rs. 42,000
	Rs. 4,64,000.

Problem No. 6 : On March 31.2010, Winn Company traded in an old machine having a carrying amount of Rs. 16,800, and paid cash difference of Rs. 6,000 for a new machine having a total cash price of Rs. 20,500. On March 31, 2010, what amount of loss should Winn Company recognize on this exchange?

Solution :

As per Para 2.2. ol AS-10 (refer point 10.3-3) - When a fixed asset is acquired in exchange or in part exchange for another asset, the cost of the asset acquired should be recorded either at fair market value or at the net book value of the asset given up, adjusted for any balancing payment or receipt of cash or other consideration. The cash price of the new machine represents its fair market value (FMV). The FMV of the old machine can be determined by subtracting the cash portion of the purchase price (Rs. 6,000) from the total cost of the new machine. Rs. 20,500 - Rs. 6,000 = Rs. 14,500. Since the book value of the machine (Rs. 16,800) exceeds its FMV on the date of the trade in (Rs. 14,500), the difference of Rs. 2,300 must be recognized as a loss, however, if the FMV of the old machine had exceeded its book value, the gain would not be recognized.

Problem No. 7 : A building suffered uninsured fire damage. The damaged portion of the building was refurbished with higher quality materials. The cost and related accumulated depreciation of the damaged portion are identifiable. To account for these events, the owner should

(a) Reduce accumulated depreciation equal to the cost of refurbishing.

(b) Record a loss in the current period equal to the sum of the cost of refurbishing and the carrying amount of the damaged portion of the building.

(c) Capitalize the cost refurbishing and record a loss in the current period equal to the carrying amount of the damaged portion of the building.

(d) Capitalize the cost of refurbishing by adding the cost to the carrying amount of the building.

Solution :

(c) When an entity suffers a casualty loss to an asset; the accounting loss is recorded at the net carrying value of the damaged asset, if known. In this case, the cost and related accumulated depreciation are identifiable. The entity should therefore recognize a loss in the current period equal to the carrying amount of the damaged portion of the building (refer point 10.8). The refurbishing of the building, which is an economic event separate from the fire damage, should be treated similarly as the purchase of other assets or betterments. The cost of refurbishing the building should therefore be capitalized and depreciated over the shorter- of the refurbishment's useful lives or the useful life of the building.

Loss	Dr.	...	
Ace, Depreciation	Dr.	...	
To Building			...
Building	Dr.	...	
Cash			....

Therefore, answer (c) is correct and answer (b) is incorrect. Answer (a) is incorrect because in order to reduce the accumulated depreciation account, the useful life ot the asset must be extended. In this case, there is no mention of this fact. Answer (d) is incorrect because it fails to recognize the casualty loss and properly remove file cost and accumulated depreciation on the damaged portion of the building from the accounting records.

Note : If the components of the damaged portion were not identifiable, the following entry would be made:

Loss	Dr.	...	
Cash			....

Problem No. 8 - Rawat & Co. Ltd. incurred costs to modify its building and to rearrange its production line. As a result, an overall reduction in production costs is expected. However, the modifications did not increase the building's market value, and the rearrangement did not extend the production line's life.

Should the building modification costs and the production line rearrangement costs be capitalized?

	Building modification costs	**Production line rearrangement costs**
(a)	Yes	No
(b)	Yes	Yes
(c)	No	No
(d)	No	Yes

Solution :

(b) As per Para 12.1 of AS-10, (refer point 10.6) - Only expenditure that increases the future benefits from the existing asset beyond its previously assessed standard of performance is included in the gross book value, e.g., an increase in capacity. In this case future benefits from the existing asset appear to have increased beyond its previously assessed standard of performance as there is over all reduction in production cost which is expected. Therefore both the building modification and production line rearrangement contributed to the improved efficiency in the production process. Therefore, both costs should be capitalized and answer (b) is correct.

Problem No. 9 : A conveyor system was capitalized on 01-01-2006 with value of Rs. 41.37 crores. The break-up of the capital cost was as follows :

Civil & Mechanical structure	11.72
Driving units and pluming	05.40
Rope	02.83
Belt	11.17
Safely and electrical equipments	06.15
Other accessories	04.10
	41.37

During the financial year 2009-10 due to wear and tear, the rope used in the conveyor system was replaced by a new one at cost, at Rs. 8 crores. As new rope did not increase the capacity and is a component of the total assets. The company charged the full cost of the new rope to repairs and maintenance. Old rope continues to appear in the book hoi account and is charged with depreciation every year.

Whether the above accounting treatment is correct. If not, give the correct accounting treatment with explanation.

Solution :

As per Para 23 of AS-10 (refer point 10.6) - Subsequent expenditure relating to an item of fixed asset should be added to its book value only of it increases the future benefits from the existing asset beyond its previously assessed standard of performance, in the instant case, the new replaced rope does not increase the future benefits from the assets beyond their previously assessed performance, therefore cost of replacement of rope should be charged to revenue, however in doing so the estimated scrap value of the old rope should be deducted from the cost of new rope.

Problem No. 10 : One customer from whom Rs. 5 lakhs are recoverable for credit sales given a motor car in full settlement of dues. The directors estimate that the market value of the motor car transferred is Rs. 5.25 lakhs. As on the date of the balance sheet the car has not been registered in the name of the auditee. As an auditor, what would you do in this situations?

Solution :

The motor car has been acquired in exchange for another assets i.e. receivables. The fair value of motor car is Rs. 5.25 lakhs and that of receivable Rs. 5 lakhs. As per AS-10 the asset acquired in an exchange of assets should be valued at the fair market value of assets acquired or the asset given up, whichever is more clearly evident. Here fair market value of the assets given up obviously more clearly evident. Hence, the motor car should he valued at Rs. 5 lakhs. Also the motor car should be recognised as an asset even though it is not yet registered in auditec's name. This is because legal title is not necessary for an asset to exist. What is necessary is control as per the framework for preparation and presentation

of financial statements. Applying substance over form we find since price has been settled, the auditce has control, hence it should be reflected as an asset along with a note to the effect that the registration in auditec name is pending.

Problem No. 11 : A publishing company undertook repair and overhauling of its machinery at a cost of Rs. 2.50 lakhs to maintain them in good condition and capitalized the amount, as it is more than 25% of the original cost of the machinery. As an auditor, what would you do in this situation? (C.A. Inter, Nov. 2002)

Solution :

Size of the expenditure is not the criteria to decide whether subsequent expenditure should be capitalized. The important question is whether the expenditure increases the expected future benefits from the asset beyond its pre-assessed standard of performance as per AS- 10. Only then it should capitalize. Since in this case, only the benefits are maintained at existing level, the expenditure should not he capitalized. If under the circumstances the amount is material the auditor should qualify his report.

Problem No. 12 : A company has scrapped a semi-automatic part of a machine (not writtenoff) and replaced with a more expensive fully automatic part, which has doubled the output of the machine. At the same time the machine was moved to more suitable place in the factory, which involved the building of new foundation in addition to the cost of dismantling and re-erection. The company wants to charge fhe whole expenditure to revenue. As an auditor, what would you do in this situation? (C.A. Inter, Nov. 2011)

Solution :

If the subsequent expenditure increases the expected future benefits from the asset beyond its pre-assessed standard of performance then as per AS-10 it should be capitalized. Otherwise it should he expensed. In this case, the replacement of semi-automatic part with a fully automatic part has doubled the output of the machine thus, it has increased future benefits beyond the machines' pre-assessed standard performance, hence this expenditure should be capitalized as part of cost of the machine. However, the expenses for shifting the machine and building of a new foundation in addition to the cost of dismantling and re-erection do not contribute to any new future benefits from the existing asset. They only serve to maintain performance of the machine. Hence, this cost should he charged to revenue.

Problem No. 13 : NDA Limited purchased a machine of Rs. 20 lakhs including excise duty of Rs. 4 lakhs. The excise duty is cenvatable under the excise laws. The enterprise intends to avail CENVAT credit and it is reasonably certain to utilize the same within reasonable time. How should the excise duty of Rs. 4 lakhs be treated?

Solution :

Year of acquisition   **(Rs in lakhs)**

Machine Account	Dr.	16	
CENVAT Credit Receivable Account	Dr.	2	
CENVAT Credit Deferred Account	Dr.	2	
To Supplier's Account	Dr.		
Next Year			20
CENVAT credit receivable Account	Dr.	2	
To CENVAT credit deferred Account			2

Problem No. 14 : Is Project under sale fixed or current asset?

Solution :

According to para 24 of AS-10, Accounting for Fixed Assets. Material items retired from active use and held for disposal should be stated at the lower of their net book value and net realizable value and shown separately in the financial statements.

In view of the above, the ASB opined that project under sale, which was originally treated, as fixed asset would continue to be a fixed asset even if it is under sale and will not, therefore, be classified as a current asset. However, if an enterprise were a dealer of projects, then the project under sale would be an inventory and will be classified as a current asset.

Problem No. 15 : A Company transferred land from fixed assets to current assets at market price and adjusted the excess value under Capital Reserve instead of Revaluation Reserve. In subsequent years, the value was written down gradually as "decline in market" whether unusual accounting?

Solution :

The treatments in different circumstances as clarified by Accounting Standard Board (ASB) are as follows:

(A) In case the intention of the enterprise is to become a dealer of the asset, which was there to treated as a fixed asset, it is permissible to transfer such assets to current assets. With regard to valuation of such assets, the following alternatives are available :

- Fixed assets reclassificd, as current assets Should be valued at their carrying amount or at the net realisable value, whichever is lower. In this case, no appreciation would be recognised either as capital reserve or the revaluation reserve.

- It would be appropriate to value assets which were there to classified as fixed assets at their market price in order to determine the correct profit, on sale of such assets in the ordinary course of business. The excess of market value over the carrying amount at the date of reclassification can be transferred to revaluation reserve.

The Board also noted another view that the question of revaluation reserve arises in a situation where a fixed asset is revalued and continues to be a fixed asset. However in case an asset, which was originally classified as a fixed asset and is now classified as current asset, the excess can be transferred to a capital reserve instead of revaluation reserve.

In support of this view, it is argued that the nature of revaluation reserve and capital reserve is the same, as both cannot be used for distribution on dividend. The 'revaluation reserve' is covered by the definition of 'capital reserve' as given in Part 111 of Schedule VI to the Companies Act, 1956. The relevant paragraph of Part III is reproduced below:

"The expression 'capital reserve shall be not include any amount regarded as free for distribution through the profit and loss account' and the expression 'revenue reserve' shall mean any reserve other than a 'capital reserve'

For subsequent accounting, the amount arrived at as per above on the date of re-classification would be treated as cost of the current assets for applying AS-2 which requires that inventories should be valued at cost or net realizable value whichever is lower.

(B) In case the intention is not to deal in the assets which were thereto treated as fixed assets, but assets retired from active use and held for disposal, these should continue to be classified as fixed assets and treated as per paragraph 24 oF AS- 10 which requires that such items should be stated at the lower of their net book value and net realisable value and shown separately in the financial statements.

Problem No. 16 : ABC Ltd. imported a machine from Germany at a cost of Euros 150,000. The exchange rate at the time of import was Rs. 55 for 1 Euro. Customs duty was paid at 25% on its cost. The customs department applied a standard exchange rate of Rs. 52 for I Euro for the purpose of computation. Other port charges, inward transport and octroi amounted to Rs. 2 lakhs.

An engineer was invited from Germany for installation. His fees and expenses came to Rs. 3 lakhs in rupees plus 10,000 Euros. This was remitted at Rs. 56 for 1 Euro.

A loan of Rs. 50 lakhs was taken for the acquisition of the machine at an interest of 8% per annum.

The loan was disbursed on 1st September. 2008. The exchange rate was Rs. 55.80 for 1 Euro on this date.

The machine wns installed and put to commercial use on 1st Fcbruarv, 2009.

Depreciation is charged on straight-line basis in the books of account at 13.91% per annum.

The exchange rate on 31st March. 2009 was Rs. 57 for 1 Euro. The exchange rate on 31st March, 2010 was Rs. 59 for 1 Euro.

10% of the loan was repaid on 1st October, 2009. The exchange rate was Rs. 57.75 on this day.

From the above information work out the following.

  (i) Original cost of the machine in the books of account :

 (ii) Depreciation for the financial year ended 31st March, 2009 :

(iii) Book value as on 31st March, 2009 :

 (iv) Exchange rate differences if any charged to profit and loss for the financial year ended 31st March, 2009;

  (v) Depreciation for the financial year ended on 31st March, 2010;

 (vi) Book value as on 31st March, 2010;

(vii) Exchange rate difference if any to be charged to profit and loss for the financial year to end 31st March, 2010

Note : Apply the revised and latest accounting standards as applicable in India.

(i) Original cost of machine in the books of account : (Rs.)

Purchase Price	Euro 150,000	@ Rs. 55	82, 50,000
Custom Duty	Euro 37,500	@ Rs. 52	19,50,000
Other Charges			2,00,000
Engineer's Rupee Payments			3,00,000
Engineer's Euro Payments	Euro 10,000	@ Rs. 56	5,60,000
Interest on Loan	Rs. 50,00,000	8%	1,66,667
		Total Cost :	1,14,26,667

(ii) Depreciation for the financial year ended 3 1-03-2009 (Rs.)
    @ 13.91% per annum on Rs. 1,14,26,667 for two months   2,64,908

(iii) Book Value as on 31-03-2009: (Rs. 1,14,26,667-2,64,908)   1,11,61,759

(iv) Exchange fluctuation expense for the financial year ended
    31-03-2009: is *NIL*, as the loan was denominated in rupees.
    Hence, no fluctuation is applicable.

(v) Depreciation for the year to end 31-03-2010 @ 13.91% Per annum   15, 89,449

(vi) Book Value as on 31-03-2010: (Rs. 1,11,61,759- 15.89,449)   95,72,310

(vii) Exchange fluctuation expense for financial year ended
    31-03-2010: is *NIL*, as the loan was denominated in rupees.
    Hence, no fluctuation is applicable.

Problem No. 17 : Ltd. purchased machinery from K Ltd. on 30-9-2008. The price was 370.44 lakhs before charging 8% sales tax and giving a trade discount of 2% on the quoted price. Transport charges were 0.25% on the quoted price and installation charges come to 1% on the quoted price.

A loan of Rs. 300 lakhs was taken from the bank on which interest at 15% per annum was to be paid. Expenditure incurred on the trial run was Material Rs. 35.000, wages Rs. 25,000 and Overheads Rs. 15,000.

Machinery was ready for use on 01.12.2008. However it was actually put to use only on 1-5-2009. Find out the cost of the machine and suggest the accounting treatment for the expenses incurred in the interval between the dates 1 -12-2008 to 1-5-2009. The entire loan amount remained unpaid on 1-5-2009.

Solution :

Calculation of cost of Machine as per AS-10

Price of Machine	370.44
Less : Trade discount 2%	7.41
	363.03
Add : Sale Tax 8%	29.04
	392.07
Transport Charges 0.25% on Rs. 370.44	0.93
Installation Charges 19% on Rs. 370.44	3.70
	396.70

Calculation of borrowings cost -

30-09-2008 to 01-12-2008 (presumed to be qualilying asset)

$300 \times 15 / 100 \times 2 / 12$	7.50
	404.20
Add : Expenses on trial run	0.75
Total Cost	**404.95**

As per AS-10, the capitalization of interest should cease when substantially all the activities necessary for intended use are completed. Therefore interest for the period 1-12-2008 to 1-5-2009 should be expensed.

EXERCISES

1) How would you deal with the following situations?

- The surplus arising in revaluation of land and building has been credited to the profit & loss account to the extent of depreciation charged there on previous year. It is argued that to this extent, depreciation need not have been charged in these years.

  [Ans. : No]

- Interest on substantial loans taken specifically to acquire certain fixed assets is being capitalized even after the commencement of commercial production. The management argues that the interest is attributable exclusively to those fixed assets and should therefore be capitalized.

  [Ans. : No]

- The company has constructed a boiler for use in its nevw factory. A substantial portion of the overheads has been charged to the cost of the boiler. Thus, the cost of the self-constructed boiler is almost double the market price of a similar boiler.

  [Ans. : Not correct see paras 10 & 9 of AS-10]

- A fixed asset costing Rs. 1,00,000 was revalued at Rs. 1,50,000 afrer three years of use, at that time; its book value was Rs. 70,000 (SLM @ 10%). The asset is now sold for Rs. 1,40,000. Its book value at the time of sale is Rs. 94,000. The management wishes to credit a sum of Rs. 1,26,000 as profit from the sale of the asset by transferring the sum of Rs. 80,000 from revaluation reserve.
[Ans. : No]
- As per report of valuation of existing fixed assets, book value of the net assets of the enterprise is much lower than their market value. The difference between book value and market value is accounted for as goodwill.
[Ans : No]
- The enterprise had earlier installed its main manufacturing machine on the ground floor of the factory. The company later modified its production process, Which necessitated the installation of the said machine on the first floor. The company, therefore, constructed the entire first door and considering this construction as a foundation tor machine, debited its cost to the plant and machinery account.
[Ans. : No]

2) A public limited company whose main object as stated in its memorandum of association is to purchase, acquire, contract, develop, cultivate and sell, agricultural and urban land, buys large plots of virgin lands, develops and cultivates them and sells them in small plots. Land purchased by the company and cost of the development has been consistent grouped under fixed assets in its balance sheet. **Comment**
[Ans. : No]

3) Discuss the accounting treatment of the following :
- Fixed assets acquired in exchange for other assets.
- Fixed asset acquired on hire-purchase basis.
- Fixed asset owned jointly with other.

4) What is meant by "revaluation of fixed assets"? What are the various bases on which fixed assets can be revalued? Where a fixed asset is revalued, how would the following items be dealt with in the accounts?
- Surplus arising on revaluation
- Depreciation on the revalued asset
- Gain or loss on disposal of the revalued asset.

5) How would you deal?
"The company has sold some old machinery for Rs. 1 crore. The details of the cost of such machinery are not available since the entire recording relating to fixed asset has been destroyed in on earthquake?

6) A newly set up Private Ltd. manufacturing company has incurred following expenditure for the acquisition of plant & machinery

(a) Foreign tour expenses of directors for purchasing plant & machinery.

(b) Technical staff's salary for erection of plant & machinery.

(c) Non-technical staff's salary during the period of installation of plant & machinery

(d) Other sundry expenses such as stationery, printing, postage, telegram and telephone and local conveyance charge etc.

The company intends to capitalize the above expenses. Is the company justified? State with reasons.

Ans. : (a) Yes (b) Yes (c) No (d) No

7) Comment

Z Ltd. acquired a car for its Managing Director on hire purchase basis. The interest payable as well as penalty payable for late payment of instalment was added to the cost of car.

Ans. : Not correct

8) AD Softex (India) Ltd. acquired a machine from USA, purchase price US$1,00,000 exchange rate on the date of acquisition US$1 = 42.80. Transportation cost USD 5000, Custom duty @ 10% against which the company is entitled to enioy duty drawback. Installation expenses Rs. 1,50,000, technical fees for installation USD 1000 (exchange rate 43). Expenses for trial run Rs. 50.000 income from selling products obtained in the process of trial run Rs. 20,000. Find out cost of fixed assets.

Ans. : Rs. 47.17 lakhs

9) AD Softex (India) Ltd. acquired a plant on 1-4-2009 for Rs. 200 lakhs. AD softex (India) Ltd. charges straightline depreciation on the basis of estimated useful life of the, plant at 10 years and scrap value at the end 2.5%. At the beginning of the 5th year the asset was revalued at 10% of the WDV and the revaluation profit was transferred to Revaluation Reserve. The excess depreciation arising out of revaluation was adjusted by taking transfer from revaluation reserve. While charging depreciation after revaluation estimated remaining useful life was assumed to be 6 years and scrap realization was expected to be 2.5% of the revalued figure. At the beginning of the 8 years the company found the asset useless and, accordingly, had decided to retire it. On the date of retirement the estimated realisable value of the asset is Rs 6,50,000.

Find out the loss on retirement of the asset.

Ans. : Loss Rs. 56.025 lakhs (Balance of Revaluation Reserve also have been credited to P&L A/c.)

Advanced Problems

10) A public limited company has taken the loan of Rs. 90,28.800 from ICICI for the purchase of fixed assets and the total cost of fixed asset is given below:

Cost of Purchase		102,04,954.00
Pre-operarive expenses capitalized		
Capitalized Interest	1,87,003.00	
Other pre-operative Expenses	8.72,942.00	10,59,945.00

Details of the loan amount due to ICICI as on 3 1 -3-2009 were

(1) Principal amount	90,28,800
(2) Capitalized pre-delivery interest	1,00,994
(3) Other normal interest	62,89,142
(4) Penal Interest	19,93,580

The Govt. of India provided a rehabilitation relief to company for the waiver of loan and interest under the waiver scheme -

(i) All penal interest and normal (including capitalized pre-delivery interest) and 70% of the outstanding principal.

(ii) Balance 30% of the outstanding principal would be paid.

The company has accounted for the amounts waived as follows -

(a) The outstanding principal amount waived by ICICI {i.e. Rs. 63,20,160) has been credited to capital reserve account by debit to term loan account.

(b) The capitalized pre-delivery interest, other normal interest and penal interest waived, amounting to Rs. 83,83,716 have been offset against the debit balance of profit and loss account as on 3 1-3-2009 without crediting the same to the current year's profit and loss account.

Comment whether the accounting treatment of the company is correct.

Ans : a & b not correct

11) A public sector company decided to procure Diesel Generating (DG) sets. To finance the acquisition of DG sets, the Govt. of India sanctioned Rs. 29 crores (out of which 50% as equity and 50% as loan). The process of placement of orders for procurement of DG sets started. During the intervening period, Rs. 29 crores was invested temporally in short-term deposit. Following interest was received on investment of Rs. 29 crores.

Interest received from investment of Rs. 14.5 crores (loan)

2007-08	12 lakhs
2008-09	77 lakhs
2009-10	100 lakhs
	189 lakhs

Interest received from investment of Rs. 14.5 crores (Equity)

2007-08	14 lakhs
2008-09	86 lakhs
2009-10	120 lakhs
	220 lakhs

The company has followed the following accounting method :

1. Interest in relation of loan amount (i.e. Rs. 189 lakhs). Net Interest (i.e. interest payable to Govt. of India less 189) has been debited to capital work-in-progress.

2. Interest in relation of equity amount (i.e. 220 lakhs). The interest was included under the miscellaneous income. Is the treatment is correct?

Ans. : 1. Correct 2. Wrong.

12) On July 1, 2009 Town co. Purchased for Rs. 5,40,000 a warehouse building and the land on which it is located. The following data were available concerning the property :

	Current appraised Value (Rs.)	Seller's original Cost (Rs.)
Land	200,000	140,000
Warehoused building	300,000	280,000
	500,000	420,000

Town Co. should record the land at

(a) Rs. 140.000 (b) Rs. 180,000 (c) Rs. 200,000 (d) Rs. 216,000

Ans. : (d)

13) During 2011, King Company made the following expenditures relating to its plant building:

Continuing and frequent repairs	Rs. 40,000
Repainted the plant building	Rs. 10,000
Major improvement to the electrical	
Wiring system	Rs. 32,000
Partial replacement of roof tiles	Rs. 14,000

How much should be charged to repair and maintenance expenses in 2011?

(a) Rs. 96,000   (b) Rs. 82,000

(c) Rs 64,000   (d) Rs. 54,000

Ans. : (c)

14) On June 18, 2010, Dell Printing co. incurred the following costs for one of its printing presses.

	Amount (Rs.)
Purchase of collating and stapling attachment	84,000
Installation of attachment	36,000
Replacement parts for overhaul of press	26,000
Labour and overhead in connection with overhaul	14,000

The overhaul resulted in a significant increase in production. Neither the attachment nor the overhaul increased the estimated useful lile of the press. What amount of the above costs should be capitalized?

    (a)　Re. 0　　　　　　　　(b) Rs. 84,000

    (c) Rs. 120,000　　　　　　(d) Rs. 160,000

Ans. : (d)

15) On January 2, 2010, Induga Ltd. bought machinery under a contract that required a down payment of Rs. 10,000, plus 24 monthly payments of Rs. 5,000 each for total cash payment of Rs. 1,30,000. The cash equivalent price of the machinery was Rs. 1,10,000. The machinery was estimated to have useful life of 10 years and salvage value of Rs. 5,000. Induga Ltd. uses straight-line depreciation. In its 2010 income statement, what amount should Induga Ltd. report as depreciation for the machinery?

    (a) Rs. 10,500　　　　　　(b) Rs. 11,000

    (c) Rs. 12,500　　　　　　(d) Rs. 13,000

Ans. : (a)

1.8 AS -14 : Accounting for Amalgamation [Effective Date: 1st April, 1995]

Introduction

Companies have always tried to grow through the development of new products and expansion of existing products in the new potential markets. In many cases, however, the desired growth can be achieved through amalgamation (merger and acquisition).

There are generally three common ways in which companies can amalgamate together to gain advantage in their market. They are as under:

Horizontal It is an amalgamation that takes place between two companies in the same line of business. For example, when a tea company amalgamates with another tea company. The main purpose of horizontal amalgamation is the acquisition of a competitor, by either companies, in the same line of business, which increases the market share and reduce competition in one stroke.

Vertical It is an amalgamation that takes place when a company amalgamates with a supplier or a customer. Both strengthen the amalgamated company's competitive position and may enable it to diversify.

Conglomerate Conglomerate is a diversified group of companies. In a conglomerate amalgamation, the amalgamating companies are in totally unrelated lines of business. The main purpose of conglomeration is diversification of risks.

The main motives for amalgamation are:
  (i) achieving economies of scale;
 (ii) encouraging diversification;
(iii) rapidity in market entry;
(iv) enhancing operating efficiency;
 (v) acquiring technology, marketing channels etc.
(vi) management effectiveness can be availed of through superior management talent.

Scope

This statement deals with accounting for amalgamations and the treatment of any resultant goodwill or reserves. This statement is directed principally to companies although some of its requirements also apply to financial statements of other enterprises.

This statement does not deal with the *acquisition of whole or part of the shares* or whole or part of the assets of another company. The distinguishing feature of an acquisition is that the acquired company is not dissolved.

Definitions

The following terms are used in this statement with the meanings specified:w :
 (a) *Amalgamation* means an amalgamation pursuant to the provisions of the Companies Act, 1956 or any other statute which may be applicable to companies.
 (b) *Transferor company* means the company which is amalgamated into another company.
 (c) *Transferee company* means the company into which a transferor company is amalgamated.

Example:

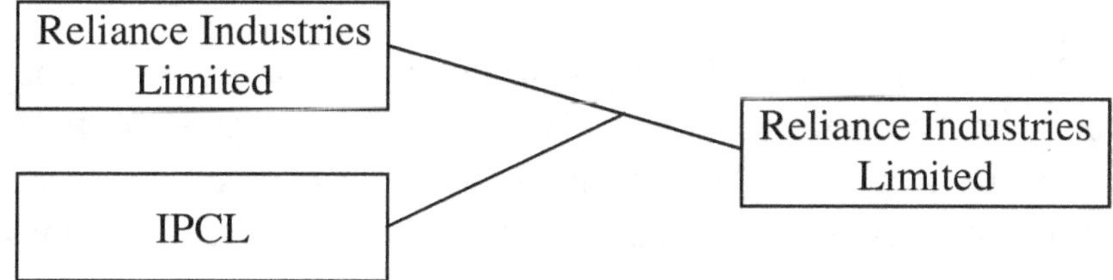

Here, IPCL is the transferor company and Reliance Industries Ltd. is the transferee company.
 (d) *Reserve* means the portion of earnings, receipts or other surplus of an enterprise (whether capital or revenue) appropriated by the management for a general or a specific purpose other than a provision for depreciation or diminution in the value of assets or for a known liability.

(e) *Amalgamation in the nature of merger* is an amalgamation which satisfies all the following conditions.

   (i)   All the assets and liabilities of the transferor company become, after amalgamation, the assets and liabilities of the transferee company.

   (ii) Shareholders holding not less than 90% of the face value of the equity shares of the transferor company (other than the equity shares already held therein, immediately before the amalgamation, by the transferee company or its subsidiaries or their nominees) become equity shareholders of the transferee company by virtue of the amalgamation.

   (iii) The consideration for the amalgamation receivable by those equity shareholders of the transferor company who agree to become equity shareholders of the transferee company is discharged by the transferee company wholly by the issue of equity shares in the transferee company, except that cash may be paid in respect of any fractional shares.

   (iv) The business of the transferor company is intended to be carried on, after the amalgamation, by the transferee company.

   (v) No adjustment is intended to be made to the book values of the assets and liabilities of the transferor company when they are incorporated in the financial statements of the transferee company except to ensure uniformity of accounting policies.

(f) *Amalgamation in the nature of purchase* is an amalgamation which does not satisfy any one or more of the conditions specified in sub-paragraph (e) above

(g) *Consideration for the amalgamation* means the aggregate of the shares and other securities issued and the payment made in the form of cash or other assets by the transferee company to the shareholders of the transferor company.

(h) *Fair value* is the amount for which an asset could be exchanged between a knowledgeable, willing buyer and a knowledgeable, willing seller in an arm's length transaction.

(i) *Pooling of interests* is a method of accounting for amalgamations the object of which is to account for the amalgamation as if the separate businesses of the amalgamating companies were intended to be continued by the transferee company. Accordingly, only minimal changes are made in aggregating the individual financial statements of the amalgamating companies.

Types of Amalgamation

An amalgamation may be either -

(a) an amalgamation in the nature of merger, or

(b) an amalgamation in the nature of purchase.

If *all* the *five* conditions stated in paragraph (e) of definitions are satisfied then it will be treated as an amalgamation in the nature of merger.

If one of the five conditions is not satisfied, it will be treated as amalgamation in the *nature of purchase.*

Methods of Accounting for Amalgamations

There are two methods of accounting for amalgamations:
  (i) the Pooling of Interest Method
 (ii) the Purchase Method

It should be noted that the accounting standard deals with the accounting procedures only in the books of the transferee company.

When an amalgamation is considered to be an amalgamation in the nature of merger, it should be accounted for under the pooling of interests method.

Amalgamation

Amalgamation means an amalgamation as per the provision of Companies Act, 1956 or any other law applicable to Companies. Sections 391 to 394 of Companies Act, 1956 governs the provisions of amalgamation.

Accounting standard in case of amalgamation

This Accounting Standard deals with accounting to be made in the books of Transferee Company in case of amalgamation.

This Accounting Standard is *not applicable* to cases of acquisition of shares when one company acquires / purchases the share of another company and the acquired company is not dissolved and its separate entity continues to exist.

The standard is applicable where acquired company is dissolved and separate entity ceased to exist. The Company acquired is called Transferor Company (selling company). The acquiring company, which is purchasing the business of acquired company, is called Transferee Company (purchasing company).

Purchase consideration

As the Transferee company (purchasing company) is purchasing business of Transferor Company, the transferee company shall pay purchase consideration to the transferor company.

Consideration for the amalgamation means total of the shares and other securities issued and payment made in form of cash or other assets by the transferee company to shareholders of the transferor company.

Types of amalgamation

As per this standard there are two types of amalgamation :
- Amalgamation in the nature of merger.
- Amalgamation in the nature of purchase.

Amalgamation in the nature of merger - An amalgamation is in the nature of merger if following conditions are satisfied :

- All assets and liabilities of Transferor Company are taken over by the transferee company.
- The shareholders holding at least 90% or more of the equity shares of the transferor company become the equity shareholder of the transferee company (shares already held by the transferee com-pany and its subsidiaries are not counted for the purpose of 90% or more limit).
- Consideration for the amalgamation is paid in equity shares by the transferee company to the equity shareholder of the transferor company (except fractional shares can be paid in cash).
- Business of the transferor company is intended to be carried on by the transferee company.
- No adjustment is made in the book values of the assets and liabilities of the transferor company by way of revaluation or otherwise, except the adjustments to ensure uniformity of accounting policies. For example, if transferor company follows the straightline method of depreciation for the fixed assets whereas the transferee company follows the diminishing balance method of depreciation, the transferee company can adjust the book value of fixed assets of the transferor company in the books of transferee company only for the difference of depreciation between straightline method and diminishing balance method. Such adjustment in the book value of fixed assets will not be treated as revaluation.

Amalgamation in the nature of purchase - An amalgamation will be considered in the nature of purchase if any of the conditions regarding .amalgamation in the nature of merger is not satisfied.

Accounting Method

How the accounting for purchased assets and liabilities shall be made in the books of Transferee Company is also prescribed by this standard. As per the standard the accounting methods to be followed are as under :
- in case of merger-pooling interest method
- in case of purchase-purchase method
    It should be noted that AS-14 does not mention at all, how accounting is to be made

in Transferor Company's books, and therefore accounting as per common practice has to be done in the books of Transferor Company irrespective of the type of amalgamation.

Pooling interest method -

- In preparing the financial statement le. balance sheet of the Transferee Company after amalgamation - line by line addition of respective assets and liabilities of transferor and transferee company should be made except for share capital.
- The difference between purchase consideration paid by the transferee company to the transferor company and the amount of share capital (equity + preference capital) of the transferor company should be adjusted with reserves.
- Reserves mean the portion of earning, for example, profit & loss account, general reserve, capital reserves.
- If purchase consideration is more than the share capital of the transferor company (equity + preference share capital), then amount shall be debited to reserves, if reverse is the case, the difference is credited to reserves.

Purchase Method -

- If any of the conditions of merger is not satisfied, then the amalgamation shall be classified as purchase, therefore the purchase method of accounting shall be followed in the books of transferee company.
- As per the purchase method in the books of transferee company assets and liabilities shall be recorded at the value at which these assets and liabilities are taken over by the transferee company from the transferor company; certainly asset do not include fictitious assets and liabilities do not include inside/internal liabilities i.e. reserves and surplus.
- If purchase consideration exceeds the net assets taken over (Net Assets = Assets at their agreed value less liabilities at agreed value), the difference is debited to Goodwill account. If purchase consideration is less than the net assets taken over, the difference is credited to capital reserve.

Statutory Reserves

Statutory Reserves are those reserves, which are created as per the particular statute/ law, under that law, the reserve is created and this law puts some restriction on utilisation and maintenance of reserves for a particular period.

- Separate accounting adjustment / entry is not required tor statutory reserves in the case of merger as all reserves are also recorded in the transferee book including statutory reserves.
- However in case of amalgamation by way of purchase, the reserves being internal liabilities, are not recorded in the books of transferee as per the purchase method.

- Therefore in the case of purchase to comply with the requirements of particular statute, the statutory reserves created in the books of transferor company is to be maintained for some more years in the transferee company books. As per the standard to fulfil the requirement of maintenance of statutory reserves the transferee company shall record the statutory reserves in its books by debiting to amalgamation adjustment account and crediting statutory reserve.
- Amalgamation adjustment account shall be disclosed in balance sheet under the head of "Misc. Expenditure" and statutory reserves under the head "Reserves and surplus".
- When the maintenance of statutory reserves is no longer required, the entry passed should be reversed

Statutory Reserves	Dr.
    To Amalgamation Adjustment Account

Treatment of Goodwill arising on Amalgamation

Goodwill arising on amalgamation represents a payment made in anticipation of future income and it is appropriate to treat it as an asset to be amortised to income on a systematic basis over its useful life. Due to the nature of goodwill, it is frequently difficult to estimate its useful life with reasonable certainty. Such estimation is, however, made on a prudent basis. Accordingly, it is considered appropriate to amortize goodwill over a period not exceeding five years unless a somewhat longer period can be justified. The requirement of AS-26 intangible asset regarding amortization shall not apply to such goodwill.

Disclosure

In first financial statement of transferee company the following disclosures for all amalgamation should be made:
- Names and general nature of business of amalgamating companies.
- Effective date of amalgamation.
- Method of accounting used.
- Particulars of scheme sanctioned under a statute.

Amalgamation accounted under pooling interest method - description and number of shares issued, difference between consideration and net assets acquired. Amalgamtion accounted under purchase method -
- Consideration for the amalgamation.
- Difference between consideration and net assets acquired and treatment thereof including period of amortization of goodwill.

Different Treatment of Reserve - Sometimes the scheme of amalgamation sanctioned under a statute i.e. Companies Act, 1956 or any other statute prescribes a different treatment to be given to reserves of the transferor company after the amalgamation as compared to AS-14 in such case following disclosures should be made :

1. A description of the accounting treatment given to the reserves and the reasons for following a treatment different from that prescribed in AS -14.

2. Deviations in the accounting treatment given to the reserves as prescribed by the scheme of amalgamation sanctioned under the statute as compared to the requirements of AS-14 that would have been followed had no treatment been prescribed by the scheme.

3. The financial effect, if any, arising due to such deviation.

Significant differences among AS-14, IFRS-3 and US GAAP

- IFRS-3 allows only **Purchase Method**. Option of pooling method given under IFRS/IAS-22 has been withdrawn whereas AS-14 allows both pooling of Interest Method and Purchase Method.

- IFRS-3 requires valuation of assets and liabilities at **fair value** whereas AS-14 requires valuation at carrying value.

- IFRS-3 requires Goodwill to be tested for impairment whereas AS-14 requires amortization of Goodwill.

- IFRS-3 requires recognition of negative goodwill immediately in profit and loss account whereas AS-14 requires it to be credited to Capital Reserve.

- IFRS-3 reverse acquisition is accounted assuming acquirer is the acquiree whereas AS-14 does not deal with reverse acquisition.

- IFRS-3 requires valuation of financial assets to be dealt with as per IFRS/IFRS/IAS-39 whereas AS-14 contains no such similar provision.

- Under IFRS-3, provisional values can be used provided they are updated retrospectively within 1 2 months with actual values whereas there is no such provision in AS- 14.

- Under US GAAP, FASB-141 has also been revised and the enterprises can no longer use the pooling of interest method. FAS-142 under US GAAP does not require any amortization of goodwill, as it does not treat it as a wasting asset. FAS- 1 42 now requires goodwill to be written off when impaired.

- Under IFRS, the useful life of goodwill is indefinite hence not amortised. Under AS-14 the amortisation should not exceed 5 years, unless a somewhat longer period is justified.

PROBLEMS

Problem No. 1 : Balance Sheet as on 31 March, 2010

Liabilities	A Ltd.	B Ltd.	Assets	A Ltd.	B Ltd.
Equity Share Capital			Land and Buildings	25,00	15,50
(Rs. 10 per share)	50,00	30,00	Plant and Machinery	32,50	17,00
14% Preference Share			Furniture and Fittings	5,75	3,50
Capital (Rs. 100 each)	22,00	17,00	Investments	7,00	5,00
General Reserve	5,00	2,50	Stock	1 2,50	9,50
Export Profit Reserve	3,00	2,00	Debtors	9,00	10,30
Investment Allowance	-	100	Cash & Bank	7,25	5,20
Reserve					
Profit and Loss Account	7,50	5,00			
13% Debentures	5,00	3,50			
(Rs. 100 each)					
Trade Creditors	4,50	3,50			
Other Current Liabilities	2,00	1,50			
	99,00	66,00		99,00	66,00

A Ltd. takes over B Ltd. on 1 0 April, 2010. The purchase consideration is discharged as follows :

(i) Issued 3,50,000 equity shares of Rs. 10 each at par with the equity shareholders of B Ltd.

(ii) Issued 15% preference shares of Rs. 100 each to discharge the preference shareholders of B Ltd. at 10% premium.

(iii) The debenture holders of B Ltd. will be converted into equivalent number of debentures of A Ltd.

(iv) The statutory reserves of B Ltd. are to be maintained for two more years.

Show the opening entries and the opening balance sheet of A Ltd. after amalgamation on the assumption that

(a) the amalgamation is in the nature of the merger.

Solution :

Amalgamation in the nature of merger : Balance Sheet of A Ltd.

Liabilities	Rs.	Assets	Rs.
Equity Share Capital (Rs. 10 each)	85,00	Land and Buildings	40,50
15% Preference Share Capital (Rs. 100)	18,70	Plant and Machinery	49,50
14% Preference Share Capital (Rs. 100)	22,00	Furniture and Fittings	9,25
General Reserve	80	Investments	12,00
Export Profit Reserve	5,00	Stock	22,00
Investment Allowance Reserve	1,00	Debtors	19,30
Profit and Loss Account	12,50	Cash & Bank	12,45
13% Debentures (Rs. 100 each)	8,50		
Trade Creditors	8,00		
Other Current Liabilities	3,50		
	1,65,00		1,65,00

'The difference between the amount recorded as share capital issued and the amount of share capital of transferor company should be adjusted in reserves. Thus, General Reserve = Rs. '000 [7,50 - (53,70 - 47,00)] = Rs. 80

Purchase Consideration

To Equity Shareholders of B Ltd.	35,00
To Preference Shareholders of B Ltd.	18,70
	53.70

Problem No. 2 : A Ltd. and B Ltd. were amalgamated on and from 1st April, 2010. A new company C Ltd. was formed to take over the business of the existing companies. The Balance Sheets of A Ltd. and B Ltd. as on 31st March, 2010 are given below: (Rs. in lakhs)

Liabilities	A Ltd.	B Ltd.	Assets	A Ltd.	B Ltd.
Share Capital			Fixed Assets		
Equity Shares, of	800	750	Land & Building	550	400
Rs. 100 each					
12% Pref. Shares of	300	200	Plant & Machinery	350	250
Rs. 100 each			Investments	150	50
Reserives and Surplus			Current Assets,		
Revaluation Reserve	150	100	Loans and Advances		
General Reserve	170	150	Stock	350	250

Liabilities	A Ltd.	B Ltd.	Assets	A Ltd.	B Ltd.
Investment Allowance Reserve	50	50	Sundry Debtors	250	300
P & L Account	50	30	Bills Receivable	50	50
Secured Loans:			Cash and Bank	300	200
10% Debentures (Rs. 100 each)	60	30			
Current Liabilities and Provisions					
Sundry Creditors	270	120			
Bills Payables	150	70			
	2,000	1,500		2,000	1,500

Additional Information:

(1) 10% Debenture holders of A Ltd. and B Ltd, are discharged by C Ltd. issuing such number of its 15% Debentures of Rs. 100 each so as to maintain the same amount of interest.

(2) Preference shareholders of the two companies are issued equivalent number of 15% preference shares of C Ltd. at a price of Rs. 150 per share (face value Rs. 100).

(3) C Ltd. will issue 5 equity shares for each equity share of A Ltd. and 4 equity shares for each equity share of B Ltd. The shares are to be issued @ Rs. 30 each, having a face value of Rs. 10 per share.

(4) Investment allowance reserve is to be maintained for 4 more years.

Prepare the Balance Sheet of C Ltd. as on 1st April, 2010 after the amalgamation has been carried out on the basis of amalgamation in the nature of purchase.

Solution.

Balance Sheet of C Ltd. As at 1st April, 2010

Liabilities	Amount	Assets	Amount
Share Catpital		**Fixed Assets**	
70,00,000 Equity Shares of Rs.10 each	700	Goodwill	20
5.00.000 Preference shares of Rs. 100 each	500	Land and Building	950
(all the above shares are allotted as Fully		Plant and Machinery	600
paid up pursuant to contracts without		Investments	200
payment being received in cash)			

Liabilities	Amount	Assets	Amount
Reserve and Surplus		**Current Assets, Loans and Advances**	
Share Premium Account	1650	A. Current Assets	
Investment Allowance Reserve	100	Stock	600
Secured Loans		Sundry debtors	550
15% Debentures	60	Cash and Bank	500
Unsecured Loans	-	B. Loans and Advances	
		Bills Receivable	100
Current Liabilities and Provisions		**Miscellaneous Expenditure**	
A. Current Liabilities		(to the extent not	
Acceptances	220	written off or adjusted)	
Sundry Creditors	390	- Amalgamation	100
B. Provisions		Adjustment Account	
	3620		3620

Working Notes :

(Rs. in lakhs)

	A. Ltd.	B. Ltd
(1) Computation of Purchase Consideration		
(a) Preference Shareholders	450	300
(b) Equity Shareholders	1200	900
	1650	1200
(2) Net Assets Taken Over		
Assets Taken Over :		
Land and Building	550	400
Plant and Machinery	350	250
Investments	150	50
Stock	350	250
Sundry Debtors	250	300
Bills Receivable	50	50
Cash and Bank	300	200
	2000	1500

Less : Liabilities taken over :				
Debentures	40		20	
Sundry Creditors	270		120	
Bills Payable	150	460	70	210
Net Assets taken over		1540		1290
Purchase consideration		1650		1200
Goodwill		110		
Capital Reserve				90

Note : Since Investment Allowance Reserve is to be maintained for 4 years, it is carried forward by a corresponding debit lo Amalgamation Adjustment Account in accordance with AS-14.

Problem No. 3 : Three subsidiary companies viz,. Company A, B and C, are being merged into another company, viz., Company D. The transferor and transferee companies have received approvals for merger from respective High Courts in January and February, 2010 respectively.

Required :

(a) What is the nature of the 'reserves' (whether capital or general reserves) for the purpose of AS-14 (Para 35) and for the purpose of giving effect to the scheme of amalgamation of the Company D in its books of account ?

(b) Whether such reserves are available for the purpose of distribution to shareholders as dividends and/or bonus shares.

Solution :

(a) The difference between the issued share capital of the transferee company and the share capital of the transferor companies should be treated as capital reserve for the purpose of Para 35 of AS-14 and for the purpose of giving effect to the scheme of amalgamation of Company D in its books of account.

(b) Reserve created on amalgamation is not available for the purpose of distribution to shareholders as dividend and/or bonus shares.

EXERCISES

1) NDA Corp acquired all the assets and liabilities of Induga Corp for consideration of Rs. 50 crores. However Induga Corp was not dissolved and continued to exist. NDA Corp want to know whether acquisition accounting should be made as per AS-14.

2) What is merger as per AS-14? What method of accounting is suggested in merger?

3) Goodwill arising on acquisition as per AS-14 is to be treated as per AS-26.

1.9 AS - 21 : Consolidated Financial Statement

Objectives

The objective of this statement is to present financial statements of a parent and its subsidiary(ies) as a single economic entity. In other words the holding company and its subsidiary(ies) are treated as one entity for the preparation of these consolidated financial statements. Consolidated profit/loss account and consolidated balance sheet are prepared for disclosing the total profit/loss of the group and total assets and liabilities of the group. As per this accounting standard, the consolidated balance sheet if prepared should be prepared in the maner prescribed by this statement.

What is parent

A parent is an enterprise that has one or more subsidiaries.

What is subsidiary

It is an enterprise that is controlled by another enterprise know parent.

Control

Control can be exercised directly or indirectly (through subsidiary) by purchasing more than 50% of the voting power of an enterprise or by-controlling composition of board of directors/governing body. Generally it is done by purchasing more than 50% of the equity shares (voting, power) of an enterprise.

Format of consolidated Financial Statements

These are prepared/presented in the same format as that followed by the parent for preparation of its separate financial statements.

Application of other accounting standards in preparation of consolidated financial statements.

As per this accounting standards while preparing the consolidate financial statements, the other accounting standards shall apply in the same manner as they apply in preparing the separate financial statements.

Accounting for investments made by parents in its subsidiary (ies) while preparing separate financial statements - A parent should account for the investment in subsidiary(ies) in accordance with AS-13. *"Accounting for investments"*. As per Accounting Standard-13, the investment made by a parent in subsidiary(ies) should be recorded at cost.

Consolidated financial statements are no substitute for separate financial statements

Consolidated financial statements are not the substitute for separate financial statements of a parent and its subsidiary(ies). In other words, a parent and its subsidiary(ies) shall prepare separate financial statements as per governing law. The consolidated financial statement rnadc by a parent is in addition to the separate financial statements.

Scope of consolidated financial statement

A parent, which is required to prepare the consolidated financial statements, should consolidate the financial statements of all its subsidiary(ies), whether domestic or foreign.

Exceptions

Consolidated financial statements are not required to be prepared even if parent-subsidiary(ies) relationship exists when -

- A parent acquires the control (investment in subsidiary), which is intended to be temporary as the investment (control) is to be disposed in the near future.
- The subsidiary operates under severe long-term restrictions and due to this its ability to transfer the funds to parent is significantly weakened.

Dissimilar activities of parent and its subsidiaries cannot be the ground for non-consolidation of financial statements.

Consolidation procedure

In preparing consolidated financial statements the financial state-ments (Balance sheet and profit/loss account) of the parent and its subsidiaries should be combined/added on line by line basis by adding the like items of assets, like ilems of liabilities, like items of income and expense.

- The cost of investment of parent in each subsidiary should be cancelled/eliminated with parent's portion of equity of each subsidiary on the date on which the investment was acquired in each subsidiary. Parents portion of equity means share of parent (holding) in equity share capital of subsidiary + share in reserve and surplus of the subsidiary on the date of acquisition of share. In other words, parent's portion of equity in each subsidiary(ics) on the date of acquisition is paid up share capital held by holding + Share of pre-acquisition profits.
- If cost of investment in a subsidiary exceeds the parent's (holding portion of equity i.e. paid up capital held by the holding + share, pre-acquisition profits on the date of consolidation, the excess debited in goodwill, and such goodwill arising due to consolidate procedure should be shown as an asset in consolidated financi statement.
- When the cost of investment in subsidiary is less than the paid equity capital held by holding (parent) + share of pre-acquisition profits, the difference is credited to capital reserve and this capital reserve is shown in consolidated financial statement under the head 'Reserve and surplus'.
- Minority interest - should be calculateda and shown in the consolidated financial statements separately in separate head. Minority interest means the portion of net assets of subsidiary on the date consolidation not controlled by the parent itself or

through subsidiary. Minority interest - paid up equity capital held outsider (outside the group) + share of 'reserve and surplus' ***on the date of consolidation***. Preference share capital not held by parent or group is also shown along with minority interest.

- While calculating minority interest, share of minority in net profit of consolidated subsidiaries for the reporting period should calculated and charged against the consolidated profit: consequently balance profit after charging minority interest represent the parent (holding Co.) share in profit which will be shown unde the head 'Reserve & surplus' in consolidated balance sheet.
- Intra-group balances and transactions i.e. inter-company debtor / creditors inter-company purchases/sales and resulting unrealized profit shall be eliminated in full.

Unrealised losses - Unrealized losses from intra-group transactions should also be eliminated if recoverable amount is more than cost of transactions, for example, if X Ltd. (holding Co.) sells good costing Rs. 5,00,000 to its subsidiary Y Ltd. at Rs. 4,00,000 and on the date of consolidation. The goods are lying in stock of Y Ltd. The recoverable amount of stock is-Rs. 5,50,000; as the recoverable amount is more than the cost of the transaction, the unrealized loss of Rs. 1,00,000 should eliminated by adding to stock and adding to consolidated profit and loss account in consolidated Balance Sheet.

It should be noted that if unrealized losses are on account of intra-group sale/purchase of assets - the recoverable amount shall have the meaning as described in accounting standard on "impairment of assets".

Consolidation when different reporting date - Financial state-ment of parents and its subsidiary used for consolidation are generally of same date, however when reporting dates are different and it is not practical to prepare the financial statements of subsidiary of the same date, the different reporting date financial statement can be consolidated making adjustment for the effects of significant transactions that occur between those dates and parent financial statements provided difference is not more than **six months**. If parent and its subsidiaries are following different accounting policies, the consolidated financial statement should be prepared using uniform accounting policies, if it is not practicable, then the items in which different accounting policies have been followed should be disclosed.

Disposal of investment in a subsidiary

The difference between the proceeds from the disposal of investments in a subsidiary and the carrying amount of its assets less liabilities as of the date of disposal is recognized in the consolidated statement of profit and loss as the profit or loss on the disposal of the investment in a subsidiary.

Successive purchase of shares in a subsidiary by the parent

If an enterprise purchases two or more times the investment of other enterprises and eventually obtains control of the other enterprise the consolidated financial statement is prepared from the date on which holding subsidiary relationship is established. Further, in such cases goodwill or capital reserve on consolidation should be determined on step by step basis, however if small investments are made over a period of time, then the date of latest major investment which resulted in control, should be considered as date of investment for all successive purchases and, accordingly, calculation of goodwill/capital reserve should be made.

Minority interest is in negative

When minority interest comes in negative (minus), this should be adjusted against majority interest. In other words, negative minority interest will not be shown in consolidated balance sheet. If the subsidiary subsequently reports profits, all such profits should be allocated to majority interest until minority share of losses previously absorbed by majority has been recovered.

Arrears of cumulative preference share of a subsidiary

If the subsidiary has arrears of cumulative preference shares which are held outside the group, then the holding company share of profits is calculated after charging the arrear of cumulative preference dividend of a subsidiary, whether declared or not.

Disclosure

Following disclosure should be made in consolidated financial statements :
- List of all subsidiaries.
- Proportion of ownership interest
- Nature of relationship between parent and subsidiary whether direct control or control through subsidiaries.
- Name of the subsidiary of which reporting date are different.
- The fact for different accounting policies applied for preparation consolidated financial statements.
- If consolidation of particular subsidiary has not been made as the grounds allowed in accounting standards the reason for consolidating should be disclosed.

Explanation/Guidance issued by the ICAI

The ICAI has issued the following clarification on AS-21 :

One subsidiary has two parents

If an enterprise is controlled by two enterprises - one controls by virtue of majority voting power and the other controls by virtue of controlling of the composition of the Board of Directors. In this case there will be two parent / holding enterprises of one subsidiary. The question arises which enterprises should consolidate the financial statement of the The ICAI has clarified that both the enterprises (Holding) should consolidate the financial statements of the same subsidiary enterprise.

Tax expense

It is clarified by the ICAI that Tax expense appearing in the separate financial statements of parent and subsidiaries do not require adjustments for the purpose of consolidation and therefore simply aggregated in consolidated financial statements.

Voting power shares are held as stock in trade

It is clarified that where an enterprise owns majority of voting power virtue of ownership of the share of another enterprises and all the shares held as stock in trade with a view to their subsequent disposal in the near future then control will be considered temporary (para 21.9) therefore no consolidation of financial statements are required to be prepared.

Notes and Information Disclosed in Separate Financial Statement The ICAI has clarified that for preparing consolidated financial statemeals following notes and statutory information disclosed in financial statements of the parent and/or subsidiary need not to be included in the consolidated financial statements as these notes and statutory information are not having any effect on the true and fair view of the consolidated financial statements:

- Source from which bonus shares are issued, e.g., capitalization of profits or Reserves or from Share Premium Account.
- The name(s) of the small scale industrial undertaking(s) to whom the company owes a sum exceeding Rs. 1 lakh, which is outstanding for more than 30 days,
- A statement of investments (whether shown under Investment or under Current Assets as stock-in-trade) separately classifying trade investments and other investments, showing the names of the bodies corporate (indicating separated the names of the bodies corporate under the same management) in whose shares or debentures, investments have been made (including all investments, whether existing or not, made subsequent to the date as at which the previous balance sheet was made out) and the nature and extent of the investment so made in each such body corporate.
- Quantitative information in respect of sales, raw materials consumed, Opening and closing slocks of goods produced/traded and purchases made, wherever applicable.
- A statement showing the computation of net profits in accordance with section 349 of the Companies Act, 1956, with relevant details of the calculation of the commissions payable by way of percentage of such profits to the directors (including managing directors) or manager (if any).
- In the case of manufacturing companies, quantitative information in regard to the

licensed capacity- (where licence is in force); the installed capacity; and the actual production.

- Value of imports calculated on C.I.F. basis by the company during the financial year in respect of : -
    (i) Raw materials;
    (ii) Components and spare parts;
    (iii) Capital goods;
- Expenditure in foreign currency during the financial year on account of royalty, know-how, professional and consultation fees, interest, and other matters;
- Value of imported raw materials, spare parts and components consumed during the financial year and the value of all indigenous raw materials, spare parts and components similarly consumed and the percentage of each to the total consumption;
- The amount remitted during the year in foreign currencies account of dividends, with a specific mention of the number of non resident shareholders, the number of shares held by them on which dividends were due and the year to which the dividends related:
- Earnings in foreign exchange classified under the following head namely : -
    1. Export of goods calculated on F.O.B. basis;
    2. Royalty, know-how, professional and consultation fees;
    3. Interest and dividend;
    4. Other income, indication the nature thereof.

Applicability of Accounting Standard to an Unlisted Indian Company - The Council of the Institute of Chartered Accountants of India has issue an Announcement that in case the Indian company, which is a subsidiary the listed foreign company, it would also considered as a Level - I enterprise for the reason that it is a subsidiary of another Level-I enterprise. In case the parent foreign company is not required to prepare its financial statements as per the Indian GAAPs, its India subsidiary would not be considered to be a Level-I enterprise provided it does not meet any other criteria for becoming Level-I enterprise as per the said scheme.

Transitional provisions

On the first occasion that consolidated financial statements presented, comparative figures for the previous period need not presented. In all subsequent years full comparative figures for previous period should be presented in the consolidated financial statements.

Significant differences among AS, IFRS/IAS and US GAAP

Control - As per AS-21, the definition of "Control" includes indirect control which may exist without majority holding. IAS-27 defines "Control" as the power to govern the financial and operating policies enterprise so as to obtain benefits from activities. As per

US GAAP (SAFS 94 and ARB 51), only majority owned undertakings are considered as subsidiaries.

Requirements - As per AS-21, consolidated financial statements required in addition to, and not in lieu of, separate financial stateme if the enterprises are required to prepare the consolidated financial statements under any statute. Presently the listed companies are quired to prepare consolidated financial statements. IAS-27 and the GAAP compulsorily require preparing consolidated financial statemt unless it is itself a wholly owned subsidiary.

US GAAP (Statement 94) does not permit parent company only financial statements to be issued as general purpose financial statements. This is a significant difference from the practice in any other countries in the world where there is a requirement to publish the parent financial statements separately, as a result, American companies provide less information than companies in many other countries.

Goodwill - As per AS-21, goodwill or capital reserve is determined on historical cost basis; no prescription for amortization of goodwill. As per IAS-27, goodwill or capital reserve is determined on the basis of assets or liabilities considered at their fair value; amortization is also provided.

Differential period - As per AS-21, differential period between dates of parent and subsidiary, if do not coincide should not exceed six months which is in line with the requirement of section 212 of the Companies Act, 1956. As per IAS-27 and US GAAP, differential should not exceed three month.

Other statutory requirements - In India, the Indian Companies Act, 1956, prescribes under section 212 the requirements for disclosure which are in addition to the requirement of the disclosure as per AS-21. There are no corresponding statutory requirements under US GAAP.

Deferred tax - Both IAS-27 and US GAAP require that if income-taxes have been paid on inter-company profits on assets remaining within the group, those taxes are deferred until the related assets are sold in an arm's length transaction. This principle does not apply under Indian GAAP.

Investment in subsidiary - IAS-27 also provides guidance for accounting for investment in subsidiaries in a parent's separate financial statements. IAS-27 requires that a parent's investment in a subsidiary to be accounted for in the parent's separate financial statements (a) at cost, (b) using the equity method as described in IAS-28 or (c) as available for sale of financial assets as described in IAS-39. Under AS-21, in a parent's separate financial statements, investments in subsidiary should be - accounted for in accordance with AS-13. "Accounting for investment", which is cost as adjusted for any permanent diminution in value of those investment.

Exception of consolidation - AS-21 provides that a subsidiary should be excluded from consolidation when it operates under severe long-term restrictions which significantly impair its ability to transfer funds to the parent. However, IAS-27 specifically provides that consolidation is required till control is not lost for such subsidiary. US GAAP does not prescribe such condition for exclusion from consolidation, however, US GAAP (FAS 94) provides that if the subsidiary operates under foreign exchange restrictions, controls or other government-imposed uncertainties which cast significant doubt on the parent's ability to control the subsidiary (FAS 94.13).

PROBLEMS

Problem No. 1 : The summarized Balance Sheet of A Ltd. and B Ltd. are as follows : Balance Sheet as on 31 st March, 2010.

Libilities	A Ltd.	B Ltd
Equity shares	6,00,000	4,00,000
6% preference shares	-	1,00,000
General Reserve	1,60,000	80,000
Profit & Loss Account	20,000	25,000
Bills Payable	1,30,000	1,20,000
Creditors	2,30,000	2,85,000
Proposed dividend	60,000	40,000
	12,00,000	10,50,000
Assets :	**A Ltd.**	**B Ltd**
Goodwill	-	20,000
Fixed Assets	3,50,000	2,50,000
Investment	3,60,000	90,000
Stock	2,20,000	3,60,000
Debtors	2,10,000	2,50,000
Bills Receivable	40,000	35,000
Cash	20,000	45,000
	12,00,000	10,50,000

A Ltd. purchased interest in B Ltd. by acquiring ils 3/4th equity share capital at a premium of 20% on 1st April, 2009. Prepare a consolidated balance sheet in the books of A Ltd. as on 31st March, 2010. The following further information is to be taken into account:

- Profit and loss account of B Ltd. includes an amount of Rs. 20,000 brought forward from the year 2008-09.

- Creditors of A Ltd. include an amount of Rs. 12,000 for purchases from B Ltd., which are still unsold. B Ltd. sells goods at 20% above cost.
- B Ltd. remitted a cheque for Rs. 10,000 on 31st March, 2010 which was received by A Ltd. in the month of April 2010.
- Bills receivable worth Rs. 20,000 out of total bills receivable of Rs. 25,000 received from B Ltd. were discounted by A Ltd. and B Ltd. had endorsed to its creditors all the bills receivable received from A Ltd. amounting to Rs. 15,000.
- The directors of A Ltd. and B Ltd. have proposed a dividend of 10% on equity share capital for the year 2009-10.

Solution :

Consolidation of Balance Sheet of A Ltd. and its subsidiary B Ltd.

1. Parents (holding company) A Ltd. portion of equity in subsidiary B Ltd. on the date of acquisition to be cancelled with the investment in subsidiary for this we have to make analysis of profit into pre-acquisition and post acquisition

	Pre-acquisition Profit	Post acquisition Profit
Profit / Loss A/c	20,000	5,000
G.R.	80,000	-
	1,00,000	5,000
Minority Interest 1/4	25,000	1,250
	75,000	3,750

Note : Profit or loss, reserves balance of subsidiary on the date of consolidation has to be analysed between pre and post acquisitions.

Cost of Control

Cost of investment in subsidiary to be cancelled with holding company portion of equity

Cost of investment in subsidiary		3,60,000
Paid up share capital held by holding	3,00,000	3,75,000
Pre-acquisition profit share	75,000	
Capital Reserve		15,000

Minority interest

Paid-up value of shares held by minority		1,00,000
Share in reserves & surplus		
Pre-acquisition	25,000	
Post acquisition	1,250	26,250
		1, 26,250
		1,00,000 2,26,250

Consolidated Balance Sheet of A Ltd. and its subsidiary B Ltd. on 31st March, 2010

Liabilities	Rs.	Assets		Rs.
Equity Share Capital	6,00,000	Goodwill	20,000	
General Reserve	1,60,000	Less : C.R. on		
Profit & Loss A/c 20,000		Consolidation	15,000	5,000
Share from Subsidiary 3,750		Fixed Assets		
		(3,50,000 + 2,50,000)		6,00,000
Less : Unrealized profit 2,000	21,750	Investment (other		
		than in subsidiary)		90,000
Bills Payable (1,30,000 +				
1.20,000 - 5,000)	2,45,000	Stock	5,80,000	
Creditors (2,30,000 +	5,03,000	Less : Unrealized	2,000	578,000
2,85,000-12,000)		profit 12000 X 1 /6		
Proposed Dividend	1,00,000	Debtors	4,60,000	
Minority interest	2,26,250	Less: Inter Company		
		debts	12,000	
			4.48,000	
		Less : Cheque in transit 10.000		4,38,000
		Bills Receivable	75,000	
		Inter company B/R	5,000	70,000
		Cheque in transit		10,000
		Cash		65,000
	18,56,000			18,56,000

Note:

- Consolidation done by line-by-line addition of respective assets & liabilities^
- Inter-company profits from stock eliminated 100%.
- Inter-company debtors, B/R eliminated.
- Minority interest shown separately

Problem No. 2 : NDA Ltd. own 75% of the voting power share of Induga Ltd. on 1-4-2009 for Rs. 2,000,000. The net asset of Induga Ltd. on 1 -4-2009 was Rs. 2,000,000. On 1-10-2010 the investment in Induga Ltd. was sold for Rs. 3,100,000. The net asset Induga Ltd. on 31-3-2010 and 30-9-2010 was Rs. 3,000,000 and Rs. 3,200,000 respectively, the difference representing the profit for the six month period ended on 30-9-2010. Calculate the profit/loss on disposal of the investment in subsidiary to be recognised in the consolidated profit & loss account.

Solution :

Net Assets of Induga Ltd.		**Amount (Rs.)**
(Subsidiary) on the date of disposal (1-10-2010)		3,200,000
Less: Minority interest 25%		800,000
NDA (parents) shares in Induga Ltd.		2,400,000
Proceeds from disposal of subsidiary		3,100,000
Less: Parents share in the net assets of the subsidiary		
(75% of Rs. 3,200,000)		2,400,000
		700,000
Less: Goodwill in consolidated Balance Sheet		
(cost of investment)	2,000,000	
Less: 75% of net assets	Rs. 1,500,000	500,000

Gain on disposal to be recognized in consolidated profit & loss A/c Rs. 200,00

Problem No. 3 : NDA Ltd. made the following purchases of shares in Induga Ltd.:

Date	Number of shares purchased	Cost	Balance of Induga Ltd.'s reserve
1-3-2005	10,000	25	120
5-5-2007	5,000	15	140
1-4-2009	45,000	200	160

The final accounts of NDA Ltd. and Induga Ltd. for the year 2009 were as follows:

(a) Profit and loss accounts for the year ended 3 1st December, 2009

		(Rs. in '000)
	NDA Ltd.	**Induga Ltd.**
Profit before tax	200	120
Tax	60	40
Profit after tax	140	80
Beginning retained profit	160	160
Ending retained profit	300	240

(b) Balance sheet as at 31st December, 2009

		(Rs. in '000)
	NDA Ltd.	**Induga Ltd.**
Land	500	300
Investment in Induga Ltd.	240	—
Current assets	60	150
	800	450
Share capital, par value of Re.1	400	100
Retained profit	300	240
Current liabilities	100	110
	800	450

The final accounts of NDA Ltd. and Induga Ltd. for the year 2010 are as tollows

(a) Profit and loss accounts for the year ended 31st December, 2010

		(Rs. in '000)
	NDA Ltd.	**Induga Ltd.**
Profit before tax	100	90
Tax	30	30
Profit after tax	70	60
Beginning retained profit	300	240
Ending retained profit	370	300

(b) Balance sheets at 31st December, 2010

	NDA Ltd.	(Rs. in 000's) Induga Ltd.
Land	500	300
Investment in Induga Ltd.	240	-
Current assets	210	150
	950	450
Share capital, par value of Re.1	400	100
Retained profit	370	300
Current liabilities	180	50
	950	450

Induga Ltd.'s land was revalued of Rs. 3,10,000 on 1st March, 2005 revalued Rs. 3,20,000 on 5th May, 2007 and Rs. 3,40,000 on 1st April, 2009.

The group amortises goodwill on consolidation on a straight-line basis over a period of five years. A full year's amortisation is provided if the goodwill exists for more than six months during the year.

Each of the share acquisition transactions is considered to be significant, therefore the step-by-step method is to be used.

The group uses the whole-year approach in presenting the consolidated profit at loss account.

Required : Prepare the consolidated profit and loss account and consolidate balance sheet for NDA Ltd. and its subsidiary for the years 2009 and 2010 also pass consolidated journal entries.

Solution : Consolidated accounts.

NDA Ltd. and its subsidiary consolidated Profit & Loss Account
for the year ended 31-12-2009

	(Rs. in '000)
Profit before tax (200+120-12 Goodwill amortisation)	308
Tax	100
Profit after tax	208
Minority interest (80 × 40%)	32
Profit before pre-acquisition profit	176
Pre-acquisition profit	9
Profit attributable to shareholders	167
Beginning retained profit (160-91-64+160)	165
Ending retained profit	332

NDA Ltd. and its subsidiary consolidated Balance Sheet as at 31-12-2009

(Rs. in 000's)

Goodwill on consolidation	48
Land	840
Current assets	210
	1098
Share capital	400
Retained profit	332
Revaluation reserve	4
Minority interest	152
Current liabilities	210
	1,098

For 2010

(I)   Consolidated journal entries

Amt. (Rs.)

(a)	Share capital	Dr.	60,000	
	Beginning retained profit	Dr.	1,00,000	
	Land	Dr.	20,000	
	Goodwill on consolidation	Dr.	60,000	
	To Investment in Induga Ltd.			2,40,000
	(Elimination of investment account)			
(b)	Profit before tax	Dr.	12,000	
	Beginning retained profit	Dr.	12,000	
	To Goodwill on consolidation			24,000
	(Amortization of goodwill)			
(c)	Profit & Loss A/c	Dr.	24,000	
	To Minority Interest			24,000
	(Minority interest in profit)			
(d)	Share capital	Dr.	40,000	
	Land A/c	Dr.	16,000	
	Beginning retained profit		96,000	
	To Minority Interest			1,52,000
	(Minority interest)			
(e)	Land A/c	Dr.	4,000	
	To Revaluation Reserve			4,000

(II) Consolidation worksheet

(Rs. in 000's)

	NDA Ltd	Induga Ltd.	Adjustments Dr.	Cr.	Consolidated Balances
Profit before tax	100	90	12		178
Tax	30	30			60
Profit after tax	70	60			118
Minority interest	-	-	24		24
Group profit	-	-			94
Beginning	300	240	100		
Retained Profit			12		
			96		332
Ending retained profit	370	300			426
Goodwill	-	-	60	24	36
Land	500	300	40		840
Investment	240	-		240	-
Current assets	210	150			360
Share Capital	400	100	60		
			40		400
Retained profit	370	300			426
Current liabilities	180	50			230
Minority Interest	-	-	24		
			152		176
Revalued reserve			4		4

(III) Consolidated accounts

NDA Ltd. and its subsidiary consolidated Profit & Loss Account for the year ended 31-12-2010

(Rs. in '000)

Profit before tax	178
Tax	60
Profit after tax	118
Minority interest	24
Profit attributable to shareholders	94
Beginning retained profit	332
Ending retained profit	426

NDA Ltd. and its subsidiary consolidated Balance Sheet as at 31-12-2010

(Rs. in '000)

Goodwill on consolidation	36
Land	840
Current assets	360
	1,236
Share capital	400
Retained profit	426
Revaluation reserve	4
Minority interest	176
Current liabilities	230
	1,236

(1) The amount of prc-acquisition profit, valuation of land and goodwill on consolidation are determined as shown :

Pre-acquisition profit in beginning retained profit

$10\% \times$ Rs. 1,20,000 = Rs. 12,000

$5\% \times$ Rs. 1,40,000 = Rs. 7,000

$45\% \times$ Rs. 1,60,000 = Rs. 72,000

Total = Rs. 91,000

Prc-acquisition profit in current year's profit

$= 45\% \times 3/12 \times$ Rs. 80,000 = Rs. 9,000

Revaluation profit of land :

$10\% \times$ Rs. 10,000 = Rs. 1,000

$5\% \times$ Rs. 20,000 = Rs. 1,000

$45\% \times$ Rs. 40,000 = Rs. 18,000

Total = Rs. 20,000

Goodwill on consolidation :

Rs. 9,000 + Rs. 20,000)

= Rs. 2,40,000 - (Rs. 1.00,000 × 60% + Rs. 91,000

= Rs. 60,000

(2) For all subsequent years, the determination of pre-acquisition reserve, valuation of land and goodwill on consolidation will be determined as shown above.

(3) The group's 2010 beginning retained profit is, as it should, equal to the group's 2009 ending retained profit. The figure of Rs. 3,32,000 can be proved by adding NDA Ltd.'s retained profit of Rs. 3,00,000 to the group share of Induga Ltd.'s post-acquisition reserve of Rs. 44,000 [10% × (Rs. 2,40,000 - Rs. 1,20,000) + 5% × (Rs. 2,40,000 -

Rs. 1.40,000) + 45% × (Rs. 2.40,000 - Rs. 1,80,000)], less goodwill amortization of Rs. 12,000 (Rs. 60,000 × 1 /5).

(4) The Group's 2010 ending retained profit of Rs. 4,26,000 can be proved by adding NDA Ltd.'s ending retained profit of Rs. 3,70,000 to the group's interest in Induga Ltd.'s post-acquisition profit in the ending retained profit of Rs. 80,000 (Rs. 3,00,000 × 60% - Rs. 1,00,000 pre-acquisition profit), less goodwill amortization for two years of Rs, 24,000 (Rs. 60,000 × 2/5).

Problem No. 4 : H Ltd. owns 60% of S Ltd, acquired on 1st April 2010 for Rs. 90 lakhs. At that date 60% of the net assets were Rs. 80 lakhs, thereby resulting in a goodwill of Rs. 10 lakhs. The total net assets of S Ltd. on 31st March 2011 and 30th September 2011 were Rs. 1.80 crores and Rs. 2 crores respectively, the difference of Rs. 20 lakhs representing the profit for the period. On October 1, 2011, half of its investment in S Ltd. (30%) was sold for an amount of Rs. 2.50 crores. As a result on that date the subsidiary has become an associate. You are required to explain the nature of the relationship between the two companies on the relevant dates and the accounting adjustments that are necessary as a result of any change in the relationship. The profit arising on part sale of investment, carrying value of the portion unsold and good will/capital reserve that arises on change in nature of the investment may also be worked out by you.

Solution :

The profit or loss on the disposal of the part of the investment in S Ltd. and the carrying value of the investment retained would be computed as follows:

Particulars		Amt. (Rs.)
Proceeds on disposal of investment in S Ltd.		2,50,00,000
Less :		
Total net assets of S Ltd. on the date of disposal	2,00,00,000	
Less : Minority Interest in S Ltd. on the date of disposal (40% of Rs. 2 crores)	(80,00,000)	
Share of H Ltd in S Ltd on date of disposal	1,20,00,000	
Add: Goodwill on acquisition	10,00.000	
Total value of investment in CFS of H Ltd.	1,30,00.000	
Less : Carrying value of investment which is proposed to be disposed (1.30 crores × 30% ÷ 60%)	(65,00,000)	(65,00,000)
Profit on disposal of part of the investment		1,85,00,000
Carrying value of associate retained in the CFS	65,00,000	

Consequently, Rs. 65 lakhs would be considered the cost of the investment retained in H Ltd. (forming 30% equity). This amount would be used to apply the equity method of accounting as specified in AS 23 as follows :

Particulars	Amt. (Rs.)
Carrying value of investment (cost) as at October 1, 2011	65,00,000
Less:	
Share in the value of equity of S Ltd. as at the date the investment transformed from a subsidiary to an associate i.e., the date of disposal of the part of investment (30% of Rs. 2 crores)	(60,00,000)
Goodwill arising on such investment included in carrying amount of investment	5,00,000

Henceforth (after October 1, 2011) the profits arising in A Ltd. (earlier S Ltd.) will be included to the extent of 30% in the profit and loss account and investment schedule of the CFS. The carrying amount of the investment at the date that it ceases to be a subsidiary is regarded as cost thereafter. Therefore, when the subsidiary relationship ceases and in its place an associate's relationship comes into existence, the carrying amount of the investment at the date that it ceases to be a subsidiary regarded as cost of investment in the associate. Goodwill / capital reserve arising on account of the change in the nature of the investment will be computed as on the date of such change. Accordingly, when a part of the investment in a subsidiary is disposed of during the year such investment takes the form of an investment in an associate, the results of operations of the subsidiary will be included in the consolidated statement of profit and loss for the period from the beginning of the period until it ceased to be a subsidiary.

EXERCISES

1) Is it mandatory to consolidate the subsidiary financial statements with holding as per Companies Act, 1956.

2) State the circumstances when consolidation of subsidiary is not done.

3) X Ltd. is textile manufacturing company it has purchased 75% equity shares of Y Ltd., which is Software Company. X Ltd. did not consolidate the accounts of Y Ltd. on the pretext that subsidiary business is entirely different and it does not make sense to consolidate the subsidiary (Y Ltd.) accounts. Comment.

Ans. : [Contention is not correct as per AS-21]

4) While consolidating the financial statement the minority interest was calculated as (-) Rs. 50,000. The Accountant wants to show it in assets side of consolidated balance sheet. Comment.

Ans. : [Rs. 50,000 to be adjusted with majority interest]

5) How is consolidation of a subsidiary done, when, for the first time since acquisition, it has come out of the restrictions that prohibit consolidation of subsidiaries, although the acquisition of the subsidiary by the parent occurred in an earlier year?

Ans. : [From the date of acquisition only not from the date of the subsidiary was out of the restrictions.]

6) Can goodwill and capital reserve arising on consolidation of different subsidiaries be set off, or should they be recorded and disclosed at gross.

Ans. : [May be set off]

7) Is it necessary that preference dividend in respect of outstanding cumulative preference share held outside the group needs to be adjusted against profit or loss of the subsidiary in calculating holding company shares in profit of the subsidiary irrespective of the profitability of the subsidiary even if there is loss and there is no distributable profit.

Ans. : [Yes]

8) NDA Ltd. paid Rs. 1,00,000 to acquire 60% of Induga Ltd. in 2008 when Induga Ltd.'s net assets at book value were represented by share capital of Rs. 1,00,000 and retained profit of Rs. 30,000, also at this date Induga Ltd.'s land carried a book value of Rs. 1,00.000 was revalued at Rs. 1,20,000.

NDA Ltd. paid Rs. 60,000 to acquire an additional 20% of Induga Ltd. in 2010 when Induga Ltd's net assets at book value were represented by share capital of Rs. 1,00,000 and retained profit of Rs. 50,000. Also, at this date, Induga Ltd.'s land of Rs. 1,00,000 was-revalued at Rs. 1,50,000.

The group policy on goodwill is capitalization and amortisation. The goodwill is to be amortised on a straight-line basis over a period of five years, commencing from the year the subsidiary company is acquired. Calculate goodwill for 2008 and 2010 on acquisition and its amortization.

Ans. : [Goodwill 2008 - Rs. 10,000, 2010 - Rs. 20,000]

9) The balance sheets of NDA Ltd. and its subsidiaries, induga Ltd. and Sun Ltd as at 31st December, 2010 were as follows :

(Rs. in 000's)

	NDA Ltd.	Induga Ltd.	Sun Ltd
Investment, at cost			
4,000,000 share in Induga Ltd.	5,000	-	-
1,000,000 share in Sun Ltd,	1,000	-	-
Other assets	6,000	6,500	1,500
	12,000	6,500	1,500
Share capital, @ Re.1 per share	8,000	5,000	1,000
Retained profits	4,000	1,500	500
	12,000	6,500	1,500

Induga Ltd. was acquired in January 2008 when the value of its net assets represented by share capital of Rs. 50,00,000 and retained profits of Rs. 10,00,000. Sun Ltd. was acquired when it was formed in 2009.

The group amortises goodwill on consolidation on a straight-line basis over years and provides for a full year's amortisation if the goodwill exists for more the six months in the year.

On 1st January, 2011, NDA Ltd. sold all its shareholding in Induga Ltd. for cash consideration of Rs. 60,00,000.

Required : Calculate the profit or loss on disposal of shares in subsidiary from:

(a) Holding company view point

(b) From consolidated group view point

Ans. : [(a) Profit Rs. 10,00,000. (hi Profit Rs. 7,20,000]

10) The 31st December, 2009 balance sheet of NDA Ltd. arid its subsidiary, Induga; Ltd., were as follows :

(Rs. in 000's)

	NDA Ltd.	Induga Ltd
Investment, at cost		
90,000 shares in S Ltd.	300	-
Other assets	700	600
	1,000	600
Share capital, @ Re.1 per share	400	100
Retained profit	400	300
Liabilities	200	200
	1,000	600

NDA Ltd. acquired its investment in Induga Ltd. as follows :

Date	Number of share Purchase	Cost	Balance of Induga Ltd. 's retained profit
25-1-2005	20,000	40	100
21-3-2006	20,000	60	150
20-4-2007	50,000	200	200

The excess payments were for goodwill.

The group policy is to amortise goodwill on consolidation on a straight-line basis over a period of 5 years. A full year's amortisation is provided if the goodwill exists for more than six months during the year.

On 30th December, 2010, NDA Ltd. sold 30,000 of Induga Ltd.'s shares for cash consideration of Rs. 2,00,000.

The final accounts of the companies for the year 2010 were as follows :

(1) Balance sheets as at 31st December, 2010 (Rs. in '000)

	NDA Ltd.	Induga Ltd.
Investment, at cost		
60,000 shares in Induga Ltd.	200	-
Other assets	1,000	820
	1,200	820
Share capital, @ Re.1 per share	400	100
Retained profit	600	420
Liabilities	200	300
	1,200	820

(2) Profit and loss accounts for the year ended 31st December, 2010

(Rs. in '000)

	NDA Ltd.	Induga Ltd.
Profit before tax	150	180
Taxation	50	60
Profit after tax	100	120
Extraordinary item(Note 2)	100	–
Profit after tax and EI	200	120
Beginning retained profit	400	100
Ending retained profit	600	420
Profit on disposal of shares in subsidiary.		

Required : Prepare for NDA Ltd. and its subsidiary the 2009 consolidated balance sheet, and the 2010 consolidated balance sheet, and consolidated profit and loss account.

Ans : [B / S for 2009 - Total Rs. 1,324, 2010 - Rs. 1,828. Consolidation P/L A/C- Rs. 236. Goodwill in B/S 2010 Rs. 8]

CHAPTER 2

Company Final Accounts

2.1 Introduction

One of the norms of modern business dictates al business entities to prepare a set of Financial statements with a two-fold purpose - for assessing periodically profits earned and for getting conversant with the financial position of the business concern in question on a specified date. Joint stock companies, simply referred to as companies in India, are no exception to this prescription.

A Profit and loss Account and a Balance Sheet are essential for all business concerns except the single-ownership ones. In the case of joint stock companies, the Companies Act, 1956 further prescribes books of Account to be maintained and lays down the format and content of financial statments to be made. In addition, the accounts should be statutorily audited by external/s who are called Autitor/s - person or persons legally qualified to do the work. It is the auditor's duty to submit a report in the prescribed format for the shareholder's to see.

Since the introduction of the limited liability system, it has become procedural to appoiont a board of directors, through election by the sharholders, which board is supposed to protect and promote their interest to the best of its ability. However, a complete reliance on the board of directors may not be an adequate safeguard of shareholders' interest.

The Companies Act, therefore, Prescribes a few provisions under which financial Statements are to be prepared and presented. The purpose is to lay before the shareholders adequate information for enabling them to judge the performance of the company and, thus, the role of the directors during a specified period, Called the "accounting period'

As the preparation of the financial statements of a company requires the observation of the legal prescriptions, it acquires much importance for the shareholders in their efforts to assess the business unit's health.

Books of Accounts to be kept by Company

Section 209 of the Companies Act, 1956 requires that every company shall keep at its registered office proper books of account regarding -

a) All sums of money received and expended by the company and the matters in respect of which the receipt and expenditure take place.

b) All sales and purchases of goods by the company.

c) the assets and liabilities of the company; and

d) in the case of a company pertaining to any class of companies engaged in production, processing, manufacturing or mining activities, such particulars relating to utilisation of material or labour or to other items of cost as may be prescribed, if such class of companies is required by the Central Government to include such particulars in the books of account.

Proper books of account shall not be deemed to be kept with respect to the matters specified above -

a) if there are not kept such books as are necessary to give a true and fair view of the state of affairs of the company or branch office, as the case may be, and to explain its transactions; and

b) if such books are not kept on accrual basis and according to the double entry system of accounting.

The books of account of every company relating to a period of not less than eight years immediately preceding the current year together with the vouchers relevant to any entry in such books of account shall be preserved in a good order.

The books of account and other books and papers of every company shall be open to inspection by any director during business hours.

To satisfy the different requirements of the Companies Act, generally the following books of account are maintained by companies.

1. Cash book to record cash and bank transactions, discounts allowed and received.
2. Purchases Day Book to record credit Purchases.
3. Sales Day Book to record credit sales.
4. Returns Inwards Book or Sales Returns Book to record goods returned by customers.
5. Returns Outwards Book or Purchases Returns Book to record goods returned by the Company to suppliers.
6. Bills Receivable Book to record the details of Bills receivable
7. Bills Payable Book to record the details of Bills Payable.
8. Journal Proper to record opening entries, closing entries, adjustment entries and such residual transactions for which there is no separate book of primary entry.
9. General Ledger showing all accounts other than the accounts of customers and suppliers.

10. Debtors' Ledger or Customers' Ledger showing accounts of customers.
11. Creditors' Ledger or Suppliers' Ledger showing accounts of suppliers.

2.2 Statutory Books

As per the provisions of different sections of the Companies Act, the following records are also to be maintained in addition to the above books of account.

1. Register of Investments no held inthe compnay's name (Section 49)
2. Register of Charges (Section 143)
3. Register of Members (Section 150)
4. Index of Members (Section 151)
5. Register of Debenture-holders with Index (Section 152)
6. Copies of Annual Returns (Section 163)
7. Minute Books - of the G.M and of the meetings of the board and its Committees (Section 193)
8. Register of Contracts, Companies and Firms in Which Directors are Interested (Section 301)
9. Register of Directors, Managing Director, Manager and Secretary (Section 303)
10. Register of Directors' Shareholdings etc. (Section 307)
11. Register of Loans made to other companies under the same management (Section 370)
12. Register of Investments in Shares and Debentures of bodies corporate (Section 372)
13. Directors' Attendance Book (Regulation 71 of Table A)

2.3 Statistical Books

In addition to books of account and statutory books. companies usually maintain the following books which give details information regarding holding and transfer of shares and debentures, calls made on shareholders and debentureholders, interest paid to debenturholders, Share warrants issued and surrendered and such other matters not covered by the books of account and statutory books.

1. Share Application and Allotment Book
2. Share Call Book
3. Debenture Application and Allotment Book
4. Debenture Call Book
5. Register of Share Transfers;
6. Shareholders' Dividend Book
7. Debenture Interest Book;
8. Register of Cerfitication and Balance Tickets;
9. Debenture Transfer Register;
10. Register of Share Certificates;

11. Register of Probates;
12. Register of Share Warrants;
13. Register of Dividend Mandates;
14. Agenda Book;
15. Register of Sealed Documents;
16. Register of Powers of Attorney.

2.4 Annual Accounts and Balance Sheet

As per the provision of Section 210 of the Companies Act 1956, at every annual general meeting of a company held in pursuance of Section 166, the Board of Directors of the company shall lay before the company

a) a Balance Sheet as at the end of the period specified in sub - section (3); and

b) a Profit and Loss Account for that period.

In the case of a company not carrying on business for Profit, an Income and Expenditure Account shall be laid before the company at its annual general meeting instead of a Profit and Loss Account, and all references to 'Profit and Loss Account', 'Profit' and 'Loss' in this section and elsewhere in this Act, Shall be construed, in relation to such a company, as a references respectively to the 'Income and Expenditure Acount', 'The excess of income over expenditure', and 'the excess of expenditure over income'.

The Profit and Loss Account Shall relate -

a) in the case of first annual general meeting of the company. to the period beginning with the incorporation of the company and ending with a day which shall not precede the day of the meeting by more than nine months; and

b) in the case of any subsequent annual general meeting of the company. to the period beginning with the day immediatly after the period for which the account was last submitted and ending with a day. which shall not precede the day of the meeting by more than six months, or in cases where an extension of time has been granted for holding the meeting under the second provision to sub-section (I) of section 166 by more than six months and the extension so granted.

The period to which the account aforesaid relates in referred to in this Act as a 'Financial year' and it may be less or more than a calendar year but it shall not exceed fifteen months.

Form and Contents of Balance Sheet and Profit and Loss Account

Section 211 of the Companies Act. 1956 states that :

1) Every Balance Sheet of a company shall give a true and fair view of the state of affairs of the company as at the end of the financial year and shall, subject to the provisions of this section, be in the form set out in Part I of Schedule VI, or as near therto as circumstances admit or in such other form as may be approved by the Central Government either generally or in any particular case; and in preparing the Blanace

Sheet due regard shall be had, as far as may be, to the general instructions for preparation of Balance Sheet under the heading "Notes' at the end of that Part.

Provided that nothing contained in this sub- section shall apply to any insurance or banking company or any company engaged in the generation or supply of electricity or to any other class of company for which a form of Balance Sheet has been specified in or under the Act governing such class of company.

2) Every Profit and Loss Account of a company shall give a true and fair view of the profit and loss of the company for the financial year and shall, subject as aforesaid, comply with the requirements of Part II of Schedule VI,so far as they are applicable thereto

Provided that nothing contained in this sub-section shall apply to any insurance or banking company or any company engaged in the generation or supply of electricity or to any other class of company for which a form of Profit and Loss Account has been specified in or under the Act governing such class of company.

3) The Central Government may, be notification in the Official, Gazette, exempt any class of companies from compliance with any of the requirements in Schedule VI, if, in its opinion, it is necessary to grant the exemption in public interest.

Any such exemption may be granted either unconditionally or subject to which conditions as may be specified in the notification.

3A) Every profit and loss account and balance sheet of the company shall comply with the accounting standards.

3B) Where the profit and loss account and the balance sheet of the company do not comply with the accounting standards, such companies the disclose in its profit and loss account and balance sheet, the following namely.

a) the deviation from the accounting standards;

b) the reasons for such deviation; and

c) the financial effect, if any, arising due to such deviation.

3C) For the purposed of this section, the expression "accounting standards" means the standards of accounting recommended by the Institute of Chartered Accountants of India constituted under the Chartered Accountants. Act 1949 (38 of 1949) as may be prescribed by the Central Government in consultation with the National advisory Committee on Accounting Standards. established under sub-section (1) of section 210A Provided that the standard of accounting specified by the Institute of Chartered Accountants of India Shall be deemed to be the Accounting Standards unitl the accounting standards are prescribed by the Central Government under this sub-section.

4) The Central Government may, on the application or with the consent of the Board of Directors of the company, by order, modify in relation to that company any of the requirements of this Act as to the matters to be stated in the company's Balance Sheet

or Profit and Loss Account for the purpose of adapting them to the circumstances of the company.

Contents of Revised Schedule VI

1. General Instructions for Preparation of Balance Sheet and Statement of Profit and Loss of a company.
2. Form of Balance Sheet (only vertical format) with General Instructions for preparation of Balance Shet (PART - I) The privilege of having a balance Sheet under horizontal or vertical format has been done away with. Option of only one format i.e Vertical format is now available for preparation of the Balance Sheet.
3. Form of Statement of Profit and Loss with General Instructions for preparation of Statement of Profit and Loss (PART - II)
4. The general format does not apply to Insurance Companies, Banking Companies, Electricity Companies or any other company governed by a separate Act, Where a form has been specified under that Act.

2.5 Disclosures

1. The Revised Schedule VI has eliminated the concept of "Schedule' and such information is now to be furnished in the notes to accounts.
2. **Proposed Dividend :** Part I of Revised Schedule VI does not require the provision for Proposed dividend to be made and only desires disclosure of same in notes to accounts. Although Revised Schedule VI does not require provision for proposed dividend, however, the accounting Standards have an overriding effect over Revised Schedule VI and Accordingly companies will have to account for the same until revision to this effect is made in AS 4.
3. **Share Capital :** Shareholder holding more than 5% Shares specifying the number of Shares held, etc.
4. **Long Term Borrowing :** Shall be stated in descending order of maturity or conversion. Further Period and amount of continuing default as on balance sheet date in repayment of loans and interest also needs to be disclosed.
5. **Trade Receivables :** The term Sundry debtor has been replaced with trade receivables.
6. **Cash and cash equivalents :** Bank deposits with more than 12 months maturity to be disclosed separately. The difurcation of bank deposits among scheduled and non scheduled banks has been dispensed with.
7. **Contingent liabilities and commitments :** These were required to be disclosed as footnote to balance Sheet under old Schedule VI and are now required to be disclosed in notes to accounts.
8. Income or expenditure exceeding 1% of the revenue from operations or ₹ 1,00,000 whichever is higher, need to be disclosed by way of notes.
9. The limits of rounding off (on the basis of turnover) are as follows

Turnover	Rounding off
Less than 100 Crores	To the nearest hundereds, thousands, lakhs or millon, or decimals thereof
More than 100 Crores	To the nearest Lakhs, millions or Crores, or decimals therof.

10. An asset shall be classified as current when it satisfies any of the following criteria.
    a) It is expected to be realized within twelve months after the reporting date; or
    b) Used to settle a liablility for at least twelve month after the reporting date.

11. A liablility Shall be classified as current when it is due to be settled within twelve months after the reporting date;

12. Reserves & Surplus : The balance of 'Reserves and Surplus' after adjusting negative balance of surplus (Profit & Loss Account), if any, shall be shown under the head 'Reserves and Surplus' even if the resulting figure is in the negative. Earlier, any debit balance in profit and Loss Account was required to be shown as the last item on the asset side of the Balance Sheet.

13. The Old Schedule VI required Separate presentation of debtors outstanding for a period exceeding 6 months based on date on which the bill / invoice was raised whereas, the Revised Schedule VI requires separate disclosure of "trade receivables outstanding for a period exceeding six months from the date the bill / invoice is due for payment."

14. The name has been changed to "Statement of Profit and Loss" as against "Profit and Loss Account' as contained in the Old Schedule VI

2.6 Part I :   Form of Balance Sheet

Name of the Company			
Balance Sheet as at 31 March 2014			
Particulars	Note No.	As at 31 March, 2014 ₹	As at 31 March, 2013 ₹
A. **Equity and Liabilities**			
1. **Shareholder's funds**			
a. Share Capital	1		
b. Reserves and Surplus	2		
c. Money received against share Warrants			

2	**Share application money pending allotment**			
3	**Non-current liablities**			
	(a) Long-term borrowings	3		
	(b) Deferred tax liabilities (net)			
	(c) Other long-term liabilities	4		
	(d) Long-term Provisions			
4	**Current liabilities**			
	(a) Short-term borrowings	6		
	(b) Trade Payables			
	(c) Other current liabilities	7		
	(d) Short-term provisions	8		
	Total			
B	**Assets**			
1	**Non-current assets**			
	(a) Fixed assets			
	(i) Tangibls assets	9		
	(ii) Intangible assets	10		
	(iii) Capital work-in-progress			
	(iv) Intangible assets under developments			
	(v) Fixed assets held for sale			
	(b) Non-current investments	11		
	(c) Deferred tax assets (net)			
	(d) Long-term loans and advances	12		
	(e) Other non-current assets	13		
2	**Current Assets**			
	(a) Current Investments	14		
	(b) Inventories	15		
	(c) Trade receivables	16		
	(d) Cash and cash equivalents	17		
	(e) Short-term loans and advances	18		
	(f) Other current assets			
	Total			

Part II : **Form of Statment of Profit and Loss**

<table>
<tr><td colspan="4" align="center">Name of the Company</td></tr>
<tr><td colspan="4" align="center">Statement of Profit and Loss for the year ended 31 March, 2014</td></tr>
<tr>
<td colspan="2" align="center">Particulars</td>
<td align="center">Note No.</td>
<td align="center">For the year ended 31 March, 2014
₹</td>
<td align="center">For the year ended 31 March, 2013
₹</td>
</tr>
<tr><td colspan="2">A   Continuing Operations</td><td></td><td></td><td></td></tr>
<tr><td>1</td><td>Revenue from operations (gross)</td><td></td><td></td><td></td></tr>
<tr><td></td><td>Less : Excise duty</td><td></td><td></td><td></td></tr>
<tr><td></td><td>Revenue from operations (net)</td><td>20</td><td></td><td></td></tr>
<tr><td>2</td><td>Other income</td><td>21</td><td></td><td></td></tr>
<tr><td>3</td><td>Total revenue (1+2)</td><td></td><td></td><td></td></tr>
<tr><td>4</td><td>Expenses</td><td></td><td></td><td></td></tr>
<tr><td></td><td>(a) Cost of materials consumed</td><td></td><td></td><td></td></tr>
<tr><td></td><td>(b) Purchase of stock-in-trade</td><td></td><td></td><td></td></tr>
<tr><td></td><td>(c) Changes in inventories of finished goods, work-in-progress and stock-in-trade</td><td></td><td></td><td></td></tr>
<tr><td></td><td>(d) Employee benefits expense</td><td>22</td><td></td><td></td></tr>
<tr><td></td><td>(e) Finance costs</td><td>23</td><td></td><td></td></tr>
<tr><td></td><td>(f) Depreciation and amortisation expense</td><td></td><td></td><td></td></tr>
<tr><td></td><td>(g) Other expenses</td><td>24</td><td></td><td></td></tr>
<tr><td></td><td>Total expenses</td><td></td><td></td><td></td></tr>
<tr><td>5</td><td>Profit / (Loss) before exceptional and extraordinary items and tax (3-4)</td><td></td><td></td><td></td></tr>
<tr><td>6</td><td>Exceptional items</td><td></td><td></td><td></td></tr>
<tr><td>7</td><td>Profit / (Loss) before extraordinary items and tax (5 ± 6)</td><td></td><td></td><td></td></tr>
</table>

8	**Extraordinary items**			
9	**Profit / (Loss) before tax (7 ± 8)**			
10	**Tax expense :**			
	(a) Current tax expense for current year			
	(b) (Less) : MAT credit (where applicable)			
	(c) Current tax expense relating to prior years			
	(d) Net current tax expense			
	(e) Deferred tax			
11	**Profit / (Loss) from continuing operations (9 ± 10)**			
B	**Discontinuing Operations**			
12.i	Profit / (Loss) from discontinuing operations (before tax)			
12.ii	Gain / (Loss) on disposal of assets / settlement of liabilities attributable to the discontinuing operations			
12.iii	Add / (Loss) : Tax expense of discontinuing operations			
	(a) on ordinary activities attributable to the discontinuing operations			
	(b) on gain / (Loss) on disposal of assets / settlement of liabilities			
13	**Profit / (Loss) from discontinuing operations (12.i ± 12.ii ± 12.iii)**			
C	**Total Operations**			
14	**Profit / (Loss) for the year (11 ± 13)**			
15	**Earnings per equity share :**			
	(1) Basic			
	(2) Diluted			

Note 1 : Share Capital		
Particulars	**As at 31 March, 2014**	**As at 31 March, 2013**
	₹	₹
Authorized Share Capital ..... Equity Share of ₹ ... each (Pr. Yr. ... Equity Shares) .... Preference Shares of ₹ .... each (Pr. Yr. .... preference Share)		
Issued Share Capital .... Equity Share of ₹ .... each (Pr. Yr. .... Equity Shares) .... Preference Shares of ₹ ... each (Pr. Yr. .... Preference Share)		
Subscribed & Fully Paid up ..... Equity Share of ₹ ... each (Pr. Yr. .... Equity Shares) .... Preference Shares of ₹ ... each (Pr. Yr. .... preference Share)		
Subscribed & not fuliy Paid up ..... Equity Share of ₹ ... each (Pr. Yr. .... Equity Shares) .... Preference Shares of ₹ ... each (Pr. Yr. .... preference Share)		
Less : Calls Unpaid • By Directors • By Officers		
Less : Forfeited Shares (Amount ordinarily paid-up) (....... Shares (Equity / Preference) issued for a Considerations other than Cash) (.... Shares (Equity / preference) issued as Bonus Shares & for this purpose .... (Reserves) is used		
Total		

Note 2 : Reserves and Surplus

Particulars	As at 31 March, 2014	As at 31 March, 2013
	₹	₹
Capital Reserves		
Capital Redemption Reserve		
Securities Premium Reserve		
Debenture Redemption Reserve		
Revaluation Reserve		
Share Options Outstanding Account		
Other Reserves (specify the nature and purpose of reserve and the amount in respect there of)		
Total		

Note 3 : Long - term borrowings

Particulars	As at 31 March, 2014	As at 31 March, 2013
	₹	₹
Bonds / debentures		
Term loans • From banks • Form other parties		
Deferred payment liabilities		
Deposits		
Loans and advances from related parties		
Long term maturities of finance lease obligations		
Other loans and advances (specify nature)		
Total		

Note 4 : Other Long-term liabilities

Particulars	As at 31 March, 2014	As at 31 March, 2013
	₹	₹
Trade Payables		
Others		
Total		

Note 5 : Long-Term Provisions

Particulars	As at 31 March, 2014	As at 31 March, 2013
	₹	₹
Provision for employee benefits		
Others		
Total		

Note 6 : Short-term borrowings

Particulars	As at 31 March, 2014	As at 31 March, 2013
	₹	₹
Loans repayable on demand		
• From banks		
• From others parties		
Loans and advances from related parties		
Deposits		
Others loans and advances (specify nature)		
Total		

Note 7 : Other Current Liabilities

Particulars	As at 31 March, 2014 ₹	As at 31 March, 2013 ₹
Current maturities of long-term debt		
Current maturities of finance lease obligations		
Interest accrued but not due on borrowings		
Interest accrued and due on borrowings		
Income received in advance		
Unpaid dividends		
Application money received for allotment of securities and due for refund and interest accrued thereon		
Unpaid matured deposits and interest accrued thereon		
Unpaid matured debentures and interest accrued thereon		
Other payables (specify nature)		
Total		

Note 8 : Short - Term Provisions

Particulars	As at 31 March, 2014 ₹	As at 31 March, 2013 ₹
Provision for employee benefits		
Other (specify nature)		
Total		

Note 9 : Tangible Assets

Particulars	As at 31 March, 2014	As at 31 March, 2013
	₹	₹
Land		
Buildings		
Plant and Equipment		
Furniture and Fixtures		
Vehicles		
Office equipment		
Others (specify nature)		
Total		

Note 10 : Intangible Assets

Particulars	As at 31 March, 2014	As at 31 March, 2013
	₹	₹
Goodwill		
Brands / trademarks		
Computer software		
Mastheads and publishing titles		
Mining rights		
Copyrights and patents and other intellectual property rights, services and operating rights		
Recipes, formulae, models, designs and prototypes		
Licenses and franchise		
Others (specify nature)		
Total		

Note 11 : Non-current Investments

Particulars	As at 31 March, 2014	As at 31 March, 2013
	₹	₹
Investment property		
Investment in Equity Instruments		
Investment in preference shares		
Investment in Governmnet or trust securities		
Investment in debentures or bonds		
Investment in Mutual Funds		
Investment in Partnership firms		
Other Non-Current Investments (specify nature)		
Aggregate amount of quoted investments and market value thereof		
Aggregate amount of unquoted investments		
Aggregate provision for diminution in value of investments		

Note 12 : Long-term Loans and Advances

Particulars	As at 31 March, 2014	As at 31 March, 2013
	₹	₹
Capital Advances		
Security Deposits		
Loans and advances to related parties (giving details thereof)		
Other loans and advances (a) Secured, considered good (b) Unsecured, considered good (c) Doubtful		
Total		

Note 13 : Other Non-Current Assets		
Particulars	**As at 31 March, 2014**	**As at 31 March, 2013**
	₹	₹
Long Term Trade Receivable (including trade receivables on defferred credit terms)		
Others (specify nature)		
Total		

Note 14 : Current Investments		
Particulars	**As at 31 March, 2014**	**As at 31 March, 2013**
	₹	₹
Investments in equity Instruments		
Investments in Perference Shares		
Investments in Government or Trust Securities		
Investments in Debentures or Bonds		
Investments in Mutual Funds		
Investments in Partnership Firms		
Other Investments (specify nature)		
Total		

Note 15 : Inventories

Particulars	As at 31 March, 2014	As at 31 March, 2013
	₹	₹
Raw materials		
Work-in-progress		
Finished goods		
Stock-in-trade (in respect of goods acquired for trading)		
Stores and spares		
Loose tools		
Others (specify nature)		
Total		

Note 16 : Trade Receivables

Particulars		As at 31 March, 2014	As at 31 March, 2013
		₹	₹
Trade Receivable > 6 month from the due date of Payment			
Secured, considered good	××		
Unsecured considered good	××		
Doubtful	××		
	××		
Less : Provision for Bad debt	××	××	
Trade Receivable ≤ 6 month from the due date of Payment			
Secured considered good	××		
Unsecured considered good	××		
Doubtful	××		
	××		
Less : Provision for Bad debts	××	××	
Total			

Note 17 : Cash and Cash Equivalents

Particulars	As at 31 March, 2014	As at 31 March, 2013
	₹	₹
Balances with bank • Unpaid Dividend • Margin Money • Bank deposits with more than 12 months maturity		
Cheques, darfts on hand		
Cash on hand		
Others (specify nature)		
Total		

Note 18 : Short-term Loans and Advances

Particulars	As at 31 March, 2014	As at 31 March, 2013
	₹	₹
Loans and advances to related parties (giving detalis thereof) Secured, considered good　　xx Unsecured, considered good　　xx Doubtful　　xx 　　xx Less : Provision for Bad debt　　xx	xx	
Others (specify nature) Loans and advances to related parties (giving details thereof) Secured, considered good　　xx Unsecured, considered good　　xx Doubtful　　xx Less : Provision for Bad debt　　xx	xx	
Total		

Note 19 : Contingent Liabilities and Commitments

Particulars	As at 31 March, 2014	As at 31 March, 2013
	₹	₹
Contigent liabilities shall be classified as : (a) Claims against the company not acknowledged as debt (b) Guarantees (c) Other money for which the company is contingently liable		
Commitments shall be classified as : (a) Estimated amount of contracts remaining to be executed on capital account and not provided for (b) Uncalled liability on shares and other investments partly paid (c) Other commitments (specify nature)		
Total		

Note 20 : Revenue from Operations

Particulars	As at 31 March, 2014	As at 31 March, 2013
	₹	₹
In Respect to Non-finance Company Sale of Products Sale of Services Other Operating Revenues Less : Excise Duties		
In Respect to Non-finance Company Interest Other Financial Services		
Total		

Note 21 : Other Income		
Particulars	**As at 31 March, 2014**	**As at 31 March, 2013**
	₹	₹
Interest Income (other than a Finance company)		
Dividend Income		
Net Gain/Loss on Sale of Investments		
Other Non-Operating Income (net of expenses directly attributable to such income)		
Adjustment to the carrying value of Investments (Write-back)		
Net Gain/Loss on foreign currency translation and transaction (other than considered as finance cost)		
Total		

Note 22 : Employee Benefits Expense		
Particulars	**As at 31 March, 2014**	**As at 31 March, 2013**
	₹	₹
Salaries & Wages		
Contribution to Provident & Other Funds		
Expenses on Employee Stock Option Scheme (ESOP)		
And Employee Stock Purchase Plan (ESPP)		
Staff Welfare Expenses		
Total		

Note 23 : Finance Cost		
Particulars	**As at 31 March, 2014**	**As at 31 March, 2013**
	₹	₹
Interest Expense		
Other Borrowing Costs		
Applicable Net Gain/Loss of Foreign Currency translations & transactions.		
Total		

Note 24 : Other Expenses		
Particulars	**As at 31 March, 2014**	**As at 31 March, 2013**
	₹	₹
Consumption of Stores and spare parts		
Power and fuel		
Rent		
Repairs to Buildings		
Repairs to Machinary		
Insurance		
Rates & Taxes (excluding Income tax)		
Miscellaneous Expenditure		
Payment to Auditors • As Auditors • For Taxation Matters • For Company Law Matters • For Management Services • For Other Services • For Reimbursement of Expenses		
Total		

Provisions of law in relation to Transfer to Reserves [Sec. 205(2A)]

1. No dividend shall be declared or paid by a company for any financial year out of the profits of the company for that year arrived at after providing for depreciation u/s 205(2), except after the transfer to reserves of the company of the prescribed percentage of its profit for that year, not exceeding 10%.

2. Under the companies (Transfer of Profits to Reserves) Rules, 1975, the percentage of profits required to be transferred to reserves have been related to the rate of dividend proposed for the year. These are as under -

Rate of dividend	Percentage of profit required to be transfereed to reserves
Upto 10%	Nil
Exceeding 10% but not exceeding 12.5%	Not less than 2.5% of the current profits.
Exceeding 12.5% but not exceeding 15%	Not less than 5% of the current profits.
Exceeding 15% but not exceeding 20%	Not less than 7.5 of the current profits.
Exceeding 20%	Not less than 10% of the current profits.

Note :

1. Transfer to Reserve u/s 205(2A) does not include any transfer to Development Rebate Reserve, Capital or any special Reserve. The reserves contemplated are only "Free Reserve"

2. Arrears of depreciation mentioned in section 205(1) should also be provided in determining the profit for the purpose of transfer to reserves.

3. Profit for the above purpose should be (a) after tax and (b) after debit for statutory Reserve, wherever applicable.

4. The rates of dividend mentioned in the table above relate to the rates of Equity Dividend and the portion of dividend in excess of the fixed rate of dividend in respect of participating Perference shares.

5. Companies are free to carry the residual profit, irrespective of the amount, after dividend and transfer to reserves, in the Profit and Loss Account.

Managerial Remuneration

1. Total Managerial Remuneration – 11% of Net Profit computed u/s 349. Sitting Free excluded.

2. Individual Limits

   - MD, WTD or Manager - 5% to any one and 10% to all.

2.7 PROBLEMS

Problem No. 1 : Shruti Ltd., Mumbai is in the midst of finalizing its accounts for the year-ended 30th September 2012. A Profit and Loss Account has been prepared in draft, the account balances as rounded off to the nearest thousands, are listed below :

Particulars	(₹)	Particulars	(₹)
Shares Capital	25,00,000	Finished Goods	1,41,400
General Reserve	6,03,100	Stores and Spares	2,77,100
Development Rebate Reserve	6,27,100	Tools Jigs and Dies	9,18,700
Land	2,22,500	Cash Credit from Banks	30,67,200
Buildings	9,31,600	Acceptances	2,64,500
Plant and Machinary	64,28,200	Sundry Creditors	6,16,200
Furniture, Fixtures & Office Equipment	1,59,400	Other Current Liabilities	10,31,700
Vehicles	45,400	Interest Accured but not due on loans	58,900
Depreciation Reserve		Provisions for Gratuity and Pension	24,100
Building	2,19,300	Interest Accured on Deposits	200
Plant and Machinary	30,32,800	Sundry Debtors	24,23,100
Furniture	56,800	Cash in Hand	3,700
Vehicles	24,500	Bank Balance	
Loan from State government	57,500	On Current Accounts	3,900
Other Secured Loans	32,46,000	On Deposit Accounts	2,700
Fixed Deposits from Public	2,40,000	Loans and Advance	4,51,800
Unsecured Loans	1,11,400	Preliminary Expenses	800
Raw Materials and Components	42,01,400	Advance Income - Tax paid	3,48,900
Work in Progress	6,11,600	Capital Work-in-Progress	59,600
		Profit & Loss A/c (Profit for the year)	14,50,900

In arriving at the profit for the year, the following have been charged :

Particulars	₹
Depreciation	12,42,400
Salary and perquisite to Managing Director	7,200
Director's fee	400

The Authorized capital is 3,50,000 Equity shares of ₹ 100 each. The from the State Government is secured by a charge on the land, cash credits by hypothecation of stocks and book Debts and the other Secured Loans on the Buildings and Plant and Machinary.

The following adjustments are yet to be made -

(i) Investment Allownce Reserve to be created ₹ 5,40,000

(ii) Provision to be made for Income-Tax in ₹ 4,40,000

(iii) Provision to be made for Managing Director's Commission at 1% of the profits.

(iv) Proposed Dividend at 10%.

Depreciation as per section 350 of the Companies Act is ₹ 10,42,400

Required :

(i) Show the computation of commission payable to the Managing Director; and

(ii) Prepare the Balance sheet of the company, based on all the above.

Solution :

Profit and Loss Adjustment Account

Particulars	₹	Particulars	₹
To Commission to MD	16,600	By Profit for the year	14,50,900
To Investment Allownce Reserve	5,40,000	(as per Draft P & L A/c)	
To Provision for Tax	4,40,000		
To Proposed Dividends	2,50,000		
(10% × 25,00,000)			
To Balance carried to Balance Sheet	2,04,300		
	14,50,900		14,50,900

Computation of Commission to the Managing Director

Particular	₹ Amount	₹ Amount
Profit as per draft Profit and Loss Account		14,50,900
Add : Depreciation charged in the Profit and Loss Account	12,42,400	
Salary and Remuneration to Managing Director	7,200	
Director Fees	400	12,50,000
		27,00,900
Less : Depreciation u/s 350 of the Companies Act		(10,42400)
Profit u/s 349 for the purpose of Managerial Remuneration		**16,58,500**
Maximum Remuneration (5%)		82,900
Less : Salaries and Remuneration Paid (Director's Fees is excluded for this purpose)		(7200)
Maximum Commission Payable to Managing Director		**75,700**
Commission to be provided for at 1% on Net Profits **(1% of ₹ 16,585)**		16,600

Dollar Ltd		
Balance Sheet as at 30th September, 2012		
Particulars	**Note No.**	**As at 30 September, 2012** ₹
A **EQUITY AND LIABILITIES**		
1 **Shareholder's funds**		
(a) Share Capital	1	25,00,000
(b) Reserves and Surplus	2	19,74,500
(c) Money received against share warrants		
2 **Share application money pending allotment**		

3	**Non-current liabilities**		
	(a) Long-term borrowings	3	36,54,900
	(b) Deferred tax liabilities (net)		
	(c) Other long-term liabilities		
	(d) Long-term Provisions		
4	**Current liabilities**		
	(a) Short-term borrowings	4	30,67,200
	(b) Trade Payables	5	8,80,700
	(c) Other current liabilities	6	11,07,200
	(d) Short-term provisions	7	3,65,200
	Total		1,35,49,700
B	**ASSETS**		
1	**Non-current Assets**		
	(a) Fixed assets		
	(i) Tangible assets	8	44,53,700
	(ii) Intangible assets		
	(iii) Capital work-in-progress		59,600
	(iv) Intangible assets under developments		
	(v) Fixed assets held for sale		
	(b) Non-current investments		
	(c) Deferred tax assets (net)		
	(d) Long-term loans and advances		
	(e) Other non-current assets		800
2	**Current Assets**		
	(a) Current Investments		
	(b) Inventories	9	61,50,200
	(c) Trade receivables		24,23,100
	(d) Cash and cash equivalents	10	10,300
	(e) Short-term loans and advances		4,51,800
	(f) Other Current Assets		200
	Total		1,35,49,700

Note 1 : Share Capital	
Particulars	**As at 30 Sept, 2012**
	₹
Authorized Share Capital	
3,50,000 Equity Share of ₹ 100 each	35,00,000
Issued, Subscribed & Fully Paid up Shares Capital	
2,50,000 Equity Share of ₹ 100 each	25,00,000
Total	25,00,000

Note 2 : Reserves and Surplus	
Particulars	**As at 30 Sept, 2012**
	₹
General Reserves	6,03,100
Development Rebate Reserve	6,27,100
Investment allowance Reserve	5,40,000
Profit & Loss	2,04,300
Total	19,74,500

Note 3 : Long - term Borrowings	
Particulars	**As at 30 Sept, 2012**
	₹
Loan from state Govt. (Secured by Charge on assets)	57,500
Other Secured Loan (Secured by Charge on building & Plant & Machinery)	32,46,000
Fixed Deposit From Public	2,40,000
Unsecured Loans	1,11,400
Total	36,54,900

Note 4 : Short - term Borrowings

Particulars	As at 30 Sept, 2012
	₹
Cash Credit From Bank (Secured by hypothecation of Stock & book debts)	30,67,200
Total	30,67,200

Note 5 : Trade Payables

Particulars	As at 30 Sept, 2012
	₹
Acceptances	2,64,500
Trade Creditors	6,16,200
Total	8,80,700

Note 6 : Other Current Liabilities

Particulars	As at 30 Sept, 2012
	₹
Other Current Liabilities	10,31,700
Interest Accrued	58,900
MD Commission Payable	16,600
Total	11,07,200

Note 7 : Short-term Provisions

Particulars	As at 30 Sept, 2012
	₹
Provision for Taxation (4,400 - 3489)	91,100
Proposed Dividends	2,50,000
Provision for Gratuity & Pension	24,100
Total	3,65,200

Note 8 : Tangible Assets

Particulars	As at 30 Sept, 2012
	₹
Land	2,22,500
Buildings	7,12,300
Plant and Equipment	33,95,400
Furniture and Fixtures	1,02,600
Vehicle	20,900
Total	44,53,700

Note 9 : Inventories

Particulars	As at 30 Sept, 2012
	₹
Raw Material & Consumables	42,01,400
Work in progress	6,11,600
Finished goods	1,41,400
Stores & Spares	2,77,100
Tools jigs and Dies	9,18,700
Total	61,50,200

Note 10 : Cash and Cash Equivalents

Particulars	As at 30 Sept, 2012
	₹
Balances with bank on current account	3,900
Balances with bank on deposit account	2,700
Cash on hand	37,00
Total	10,300

Problem No. 2 : From the following particulars furnished by Uday Limited, Pune prepare the Balance sheet as at 31st March, 2012 as required by Part I, Schedule VI of the Companies Act.

(in ₹)

Particulars	Debit		Credit
Equity Capital (Face Value of ₹ 100)			20,00,000
Calls in Arrears		2,000	
Land		4,00,000	
Building		7,00,000	
Plant and Machinary		10,50,000	
Furniture		1,00,000	
General Reserve			4,20,000
Loan from State Financial Corporation			3,00,000
Stock : Finished goods	4,00,000		
Raw Material	1,00,000	5,00,000	
Provision for Taxation			1,36,000
Sudry Debtors		4,00,000	
Advances		85,400	
Proposed Dividend			1,20,000
Profit and Loss Account			2,00,000
Cash Balance		60,000	
Cash at Bank		4,94,000	
Preliminary Expenses		26,600	
Loans (Unsecured)			2,42,000
Sundry Creditors (for goods and expenses)			4,00,000
Total		**38,18,000**	**38,18,000**

The following additional information is also provided :

   (i) 4,000 Equity shares were issued for consideration other than cash.

  (ii) Debtors of ₹ 1,04,000 are due for more than six months from the due date of payment.

 (iii) The Balance of ₹ 3,00,000 in the loan account with state finance corporation includes 15,000 interest accured but not due.

 (iv) Balance at Bank includes ₹ 4,000 with Elite Bank Limited, which is not a scheduled Bank.

  (v) Bills Receivalbe for ₹ 5,50,000 maturing on 30th June have been discounted.

 (vi) The company had Contract for the erection of Machinary at ₹ 3,00,000 which is still incomplete.

Solution :

<table>
<tr><td colspan="4" align="center">XYZ Limited</td></tr>
<tr><td colspan="4" align="center">Balance Sheet as at 31 March, 2012</td></tr>
<tr><td colspan="2" align="center">Particulars</td><td align="center">Note No.</td><td align="center">As at 31 March, 2012</td></tr>
<tr><td></td><td></td><td></td><td align="center">₹</td></tr>
<tr><td>A</td><td>EQUITY AND LIABILITIES</td><td></td><td></td></tr>
<tr><td>1</td><td>Shareholder's funds</td><td></td><td></td></tr>
<tr><td></td><td>(a) Share capital</td><td align="center">1</td><td align="right">19,98,000</td></tr>
<tr><td></td><td>(b) Reserves and Surplus</td><td align="center">2</td><td align="right">6,20,000</td></tr>
<tr><td></td><td>(c) Money received against share Warrants</td><td></td><td></td></tr>
<tr><td>2</td><td>Share application money pending allotment</td><td></td><td></td></tr>
<tr><td>3</td><td>Non-current liabilities</td><td></td><td></td></tr>
<tr><td></td><td>(a) Long-term borrowings</td><td align="center">3</td><td align="right">5,27,000</td></tr>
<tr><td></td><td>(b) Deferred tax liabilities (net)</td><td></td><td></td></tr>
<tr><td></td><td>(c) Other long-term liabilities</td><td></td><td></td></tr>
<tr><td></td><td>(d) Long-term Provisions</td><td></td><td></td></tr>
<tr><td>4</td><td>Current liabilities</td><td></td><td></td></tr>
<tr><td></td><td>(a) Short-term borrowings</td><td></td><td></td></tr>
<tr><td></td><td>(b) Trade Payables</td><td></td><td align="right">4,00,000</td></tr>
<tr><td></td><td>(c) Other current liabilities</td><td align="center">4</td><td align="right">15,000</td></tr>
<tr><td></td><td>(d) Short-term provisions</td><td align="center">5</td><td align="right">2,56,000</td></tr>
<tr><td></td><td align="right">Total</td><td></td><td align="right">38,16,000</td></tr>
<tr><td>B</td><td>ASSET</td><td></td><td></td></tr>
<tr><td>1</td><td>Non-current assets</td><td></td><td></td></tr>
<tr><td></td><td>(a) Fixed assets</td><td></td><td></td></tr>
<tr><td></td><td>   (i) Tangible assets</td><td align="center">6</td><td align="right">22,50,000</td></tr>
<tr><td></td><td>   (ii) Intangible assets</td><td></td><td></td></tr>
</table>

		(iii) Capital work-in-progress		
		(iv) Intangible assets under developments		
		(v) Fixed assets held for sale		
	(b)	Non-current investments		
	(c)	Deferred tax assets (net)		
	(d)	Long-term loans and advances		
	(e)	Other non-current assets	7	26,600
2		**Current Assets**		
	(a)	Current Investments		
	(b)	Inventories	8	5,00,000
	(c)	Trade receivables	9	4,00,000
	(d)	Cash and cash equivalents	10	5,54,000
	(e)	Short-term loans and advances		85,400
	(f)	Other current assets		
		Total		**38,16,000**

Note 1 : Share Captial	
Particulars	**As at 31 March, 2012**
	₹
Issued Subscribed & Fully Paid up Shares Capital	
10,000 Equity Share of ₹ 100 each	20,00,000
Less : Calls Unpaid	2,000
{2,000 Equity Shares issued for a Consideration other than Cash}	
Total	**19,98,000**

Note 2 : Reserves and Surplus

Particulars	As at 31 March, 2012
	₹
General Reserves	4,20,000
Profit & Loss	2,00,000
Total	6,20,000

Note 3 : Long-term borrowings

Particulars	As at 31 March, 2012
	₹
Unsecured Loan	2,42,000
Loan from State Financial Corporation	2,85,000
Total	5,27,000

Note 4 : Other Current Liabilities

Particulars	As at 31 March, 2012
	₹
Interest accrued but not due on borrowings	15,000
Total	15,000

Note 5 : Short-term Provisions

Particulars	As at 31 March, 2012
	₹
Provision for Taxation	1,36,000
Proposed Dividends	1,20,000
Total	2,56,000

Note 6 : Tangible Assets

Particulars	As at 31 March, 2012
	₹
Land	4,00,000
Buildings	7,00,000
Plant and Equipment	10,50,000
Furniture and Fixtures	1,00,000
Total	22,50,000

Note 7 : Other Non-Current Assets

Particulars	As at 31 March, 2012
	₹
Preliminary Expenses	26,600
Total	26,600

Note 8 : Inventories

Particulars	As at 31 March, 2012
	₹
Raw Materials	1,00,000
Finished goods	4,00,000
Total	5,00,000

Note 9 : Trade Receivable

Particulars	As at 31 March, 2012
	₹
Trade Receivable > 6 month from the due date of Payment	
Unsecured considered good 1,04,000	
Less : Provision for Bad debt...	1,04,000
Trade Receivable ≤ 6 month from the due date of Payment	
Unsecured considered good 2,96,000	
Less : Provision for Bad debt....	2,96,000
Total	4,00,000

Note 10 : Cash and Cash Equivalents

Particulars	As at 31 March, 2012
	₹
Balances with bank	4,94,000
Cash on hand	60,000
Total	5,54,000

Note 11 : Contigent Liabilities and Commitments

Particulars	As at 31 March, 2012
	₹
Contigent liabilities shall be classified as :	
Other money for which the company is contingently liable	5,50,000
Commitments shall be classified as :	
Estimated amount of contracts remaining to be executed on capital account and not provide for	3,00,000
Total	8,50,000

Problem No. 3 : Following are the balance from the books Amrut Ltd Nagar as at 31st March 2013

Particulars	₹	Particulars	₹
Sales	1,33,94,000	Other Expenses	22,52,800
Depreciation	71,000	General Reserve	5,16,000
Other Income (Operation)	57,600	Sundry Debtors	11,80,000
Development Rebate Reserve	46,800	Share Capital	4,00,000
Investment Allowance Resreve	85,000	Secured Loans	2,69,600
Fixed Assets at Cost	12,77,400	Cash at Bank	6,400
Investments (Long Term)	3,800	Loan & Advances (Short term)	11,600
Interest Accrued	500	Fixed Deposits	3,20,000
Purchases (Raw Material)	89,68,000	Depreciation Reserve	5,60,000
Salaries and Wages	6,94,200	Provision for Doubtful Debts	1,200
		Sundry Creditors	22,15,500

Calculate Managing Director's Remuneration and Prepare in the proper from the profit and loss Account and Balance Sheet as at 31st March 2013 with the help of the following information.

Particulars	₹	₹
Stocks	Opening	Closing
- Raw Material and stores	10,00,400	5,00,200
- Work in progress	19,01,600	4,00,800
- Finished goods	4,98,000	16,19,000
Depreciation as per schedule XIV to the companies Act, 1956		80,000
Market value of Investments		2,900
Sundry debtors due for more than 6 months		7,200
Out of above, provision made this year for Doubtful debts		800
Included in other expenses are		
- Audior's fee for audit		1,200
- Payment to Auditors for other services		400

- Income Tax to the provided at 36.6%
- Managing Directors Remuneration is at 5% of Net Profit as per law subject to maximum of ₹ 2,40,000 p.a.
- Provide Dividends at 25% on capital and transfer the Balance of profits to general Reserve.
- Authorised capital of the company is 60,00,000 equity Shares of ₹ 100 each. Out of this 4 lakhs shares have been issued and fully paid.
- Provision for Doubtful debts is made in respect of Debotors due for more than 6 months.
- Debtors due for less than 6 months is secured to the extent of ₹ 60,000

Solution :

Fundoo Ltd			
Balance Sheet as at 31st March 2013			
	Particulars	**Note No.**	**As at 31 March, 2013**
			₹
A	**Equity and Liabilities**		
1	**Shareholder's Funds**		
	(a) Share capital	1	4,00,000
	(b) Reserves and Surplus	2	9,20,550
	(c) Money received against share Warrants		

2	**Share application money pending allotment**		
3	**Non current liabilities**		
	(a) Long - term borrowings	3	5,89,600
	(b) Deferred tax liabilities (net)		
	(c) Other Long-term liabilities		
	(d) Long - term Provisions		
4	**Current Liabilities**		
	(a) Short term borrowings		
	(b) Trade Payables		22,15,500
	(c) Other Current liabilities		2,400
	(d) Short term provisions	4	3,10,450
	Total		44,38,500
B	**Assets**		
1	**Non Current Assets**		
	(a) Fixed Assets		
	(i) Tangible assets	5	7,17,400
	(ii) Intangible assets		
	(iii) Capital work in progress		
	(iv) Intangible assets under developments		
	(v) Fixed assets held for sale		
	(b) None - Current investments		3,800
	(c) Deferred tax assets (net)		
	(d) Long term loans and advances		
	(e) Other non current assets		
2	**Current Assets**		
	(a) Current Investments		
	(b) Inventories	6	25,20,000
	(c) Trade receivables	7	11,78,800
	(d) Cash and cash equivalents		6,400
	(e) Short term loans and advances		11,600
	(f) Other current assets		500
	Total		44,38,500

	Statements of Profit and Loss for the year ended 31 March 2013		
	Particulars	**Note No.**	**For the year ended 31 March, 2013**
			₹
A	**Continuing Operations**		
1	**Revenue from operations (gross)**	8	1,34,51,600
	Less : Excise duty		
	Revenue from Operations (net)		1,34,51,600
2	**Other income**		
3	**Total revenue (1 + 2)**		1,34,51,600
4	**Expenses**		
	(a) Cost of materials consumed	9	94,68,200
	(b) Purchase of stock in trade		
	(c) Changes in inventories of finished goods, work in progress and stock in trade		3,79,800
	(d) Empolyee benefits expense	10	6,96,600
	(e) Finance costs		
	(f) Depreciation and amortisation expense		71,000
	(g) Other expenses	11	22,52,800
	Total expenses		1,28,68,400
5	**Profit / (Loss) before exceptional and extraordinary items and tax (3 -4)**		5,83,200
6	**Exceptional items**		
7	**Profit / (Loss) before extraordinary items and tax (5 ± 6)**		5,83,200
8	**Extraordinary items**		
9	**Profit / (Loss) before tax (7 ± 8)**		5,83,200
10	**Tax expenses :**		
	(a) Current tax expense for current year		2,10,450

	(b) (Less) : MAT credit (where applicable)		
	(c) Current tax expense relating to prior years		
	(d) Net current tax expense		
	(e) Deferred tax		
11	**Profit / (Loss) From continuing operations (9 ± 10)**		3,72,750
B	**Discountinuing Operations**		
12.i	Profit / (Loss) from discontinuing operations (before tax)		
12.ii	Gain / (Loss) on disposal of assets / settlement of liabilities attributable to the discontinuing operations		
12.iii	Add / (Loss) : Tax expense of discontinuing operations		
(a)	On ordinary activities attributable to the discontinuing operations		
(b)	On gain / (Loss) on disponsal of assets / settlement of liabilities		
13	**Profit / (Loss) from discontinuing Operations (12i ± 12.ii ± 12.iii)**		
C	**Total Operations**		
14	**Profit / (Loss) for the year (11 ± 13)**		3,72,750
15	**Earnings per equity share :** (1) Basic (2) Diluted		

Working Notes :

1. Other expenses		22,52,800
(-) Provision for doubtful debts		800
(-) Auditors Remuneration		
Audit fees	1200	
Other Service	400	
		(1600)
		22,50,400

2. Profit u/s 349

Net Profit before MD remuneration	5,85,600
+ Depreciation	71,000
+ Prov. for BD	800
(-) Dep. Sch. XIV	80,000
	5,77,400
5% of 5,77,400	28,870

    Subject of Max of 2400

3. Prov for doubtful debt is not allowad under income tax.

Let us assume depreciation under income tax is ₹ 80,000 i.e. similar to depreciation under companies Act.

Taxable Profit

Profit before to as per books	5,83,200
+ Dep. Charged in books	71,000
+ Prov.for BD (not allowed in IT)	300
(-) Dep. under IT Act	80,000
	5,75,000
36.6% of 5,75,000	2,10,450

Note 1 : Share Capital

Particulars	As at 31 March, 2013
	₹
Authorized Share Capital 6,00,000 Equity Share of ₹ 100 each	6,00,000
Issued Subscribed & Fully Paid up Shares Capital 4,00,000 Equity Share of ₹ 100 each	4,00,000
Total	4,00,000

Note 2 : Reserves and Surplus

Particulars	As at 31 March, 2013
	₹
Development Rebate Reserve	46,800
Investment Allowance Reserve	85,000
General Reserve	5,16,000
Profit & Loss	2,72,750
Total	9,20,550

Note 3 : Long - term Borrowings

Particulars	As at 31 March, 2013
	₹
Secured Loan	2,69,600
Unsecured Loan	3,20,000
Total	5,89,600

Note 4 : Short - term Provisions

Particulars	As at 31 March, 2013
	₹
Provision for Tax	2,10,450
Proposed Dividend	1,00,000
Total	3,10,450

Note 5 : Tangible Assets

Particulars	As at 31 March, 2013
	₹
Fixed Assets at Cost	12,77,400
Less : Depreciation Reserve	5,60,000
Total	7,17,400

Note 6 : Inventories

Particulars	As at 31 March, 2013
	₹
Raw Material & Stores	5,00,200
Work in progress	4,00,800
Finished goods	16,19,000
Total	25,20,000

Note 7 : Trade Receivables

Particulars	As at 31 March, 2013
	₹
Trade Receivables > 6 month from the due date of Payment Unsecured Considered good 7200 Less : Provisiong for Bad debt 1200	6000
Trade Receivables < 6 month from the due date of Payment secured considered good 6,00,000 Unsecured considered good 5,72,800	11,72,800
Total	11,78,800

Note 8 : Revenue from Operations

Particulars	As at 31 March, 2013
	₹
Sales of Products	1,33,94,000
Other Operating Revenues	57,600
Total	1,34,51,600

Note 9 : Cost of Material Consumed

Particulars	As at 31 March, 2013
	₹
Raw Material Purchases	89,68,000
Opening Stock of Raw Material	10,00,400
Less : Closing Stock	5,00,200
Total	94,68,200

Note 10 : Employees Benefit Expenses

Particulars	As at 31 March, 2013
	₹
Salaries and Wages	6,94,200
MD Remuneration	2,400
Total	6,96,600

Note 11 : Other Expenses

Particulars		As at 31 March, 2013
		₹
Auditors Remuneration		
For Audit	1200	
For Other Services	400	1,600
Provision for Baddebts		800
Other Expenses (WN1)		22,50,400
Total		22,52,800

Problem No. 4 : Prepare a Balance Sheet of Kartiki Ltd, Nasik as at 31st March, 2012 required under schedule VI of the companies Act, 1956, from the following information of Honeymoon Ltd.

Particulars	Amount (₹)	Particulars	Amount (₹)
Terms Loans (Secured)	20,00,000	Investments (Long term)	4,50,400
Sundry Creditors	22,90,000	Loss for the year	6,00,000
Advances	7,44,000	Sundry Debtors	24,50,000
Cash and Bank Balances	5,50,000	Miscellaneous expenses	1,16,000
Staff Advances	1,10,000	Loan from debtors	4,00,000
Provision for Taxation	3,40,000	Provision for doubtful debtors	40,400
Securities Premium	9,50,000	Stores	8,00,000
Loose Tools	1,00,000	Fixed assets (WDV)	1,03,00,000
General Reserve	41,00,000	Finished goods	15,00,000
Capital work in progress	4,00,000		

Additional Information :

i) Share Capital Consists of :
- 60,000 Equity shares of ₹ 100 each fully paid up.
- 20,000 10% Redeemable preferences shares of ₹ 100 each fully paid up.

ii) Depreciation on assets ₹ 10,00,000

Solution :

		Balance Sheet as at 31 March, 2012		
		Particulars	**Note No.**	**As at 31 March, 2012**
				₹
A		**EQUITY AND LIABILITIES**		
1		**Shareholder's funds**		
		(a) Share capital	1	80,00,000
		(b) Reserves and Surplus	2	44,50,000
		(c) Money received against share warrants		
2		**Share application money pending allotment**		

3	**Non-current liabilities**		
	(a) Long-term borrowings	3	20,00,000
	(b) Deferred tax liabilities (net)		
	(c) Other long-term liabilities		
	(d) Long-term Provisions		
4.	**Current liabilities**		
	(a) Short-term borrowings	4	4,00,000
	(b) Trade Payables		22,90,000
	(c) Other current liabilities		
	(d) Short-term provisions	5	3,40,000
	Total		1,74,80,000
B	**ASSETS**		
1	**Non-current assets**		
	(a) Fixed assets		
	(i) Tangible assets		1,03,00,000
	(ii) Intangible assets		
	(iii) Capital work-in-progress		4,00,000
	(iv) Intangible assets under developments		
	(v) Fixed assets held for sale		
	(b) Non-current investments		4,50,400
	(c) Deferred tax assets (net)		
	(d) Long-term loans and advances		
	(e) Other non-current assets	6	1,16,000
2	**Current Assets**		
	(a) Current Investments		
	(b) Inventories	7	24,00,000
	(c) Trade receivables	8	24,09,600
	(d) Cash and cash equivalents		5,50,000
	(e) Short-term loans and advances	9	8,54,000
	(f) Other current assets		
	Total		1,74,80,000

Note 1 : Share Capital

Particulars	As at 31 March, 2012
	₹
Issued, Subscribed & Fully Paid up Shares Capital	
60,000 Equity Share of ₹ 100 each	60,00,000
20,000 Redeemable Preference Share of ₹100 each	20,00,000
Total	80,00,000

Note 2 : Reserves and Surplus

Particulars	As at 31 March, 2012
	₹
General Reserves	41,00,000
Securities Premium	9,50,000
Profit & Loss A/c	6,00,000
Total	44,50,000

Note 3 : Long-term borrowings

Particulars	As at 31 March, 2012
	₹
Term Loan (Secured)	20,00,000
Total	20,00,000

Note 4 : Short-term Borrowings

Particulars	As at 31 March, 2012
	₹
Loan from Debtors	4,00,000
Total	4,00,000

Note 5 : Short-term Provisions

Particulars	As at 31 March, 2012
	₹
Provision for Taxation	3,40,000
Total	3,40,000

Note 6 : Other Non Current Assets

Particulars	As at 31 March, 2012
	₹
Misscellaneous expenses	1,16,000
Total	1,16,000

Note 7 : Inventories

Particulars	As at 31 March, 2012
	₹
Loose Tools	1,00,000
Stores	8,00,000
Finished Goods	15,00,000
Total	24,00,000

Note 8 : Trade Receivables

Particulars		As at 31 March, 2012
		₹
Trade Receivables		
Unsecured considered good	24,50,000	
Less : Provision for Bad debt	40,400	24,09,600
Total		24,09,600

Note 9 : Short term Loans & Advances	
Particulars	**As at 31 March, 2012**
	₹
Staff Advances	1,10,000
Other Advances	7,44,000
Total	8,54,000

Problem No. 5 : Following balance are extracted from the books of the Omkar Industries Ltd, Satara as at 31 st Dec. 2013.

Particulars	Debit	Credit
Sales		27,60,000
Purchases of Materials	12,18,000	
Share capital fully paid		1,00,000
Land purchased in the year as stock	73,000	
Leasehold premises	42,000	
Creditors		4,63,000
Debtors	7,35,000	
Directors Salaries	39,000	
Wages	1,11,000	
Work in progress on 1st january	2,10,000	
Sub contractors cost	8,94,000	
Equipment, Fixtures and fittings at cost on 1st January	2,64,000	
Stock on 1st January	59,000	
Profit and Loss Account, Credit Balaance on 1st January		1,28,000
Secured Loan		1,12,000
Bank Overdraft		1,05,000
Interest on loan and overdraft	22,000	
Depreciation on Equipment on 1st January		1,64,000
Administration Expenses	1,47,000	
Office Salaries	18,000	
Total	**38,32,000**	**38,32,000**

The following further information is furnished to you.

i) On 31st December, Stock in Hand including the land acquired during the year, is valued at 1,42,000 Work progress at that date is valued at 1,40,000

ii) On 1st July, the company moved to a new premise. The premise was taken on a 12 years lease and the lease premium paid amounted to 42,000 The company used sub contract Labour of 40,000 and Materials at cost of 38,000 in the refurbishment of the said premises. These are to be considered as part of the cost leasehold premises.

iii) A review of the Debtors reveals specific doubtful debts of ₹ 35,000 among dues outstanding for more than 6 months and the Directors wish to provide for these together with a provision of 2% of the balance Debtors.

iv) Depreciation on equipment, fixtures and fittings is provided at 15% on the written down value.

v) Uner the income tax Rules, the Depreciation on the companys assets amounts to ₹ 25,000

vi) Elite Ltd. sued Hexa Industries Ltd. for supplying defective materials, which has been written off as valueless. The Directors are confident that Hexa Industries Ltd. will agree for a settlement of ₹ 50,000

vii) The Directors propose a dividend of 25%

viii) ₹ 20,0000 is to be provided as Audit Fee.

ix) The company will provide 10% of Pre-tax Profit as Bonus to Employees in the books before charging Bonus.

x) Income Tax to be provided at 50% of the profits.

xi) Debtor of ₹ 300 had remained outstanding for more than 6 months.

You are required.

1. To prepare the company's Financial Statements for the year ended 31st December as near as possible to proper form of Company Final Accounts; and

2. To prepare a set of Notes to Accounts including significant accounting policies.

Solution :

<table>
<tr><td colspan="4" align="center">Elite Ltd</td></tr>
<tr><td colspan="4" align="center">Balance Sheet as at 31st December 2013</td></tr>
<tr><td colspan="2" align="center">Particulars</td><td>Note No.</td><td align="center">As at 31 Dec, 2013</td></tr>
<tr><td colspan="2"></td><td></td><td align="center">₹</td></tr>
<tr><td>A</td><td>Equity and Liabilities</td><td></td><td></td></tr>
<tr><td>1</td><td>Shareholder's funds</td><td></td><td></td></tr>
<tr><td></td><td>(a) Share Capital</td><td></td><td>1,00,000</td></tr>
<tr><td></td><td>(b) Reserves and Surplus</td><td>1</td><td>1,89,000</td></tr>
<tr><td></td><td>(c) Money received against share Warrants</td><td>-</td><td></td></tr>
<tr><td>2</td><td>Share application money pending allotment</td><td></td><td></td></tr>
<tr><td>3</td><td>Non - current liabilities</td><td></td><td></td></tr>
<tr><td></td><td>(a) Long term borrowings</td><td>2</td><td>2,17,000</td></tr>
<tr><td></td><td>(b) Deferred tax liabilities (net)</td><td></td><td></td></tr>
<tr><td></td><td>(c) Other long-term liabilities</td><td></td><td></td></tr>
<tr><td></td><td>(d) Long-term Provisions</td><td></td><td></td></tr>
<tr><td>4</td><td>Current liabilities</td><td></td><td></td></tr>
<tr><td></td><td>(a) Short term borrowings</td><td></td><td></td></tr>
<tr><td></td><td>(b) Trade Payables</td><td></td><td>4,63,000</td></tr>
<tr><td></td><td>(c) Other Current liabilities</td><td>3</td><td>44,000</td></tr>
<tr><td></td><td>(d) Short - term provisions</td><td>4</td><td>1,55,000</td></tr>
<tr><td colspan="2" align="center">Total</td><td></td><td>11,68,000</td></tr>
<tr><td>B</td><td>Assets</td><td></td><td></td></tr>
<tr><td>1</td><td>Non - Current Assets</td><td></td><td></td></tr>
<tr><td></td><td>(a) Fixed assets</td><td></td><td></td></tr>
<tr><td></td><td>   (i) Tangible assets</td><td>5</td><td>2,00,000</td></tr>
<tr><td></td><td>   (ii) Intangible assets</td><td></td><td></td></tr>
</table>

		Particulars	Note	
		(iii) Capital work in progress		
		(iv) Intangible assets under developments		
		(v) Fixed assets held for sale		
	(b)	Non current investments		
	(c)	Deferred tax assets (net)		
	(d)	Long - term loans and advances		
	(e)	Other non - current assets		
2		**Current Assets**		
	(a)	Current Investments		
	(b)	Inventories	6	2,82,000
	(c)	Trade receivables	7	6,86,000
	(d)	Cash and cash equivalents		
	(e)	Short - term loans and advances		
	(f)	Other Current assets		
		Total		11,68,000

		Elite Ltd		
		Statement of Profit and Loss for the year ended 31 December 2013		
		Particulars	**Note No.**	**For the year ended 31 Dec, 2012**
				₹
A		Continuing Operations		
1		Revenue from operations (gross)		27,60,000
		Less : Excise duty		
		Revenue from operations (net)		27,60,000
2		Other income		
3		Total revenue (1 + 2)		27,60,000

4	**Expenses**		
	(h) Cost of materials consumed	8	11,80,000
	(i) Purchase of stock in trade		73,000
	(j) Changes in inventories of finished goods, work in progress and stock in trade	9	13,000
	(k) Employee benefits expense	10	1,92,000
	(l) Finance costs		22,000
	(m) Depreciation and amortisation expense		20,000
	(n) Other expenses	11	10,70,000
	Total expenses		25,70,000
5	**Profit / (Loss) before exceptional and extraordinary items and tax (3 - 4)**		2,16,000
6	**Exceptional items**		
7	**Profit / (Loss) before extraordinary items and tax (5 ± 6)**		2,16,000
8	**Extraordinary items**		
9	**Profit / (Loss) before tax (7 ± 8)**		2,16,000
10	**Tax expense**		
	(a) Current tax expense for current year		1,30,000
	(b) (Less) : MAT Credit (Where applicable)		
	(c) Current tax expense relating to prior years		
	(d) Net Current tax expense		
	(e) Deferred tax		
11	**Profit / (Loss) From continuing operations (9 ± 10)**		86,000
B	**Discontinuing Operations**		
12.i	Profit / (Loss) From discontinuing operations (before tax)		
12.ii	Gain / (Loss) on disposal of assets / Settlement of liabilities attributable to the discontinuing operatiosn		
12.iii	Add / (Loss) : Tax expense of discontinuing operations		

	(a) On ordinary activities attributable to the discontinuing operations		
	(b) on gain / (Loss) on disposal of assets / settlement of liabilities.		
13	**Profit / (Loss) From discontinuing Operations (12.i ± 12.ii ± 12.iii)**		
C	**Total Operations**		
14	**Profit / (Loss) For the year (11 ± 13)**		86,000
15	**Earnings per equity share** (1) Basic (2) Biluted		

Working Notes :

1. Calculation of Depreciation

Furniture (Equipment, fixture & Fittings) Cost	2,64,000
(-) Depreciation	1,64,000
	1,00,000
Depreciation 100 × 15%	= 15,000
Lease hold premises	
Lease Rent	42,000
+ Refurbishment	
Material	38,000
Subcontract	40,000
	1,20,000

$$\text{Annual depreciation } \frac{\cos t}{\text{life}} = \frac{1,20,000}{12,000} = \quad = 10,000$$

$$\text{Depreciation for Current year} = 10 \times \frac{6,000}{12} = \quad = 5000$$

2. Provision for doubtful debts

Specific Provision	35,000
+ Other Prov. (7,35,000 - 35,000) × 2%	14,000
	49,000

3. **Profit before bonus to employees** = 5,55,000 - (39,000 + 22,000 + 1,47,000 + 18,000 + 20,000 + 49,000 + 20,000) =   2,40,000

    Bonus = 10% of 2,40,000 =   24,000

4. **Taxable Profit**

Profit before tax (as per books)	2,16,000
+ Dep. As per books	20,000
(-) Dep. As per IT Rules	25,000
+ provision of doubtful	49,000
Taxable profit	2,60,000
Tax = 2,60,000 × 50%	1,30,000

5. **Transfer to reserve :**

Profit before tax	2,16,000
Tax	1,30,000
PAT	86,000
Transfer to reserve @ 10%	9000
	77,000
Proposed Dividend	25,000
Transfered to B/S	52,000

Note 1 : Reserves and Surplus

Particulars	As at 31 Dec, 2013
	₹
Profit & Loss (128 + 52)	1,80,000
General Reserve	9000
Total	1,89,000

Note 2 : Long - term Borrowings

Particulars	As at 31 Dec, 2013
	₹
Bank Overdraft	1,05,000
Secured Loan	1,12,000
Total	2,17,000

Note 3 : Ohter Current Liabilities

Particulars	As at 31 Dec, 2013
	₹
Audit Fees Payable	20,000
Bonus Payable	24,000
Total	44,000

Note 4 : Short term Provisions

Particulars	As at 31 Dec, 2013
	₹
Provision for Taxation	1,30,000
Proposed Dividends	25,000
Total	1,55,000

Note 5 : Tangible Assets

Particulars		As at 31 Dec, 2013
		₹
Leasehold Premises	42,000	
Add : Sub - Contract Labour	40,000	
Add : Material Consumed	38,000	
	1,20,00	
Less : Depreciation	5000	1,15,000
Equipment (Gross Block)	2,64,000	
Less : Depreciation	1,79,000	85,000
Total		2,00,000

Note 6 : Inventories

Particulars	As at 31 Dec, 2013
	₹
Work in progress	1,40,000
Finished goods	1,42,000
Total	2,82,000

Note 7 : Trade Receivables

Particulars		As at 31 Dec, 2013
		₹
Trade Receivables > 6 month from the due date of Payment		
Unsecured considered good	2,65,000	
Doubtful	35,000	
Less:Provision for Bad debt (35,000 + 5,300)	40,300	2,59,700
Trade Receivables < 6 month from the due date of Payment		
Unsecured Considered good	4,35,000	
Less: Provision for Bad debt	8,700	4,26,300
Total		6,86,000

Note 8 : Cost Of Material Consumed

Particulars	As at 31 Dec, 2013
	₹
Raw Material	12,18,000
Less : Material used in refurnishment of new premises	38,000
Total	11,80,000

Note 9 : Changes in Inventories of Finished Goods, WIP & Stock in Trade

Particulars	As at 31 Dec, 2013
	₹
Opening Finished Goods	59,000
WIP	2,10,000
Closing Finished Goods	1,42,000
WIP	1,40,000
Total	13,000

Note 10 : Employees Benefit Expenses

Particulars	As at 31 Dec, 2013
	₹
Wages	1,11,000
Bonus to employees	24,000
Directors salary	39,000
Officer Salaries	18,000
Total	1,92,000

Note 11 : Other Expenses

Particulars	As at 31 Dec, 2013
	₹
Subscontractors Cost (894 - 40)	8,54,000
Administration Expenses	1,47,000
Provision for Bad Debt	49,000
Payment to Auditors	20,000
Total	10,70,000

Problem No. 6 : From the following particulars of Sunrise Limited Pune you are required to calculate the managerial Remuneration in the following situations.

(i) There is only one Whole Time Director.

(ii) There is two Whole Time Directors.

(iii) There are two Whole Time Directors, a part time Director and a Manager.

Liabilities	₹
Net Profit before Income Tax and Managerial Remuneration, but after depreciation and Provision for repairs	87,04,100
Depreciation provided in the books	31,00,000
Provision for Repairs for Machinery during the year	2,50,000
Depreciation Allowable under Schedule XIV	26,00,000
Actual expenditure incurred on Repairs during the year	1,50,000

Solution : Computation of Net Profits u/s 349 of the Companies Act.

Net Profit before Provision for Income tax and Managerial Remuneration, but after Depreciation and Provision for Repairs		87,04,100
Add : Depreciation Provided in the Books	31,00,000	
Provision for Repairs of Machinery	2,50,000	33,50,000
		1,20,54,100
Less : Depreciation allowable under Schedule XIV	26,00,000	
Actual Expenditure income on Repairs	1,50,000	27,50,000
Net Profit under Section 349		**93,04,100**

Note : Excess Provision over and above actually incurred shall be added back in determining the Net Profits.

Computation of Managerial Remuneration u/s 309

Situation	% of Remuneration	Managerial remuneration
One Whole Time Director	5%	4,65,205
Tow Whole Time Directors	10%	9,30,410
Two Whole Time Directors and Part Time Director and a Manager	11%	10,23,451

Problem No. 7 : The following extract of Balance Sheet Abhishek Ltd sangli as at 31 st March was obtained.

Liabilities	₹
Authorised Capital :	
10,000 14% Preference shares of ₹ 100 each	10,00,000
1,00,000 Equity Shares of ₹ 100 each	1,00,00,000
	1,10,00,000
Issued and Subsecribed Capital.	
7,500 14% Prefernce Sheres of ₹ 100 each fully paid	7,50,000
60,000 Equity Shares of ₹ 100 each ₹ 80 paid up	48,00,0000
Share Suspense Accoung	10,00,000
Reserves and Surplus	
Capital Reserves(60% is Revaluation Reserve)	1,25,000
Securities Premium	25,000
Secured Loans : 15% Debentures	32,50,000
Unsecured Loans :	
Public Deposits	1,85,000
Cash credit from SBI	2,30,000
Current Liabilities : Surdry Credtitors	1,72,500

Assets	₹
Investment Shares, Debentures etc	37,50,000
Profit and Loss Account	7,62,500
Preliminary Expenses not written off	27,500

Share Suspense Account represents application money received on shares the allotment of which is not yet made. Abhishek Ltd has been sustaining losses for the last few years. The company has only one Whole - Time Director. Find out how much remuneration can the company pay to its managerial person as per the provision of Part II of Schedule XIII to the Companies Act, 1956 Would your answer differ if Abhishek Ltd. is an Investment Compay?

Solution :

Computation of Effective Capital

If Abhishek Ltd is treated as an	Non-Invt. Company	Investment Company
Paid up Share Capital		
15,000 14 % Preference Shares	7,50,000	7,50,000
1,20,000 Equity Shares	4,80,000	4,80,000
Add : Capital Reserve (Excluding Revaluation Reserve 60%)	50,000	50,000
Securities Premium	25,000	25,000
15% Debentures	32,50,000	32,50,000
Public Deposits (Repayable after one year)	1,85,000	1,85,000
(A)	**90,60,000**	**90,60,000**
Less : Items for deduction		
Investment (deducted for a Non Investment as company) Per Expln 1 to Part II of Schedule XIII	37,50,000	-
Profit and Loss Account (Dr. Balance)	7,62,500	7,62,500
Preliminary Expenses no written off	27,500	27,500
(B)	**45,40,000**	**7,90,000**
Effective Capital (A - B)	**45,20,000**	**82,70,000**
Slab under which the efective capital falls	Less : than ₹ 1 Crore	₹ 1 Crore or more, but less than ₹ 5 Crores

Maximum Remuneration and conditions to be fulfilled

If Abhishek Ltd is treated as an	Non-Invt. Company	Investment Company
Slab under Which the Effective Capital Falls - Determined above	Less than ₹ 1 Crore	₹ 1 Cror or less More, but than ₹ 5 Crores
Part II (1) (A) of Schedule XII : 2 Conditions to be fulfilled Monthly Remuneration Shall not exceed	37,500	50,000
Annual Managerial Remuneration not to exceed	4,50,000	6,00,000
Part II (1) (B) of Schedule XIII : 4 Conditions to be fulfilled Monthly Remuneration Shall not exceed	75,000	1,00,000
Annual Managerial Remuneration not to exceed	9,00,000	12,00,000

The conditions to be fulfilled are as under Part II (1) (A) First 2 Conditions Part II (1) (B) - all 4 Conditions

- Approval of Remuneration Committee by a resolution

- Company Should not default in repayment of its Debts (including Public Deposits & Debentures) or Interest thereon for Continuous period of 30 days or more in the preceding financial year before the appointment of such Managerial Person.

- Special Resoultion at Company's General Meeting, Authorizing Payament of Remuneration for a period not exceeding a period of three years.

- Statement Containing the particulars Prescribed under Schedule XIII Part II (10) (B) to be sent to Shareholders, along with Notice to General Meeting.

Problem No. 8 : Bright Pune Ltd was incorporated on 1st April to take over the running business of Shri Rockey. The purchase consideration was satisfied by allotment of.

(i) 20,000 Equity Shares of ₹ 10 each at par.

(ii) 10,000 10% Redeemable Preference Shares ₹ 10 each at par, redeemable on 31.03.2010

(iii) ₹ 50,000 paid in cash.

The company issued a prospectus for raising by issue of 30,000 equity shares of ₹ 10 each at par and 15,000 10% Redeemable preference Shares of ₹ 10 each, at par The entrie amount in respect of the issue was received by 30th june, except Final call of ₹ 2.50 per share on 1000 shares issued to Shri Rockey, a Director. Underwriting commission at 2% on Equity Shares and at 3% preference Shares were paid to a merchant banker.

The Preliminary Expenses were estimated at ₹ 50,000 in the prospectus but the actual expenses incurred were as under.

Solicitor's Fee	₹ 10,000
Printingof Memorandum	₹ 15,000 (of which ₹ 5000 remained unpaid)
Stamping and Registration	₹ 20,000
Advertisement Expenses	₹ 30,000

The Company Purchased a plot of land for ₹ 75,000 Further, it advanced ₹ 1,00,000 for construction of office Building and ₹ 1,50,000 to a supplier, being 40% of contract price for supply of Machinery. A part of the investments taken over from Shri. Rockey was sold for ₹ 50,000 (₹ 5,000 in excess of their book value)

Prepare a Receipts and Payments Account and other relevant information to be included in the Statutory Report pursuant to Sec. 165 of the Companies Act. 1956 in respect of Roadshow Ltd made upto 30th June

Solution :

Extracts from the Statutory Report of Bright Ltd.
(Pursuant to Section 165 of Companies Act, 1956)

1. Receipts and Payment A/c upto 30th June

Receipts	₹	Payments	₹	₹
Shares :	2,97,500	Vendor (Shri Rocky)		50,000
- Equity Shares		Preliminary Expenses :		
(3,00,000 - 2,500)	1,50,000	(a) Underwriting Commission :		
- 10% Redeemable	50,000	Equity Shares (2% on 3,00,000)	6000	
Pref. Shares		- Pref. Shares (3% on 1,50,000)	4,500	
		(b) Solicitor's Fees	10,000	
		(c) Printing of Memorandum	10,000	
		(d) Stamoping and Registration	20,000	
		(e) Advertisement	30,000	80,500
		Capital Expenditure :		
		Land		75,000
		Building (Advance)		1,00,000
		Machinery (Advance)		1,50,000
		Closing Balance		42,000
Total	**4,97,500**	**Total**		**4,97,500**

2. Financial Information for inclusion in the statutory Report

(a) Shares Allotted subject to payment there of in Cash

Particulars	No of Shares	Nominal value of each Share	Amount received upto 30th june
Equity Shares	30,000	10	2,97,500
10% Redeemable Preference Shares	15,000	10	1,50,000

(b) Shares allotted as fully paid up otherwise than in cash (to Vendor for purchase of running business)

Particulars	No of Shares	Nominal value of each Share	Amount received upto 30th june
Equity Shares	20,000	10	2,00,000
10% Redeemable Preference Shares	10,000	10,	1,00,000

(c) Preliminary Expenses

Particulars	Preliminary Expenses actually incurred up to 30th june
Solicitor's Fee	10,000
Printing of Memorandum	15,000
Stamping	20,000
Advertisement Expensese	30,000
Total	**75,000**

Preliminary Expenses as estimated in the prospectus: **50,000**

(d) Particulars of Contracts entered into by the Company

    (a) The Company has advanced ₹ 1,00,000 for construction of Office Building.

    (b) The Company has entered into a contract for supply of Machinery costing ₹ 3,75,000 against which a sum of ₹ 1,50,000 has been advanced, being 40% of contract Price.

(e) Arrears due on calls from Directors Shri Rocky, Director ₹ 2,500 is due.

2. 8 EXCERCISE

1. From the following particulars furnished by XYZ Limited, Pune prepare the Balance sheet as at 31st March, 2014 as required by Part I, Schedule VI of the Companies Act.

(in ₹)

Particulars		Debit	Credit
Equity Capital (Face Value of ₹ 100)			10,00,000
Calls in Arrears		1,000	
Land		2,00,000	
Building		3,50,000	
Plant and Machinary		5,25,000	
Furniture		50,000	
General Reserve			2,10,000
Loan from State Financial Corporation			1,50,000
Stock : Finished goods	2,00,000		
Raw Material	50,000	2,50,000	
Provision for Taxation			68,000
Sudry Debtors		2,00,000	
Advances		42,700	
Proposed Dividend			60,000
Profit and Loss Account			1,00,000
Cash Balance		30,000	
Cash at Bank		2,47,000	
Preliminary Expenses		13,300	
Loans (Unsecured)			1,21,000
Sundry Creditors (for goods and expenses)			2,00,000
Total		**19,09,000**	**19,09,000**

The following additional information is also provided :

(i) 2,000 Equity shares were issued for consideration other than cash.

(ii) Debtors of ₹ 52,000 are due for more than six months from the due date of payment.

(iii) The Balance of ₹ 1,50,000 in the loan account with state finance corporation includes 7,500 interest accured but not due.

(iv) Balance at Bank includes ₹ 2,000 with Elite Bank Limited, which is not a scheduled Bank.

(v) Bills Receivalbe for ₹ 2,75,000 maturing on 30th June have been discounted.

(vi) The company had Contract for the erection of Machinary at ₹ 1,50,000 which is still incomplete.

2. Prepare a Balance Sheet of Sneha Ltd, Nasik as at 31st March, 2014 required under schedule VI of the companies Act, 1956, from the following information of Honeymoon Ltd.

Particulars	Amount (₹)	Particulars	Amount (₹)
Terms Loans (Secured)	10,00,000	Investments (Long term)	2,25,200
Sundry Creditors	11,45,000	Loss for the year	3,00,000
Advances	3,72,000	Sundry Debtors	12,25,000
Cash and Bank Balances	2,75,000	Miscellaneous expenses	58,000
Staff Advances	55,000	Loan from debtors	2,00,000
Provision for Taxation	1,70,000	Provision for doubtful debtors	20,200
Securities Premium	4,75,000	Stores	4,00,000
Loose Tools	50,000	Fixed assets (WDV)	51,50,000
General Reserve	20,50,000	Finished goods	7,50,000
Capital work in progress	2,00,000		

Additional Information :

i) Share Capital Consists of :
- 30,000 Equity shares of ₹ 100 each fully paid up.
- 10,000 10% Redeemable preferences shares of ₹ 100 each fully paid up.

ii) Depreciation on assets ₹ 5,00,000

3. Medha Mumbai Ltd., is in the midst of finalizing its accounts for the year-ended 30th September. A Profit and Loss Account has been prepared in draft, the account balances as rounded off to the nearest thousands, are listed below :

Particulars	(₹ 000's)	Particulars	(₹ 000's)
Shares Capital	25,000	Finished Goods	1,414
General Reserve	6,031	Stores and Spares	2,771
Development Rebate Reserve	6,271	Tools Jigs and Dies	9,187
Land	2,225	Cash Credit from Banks	30,672
Buildings	9,316	Acceptances	2,645
Plant and Machinary	64,282	Sundry Creditors	6,162
Furniture, Fixtures & Office Equipment	1,594	Other Current Liabilities	10,317
Vehicles	454	Interest Accured but not due on loans	589

Particulars	(₹ 000's)	Particulars	(₹ 000's)
Depreciation Reserve		Provisions for Gratuity and Pension	241
Building	2,193	Interest Accured on Deposits	2
Plant and Machinary	30,328	Sundry Debtors	24,231
Furniture	568	Cash in Hand	37
Vehicles	245	Bank Balance	
Loan from State government	575	On Current Accounts	39
Other Secured Loans	32,460	On Deposit Accounts	27
Fixed Deposits from Public	2,400	Loans and Advance	4,518
Unsecured Loans	1,114	Preliminary Expenses	8
Raw Materials and Components	42,014	Advance Income - Tax paid	3,489
Work in Progress	6,116	Capital Work-in-Progress	596
		Profit & Loss A/c (Profit for the year)	14,509

In arriving at the profit for the year, the following have been charged :

Particulars	₹
Depreciation	12,424
Salary and perquisite to Managing Director	72
Director's fee	4

The Authorized capital is 3,50,000 Equity shares of ₹ 100 each. The from the State Government is secured by a charge on the land, cash credits by hypothecation of stocks and book Debts and the other Secured Loans on the Buildings and Plant and Machinary.
The following adjustments are yet to be made -
   (i) Investment Allownce Reserve to be created ₹ 5,400
   (ii) Provision to be made for Income-Tax in ₹ 4,400
   (iii) Provision to be made for Managing Director's Commission at 1% of the profits.
   (iv) Proposed Dividend at 10%.
      Depreciation as per section 350 of the Companies Act is ₹ 10,424

Required :
   (i) Show the computation of commission payable to the Managing Director; and
   (ii) Prepare the Balance sheet of the company, based on all the above.

4. Following are the balance from the books Vaishali Ltd Nagar as at 31st March 2014.

(₹ in 000's)

Particulars	(₹ 000's)	Particulars	(₹ 000's)
Sales	13,39,400	Other Expenses	2,25,280
Depreciation	7,100	General Reserve	51,600
Other Income (Operation)	5,760	Sundry Debtors	1,18,000
Development Rebate Reserve	4,680	Share Capital	40,000
Investment Allowance Resreve	8,500	Secured Loans	26,960
Fixed Assets at Cost	1,27,740	Cash at Bank	640
Investments (Long Term)	380	Loan & Advances (Short term)	1,160
Interest Accrued	50	Fixed Deposits	32,000
Purchases (Raw Material)	8,96,800	Depreciation Reserve	56,000
Salaries and Wages	69,420	Provision for Doubtful Debts	120
		Sundry Creditors	2,21,550

Calculate Managing Director's Remuneration and Prepare in the proper from the profit and loss Account and Balance Sheet as at 31st March 2014 with the help of the following information.

Particulars	₹	₹
Stocks	Opening	Closing
- Raw Material and stores	1,00,040	50,020
- Work in progress	1,90,160	40,080
- Finished goods	49,800	1,61,900
Depreciation as per schedule XIV to the companies Act, 1956		8,000
Market value of Investments		290
Sundry debtors due for more than 6 months		720
Out of above, provision made this year for Doubtful debts		80
Included in other expenses are		
- Audior's fee for audit		120
- Payment to Auditors for other services		40

- Income Tax to be provided at 36.6%
- Managing Directors Remuneration is at 5% of Net Profit as per law subject to maximum of ₹ 2,40,000 p.a.
- Provide Dividends at 25% on capital and transfer the Balance of profits to general Reserve.
- Authorised capital of the company is 6 lakhs equity Shares of ₹ 100 each. Out of this 4 lakhs shares have been issued and fully paid.
- Provision for Doubtful debts is made in respect of Debtors due for more than 6 months.
- Debtors due for less than 6 months is secured to the extent of ₹ 60,000

5. Following balance are extracted from the books of the Rajesh Industries Ltd, Satara as at 31 st Dec. 2013

(₹ in 000's)

Particulars	Debit	Credit
Sales		2,760
Purchases of Materials	1,218	
Share capital fully paid		100
Land purchased in the year as stock	73	
Leasehold premises	42	
Creditors		463
Debtors	735	
Directors Salaries	39	
Wages	111	
Work in progress on 1st january	210	
Sub-contractors cost	894	
Equipment, Fixtures and fittings at cost on 1st January	264	
Stock on 1st January	59	
Profit and Loss Account, Credit Balance on 1st January		128
Secured Loan		112
Bank Overdraft		105
Interest on loan and overdraft	22	
Depreciation on Equipment on 1st January		164
Administration Expenses	147	
Office Salaries	18	
Total	**3,832**	**3,832**

The following further information is furnished to you.

i) On 31st December, Stock in Hand including the land acquired during the year, is valued at ₹ 1,42,000 Work progress at that date is valued at ₹ 1,40,000.

ii) On 1st July, the company moved to a new premise. The premise was taken on a 12 years lease and the lease premium paid amounted to ₹ 42,000 The company used sub contract Labour of ₹ 40,000 and Materials at cost of ₹ 38,000 in the refurbishment of the said premises. These are to be considered as part of the cost leasehold premises.

iii) A review of the Debtors reveals specific doubtful debts of ₹ 35,000 among dues outstanding for more than 6 months and the Directors wish to provide for these together with a provision of 2% of the balance Debtors.

iv) Depreciation on equipment, fixtures and fittings is provided at 15% on the written down value.

v) Uner the income tax Rules, the Depreciation on the companys assets amounts to ₹ 25,000

vi) Elite Ltd. sued Hexa Industries Ltd. for supplying defective materials, which has been written off as valueless. The Directors are confident that Hexa Industries Ltd. will agree for a settlement of ₹ 50,000

vii) The Directors propose a dividend of 25%

viii) ₹ 20,000 is to be provided as Audit Fee.

ix) The company will provide 10% of Pre-tax Profit as Bonus to Employees in the books before charging Bonus.

x) Income Tax to be provided at 50% of the profits.

xi) Debtor of ₹ 300 had remained outstanding for more than 6 months.

You are required.

1. To prepare the company's Financial Statements for the year ended 31st December as near as possible to proper form of Company Final Accounts; and

2. To prepare a set of Notes to Accounts including significant accounting policies.

CHAPTER 3

Company Liquidation Accounts

A) Preparation of Liquidators Final Statement of Account

    3.1 Meaning of Liquidation

    3.2 Modes of Winding Up

    3.3 Consequences of Liquidation

    3.4 Preparation of Liquidator's Final Statement of Account

    3.5 Problems

    3.6 Exercises

B) Preparation of Statement of Affairs and Deficiency Account

    3.7 Form No. 57

    3.8 Problems

    3.9 Exercises

A) PREPARATION OF LIQUIDATORS FINAL STATEMENT OF ACCOUNT

A limited company is an artificial person created by law. Its existence is not perpetual. As the company is formed by law, it is dissolved through the process laid down by the law. The company cannot have a natural death. A solvent or insolvent company can be liquidated or dissolved. It can be brought to an end, if the directors of the company desire to dissolve the company. On dissolution, the company's name shall be struck off by the Registrar from the Register of the Company and he shall also get the fact published in the Official Gazette.

3.1 Meaning of Liquidation:

Liquidation or winding up of a company is a process by which the dissolution of a company is brought about and its property is administered for the benefits of its creditors and members. An administrator called liquidator is appointed to carry out the work related to liquidation and he is vested with the control of the company. Assets are realised, calls-in-arrears are collected, besides uncalled capital, if any, is called up, if necessary. Debts are paid off and finally the surplus, if any, is distributed among the members of the company in accordance with their rights. Thus, liquidation or winding up ultimately leads to dissolution of a company.

3.2 Modes of Winding Up

A Company can be liquidated in any of the following three ways :
1) Compulsory winding up.
2) Voluntary winding up.
3) Winding up under the supervision of Court.

1) Compulsory Winding Up :

The winding up of a Company by an order of the Court is known as compulsory winding up. According to Section 433 of the Company's Act, the Court may order for the compulsory winding up of a company in the following circumstances –
1) If the company passes a special resolution for winding up.
2) If the company is insolvent.
3) If the company commits a default in holding a statutory meeting.
4) If the company does not commence its business within a year of its incorporation or suspends business for a year.
5) If the company is unable to pay its debts.
6) If the number of the members of a company falls below 7 in case of a public company and 2 in case of a private company.
7) If the court is of the opinion that it is just and equitable that the company should be wound up.

The petition for winding up to the Court can be made by the company itself, any of its creditors, a contributory, the Registrar or any person authorised by the Central Government to make such a petition.

2) Voluntary Winding Up

A liquidation without intervention of the Court is known as "voluntary liquidation". A company may be wound up voluntarily –
i) by passing an ordinary resolution in the general meeting; or –
    a)   when the period for the duration for which the company was constituted has expired or over; or –
    b)   when the event or happening on which depended the termination of the existence of the company has happened.
ii) by passing a special resolution to wind up voluntarily for any reason whatsoever.

Types of Voluntary Liquidation

There are two types of voluntary liquidation. These are as follows :
1)   Voluntary liquidation by members.
2)   Voluntary liquidation by creditors.

    1)   **Voluntary liquidation by members :** In this type, the member of the Company voluntarily decides to wind up the company. The company may be solvent and able to pay all its debts from realisation of its assets to all claimants, but members may yet want to dissolve the company.

Legal provisions regarding voluntary winding up –

1) At least two or more directors must file a statutory declaration for the winding up of a company to the Registrar.
2) The statutory declaration must be made within 5 weeks immediately preceding the date of the passing of the resolution for winding up of a company.
3) Special resolution must be passed in the general meeting of members.
4) The special resolution is to be advertised in the Official Gazette within 14 days of the passing of such resolution.
5) The company must give a notice to the liquidator within 10 days from the passing of such resolution, regarding the appointment of liquidator.
6) If the process of winding up takes more than a year, the liquidator is expected to call a meeting of the company at the end of each year and give the information in respect of its act and dealing regarding the realisation of assets.

After completing all the formalities, the decision of liquidation of the company is taken and the business of the company comes to an end.

2) Voluntary liquidation by creditors : In this case, the creditors them selves convene the meeting of voluntarily to initiate the process of winding up of the company. This meeting is convened only after the meeting of the members of the company takes place. At the meeting, the resolution of wind up the company is passed and the same is sent it to the Registrar within 10 days from the date on which such a resolution is passed. A voluntary liquidation by creditor's may be initiated only if the company is not in a position to pay off its liabilities.

3) Winding up under the supervision of the Court : According to Section 522 of the companies Act, at any time, after a company has passed a resolution for voluntary winding up, the court may make an order that the voluntary winding up shall continue subject to the supervision of the Court. Such an order is passed by the Court on the application of any creditor or contributory or liquidator or the company itself under the following circumstances –

i) The liquidator under voluntary winding up is prejudiced or is negligent in collecting the assets of a company.
ii) The resolution for winding up was obtained by fraud.

3.3 Consequences of Liquidation (Effects of Liquidation)

The following are the consequences which generally follow a company's winding up decision :-

1) An official designated as a liquidator will take over the administration of the Company. In case of compulsory winding up, the official liquidator attached to High Court

functions as a liquidator of the company. In case of voluntary winding up, such an official is appointed by the members or the creditors depending upon members or creditor's voluntary winding up.

2) The powers of the Board of Directors will terminate and will not vest in the liquidator.

3) The winding up order or resolutions of voluntary winding up shall operate as a notice of discharge to all members of the company. The members of the company will be termed as contributories on the commencement of company's winding up. The liquidator will prepare a list of all such contributories who may be made liable to contribute towards the company on account of deficiency in the assets of the company. In case there is a surplus in the asset, the liquidator shall prepare a list of those members, who are entitled to share this surplus. The term contributory include members of both the above categories.

4) The liquidator will realise the assets of the company and distribute the proceeds among various claimants.

3:4 Preparation of Liquidator's Final Statement of Account

After the winding up of the company, the main duty of the liquidator is to collect the assets of the company and realise them and distribute the money so realised among right claimants. For this purpose, he maintains a cash book for recording the receipts and payments and is required to submit an abstract of the cash book to the Court in case of compulsory winding up, and to the Company in case of voluntary winding up. The liquidator is also required to prepare an account of winding up known as "Liquidator's Final Statement of Account" after the affairs of the Company are fully wound up. This account takes the form of Cash Account and the following receipts and payments are shown in this account –

Receipts:

During the process of winding up, the liquidator receives the amount from :
1) Realisation of assets of the Company.
2) Realisation from debtors of the Company.
3) Surplus from fully secured creditors.
4) Contribution received from directors and officers of the Company.
5) Calls made and received from contributers.

Payment:

On the credit side of this account, he records the payments made in the following priority order :
1) Payment to fully secured creditors.
2) Payment of legal expenses.
3) Liquidator's remuneration.
4) Liquidation expenses or cost of winding up.

5) Payment to preferential creditors.
6) Payment to debentureholders including outstanding interest and other creditors having a floating charge on the assets of the Company.
7) Payment to unsecured creditors.
8) Payment to shareholders.
   a) Preference shareholders.
   b) Equity shareholders

Proforma of Liquidator's Final Statement of Account is as follows :-

Form No. 156

(See Rule 329)

Companies Act, 1956

* Strike out what does not apply

* Here state whether the winding up is a members' or creditors' voluntary winding up or a winding up under the supervision of the Court. If under the supervision of the Court, mention the number of the petition in which the order was made and the date of the order.

Liquidator's Statement of Account of the Winding up

(Members' / Creditors' Voluntary Winding up)

(Pursuant to Section 318 / 497)

1. Name of the Company ...... Ltd.
2. Nature of proceeding :
3. Date of commencement of the winding up :
4. Name and address of the Liquidator :

   Statement showing how the winding up has been conducted and the property of the Company has been disposed off from .... 20.... (commencement of winding-up) to ...... 20.... (Close of winding up.)

Receipts	Estimated Value Rs. P.	Value realised Rs. P.	Payments	Rs. P.	Payments Rs. P.
Assets :			Legal charges		
Cash at Bank			Liquidator's remuneration :		
Cash in Hand			When applicable -		
Marketable Securities			% on Rs. .... realised		
Bills Receivable			% on Rs. .... distributed		
Trade Debtors			Total	.....	
Loans and Advances					
Stock-in-trade					
Work-in-progress					

Receipts	Estimated Value Rs. P.	Value realised Rs. P.	Payments	Rs. P.	Payments Rs. P.

Freehold property
Leasehold property
Plant and Machinery
Furniture, Fittings,
    Utensils, etc.
Patents, Trade Marks etc.
Investments other than
    Marketable Securities
Surplus from Securities
Unpaid Calls at commen-
    cement of winding up
Amounts receivable from
    calls on contributories
    made in the winding up
Receipts as per Trading
    Account
Other property, viz...
 	
        Total
 	
Less
    Payments to redeem
      securities
    Costs of execution
    Payments as per
      Trading Accounts
			(By whom fixed ......)
			Auctioneers' and Valuers'
			    charges
			Liquidation expenses
			Costs of possession and
			    maintenance of estate
			Costs of notices in Gazette
			    and newspapers
			    Incidental outlay
			    (establishment charges
			    and other expenses of
			    liquidation)
			Total costs and charges
			i) Debentureholders :
			    Payment of Rs. .... per
			    Rs. ..... debenture
			    Payment of Rs. .... per
			    Rs. ..... debenture
			    Payment of Rs. .... per
			    Rs. ..... debenture
			ii) Creditors :
			    ...... * Preferential
			    ...... * Unsecured :
			    Dividend(s) .... P. in the
			      rupee on Rs.
			    (The estimate of the
			    amount expected to rank
			    for dividend was Rs. .....)
			iii)Returns to contributories :
			    (Equity and preferential
			    shareholders)
			    .... P. per rupee ....*share ....
			    .... P. per rupee ....*share ....
			    .... P. per rupee ....*share ....
			Add balance		

Explanations of some important item and order of payment

1) Legal Expenses:

The expenses which are incurred by the Company during the period of its winding up on meeting the legal requirements are known as legal expenses.

2) Liquidator's Remuneration:

A liquidator gets his remuneration in the form of commission based on assets realised and payment made to creditors or contributories. This remuneration is fixed in the general meeting of members. The liquidator gets the following type of remuneration –

a) Fixed remuneration.

b) Commission on realisation of assets.

c) Commission on payment to –

i) Unsecured creditors.

ii) Equity shareholders.

a) Fixed remuneration : A fixed amount may be given as a commission or remuneration to the liquidator.

b) Commission on realisation of assets : Realisation of assets means the amount receivable from sale of assets of the Company. While calculating the commission on realisation of asset, the following points must be taken into consideration :

i) The amount of cash in hand and cash at bank are not included in the realisation proceeds. If it is specially mentioned that these should be included, only then, they are to be included in the realisation proceeds.

ii) The liquidator gets commission on the surplus from the asset given to creditors after making payment to secured creditors. The liquidator makes an effort for realising the surplus from such asset from secured creditors. However, if he sells the asset himself, he gets commission on the total proceeds of such assets.

iii) Commission on Unsecured Creditors.

The creditors who have not been given any asset of the company as a security are called unsecured creditors. As the preferential creditors are unsecured, the amount of preferential creditor is also included in the unsecured creditors. But, if it is specially mentioned that, the commission is payable excluding preferential creditors, then the commission of liquidator is to be charged only on the amount paid to unsecured creditor.

If the amount is sufficient to make payment of unsecured creditors, the commission is charged after making the payment of unsecured creditors.

For example : Suppose the amount available is Rs. 40,000 and unsecured creditors are Rs. 30,000, and the rate of commission is 2%, the commission will be charged on Rs. 30,000 i.e. $\dfrac{30,000 \times 2}{100}$ = Rs. 600. Thus, the unsecured creditors will be paid Rs. 30,000 and the liquidator will be paid a commission of Rs. 600.

If cash is insufficient

If cash is not sufficient to pay secured creditors / contributories and the remuneration to liquidator, the remuneration is calculated as under :-

Suppose liquidator's remuneration is fixed at 2% on the amount paid to unsecured creditors, unsecured creditors are Rs. 30,000 and the cash available is Rs. 30,294. If Rs. 30,000 are to be paid to unsecured creditors, the liquidator must get Rs. 600 at 2% on the payment of Rs. 30,000 to unsecured creditors. But after the payment of Rs. 30,000, cash available is only Rs. 294 and as such Rs. 600 cannot be paid to liquidator. Hence, in such a case, the remuneration is calculated by using the following formula :

$$\text{Liquidator's Remuneration} : \frac{\text{Cash available for unsecured Creditors} \times \% \text{ of commission}}{100 + \% \text{ of commission}}$$

Cash		Cash	Remuneration
102	:	30,294	2% i.e. Rs. 2

$$= \frac{30,294 \times 2}{102} = \text{Rs. } 594$$

Rs. 30,294 less Rs. 594 = Rs. 29,700 cash available for payment to unsecured creditors and 2% of 29,700 is Rs. 594.

Thus, in such a case, the rate of remuneration is to be added to 100 and then remuneration is calculated on cash available as shown above.

iv) Commission on payment to equity shareholder

Sometimes, instead of giving a commission on amount paid to unsecured creditors, the liquidator is paid a commission on the amount paid to equity shareholders. If the amount available is sufficient to make the payment of Equity shareholder's capital, commission is charged on the principle of 'Berere charging' but if the amount is net sufficient to make capital payment of equity shareholder's capital the commission is charged on the principle of 'After charging' and the balance will be paid to equity shareholders.

3) Liquidation expenses :

After the payment of liquidator's remuneration, liquidation expenses or cost of winding up is paid. Liquidation expenses include cost of possession and maintenance of estate and cost of notices in Gazette and newspapers.

4) Fully secured creditors :

Fully secured creditors are those creditors, whose amount of loan is fully secured. They are given asset as a security and generally the realisable value of this asset is more than the amount of loan.

For example : If the amount of loan is Rs. 30,000 and the value of asset is Rs. 50,000, the creditors are termed as fully secured creditors.

Generally, the payment made to the fully secured creditor and the amount realised from the sale of security are not shown in the liquidator's final statement of account. The fully secured creditors recover the amount of asset and hand over the surplus to the liquidator. This surplus is shown in the liquidator's final statement of account.

Partly secured creditors : If the amount realised from the security is less than the claim of the creditor, his unsatisfied balance is added to the unsecured creditor.

For example : If the claim of a creditor is for Rs. 15,000 and the amount realised from the security is Rs. 10,000, the unsatisfied balance of claim Rs. 5,000 is added to unsecured creditors. Such creditors are treated as partly secured creditors.

5) Preferential Creditors :

The following are the preferential creditors who are paid after meeting the cost of winding up including the liquidator's remuneration but in priority to all other debts :

i) All revenue taxes, ceases and rates due and payable by the Company to the Government or local authority within 12 months before the date of commencement of winding up.

ii) All wages or salaries of any employee due for the period not exceeding 4 months, within 12 months before the commencement of winding up and any compensation payable to any workmen under any of the provisions of Chapter V(A) of the Industrial Disputes Act, 1947, provided the amount payable to any one claimant will not exceed Rs. 1,000.

iii) All accrued holiday remuneration becoming payable to an employee on account of the termination of his employment before or on account of winding up.

(Note : Persons who advance money for the purpose of preferential payment under (ii) and (iii) above will be treated as preferential creditors)

iv) Unless the company is being wound up voluntarily for the purpose of reconstructions or amalgamation, all contributions payable during the 12 months previous to winding up, by the company as the employer of any person, under Employee's State Insurance Act, 1948, or any other law for the time being in force.

v) All sums due as compensation under Workmen's Compensation Act, 1923.

vi) All sums due to any employee from a provident fund, a pension fund, a gratuity fund or any other fund for the welfare of the employees maintained by the Company.

vii) The expenses of any investigation held under Sections 235 or 237, insofar as they are payable by the Company.

If the cash is insufficient to pay in full all the preferential creditors, then the cash available is paid proportionately to all of them.

6) Debentureholders and creditors having floating charge :

When no specific asset of the Company is given as security to debentureholders or creditors but all assets of the Company are given as a security to them, they are called as debentureholders and creditors having a floating charge. They have no right to sell any specific asset and get the amount realised for their loans. They will rank as unsecured and will be paid after the payment of preferential creditors.

7) Interest on Debentures :

If the company is solvent, interest is paid upto the date of actual payment of principal, and if the company is insolvent, the interest is payable only upto the date of the commencement of winding up.

8) Payment to unsecured creditors :

After the payment to debentureholders, unsecured creditors rank for payment. Unsecured creditors may get full amount of their claim, if the surplus is available. On the other hand, if sufficient cash is not available, they may get part payment for the settlement of their dues.

9) Payment to Contributories :

The contributories in the event of winding up of a company may be :
i) Preferential shareholders.
ii) Equity shareholders.

Payment to preferential shareholders with arrears of dividend :

Preference shareholders have a preference to receive their capital and dividend over equity shareholders. While paying the dividend on preference shares, the following points should be taken into account –
  i) No dividend is payable for the period falling after commencement of winding up. It means arrears of dividend upto the date of commencement of winding up are only considered.
  ii) If dividend was declared but not paid, it is to be paid as debt of the Company and not as arrears and it is paid in priority of returns of even preference share capital.
  iii) If dividend is in arrears and has not been declared, it is paid only if there remains any surplus after repayment of equity share capital in full.

However, if the Articles state that arrears of dividend on preference shares are to be paid before anything is paid to equity shareholders, the payment of dividend is to be made accordingly. In this case, if it is felt necessary, the required amount is collected by making a call on partly-paid equity shares.

10) Payment to Equity Shareholders

After having paid all the claims of preference shareholders, all the cash available is paid to equity shareholders. If there are various types of equity shares i.e. fully paid and partly paid equity shares, but no provision is made for giving priority to any class of them, the excess amount paid on any share then is returned first and the balance is distributed proportionately among all classes of shares.

Calls on partly paid shares :

If the amount available by realisation of assets is not sufficient to pay the claims of all claimants, the liquidator can make a call on these shares which are partly paid up.

Calls-in-Advance :

Sometimes, some equity shareholders pay the amount without the call being made by the Company, Such an amount is called as "Calls-in-advance". In case of winding up of the Company, the amount of calls-in-advance will be paid before making the payment to equity shareholders.

3.5 PROBLEMS

Problem No. 1 : Poona Ltd. passed a resolution to wind up voluntarily on 30th June, 2014, when its Balance Sheet stood as under :-

Balance Sheet as on 30-6-2014

Liabilities	Rs.	Assets	Rs.
Share Capital :		Land	50,000
Authorised and Subscribed		Plant & Machinery	1,15,000
1,000, 6% Preference Shares		Patents	30,000
of Rs. 100 each	1,00,000	Stock at Cost	27,500
500 Equity Shares of Rs. 100	-	Sundry Debtors	55,000
each, Rs. 75 paid-up	37,500	Cash at Bank	15,000
1,500 Equity Shares of Rs. 100	-	Profit & Loss A/c	60,000
each, Rs. 60 paid-up	90,000		
5% Debentures (Floating			
charge on all assets)	50,000		
Interest on Debentures	2,500		
Creditors	65,000		
Income Tax	7,500		
	3,52,500		3,52,500

a) The preference dividends were in arrears for two years. The arrears are payable on liquidation as per the Articles of Company. Creditors include a loan of Rs. 25,000 on the mortgage of land.

b) The Assets realised is as follows :
Land Rs. 60,000; Plant and Machinery Rs. 87,500; Patents 27,500; Stock Rs. 30,000 and Sundry Debtors Rs. 40,000.

c) The Expenses of Liquidation amounted to Rs. 5,450.

d) The liquidator is entitled to a commission of 3% on all assets realised and 2% on amounts distributed among unsecured creditors except preferential creditors.

e) All payments were made on 31st December, 2014.

You are required to prepare Liquidator's Statement of Account.

Solution

Liquidator's Final Statement of Account

Receipts		Rs.	Payments		Rs.
To Cash at Bank		15,000	By Liquidator's Remuneration		
To Assets Realised			3% × 2,45,000 =	7,350	
Land	60,000		2% × 40,000 =	800	8,150
Plant and Machinery	87,500		By Liquidation Expenses		5,450
Patents	27,500		By Preferential Creditors (Income tax)		7,500
Stock	30,000		By Debentureholders together		
Debtors	40,000	2,45,000	with interest upto 31-12-08		53,750
			(50,000 + 2,500 + 1,250)		
			By Unsecured Creditors		40,000
			By 6% Preference Shareholders		
			Dividend	12,000	
			Capital	1,00,000	1,12,000
			By Equity Shareholders holding		
			500 shares of Rs. 100 each		
			Rs. 75 paid up		
			(Rs. 15 per share refunded)		
			(500 × 15)		7,500
			By Equity Shareholders holding		
			2,000 shares of Rs. 100 each		
			Rs. 60 paid up		25,650
			(Paid Rs. 12.825 per share)		
			(2000 × 12.825)		
		2,60,000			2,60,000

Notes :

1) Income tax is treated as preferential creditors.

2) Payment to equity shareholders.

	Rs.
Total amount Realised	2,60,000
Less : Paid to claimant except equity shareholders	2,26,850
Amount payable to equity shareholders	33,150
Less : Amount paid to 500 equity shareholders of Rs. 75 each Rs. 15 per share refunded	7,500
Balance paid to all	25,650
Equity shareholders at Rs. 12.825 per share (12.825 × 2,000)	25,650

Problem No. 2 : The Breakfast Food Ltd. went into voluntary liquidation on 31st December, 2013. Its Balance Sheet as on that date was as under :

	Rs.		Rs.
5,000 Preference Shares		Land & Building	2,50,000
of Rs. 100 each	5,00,000	Machinery and Plant	6,25,000
2,500 Equity Shares of		Patents	1,00,000
Rs. 100 each, Rs. 75 paid-up	1,87,500	Stock	1,37,500
7,500 Equity shares of		Debtors	2,75,000
Rs. 100 each, Rs. 60 paid-up	4,50,000	Cash	75,000
5% Mortgage Debentures	2,50,000	Profit & Loss A/c	2,80,000
Interest Outstanding on above	12,500	Discount on Debentures	20,000
Creditors	3,62,500		
	17,62,500		**17,62,500**

The Liquidator is entitled to a commission of 3% on all assets realised and surplus from security except cash and 2% on the amount distributed among the unsecured creditors other than preferential creditors. Creditors include preferential creditors Rs. 37,500 and loans for Rs. 1,25,000/- secured by mortgage on Land and Building.

Assets realised as under :

Land and Building Rs. 3,00,000/-, Machinery and Plant Rs. 5,00,000/-, Patents Rs. 75,000/- Stock Rs. 1,50,000, Debtors Rs. 2,00,000/- Expenses of liquidation amounted to Rs. 17,250 and legal expenses Rs. 10,000/-

Prepare liquidator's final statement of Account. (P.U.)

Solution :

Liquidator's Final Statement of Account

Receipts	Rs.	Payments		Rs.
To Cash at Bank	75,000	By Legal Expenses		10,000
To Sundry Debtors	2,00,000	By Liquidator's Remuneration		
To Stock	1,50,000	3% on Rs. 11,00,000 =	33,000	
To Patents	75,000	2% on Rs. 2,00,000 =	4,000	37,000
To Machinery and Plant	5,00,000	By Cost of liquidation		17,250
To Surplus from Land and Building	-	By Preferential Creditors		37,500
(3,00,000 - 1,25,000)	1,75,000	By Debentureholders having		
		floating charge - principal 2,50,000		
		Interest Outstanding	12,500	2,62,500
		Unsecured Creditors (3,62,500		
		- 37,500 - 1,25,000)		2,00,000
		By Preference shareholders		
		capital	5,00,000	5,00,000
		By Equity Shareholders Rs. 15		
		per share on 2,500 shares	37,500	
		All shareholders	73,250	1,10,750
		(on 10,000 shares)		
	11,75,000			**11,75,000**

Note :

1) Liquidator's Remuneration on assets realised

Land and Building (3,00,000 - 1,25,000)	1,75,000
Plant and Machinery	5,00,000
Patents	75,000
Stock	1,50,000
Debtors	2,00,000
Total assets realised	11,00,000

Problem No. 3 : Following is the Balance Sheet of Reena Ltd., as on 30th June, 2013

Balance Sheet

Liabilities	Rs.	Assets	Rs.
Share Capital :	-	Land and Building	75,000
1,500, 8% Preference Shares	-	Plant and Machinery	1,80,000
of Rs. 100 each	1,50,000	Furniture	30,000
4,500 Equity Shares of Rs. 100	-	Fitting	15,000
each Rs. 50 paid-up	2,25,000	Moulds	1,50,000
6% Debentures (having a	-	Stock	75,000
floating charge on all assets)	1,20,000	Debtors	37,500
Outstanding Debenture Interest	7,200	Cash in Hand	1,500
Sundry Creditors :	-	Profit and Loss A/c	1,12,500
On Mortgage of Plant			
and Machinery	90,000		
Preferential	9,300		
Unsecured	75,000		
	6,76,500		**6,76,500**

The company went into voluntary liquidation as on the above Balance Sheet date. Preference dividend was in arrears for one year and as per the Articles of the company, it was to be paid.

The Liquidator realised the assets as under :-

Land and Building	-	1,50,000
Plant and Machinery	-	1,65,000
Moulds	-	1,27,500
Furniture	-	18,000
Stock	-	63,000
Debtors	-	31,500

Fittings were worthless.

The Liquidation Expenses amounted to Rs. 8,190.

The liquidator is entitled to a remuneration at 2% on the assets realised, 2% on the amount distributed to unsecured creditors and 10% on the amount returned to equity shareholders. In addition to the above liabilities, the liquidtor had to pay Rs. 2,700 as repairs bill of Plant and Machinery.

The Liquidator made payments on 31st December, 2013. Prepare, Liquidator's Final Statement of Accounts.   (P.U.)

Solution

Liquidator's Final Statement of Account

Receipts	Rs.	Payments	Rs.
To Cash Balance	1,500	By Liquidator's Remuneration	
		on Assets Realised	
To Assets Realised 5,55,000		2% × 5,50,000 = 11,100	
Less : Secured Creditors 90,000	4,65,000	on Unsecured Creditors	
		2% × 87,000 = 1,740	
		on Equity Shareholders	
		10% × 59,700 = 5,970	18,810
		By Liquidation Expenses	8,190
		By Preferential Creditors	9,300
		By Debentures together	
		with interest upto	
		31st Dec., 2008	1,30,800
		By Unsecured Creditors	77,700
		By Preference Shareholders	
		Dividend 12,000	
		Capital 1,50,000	1,62,000
		By Equity Shareholders	59,700
	4,66,500		4,66,500

Notes : Remuneration to Liquidator :

i) Preferential creditors, being unsecured are taken into consideration. Amount due for repairs is also included in unsecured creditors.

ii) Cash in hand is not considered while taking the assets realised. As Plant and Machinery is realised by the liquidator himself, it is considered for calculation and remuneration.

Problem No. 4 : Swati Co. Ltd. passed a resolution to wind up voluntarily on 31st March, 2014, when its Balance Sheet stood as follows :

Liabilities	Rs.	Assets	Rs.
Share Capital :		**Fixed Assets :**	
8,000 Preference Shares of Rs.10 each	80,000	Freehold Property	80,000
12,000 Equity Shares of Rs. 10 each fully paid	1,20,000	Plant and Machinery	70,000
Secured Loan :		**Current Assets :**	
5% Debentures secured		Stock	80,000
on Freehold Property	60,000	Cash	250
Current Liabilities :		Debtors	59,750
Bank Overdraft	30,000	Profit and Loss A/c	73,000
Trade Creditors	68,500		
Preferential Creditors	4,500		
(Dividend on Preference Shares was in arrears for 3 years at 6%p.a.)			
	3,63,000		3,63,000

Freehold property was sold for Rs. 1,00,000, Plant and Machinery realised Rs. 60,000. Stock realised Rs. 75,000 and Debtors realised Rs. 50,000. Debentures were paid off out of the sale proceeds of freehold property. Cost of liquidation was Rs. 5,000 and liquidator's remuneration was fixed at Rs. 2,531 plus 2% on all assets realised except cash and 10% on the amount returned to equity shareholders.

Prepare the liquidator's final statement of the account. (P. U.)

Solution : **Liquidator's Final Statement of Account**

Receipts	Rs.	Payments		Rs.
To Cash	250	By Legal Expenses		
To Debtors	50,000	By Liquidator's Remuneration		
To Stock	75,000	Fixed =	2,531	
To Plant and Machinery	60,000	2% on Rs. 2,85,000 =	5,700	
To Surplus from Freehold		10% on Rs. 13,290 =	1,329	9,560
Property (1,00,000-60,000)	40,000	By Liquidation Expenses		5,000
		By Preferential Creditors		4,500
		By Unsecured Creditors		
		Bank Overdraft	30,000	
		Trade Creditors	68,500	98,500
		By Preference		
		Shareholders capital	80,000	
		Dividend Arrears	14,400	94,400
		By Equity Shareholders		13,290
Tatal Rs.	2,25,250			2,25,250

Notes :

1) **Liquidator's remuneration on payment to equity shareholders :**
   Balance available after payment of preference shareholders :
   2,25,250 - 2,10,631 = Rs. 14,619/-
   Commission = 14,619 × 10/110 = Rs. 1,329.
   Net Balance to be paid to equity shareholders = 14,619 - 1,329 = Rs. 13,290/-
   Thus 10% of Rs. 13,290 = Rs. 1,329/-

2) Debentureholders are secured. Their payment is not shown in the Liquidator's Final Statement of Account.

Problem No. 5 : Following was the Balance Sheet of Star Ltd., as on 31st March, 2014.

Balance Sheet

Liabilities	Rs.	Assets	Rs.
Share Capital :		Land and Building	2,00,000
2,000, 10% Preferences Shares		Plant and Machinery	1,50,000
of Rs. 100 each, fully paid	2,00,000	Furniture	20,000
3,000 Equity Shares of Rs. 100		Stock	1,00,000
each, Rs. 90 paid-up	2,70,000	Debtors	1,20,000
1,000 Equity Shares of Rs. 100		Bills Receivable	20,000
each, Rs. 85 paid-up	85,000	Cash in Hand	5,000
7% Debentures (floating charge		Profit and Loss A/c	2,40,000
on all assets)	1,00,000		
Creditors	2,00,000		
	8,55,000		8,55,000

The Company went into voluntary liquidation as on above date.

The preference share dividend was in arrears for two years and as per the Articles, it was to be paid before returning the equity share capital.

The debenture interest was paid upto 31st March, 2014. However, the debentureholders were repaid on 30th Sept., 2014

Included in the sundry creditors, a loan of Rs. 20,000 secured on the hypothecation of Plant and Machinery and preferential creditors of Rs. 10,000.

The liquidator realised the assets as follows : Land and Building Rs. 1,90,000; Plant and Machinery Rs. 1,30,000; Furniture Rs. 10,000, Stock Rs. 90,000; Debtors Rs. 1,15,000; Bills Receivable Rs. 14,000.

Legal charges on liquidation Rs. 2,000 and liquidation expenses Rs. 1,300. The liquidator's remuneration was fixed at Rs. 500 plus 2.5% on the amount realised by him, plus 2% on the amount distributed to unsecured creditors, including preferential creditors. The liquidator made all payments on 30th Sept., 2014.

Prepare Liquidator's Final Statement of Account. (P.U.)

Solution

Liquidator's Final Statement of Account

Receipts		Rs.	Payments		Rs.
To Cash		5,000	By Legal Expenses		2,000
To Assets realised	5,49,000		By Liquidator's Remuneration		
Less : Paid to	20,000	5,29,000	Fixed	500	
Secured Creditors			On Assets Realised		
			2.5% × 5,49,000	13,725	
			On Unsecured Creditors		
			2% × 1,80,000	3,600	17,825
To Calls received on			By Liquidation Expenses		1,300
Equity Shares			By Preferential Creditors		10,000
on 3,000 × 1.406		4,218	By Debentures	1,00,000	
on 1,000 × 6.407		6,407	Interest	3,500	1,03,500
			By Unsecured Creditors		1,70,000
			By Preference Shareholders		
			Dividend	40,000	
			Capital	2,00,000	240,000
		5,44,625			5,44,625

Note : Call to be made on Equity Shares.

Face value of equity shares Rs. 4,00,000; paid-up value Rs. 3,55,000 + Rs. 10,625, falling short to pay preference shareholders. Hence, the total deficiency is Rs. 3,65,625. Hence, each shareholder is required to lose Rs. 91.406 as under :

$$\frac{3,65,625}{4,00,000} \times 100 = 91.40625$$

Thus, shareholder who has paid Rs. 85 has to pay Rs. 6.407 and shareholder who has paid Rs. 90 has to pay 1.406 (.001 is adjusted instead of taking exact figure ·40625)

Problem No. 6 : The Oversmart Co. Ltd. went into liquidation on 31st December, 2013, when the following Balance Sheet was prepared:

Balance Sheet as on 31ˢᵗ December, 2013

Liabilities		Rs.	Assets	Rs.
Share Capital :			**Fixed Assets :**	
Authorised :			Goodwill	50,000
30,000 shares of			Leasehold Property	48,000
Rs. 10 each		3,00,000	Plant and Machinery	65,500
Issued and Paid up :			**Current Assets :**	
19,500 shares of			Stock on Hand	56,800
Rs. 10 each		1,95,000	Sundry Debtors	64,820
Unsecured loans :			Cash in Hand	2,500
Bank Overdraft		12,000	Profit and Loss A/c	98,680
Current Liabilities :				
Sundry Creditors				
Preferential	24,200			
Partly Secured	55,310			
Unsecured	99,790	1,79,300		
		3,86,300		3,86,300

The liquidator realised the assets as follows :

Leasehold property which was used in the first instance to pay partly secured creditors pro-rata Rs. 35,000.

Plant and Machinery	Rs. 51,000
Stock in Hand	Rs. 39,000
Sundry Debtors	Rs. 58,500

The expenses of liquidation amounted to Rs. 1,000 and the remuneration of the liquidator was agreed at 2.5% on the amount realised including cash and 2% on the amount paid to the unsecured creditors, including preferential creditors.

Prepare the liquidator's Final Statement of Accounts showing distribution.   (P.U.)

Solution :   **Liquidator's Final Statement of Accounts.**

Receipts	Rs.	Payments		Rs.
To Cash in Hand	2,500	By. Legal Expenses		
To Sundry Debtors	58,500	By Liquidator's Remuneration		
		on Assets Realised		
To Stock in Hand	39,000	2.5% on creditor 1,86,000 =	4,650	
To Plant and Machinery	51,000	2% on 24,200 =	484	
		2% on 1,18,300 =	2,366	7,500

Receipts	Rs.	Payments		Rs.
		By Liquidation Expenses		1,000
		By Debenture holders having floating charge		–
		By Preferential Creditors		24,200
		By Unsecured Creditors		
		Creditors	99,790	
		Unsatisfied Claim	20,310	
		Bank Overdraft	12,000	
		(See Note 2)		
			1,32,100	1,18,300
	1,51,000			1,51,000

Note :

1) Liquidator's Remuneration

2.5% on Assets Realised

Assets Realised	Rs.
Leasehold Property	35,000
Plant and Machinery	51,000
Stock	39,000
Debtors	58,500
Cash	2,500
	1,86,000

2.5% on 1,86,000 = Rs. 4,650

2) Commission on Payment to unsecured creditors.

	Rs.
Total amount Realised	1,51,000
Less : (Preferential Crs. + commission + liquidation exps)	
= 24,200 + 4,650 + 484 + 1,000 =	30,334
Balance available for unsecured creditors.	1,20,666
But actual unsecured creditors are	
Rs. 99,790 + 20,310 + 12,000 =	1,32,100

As the available cash is insufficient for payment to unsecured creditors, the commission to be paid on unsecured creditors will be calculated as under :

$$= \frac{\text{Balance available} \times \% \text{ of commission}}{100 + 2}$$

$$= \frac{1,20,666 \times 2}{102} = \text{Rs. } 2,366$$

	Rs.
Balance of Cash available	1,20,666
Less : Commission to be paid	2,366
Unsecured Creditors	1,18,300

Problem No. 7 : On 1st April, 2014 'P' Ltd., went into voluntary liquidation. The position at the commencement of winding up was as follows :

Balance Sheet as on 1-4-2014

Liabilities		Rs.	Assets	Rs.
Paid-up Capital :			Building	2,10,000
1,000, 8% Preference Shares			Debtors	65,000
of Rs. 100 each		1,00,000	Stock	35,000
1,500 Equity Shares of			Cash	8,775
Rs. 100 each		1,50,000	Machinery	50,000
5% Debentures (having a			Furniture	40,000
floating charge)	1,00,000		Profit and Loss A/c	46,225
Interest Accrued	2,500	1,02,500		
Sundry Creditors	63,500			
Bank Overdraft	30,000			
Trade Debts				
Income Tax for				
Assessment Year				
2013-14	5,000			
Rates	3,500			
Electricity	500	1,02,500		
		4,55,000		4,55,000

The liquidator realised the following amounts :

Buildings Rs. 4,00,000; Debtors Rs. 57,000; Stock Rs. 25,000; Machinery Rs. 36,000; Furniture Rs. 32,000.

The liquidator's remuneration was 5% on the amount realised by him and 1% on the amounts paid to unsecured creditors. His expenses amounted to Rs. 2,000, 5% debentures were paid on 1st July, 2014. In the event of liquidation, the preference shareholders were entitled to 10% of any surplus, left after discharging all liabilities and costs, the balance belonging to the equity shareholders.

Prepare the Liquidator's Final Statement of Account.

Solution :

Liquidator's Final Statement of Account.

Receipts	Rs.	Payments		Rs.
To Cash	8,775	By Liquidator's remuneration		
To Assets realised	5,50,000	5% × 5,50,000 =	27,500	
		1% × 1,02,500 =	1,025	28,525
		By Liquidation Expenses		2,000
		By Debentureholders		
		(together with interest)		1,03,750
		By Unsecured Creditors		1,02,500
		By Preference Shareholders		1,07,200
		(See Note)		
		By Equity Shareholders		2,14,800
		(See Note)		
	5,58,775			5,58,775

Note : Payment to Preference Shareholders and equity Shareholders

		Rs.
Total Cash Received		5,58,775
Less : Total Cost and liabilities		
(28,525 + 2,000 + 1,03,750 + 1,02,500)		2,36,775
Surplus		3,22,000
Paid Preference shareholders and equity shareholders		
(1,00,000 + 1,50,000)		2,50,000
		72,000
Preference Shareholders get Rs.	1,00,000	- 7,200
+ 10% of 72,000	7,200	64,800
	1,07,200	

Balance Rs. 64,800 will be paid to equity shareholders. They get
Rs. 1,50,000 + 64,800 = 2,14,800.

Problem No. 8 : The following is the position of "X" Ltd. as on 30th June, 2014 on which date the company is taken into voluntary liquidation.

Particulars	Rs.	Rs.
Share Capital - Issued and Subscribed		
2,500 Preference shares of Rs. 100 each fully paid		2,50,000
20,000 Equity shares of Rs. 10 each fully paid		2,00,000
Land and building	75,000	
Machinery	1,00,000	
Furniture	5,000	
Vehicles	15,000	
Secured Loans -		
From Bank against mortgage of Land and Buildings		50,000
Others against a floating charge on the		
Company's undertaking		25,000
Cash	5,000	
Other current assets	2,50,000	
Sundry Liabilities		25,000
Profit and Loss A/c	1,00,000	
	5,50,000	5,50,000

The realisation were :

1) Land and Buildings (realised by Bank) for Rs. 60,000.

2) Machinery Rs. 90,000

3) Furniture Rs. 5,000

4) Vehicles Rs. 20,000

5) Other current assets Rs. 2,25,000.

Sundry liabilities included preferential claims of Rs. 2,500. The liquidator is entitled to a fixed remuneration of Rs. 125 increased by 1% of the amounts disbursed to unsecured creditors (excluding preferential claims) and $\frac{1}{4}$% of the amounts realised by him in respect of company's assets.

You are required to show the liquidator's final statement of account to record his dealings.

Liquidator's Final Statement of Account

Receipts	Rs.	Payments		Rs.
To Cash in Hand	5,000	By Legal Expenses		–
To Assets Realised :		By Liquidator's remuneration :		
Current Assets	2,25,000	Fixed	125	
Machinery	90,000	On Assets realised		
Furniture	5,000	¼% on 3,40,000	850	
		On Unsecured Creditors		
Vehicles	20,000	1% on 22,500	225	1,200
Surplus Received from		By Liquidation Expenses		–
Land and Buildings (60,000-50,000)	10,000	By Preferential Creditors		2,500
		By Secured Creditors		
		having floating charge		25,000
		By Unsecured Creditors		22,500
		By Preference Shareholders		2,50,000
		By Equity Shareholders		53,800
	3,55,000			3,55,000

Notes :

1) Liquidator's remuneration on realisation of assets is calculated on those assets only which are realised by liquidator except cash in hand. As land and buildings are realised by Bank, it is not considered. (i.e. Rs. 90,000 + 5,000 + 20,000 + 2,25,000 = Rs. 3,40,000)

2) Liquidator's commission (remuneration) on payment to unsecured creditors is calculated on the amount excluding preferential creditors.
   (unsecured Creditors 2,500 = Rs. 25000 - Preferential Creditors 2500 = 22,500)

3) Payment to secured creditors is not shown in the liquidator's statement.

Problem No. 9 : Following was the Balance Sheet of Alpha Ltd., as on 31st December, 2013

Liabilities	Rs.	Assets	Rs.
Share Capital :		Goodwill	2,24,000
2,000, 8% Preference Shares		Land and Building	4,36,000
of Rs. 100 each fully paid	2,00,000	Plant and Machinery	1,80,000
4,000 Equity Shares of Rs. 100		Furniture	20,000
each, Rs. 80 paid-up	3,20,000	Office Equipments	40,000
6,000 Equity Shares of Rs. 100		Stock	1,98,000
each, Rs. 70 paid-up	4,20,000	Debtors	1,70,000

Liabilities	Rs.	Assets	Rs.
8% Debentures (having a		Bills Receivable	44,000
Floating charge on all assets)	2,00,000	Cash in Hand	16,000
Debentures Interest	8,000	Profit and Loss A/c	1,40,000
Creditors	3,20,000		
	14,68,000		14,68,000

The company went into voluntary liquidation as on that date :

a) The preference dividend was in arrears for 3 years and as per the articles it was to be returned before returning equity capital.

b) Sundry creditors include a loan of Rs. 80,000 secured on the hypothecation of plant and Machinery and preferential creditors of Rs. 20,000.

c) The liquidator realised the assets as follows :
Land and Building Rs. 4,30,000; Plant and Machinery Rs. 1,00,000; Office Equipments Rs. 25,000; Furniture Rs. 16,000; Stock Rs. 1,40,000; Debtors Rs. 1,20,000 and Bills Receivable Rs. 28,000

d) Legal Charges on Liquidation amounted to Rs. 2,000. The liquidation expenses were Rs. 5,200. The Liquidator's remuneration was fixed at Rs. 2,000 plus 2% on sale of assets, plus 4% on the amount distributed to unsecured creditors.

e) There was a typewriter which was completely written off from the books of accounts but liquidator sold it for Rs. 1,000, which was not included in the amount of office equipments above.

Prepare Liquidator's statement of account if the amounts were paid on 31st March, 2014 (P.U.)

Liquidator's Final Statement of Account

Receipts	Rs.		Payments	Rs.	
To Cash in hand		16,000	By Legal Expenses		2,000
To Assets realised :			By Liquidator's		
Land and Building	4,30,000		Remuneration :		
Office Equipments			Fixed	2,000	
including Typewriter	26,000		On Sales of Asset		
Furniture	16,000		8,60,000 × 2%	17,200	
Stock	1,40,000		On Unsecured Creditors		
Debtors	1,20,000		2,40,000 × 4%	9,600	28,800
Bills Receivable	28,000		By Liquidation Expenses		5,200
Plant and Machinery			By Preferential Creditors		20,000

Receipts		Rs.	Payments		Rs.
Balance after payment			By Debentureholders 2,00,000		
to Secured Creditors	20,000	7,80,000	Interest upto 31-8-2014 12,000		2,12,000
			By Unsecured Creditors		2,20,000
			By Preference Shareholders		
			Capital	2,00,000	
			Dividend Arrears	48,000	2,48,000
			By Equity Shareholders holding 4,000 shares on which Rs. 80 per share are paid are refunded @ Rs. 10 per share to make them Rs. 70 per share paid.		40,000
			By Equity Shareholders holding 10,000 shares, Rs. 2 per share are refunded		20,000
		7,96,000			7,96,000

Notes :

1) Liquidator realised following assets.

	Rs.
Land and Building	4,30,000
Plant and Machinery	1,00,000
Office Equipment including Typewriter	26,000
Furniture	16,000
Stock	1,40,000
Debtor	1,20,000
Bills Receivable	28,000
Total	8,60,000

2) Liquidator's remuneration on unsecured creditors is calculated on the amount including preferential creditor and excluding secured creditors.

Problem No. 10 : Mr. Raj was appointed as the liquidator of Badluck Ltd., on 1st January, 2014, on which date Balance Sheet of the Company stood as under :

Balance Sheet
as at 1ˢᵗ January, 2014

Liabilities		Rs.	Assets	Rs.
Share Capital :			**Fixed Assets :**	90,000
10,000 Equity Shares			**Current Assets :**	
of Rs. 10 each, Rs. 8 per			Loans and Advances	20,000
share called-up	80,000		**Miscellaneous Expenditure :**	
Less : Calls-in-arrears	5,000	75,000	Profit & Loss A/c	37,000
5,000, 6% Cumulative				
Preference Shares of				
Rs. 10 each		50,000		
Secured Loan		10,000		
Current Liabilities :				
(including unpaid Income Tax				
Rs. 2,000)		12,000		
Contingent Liability				
Arrears of Cumulative				
Preference Dividend				
Rs. 9,000				
		1,47,000		1,47,000

The calls-in-arrears were duly collected. The assets realised Rs. 82,000. The liquidation expenses amounted Rs. 2,980. The remuneration of the liquidator was fixed at Rs. 2,000 plus 2% of the amount distributed among the equity shareholders.

You are required to prepare the liquidator's final statement of Account.

Solution

Liquidator's Final Statement of Account

Receipts	Rs.	Payments		Rs.
To Assets Realised	82,000	By Secured Loan		10,000
To Loans and Advances	20,000	By Liquidator's Remuneration		
To Calls in Arrears	5,000	Fixed	2,000	
		2% on 20,068	412	2,412
		By Liquidation Expenses		2,980
		By Preferential Creditors		2,000
		(Income Tax)		
		By Unsecured Creditors		10,000

Receipts	Rs.	Payments		Rs.
		By Preference Shareholders		
		Dividend Arrears	9,000	
		Capital	50,000	59,000
		By Equity Shareholders		20,608
	1,07,000			1,07,000

Note :

(i) It is presumed that Loans and Advances are recovered in full; (ii) the preference share dividend was declared and as such ranks for payment before paying anything to equity shareholder :

Problem No. 11 : The Breakfast Food Ltd., went into voluntary liquidation on 31st March, 2014.

Balance Sheet as on 31-3-2014

Liabilities	Rs.	Assets	Rs.
Share Capital :		Land and Building	2,50,000
5000, 6% Cumulative Preference		Plant and Machinery	6,25,000
Shares of Rs. 100 each	5,00,000	Patents	1,00,000
2,500 Equity Shares of		Stock	1,37,500
Rs. 100 each, Rs. 75 paid	1,87,500	Sundry Debtors	2,75,000
7,500 Equity Shares of 100 each		Cash at Bank	75,000
Rs. 60 paid	4,50,000	Profit and Loss A/c	2,80,000
5% Mortgage Debentures	2,50,000	Discount on Issue of Debentures	20,000
Interest Outstanding	12,500		
Creditors	3,62,500		
	17,62,500		17,62,500

The liquidator is entitled to a commission of 3% on all assets realised except cash and 2% on amounts distributed among unsecured creditors other than preferential creditors. Creditors include preferential creditors Rs. 37,500 and a Loan for Rs. 1,25,000 secured by a mortgage on land and buildings. The preference dividends were in arrears for two years. The assets realised, as follows:

Land and Building Rs. 3,00,000; Machinery and Plant Rs. 5,00,000; Patents Rs. 75,000; Stock Rs. 1,50,000; Sundry Debtors Rs. 2,00,000. The expenses of liquidation amounted to Rs. 17,250 and legal expenses Rs. 10,000.

Prepare the Liquidator's Final Statement of Account.

Solution **Liquidator's Final Statement of Account**

Receipts		Rs.	Payments		Rs.
To Bank Balance		75,000	By Legal Expenses		10,000
To Assets realised			By Liquidator's Remuneration		
Machinery and Plant	5,00,000		12,25,000 × 3% =	36,750	
Patents	75,000		2,00,000 × 2% =	4,000	40,750
Stock	1,50,000		By Liquidation Expenses		17,250
Debtors	2,00,000	9,25,000	By Preferential Creditors		37,500
To Surplus from			By Debentureholders		2,62,500
secured Creditor		1,75,000	By Unsecured Creditors		2,00,000
			By Preference Shareholders		5,00,000
			By Equity Shareholders		
			holding 2,500 shares on which		
			Rs. 75 per share were paid,		
			Rs. 15 per share refunded		37,500
			By Equity Shareholders		
			holding 10,000 shares refunded		
			Rs. 6.95 per share		69,500
		11,75,000			11,75,000

Problem No. 12 : Following balances appeared in the book of Goodluck Ltd., as on 1st April, 2014.

Land and Building	2,00,000
Plant and Machinery	5,80,000
Stock	1,10,000
Debtors	2,20,000
Cash at Bank	60,000
Profit and Loss A/c	30,000
	12,00,000

Less Liabilities -

9% Debentures (having floating charge on all assets)	2,00,000	
Creditors	2,90,000	4,90,000
		7,10,000

Share Capital (paid-up)

a) 2,000, 6% Preference Shares of Rs. 100 each	2,00,000
b) 2,000, Equity Shares of Rs. 100 each, Rs. 75 per share paid-up	1,50,000
c) 6,000 Equity Shares of Rs. 100 each, Rs. 60 per share paid-up	3,60,000
	7,10,000

The Company went into voluntary liquidation on 1-4-2014.

The assets were realised as under :

Land and Building Rs. 2,40,000, Plant and Machinery Rs. 4,60,000, Stock Rs. 1,20,000 and Debtors Rs. 1,60,000

The preference dividends were in arrears for two years. Creditors include :

a) Rs. 30,000 preferential

b) Rs. 1,00,000 loan on the mortgage of land and buildings.

Cost of liquidation Rs. 13,800

Liquidator's Remuneration -

a) 3% on all assets realised except Cash at Bank, and

b) 2% on distribution to unsecured creditors.

Prepare the liquidator's statement of account assuming that the payment was made on 30th September, 2014.

Solution :   **Liquidator's Final Statement of Account**

Receipts	Rs.	Payments		Rs.
To Cash at Bank	60,000	By Legal Expenses		
To Debtors	1,60,000	By Liquidator's Remuneration		
To Stock	1,20,000	3% on Rs. 9,80,000 =	29,400	
To Plant	4,60,000	2% on Rs. 1,90,000 =	3,800	33,200
To Surplus from Land and		By Liquidation Expenses		13,800
Buildings (2,40,000 - 1,00,000)	1,40,000	By Debenture having a floating		
		charge on assets	2,00,000	
		Interest Accrued for		
		6 months	9,000	2,09,000
		By Preferential Creditors		30,000
		By Unsecured Creditors		1,60,000
		By Preference		
		Shareholders	2,00,000	
		Arrears of Dividend	24,000	2,24,000
		By Equity Shareholders		
		Rs. 15 per share on		
		2,000 shares =	30,000	
		Rs. 30 on all shares	2,40,000	2,70,000
	9,40,000			9,40,000

Note :

1) Liquidator's remuneration on payment to unsecured creditors is calculated on the amount including preferential creditors.

2) Payment to preferential creditors is shown after the payment to debenture holders having floating charge.

Problem No. 13 :

Balance Sheet of Brightless Ltd.
as on 31-3-2014

Liabilities	Rs.	Assets	Rs.
20,000, 6% Non-cumulative		Land and Building	1,90,000
Preference Shares of Rs. 10	2,00,000	Plant and Machinery	1,20,000
10,000 Equity Shares of		Patents	10,000
Rs. 10 each, Rs. 9 paid	90,000	Stock	45,000
10,000 Equity Shares of		Debtors	90,000
Rs. 10 each, Rs. 5 paid	50,000	Bank	29,950
6% Mortgage Debentures		Investment	40,000
Secured by Land and Building	1,00,000	Profit and Loss A/c	70,550
Outstanding Interest			
on Debentures	6,000		
Loan secured by Hypothecation			
of Stock	40,000		
Trade Creditors	80,000		
Creditors for Salaries	15,000		
Liability for Workmen's			
Compensation	2,000		
Owing to Government for			
Telephone and Taxes	12,500		
	5,95,500		5,95,500

The company went into voluntary liquidation on 1-4-2014 and a liquidator was appointed with a remuneration of 2% of assets realised with the exception of cash and 2% of the amount distributed amongst unsecured creditors (excluding preferential creditors). Stock realised Rs. 30,000, Land and Building Rs. 1,60,000 and other assets Rs. 2,40,000. All assets were realised and payments made on 30-9-2014.

Prepare liquidator's final statement of account assuming the expenses were Rs. 4,450.

Solution

Liquidator's Statement of Account

Receipts		Rs.	Payments		Rs.
To Bank Balance		29,950	**By Secured Creditors:**		
To Assets realised			Debentures with Interest		
Land and Building	1,60,000		upto 30-9-2008	1,09,000	
Stock	30,000		Loan	30,000	1,39,000
Others	2,40,000	4,30,000	**By Liquidator's Remuneration**		
To Call proceeds on			2% on Rs. 4,30,000	8,600	
10,000 shares on which			2% on Rs. 90,000	1,800	10,400
Rs. 5 paid (@ Rs. 2.67 per		26,700	By Liquidation Expenses		4,450
share)			By Preferential Creditors		29,500
			By Unsecured Creditors		90,000
			By Preference Shareholders		2,00,000
			By Ordinary Shareholders		13,300
			holding 10,000 shares		
			on which Rs. 9 were paid		
			(@ Rs. 1.33 per share)		
		4,86,650			4,86,650

Notes :

1. Loan creditor for Rs. 40,000 was given security of stock, which realised Rs. 30,000. Therefore, uncovered balance of debt Rs. 10,000 is added to unsecured creditors.

2. After payment of unsecured creditors, cash available is Rs. 1,86,600. As the pref. shares have priority for repayment of capital, necessary calls must be made on equity shares and the preference shareholders must be paid. On 10,000 equity shares of Rs. 10 each Rs. 9 are paid, whereas on other 10,000 Equity Shares Rs. 5 paid. Therefore, to pay Preference shareholders in full and to bring the paid-up capital on equity shares to equal, a call of Rs. 2.67 is required to be made on 10,000 equity shares on which Rs. 5 were paid. The amount of call is arrived at as under :

Paid amount on equity shares (90,000 plus 50,000)	1,40,000
Amount falling short to pay preference shareholders	13,400
Total amount required	1,53,400

   Hence, the total deficiency Rs. 1,53,400 is to be divided between 20,000 equity shares. The deficiency per share comes to Rs. 7.67 which means Rs. 2.67 to be called on 10,000 equity shares on which Rs. 5 were paid and the other 10,000 equity shares on which Rs. 9 were paid are to get Rs. 1.33 so that the loss suffered by them per share will also be 7.67.

3.6 EXERCISES

A) Objective type questions

Fill in the gaps :

1) Liquidation means ...... of a company
2) Liquidation without intervention of the Court is known as ......
3) For passing a special resolution, a notice of ...... days must be given.
4) The creditors who receive full amount of loan are called as ......
5) The creditors who are paid prior to any payment to unsecured creditors are known as ......

Ans. : 1) dissolution 2) voluntary liquidation 3) 14   4) fully secured creditors 5) Preferential creditors.

B) State whether the following statements are True or False

1) Voluntary liquidation is done with the help of Court.
2) Liquidator gets commission on assets realised by him.
3) Compulsory liquidation is done with the help of Court.
4) Equity shareholders receive their dues before preference shareholders.
5) A Liquidator is appointed for liquidation of a company.

Ans. : 1) False 2) True 3) True 4) False 5) True

PROBLEMS :

1) Ahmednagar Ltd. passed a resolution to wind up voluntarily on 30th June, 2014, when its Balance Sheet stood as under :-

Balance Sheet

Liabilities	Rs.	Assets	Rs.
Share capital		Land	1,00,000
Authorised and		Plant and Machinery	2,30,000
Subscribed 2000, 6% Preference		Patents	60,000
shares of Rs. 100 each	2,00,000	Stock at Cost	55,000
1,000 Equity Shares of Rs. 100		Sundry Debtors	1,10,000
each, Rs. 75 paid	75,000	Cash at Bank	30,000
3,000 Equity Shares of Rs.100		P and L A/c	1,20,000
each, Rs. 60 paid	1,80,000		
5% Debentures (Floating			
charge on all assets)	1,00,000		
Interest on Debenture	5,000		
Creditors	1,30,000		
Income Tax	15,000		
	7,05,000		7,05,000

a) The preference dividends were in arrears for two years. The arrears are payable on liquidation as per the Articles of Company. Creditors include a loan for Rs. 50,000 on the mortgage of land.

b) The assets realised is as follows :
Land Rs. 1,20,000, Plant and Machinery Rs. 1,75,000, Patents Rs. 55,000, Stock Rs. 60,000 and Sundry Debtors Rs. 80,000

c) The expenses of liquidation amounted to Rs. 10,900.

d) The liquidator is entitled to a commission of 3% on all assets realised and 2% on amounts distributed among unsecured creditors.

e) All payments were made on 31st December, 2014. You are required to prepare Liquidator's Statement of Account. (P.U.)

Answer : Total of Liquidator's Account Rs. 4,70,000

2. Altra-optimist Ltd., went into voluntary liquidation on 31st March, 2014. The following Balance Sheet was prepared.

Liabilities	Rs.	Assets	Rs.
Subscribed Capital :		Goodwill	40,000
19,500 Equity Shares of		Patents	10,000
Rs. 10 each fully paid	1,95,000	Freehold Building	48,000
Sundry Creditors :		Plant	65,500
Preferential	24,200	Stock-in-trade	56,800
Partly Secured		Sundry Debtors	64,820
(Against Freehold Property)	55,310	Bills Receivable	2,500
Unsecured	99,790	Profit and Loss A/c	98,680
Bank Overdraft (Unsecured)	12,000		
	3,86,300		3,86,300

The Liquidator realised the assets as follows :

a) Freehold Property (used to pay partly secured creditors)   Rs. 35,000

b) Plant   Rs. 51,000

c) Stock in Trade   Rs. 39,000

d) Bills Receivable   Rs. 2,500

e) Debtors   Rs. 58,500

The expenses of liquidation amounted to Rs. 1,000 and the Liquidator's remuneration was agreed at 2½% on the amount realised and 2% on the amount paid to unsecured creditors.

You are required to prepare :

1. Liquidator's Final Statement of Account.

2. The Working of Liquidator's remuneration.

Ans : Total of Liquidator's A/c Rs. 1,51,000

3. From the following information relating to Star Company Ltd., prepare Liquidator's Final Statement of Account.

   1. Share Capital :

      (a) 1,000, 6% Preference Shares of Rs. 100 each fully paid.

      (b) 40,000 'A' Equity Shares of Rs. 10 each fully paid

      (c) 30,000 'B' Equity Shares of Rs. 10 each, Rs 8 paid.

      (d) 20,000 'C' Equity Shares of Rs. 5 each, Rs. 3 paid up

   2. Debentures of Rs. 50,000

   3. Creditors –

      Preferential Creditors Rs. 20,000

      Unsecured Creditors Rs. 70,000

      The preference dividends were in arrears for two years.

   The Assets realised Rs. 3,20,000

   Cost of liquidation amounted to Rs. 4,000 and the liquidator's remuneration is fixed at 5% on assets realised. (P.U.)

Ans. : Total of Liquidator's Final Statement of Account Rs. 3,40,000

4. The Mumbai Co. Ltd. went into voluntary liquidation on 31st March, 2014 with the following assets and liabilities :-

	Rs.
Cash in Hand	750
Stock which realised	29,600
Book Debts which realised	49,200
Furniture which realised	1,050
Investments lodged with the Bank against	
Overdraft which were sold by the Bank for -	4,900
Unsecured Creditors	53,775
Preferential Creditors	5,295
Bank Overdraft	4,000
6% Debentures secured by a floating charge on the	
undertaking interest paid on 30th September, 2013	44,000

The excess amount realised by the Bank was remitted to the Liquidator. Debentures were paid off on 20th Sept., 2014 together with interest to the date of winding up and a first and final dividend distributed to the creditors.

The Liquidator's remuneration is to be calculated at 3% on the net amount realised (including cash in hand but excluding the amount paid to the secured creditors out of the proceeds of the security) and 2% on the amount distributed to the Unsecured creditors excluding preferential creditors. The expenses of winding up amounted to Rs. 1,014.75.

Prepare the Liquidator's Final Statement of Account showing the rate and the amount of the final dividend payable to the unsecured Creditors.

Ans : Liquidator's Statement : Rs. 81,500

5. A Limited Company passed a resolution to wind up voluntarily on 31st March, 2014, when its Balance Sheet stood as follows :

Liabilities	Rs.	Assets	Rs.
Share Capital :		**Fixed Assets :**	
Issued and Subscribed :		Freehold Property	80,000
8,000 Preference Shares	80,000	Plant and Machinery	70,000
12,000 Equity Shares	1,20,000	**Current Assets :**	
Secured Loans :		Stock	80,000
5% Debenture secured		Cash	250
on Freehold Property	60,000	Debtors	59,750
Current Liabilities :		Profit and Loss A/c	70,000
Bank Overdraft	30,000		
Trade Creditors	65,500		
Income Tax	4,500		
	3,60,000		3,60,000

The interest on debentures is paid upto 31-3-2013 but dividend on preference shares @ 6% is in arrears for three years.

The Freehold Property was sold for Rs. 1,00,000, Plant and Machinery realised Rs. 60,000, Stock Rs. 75,000 and Debtors realised Rs. 50,000, The debentures were paid off out of sale proceeds of assets. Cost of liquidation was Rs. 5,000 and the Liquidator's remuneration was fixed at Rs. 2,530 plus 2% on the amount realised and 10% on the amount returned to equity shareholders.

The Company's Articles give the Preference Shares priority over Equity Shares both for dividend and capital. Draft the Liquidator's Final Statement of Account to show the distribution.

Ans. : Total of Liquidator's A/c Rs. 2,85,250

6. The position of Goodluck Ltd. in liquidation is as follows :

Balance Sheet

Liabilities	Rs.	Assets	Rs.
Share Capital :		Cash	1,16,000
1,000, 6% Preference Shares of		(Left after paying all other	
Rs. 100 each fully paid	1,00,000	Liabilities and Liquidation Expenses)	
1,000 Equity Shares of		Deficiency	66,000
Rs. 50 each fully paid	50,000	(Excluding Arrears of one year's	
1,000 Equity Shares of Rs. 40 each,		dividend on Preference Shares)	
Rs. 30 per Share called 30,000			
Less : Calls in Arrears 4,000	26,000		
Calls in Advance	6,000		
	1,82,000		1,82,000

Prepare Liquidator's Final Statement of Account presuming that the Articles of Association provide for payment of preference dividend in arrears before payment to Equity Shareholders.

Ans. : Total of Liquidator's Final Statement of Account - Rs. 1,22,000.

7. A Company passed a Special Resolution for voluntary winding on 31st March, 2014, when its Balance Sheet stood as under :-

Balance Sheet

Liabilities	Rs.	Assets	Rs.
Share Capital :		Plant and Machinery	4,00,000
5,000 Equity Shares of Rs. 100		Fittings and Furniture	1,000
each fully paid	5,00,000	Stock in trade	50,000
1,000 Equity Shares of		Debtors	1,50,000
Rs.100 each,		Cash in Hand	5,000
Rs.75 called up and paid-up	75,000	Profit and Loss A/c	4,21,000
1,000, 6% Cumulative Preference			
Shares of Rs. 100 each			
fully paid-up	1,00,000		
7% Debentures (secured on			
Plant and Machinery)	1,00,000		
Unsecured Creditors	2,52,000		
	10,27,000		10,27,000

Dividend on preference shares remained unpaid for full one year. Interest (payable annually on December 31) on debentures was paid upto December 31, 2013. Unsecured creditors included Rs. 2,000 of preferential Creditors.

Plant and Machinery realised Rs.3,60,000, Stock Rs.1,00,000 and Debtors Rs.1,40,000. Furniture and Fitting realised nothing. The expenses of winding up amounted to Rs.19,500.

The Liquidator's remuneration is to be @ 4% on realisation of assets and @2% on distribution among unsecured creditors excluding preferential Creditors. The winding up was completed on 30th June, when the Debentures were repaid. The necessary call was made and received in full from all shareholders.

Please draw up the Liquidator's Statement of Account.

Answer :- Total – Liquidator's Final statement of Account Rs. 5,06,500

8. The following is the position as on 31-12-2013 of Overwise Ltd., which goes into voluntary liquidation as on that date:

Liabilities	Rs.	Assets	Rs.
Share Capital :		Fixed Assets	90,000
3,000 Equity Shares		Stock	2,40,000
of Rs.50 each	1,50,000	Debtors	1,80,000
100 Preference Shares		Cash at Bank	10,000
of Rs.100 each	10,000	Loans and Advances	40,000
General Reserve	10,000		
Loan from Strong Bank			
Ltd. (Secured)	20,000		
5% Debentures (Secured)	2,80,000		
Creditors	90,000		
	5,60,000		5,60,000

The following information is given:

a) The loan from Strong Bank Ltd., is secured by first charge on fixed assets.

b) 5% debentures are secured by pledge of goods, hypothecation of all current assets and a second charge on fixed assets.

c) Creditors include preferential creditors of Rs. 20,000. On 15-1-2014, stocks are sold. Stocks in the pledge/godown realised Rs. 1,40,000 and other stocks were sold for Rs. 40,000. On 31-1-2014, expenses of liquidation amounting to Rs.300 are met and fixed assets are sold for Rs.1,30,000 on 15-2-2014, all other current assets realised for Rs.1,91,000 and liquidator's remuneration amounting to Rs.700 are paid.

There was a moped which was completely written off from the books of accounts but Liquidator sold it for Rs.1,000 which was not included in the amount of fixed assets above.

In addition to the above liabilities, the Liquidator had to pay Rs. 1,500 as repair bill of Plant and Machinery.

Prepare Liquidator's Cash Account and Liquidator's Final Statement of Account presuming that all payments are made in order of preference on earliest availability of cash.

Ans :- Total of Liquidator's Final statement of Account Rs. 2,12,000

9) A Company passed a special Resolution for winding up on 31st March, 2014, when its Balance Sheet stood as under:

Liabilities	Rs.	Assets	Rs.
Share Capital -		Plant and Machinery	2,00,000
2,500 Equity Shares of		Furniture and Fittings	500
Rs.100 each fully paid	2,50,000	Stock-in-trade	25,000
500 Equity Shares of		Debtors	75,000
Rs.100 each, Rs. 75		Cash in Hand	2,500
per share called and paid-up	37,500	Profit and Loss A/c	2,10,500
500, 6% Cumulative			
Preference Shares of Rs.100			
each fully paid	50,000		
7% Debentures (Secured on			
Plant and Machinery)	50,000		
Unsecured Creditors	1,26,000		
	5,13,500		5,13,500

Dividend on preference shares remained unpaid for full year. Interest (payable annually on December 31) on debentures was paid upto December 31, 2013. Unsecured creditors include Rs. 1,000 of preferential creditors.

Plant and Machinery realised Rs.1,80,000/-, Stock Rs.50,000/- and Debtors Rs. 70,000/- Furniture and fittings realised nothing.

The expenses of winding up amounted to Rs. 9,750/-

The Liquidator's remuneration is to be @ 4% on realisation of assets and at 2% on distribution among unsecured creditors excluding preferential creditors. The winding up was completed on 30th June 2014, when the debentures were repaid. The necessary call was made and received in full from all shareholders.

Please draw up the Liquidator's Account.

Ans:- Total of Liquidator's Final Statement of Account – Rs. 2,63,250

10) You are asked by a Liquidator of a Company to prepare a Statement of Account to be laid before a meeting of the shareholders from the following :-

Balance Sheet of the Company as on the date of liquidation i.e. 1-1-2014

Liabilities	Rs.	Assets	Rs.
Share Capital :		Fixed Assets	4,00,000
4,000 Equity Shares of Rs.100		Book Debts	3,00,000
each, called Rs. 80	3,20,000	Loss todate	1,00,000
1,000 Pref. Shares of Rs.100			
each, called up Rs. 70	70,000		
Secured Loans from Banks			
on Building and Machinery	1,50,000		
Trade Creditors	2,60,000		
	8,00,000		8,00,000

The assets realised as follows on 1-4-2014 : fixed assets Rs.1,00,000 book debts Rs.1,00,000, expenses paid Rs. 4,000 on 1-6-2014. Fixed Assets (final) Rs.2,00,000, Book Debts Rs.1,00,000 on 1-8-2014, book debts (final payment) Rs.50,000. The liquidator is entitled to a commission at 5% on collection and 2% on the amount paid to equity shareholders. Prepare a statement on the assumption that disbursements are made in accordance with law, as and when cash is available.

Ans :- Total of Liquidator's Statement of Account Rs. 4,00,000

B) PREPARATION OF STATEMENT OF AFFAIRS AND DEFICIENCY ACCOUNT

Where the Court has made a winding up order or appointed the official liquidator as provisional liquidator, the directors of the company must make available to the liquidator a statement as to the affairs of the company in *the prescribed form,* verified by an affidavit, and containing the following particulars, namely:

(a) the assets of the company, stating separately the cash balance in hand and at the bank, if any, and the negotiable securities, if any held by the company;

(b) its debts and liabilities;

(c) the names, residences and occupations of its creditors, stating separately the amount of secured and unsecured debts;

(d) the debts due to the company and the names, residences and occupations of the persons from whom they are due and the amount likely to be realised on account thereof.

The objective of preparation of statement of affairs is to give the liquidator a rough idea as to the financial position of the company. The statement of affairs is required in *both compulsory and voluntary* winding up. In case of compulsory winding up, the statement should be made within 21 days from the date of appointment of the provisional liquidator (or in the absence of such an appointment, from the 'date of commencement of winding up). The Court of the Official Liquidator has power to extend the time upto 3 months.

3.7 FORM No. 57

(See rule 127)

In the High Court at ....

[(Or)] In the District Court of. ....

Original Jurisdiction

In the matter of the companies Act, 1956

and

In the matter of .... (Give the name of the Company (In liquidation)

Company Petition No..................... of 20..............

Statement of Affairs under Section 454

Statement of affairs of the above-named company as on the .... day of 20.................. the date of the winding-up order [or the order appointing Provisional Liquidator or the date directed by the Official Liquidator].

I/We .... of .... do solemnly affirm and say that the statement made overleaf and the several lists hereunto annexed marked 'A' to I are to the best of my/ our knowledge and belief a full, true and complete statement as to the affairs of the above-named company, on the .... day of .... 20.......... the date of the winding-up order [or the order- appointing Provisional Liquidator or the date directed by the Official Liquidator], and that the said company carries/carried on the following business:

[Here set out nature of company's business.]   Signature(s)

Solemnly affirmed at .... this .... day of .... 20....

Before me

Commissioner for Oaths

The commissioner is particularly requested, before swearing the affidavit, to ascertain that the full name, address and description of the deponent are stated, and to initial any crossings-out or other alterations in the printed form. A deficiency in the affidavit in any of the above respects will entail its refusal by the Court and will necessitate its being re-sworn.

NOTE : The several lists annexed are not exhibits to the affidavit.

STATEMENT OF AFFAIRS AND LISTS TO BE ANNEXED

Statement as to the affairs of .... Ltd. on the .... day of .... 20....... being the date of the winding-up order (or order appointing Provisional Liquidator on the date directed by the Official Liquidator as the case may be) showing assets at estimated realisable values and liabilities expected to rank :-

Particulars	Estimated Realisable Values (Rs)
Assets not specifically pledged (as per list 'A')	
Balance at Bank	
Cash in Hand	
Marketable Securities	
Bills Receivable	
Trade Debtors	
Loans and Advances	
Unpaid Calls	
Stock-in-trade	
Work-in-progress	
....	
....	
Freehold Property. Land and Buildings	
Leasehold Property	
Plant and Machinery	
Furniture, Fittings. Utensils, etc.	
Investments other than marketable securities	
Livestock	
Vehicles, etc.	
Other property, viz.	
....	
....	
*** Assets specifically pledged (as per list 'B')**	

	(a) Estimated - Realisable Value (Rs)	(b) Due to Secured Creditors (Rs)	(c) Deficiency Ranking as Unsecured (Rs)	(d) Surplus carried 10 last column (Rs)
Freehold Property				
Rs				

    * Note : All assets specifically mortgaged, pledged or otherwise given as security should be included under this head. In the case of goods given as security, those in possession of the company and those not in possession should be separately set out.

Particulars			Estimated Realisable Values (Rs)
Estimated surplus from assets specifically pledged			
Estimated total assets available for preferential creditors, debenture holders secured by a floating charge, and unsecured creditors** (carried forward)			Rs
Summary of Gross Assets			
		(d) Rs.	
Gross realisable value of assets specifically pledged .... Other Assets			
Gross Assets **(Rs)**			
Estimated total assets available for preferential creditors, debenture holders secured by a floating charge, and unsecured creditors** (brought forward).			
	Liabilities		**Rs**
(e) Gross Liabilities Rs.	(to be deducted from surplus or added to deficiency as the case may be.) Secured creditors (as per List 'B') to the extent to which claims are estimated to be covered by assets specifically pledged [item(a) or (b) on preceding page, whichever is the less] (Insert in 'Gross Liabilities' column only) Preferential creditors (as per List'C') .... Estimated balance of assets available for Debenture holders secured by a floating charge and unsecured creditors** .... Debenture Holders secured by a floating charge (as per List 'D') .... Estimated Surplus Deficiency as regards Debenture Holders** .... Unsecured Creditors (as per List 'E')		Rs

	Liabilities	**Rs**
	Estimated unsecured balance of claims of creditors partly secured en specific assets, brought from preceding page(c)	
	Trade Accounts	
	Bills Payable	
	Outstanding Expenses	
	Contingent Liabilities (state nature)	
	Estimated Surplus / Deficiency as regards Creditors	
	(Being difference between Gross Assets brought from preceding page (d) and Gross Liabilities as per column (e)]	
	Issued and Called-up Capital:	
	.... preference shares of .... each .... called-up	
	(as per List 'F')	
	.... equity shares of .... each .... called-up	
	(as per List 'G')	
	....	
	....	
	Estimated Surplus/Deficiency as regards Members**	
	(as per List 'H')	

** These figures must be read subject to the following notes:

  (1) (f) There is no unpaid capital liable to be called-up. or

        (g) The nominal amount of unpaid capita! liable to be called-up is Rs .... estimated to produce Rs .... which is/is not charged in favour of Debenture Holders (Strike out (f) or (g)).

  (2) The estimates are subject to costs of the winding and to any surplus or deficiency on trading Pending realisation of the assets.

LIST 'A' — ASSETS NOT SPECIFICALLY PLEDGED

Statement of Affairs — List 'A'

Full particulars of every description of property not specifically pledged and not included in any other List are to be set forth in this list.

	Full statement and nature of property	Book value Rs. P.	Estimated to produce Rs. P.
State name of bankers	Balance at Bank		
	Cash in Hand		
	Marketable Securities, viz., ...		
	Bills Receivable (as per Schedule I)		
	Trade Debtors (as per Schedule II)		
	Loans and Advances (as per Schedule III)		
	Unpaid Calls (as per Schedule IV)		
State nature	Stock-in-Trade (as per Schedule V)		
State nature	Work-in-Progress		
	Freehold property, viz..............................		
	Leasehold property, viz		
	Plant and Machinery, viz.		
	Furniture, Fittings, Utensils, etc.		
	Patents, Trade Marks, etc., viz		
	Investments other than Marketable Securities, viz.		
	Livestock, Vehicles, etc		
	Other Property, viz.		

Signature Dated.............. 20 ....

SCHEDULE I — BILLS OF EXCHANGE, PROMISSORY NOTES, ETC., ON HAND AVAILABLE AS ASSETS

Statement of Affairs: Schedule I to List 'A'

The names to be arranged in alphabetical order and numbered consecutively.

Sr. No.	Name of Acceptor of bill or note	Address, etc.	Amount of bill or note Rs P	Date when due	Estimated to produce Rs P	Particulars of any property held as security for pay-ment of bill or note

Signature Dated.............. 20 ....

SCHEDULE II — TRADE DEBTORS
Statement of Affairs: Schedule II to List 'A'

The names to be arranged in alphabetical order and numbered consecutively.

Note : If the debtor to the company is also a creditor, but for a less amount than his indebtedness, the gross amount due to die company and the amount of the contra account should be shown in die third column, and the balance only be inserted under the heading 'Amount of debt' thus :   Rs   P

Due to the company
Less: Contra Account
No such claim should be included in List 'E'

| Sr. No. | Name | Resid- ence and occupa- tion | Amount of Debt | | | Folio of ledger or other book where parti- culars to be found | When Contracted | | Estimated to | Particulares of any securities held for debt |
			Good	Doubtful	Bad		Month	Year		
			Rs P	Rs P	Rs P				Rs P	

Signature   Dated............... 20 ....

SCHEDULE III — LOANS AND ADVANCES
Statement of Affairs : Schedule III to List 'A'

Serial No.	Date of Advance	Name and address of person to whom advanced	Amount due	Estimated to realise	Particulars of security, if any	Folio of ledger or other book where particulars to be found
			Rs P	Rs P		

Signature   Dated............... 20 ....

SCHEDULE IV — UNPAID CALLS

Statement of Affairs : Schedule IV to List 'A'

The names to be arranged in alphabetical order and numbered consecutively.

Consecutive No.	No. in Share Register	Name of Shareholder	Address	No. of Shares Held	Amount of Call per Share Unpaid Rs P	Total Amount Due Rs P	Estimated to Realise Rs P

Signature   Dated............... 20 ....

SCHEDULE V — STOCK IN TRADE

Statement of Affairs : Schedule V to List 'A'

Serial No.	Description	Quantity	Book Value Rs P	Estimated to Realise Rs P

Signature   Dated............... 20 ....

SCHEDULE VI — DEBTS DUE FROM CONTRIBUTORS

(other than unpaid calls)

Statement of Affairs: Schedule VI to List 'A'

Consecutive No.	No. in Share Register	Name of Share-holders	Address	Nature & Particulars of the Debt	Amount Due Rs P	Security Held, if any for the debt	Serial No. in Schedule I, II or III as We case may be where the debt is included

Signature   Dated............... 20 ....

LIST 'B' —ASSETS SPECIFICALLY PLEDGED AND CREDITORS FULLY OR PARTLY SECURED

(Not including Debenture Holders secured by a floating charge)
The names of the secured creditors are to be shown against the assets
on which their claims are secured, numbered consecutively,
and arranged in alphabetical order as far as possible
Statement of Affairs List 'B"

Particulars of assets specifically pledged*	Date when security	Estimated Value of security	No.	Name of Creditor	Address & occupation	Amount of dabt	Deat when contracted	Consideration	Balance of debt unsecured carried to list 'E'	Estimeted surplus form security
		Rs P				Rs P			Rs P	Rs P

Signature   Dated............... 20 ....

All assets specifically mortgaged, pledged or otherwise given as security should be set out: goods given as security but in possession of the company and goods not in possession should be separately set out.

LIST 'C' — PREFERENTIAL CREDITORS FOR RATES, TAXES, SALARIES, WAGES AND OTHERWISE

The names to be arranged in alphabetical order and numbered consecutively
Statement of Affairs List 'C'

No.	Name of Creditor	Address & occupation	Nature of claim	Period during which claim accrued due	Date when due	Amount of claim	Amount payable in full	Balance not perferential carried of list 'E'

Signature   Dated............... 20 ....

LIST 'D' — LIST OF DEBENTURE HOLDERS SECURED
BY A FLOATING CHARGE

The names to be arranged in alphabetical order and numbered consecutively. Separately
Lists must be furnished of holders of each issue of Debentures, should more than one
issue have been made Statement of Affairs List 'D'

No.	Name of Holder	Address	Amount Rs P	Description of assets over Which security extends

Signature   Dated............... 20 ....

LIST 'E' — UNSECURED CREDITORS

The names to be arranged in alphabetical order and numbered consecutively
Statement of Affairs List 'E'

Note :

(1) When there is a contra account against the creditor less than his claim against the
company, the amount of the creditor's claim and the amount of the contra account
should be shown in the third column and the balance only inserted under the heading
'Amount of Debt' thus:

                                                   Rs   P

                  Total amount of claim...............

                  Less: Contra Account...............

No such set-off should be included in Schedule I attached to List 'A'

(2) The particulars of any Bills of Exchange and Promissory Notes held by a creditor
should be inserted immediately below the name and address of such creditor.

No.	Name	Address and occupation	Amount of debt		Date when contracted		Follo of ledger of other book where particulars to be found	Consideration
			Rs	P	Month	Year		
	Unsecured balance of creditors partly secured - brought from List 'B' Balance not preferention of preferential creditors - brought from List 'C'							

Signature   Dated............... 20 ....

LIST 'F' — LIST OF PREFERENCE SHAREHOLDERS
The names to be arranged in alphabetical order and numbered consecutively
Statement of Affairs List 'F'

Consecutive Number	Register number	Name of shareholder	Address	Nominal amount of share	Number of shares held	Amount per share called-up Rs P	Total amount called-up Rs P

Signature   Dated............... 20 ....

LIST 'G' — LIST OF EQUITY SHAREHOLDERS
The names to be arranged in alphabetical order and numbered consecutively
Statement of Affairs List 'G'

Consecutive Number	Register number	Name of shareholder	Address	Nominal amount of share	Number of shares held	Amount per share called-up Rs P	Total amount called-up Rs P

Signature   Dated............... 20 ....

LIST 'H' — DEFICIENCY OR SURPLUS ACCOUNT
Statement of Affairs List 'H'

The period covered by this Account must commence on a date not less than 3 years before the date of the winding-up order [or] the order appointing Provisional Liquidator, or the date directed by the Official Liquidator [or], if the company has not been incorporated for the whole of that period, the date of formation of the company, unless the Official Liquidator otherwise agrees,

	Rs
Items contributing to deficiency (or Reducing Surplus):	
1. Excess (if any) of Capital and Liabilities over Assets on the .... 20..... as shown by Balance Sheet (copy annexed)	
2. Net dividends and bonuses declared during the period from .... 20...-. to the date of the statement	
3. Net trading losses (after charging items shown in note below) for the same period	

	Rs
4. Losses other than trading losses written off or for which provision has been made in the books during the same period (give particulars or annex schedule)	
5. Estimated losses now written off or for which provision has been made for the purpose of preparing the statement (give particulars or annex schedule)	
6. Other items contributing to deficiency or reducing Surplus	

Items reducing Deficiency (or contributing to Surplus) :

  7. Excess (if any) of assets over capital and liabilities on the ....
     (copy annexed)

  8. Net trading profits (after charging items shown in note below) for the period from .... 20..... to the date of statement

  9. Profits and income other than trading profits during the same period (give particulars or annex schedule).

  10. Other items reducing Deficiency or contributing to Surplus ....

Deficiency/Surplus as shown by Statement

Note as to Net Trading Profits and Losses:

Particulars are to be inserted here (so far as applicable) of the items mentioned below, which are to be taken into account in arriving a! the amount of net trading profits or losses shown in this account

Provisions for depreciation, renewals or diminution in value of fixed assets

Charges for Indian Income-tax and other Indian taxation on profits

Interest on debentures and other fixed loans

Payments to directors made by the company and required by law to be disclosed in the accounts

Exceptional or non-recurring expenditure	Rs
Exceptional or non-recurring receipts	Rs
Balance, being other trading profits or losses	Rs
Net trading profits Losses as shown in Deficiency or	
Surplus Account above	Rs

Signature   Dated............... 20 ....

3.8 PROBLEMS

Problem No. : 1 - Unstable Ltd. went into compulsory liquidation. Their summarised Balance Sheet as at 31st March, 2014 appears as under:

Liabilities	Rs.	Assets	Rs.
2,50,000 Equity Shares of Rs 10 each	25,00,000	Land and Buildings	5,00,000
		Other Fixed Assets	20,00,000
Secured Debentures (security Land and Buildings)	10,00,000	Current Assets	45,00,000
		Profit and Loss Account	20,00,000
Unsecured Loans	20,00,000		
Trade Creditors	35,00,000		
	90,00,000		90,00,000

Contingent liabilities are :

	Rs
for Bills Discounted	1,00,000
for Excise duty demands	1,50,000

On investigation, it is found that the contingent liabilities are certain to devolve and that the assets are likely to be realised as follows:

	Rs
Land and Buildings	11,00,000
Other Fixed Assets	18,00,000
Current Assets	35,00,000

Taking the above into account, prepare the Statement of Affairs. *[C.A. (inter) — Adapted]*

Solution : Statement of Affairs of Unstable Ltd. as at 31st March, 2014

(all figures in Rupees)

Assets	Estimated Realisable Values (Rs)
Assets not Specifically Pledged (as per List A)	
Other Fixed Assets	18,00,000
Current Assets	35,00,000
	53,00,000

Assets					Values (Rs)
Assets Specifically Pledged (as per list B)					
	(a) Estimated - Realisable Value (Rs)	(b) Due to Secured Creditors (Rs)	(c) Deficiency RanKing as Unsecured (Rs)	(d) Surplus carried 10 last column (Rs)	
Land and Buildings	11,00,000	10,00,000	---	1,00,000	1,00,000

	Rs
Estimated Surplus from Assets Specifically Pledged	54,00,000
Estimated Total Assets Available for Preferential Creditors, Debentureholders Secured by Floating Charge and Unsecured Creditors	
Summary of Gross Assets	Rs
Gross Realisable Value of Assets Specifically Pledged	11,00,000
Other Assets	53,00,000
Gross Assets	64,00,000

Liabilities		Rs
Gross Liabilities	(To be deducted from surplus or added to deficiency as the case may be)	
10,00,000	Secured Creditors (as per List 'B') to the extent to which Claims are estimated to be covered by Assets specifically pledged	
1,50,000	*Preferential Creditors (as per List 'C')	1,50,000
	Estimated Surplus available for Unsecured Creditors	52,50,000
	Unsecured Creditors (as per List 'E')	
20,00,000	Unsecured Loans	20,00,000
35,00,000	Trade Creditors	35,00,000
1,00,000	Contingent Liability on Bills Discounted	1,00,000
67,50,000	**Estimated Deficiency as regard Creditors**	3,50,000
	(Being the difference between gross assets and gross liabilities, i.e., Rs 64,00,000 - 67,50,000)	
	2,50.000 Equity Shares of Rs 10 each (as per List 'G')	25,00,000
	Estimated Deficiency as regard Members	28,50,000

***Tutorial Note :** Contingent liabilities for excise demand will be treated as Preferential Creditors.

Problems No. : 2 - X Co. Lid. went into voluntary liquidation on 1st April. 2014. The following balances are extracted from its books on that date :

Liabilities	Rs.	Assets	Rs.
Share Capital :		Machinery	90,000
2,40,000 Equity Shares of		Leasehold Properties	1,20,000
Rs. 10 each	2,40,000	Stock	3,000
Debentures (Secured	1,50,000	Debtors	1,50,000
by floating charge)		Investments	18,000
Overdraft	54,000	Cash in Hand	3,000
Creditors	60,000	Profit and Loss Account	1,20,000
	5,04,000		5,04,000

The following assets are valued as under

	Rs.
Machinery	1,80,000
Leasehold Properties	2,18,000
Investments	12,000
Stock	6,000
Debtors	1,40,000

The bank overdraft is secured by deposit of title deeds of leasehold properties. There were preferential creditors of Rs 3,000 which were not included in Creditors Rs 60,000.

Prepare a Statement of Affairs to be submitted to the meeting of member / creditors.

[C.A. (Inter) — November, 1992]

Solution : **Statement of Affairs of X Co. Ltd. as at 1st April, 2014**

Assets	Estimated Realisable Values (Rs)
Assets not Specifically Pledged (as per List A)	
Cash in Hand	3,000
Investments	12,000
Debtors	1,40,000
Stock	6,000
Machinery	1,80,000
	3,41,000

Assets					Values (Rs)
Assets Specifically Pledged (as per list B)					
	(a) Estimated - Realisable Value (Rs)	(b) Due to Secured Creditors (Rs)	(c) Deficiency RanKing as Unsecured (Rs)	(d) Surplus carried to last column (Rs)	
Leasehold Property	2,18,000	54,000	---	1,64,000	1,64,000

Assets		Values (Rs)
Estimated Surplus from Assets Specifically Pledged		5,05,000
Estimated Total Assets Available for Preferential Creditors, Debentureholders Secured by Floating Charge, and Unsecured Creditors		
Summary of Gross Assets	**Rs**	
Gross Realisable Value of Assets Specifically Pledged	2,18,000	
Other Assets	3,41,000	
Gross Assets	5,59,000	

	Liabilities	Rs
Gross Liabilities	(To be deducted from surplus or added to deficiency as the case may be)	
54,000	Secured Creditors (as per List 'B') to the extent to which Claims are estimated to be covered by Assets specifically pledged	
3,000	*Preferential Creditors (as per List 'C')	3,000
	Estimated Balance of Assets available for Debentureholders secured in Floating charge, and Unsecured Creditors	5,02,000
1,50,000	Debentures	1,50,000
	Estimated Surplus available for Unsecured Creditors	3,52,000
	Unsecured Creditors (as per List 'E')	
60,000	Creditors	60,000
2,67,000	**Estimated Surplus as regard Creditors**	2,92,000
	(Being difference between gross assets and gross liabilities, i.e. Rs 5,59,000 - 2,67,000)	2,40,000
	24,000 Equity Shares of Rs 10 each (as per List 'G')	
	Estimated Surplus as regards Members	52,000

Problem No. 3 : Bad Luck Ltd. went into compulsory liquidation on 30th June, 2014. From the following particulars prepare a Statement of Affairs in the present statutory form as far as possible :

Particulars	Rs
Equity Share Capital —20,000 Equity Shares of Rs 10 each, Rs 5 paid-up	1,00,000
7% Preference Share Capital — 20,000 Shares of Rs 10 each fully paid	2,00,000
6% First Mortgage Deb. secured by a Floating Charge upon the whole	1,50,000
of the assets of the company except un-called capital	
Fully Secured Creditors (value of Securities Rs 35,000)	30,000
Partly Secured Creditors (value of Securities Rs 10,000)	20,000
Preferential Creditors for rent, taxes, salaries and wages	6,000
Bills Payable	1,00,000
Unsecured Creditors	70,000
Bank Overdraft	10,000
Bills Receivable in Hand	15,000
Bills Discounted (one bill for Rs 10,000 estimated to be bad)	30,000
Investments in shares: Estimated value Rs 35,000	50,000
(deposited with secured creditors)	
G.P. Notes: estimated value Rs 10,000	15,000
(deposited with partly secured creditors)	
Book Debts: Rs	
Good 10,000	
Doubtful (estimated to produce 50 paisa in the rupee) 7,000	
Bad 6,000	23,000
Land and Building (estimated to produce Rs 1,00,000)	1,50,000
Stock-in-trade (estimated to produce Rs 40,000)	50,000
Machinery and Tools (estimated to produce Rs 2,000)	5,000
Cash in Hand	100

Solution : Statement of Affairs of Bad Luck Ltd. as at 30th June, 2014

Assets	Estimated Realisable Values (Rs)
Assets not Specifically Pledged (as per List A)	
Cash in Hand	100
Bills Receivable	15,000
Trade Debtors	13,500
Stock-in-Trade	40,000
Land and Buildings	1,00,000
Plant and Machinery	2,000
	1,70,600

Assets Specifically Pledged (as per list B)

	(a) Estimated - Realisable Value (Rs)	(b) Due to Secured Creditors (Rs)	(c) Deficiency RanKing as Unsecured Creditors (Rs)	(d) Surplus carried 10 last column (Rs)	
Investments in Shares	35,000	30,000	-	5,000	
G.P. Notes	10,000	20,000	10,000	-	5,000

	Estimated Realisable Values (Rs)
Estimated Surplus from Assets Specifically Pledged	1,75,600
Estimated Total Assets Available for Preferential Creditors,	
Debentureholders Secured by Floating Charge, and	
Unsecured Creditors carried forward	

Summary of Gross Assets	**Rs**
Gross Realisable Value of Assets Specifically Pledged	45,000
Other Assets	1,70,600
Gross Assets	2,15,600

	Liabilities	Rs
Gross Liabilities	(To be deducted from surplus or added to deficiency as the case may be)	
40,000	Secured Creditors (as per List 'B') to the extent to which Claims are estimated to be covered by Assets specifically pledged	
6,000	*Preferential Creditors (as per List 'C')	6,000
	Estimated Surplus available to Debentureholders secured by Floating charge, and Unsecured Creditors	1,69,600
1,50,000	Debentureholders secured by a Floating Charge (as psr List 'D')	1,50,000
	Estimated Surplus available to Unsecured Creditors	19,600
	Unsecured Creditors (as per List 'E')	
10,000	Partly secured creditors (deficiency ranking as unsecured)	10,000
70,000	Unsecured creditors	70,000
1,00,000	Bills Payable	1,00,000
10,000	Bank Overdraft	10,000
10,000	Contingent Liability (for bills discounted)	10,000
3,96,000	**Estimated Deficiency as regards Creditors**	1,80,400
	[Being the difference between gross assets and gross liabilities i.e.Rs 2,15,000 -Rs 3,96,000]	
	20,000 Preference Shares of Rs 10 each fully called-up (as per List 'F')	2,00,000
	20,000 Equity Shares of Rs 10 each, Rs 5 called-up	1,00,000
	Estimated Deficiency as regards Members (as per List 'H')	4,80,400

Problems No. 4 :

A winding up order has been issued against M Ltd.

The following information is obtained with regard to the assets and liabilities as on 30 June, 2014 :

Particulars	Rs.	Particulars	Rs.
Freehold premises (book value Rs 4,50.000) valued at	3,75,000	Bank overdraft — unsecured	58,125
		Cash in Hand	825
First mortgage of		Stock (at cost Rs 50,850)	
freehold premises	3,00,000	estimated to realise	33,900
Second mortgage of	1,12,500	Issued Capital :	
freehold premises		Equity Shares of Rs 10	
8% debentures carrying a	1,50,000	each fully called-up	1,50,000
floating charge on the		Calls-in-arrears, Rs 3,000	
undertaking, interest due		estimated to realise	1,500
1st September and 1st April		Unsecured creditors	2,96,250
and paid on due dates		Contingent liability in respect	
Managing Director's emoluments	22,500	of a claim for damages	
(6 months)		Rs 37,500 - estimated	
Staff salary unpaid (one month)	16,050	to be settled for	18,000
Trade debtors		Income-tax liability	
Good	31,500	For 30 June, 2012	5,250
Doubtful	12,900	For 30 June, 2013	1,275
(estimated to realise 50%)		For 30 June, 2014	2,700
Bad	72,750		
Plant and machinery			
(book value Rs 2,47,500)			
estimated to realise	1,74,000		

The Reserves of the company on 1st July 2013 amounted to Rs 7,500.
You are required to prepare :
(i) Statement of Affairs, and (ii) Deficiency Account.   *[C.A. - Adopted]*

Solution : **Statement of Affairs of M Ltd. as at 30th June, 2014**

Assets	Estimated Realisable Values (Rs)
Assets not Specifically Pledged (as per List A)	
Cash in Hand	825
Trade Debtors (Rs 31,500 + 50% of Rs 12,900)	37,950
Unpaid Calls	1,500
Stock	33,900
Plant and Machinery	1,74,000
	2,48,175

Assets Specifically Pledged (as per list B)

	(a) Estimated - Realisable Value (Rs)	(b) Due to Secured Creditors (Rs)	(c) Deficiency RanKing as Unsecured (Rs)	(d) Surplus carried to last column (Rs)	
Freehold Premises	3,75,000	3,00,000	---	---	
Second Mortgage on above	---	1,12,500	37,500	---	---

	Estimated Realisable Values (Rs)
Estimated Total Assets Available for Preferential Creditors, Debentureholders Secured by Floating Charge, and Unsecured Creditors carried forwards	2,48,175

Summary of Gross Assets	**Rs**
Gross Realisable Value of Assets Specifically Pledged	3,75,000
Other Assets	2,48,175
Gross Assets	6,23,175

	Liabilities	Rs
Gross Liabilities	(To be deducted from surplus or added to deficiency as the case may be)	
3,75,000	Secured Creditors (as per List 'B') to the extent to which Claims are estimated to be covered by Assets specifically pledged	
20,025	Preferential Creditors (as per List 'C'} [Note 2]	20,025
	Estimated Surplus available to Debenturehnlders secured by Floating charges, and Unsecured Creditors	2,28,150
1,53,000	Debentureholder secured by a Floating Charge (as per List 'D') [Rs. 1,50,000 + Rs. 3,000 (interest)]	1,53,000
	Estimated Surplus available to Unsecured Creditors	75,150
	Unsecured Creditors (as per List 'E')	
37,500	Partly secured creditors (deficiency ranking as unsecured)	37,500
2,96,250	Unsecured Creditors	2,96,250
27,750	Outstanding Director's Emoluments and Taxes (Rs 22,500 + Rs 5,250)	27,750
58,125	Bank Overdraft	58,125
18,000	Contingent Liability in respect of a Claim for Damages	18,000
9,65,650	**Estimated Deficiency as regard Creditors**	3,62,475
	15,000 Equity Shares of Rs 10 each fully called up less calls in arrears Rs 1,500	1,48,500
	Estimated Deficiency as regards Members (as per List H)	5,10,975

List H — Deficiency Account

	Rs
A. Items contributing to Deficiency	
1. Excess of Capital and Liabilities over assets on 1st July, 2013	----
2. Dividend and Bonus declared	----
3. Net trading losses after charging depreciation, taxation, interest on debentures, etc. (Note 1)	2,55,825
4. Losses other than trading losses	----
5. Estimated losses now written off Rs	
Freehold Premises 75,000	
Trade Debtors 79,200	
Plant and Machinery 73,500	
Stock 16,950	
Claim for Damages 18,000	2,62,650
6. Any other item	----
	5,18,475
B. Items Reducing Deficiency	
7. Excess of Assets over Capital and Liabilities as on 1st July, 2013	7,500
8. Net Trading Profit	----
9. Profits and Incomes other than Trading Profit	----
10. Other Items	----
Deficiency as explained in the Statement of Affairs	5,10,975

Working Notes :   **(1) Balance Sheet as at 30th June, 2014**

Liabilities	Rs.	Assets	Rs.
15,000 Equity Shares of Rs 10 each	1,50,000	Freehold Premises	4,50,000
		Plant and Machinery	2,47,500
Less: Calls-in-Arrears	3,000	Sundry Debtors (Rs 31,500 +	1,17,150
	1,47,000	12,900 + 72,750)	
Reserve —1.7.2013	7,500	Stock	50,850
1st Mortgage	3,00,000	Cash	825
2nd Mortgage	1,12,500	Profit and Loss Account	2,55,825
8% Debentures	1,50,000		

Liabilities	Rs.	Assets	Rs.
Interest on Debentures for 3 months	3,000		
Unsecured Creditors	2,96,250		
Director's Remuneration due	22,500		
Staff Salary Outstanding	16,050		
Bank overdraft	58,125		
Liability for I.T	9,225		
	11,22,150		11,22150

(2) Preferential Creditors

	Rs
Income tax : 2012-13	1,275
2013-14	2,700
Staff Salary	16,050
	20,025

It should be noted that the tax which becomes payable within 12 months of the relevant date will be preferential claim even though it relates to an earlier period.

(3) Managing Director's remuneration has not been classified as preferential creditors as he is an officer and not an employee.

Problems No. 5 : Insol Ltd. is to be liquidated. Their summarised Balance Sheet as at 30th September, 2014, appears as under:

Liabilities	Rs.	Assets	Rs.
2,50,000 equity shares of Rs. 10 each	25,00,000	Land and Buildings	5,00,000
		Other fixed assets	20,00,000
Secured debentures (on land and buildings)	10,00,000	Current assets	45,00,000
		Profit and Loss A/c	20,00,000
Unsecured loans	20,00,000		
Trade creditors	35,00,000		
	90,00,000		90,00,000

Contingent liabilities are:

For bills discounted	1,00,000
For excise duty demands	1,50,000

On investigation, it is found that the contingent liabilities are certain to devolve and that the assets are likely to be realised as follows:

	Rs.
Land and Buildings	1,00,000
Other fixed assets	18,00,000
Current assets	35,00,000
Taking the above into account, prepare the statement of affairs.	*(C.A. Inter)*

Solution :

Statement of Affairs of INSOL Ltd. (In Liquidation)

as on 30th Sep., 2014

Assets	Estimated Realisable Values (Rs)
Assets not Specifically Pledged (as per List A)	
Other fixed assets	18,00,000
Current assets	35,00,000
	53,00,000
Assets Specifically Pledged (as per list B)	

	(a) Estimated - Realisable Value (Rs)	(b) Due to Secured Creditors (Rs)	(c) Deficiency RanKing as Unsecured (Rs)	(d) Surplus carried to last column (Rs)	
Land & Building	11,00,000	10,00,000	---	1,00,000	1,00,000

	Estimated Realisable Values (Rs)
Estimated Total Assets Available for Preferential Creditors,	54,00,000

Summary of Gross Assets

	Rs
Gross Realisable Value of Assets Specifically Pledged	11,00,000
Other Assets	53,00,000
Gross Assets	64,00,000

Gross Liabilities	Liabilities	Rs
10,00,000	Secured Creditors (as per List 'B') to the extent to which Claims are estimated to be covered by Assets specifically pledged	
1,50,000	Preferential Creditors (as per List 'C')	1,50,000
		52,50,000
	Unsecured Creditors (as per list E)	
20,00,000	Unsecured Loans	20,00,000
35,00,000	Trade Creditors	35,00,000
1,00,000	Contingent Liability on Bills Discounted	1,00,000
67,50,000	Estimated deficiency as regards creditors (67,50,000 - 64,00.000)	3,50,000
	2,50,000 Equity shares of Rs. 10 each; (as per list G)	25,00,000
	Estimated deficiency as regards members	28,50,000

Problem No. 6 : X Co. Ltd. went into voluntary liquidation on 1st April, 2014. The following balances are extracted from its books on that date:

	Rs.		Rs.
Capital :		Machinery	90,000
24,000 Equity Shares of	2,40,000	Leasehold properties	1,20,000
Rs 10 each		Stock	3,000
Debentures (secured by	1,50,000	Debtors	1,50,000
floating charge)		Investments	18,000
Bank overdraft	54,000	Cash in hand	3,000
Creditors	60,000	Profit and loss account	1,20,000
	5,04,000		5,04,000

The following assets are valued as under :

	Rs.
Machinery	1,80,000
Leasehold properties	2,18,000
Investment	12,000
Stock	6,000
Debtors	1,40,000

The bank overdraft is secured by deposit of title deeds of leasehold properties. There were preferential creditors Rs, 3,000 which were not included in creditors Rs. 60,000.

Prepare a statement of affairs to be submitted to the meeting of members/creditors. *(C.A. Inter)*

Solution:

Statement of Affairs of X Co. Ltd on the 1st day of April, 2014

Assets					Estimated Realisable Values (Rs)
Assets not Specifically Pledged (as per List A)					
Cash in hand					3,000
Investments					12,000
Debtors					1,40,000
Stock					6,000
Machinery					1,80,000
					3,41,000
Assets Specifically Pledged (as per list B)					
	(a) Estimated - Realisable Value (Rs)	(b) Due to Secured Creditors (Rs)	(c) Deficiency RanKing as Unsecured (Rs)	(d) Surplus carried to last column (Rs)	
Leasehold property	2,18,000	54,000	---	1,64,000	1,64,000
Estimated surplus from assets specifically pledged					
Estimated Total Assets Available for Preterential Creditors, debentureholders secured by floating charge, and unsecured creditors.					5,05,000

	Rs
Summary of Gross Assets	
Gross Realisabie Value of Assets Specifically Pledged	2,18,000
Other Assets	3,41,000
Gross Assets	5,59,000

	Liabilities	Rs
Gross Liabilities	(To be deducted from surplus or added to deficiency as the case may be)	
54,000	Secured Creditors to the extent to which Claims are estimated to be covered by Assets specifically pledged	
3,000	Preferential Creditors (as per List 'C') [Note 2]	3,000
	Estimated balance of assets available for Debenturehnlders secured by Floating charges and Unsecured Creditors	5,02,000
1,50,000	Debentureholder as per List 'D'	1,50,000
	Estimated Surplus as regard debenture holders	3,52,000
60,000	Creditors unsecured as per list E	60,000
2,67,000		
	Estimated Deficiency as regard Creditors (being difference between gross assets and gross liabilities)	2,92,000
	Issued and called up capital :	
	24,000 Equity Shares of Rs 10 each as per list F	2,40,000
	Estimated Surplus as regard members	52,000

Problem No. 7 : Shri Chopra is appointed liquidator of Moon Company Limited, in voluntary liquidation, on 1st July 2014. Following balances are extracted from the books on that date;

	Rs.		Rs.
Capital:		Machinery	45,000
24,000 shares of Rs. 5 each	1,20,000	Leasehold properties	60,000
Reserve for Bad Debts	15,000	Stock in Trade	1,500
Debentures	75,000	Book Debts	90,000
Bank Overdraft	27,000	Investments	9,000
Liabilities for purchases	30,000	Calls-in-Arrear	7,500
		Cash in hand	1,500
		Profit and Loss account	52,500
	2,67,000		2,67,000

You are required to prepare a statement of affairs to be submitted to the meeting of the creditors. The following assets are valued as under:

Machinery	Rs.	90,000
Leasehold Properties	Rs.	1,09,000
Investments	Rs.	6,000
Stock-in-trade	Rs.	3,000

Bad Debts are Rs. 3,000 and the doubtful debts are Rs. 6.000 which are estimated to realise Rs. 3.000. The bank overdraft is secured by deposit of title deeds of leasehold properties. Preferential creditors are Rs. 1,500. Telephone rent outstanding is Rs. 120. *(C.A. Inter)*

Solution:

Statement of Affairs of Moon Co. Ltd. as on 1st July, 2014

Assets	Estimated Realisable Values (Rs)
Assets not Specifically Pledged (as per List A)	
Cash in hand	1,500
Marketable Securities.	6,000
Calls in arrear	7,500
Trade Debtors	84,000
Stock in trade	3,000
Machinery	90,000
Assets Specifically Pledged (as per list B)	1,92,000

Particulars	Estimated - Realisable Value (Rs)	Due to Secured Creditors (Rs)	Deficiency RanKing as Unsecured (Rs)	Surplus carried to last column (Rs)	
Leasehold properties	1,09,000	27,000	---	82,000	82,000

Estimated surplus from assets specifically pledged		
Estimated total assets available for preferential creditors, debenture-holders having a floating charge & unsecured creditors c/d.		2,74,000

Summary of Gross Assets	**Rs.**
Gross Receivable Value of Assets Specifically Pledged	1,09,000
Other Assets	1,92,000
Gross Assets	3,01,000

Estimated total assets available for preferential creditors debenture-holders having a floating charge and unsecured creditors, brought forward

Gross Liabilities	Liabilities		Rs
27,000	Secured Creditors as per List 'B' to the extent to which Claims are estimated to be covered by Assets specifically pledged		
1,500	Preferential Creditors (as per List 'C')		1,500
	Estimated balance of assets available for debentureholders secured by Floating charges and Unsecured Creditors[1]		2,72,500
75,000	Debentureholder secured by a floating charge as per List 'D'		75,000
	Estimated Surplus as regard debentureholders		1,97,500
30,120	Unsecured Creditors (as per list E)		
	Liability for purchase	30,000	
	Outstanding Expenses - telephone rent	120	30,120
1,33,620			
	Estimated Deficiency as regard Creditors being the difference between gross assets and gross liabilities		1,67,380
	Issued and called up capital :		
	24,000 Equity Shares of Rs 5 each, fully paid as per list G		1,20,000
	Surplus as regards contributories		47,380

Problems No. 8 : A winding up order has been issued against M. Ltd. The following information is obtained with regard to the assets and liabilities as on 30th June, 2014:

	Rs.
Freehold premises (book value Rs. 4,50,000) valued at	3,75,000
First Mortgage of Freehold premises	3,00,000
Second Mortgage of Freehold premises	1,12,500
8% Debentures carrying a floating charge on the undertaking, interest due 1 st September and 1 st April, and paid on due dates	1,50,000
Managing Director's emoluments (6 months)	22,500
Staff Salary unpaid (one month)	16,050

These figures must be read subject to the following notes:

  (a) There is no unpaid capital liable to be called up.

  (b) The estimates are subject to costs of the winding-up and to any surplus or deficiency on trading pend realisation of the assets.

Trade Debtors	Good	31,500
	Doubtful (estimated to realise 50%)	12,900
	Bad	72,750

Plant and Machinery (Book value Rs. 2,47,500) Estimated to realise — 1,74,000

Bank Overdraft: Unsecured — 58,125

Cash in hand — 825

Stock (at cost: Rs. 50,850) Estimated to realise — 33,900

Issued Capital:

Equity Shares of Rs. 10 each fully called up — 1,50,000

Calls in arrear, Rs. 3,000, Estimated to realise — 1,500

Unsecured Creditors — 2,96,250

Contingent Liability in respect of a claim for damages Rs. 37,500
estimated to be settled for — 18,000

Income-lax Liability:

For 30-6-2012	5,250
For 30-6-2013	1,275
For 30-6-2014	2,700

The Reserves of the Company on 1-7-2013 amounted to Rs. 7,500.

You are required to prepare:

   (i)   Statement of Affairs and

   (ii) Deficiency Account.   (C.A.)

Solution:

i) Statement of Affairs of M Ltd. (in liquidation) as on 30th June, 2014

Assets	Estimated Realisable Values (Rs)
Assets not Specifically Pledged (as per List A)	
Cash in hand	825
Trade debtors	37,950
Unpaid calls	1,500
Stock	33,900
Plant and Machinery	1,74,000

Assets not Specifically Pledged (as per list B)

	Estimated - Realisable Value (Rs)	Due to Secured Creditors (Rs)	Deficiency RanKing as Unsecured (Rs)	Surplus carried to last column (Rs)	
Freehold premises Second mortgage on above	3,75,000 ---	3,00,000 1,12,500	--- 37,500	--- ---	

Estimated total assets available for preferential creditors, debenture-holders secured by a floating charge & other creditors (carried forward) — 2,48,175

Summary of Gross Assets	**Rs**
Assets specifically pledged	3,75,000
Other Assets	2,48,175
Gross Assets	6,23,175

Gross Liabilities	Liabilities	Rs
3,75,000	Secured Creditors as per List 'B' to the extent Claims are covered by Assets specifically pledged	
20,025	Preferential Creditors as per List 'C'	20,025
		2,28,150
	Estimated balance of assets available for debentureholders having a Floating charges and Unsecured Creditors[1]	
1,53,000	Debentureholder secured by floating charge as per List 'D'	1,53,000
	Estimated Surplus as regard debentureholders	75,150
37,500	Unsecured Creditors as per list E	
	Estimated unsecured balance of claims *Rs.*	
	of partly secured creditors 37,500	
2,96,250	Trade creditors 2,96,250	
27,750	Outstanding expenses and taxes (5,250 + 22,500) 27,750	
58,125	Bank overdraft 58,125	
18,000	Contingent liability, for claim for damages 18,000	
9,85,650		4,37,625

These figures must be read subject to the following notes:
   (a)   There is no unpaid capital liable to be called up.
   (b)   The estimates are subject to costs of the winding-up and to any surplus or deficiency on trading pend realisation of the assets.

	Liabilities	Rs
	Estimated deficiency as regards creditors, being the excess'of gross liabilities over gross assets	3,62,475
	Issued and called up capital 15,000 Equity Shares of Rs. 10 each fully called up less calls in arrear, Rs. 1,500 (As per List G)	1,48,500
	Estimated deficiency as regards contributories	5,10,975

List-H-Deficiency Account

		Rs
Items contributing to deficiency (or reducing surplus):		
1.	Excess of Capital and Liabilities over Assets on...	Nil
2.	Net Dividends and bonuses declared during the period	Nil
3.	Net Trading-Losses for the same period	2,55,825
4.	Losses other than trading losses written off or for which provision has been made in the books during the same period.	
5.	Estimated losses now written off or for which provision has been made for the purpose of preparing the statement. *Rs.*	
	On Freehold Premises 75,000	
	On Trade Debtors 79,200	
	On Plant and Machinery 73,500	
	On Stock 16,950	
	On Claim for damages 18,000	2,62,650
6.	Other items contributing to deficiency or reducing surplus.	Nil
	Total	5,18,475
Items reducing deficiency (or contributing to surplus):		
7.	Excess of Assets over Capital and Liabilities on 1st July, 2013	7,500
8.	Net Trading Profits for the period from	Nil
9.	Profits and income other than trading profits during the same period.	Nil
10.	Other items reducing deficiency or contributing to Surplus.	
	Total	7,500
	Deficiency as shown by statement of affairs.	5,10,975

Working Notes:

1. Preferential Creditors (List - C):

	Rs.
Income-tax liability for 30.6.2013	1,275
Income-tax liability for 30.6.2014	2,700
Staff Salary	16,050
Total	**20,025**

It has been assumed that Income-tax liability for 30.6.2012 is due for a period more than 12 months. Managing Director's emoluments are not preferential.

2. Outstanding interest on debentures for *3* months will be added in the amount payable to debenture holders.

3. Balance of P & L A/c has been calculated by preparing Balance Sheet.

Balance Sheet as at 30-6-2014

	Rs.		Rs.
Capital	1,47,000	Freehold premises	4,50,000
Reserves	7,500	Plant and Machinery	2,47,500
1st Mortgage	3,00,000	Sundry Debtors	1,17,150
2nd Mortgage	1,12,500	Stock	50,850
8% Debentures	1,50,000	Cash	825
Interest for 3 months	3,000	Profit and Loss Account	2,55,825
Sundry creditors (including managerial remuneration and salaries)	3,34,800	(Balancing figure)	
Bank overdraft.	58,125		
Provision for taxation	9,225		
	11,22,150		11,22,150

Problems No. 9 : The following particulars were extracted from the books of X Ltd. on 31st July 2014 on which date winding up order was made:

Rs.

Equity Share Capital

20,000 Shares of Rs. 10 each. Rs. 5 paid up capital	1,00,000
6% Preference share 20,000 Shares of Rs. 10 each fully paid	2,00,000
6% Debentures, secured by a floating charge upon the whole of the assets of the company, exclusive of the uncalled capital	1,50,000
Fully secured creditors (value of securities Rs. 35,000)	30,000
Partly secured creditors (value of securities Rs. 10,000)	20,000
Preferential creditors for rates, taxes, wages etc.	6,000
Bills Payable	1,00,000
Unsecured creditors (Trade Accounts)	70,000
Bank Overdraft	10,000
Bills Receivable in hand	15,000
Bills Discounted (one bill for Rs. 10,000 known to be bad)	40,000
Bock Debts Good	10,000
Doubtful (estimated to Produce 50%)	7,000
Bad	6,000
Land and Building (estimated to produce Rs. 1,00,000)	1,50,000
Stock in trade (ost'i mated to produce Rs. 40,000)	50,000
Machinery, Tools, etc. (estimated to produce Rs. 2,000)	5,000
Cash in hand	100

Make out a Statement of Affairs and Deficiency Account.

Solution :

Statement of Affairs of X Ltd. as on 31st July, 2014

Assets	Estimated Realisable Values (Rs)
Assets not Specifically Pledged (as per List A)	
Cash in hand	100
Bill Receivable	15,000
Debtors	13,500
Stock in Trade	40,000
Land and Building	1,00,000
Machinery, Tools etc.	2,000

Assets Specifically Pledged (as per list B)					
	Estimated - Realisable Value (Rs)	Due to Secured Creditors (Rs)	Deficiency RanKing as Unsecured (Rs)	Surplus carried to last column (Rs)	
	35,000	30,000	---	5,000	
	10,000	20,000	10,000	---	

	Rs
Estimated surplus from Assets Specifically Pledged	5,000
Estimated total Assets available for Preferential creditors, debenture holders secured by a floating charge, and unsecured creditor: (carried forward) Rs.	

Summary of Gross Assets (d)

	Rs
Gross realisable value of Assets Specifically Pledged	45,000
Other Assets	1,70,600
Gross Assets Rs.	2,15,600

Estimated total assets available for Preferential Creditors, Debenture holders secured by a floating charge and unsecured creditors (brought forward) — 1,75,600

Gross Liabilities	Liabilities	Rs
Rs.	(To be deducted from surplus or added to deficiency as the case may be)	
40,000	Secured Creditors (as per list B) 10 the extent to which claims are estimated to be covered by assets specifically pledged	
6,000	Preferential Creditors (as per list C)	
1,69,000	Estimated balance of assets available for Debenture holders secured by a floating charge and unsecured creditors.	6,000
		1,69,600
1,50,000	Debentures holders secured by a floating charge (as per list 'D')	1,50,000
	Estimated surplus as regards Debenture holders Unsecured creditors (as per list 'E')	19,600

	Liabilities		Rs
10,000	Estimated unsecured balance of claims of creditors party secured on specific assets [Item (c) above]	10,000	
70,000	Trade Accounts	70,000	
1,00,000	Bill Payable	1,00,000	
10,000	Bank overdraft	10,000	
40,000	Contingent Liabilities (re-bills discounted)	10,000	
4,26,000			2,00,000
	Estimated Deficiency as regards creditors (being difference between Gross Assets and Gross Liabilities)		1,80,400
	Issued and Called up Capital		
	20,000 6% Preference Share of Rs. 10 each.		
	Rs. 10 Called up (as per list 'F')	2,00,000	
	2,00,000 Equity shares of Rs. 10 each Rs. 5		
	Called up (as per list 'G')	1,00,000	3,00,000
	Estimated Deficiency as regard members (as per list H)		4,80,400

List-H-Deficiency Account

		Rs
Items contributing to deficiency (or reducing surplus);		
1.	Excess of Capital and Liabilities, over assets on 31st July, 2014.	3,97,900
2.	Net dividends and bonuses declared during the period.	Nil
3.	Net Trading Losses for the same period.	Nil
4.	Losses other than trading losses written off or for which provision has been made in the books during the same period.	Nil
5.	Estimated losses now written off or for which provision has been made for the purpose of preparing the statement.	
	On Land and Building 50,000	
	On Machinery, Tools etc. 3,000	
	On Stock in Trade 10,000	
	On Book Debts 9,500	
	On Bills Discounted 10,000	82,500
6.	Other items contributing to deficiency or reducing surplus	Nil
	Total	4,80,400

	Rs
Items reducing deficiency for contributing to surplus):	
7. Excess of Assets over Capital and Liabilities on	Nil
8. Net Trading Profits for the period from	Nil
9. Profits and.income other than trading profits during the same period.	Nil
10. Other items reducing deficiency or contributing to surplus.	Nil
Total	Nil
Deficiency as shown by Statement of Affairs	4,80,400

Note:

The details of profits, losses, dividend etc. are to be given for a minimum period of 3 years in the Deficiency Account. Due to lack of information in the question, accumulated losses as on the date of winding up i.e. 31st July. 2014 have been shown. The amount of loss will be calculated by preparing trial balance as on 31st July. 2014.

Trial Balance as on 31st July, 2014

Particulars	Rs.	Particulars	Rs.
Book Debts	23,000	Equity Share Capital	1,00,000
Land and Building	1,50,000	Preference Share Capital	2,00,000
Stock in Trade	50,000	Debentures	1,50,000
Machinery, Tools etc.	5,000	Fully Secured Creditor	30,000
Cash in hand	100	Partly Secured Crs.	20,000
Security (with fully	35,000	Preferential Creditors	6,000
secured creditors)		Bills Payable	1,00,000
Security (with partly	10,000	Unsecured Creditors	70,000
secured creditors)		Bank Overdraft	10,000
Bills Receivable	15,000		
Excess of Capital and			
Liabilities over			
Assets (Balancing figure)	3,97,900		
Total	6,86,000		6,86,000

Problems No. 10 : On 31st December, 2013, a compulsory order for winding up was made against. X Company Ltd., the following particulars being disclosed.

	Book Value Rs.	(Estimated to Produce) Rs.
Cash in hand	100	100
Debtors	4,000	3,600
Land and Buildings	60,000	48,000
Furniture & Fixtures	20,000	20,000
Unsecured Creditors	20,000	
12% Debentures:		
Secured on Land and Buildings	42,000	
Secured by floating charge	10,000	
Preferential Creditors	4,000	
Share Capital (3,200 shares of Rs. 100 each)	3,20,000	

Liability for bills discounted was Rs. 16,000 estimated to rank at Rs. 6,000. Other contingent liabilities were Rs. 14,000 estimated to rank at Rs. 12,000.

There is a contingent liability for workmen's compensation expected to rank Rs. 2,000.

As on 1.1.2010 Company had a debit balance in P/L Account amounting to Rs. 50,000 and preliminary expenses amounting to Rs. 30,000. There was a balance of Rs. 1,00,000 in share premium on the same date.

During 2010 Company earned a profit of Rs. 1.20,000 before interest on debentures @ 12% on Rs. 52,000, provision for depreciation amounting Rs. 30,000, and income Tax Rs. 25,000. Company paid a dividend @ 15% for 2010. Company suffered a total Loss of Rs. 1,45,000 in 2011 and 2012 after interest on Debenture amounting to Rs. 6,240 p.a. and provision it depreciation amounting to Rs. 25,000 and 20,000 for 2011 and 2012 respectively. Proper accounts have not been prepared for 2013.

Prepare Statement of Affairs and Deficiency Account.

Solution :

Statement of Affairs of X Co. Ltd, as on 31st Dec. 2013

Assets	Estimated Realisable Values (Rs)
Assets not Specifically Pledged (as per List A)	
Cash in hand	100
Debtors	3,600
Furniture and Fixtures	20,000
Assets Specifically Pledged (as per list B)	

	(a) Estimated - Realisable Value (Rs)	(b) Due to Secured Creditors (Rs)	(c) Deficiency RanKing as Unsecured (Rs)	(d) Surplus carried to last column (Rs)
Land and building	48,000	42,000	---	6,000

	Estimated Realisable Values (Rs)
Estimated surplus from assets specifically pledged	6,000
Estimated total assets available for Preferential Creditors, Dcbentureholders secured by a floating charge of unsecured Creditors	29,700
Summary of Grass Assets.	
Gross realisable value of assets specifically pledged 48,000	
Other Assets (29700 - 6,000) 23,700	
Gross Assets 71,700	

Gross Liabilities	Liabilities	Rs
	(To be deducted from surplus or added to Deficiency as the case may be)	
42,000	Secured Creditors (As per List 'B') to the extent to which claims are estimated to be covered by Assets specifically Pledged.	6,000
6,000	Preferential Creditors (As per List 'C')	
	Estimated balance of assets available for debentures secured by floating charge and unsecured Creditors.	23,700
10,000	Debentures secured by floating charge (As per List 'D')	10,000

	Liabilities	Rs
	Estimated Surplus as regards debentures secured by floating charge.	13,700
38,000	Unsecured Creditors (As per List 'E')	38,000
96,000	Estimated Deficiency as regards creditors (being the difference between Gross Liabilities and Gross Assets)	24,300
	Issued and Called up Capita! (List F & 'G')	3,20,000
	Estimated deficiency as regards contributories (List 'H')	3,44,300

List - H - Deficiency Account

Items contributing to deficiency (or reducing surplus) :

1. Excess of Capital and Liabilities over assets on — Nill
2. Net dividends and bonuses declared during the period from 1.1.2010 to the date of statement. — 48,000
3. Net Trading Losses for the same period (after charging items shown in Note below) 2011 and 2012 Rs. 1,45,000 / 2013 Rs. 1,97,660 — 3,42,660
4. Losses other than trading losses written off or for which provision has been made in the books during the same period. — Nil
5. Estimated losses now written off or for which provision has been made for the purpose of preparing the statement.

Bad Debts	400
Decrease in value of Land and Building	12,000
Liability for Bills discounted	6,000
Other contingent liabilities	12,000
Workmen's compensation	2,000

— 32,400

6. Other items contributing to deficiency or reducing surplus. — Nil

Total — 4,23,060

Items reducing deficiency (or contributing to surplus):

7. Excess of assets over capital and liabilities on 1.1.2010 — 20,000
8. Net Trading profits for the period from 1.1.2010 to the date of statement (after charging items shown in note below) for 2010 — 58,760
9. Profits and income other than trading profits during the same period. — Nil
10. Other items reducing deficiency or contributing to surplus. — Nil

Total — 78,760

Deficiency as shown by Statement of Affairs — 3,44,300

	Rs.
Notes to Net Trading Profits and Losses:	
Provision for depreciation, renewals or diminution in value of fixed assets.	75,000
Charges for Indian Income Tax and other Indian taxation on profits	25,000
Interest on Debentures and other fixed loans	24,960
Balance being other trading profits and losses	1,58,940
Net trading losses as shown in Deficiency Account	2,83,900

Working Notes:

1. Unsecured Creditors (List-E)   Rs.

Creditors as per books	20,000
Bills discounted	6,000
Other contingent liabilities	12,000
Total	38,000

2. Preferential Creditors (List-C)

Creditors as per books	4,000
Contingent liability for workmen's compensation.	2,000
Total	6,000

3. Excess of Assets over Capital and Liabilities as on 1.1.2010

Share Premium	1,00,000
Less : Debit balance of P/L A/c & Preliminary Expenses	80,000
	20,000

4. Net Trading Profit for 2010 :

Profit as given		1,20,000
Less : Interest on Debentures	6,240	
Depreciation	30,000	
Income Tax	25,000	
Net Trading Profit	61,240	
		58,760

5. Profit or loss for 2013 is not given in the question. Therefore, this will be calculated by preparing a trial balance. Before preparing trial balance, a Reserve and Surplus Account will be prepared to find out the balance of reserve and surplus as on 1.1.2013.

Reserve and Surplus Account

Date	Particulars	Rs.	Date	Particulars	Rs.
1.1.2010	To P/L A/c	50,000	1.1.2010	By Share Prem.	1,00,000
	To Preliminary		31.12.2010	By Net Profit	58,760
	Expenses	30,000	31.12.2012	By Balance	1,14,240
	To Dividend for 2010-	48,000			
	To Net Loss				
	for 2011 & 2012	1,45,000			
		2,73,000			2,73,000

Dr.   **Trial Balance as on 31.12.2013**

Particulars	Rs.	Particulars	Rs.
Cash in hand	100	Unsecured Credit.	20,000
Debtors	4,000	Debentures	52,000
Land and Building	60,000	Preferential Crs.	4,000
Furniture & Fixtures	20,000	Share Capital	3,20,000
Debit balance of Reserve and surplus as on 31.12.2012	1,14,240		
Loss for 2013 (Balancing figure)	1,97,660		
	3,96,000		3,96,000

Note : Contingent liabilities will not be taken in the trial balance. Interest on debentures for 4 years has been taken in 'Notes as to Net Trading Profits and Losses; including for 2012. But amount of depreciation for 2013 has been ignored as there is no information given.

3.9 EXCERCISES

1. What is meant by liquidation of a company ? Describe various modes of winding up.
2. Give a proforma of the Statement of Affairs and the Deficiency/Surplus Account with imaginary figures.
3. Write short notes on Deficiency Account.   **(C.A.-May 87)**
4. What do you mean by the term contributories ? Describe the various types of contributories and their liabilities.
5. Explain Preferential Creditors as given under Indian Companies Act.
6. Write note on 'Over-riding Preferential Payment under section 529A of the Companies Act.   **(CA. Inter May 2000)**
7. What are the contents of 'Liquidators' Statement of Account'? How frequently does a

liquidator has to submit such statement. **(C.A. Inter Nov. 1999)**

8. What is meant by 'B List of Contributories' what is the liability of contributories included in this list. (C.A. Inter May 2001, Nov. 2008)

PROBLEMS

A) Statement of Affairs & Deficiency Account

1. The following information was extracted from the books of a limited company on December 31. 2013. on which date a winding up order was made:

	Rs.
Ordinary share capital :	
2,000 shares of Rs. 10 each	20,000
6% preference shares capital:	
3.000 shares of Rs. 10 each	30,000
Calls in arrear estimated to produce Rs. 200	400
5% First Mortgage debentures secured by the floating charge on the whole of the assets of company (interest paid to date)	20,000
Creditors fully secured (value of securities Rs. 4,000)	3,500
Creditors partly secured (value of securities Rs. 2,000)	4,000
Preferential creditors for wages, rates and taxes, etc.	750
Unsecured creditors	27,000
Bank overdraft, secured by a second charge on the whole of the assets of the company	2,000
Cash in hand	120
Book Debts : Good	3,800
Doubtful (estimated to produce Rs. 300)	800
Bad	450
Stock-in-trade (estimated to produce Rs. 6,000)	7,200
Freehold land and buildings (estimated to produce Rs. 18,500)	21,000
Plant and Machinery (estimated to produce Rs. 6,300)	6.000
Fixtures and fittings (estimated to produce Rs. 800)	1,200

You are required to prepare a Statement of Affairs of the company.

Ans. : Deficiency as regards creditors Rs. 15,230;

Deficiency as regards contributories Rs. 65,030

Hint : Bank Overdraft will be shown under list 'D'

2. The following information relates to Catastrophe Ltd. which was wound up on April 1, 2014.

	Rs.	Rs.
Share Capital :		
10,000 8% Preference shares of Rs. 100 each fully paid		10,00,000
5,00,000 Equity shares of Rs. 5 each fully called	25,00,000	
Less: Call in arrears	10,000	24,90,000
		34,90,000
Liabilities		
Secured Loan (on 1 st Mortgage of Land and buildings)		1,50,000
Secured Loan (on floating charge of the Company's undertakings)	8,00,000	
Unsecured Creditors (including preferential items Rs. 60,000)	21,60,000	31,10,000
		66,00,000

Assets	**Estimated to realize Rs.**	**Book Value Rs.**
Land and Buildings	1,80,000	3,00,000
Plant and Machinery	12,00,000	15,00,000
Furniture	50,000	30,000
Vehicles	50,000	10,000
Stock	4,00,000	8,00,000
Book Debts		
Good		8,28,000
Doubtful	1,00,000	1,50,000
Bad		40,000
Bills receivable	90%	20,000
Loans (considered bad)		1,00,000
Cash		12,000
Bank		10,000

(**Note:** Bills discounted and awaited maturity Rs. 20,000 of which Rs. 10,000 is expected to be dishonoured.)

Prepare Statement of Affairs:

    (a) as regards creditors; and

    (b) as regards contributories   (C,A.)

Ans.: Deficiency as regards creditors Rs. 2,62,000; Deficiency as regards contributories Rs, 37,62,000;)

Hint : It has been assumed that calls in arrears are realisable in full.

Bills discounted expected to be dishonoured will be added with unsecured creditors.

3. The following particulars-were extracted from the books of Manish Ltd., on 31st March, 2014, on which date a winding-up order was made:

	Rs.		Rs.
Equity Share Capital:			
20,000 Shares of Rs. 10 each			
Rs. 5 called up	1,00,000	Rates & Taxes	2,000
Calls in arrear (Rs. 6,000)		Wages & Salaries	4,000
estimated to produce	5,000	Bills payable	90,000
16% Preference share capital		Creditors	80,000
20,000 Shares of Rs. 10		B/R in hand	12,000
each fully called up and paid up	2,00,000	Debtors : Good	13,000
15% Debentures secured by first		Doubtful (estimated to	
floating charge	1,50,000	produce 50%)	7,000
Bank overdraft secured by second		Bad	6,000
floating charge	15,000	Bills discounted Rs. 30,000	
Fully secured creditors (secured on		likely to rank	10,000
investments)	30,000	Contingent liability Rs. 15,000	
Partly secured creditors (secured on		likely to be paid	7,000
investments)	20,000	Land and building (estimated to	
Investments (with fully secured		produce Rs. 1,00,000)	1,40,000
creditors Rs. 40,000)		Stock-in-trade (estimated to	
estimated to realise	35,000	produce Rs. 40,000)	60,000
Investments (with partly secured		Machinery estimated to produce	2,000
creditors Rs. 25,000)		Cash in hand and at Bank	200
estimated to realise	10,000		

You are required to prepare a Statement of Affairs and Deficiency Account. No journal entry for rent payable Rs. 2,500 was made so far.

Ans.: Deficiency as regards contributories Rs. 4,88,800.

Hint : Prepare trial balance, balancing figure Rs. 3,79,800 shall be shown as excess of capital and liabilities over assets in Deficiency Account.

Preferential Creditors : Rs. 6,000; Contingent liability of Rs. 17,000 will be added with unsecured creditors. Bank Overdraft of Rs. 15.000 will be shown under list D.

4. From the following particulars prepare a Statement of Affairs and the Deficiency Account for submission to the official liquidator of the Equipments Ltd. which went into liquidation on December 31, 2014.

		Rs.
3,000 Equity Shares of Rs. 100 each, Rs. 80 paid		2,40,000
6%, 1,000 Preference Shares of Rs. 100 each fully paid	1,00,000	
Less calls in arrear (expected to produce)	5,000	95,000
5% Debentures having a floating charge on the assets (Interest paid up to June 30, 2014)		1,00,000
Mortgage on Land and Buildings		80,000
Trade creditors		2,65,500
Owing for wages to 15 Workmen		20,000
Secretary's salary (@ Rs. 500 p.m.) owing		3,000
Managing Director's Salary (@ Rs. 1,500 p.m.) owing		6,000

Assets	Estimated to Produce Rs.	Book Value Rs.
Land and Buildings	1,30,000	1,20,000
Plant	1,30,000	2,00,000
Tools	4,000	20,000
Patents	30,000	50,000
Stock	74,000	87,000
Book Debts	60,000	90,000
Investments (in the hands of bank against an overdraft of Rs. 1,90,000)	1,70,000	1,80.000

On 31st December, 2009 the Balance Sheet of the company showed a general reserve of Rs. 40,000 accompanied by a debit balance of Rs. 25,000 in the Profit and Loss Account. In 2010 the company made a profit of Rs. 40,000 and declared a dividend of 10% on equity shares. The company suffered a total loss of Rs. 1,09,000 besides loss of stock due to fire of Rs. 40,000 during 2011, 2012 and 2013 - For 2014 accounts were not made.

The cost of winding up is expected to be Rs. 15,000.

Ans. : Deficiency as regards creditors: Rs. 64,000; as regards contributories Rs. 4,04,000 ; Difference in Trial Balance Rs. 1,31,300.

Hint: 1. Cost of winding up will not be shown in the statement of affairs or deficiency account. It will be shown as a footnote only.

2. Trial balance will be prepared to find out loss or profit for 2014. The difference in trial balance being Rs. 1,31,300 will be treated as loss for 2014 and shown in deficiency account.

3. Preferential Creditors are Rs. 22,000. Managing Director's salary is not preferential.

4. In 2010 an equity dividend has been paid, therefore, it is implied that preference dividend has also been paid for that year.

5. As workers' claims are ovenriding preferential creditors, total wages of Rs. 20,000 are preferential. But Secretary's salary will be preferential for 4 months to the extern of Rs. 2,000.]

5. A Ltd. went into liquidation on 31st March. 2014 when its position was as under:

Liabilities	Rs.	Assets	Rs.
20,000 Equity Shares of Rs. 10 each Rs. 8 oer share called up	1,60,000	Factory shed (Rs. 50,000) Plant and Machinery	70,000
Less Calls in arrears	5,000	(Rs. 85,000)	1,00,000
	1,55,000	Furniture (Rs. 7,000)	12,000
11% Preference Shares of Rs. 100 each fully paid-up	1,00,000	Investments (Rs. 18,000) Stock (Rs. 55,000)	20,000 65,000
13% Debentures (secured by a floating charge on all assets other than calls in arrears')	75,000	Debtors (Rs, 1,50,000) Cash Preliminary expenses	1,85,000 10,000 8,000
Bank overdraft (secured against hypothecation of stock)	40,000	Profit & Loss Account	1,00,000
Loan from ICIC1 (Secured by a second charge on plant and machinery)	1,00,000		
Trade creditors	60,000		
Out standing expenses	40,000		
	5,70,000		5,70,000

Contingent Liabilities : i) Preference Dividends Rs. 22,000

ii) Bills discounted Rs. 15,000

Estimated realisable values of assets have been indicated in brackets. Three years earlier, the company had a general reserve of Rs. 15,000. The company earned a profit of Rs. 30,000 for one of the three years. Rs. 25,000 had been paid as Income tax in this period and a dividend of 10% on equity shares paid in one of the years. For another year, the company incurred a loss of Rs. 8,000. Rs. 4,500 out of the outstanding expenses is preferential. Bills discounted are likely to be dishonoured to the tune of Rs. 8,000.

Prepare Statement of Affairs and Deficiency Account on the basis that the company decides on a voluntary liquidation. **(I. C.W.A.)**

(Ans.: Surplus as regards creditors Rs. 57,000; Deficiency as regards contributories Rs. 2,25,000; including arrears of Preference dividend)

Hint : (i) Equity dividend @ 10% on Rs. 1,55,000 i.e. Rs. 15,500 will be shown in Deficiency Account. It is implied Preference dividend @ 11 % on Rs. 1,00,000 has also been paid for the year for which equity dividend has been paid,

(ii) It has been assumed that calls in Arrears are recoverable in full.

B) Liquidations Final Statement of Account

6. Before paving the creditors totaling Rs. 3,04,000 the liquidators of a company were left with Rs. 1,25,000. The shares of the company were as follows:

   1. 3,000 9% preference shares of Rs. 100 each. Rs. 80 paid.

   2. 2,000 Equity shares of Rs. 100 each Rs. 60 paid, and

   3. 3,000 equity shares of 100 each Rs. 75 said.

   What will be the call on the preference shares?

   (Ans : @ Rs. 8 on 3,000 Preference Shares)

7. In a company where the shares are as mentioned in the above question, the liquidator is left with Rs. 2,20,000 after paying off creditors. What will be the call on shares :

   (Ans. : Call on 2000 Equity shares @ Rs. 13 and refund or. 3000 shares @ Rs. 2, Rs. 240000 will be refunded to Preference share holders)

8. The position of a Company on its liquidation is as under:

   1. Issued and Paid up Capital:

      2,000 11 % Preference shares of Rs. 100 each fully paid

      2,000 Equity shares of Rs. 100 each, Rs. 80 paid.

      1,500 Equity shares of Rs. 50 each Rs. 30 per share paid.

   2. Calls in arrears are Rs. 5,000 whereas calls received in advance is Rs. 4,000.

   3. Preference dividends are in arrears for one year.

   4. Amount left with the liquidator after discharging all liabilities is Rs. 3,01,000.

   5. The Company's Articles provide for payment of arrear of preference dividends in priority to return of Equity Capital.

   You are required to prepare the Liquidator's Final Statement of Accounts, with the above information.

   (Ans. : Refund to Equity shareholders on 2000 Equity Shares @ Rs, 40)

CHAPTER 4

Computerized Accounting Practices

4.1 Inventory Accounting
4.2 Payroll Accounting
4.3 MIS Reports
4.4 Exercises

4.1 Inventory Accounting

4.1.1 Meaning of Inventory

The raw materials, work-in-process goods and completely finished goods that are considered to be the portion of a business's assets those are ready or will be ready for sale. Inventory represents one of the most important assets that most businesses possess, because the turnover of inventory represents one of the primary sources of revenue generation and subsequent earnings for the company's shareholders/owners.

4.1.2 Importance of Inventory:

- Inventories typically represent the largest current asset of manufacturing and retail firms. Inventory should be considered a "high-risk" asset.
- For many companies, inventories are a significant portion of total assets as well.
- Inventory accounting methods and management practices can become profit-enhancing tools.
- Inventory effects on profits are more noticeable when business activity fluctuates
- Topics: Types of inventory, Basic cost flow assumptions, Valuation issues and Estimation methods

4.1.3 Inventory Categories:

- Inventories consist of costs that have been incurred in an earnings process that is held as an asset until the earnings process is complete.
- Inventory may include a wider range of costs incurred and held in an inventory account for matching against revenue that will be recognized later.
- Items that may be capital assets to one company may be inventory to another.
- The major classifications of inventories depend on the operations of the business.
- **Merchandise inventory**: Goods on hand purchased by a retailer or a trading company such as an importer or exporter for resale.

- **Production inventory:**
  - Raw materials inventory - Tangible goods purchased or obtained in other ways (e.g., by mining) and on hand for direct use in the manufacture or further processing of goods for resale. Parts or subassemblies manufactured before use are sometimes classified as component parts inventory.
  - Work-in-process inventory - Goods or natural resources requiring further processing before completion and sale. Work-in-process inventory includes the cost of direct material and direct labor incurred to date, and usually some allocation of overhead costs.
- **Finished goods inventory** - Manufactured or fully processed items completed and held for sale. Finished goods inventory cost includes the cost of direct material, direct labor, and allocated manufacturing overhead related to its manufacture.
- **Production supplies inventory** - Items on hand, such as lubrication oils for the machinery, cleaning materials, as well as small items that make up an insignificant part of the finished product, such as bolts or glue.
- **Contracts in progress** - The accumulated costs of performing services required under contract.
- **Miscellaneous inventories** - Items such as office, janitorial, and shipping supplies. Inventories of this type are typically used in the near future and may be recorded as selling or general expense when purchased instead of being accounted for as inventory.

4.1.4 Definition of 'Inventory Accounting'

1. The body of accounting that deals with valuing and accounting for changes in inventoried assets. Changes in value can occur for a number of reasons including depreciation, deterioration, obsolescence, change in customer taste, increased demand, and decreased market supply and so on.
2. It is a requirement of GAAP that inventory is properly accounted for according to a very particular set of standards, so as to limit the potential of overstating profit by understating inventory value, and to limit the potential to overstate a company's value by overstating the value of inventory which has in fact materially depreciated in value.

4.1.5 Inventory Accounting with Tally:

Inventory accounting includes recording stock details, the purchase of stock, the sale of stock, stock movement between storage Locations or Godowns, and providing information on stock availability. With Tally it is possible to integrate the inventory and accounting systems so that financial statements reflect the closing stock value from the inventory system.

The inventory system operates in much the same way as the accounting system.

- First we set up the inventory details, which is a similar operation to creating the chart of accounts although, in this case, there are **No pre-defined set of stock groups**.

- Second, we create the individual stock items, which is similar to setting up the ledgers.
- Finally, we are ready to use vouchers to record the various stock transactions.

As the two systems are so similar, we will have little difficulty in using the inventory system but there are some additional features and new terminology.

Inventory Masters

In a newly created company – the inventory info. Menu comprises of these Masters, namely Stock Groups, Stock Categories, VAT Commodity, Stock Items, Unit of Measure, Godown, Voucher Types.

Maintain Stock Categories & Maintain Multiple Godowns (Also known as Locations) can be activated from F11 – Company Features → F2 Inventory Features → Storage Classification.

Stock Items

Stock Item refers to goods in which we deal — that is, goods that we manufacture or trade (sell and purchase). It is the primary inventory entity. Similar to ledgers being used in accounting transactions — we have to use Stock Items in Inventory transactions. Therefore, Stock Items are important in Inventory like how Ledgers are important in Accounting.

While creating Stock Item with Advance Entries in Masters we view few of these options.

Remarks

This is more to help identify the product or its usage when we look at its details. For example, we may create a stock item 'Printer Cable Type A' under Stock Group 'Printer Cables' and Stock Category 'Bi-tronic cables'. Given additional information here, e.g., particulars of printers and other devices that can use this cable. Stock item will give these remarks, which will help us to decide/advise whether the item is suitable for a particular requirement of Inventory.

Alter Change Standard Rates

If we wish to specify standard purchase and sales rates for the item, select **Yes.** Standard rates enable valuation of inventory at standard purchase or standard sales price. Moreover, these prices come up by default during transaction entry, (but they can be overridden with adequate authority). The standards are set to be effective from specified dates and they continue to be used at these rates until the next date where the standard rate changes.

For example, suppose we have our inventory based on standard cost or market valuation based on standard price. For valuation on any date between 1 April and 30 June 2014, the rate specified against applicable from 1-April-2014 would be only considered.

During transaction entry for any day during this period, this rate will be brought up by default.

Behaviour Cost Method :

The method using which stocks will be valued. The value arrived will be the stock value in the books. This method considers Purchase costs only. Tally permits different valuation methods for different items – it does not restrict us to one method of valuation only for all items. Hence, select the appropriate costing method. It would be interesting to know the value of our stock, both on cost as well as sale basis. It could give us comfort with the knowledge of approximate profit margins lying in the stocks. The various choices are – At Zero Cost, Average Cost, FIFO, FIFO Perpetual, Last Purchase Cost, LIFO Annual, LIFO Perpetual, Monthly Average Cost and Standard Cost.

Market Valuation Method : This method considers sale price only for valuation of stocks. The method selected, does not however, get used for standard reporting. The four choices available are : At Zero Price, Average Price, and Last Sale Price & Standard Price.

Ignore Difference due to Physical Counting : We can enter our physical stock in tally by using a physical stock voucher. There may be difference in the actual stock as per books and physical stock. We can change the option to Yes if we want to ignore the difference between the book stock and physical stock. However, it is recommended that we should not ignore the difference so that tally takes the physical stock for the next period.

Ignore Negative Balances : By default this option is No. This means that Tally would warn us if there is any shortfall in stock while making a sales entry. However, we can continue making the entry. We can change the option to Yes if do not need the warning.

Treat all Sales as New Manufacture : By default this option is No. Set this option to Yes if you want to treat all sales as new manufacturing. This means that you do not have pass entries for goods manufactured. It would automatically treat the goods as manufactured when we sell them.

Treat all Purchases as consumed : By default the option is set to No. If the option is changed to Yes, it would automatically convert all purchases to Issues. Hence all the materials purchased would be considered as issued for consumption and there would be not material in hand.

Treat All Rejection Inward as Scrap - By default the option is No. This is useful when rejected could cannot be sold back and have to be scrapped. Changing this option to Yes would allow us to treat all rejected goods as scrap and will not come in our stock.

Allow use of expired Batches - By default this option is No. It will not allow us to invoice the stock items which have expired. We can change this option to Yes, if required.

Stock Groups

Similar to Groups in Accounting Masters - these are provided for the purpose of classification of stock items. Classification is done based on some common behavior. Grouping stock items enables easy identification and reporting of stock items in statements. For example, items of a particular brand can be grouped together so that you can get the inventory details of all items of that brand. It is not necessary to group items but we can create sub-groups of Stock Groups for deeper analysis.

While creating Stock Groups we view **Can quantities of items be ADDED?**

This field pertains to information on measuring the units of the stock items that we would categories under the Stock Group. The stock item created under the group should have similar units to be 'addable'. We obviously would not want to add Kgs with Pcs [Where we have a group like 'Consumables' and items like 'grease' and 'cloth' which are measured in kg and metres respectively]. We select yes here because we want to create items like floppy disks and disk drive etc. which at this point we feel would be addable and the total meaningful. We may later Set it to No, if we find that the totals do not make sense. It is possibly, easier to set it to No initially and later set it to Yes on assessing the item units in the group.

The Stock Items categorized under the group should have similar units for them to be added up. We cannot add quantities in **Kgs** to quantities in **Pcs**.

Stock Categories

This is a feature, which offers a parallel classification of stock items. Like Stock Groups, classification is done based on some similar behavior. The advantage of categorizing items that Tally allows us to classify stock items (based on functionality) together — across different stock groups, enabling us to obtain reports on alternatives or substitutes for a stock item.

Note : – *Stock items do not have to be compulsory classified under Stock Categories.*

Locations/Godowns

A place where stock items are stored is referred to as Godowns. We can specify where the stock items are kept, e.g. warehouse, shelf or rack etc., and obtain stock reports for each Godown, and account for movement of stock between locations/Godowns.

Units of Measure

Stock Items are mainly purchased and sold on the basis of quantity. The quantity is measured by units. In such a case, it is necessary to create the Unit of Measure. Unit of Measure can be simple units such as nos., – metres, kilograms, pieces, or compound units, e.g. box of 10 pieces. Create the Units of Measure before creating the Stock Items.

Besides Simple Units we can also create Compound Units. A Compound Unit is a relation between two simple units. Hence, before we create a compound unit, ensure that the two simple units have been previously created. In the example here, we use dozens as another simple unit (created as we did nos.) Now we must give the relation between dozens and numbers as one dozen equals twelve numbers.

4.2 Payroll Accounting

4.2.1 Introduction

A payroll is the list of the employees and the payments due to each employee for specific pay period. A pay period is the amount of time over which an employee is paid. Most business use weekly, biweekly (every two weeks)or monthly pay periods.

The payroll expenses is a major expenses for most companies, to compute salary expenses, most businesses set up a payroll system for recording and reporting employees earnings information. A well designed payroll system achieve two goals:

1. The collection and processing of all information needed to prepare and issue payroll checks

2. The generation of payroll records needed for accounting purposes and for reporting government agencies, managements and others.

Business with many employees often hire a payroll clerk. The payroll clerk responsible for preparing the payroll

- Makes sure employees are paid on time
- Makes sure each employees is paid the correct amount
- Completes payroll records
- Submit payroll reports, and
- Pays payroll taxes

All payroll system has certain task in common, as shown in following figure

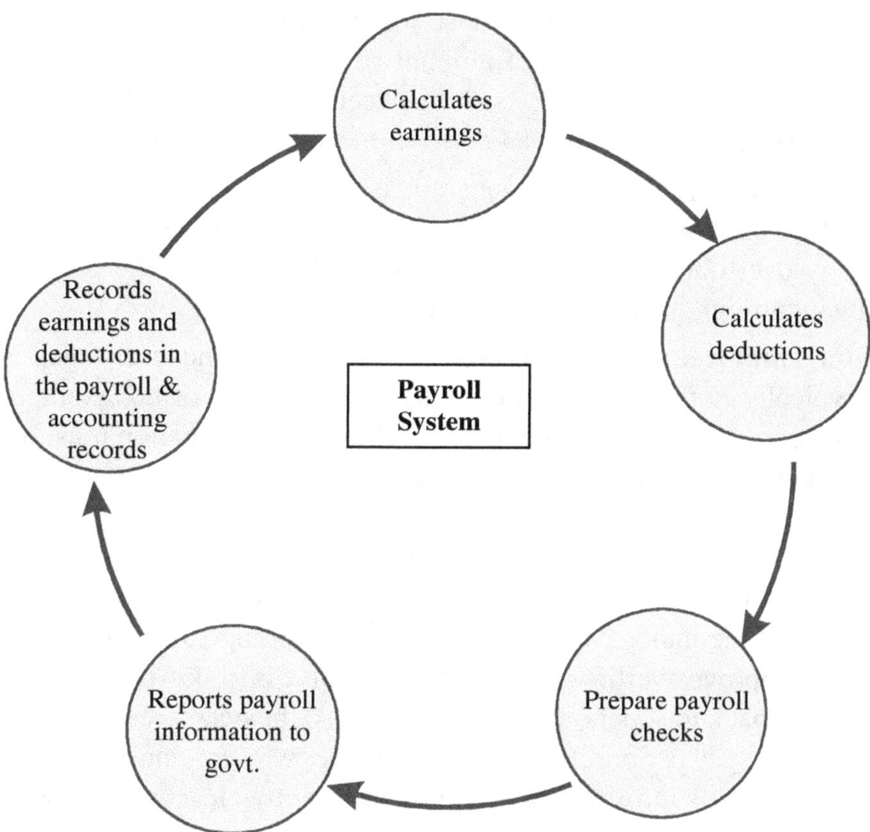

4.2.2 Payroll Accounting Process

This point provides an overview of how the payroll process typically functions, using either a payroll supplier, an in-house payroll process assisted by computer systems, or an in-house system in which everything is processed entirely by hand. Following is the process of creating a payroll system.

Creating a Payroll System

1. Set up new employees. New employees must fill out payroll-specific information as part of the hiring process, such as the form and medical insurance forms that may require payroll deductions. Copies of this information should be set aside in the payroll department in anticipation of its inclusion in the next payroll.

2. Collect time card information. Salaried employees require no change in wages paid for each payroll, but an employer must collect and interpret information about hours worked for nonexempt employees. This may involve having employees scan a badge through a computerized time clock, punch a card in a stamp clock, or manually fill out a time sheet.

3. Verify time card information. Whatever the type of data collection system used in the previous step, the payroll staff must summarize this information and verify that employees have recorded the correct amount of time. This typically involves having supervisors review the information after it has been summarized, though more advanced computerized timekeeping systems can perform most of these tasks automatically.

4. Summarize wages due. This generally is a straightforward process of multiplying the number of hours worked by an employee's standard wage rate. That said, it can be complicated by overtime wages, shift differentials, bonuses, or the presence of a wage change partway through the reporting period.

5. Enter employee changes. Employees may ask to have changes made to their paychecks, typically in the form of alterations to the number of tax exemptions allowed, pension deductions, or medical deductions. Much of this information must be recorded for payroll processing purposes, since it may alter the amount of taxes or other types of deductions.

Compiling time cards, determining who earned overtime hours, and gathering supervisory approval of those hours is a common last minute rush job prior to completing the payroll. One of the major payroll bottlenecks is locating supervisors, who have other things to do than approve overtime hours. One alternative is to skip the supervisory approval and instead report back to supervisors after the fact, so they can see the hours charged on a trend line of multiple pay periods. If there are employees who continually record an excessive amount of overtime, this information becomes abundantly clear in the report. Supervisors can then use this information to work with specific repeat offenders, possibly issuing a blanket order never to work overtime.

6. Calculate applicable taxes. The payroll staff must either use IRS supplied tax tables to manually calculate tax withholdings or have a computerized system or a supplier determine this information. Taxes will vary not only by wage levels and tax allowances taken, but also by the amount of wages that have already been earned for the year-to-date

7. Calculate applicable wage deductions. There are both voluntary and involuntary deductions. Voluntary deductions include payments into pension and medical plans; involuntary ones include garnishments and union dues. These can be made in regular amounts for each paycheck, once a month, in arrears, or prospectively. The payroll staff must also track goal amounts for some deductions, such as loans or garnishments, in order to know when to stop making deductions when required totals have been reached.

8. Account for separate manual payments. Inevitably there will be cases where the payroll staff has issued manual paychecks to employees between payrolls. This may have been done to rectify an incorrect prior paycheck; for an advance; or perhaps because of a termination. Whatever the reason, the amount of each manual check should be included in the regular payroll, at least so that it can be included in the formal payroll register for reporting purposes, and sometimes to ensure that the proper amount of employer-specific taxes are withheld to accompany the amounts deducted for the employee.

9. Create payroll register. Summarize the wage and deduction information for each employee on a payroll register; this can then be used to compile a journal entry for inclusion in the general ledger, to prepare tax reports, and for general research purposes. This document is always prepared automatically by payroll suppliers or by in-house computerized systems.

10. Verify wage and tax amounts. Conduct a final cross-check of all wage calculations and deductions. This can involve a comparison to the same amounts for prior periods or a general check for both missing information and numbers that are clearly out of line with expectations.

11. Print paychecks. Print paychecks, either manually on individual checks or, much more commonly, on a computer printer, using a standard format that itemizes all wage calculations and deductions on the remittance advice. Even when direct deposits are made, a remittance advice should be printed and issued.

12. Enter payroll information in the general ledger. Use the information in the payroll register to compile a journal entry that transfers the payroll expense, all deductions, and the reduction in cash to the general ledger.

13. Send out direct deposit notifications. If a company arranges with a local bank to issue payments directly to employee accounts, a notification of the accounts to which payments are to be sent and the amounts to be paid must be assembled, stored on tape or other media, and sent to the bank.

14. Deposit withheld taxes. The employer must deposit all related payroll tax deductions and employer-matched taxes at a local bank that is authorized to handle these transactions. The IRS imposes a rigid deposit schedule and format for making deposits that must be followed in order to avoid penalties.

15. Issue paychecks. Paychecks should, at least occasionally, be handed out directly to employees, with proof of identification required; this is a useful control point in larger companies where the payroll staff may not know each employee by name and where there is, therefore, some risk of paychecks being created for people who no longer work for the company.

16. Issue government payroll reports. The government requires several payroll-related reports at regular intervals, which require information on the payroll register to complete.

4.3 Management Information System or Reports (MIS)

4.3.1 Introduction

The concept of the MIS has evolved over a period of time comprising many different facets of the organisational functions. MIS is a necessity of all the organisations.

The initial concept of MIS was to process data from the organisation and present it in the form of reports at regular intervals. The system was largely capable of handling the data form collection to processing. It was more impersonal, requiring each individual to pick and choose the processed data and use it for his requirements. This concept was further modified when a distinction was made between data and information. The information is a product of an analysis of data. This concept is similar to a raw material and the finished product. What is needed is an information and not a mass of data. However, the data can be analysed in a number of ways, producing different shades and specifications of the information as product. It was, therefore, demanded that the system concept should be an individual-oriented, as each individual may have a different orientation towards the information. This concept was further modified, that the system should present information in such a form and format that it creates an impact on its user, provoking a decision, an action or an investigation. It was later realised that even though such an impact was a welcome modification, some sort of selective approach was necessary in the analysis and reporting. Hence, the concept of exception reporting was imbibed in MIS. The norm for an exception was necessary to evolve in the organisation. The concept remained valid till and to the extent that the norm for an exception remained true and effective. Since the environment turns competitive and is ever changing, fixation of the norm for an exception becomes a futile exercise at least for the people in the higher echelons of the organisation. Th concept was then evolved that the system should be capable of handling needbased exception reporting. This need may be either of an individual or a group of people. This called for keeping all data together in such a form that it can be accessed by anybody and can be processed to suit his needs. The concept is that the data is one but it can be viewed by different individuals in different ways. This gave rise to the concept of DATABASE, and the MIS based on the DATABASE proved much more effective.

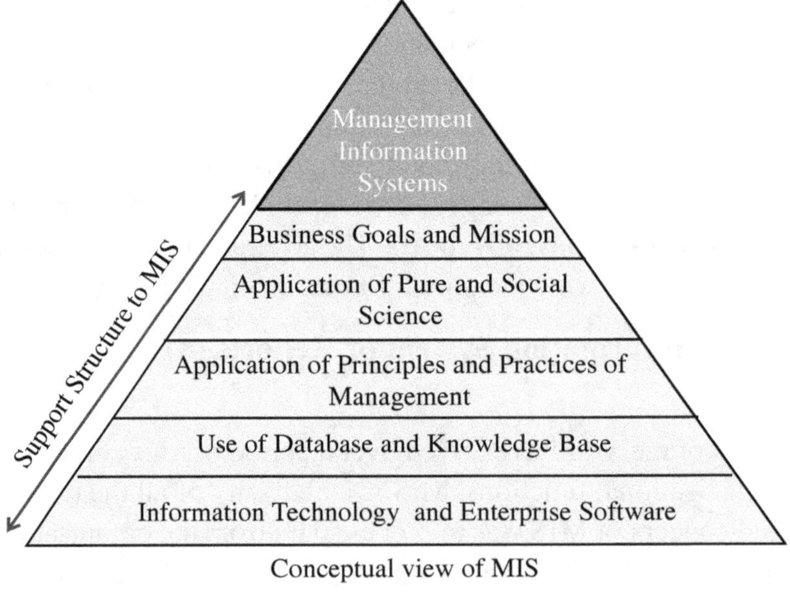

Conceptual view of MIS

4.3.2 MIS : Definition

The management Information System (MIS) is a concept of the last decade or two. It has been understood and described in a number of ways. It is also popularly known as the Information System, the Information and Decision System, the Computer-based Information System.

The MIS has more than one definition, some of which are given below.

1. The MIS is defined as a system which provides information support for decision making in the organisation.
2. The MIS is defined as an integrated system of man and machine for providing the information to support the operations, the management and the decision-making function in the organisation.
3. The MIS is defined as a system based on the database of the organisation evolved for the purpose of providing information to the people in the organisation.
4. The MIS is defined as a Computer-based Information System.

Though there are a number of definitions, all of them coverage on one single point, i.e. the MIS is a system to support the decision-making function in the organisation. The difference lies in defining the elements of the MIS. However, in today's world, the MIS is a computerised business processing system generating information for the people in the organisation to meet the information needs for decision-making to achieve the corporate objectives of the organisation.

4.3.3 Objectives of MIS

The overarching objective of MIS is to ensure long-term survival of the organisation. The system handles data, information and knowledge which are critical resources for effective decision-making and control of operations. The other specific objectives of MIS is any organisation are :

- To build competency of the organisation
- To enable the organisation to gain strategic advantage
- To reduce cost of operations and improve employee productivity
- To enhance decision effectiveness.
- To improve team collaboration.
- To increase organisation's reach, and
- To integrate the organisation through seamless information flowas and enable effective management of its operations.

  To achieve the above objectives an MIS of any organisation has to do the following :
- Aligning MIS objectives with organisation's objectives.
- Identifying need for information and system support for users
- Designing and implementing system to meet such needs

- Business process redesigning to radically improve business efficiency
- Developing and populating databases with transaction data
- Collecting relevant data, in addition to transaction data, from inside or outside the organisation to support higher level information needs
- Generating information to meet user needs to make effective decisions or planning or control actions.
- Communicating such information and extending data analysis facility to decision makers in the organisation.
- Designing and implementing security measures for protecting data and other resources of the system

4.3.4 Functions of MIS

The Management Information Department in an organisation provides a variety of services relating to computer and telecommunications services, application software design and development, and software training to user departments. These services encompass personal computers, networks, printers, servers, and more. The MIS department consults with other departments to analyse and select proper IT solutions for specific applications, provides internet access, computer training and support, and mobile computing solutions for user departments. Some of the specific functions are given below :

- Data gathering and storage
- Data processing
- Information reporting
- Information support to users
- Communication of information
- Database design and maintenance
- Network design and maintenance, and
- Protection of information resources

4.3.5 Impact of the Management Information System

Since the MIS plays a very important role in the organisation, it creates in impact on the organisations functions, performance and productivity.

The impact of MIS on the functions is in its management. With a good MIS support, the management of marketing, finance, production and personnel becomes more efficient. The tracking and monitoring of the functional targets becomes easy. The functional managers are informed about the progress, achievements and shortfalls in the activity and the targets. The manager is kept alert by providing certain information indicating and probable trends in the various aspects of business. This helps in forecasting and long-term perspective planning. The manager's attention is brought to a situation which is exceptional in nature, inducing him to take an action or a decision in the matter. A disciplined information reporting system creates a structured database and a knowledge base for all the people in the organisation. The information is available in such a form that it can be used straight away or by blending and analysis, saving the manager's valuable time.

The MIS creates another impact in the organisation which relates to the understanding of the business itself. The MIS begins with the definition of a data entity and its attributes. It uses a dictionary of data, entity and its attributes. It uses a dictionary of data, endtity and attributes, respectively, designed for information generation in the organisation. Since all the information systems use the dictionary, there is common understanding of terms and terminology in the organisation bringing clarity in the communication and a similar understanding of an event in the organisation.

The MIS calls for a systemisation of the business operations for an effective system design. This leads to streamlining of the operations which complicates the system design. It improves the administration of the business by bringing a discipline in its operations as everybody is required to follow and use system and procedures. This process brings a high degree of professionalism in the business operations.

Since the goals and objectives of the MIS are the products of business goals and objectives, it helps indirectly to pull the entire organisation in one direction towards the corporate goals and objectives by providing the relevant information to the people in the organisation.

A well designed system with a focus on the manager makes an impact on the managerial efficiency. The found of information motivates an enlightened manager to us a variety of tools of the management. It helps him to resort to such exercises as experimentation and modelling. The use of computers enables him to use the tools and techniques which are impossible to use manually. The readymade packages make this task simpler. The impact is on the managerial ability to perform. It improves the decision-making ability considerably.

Since the MIS works on the basic system such as transaction processing and databases, the drudgery of the clerical work is transferred to the computerised system, relieving the human mind for better work. It will be observed that a lot of manpower is engaged in this activity in the organisation. If you study the individual's time utilisation and its application, you will find that seventy percent of the time is spent in recording, searching, processing and communicating. This is very large overhead in the organisation. The MIS has a direct impact on this overhead. It creates an information based work culture in the organisation.

4.4 EXCERCISES

1. What is Inventory Accounting? Explain its importance.
2. State the different types of Inventory Categories.
3. Explain the Inventory Accounting with Tally.
4. What is Payroll Accounting? Explain the Process of Payroll Accounting.
5. What is Management Information System? Explain its Impact.

CHAPTER 5

Accounting for Amalgamation, Absorption and External Reconstruction of Companies

5.1 Meaning of Amalgamation, Absorption and External Reconstruction.
5.2 Vendor and Purchasing Companies.
5.3 Methods of Calculation of P.C.
5.4 Accounting Entries.
5.5 Problems on Amalgamation.
5.6 Problems on Absorption.
5.7 Problems on External Reconstruction.
5.8 AS 14 and Amalgamation.
5.9 Exercises.

Very often companies carrying on similar businesses combine with each other to obtain the economics of large scale production or to avoid the effects of cut-throat competition or to earn the benefits of monopoly. Amalgamation, absorption or reconstruction is the form of business combination. Thus, combination of two or more businesses may be done by amalgamation or absorption.

5.1 Meaning

a) Amalgamation :

The term amalgamation means taking over of the business of two or more companies by newly formed company for this purpose. The existing company or companies are liquidated and their separate legal existence comes to end. The new company is formed to take over the assets and liabilities of amalgamating companies.

For example : Jay Ltd and Vijay Ltd are dissolved and merged into a new company Jayvijay Ltd. In other words Jayvijay company is newly formed to take over the business of Jay Ltd and Vijay Ltd. In short, the companies whose business are taken over, are wound up and a new company is formed.

b) Absorption :

The term absorption means taking over the business of one or more companies by a company already in existence.

In case of amalgamation a new company is formed to take over the business of one or more companies while in case of absorption, no new company is formed. According to companies Act 1956, the term amalgamation includes absorption. The same view has been taken by various courts in our country.

For example : A Ltd, an existing company, takes over the business of B Ltd.

This is the case of absorption. In this case, no new company is formed. A Ltd is already in existence and has taken over the business of B Ltd.

c) External Reconstruction :

Reconstruction may be external or internal. Internal reconstruction means reduction of a capital of a company which is to be reconstructed. External reconstruction takes place when a new company with the same or similar name is formed to take over the business of existing company. In this case new company must be formed and if the business is taken over by an old company. It is the case of absorption and not external reconstruction.

In short, in external reconstruction a new company is floated to take over the business of the vendor company. The idea behind such a reconstruction is that substantially the same business shall be carried on by the same persons.

For example : Navin Ltd, a newly formed company has acquired the business of 'x' Ltd. (an existing company) to take over the assets and liabilities of 'x' Ltd. This is the case of external reconstruction.

In case of external reconstruction, generally the business of both companies are similar and new company is formed to avoid the losses of over capitalisation or business losses.

In short Amalgamation, Absorption and External Reconstruction described as under.

1) Amalgamation   : **Minimum two liquidations and one formation.**
2) Absorption   : **One liquidation and no new formation.**
3) External Reconstruction : **One liquidation and one formation (new company)**

In above cases, there is at least one liquidation and the business of liquidating company is taken over either by new company or an existing company. Hence, accounting entries to be passed under each of three cases are common in the books of vendor and purchasing company.

5.2 Vendor and Purchasing Companies :

The companies involved in case of amalgamation, absorption or external reconstruction can be classified, for accounting purposes, as follows.

(a) Vendor company or companies : In case of amalgamation, the companies to be amalgamated are the vendor companies. Similarly, in case of absorption the company is to be absorbed is the vendor company. In case of external reconstruction, the company to be reconstructed is the vendor company. The vendor companies are to be wound up after sale of their business.

(b) Purchasing Company / Vendee Company : The company purchasing or taking over the business is called as purchasing company or vendee company. It may be already an existing company as is the case with or absorption or a newly formed company as is the case with external reconstruction or amalgamation. The purchasing company acquires the business of vendor company is a purchasing company. It is transferee or vendee company.

Purchase Consideration :

Purchase consideration is the amount which is paid by the purchasing company for the purchase of business of the vendor company. It may, however be noted that, it is not necessary for the purchasing company to take over all assets and liabilities of the vendor company. It may take over all or some of the assets at such values as may be mutually agreed. Similarly it may take over all or some or none of the liabilities of the vendor company.

In order to have a clear understanding about the concept of purchase consideration, students are advised to note the following points.

(1) Purchase or Taking over of the business : The term 'taking over of business' indicates taking over of all assets and all third party liabilities of the vendor company. Sometimes it may be mentioned as "agreed to take over all liabilities". It means that along with liabilities the purchasing company is ready to accept all assets of the company.

(2) Trade Liabilities and Liabilities : The term "Trade Liabilities" means liabilities which are incurred on account of purchasing and selling of goods. For example : Trade creditors and Bills payable. On the other hand the term 'Liabilities' is wider than the term trade creditors. In includes all outsiders or third party liabilities. Such as Sundry Creditors, Bills Payable, Bank Overdraft, Debentures, Outstanding Salaries, Outstanding Expenses, Loan taken etc.

Here, it should be noted that shareholder's claims against the company such as share capital, general reserve, dividend equilisation reserve and all funds are included in the term liabilities.

(3) Taking Over Liabilities and Paying off Liabilities : There is a difference between 'taking over' of the liability and 'paying off' a liability. If it is stated that it is agreed to take over liabilities, it means liabilities are not to be paid immediately, but they are recorded in the books of purchasing company along with the assets taken over.

In case the purchasing company has agreed 'to pay a liability' it means (i) The liability is immediately payable and (ii) it is payable through the vendor company. In other words, the purchasing company will pay sufficient money to vendor company for paying of such liability which the purchasing company has agreed to pay. The amount so paid will become a part of purchase consideration. Such liability will not appear in the balance sheet of the purchasing company, prepared after acquiring the business of the vendor company.

5.3 Methods of Calculation of Purchase Consideration :

Purchase consideration can be calculated by different method. The method to be adopted by the student in the examination problem will depend upon the information given in the problem. Following are the different methods of calculating purchase consideration.

1) Lump Sum Amount or Direct Ascertain Method : When the purchasing company agrees to pay lump sum or fixed amount to vendor company, it is called a lump sum payment of purchase consideration. As the amount of purchase consideration is given in the problem, calculations for purchase consideration are not required. If purchase consideration is ageed at Rs. 200,000; then purchase consideration will be taken as Rs. 200,000.

2) Net Asset Method : In case of this method, purchase consideration is calculated by finding out the net assets or worth of the company. The term net assets refers to vendor company's assets less liabilities taken over by the purchasing company. For this purpose assets and liabilities are to be taken at the value mutually agreed. The purchase consideration is calculated as follows.

Purchase consideration = Assets Taken over - Liabilities taken over

Balance Sheet of 'X' Ltd.

Liabilities	Rs.	Assets	Rs.
Share capital	60,000	Goodwill	28,000
5% Debentures	10,000	Land and building	16,000
Sundry creditors	6,000	Plant and machinery	28,000
Bank overdraft	4,000	Stock	16,000
Bills payable	10,000	Debtors	8,000
General Reserve	10,000	Cash	2,000
		Preliminary Expenses	2,000
	1,00,000		1,00,000

Suppose
  (i) B Ltd takes over the business of A Ltd.
 (ii) The value agreed for various assets : Goodwill Rs. 22000, Land and Building Rs. 25000, Plant and Machinery Rs. 24000, Stock Rs. 13000 and Debtors Rs. 8000.
(iii) B Ltd does take over cash but agrees to pay sundry creditors Rs. 5000, Bills payable Rs. 8000 and Bank overdraft Rs. 5000.

Purchase consideration is to be paid as under by B Ltd. 5000 equity shares of Rs. 10 fully paid, 200, 6% debentures of Rs. 100 each and the balance in cash.

Solution :

Calculation of purchase consideration
value of assets taken over by B Ltd.

	Rs.
Goodwill	22,000
Land and Building	25,000
Plant and Machinery	24,000
Stock	13,000
Debtors	8,000
	92,000

Less liabilities taken over by B Ltd.	Rs.	
Creditors	5,000	
Bills-payable	8,000	
Bank overdraft	5,000	18,000
Purchase consideration		74,000

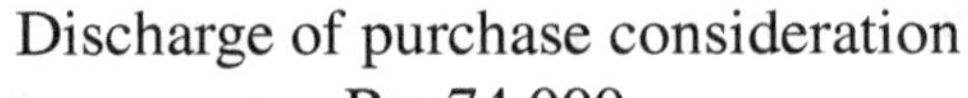

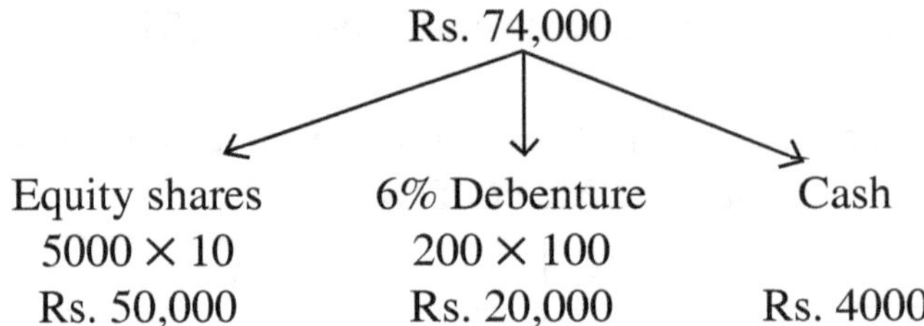

Important Notes :

While calculating purchase consideration the following points should be taken into consideration.

(1) Only agreed value of those assets are added, which have been taken over by purchasing company.

(2) Fictitious assets and expenses not written off as debit balance of profit and loss account, preliminary expenses, discount on issue of shares or debentures, underwritting commission will not be taken over by the purchasing company and therefore are not added. As these are losses, they should be borne by equity shareholders of old companies.

(3) Goodwill is an intangible asset and its agreed value is added, if taken over by purchasing company.

(4) Only agreed value of those liabilities is deducted which are taken over by purchasing company. These are third party or outsiders liabilities. They include Sundry creditors, Bills payable, Bank overdraft, Outstanding expenses etc. If these liabilities are not taken over by purchasing company, these will be paid off by vendor company.

(5) Undistributed profits like credit balance of profit and loss account, reserve fund, general reserve, sinking fund, share premium, capital Reserve are not deducted. These are transferred to equity shareholders account.

(6) When the expressions 'business' is taken over by the purchasing company is given, then all assets including cash in hand and cash at bank but excluding expenses or losses not written off are taken over and liabilities to outsiders are deducted. Staff provident fund, employee's profit sharing fund and other liabilities to employees of the company are treated as liabilities to outsiders.

(7) Debentures will be paid by the purchasing company separately under payment method or will be taken over by the purchasing company. Of course, it is ultimate liability of vendor company to pay off, if not taken over by purchasing company.

(8) Share capital, both equity and preference, will not be taken over by the purchase company. The amount of purchase consideration is paid to equity and preference shareholders.

3) Net Payment Method :

Under this method, purchasing company agrees to make payment in the form of shares /

debentures / cash to the shareholders / debentureholder / creditors of the vendor company. Thus, the total of all those different forms of payment is the purchase consideration.

The above concept will be clarified with the help of following example.

The following is the balance sheet of 'X' Ltd.

Balance Sheet

Liabilities	Rs.	Assets	Rs.
Share capital		Sundry Assets	3,58,000
15000 equity shares		Profit & Loss A/C	50,000
of Rs. 10 each.	150,000	Commission on Shares	20,000
10000, 6% preference			
shares of Rs. 10 each	1,00,000		
500, 5% debentures	50,000		
of Rs. 100 each			
Bank overdraft	28,000		
Sundry creditors	1,00,000		
	4,28,000		4,28,000

The business of 'X' Ltd is amalgamated with the business of 'Y' Ltd and formed a new company 'A' Ltd on the following terms.

(i) Pay debentureholders at a premium of 10% by issue of 6% preference shares of the face value of Rs. 10 each in A Ltd.

(ii) Issue one equity share of Rs. 10 each and make payment of Rs. 5 in cash in exchange of every two equity shares in Y Ltd.

(iii) Preference share holders to be issued 7% debentures in Y Ltd.

(iv) Sundry creditors to receive 90% of the sum due to them in fully paid equity shares of Rs. 10 each in 'Y' Ltd. in full settlement of their claims.

Calculate the purchase consideration

Solution :

Calculation of purchase consideration

Whom payable	What payable	How payable	Amt. Rs.
(i) 5% Debenture holders	6% preference Shares	50000 + 10% premium = 50000 + 5000	55000
(ii) Equity Share holders	Equity Share	One share for two old shares i.e.: 2:1, old shares 15000 New shares 7500	
Equity share holders	cash	7500 × 10 = 75000 7500 × 5 = 37500	1,12,500

(3) 6% preference Shareholders	7% debentures	Equal Amount i.e. 1,00,000	1,00,000
(4) Sundry creditors	Equity Shares	90% of 1,00,000 i.e. Rs. 90,000	90,000
		Purchase consideration	3,57,500

Creation of Goodwill or Capital Reserve :

Under lumpsum method and payment method of purchase consideration goodwill or capital reserve may be created. The goodwill is the difference between assets and liabilities taken over and purchase price. It is determined as follows.

Purchase Price (P.C.)   ×××
Add Liabilities taken over   ×××
Less. total of assets taken over ×××

Goodwill   – – –

Capital Reserve :-

If the total of assets taken over are more than the liabilities taken over and purchase price, there is a capital reserve. It is determined as follows.

Total of assets taken over   ×××
Less
(1) Purchase price   ×××
(2) Liabilities taken over   ×××   ×××

Capital Reserve   – – –

4) Share Exchange Method :

In case of this method, the purchase consideration is ascertained on the basis of the ratio in which the shares of purchasing company are to be exchanged for the shares of the vendor company. This exchange ratio is generally determined on the basis of the value of each company's share.

Example :- A Ltd has a share capital of Rs. 1.00 lakh, divided into shares of Rs. 10 each. Its business has been taken over by B Ltd. The purchase consideration is to be satisfied by exchanging shares on the basis that each share of A Ltd. has a market value of Rs. 15 while that of B Ltd has a market value of Rs. 30.

In this case the comparison of the market values of the shares of two companies show that two shares of A Ltd. are equal to one share of B Ltd. This means B Ltd will issue 5000 shares at Rs. 30 each to A Ltd. as purchase consideration. Purchase consideration, therefore, amounts to Rs. 1.50 lakhs (i.e. 5000 × 30).

In case it is desired that the entries are to be made at par, the purchase consideration amounts to Rs. 50000 (i.e. 5000 × 10) only.

Note : While issuing shares to individual shareholders of the selling company, these may be in fraction. A company cannot issue shares in fractions but it can issue fractional certificates or coupons or pay cash for the fraction.

Settlement of Purchase Consideration : The purchasing company may satisfy the purchase consideration in different forms viz. by issue of equity or preference shares of purchasing company or by issue of debentures of purchasing company or by paying cash payment.

Treatment to Funds : In business, variety of funds are created. These funds may be undistributed or accumulated profits or third party liabilities.

(i) Undistributed or Accumulated Profits : Undistributed or accumulated profits belong to shareholders and therefore, they are credited to equity shareholders account. Examples of such funds are as follows :

Reserve fund, General Reserve, Workmen's Compensation fund, Capital Reserve, Sinking Fund, Dividend Equalisation Fund, Share Premium Account, Forfeited Shares Account, Workers Welfare Fund, Fire Insurance Fund, Debenture Redemption Fund, Contingency Reserve etc.

(ii) Third Party or Outsiders Liabilities : The amounts payable to third party or outsiders are treated as third party liabilities. Examples of such funds are as follows :

Employees Profit Sharing Fund, Workmen's Saving Account, Premium On Redemption Of Debentures, Provident Fund, Pension Fund, Superannuation Fund etc.

5.4 Accounting Entries :

There is no difference regarding recording of transaction is the books of account whether, it is a case of Amalgamation, Absorption or External Reconstruction. In each case there are two parties involved i.e. the vendor company or companies and the purchasing company. In the following pages, we are giving the accounting entries to be passed in the books of both the vendor company and the purchasing company.

Entries in the books of Vendor company : Since the vendor company has to wind up its business; it will dispose off all its assets, make payment of all of its liabilities and distribute the surplus if any among its shareholders. The accounting entries to be passed in its books are as follows :

1) For a transfer of assets :

Realisation Account   ...Dr.

    To Sundry Assets

(Each asset should be credited individually at its book value. All assets have to be transferred. Of course, cash will not be transferred, if it has not been taken over by the purchasing company. Similarly, fictitious assets such as debit balance in the profit and loss account, preliminary expenses, etc. will not be transferred. such assets will be directly transferred to the equity shareholders account. The objective of passing this entry is to close accounts of all assets.)

2) For transfer of liabilities :

Sundry liabilities A/c ...Dr.

   To Realisation Account

(Each liability should be debited individually at its book value. Only such liabilities are to be transferred which have been taken over by the purchasing company. Items representing shareholders' funds do not constitute liabilities for this purpose).

3) For purchase consideration due :

Purchasing company A/c ...Dr.

   To Realisation Account

(With the amount of purchase consideration)

4) For receipt of purchase consideration :

Shares in the purchasing company A/c ...Dr.

Debentures in the purchasing company A/c ...Dr.

Bank A/c ...Dr.

   To purchasing company

(The shares and debentures are to be recorded at the price at which they have been received from the purchasing company).

5) For Payment of liabilities not taken over by the purchasing Co.

Sundry liabilities (not taken over) A/c ...Dr.

   To Bank / Shares in purchasing company A/c

(Liabilities not taken over by the purchasing company will be paid by the vendor company. Any profit or loss on payment of such liability will be transferred to realisation account.)

6) For money due to preference shareholders :

Preference share capital account ...Dr.

   To preference shareholders A/c

7) For payment to preference shareholders :

Preference shareholders Account ...Dr.

   To Bank / Shares in the purchasing company A/c

(In case preference shareholders are paid less or more than what is due to them as per the books of the vendor company, any profit or loss on payment to them will be transferred to the realisation account. Alternatively, the amount may be transferred to equity shareholders account.)

8) For liquidation expenses. There can be three situations :

(a) The vendor company may have to meet the liquidation expenses. In such a case, the entry will be as follows :

Realisation Account   ...Dr.
    To Bank A/c

(b) The purchasing company may agree to pay to the vendor company a fixed amount by way of liquidation expenses. In such a case, the amount payable as liquidation expenses will be included in the amount of purchase consideration. On payment of such expenses by the vendor company, entry as given in (a) above will be passed in the books of the vendor company.

Alternatively, these liabilities may also be transferred to realisation account and paid through that account. This method is not popular.

(c) The purchasing company may agree to reimburse the vendor company to the extent of liquidation expenses incurred by it. In such a case, the following entries will be passed:

(i) On payment of liquidation expenses :
Purchasing Company A/c   ...Dr.
    To Bank A/c

(ii) On reimbursement from the purchasing company :
Bank Account   ...Dr.
    To purchasing company A/c

Alternatively, in cases (b) and (c); no entry may be passed in the books of the vendor company. However, this is not adviseable.

9) For transfer of profit on realisation :
Realisation Account   ...Dr.
    To Equity Shareholders' A/c.
In case of loss the entry will be reversed.

10) For transfer of Equity Share Capital etc.
Equity Share Capital A/c   ...Dr.
General Reserve A/c   ...Dr.
Accumulated profits A/c   ...Dr.
    To Equity Shareholders A/c.

11) For transfer of fictitious assets :
Equity Shareholders' A/c   ...Dr.
    To Profit and Loss A/c. (Debit balance)
    To Preliminary Expenses A/c.
    To Expenses on Issue of Shares A/c.

12) For payment to Equity Shareholders :
Equity Shareholders A/c   ...Dr.
    To Shares in purchasing company A/c
    To Bank A/c

Entries in Books of the Purchasing Company

1) For purchase consideration due :
Business Purchase A/c ...Dr.
   To liquidator of vendor company A/c
(With the amount of purchase consideration).

2) For taking over assets and liabilities :
Assets (Taken over) A/c ...Dr.
   To Liabilities (Taken over) A/c
   To Business Purchase A/c.
(Each asset and liability is to be debited or credited individually at the values taken over and not at the values at which they are appearing in the books of the vendor company. Goodwill if any, appearing in the vendor company's books, should not be recorded here. In case, the value of net assets is more than the amount of purchase consideration, the balance should be credited to capital reserve. In case the purchase consideration is more than the value of the net assets, the balance should be debited to goodwill.)

3) For payment of purchase consideration.
Liquidator of Vendor Company A/c ...Dr.
   To Share Capital A/c
   To Share Premium A/c
   To Debentures A/c
   To Bank A/c
(In case the shares or debentures have been issued at premium or discount, the relevant premium or discount account should be credited or debited, as the case may be)

4) For Liquidation Expenses : The entry for liquidation expenses, when payable by the purchasing company, is as follows :

(i) If the purchasing company agrees to pay a fixed amount by way of liquidation expenses to the vendor company. In such a case the amount of liquidation expenses will be included in the purchase consideration and no separate entry will be required.

(ii) If the purchasing company agrees to reimburse the vendor company to the extent of liquidation expenses. In such a case the amount of liquidation expenses will not be included in the amount of purchase consideration. The following entry will be passed separately on payment of such expenses :

Goodwill / capital Reserve A/c ....Dr.
   To Bank A/c

(The amount of liquidation expenses will be debited to goodwill or capital reserve account, as calculated under entry (2) discussed above.)

5.5 Problems on Amalgamation

Problem No. 1 : X Ltd. and Y Ltd. are two companies carrying on business in the same line of activity. Their balance sheets as on 31-3-2014 are given.

Balance Sheet
As on 31st March, 2014

Liabilities	X Ltd.	YLtd.	Assets	X Ltd.	Y Ltd.
Fully paid up Equity shares of Rs. 10 each	6,00,000	2,00,000	Land & Building	1,00,000	
			Plant & Machinery	7,00,000	3,00,000
			Investments	1,00,000	--
General Reserve	4,00,000	2,00,000	Stock	9,00,000	4,00,000
Secured Loan	6,00,000	1,00,000	Debtors	3,00,000	1,00,000
Current Liabilities	6,00,000	4,00,000	Cash at bank	1,00,000	1,00,000
	22,00,000	9,00,000		22,00,000	9,00,000

The two companies decide to amalgamate into XY Ltd. The following further information is given :

1) X Ltd. holds 8,000 shares in Y Ltd. Rs. 12.50 each.
2) All assets and liabilities of the two companies, except investments are taken over by XY Ltd.
3) Each share in Y Ltd. is valued @ Rs. 25 for the purpose of the amalgamation.
4) Shareholders in X Ltd. and Y Ltd. are paid-off by issuing to them sufficient number of equity shares of Rs. 10 each in XY Ltd. as fully paid up at par.
5) Each share in X Ltd. is valued @ Rs. 15 for the purpose of the amalgamation.
   Show journal entries to close the books of both the companies and Balance Sheet after amalgamation.

Solution :

Statement of purchase consideration

Discharge of P.C.	X Ltd. Rs.	Y Ltd. Rs.	Particulars	X Ltd. Rs.	Y Ltd. Rs.
60000 shares of Rs. 15 each	9,00,000		Assets taken over Land & Building	1,00,000	-
			Plant & Machinery	7,00,000	3,00,000
20000 shares			Debtors	3,00,000	1,00,000
of Rs. 25 each		5,00,000	Stock	9,00,000	4,00,000
			Cash in hand	1,00,000	1,00,000
			Less : Liabilities taken	21,00,000	9,00,000
			Current Liabilities	6,00,000	4,00,000
			Secured Loan	6,00,000	1,00,000
			Goodwill	9,00,000	4,00,000
			(Balancing figure)	-	1,00,000
	9,00,000	5,00,000		9,00,000	5,00,000

Journal Entries in the books of 'X' Ltd.

Particulars		Debite Rs.	Credit Rs.
Realisation A/c	Dr.	21,00,000	
To land & building A/c			1,00,000
To plant & machinery A/c			7,00,000
To stock A/c			9,00,000
To debtors A/c			3,00,000
To cash at bank A/c			1,00,000
(Being assets taken over by XY Ltd. transferred to Realisation A/c).			
Secured Loans A/c	Dr.	6,00,000	
Current Liabilities A/c	Dr.	6,00,000	
To Realisation A/c			12,00,000
(Being the liabilities taken over by XY Ltd. transferred to realisation account.)			
XY Ltd. A/c	Dr.	9,00,000	
To Realisation A/c			9,00,000
(Being purchase consideration agreed to be paid by XY Ltd.)			
Shares in XY Ltd. A/c	Dr.	2,00,000	
To investment A/c			1,00,000
To sundry shareholders A/c			1,00,000
(Being the receipt of shares in XY Ltd., on liquidation of Y Ltd. profit transferred to sundry shareholders A/c.)			
Shares in XY Ltd. A/c	Dr.	9,00,000	
To XY Ltd. A/c			9,00,000
(By the receipt of shares from XY Ltd. on account of purchase consideration.)			
Share capital A/c	Dr.	6,00,000	
General Reserve A/c	Dr.	4,00,000	
To sundry shareholders A/c			10,00,000
(Being the transfer of share capital general reserve to sundry shareholders A/c.)			
Sundry shareholders A/c	Dr.	11,00,000	
To shares in XY Ltd.			11,00,000
(Being the distribution of shares in XY Ltd. among the shareholders.)			

Journal Entries in the books of Y Ltd.

Particulars		Debite Rs.	Credit Rs.
Realisation A/c	Dr.	9,00,000	
To plant & machinery A/c			3,00,000
To stock A/c			4,00,000
To debtors A/c			1,00,000
To cash A/c			1,00,000
(Being the assets taken over by XY Ltd. transferred to Realisation Account.)			
Secured Loans A/c	Dr.	1,00,000	
Current Liabilities A/c	Dr.	4,00,000	
To Realisation A/c			5,00,000
(Being the liabilities taken over by XY Ltd. transferred to realisation A/c.)			
XY Ltd. A/c	Dr.	5,00,000	
To Realisation A/c			5,00,000
(Being purchase consideration agreed to be paid by XY Ltd.)			
Share capital A/c	Dr.	2,00,000	
General Reserve A/c	Dr.	2,00,000	
Realisation A/c	Dr.	1,00,000	
To sundry shareholders A/c			5,00,000
(Being the share capital, general reserve & profit on realisation transferred to sundry shareholders A/c.)			
Shares in XY Ltd. A/c	Dr.	5,00,000	
To XY Ltd. A/c			5,00,000
(Being the receipt of shares from XY Ltd. on account of purchase consideration.)			
Sundry shareholders A/c	Dr.	5,00,000	
To shares in XY Ltd. A/c			5,00,000
(Being the distribution of shares in XY Ltd. among the shareholders.)			

Balance Sheet of XY Ltd. as on 1-4-2014

Liabilities	Rs.	Assets	Rs.
Share capital		Cash at Bank	2,00,000
6000 shares		Land & building	1,00,000
of Rs. 15 each	9,00,000	Plant & machinery	10,00,000
20000 shares		Stock	13,00,000
of Rs. 25 each	5,00,000	Goodwill	1,00,000
Current liabilities	10,00,000	Debtors	4,00,000
Secured Loan	7,00,000		
	31,00,000		31,00,000

Problem No. 2 : The following are Balance Sheets of A Ltd. and B Ltd as on 31st December 2013 which are amalgamated to form a new company AB Ltd.

Liabilities	A Ltd.	B Ltd.	Assets	A Ltd.	B Ltd.
Authorised & Issued			Sundry assets	4,80,000	3,22,000
capital Equity shares			Freehold property	2,00,000	1,00,000
of Rs. 10 each	5,00,000	3,00,000	Investments	50,000	20,000
5% Debentures	2,00,000	1,00,000	Debtors	2,50,000	1,50,000
Reserve Fund-	–	50,000	Preliminary		
Profit & Loss A/c	30,000	20,000	Expenses	20,000	8,000
Mortgage Loan Secured					
on Freehold property	50,000				
Sundry creditors	2,20,000	1,30,000			
	10,00,000	6,00,000		10,00,000	6,00,000

The purchase consideration consisted of :

1) The discharge of the debentures of A Ltd. and B Ltd. by the issue of equivalent amount of 6% debentures in AB Ltd.
2) The assumption of the liabilities of both companies, and
3) The issue of equity shares of Rs. 10 each at a premium of Rs. 2 per share in AB Ltd. For the purpose of the amalgamation the assets are to be revalued as under :

	A Ltd. Rs.	B Ltd. Rs.
Goodwill	1,00,000	75,000
Sundry assets	4,10,000	2,80,000
Freehold property	2,60,000	1,40,000
Investments	51,000	20,000
Debtors	2,25,000	1,35,000

Close the books of A Ltd. and B Ltd. and Balance Sheet of AB Ltd.

Solution :

Calculation of Purchase Consideration

Particulars	A Ltd.		B Ltd.	
	Rs.	Rs.	Rs.	Rs.
Assets taken over -				
Goodwill		1,00,000		75,000
Sundry Assets		4,10,000		2,80,000
Freehold property		2,60,000		1,40,000
Investments		51,000		20,000
Debtors		2,25,000		1,35,000
		10,46,000		6,50,000
Less liabilities taken over				
Mortgage loan	50,000			
Sundry creditors	2,20,000	2,70,000	1,30,000	1,30,000
		7,76,000		5,20,000

Payment of purchase consideration

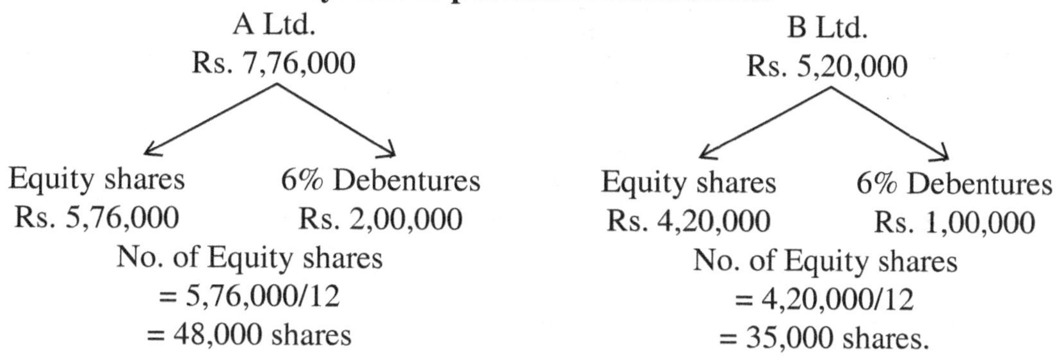

In the books of A Ltd.

Dr.   **Realisation A/c**   **Cr.**

	Rs.		Rs.
To Sundry Assets (Book Value)	9,80,000	By Sundry Liabilities (Book Value)	
To Equity Shareholders A/c (Profit) (Bal. fig.)	66,000	Mortgage loan	50,000
		Sundry Creditors	2,20,000
	–	By AB Ltd A/c (P.C.)	7,76,000
	10,46,000		10,46,000

Dr. **AB Co. Ltd. A/c** **Cr.**

	Rs.		Rs.
To Realisation A/c	7,76,000	By 6% Debentures in AB Ltd.	2,00,000
	–	By Equity Shares in AB Ltd.	5,76,000
	7,76,000		7,76,000

Dr. **6% Debentures in AB Ltd. A/c** **Cr.**

	Rs.		Rs.
To AB Ltd. A/c	2,00,000	By 5% Debentureholder A/c	2,00,000
	–		–
	2,00,000		2,00,000

Dr. **Equity shares in AB Ltd. A/c** **Cr.**

	Rs.		Rs.
To AB Ltd. A/c	5,76,000	By Equity Shareholder A/c	5,76,000
	–		–
	5,76,000		5,76,000

Dr. **5% Debentureholders A/c** **Cr.**

	Rs.		Rs.
To 6% Debentures in AB Ltd.	2,00,000	By 5% Debentures A/c	2,00,000
	–		–
	2,00,000		2,00,000

Dr. **Equity Shareholders A/c** **Cr.**

	Rs.		Rs.
To Equity Shares in AB Ltd.	5,76,000	By Equity Share Capital A/c	5,00,000
To Preliminary Expenses A/c	20,000	By Profit & Loss A/c	30,000
	–	By Realisation A/c	66,000
	5,96,000		5,96,000

In the books of B Ltd.

Dr.		Realisation A/c		Cr.
	Rs.			**Rs.**
To Sundry Assets (Book Value)		By Sundry Liab.(Book Value)		
Sundry Assets 3,22,000		Sundry Creditors		1,30,000
Freehold Property 1,00,000		By AB Ltd A/c (P.C.)		5,20,000
Investments 20,000				
Debtors 1,50,000	5,92,000			
To Equity Shareholders A/c	58,000			
(Profit)	–			–
	6,50,000			6,50,000

Dr.		AB Ltd. A/c		Cr.
	Rs.			**Rs.**
To Realisation A/c	5,20,000	By 6% Debentures in AB Ltd.		1,00,000
	–	By Equity Shares in AB Ltd.		4,20,000
	5,20,000			5,20,000

Dr.		6% Debentures in AB Ltd. A/c		Cr.
	Rs.			**Rs.**
To AB Ltd. A/c	1,00,000	By 5% Debentureholder A/c		1,00,000
	–			–
	1,00,000			1,00,000

Dr.		5% Debentureholders A/c		Cr.
	Rs.			**Rs.**
To 6% Debentures in AB Ltd.	1,00,000	By 5% Debentures A/c		1,00,000
	–			–
	1,00,000			1,00,000

Dr.		Equity Shares in AB Ltd. A/c		Cr.
	Rs.			**Rs.**
To AB Ltd. A/c	4,20,000	By Equity Shareholder A/c		4,20,000
	–			–
	4,20,000			4,20,000

Dr.   **Equity Shareholders A/c**   **Cr.**

	Rs.		Rs.
To Equity Shares in AB Ltd.	4,20,000	By Equity Share Capital A/c	3,00,000
To Preliminary Expenses A/c	8,000	By Reserve Fund	50,000
		By Profit & Loss A/c	20,000
	–	By Realisation A/c (Profit)	58,000
	4,28,000		4,28,000

Balance Sheet of AB Ltd. as on 1st January 2014

Liabilities	Rs.	Assets	Rs.
Share capital		Goodwill	1,75,000
83000 Equity shares		Sundry Assets	6,90,000
of Rs. 10 each.	8,30,000	Freehold property	4,00,000
Share premium	1,66,000	Investments	71,000
6% Debentures	3,00,000	Debtors	3,60,000
Mortgage Loan			
(Secured on Freehold property)	50,000		
Sundry Creditors	3,50,000		
	16,96,000		16,96,000

Problem No. 3 : A Co. Ltd. and B Co. Ltd agree to amalgamate and form a third company C Co. Ltd. which will take over all the assets and liabilities of the two existing companies.

In the case of A Co. Ltd. the assets and liabilities are to be taken over at book values for shares in C Co. Ltd. at the rate of 5 shares in C Co. Ltd. at a premium of 10% for every 4 shares in A Co. Ltd.

In the case of B co. Ltd.

i) The Debentures of B Co. Ltd. would be paid off by the issue of an equal number of debentures in C Co. Ltd. at a discount of 10%.

ii) The holders of 6% preference shares of B Co. Ltd. would be allotted 4 (four) 7% preference shares in C Co. Ltd. for every 5 (five) preference shares held in B Co. Ltd.

iii) The equity shareholders would be allotted sufficient shares to cover the balance on their accounts after adjusting assets values by reducing plant and machinery by 10% & Providing 5% on sundry debtors. Equity shares to B Co. Ltd. were also issued at 10% premium.

The summarised Balance sheet of A Co. Ltd. and B Co. Ltd. on the date of amalgamation were as follows :

Liabilities	'A' Co. Ltd. Rs.	'B' Co. Ltd. Rs.	Assets	'A' Co. Ltd. Rs.	'B' Co. Ltd. Rs.
Equity shares of Rs. 10 each	4,00,000	5,00,000	Plant and Machinery	8,00,000	8,00,000
6% Preference shares of Rs. 100 each	–	3,00,000	Stock	65,000	60,000
			Sundry debtors	95,000	50,000
4% Debentures	–	2,00,000	Cash and bank		
profit & Loss A/c	5,00,000	–	Balances	65,000	40,000
Contingency Reserve	50,000	–	P & L A/c	–	1,40,000
Sundry Creditors	75,000	90,000		–	–
	10,25,000	10,90,000		10,25,000	10,90,000

Prepare necessary Ledger accounts in the books of A Co. Ltd. and B Co. Ltd. and opening balance sheet in C Co. Ltd. and also calculate the purchase consideration.

Solution :

Statement of Purchase Consideration

A Co. Ltd.

Whom payable	What and How payable		Rs.
1. Equity shareholders	i)	Equity Shares (For every 4 shares 5 shares in C Ltd. Hence for 40,000 shares in A Ltd. 50,000 shares in C Ltd. Face value of 50,000 shares @ Rs. 10)	5,00,000
	ii)	Premium @ 10%	50,000
		Purchase Price	5,50,000

B Co. Ltd.

Whom payable	What and How payable		Rs.
1. Equity Shareholder	i)	Equity Shares (On the basis of final amount due on their account. The amount due is arrived at as under.) Share Capital	5,00,000
	ii)	Discount from Debentures Repayment	20,000
	iii)	Discount of 6% pref. shareholders Repayment	60,000
			5,80,000

	Less :		
	i) Depreciation of plant and machinery	80,000	
	ii) Provision for Doubtful Debts	2,500	
	iii) Profit & Loss A/c	1,40,000	
		2,22,500	
2. 6% Pref. Shareholders	i) 7% Preference shares For every 5 shares four 7% pref. shares. Hence for 3,000 pref. shares 2,400 7% pref. shares of Rs. 100 each.		2,40,000
3. 4% Debenture-holders	i) Debentures Equal number of debentures at 10% discount Hence for Rs. 2,00,000 Debentures		1,80,000
	Purchase price		7,77,500

In the Books of 'A' Co. Ltd.

Dr.   **Realisation A/c**   **Cr.**

	Rs.		Rs.
To Sundry Assets		By Sundry Liab. A/c (Book value)	
(Book value)		(Sundry Creditors)	75,000
Plant & machinery	8,00,000	By 'C' Co. Ltd. A/c	5,50,000
Stock	65,000	By Equity shareholder A/c	4,00,000
Debtors	95,000	(Bal. Fig.)	
Cash	65,000		–
	10,25,000		10,25,000

Dr.   **'C' Co. Ltd. A/c**   **Cr.**

	Rs.		Rs.
To Realisation A/c	5,50,000	By Equity shares in 'C' Ltd.A/c	5,50,000
	–		–
	5,50,000		5,50,000

Dr.   **Equity shares in 'C' Co. Ltd. A/c**   **Cr.**

	Rs.		Rs.
To 'C' Co. Ltd. A/c	5,50,000	By Equity shareholders A/c	5,50,000
	–		–
	5,50,000		5,50,000

Dr.   **Equity shareholders A/c**   **Cr.**

	Rs.		Rs.
To Equity shares 'C' Co. Ltd.	5,50,000	By Equity shareholders A/c	4,00,000
To Realisation A/c	4,00,000	By Contingency Reserve A/c	50,000
	–	By Profit & Loss A/c	5,00,000
	9,50,000		9,50,000

In the Books of 'B' Co. Ltd.

Dr.   **Realisation A/c**   **Cr.**

	Rs.		Rs.
To Sundry Assets (Book value)		By Sundry Liab. A/c (Book value) (Sundry Creditors)	90,000
Plant & machinery	8,00,000	By Debentureholders A/c (Discount)	20,000
Stock	60,000	By Pref. Shareholders A/c (Discount)	60,000
Sundry Debtors	50,000	By 'C' Company Ltd. A/c (P.C.)	7,77,500
Cash & Bank	40,000	By Equity shareholders A/c (Loss)	2,500
	–		
	9,50,000		9,50,000

Dr.   **'C' Co. Ltd. A/c**   **Cr.**

	Rs.		Rs.
To Realisation A/c	7,77,500	By Debentures in 'C' Co. Ltd. A/c	1,80,000
		By 7% preference shares in 'C' Co. Ltd. A/c	2,40,000
	–	By Equity shares in 'C' Co. Ltd. A/c	3,57,500
	7,77,500		7,77,500

Dr.   **7% Pref. shares in 'C' Co. Ltd. A/c**   **Cr.**

	Rs.		Rs.
To 'C' Co. Ltd. A/c	2,40,000	By 6% pref. shareholders A/c	2,40,000
	–		–
	2,40,000		2,40,000

Dr.   **Debentures in 'C' Co. Ltd. A/c**   **Cr.**

	Rs.		Rs.
To 'C' Co. Ltd. A/c	1,80,000	By 4% Debentureholders A/c	1,80,000
	—		—
	1,80,000		1,80,000

Dr.   **6% Pref. Shareholders A/c**   **Cr.**

	Rs.		Rs.
To 7% Pref. shares in 'C' Co. Ltd. A/c	2,40,000	By 6% pref. share Capital A/c	3,00,000
To Realisation A/c	60,000		—
	3,00,000		3,00,000

Dr.   **4% Debentures A/c**   **Cr.**

	Rs.		Rs.
To Debentureholders A/c	2,00,000	By Balance b/d	2,00,000
	—		—
	2,00,000		2,00,000

Dr.   **4% Debentureholders A/c**   **Cr.**

	Rs.		Rs.
To Debentures in 'C' Co. Ltd.A/c	1,80,000	By 4% Debentures A/c	2,00,000
To Realisation A/c (Bal. fig.)	20,000		—
	2,00,000		2,00,000

Dr.   **Equity shareholders A/c**   **Cr.**

	Rs.		Rs.
To Realisation A/c	2,500	By Equity share capital A/c	5,00,000
To Profit & Loss A/c	1,40,000		
To Equity shares in 'C' Co. Ltd. A/c	3,57,500		
	5,00,000		5,00,000

In the Books of 'C' Co. Ltd.
Balance Sheet as on...

Liabilities	Rs.	Assets		Rs.
Share Capital		**Fixed Assets**		
Authorised,		Plant & Machinery		15,20,000
Issued, Subscribed and		**Current Assets**		
Paid-up Capital		Stock		1,25,000
82,500 Equity shares of		Sundry Debtors	1,45,000	
Rs. 10 each	8,25,000	Less R.D.D.	2,500	1,42,500
7% Pref. Shares of		Cash & Bank balance		1,05,000
Rs. 10 each	2,40,000	**Miscellaneous Expenditure**		
Reserve & Surplus :		Discount on issue of		20,000
Share premium	82,500	Debentures		
Capital reserve	4,00,000			
Secured Loans				
Debentures	2,00,000			
Current liabilities				
Sundry creditors	1,65,000			
	19,12,500			19,12,500

Working Notes :

1) Since the shares are issued at 10% premium, the number of shares issued.

$$\text{is } \frac{3,57,500}{11} = 32,500 \text{ shares}$$

Rs.

i.e. Share Capital	3,25,000
Premium	32,500
	3,57,500

2) **Capital Reserve**

Value of Net assets taken from A Ltd.

	Rs.
Value of Assets	10,25,000
Less Sundry Creditors	75,000
Net assets	9,50,000
Purchase Price Paid	5,50,000
Capital Reserve	4,00,000

Problem No. 4 : Following are the balance sheets of X Ltd and Y Ltd. as on 31-12-2013

Balance Sheet of X Ltd.

Liabilities	Rs.	Assets	Rs.
6,000 Equity shares of		Land and buildings	2,00,000
Rs. 100 each	6,00,000	Plant & Machinery	3,00,000
1,000 6% Preference shares	1,00,000	Furniture	20,000
of Rs. 100 each		Stock	70,000
Contingency Reserve	20,000	Debtors	90,000
Creditors	70,000	Cash at Bank	15,000
Unclaimed Dividend	5,000	Preliminary Expenses	20,000
Contingent Liability for Bills		Discount on issue of shares	5,000
Discounted Rs. 4,000	–	Profit & Loss A/c	75,000
	7,95,000		7,95,000

Balance Sheet of Y Ltd.

Liabilities	Rs.	Assets	Rs.
7,000 Equity shares of		Freehold premises	4,00,000
Rs. 100 each	7,00,000	Plant & Machinery	2,10,000
General Reserve	18,000	Stock	29,000
Profit & Loss A/c	40,000	Debtors	1,90,000
Workmen's compensation		Cash at Bank	11,000
Fund	10,000		
Creditors	72,000		
	8,40,000		8,40,000

X Ltd. and Y Ltd. amalgamated as on 31-12-2013 and a new company Z Ltd. was formed with an authorised capital of 20,000 equity shares of Rs. 100 each. The amalgamation was agreed on the following conditions :

1) Z Ltd. took all assets of X Ltd at book values and creditors of X Ltd. The purchase consideration was discharged by issuing 3,000 equity shares of Rs. 100 each at Rs. 120 per share and the balance in cash.

2) Z Ltd., took all assets of Y Ltd. at book values except cash and also took the creditors. The purchase consideration was discharged by issuing 6,000 equity shares if Rs. 100 each at Rs. 120 per share and the balance in cash.

3) X Ltd. paid its preference capital back with arrears of preference dividend for the last two years.

4) Liability for bills discounted was settled at Rs. 2,500/-

5) Out of the unclaimed dividend Rs. 2,000 was paid to the rightful shareholders. The remaining unclaimed dividend was time barred and transferred to shareholders account.

6) Liability for workmen's compensation of Y Ltd. amounted to Rs. 7,500/-

7) The cost of liquidation of X Ltd was Rs. 5,000 and that of Y Ltd. was Rs. 6,000 which was paid by the respective companies.

   You are required to prepare :   a) Necessary accounts in the books of X Ltd.
   b) Opening entries in the books of Z Ltd.
   c) Balance Sheet of Z Ltd.

Solution :

Statement of Purchase Consideration

Particulars	X Ltd. Rs.	Y Ltd. Rs.
Sundry Assets (taken over)		
Land & Building	2,00,000	–
Plant & Machinery	3,00,000	2,10,000
Furniture	20,000	–
Stock	70,000	29,000
Debtors	90,000	1,90,000
Cash at Bank	15,000	–
Freehold Premises	–	4,00,000
	6,95,000	8,29,000
Less : Sundry Liabilities (taken over)		
Sundry Creditors	70,000	72,000
Purchase Price	6,25,000	7,57,000
Payment of Purchase Consideration		
i) 3,000 shares at Rs. 120 each - A Ltd.	3,60,000	–
ii) 6,000 shares at Rs. 120 each - B Ltd.	–	7,20,000
iii) Cash	2,65,000	37,000
	6,25,000	7,57,000

In the Books of X Ltd.

Dr.   **Realisation A/c**   **Cr.**

	Rs.		Rs.
To Sundry Assets (taken over)		By Creditors A/c	70,000
Land & Building	2,00,000	By Z Ltd. A/c	6,25,000
Plant & machinery	3,00,000	(Purchase consideration)	
Furniture	20,000	By Equity Shareholder's A/c	19,500
Stock	70,000	(Loss)	
Debtors	90,000		
Cash at Bank	15,000		
To Pref. Shareholders A/c	12,000		
(Dividend)			
To Cash A/c	2,500		
(Liability for bills discounted)			
To Cash A/c	5,000		
(Liquidation Expenses)	–		–
	7,14,500		7,14,500

Dr.   **Z Ltd. Account**   **Cr.**

	Rs.		Rs.
To Realisation A/c	6,25,000	By Shares in Z Ltd.	3,60,000
	–	By Cash	2,65,000
	6,25,000		6,25,000

Dr.   **Equity Shares in Z Ltd. A/c**   **Cr.**

	Rs.		Rs.
To Z Ltd. A/c	3,60,000	By Equity Shareholders A/c	3,60,000
	–		–
	3,60,000		3,60,000

Dr.   **Unclaimed Dividend A/c**   **Cr.**

	Rs.		Rs.
To Cash A/c	2,000	By Balance b/d	5,000
To Balance transferred to	3,000		
Equity shareholder's A/c	–		–
	5,000		5,000

Dr.   **Cash Account**   **Cr.**

	Rs.		Rs.
To Z Ltd. A/c	2,65,000	By Preference share capital A/c (Paid)	1,00,000
		By Preference dividend A/c (paid)	12,000
		By Realisation A/c (Bills discounted)	2,500
		By Unclaimed dividend A/c	2,000
		By Realisation A/c (Liquidation exp.)	5,000
		By Equity Shareholders A/c (Balancing figure)	1,43,500
	—		—
	2,65,000		2,65,000

Dr.   **Preference Shareholders Account**   **Cr.**

	Rs.		Rs.
To Cash A/c	1,00,000	By Preference share	
To Cash A/c (Dividend)	12,000	Capital A/c	1,00,000
	—	By Realisation A/c	12,000
	1,12,000		1,12,000

Dr.   **Equity Shareholder's Account**   **Cr.**

	Rs.		Rs.
To Profit & Loss A/c	75,000	By Equity Share Capital A/c	6,00,000
To Preliminary Expenses A/c	20,000	By Contingency Reserve A/c	20,000
To Discount on issue of shares A/c	5,000	By Unclaimed Dividend A/c	3,000
To Realisation A/c (Loss)	19,500		
To Shares in Z Ltd. A/c	3,60,000		
To Cash A/c	1,43,500		—
	6,23,000		6,23,000

In the Books of Y Ltd.

Dr.   **Realisation Account**   **Cr.**

	Rs.		Rs.
To Sundry Assets		By Creditors A/c	72,000
Freehold premises	4,00,000	By Z Ltd. A/c	7,57,000
Plant & machinery	2,10,000	(Purchase consideration)	
Stock	29,000	By Equity Shareholder's A/c	6,000
Debtors	1,90,000	(Loss)	
To Cash A/c	6,000		
(Liquidation Expenses)	—		—
	8,35,000		8,35,000

Dr. **Z Ltd. Account** **Cr.**

	Rs.		Rs.
To Realisation A/c	7,57,000	By Cash A/c	37,000
	–	By Shares in Z Ltd. A/c	7,20,000
	7,57,000		7,57,000

Dr. **Cash Account** **Cr.**

	Rs.		Rs.
To Balance b/d	11,000	By Workmen's	
To Z Ltd. A/c	37,000	compensation A/c	7,500
		By Realisation A/c	6,000
		(Liquidation Expenses)	
		By Equity shareholders A/c	34,500
	–	(Balancing figure)	
	48,000		48,000

Dr. **Workmen's Compensation Fund Account** **Cr.**

	Rs.		Rs.
To Cash A/c	7,500	By Balance b/d	10,000
To Equity shareholder's A/c	2,500		
(Balancing figure)	–		–
	10,000		10,000

Dr. **Equity Shareholder's Account** **Cr.**

	Rs.		Rs.
To Shares in Z Ltd. A/c	7,20,000	By Equity Share Capital A/c	7,00,000
To Realisation A/c (Loss)	6,000	By General Reserve A/c	18,000
To Cash A/c	34,500	By Profit & Loss A/c	40,000
		By Workmen's compensation	2,500
	–	Fund A/c	
	7,60,500		7,60,500

In the books of Z Ltd.
Journal Entries

Particulars		Dr. Rs.	Cr. Rs.
1. Business Purchase A/c	Dr.	13,82,000	
To Liquidator of X Ltd.			6,25,000
To Liquidator of Y Ltd.			7,57,000
(Being acquisition of the business of the two Companies as per the agreement)			
2. Land & Building A/c	Dr.	2,00,000	
Freehold premises A/c	Dr.	4,00,000	
Plant & Machinery A/c	Dr.	5,10,000	
Furniture A/c	Dr.	20,000	
Stock A/c	Dr.	99,000	
Debtors A/c	Dr.	2,80,000	
Cash at Bank	Dr.	15,000	
To Creditors A/c			1,42,000
To Business Purchase A/c			13,82,000
(Being various assets & liabilities of X Ltd. & Y Ltd. taken over)			
3. Liquidator of X Ltd. A/c	Dr.	6,25,000	
Liquidator of Y Ltd. A/c	Dr.	7,57,000	
To Equity share capital A/c			9,00,000
To share premium A/c			1,80,000
To Cash A/c			3,02,000
(Being Discharge of purchase consideration by issuing 9000 equity shares of Rs. 100 each of Rs. 120 each and balance in cash.)			

Balance Sheet of Z Ltd. as on 1-1-2014

Liabilities	Rs.	Assets	Rs.
Share capital		Land & Building	2,00,000
9000 Equity share	9,00,000	Freehold premises	4,00,000
of Rs. 100 each.		Plant & Machinery	5,10,000
Share premium Account	1,80,000	Furniture	20,000
Creditors A/c	1,42,000	Stock	99,000
Bank Overdraft	2,87,000	Debtors	2,80,000
	15,09,000		15,09,000

Problem No. 5 : Ram Ltd. and Anand Ltd. agreed to transfer their business to a new company called Ramanand Ltd. which is, formed with an authorised capital of Rs. 15,00,000 divided into 10,000 equity shares of Rs. 100 each and 5000, 9% preference shares of Rs. 100 each. The Balance Sheets of the two companies as on 31st March 2014 were as follows :

Liabilities	Ram Ltd. Rs.	Anand Ltd. Rs.	Assets	Ram Ltd. Rs.	Anand Ltd. Rs.
8,000 Equity shares of Rs. 100 each, Rs. 75 Paid	6,00,000	–	Building	5,00,000	
			Premises	–	4,50,000
			Stock	–	2,00,000
			Debtors	32,000	70,000
6,000 Equity shares of Rs. 100 each fully paid	–	6,00,000	Cash	25,000	8,000
			Machinery	1,60,000	–
Share Premium	80,000	–	Preliminary Expenses	–	22,000
General Reserve	20,000	–	Profit & Loss A/c	25,000	
Profit & Loss A/c	–	20,000			
Dividend Equidisation Fund	–	30,000			
6% Debentures	–	50,000			
Sundry Creditors	40,000	35,000			
Provident Fund	–	15,000			
R.D.D.	2,000	–			
	7,42,000	7,50,000		7,42,000	7,50,000

The terms of amalgamation were as follows :

1) Buildings to be appreciated by Rs. 1,10,000
2) Premises to be reduced to Rs. 3,30,000
3) Other assets and liabilities to be taken up at book values.
4) Shareholders of Ram Ltd. are to receive one preference share at par and three equity shares (at a premium of 10%) fully paid for every four equity shares held in Ram Ltd.
5) Shareholders of Anand Ltd. to receive two preference shares at par and two equity shares (at a premium of 10%) fully paid for every five shares held in Anand Ltd.
6) Ramanand Ltd. (New company) to discharge the debentures by issue of 8% debentures at Rs. 100 each.
7) Liquidation expenses Rs. 1000 to be borne by Ramanand Ltd. and to be adjusted to goodwill account :

Prepare :

   a) A statement showing purchase consideration of both the companies.

   b) Realisation account, shareholders' account, Debentureholders' account and New company's account in the books of Anand Ltd.

   c) Give opening journal entries of Ramanand Ltd. (New company)

Solution :

Note :

Purchase Consideration (Payment Method)

Whom Payable	What Payable	How Payable	Rs.
Ram Ltd.			
Equity shareholders	Preference Shares 9%	4 : 1 :: 8000 : 2000 (2000 × 100)	2,00,000
Equity shareholders	Equity shares	4 : 3 :: 8000 : 6000 (6000 × 100)	6,60,000
		Purchase consideration Rs.	8,60,000
Anand Ltd. :			
Equity shareholders	Preference shares 9%	5 : 2 :: 6000 : 2400 (2400 × 100)	2,40,000
Equity shareholders	Equity shares	5 : 2 :: 6000 : 2400 (2400 × 100)	2,64,000
Debentureholders	8% Debentures	–	50,000
		Purchase consideration Rs.	5,54,000

Accounts In the Books of Anand Ltd.

Dr.   **Realisation Account**   **Cr.**

	Rs.		Rs.
To Premises A/c	4,50,000	By Sundry creditors A/c	35,000
To Stock A/c	2,00,000	By Provident Fund A/c	15,000
To Debtors A/c	70,000	By Ramanand Ltd. A/c	
To Cash A/c	8,000	(P.C.)	5,54,000
	7,28,000		6,04,000
		By Equity shareholders A/c	1,24,000
	7,28,000		7,28,000

Dr. **Equity Shareholders' A/c** **Cr.**

	Rs.		Rs.
To Preliminary Exp. A/c	22,000	By Equity Share	
To Equity shares in		Capital A/c	6,00,000
Ramanand Ltd. A/c	2,64,000	By P & L A/c	20,000
To 9% pref. shares		By Dividend Equal	
in Ramanand Ltd. A/c	2,40,000	isation Fund A/c	30,000
To Realisation A/c	1,24,000		
	6,50,000		6,50,000

Dr. **Debentureholders' A/c** **Cr.**

	Rs.		Rs.
To 8% Debentures		By 6% Debentures A/c	50,000
in Ramanand Ltd. A/c	50,000		
	50,000		50,000

Dr. **Ramanand Ltd. A/c** **Cr.**

	Rs.		Rs.
To Realisation A/c	5,54,000	By Equity shares in	
		Ramanand Ltd. A/c	2,64,000
		By 9% Pref. shares	
		in Ramanand Ltd. A/c	2,40,000
		By 8% Debentures A/c	50,000
	5,54,000		5,54,000

Working Notes :

1) Provident Fund is an outside liability and transferred to the credit of Realisation A/c.
2) Preliminary expenses are losses which are transferred to Equity shareholders' A/c.
3) Liquidation expenses are paid by purchasing company. These are not recorded by vendor companies.
4) Students are advised to prepare the ledger accounts in the books of Ram Ltd.

Opening Journal Entries in the Books of Ramanand Ltd.

Particulars		L.F.	Dr. Rs.	Cr. Rs.
1) Business purchase A/c	Dr.		8,60,000	
To liquidator of Ram Ltd.				8,60,000
(Being business of Ram Ltd. acquired)				

Particulars		L.F.	Dr. Rs.	Cr. Rs.
2) Building A/c	Dr.		6,10,000	
Debtors A/c	Dr.		32,000	
Cash A/c	Dr.		25,000	
Machinery A/c	Dr.		1,60,000	
Goodwill A/c	Dr.		75,000	
To S. Creditors A/c				40,000
To R.D.D. A/c				2,000
To Business purchase A/c				8,60,000
(Being assets & liabilities taken over)				
3) Liquidator of Ram Ltd. A/c	Dr.		8,60,000	
To Equity share capital A/c				6,00,000
To Share premium A/c				60,000
To 9% preference share capital A/c				2,00,000
(Being purchase consideration paid)				
For Purchase of Business of Anand Ltd.				
4) Business, Purchase A/c	Dr.		5,54,000	
To Liquidator of Anand Ltd. A/c				5,54,000
(Being business of Anand Ltd. acquired)				
5) Premises A/c	Dr.		3,30,000	
Stock A/c	Dr.		2,00,000	
Debtors A/c	Dr.		70,000	
Cash A/c	Dr.		8,000	
Goodwill A/c	Dr.		–	
To Sundry Creditors A/c				35,000
To Provident Fund A/c				15,000
To Business Purchase A/c				5,54,000
To Capital Reserve A/c				4,000
(Being assets and liabilities of Anand Ltd. taken over)				
6) Liquidator of Anand Ltd. A/c	Dr.		5,54,000	
To Equity share capital A/c				2,64,000
To Share premium A/c				24,000
To 9% preference share capital A/c				2,40,000
To 8% Debentures A/c				50,000
(Being purchase consideration of Anand Ltd. paid)				

7) Liquidation Expenses A/c	Dr.	1,000	
To Bank A/c			1,000
(Being Liquidation Expenses paid)			
8) Goodwill A/c	Dr.	1,000	
To Liquidation Expenses A/c			1,000
(Being Liquidation expenses transferred to goodwill A/c.)			

Note :

		Rs.
Net Goodwill = Total Goodwill	=	76,000
Less capital Reserve	=	4,000
		72,000

Problem No. 6 : Following are the Balance Sheets of Anita Ltd. & Babita Ltd. as on 31st March, 2014.

Balance Sheet of Anita Ltd.

Liabilities	Rs.	Assets	Rs.
Share capital :		Land & Building	1,00,000
3,000 Equity shares		Plant & Machinery	1,50,000
of Rs. 100 each	3,00,000	Furniture	10,000
500, 6% preference		Stock	35,000
shares of Rs. 100 each	50,000	Debtors	45,000
Contingency Reserve	10,000	Cash at Bank	7,500
Creditors	35,000	Preliminary Expenses	10,000
Unclaimed Dividend	2,500	Discount on issue of shares	2,500
Contingent Liability for		Profit & Loss A/c	37,500
Bill Discounted Rs. 2,000			
	3,97,500		3,97,500

Balance Sheet of Babita Ltd.

Liabilities	Rs.	Assets	Rs.
Share capital :		Freehold Premises	2,00,000
3,500 Equity shares		Plant & Machinery	1,05,000
of Rs. 100 each	3,50,000	Stock	14,500
General Reserve	9,000	Debtors	95,000
Profit & Loss A/c	20,000	Cash at Bank	5,500
Workmen's Compensation Fund	5,000		
Creditors	36,000		
	4,20,000		4,20,000

Anita Ltd. & Babita Ltd. amalgamated as on 31st March, 2014 and a new company sunita Ltd. was formed with an authorised capital of 10,000 equity shares of Rs. 100 each. The amalgamation was agreed on the following conditions :

1. Sunita Ltd. took all assets of Anita Ltd. at book values and creditors of Anita Ltd. The purchase consideration was discharged by issuing 1,500 equity shares of Rs. 100 each Rs. 120 per share and the balance in cash.

2. Sunita Ltd. took all assets of Babita Ltd. at book values except cash and also took the creditors. The purchase consideration was discharged by issuing 3,000 Equity shares of Rs. 100 each at Rs. 120 per share and the balance in cash.

3. Anita Ltd. paid its preference capital back with arrears of preference dividend for the last two years.

4. Liability for bills discounted was settled Rs. 1,250.

5. Out of the unclaimed dividend, Rs. 1,000 was paid to the rightful shareholders. The remaining unclaimed dividend was time barred and thus transferred to shareholders account.

6. Liability for workmen's compensation of Babita Ltd. amounted to Rs. 3,750.

7. The cost of liquidation of Anita Ltd. was Rs. 2,500 and that of Babita Ltd. was Rs. 3,000, which was paid by the respective companies.

You are required to prepare :

a) Realisation Account, Sunita Ltd. A/c, Cash Account & Shareholders A/c in the books of Anita Ltd. and Babita Ltd.

b) Opening entries in the books of Sunita Ltd.

Solution :

Calculation of Purchase Consideration (Net Asset Method)

Particulars	Anita Ltd.	Babita Ltd.
Assets taken over at book values		
Land & Building	1,00,000	
Plant & Machinery	1,50,000	1,05,000
Furniture	10,000	–
Stock	35,000	14,500
Debtors	45,000	95,000
Cash at Bank	7,500	–
Freehold Premises	–	2,00,000
Total	3,47,500	4,14,500
Less Creditors	35,000	36,000
Purchase consideration	3,12,500	3,78,500
Payment of Purchase consideration		
1500 Equity shares at Rs. 100 each	1,50,000	–
3000 Equity shares at Rs. 100 each	–	3,00,000
Share premium at Rs. 20 per share	30,000	60,000
Cash	1,32,500	18,500
	3,12,500	3,78,500

In the Books of Anita Ltd.

Dr. **Realisation A/c** **Cr.**

Particulars	Rs.	Particulars	Rs.
To Land & Building A/c	1,00,000	By Creditors A/c	35,000
To Plant & Machinery A/c	1,50,000	By Sunita Ltd. A/c	3,12,500
To Furniture A/c	10,000	(Purchase price)	
To Stock A/c	35,000	By Equity shareholders A/c	9,750
To Debtors A/c	45,000	(Loss)	
To Bank A/c (transfer)	7,500		
To Bank A/c (Payments) :			
Pref. Dividend 6,000			
Liability for bills			
Discounted 1,250			
Cost of liquidation 2,500	9,750		
	3,57,250		3,57,250

Dr. **Sunita Ltd. A/c** **Cr.**

Particulars	Rs.	Particulars	Rs.
To Realisation A/c	3,12,500	By Equity shares A/c	1,80,000
		By Bank A/c	1,32,500
	3,12,500		3,12,500

Dr. **Bank A/c** **Cr.**

Particulars	Rs.	Particulars	Rs.
To Balance b/d	7,500	By Unclaimed Dividend A/c	1,000
To Sunita Ltd.'s A/c	1,32,500	By Realisation A/c (Transfer)	7,500
		By Realisation A/c (Payments)	9,750
		By Preference shareholders A/c	50,000
		By Equity shareholders A/c	71,750
	1,40,000		1,40,000

Dr. **Preference Shareholders A/c** **Cr.**

Particulars	Rs.	Particulars	Rs.
To Bank A/c	50,000	By pref. share capital A/c	50,000
	50,000		50,000

Dr. **Equity Shareholders A/c** **Cr.**

Particulars	Rs.	Particulars	Rs.
To Preliminary Expenses A/c	10,000	By Equity share capital A/c	3,00,000
To Discount on Issue of shares A/c	2,500	By Contingency Reserve A/c	10,000
To Profit & Loss A/c	37,500	By Unclaimed Dividend A/c	1,500
To Realisation A/c (Loss)	9,750		
To Equity Shares A/c	1,80,000		
To Bank A/c	71,750		
	3,11,500		3,11,500

In the Books of Babita Ltd.

Dr. **Realisation A/c** **Cr.**

Particulars	Rs.	Particulars	Rs.
To Freehold Premises A/c	2,00,000	By Creditors A/c	36,000
To Plant & Machinery A/c	1,05,000	By Sunita Ltd. A/c	3,78,500
To Stock A/c	14,500	(Purchase price)	
To Debtors A/c	95,000	By Equity shareholders A/c	3,000
To Bank A/c (Cost of Liquidation)	3,000		
	4,17,500		4,17,500

Dr. **Sunita Ltd. A/c** **Cr.**

Particulars	Rs.	Particulars	Rs.
To Realisation A/c	3,78,500	By Equity shares A/c	3,60,000
		By Bank A/c	18,500
	3,78,500		3,78,500

Dr. **Bank A/c** **Cr.**

Particulars	Rs.	Particulars	Rs.
To Balance A/c	5,500	By Realisation A/c	3,000
To Sunita Ltd. A/c	18,500	By Workmen's compensation A/c	3,750
		By Equity shareholders A/c	17,250
	24,000		24,000

Dr. **Equity Shareholders A/c** **Cr.**

Particulars	Rs.	Particulars	Rs.
To Realisation A/c	3,000	By Equity share capital A/c	3,50,000
To Equity shares A/c	3,60,000	By General Reserve A/c	9,000
To Bank A/c	17,250	By Workmen's Comp.Fund A/c	1,250
		By Profit & Loss A/c	20,000
	3,80,250		3,80,250

In the Books of Sunita Ltd.
Opening Entries

Particulars		Dr. Rs.	Cr. Rs.
Land & Building A/c	Dr.	1,00,000	
Plant & Machinery A/c	Dr.	1,50,000	
Furniture A/c	Dr.	10,000	
Debtors A/c	Dr.	45,000	
Bank A/c	Dr.	7,500	
Stock A/c	Dr.	35,000	
To Creditors A/c			35,000
To Liquidator of Anita Ltd. A/c			3,12,500
(Assets & liabilities taken over from Anita Ltd. at the values stated above.)			
Freehold Premises A/c	Dr.	2,00,000	
Plant & Machinery A/c	Dr.	1,05,000	
Stock A/c	Dr.	14,500	
Debtors A/c	Dr.	95,000	
To Creditors A/c			36,000
To Liquidator of Babita Ltd. A/c			3,78,500
(Assets & liabilities taken over from Babita Ltd. at the values of stated above.)			
Liquidator of Anita Ltd. A/c	Dr.	3,12,500	
Liquidator of Babita Ltd. A/c	Dr.	3,78,500	
To Equity share capital A/c			4,50,000
To Equity share premium A/c			90,000
To Bank A/c			1,51,000
(Issued 1,500 shares to Anita Ltd. and 3,000 shares to Babita Ltd. of Rs. 100 each at Rs. 120 per share & balance is paid in cash)			

Problem No. 7 : M Co. Ltd. and N. Co. Ltd. carry on similar business. They agreed to amalgamate. A new Co. L Ltd. is to be formed to which assets and liabilities of the existing companies with certain exceptions, are to be transferred on 31st December 2013. The balance sheets of the two companies were as follows :

Balance Sheet of M Co. Ltd.

Liabilities	Rs.	Assets	Rs.
Issued Capital		Freeholde property	1,05,000
15,000 shares of Rs. 10 each	1,50,000	Plant & Machinery	25,000
General Reserve	80,000	Motor Vehicles	10,000
Profit & Loss A/c	20,000	Stock	60,000
Sundry Creditors	75,000	Debtors	82,000
	–	Cash	43,000
	3,25,000		3,25,000

Balance Sheet of N Co. Ltd.

Liabilities	Rs.	Assets	Rs.
Issued Capital		Freeholde property	60,000
8,000 shares of Rs. 10 each	80,000	Plant & Machinery	15,000
Profit & Loss A/c	20,000	Stock	78,000
5% Debentures	60,000	Debtors	21,000
Sundry Creditors	32,000	Cash	18,000
	1,92,000		1,92,000

Assets and liabilities are to be taken over at book values with the following exceptions:

a) Goodwill of M Ltd. and N Ltd. is to be valued at Rs. 80,000 and Rs. 30,000 respectively.

b) Motor vehicles of M Ltd. are to be valued at Rs. 30,000.

c) Debentures of N Ltd. are to be discharged by the issue of 6% debentures of L Ltd. at a premium of 4%. The debtors and cash of N Ltd. are to be retained by the liquidators and the sundry creditors are to be paid out of the proceeds thereof.

Close the books of M Ltd. and N Ltd. and draw-up a Balance Sheet of L Ltd. as on 1-1-2014.

Solution :

Statement of Purchase Consideration

Particulars	M Ltd. Rs.	N Ltd. Rs.
Sundry Assets (taken over)		
Goodwill	80,000	30,000
Freehold property	1,05,000	60,000
Plant & Machinery	25,000	15,000
Motor Vehicles	30,000	–

	Rs.	Rs.
Stock	60,000	78,000
Debtors	82,000	–
Cash	43,000	–
	4,25,000	1,83,000
Less : Sundry Liabilities (taken over) Creditors	75,000	–
Purchase Price	3,50,000	1,83,000

Payment of Purchase consideration	M Ltd. Rs.	N Ltd. Rs.
i) 6% Debentures in L Ltd.	–	62,400
ii) Shares in L Ltd.	3,50,000	1,20,600

In the Books of M Ltd.

Dr.   **Realisation A/c**   **Cr.**

		Rs.		Rs.
To Sundry Assets A/c (taken over)			By Sundry Liab. A/c (taken over)	
Freehold property	1,05,000		(Sundry Creditors)	75,000
Plant & Machinery	25,000		By "L" Co. Ltd. A/c (P.C.)	3,50,000
Motor Vehicles	10,000			
Stock	60,000			
Debtors	82,000			
Cash	43,000	3,25,000		
To Equity shareholders A/c		1,00,000		
(Profit) (Bal. fig.)		–		–
		4,25,000		4,25,000

Dr.   **'L' Ltd. A/c**   **Cr.**

	Rs.		Rs.
To Realisation A/c	3,50,000	By Equity shares in L Ltd. A/c	3,50,000
	–		–
	350,000		3,50,000

Dr.   **Equity shares in L Ltd. A/c**   **Cr.**

	Rs.		Rs.
To L Ltd. A/c	3,50,000	By Equity shareholders A/c	3,50,000
	–		–
	3,50,000		3,50,000

Dr.   **Equity Shareholder's A/c**   **Cr.**

	Rs.		Rs.
To Equity shares in L Ltd. A/c	3,50,000	By Equity Share Capital A/c	1,50,000
		By General Reserve A/c	80,000
		By Profit & Loss A/c	20,000
		By Realisation A/c	1,00,000
	3,50,000		3,50,000

In the Books of N Ltd.

Dr.   **Realisation A/c**   **Cr.**

		Rs.		Rs.
To Sundry Assets A/c (Book value)			By Sundry Liab. A/c (Book value)	
Freehold property	60,000		(Sundry Creditors)	32,000
Plant & machinery	15,000		By 'L' Co. Ltd. A/c (P.C.)	1,83,000
Stock	78,000		By Cash A/c (Debtors realised)	21,000
Debtors	21,000	1,74,000		
To Cash A/c (creditors paid)		32,000		
To 5% Debentureholders A/c		2,400		
To Equity Shareholders A/c		27,600		
(Profit)				
(Bal. Fig.)		–		–
		2,36,000		2,36,000

Dr.   **'L' Co. Ltd. A/c**   **Cr.**

	Rs.		Rs.
To Realisation A/c	1,83,000	By 6% Debentures in 'L' Ltd. A/c	62,400
		By Equity shares in 'L' Ltd. A/c	1,20,600
	1,83,000		1,83,000

Dr.   **6% Debentures in 'L' Ltd. A/c**   **Cr.**

	Rs.		Rs.
To 'L' Co. Ltd. A/c	62,400	By 5% Debentureholders A/c	62,400
	–		–
	62,400		62,400

Dr.   **Equity shares in "L" Ltd. A/c**   **Cr.**

	Rs.		Rs.
To "L" Co. Ltd. A/c	1,20,600	By Equity shareholders A/c	1,20,600
	—		—
	1,20,600		1,20,600

Dr.   **Equity shareholders A/c**   **Cr.**

	Rs.		Rs.
To Equity shares in 'L' Ltd. A/c	1,20,600	By Equity share capital A/c	80,000
		By Profit & Loss A/c	20,000
To Cash A/c	7,000	By Realisation A/c	27,600
	1,27,600		1,27,600

Dr.   **5% Debentureholders A/c**   **Cr.**

	Rs.		Rs.
To 6% Debentures in 'L' Ltd. A/c	62,400	By 5% Debentures A/c	60,000
		By Realisation A/c (Bal. Fig.)	2,400
	62,400		62,400

Dr.   **Cash A/c**   **Cr.**

	Rs.		Rs.
To Balance b/d	18,000	By Realisation A/c	32,000
To Realisation A/c	21,000	By Equality shareholders A/c	7,000
	—	(Bal. Fig.)	—
	39,000		39,000

Balance Sheet of L Ltd. as on 1st Jan. 2014

Liabilities	Rs.	Assets	Rs.
Share Capital		**Fixed Assets**	
Shares	4,70,600	Goodwill	1,10,000
6% Debentures	62,400	Freehold property	1,65,000
Current Liability		Plant & Machinery	40,000
Creditors	75,000	Motor Vehicle	30,000
		Current Assets	
		Stock	1,38,000
		Debtors	82,000
		Cash	43,000
	6,08,000		6,08,000

Problem No. 8 : The following are the balance sheets of two companies Akash Ltd and Sagar Ltd. on 31 March 2014

Balance Sheet of Akash Ltd. (as on 31ˢᵗ March 2014)

Liabilities	Rs.	Assets	Rs.
Share Capital :		Good will	10,000
Equity shares of Rs. 1		Building	45,000
each fully paid	1,50,000	Machinery at cost 50,000	
Forfeited shares A/c	150	Less. Depreciation -15,000	35,000
4% Debentures	35,000	Sundry Debtors	25,850
Reserve Fund	10,000	Stock	68,276
Profit & Loss A/c	16,865	Cash at Bank	33,674
Sundry Creditors	5,785		
	2,17,800		2,17,800

Balance sheet of Sagar Ltd.
(as on 31ˢᵗ March 2014)

Liabilities	Rs.	Assets		Rs
Share Capital :		Good will		10,000
Equity Shares of Rs. 1		Building		13,000
each fully paid	39,000	Machinery at cost		11,000
5% Debentures	7,000	Sundry Debtors	10,000	
Sundry Creditors	25,700	Less : R.D.D. -	500	9,500
Bank Overdraft	600	Stock		15,200
		Profit & Loss A/c		13,600
	72,300			72,300

The two companies decided to amalgamate as on 31 st March, 2014 and a new company 'Sukhsagar Ltd' was formed with an authorised capital of Rs. 2,50,000 in shares of Rs. 1 each. The following terms were agreed.

1) The consideration was :

   a) 6 Shares of Rs. 1 each at Rs. 1.10 fully paid in the New Company in exchange of every 5 shares in Akash Ltd. and Rs. 1,000 in cash.

     On share of Rs. 1 each at Rs. 1.10 fully paid in the New Company in exchange for every 3 shares in Sagar Ltd. and Rs. 500 in cash.

   b) The debentureholders were to be allotted such debentures in the new Company bearing interest at 3.5% as would bring them the same amount of interest.

2) Akash Ltd. to pay its own cost of winding up which amounted to Rs. 300 and the cost of winding up of Sagar Ltd. is to be paid by Sukhsagar Ltd. (not to include in purchase consideration) which amounted to Rs. 200.

3) Sukhsagar Limited to take over all assets and liabilities of both companies at book values.

Prepare :

i) Realisation A/c, Sukhsagar Ltd. A/c, Equity Shares in Sukhsagar Ltd A/c, 4% Debentureholders A/c, Cash A/c and Equity Shareholders A/c in the books of Akash Limited.

ii) Open Journal entries in the books of Sukhsagar Limited.   **(March 2010 PUP)**

Solution :

Calculation of purchase consideration

Akash Ltd.	Rs	Sagar Ltd.	Rs
1) Equity Shareholders (1,80,000 × 1.10)	1,98,000	1) Equity Shareholders (13,000 Share × Rs. 1.10)	14,300
2) Cash to Eq. Shareholders	1000	2) Cash to Eq. Share holder	500
3) 4% Debenture holders 35000 × 4% = 1400 Int. 3.5 - 100 1400 ? } 40,000	40,000	3) 4% Debentureholders 7000 × 5% = 350 Int. 3.5 - 100 1400 ? } 10,000	10,000
	2,39,000		24,800

In the books of Akash Ltd.
Realisation Account

Particulars	Rs	Particulars	Rs
To Good will	10,000	By Creditors	5,785
To Buidings	45,000	By Sukhsagar Ltd.	2,39,000
To Machinery	35,000		
To Sundry debtors	25,850		
To Stock	68,276		
To Cash at bank	33,674		
To Cash A/c (Exp)	300		
To 4% Debentureholders A/c	5,000		
To Equity Shareholder A/c (Profit)	21,685		
	2,44,785		2,44,785

Sukhsagar Limited A/c

Particulars	Rs	Particulars	Rs
To Realisation A/c (P.c)	2,39,000	By Equity Share in Sukhsagar (Ltd)	1,98,000
		By Cash A/c	1,000
		By 3.5% Debenture in Sukhsagar Ltd. A/c	40,000
	2,39,000		2,39,000

Equity Shares in Sukhsagar Ltd. A/C

Particulars	Rs	Particulars	Rs
To Sukhsagar Ltd A/c	1,98,000	By Equity Shareholder A/c	1,98,000
	1,98,000		1,98,000

4% Debentureholder A/c

Particulars	Rs	Particulars	Rs
To 3.5% Debentures in Sukhsagar Ltd A/c	40,000	By 4% Debentures A/c	35,000
		By Realisation A/c	5000
	40,000		40,000

Cash A/c

Particulars	Rs	Particulars	Rs
To Sukhsagar Ltd A/c	1000	By Realisation A/c (Exp)	300
		By Equity Shareholders A/c	700
	1000		1000

Equity Shareholders Account

Particulars	Rs	Particulars	Rs
To Equity Share in Sukhsagar Ltd A/c	1,98,000	By Equity Share capital A/c	1,50,000
To Cash A/c	700	By Forfeited share a/c	150
		By Reserve Funds	10,000
		By Profit & Loss A/c	16,865
		By Realisation A/c (Profit)	21,685
	1,98,700		1,98,700

Journal Entries in the books of Sukhsagar Ltd.

Particulars	L.F.	Dr. Rs.	Cr. Rs.
1) Business Purchase A/c		2,63,800	
To Liquidator a/c			
Akash Ltd			2,39,000
To Liquidator of sagar Ltd.			24,800
2) Good will A/c	Dr.	36,985	
Building A/c	Dr.	45,000	
Machinery A/c	Dr.	35,000	
Sundry Debtor A/c	Dr.	25,850	
Stock A/c	Dr.	68,276	
Cash at Bank A/c	Dr.	33,674	
To creditor A/c			5785
To Business Purchase A/c			2,39,000
(Asset & Liabilities of Akash Ltd)			
3) Good will A/c	Dr.	2,400	
Building A/c	Dr.	13,000	
Machinery A/c	Dr.	11,000	
Sundry debtor A/c	Dr.	10,000	
Stock A/c	Dr.	15,200	
To R.D.D. A/c			500
To Creditors A/c			25,700
To Bank Overdraft			600
To Business Purchase A/c			24,800
(Asset and Liabilities of Sagar Ltd)			
4) Liquidator of Akash Ltd A/c	Dr.	2,39,000	
To Eq. Share Capital A/c			1,80,000
To share premium			18,000
To cash A/c			1000
To 3.5 % Debenture A/c (P. C. Discharge)			40,000
5) Liquidator of Sagar Ltd A/c	Dr.	24,800	
To Eq. Share Capital			13,000
To share Premium			1,300
To cash A/c			500
To 3.5% Debentures			10,000
(Discharge of Pc sagar Ltd)			
6) Good will A/c	Dr.	200	
To cash A/c			200

Scheme of Marking :

1) Calculation of Pc each 2 Marks × 2   = 4 Mark
2) Realisation A/c & Equity Shareholders A/c
    2 Marks each × 2   = 4 Mark
3) Sukhsagar Ltd A/c
    Equity Shares A/c 4% Deb.
    Holder A/c, Cash A/c
    1 mark each × 4   = 4 Mark
4) Journal entries
    entry No. 1 & 6
    1 mark each   = 2 Mark
    entry No. 2, 3, 4 & 5   = 6 Mark
    $1\frac{1}{2}$ Mark each   = 6 Mark
                           20 Mark

Problem No. 9 : The Balance Sheet of Sagar Limited and Sarita Ltd. As on 31 st March 2014 was as follows.

Balance sheet as on 31 st March, 2014

Liabilities	Sagar Ltd (Rs)	Sarita Ltd (Rs)	Assets	Sagar Ltd (Rs)	Sarita Ltd (Rs)
Share Capital :			Good will	1,80,000	-
Equity Shares of					
Rs. 100 each	5,40,000	4,00,000	Plant & Machinery	1,00,000	1,60,000
			Land & Buildings	2,60,000	1,60,000
Dividend Equilisation			Furniture	-	30,000
Reserve	20,000	-	Vehicles	-	90,000
General Reserve	24,000	-	Stock	1,60,000	1,00,000
Profit & Loss A/c	36,000	-	Debtors	80,000	20,000
Creditors	1,60,000	1,40,000	Cash in hand	20,000	10,000
Bills Payables	10,000	40,000	Cash at Bank	80,000	-
Provision for Taxation	90,000	-	Profit & Loss A/c	-	10,000
	8,80,000	5,80,000		8,80,000	5,80,000

Sagar Ltd. And Sarita Ltd. Decided to amalgamate on that date and a New Company "Mahasagar Ltd' Was formed to carry on their business on the following terms.

1) Mahasagar Ltd took all assets of Sagar Ltd. Except Debtors Cash and Bank Balances, at 10% depreciation and agreed to pay Rs. 2,00,000 for Goodwill. It also took over creditors and Bills Payables.

2) Tax Liability for 2013-14 was paid at Rs. 76,000

3) Mahasagr Ltd. took all assets of Sarita Ltd. Except Debtors and Cash. Land & Buildings and Stock were taken at 20% appreciation and other assets were taken at book values. They also agreed to take over creditors of Sarita Ltd.

4) Sarita Ltd. Paid bills payables in full.

5) Purchase Consideration was satisfied as follows. Rs. 40,000 to Sagar Ltd. And Rs. 30,000 to Sarita Ltd. The balance of Purchase Consideration was paid in equity shares of Rs. 100 each.

6) Debtors of Sagar Ltd. Sarita Ltd. Realised Rs. 76,000 and Rs. 24,000 respectively

Prepare :

i) Realisation A/c, Mahasagar Ltd A/c, Equity Shares in Mahasagar Ltd A/c, Cash A/c, Equity Shareholders A/c & Provision for Taxation A/c in the books of Sagar Ltd.

ii) Acquisition entries of Mahasagar Ltd.   **(Oct 2011 - PUP)**

Solution :

Amalgamation
Calculation of Pc Sagar Ltd.

Net Assets taken over	Rs.	Less	Liab taken over	
Good will	2,00,000		Creditors	1,60,000
Land & Bld	2,34,000		Bills Payable	1,000
Plant & Machinery	90,000			1,70,000
Stock	1,44,000			
	6,68,000		P. C.	4,98,000

Calculation of Pc Sarita Ltd.

Assets taken over		Discharge of pc	
Plant & Machinery	1,60,000	in cash	30,000
Land & Building	1,92,000	in 4220 Shares of	4,22,000
Stock	1,20,000	Rs. 100 each	
Furniture	30,000		
Vehicles	90,000		
	5,92,000		
Less Liab taken over : Creditors	1,40,000		
Pc.	4,52,000		4,52,000

In the books of Sagar Ltd.
Realisation A/c

Dr.	₹	Cr.	₹
To Sundry Assets :		By Creditors	1,60,000
Good will	1,80,000	By Bills Payables	10,000
Land & Buildings	2,60,000	By Mahasagar Ltd. (Pc)	4,98,000
Plant & Machinery	1,00,000	By cash A/c (Debtors)	76,000
Stock	1,60,000	By Equity Shareholder A/c	36,000
Debtors	80,000	(Loss)	
	7,80,000		7,80,000

Mahasagar Ltd A/c

Dr.	₹	Cr.	₹
To Realisation A/c	4,98,000	By cash A/c	40,000
(Pc)		By Equity Shares in Mahasagar	4,58,000
	4,98,000		4,98,000

Equity Shares in Mahasagar Ltd. A/c

Dr.	₹	Cr.	₹
To Mahasagar Ltd. A/c	4,58,000	By Equity Shareholder A/c	4,58,000
	4,58,000		4,58,000

Cash A/c

Dr.	₹	Cr.	₹
To Bal. B/d	20,000	By Provision for Taxation	76,000
To cah at Bank	80,000	By Equity Shareholder A/c	1,40,000
To Mahasagar Ltd. A/c	40,000		
To Realisation A/c (Debtors)	76,000		
	2,16,000		2,16,000

Equity Shareholders A/c

Dr.	₹	Cr.	₹
To Realisation A/c (Loss)	36,000	By Equity Share Capital	5,40,000
To Equity Shares in Mahasagar Ltd. A/c	4,58,000	By Dividend Eq. Reserve	20,000
To Cash A/c	1,40,000	By General Reserve	24,000
		By Profit & Loss A/c	36,000
		By Provision for Taxation	14,000
	6,34,000		6,34,000

Provision of Taxation A/c

To Cash A/c	76,000	By Bal. B/d	90,000
To Equity Shareholder A/c	14,000		
	90,000		**90,000**

Jarnal Entries in the books of Mahasagar Ltd.

Date 31-3-2014	Particulars	L.F.	Dr. Rs.	Cr. Rs.
1.	Business Purchase A/c Dr.		9,50,000	
	To Liquidator of Sagar Ltd.			4,98,000
	To Liquidator of Sarita Ltd.			4,52,000
2.	Good will A/c Dr.		2,00,000	
	Land & Building A/c Dr.		2,34,000	
	Plant & Machinery A/c Dr.		90,000	
	Stock A/c		1,44,000	
	To Creditors A/c			1,60,000
	To Bills Payable A/c			10,000
	To Business Purchase A/c			4,98,000
3.	Plant & Machinery A/c Dr.		1,60,000	
	Land & Building A/c Dr.		1,92,000	
	Stock A/c Dr.		1,20,000	
	Furniture A/c Dr.		30,000	
	Vehicles A/c Dr.		90,000	
	To Creditors A/c			1,40,000
	To Business Purchase A/c			4,52,000
4.	Liquidator of Sagar Ltd A/c Dr.		4,98,000	
	To Cash A/c			40,000
	To Equity Share capital A/c			4,58,000
5.	Liquidator of Sarita Ltd. A/c Dr.		4,52,000	
	To Cash A/c			30,000
	To Equity Share capital A/c			4,22,000

Problem No. 10 : The Balance Sheet of Kavita Ltd. and Savita Ltd. as on 31-3-2014 is as follows. A new Company was formed called Godawari Ltd. for Purchasing the business of the above two companies as on that date.

Balance Sheet
as on 31-3-2014

Liabilities	Kavita Ltd. Rs.	Savita Ltd. Rs.
Share Capital :		
1,500 Shares of Rs. 10 Each	15,000	-
800 Shares of Rs. 10 each	-	8,000
General Reserve	8,000	-
Profit and Loss	2,000	2,000
5% Debentures	-	6,000
Creditors	7,500	3,200
	32,500	19,200

Assets	Kavita Ltd. Rs.	Savita Ltd. Rs.
Building	10,500	6,000
Machinery	2,500	1,500
Motor Vehicles	1,000	-
Stock	6,000	7,800
Debtors	8,200	2,100
Cash	4,300	1,800
	32,500	19,200

The Following are the terms of Purchase of the business.

a) Good will of Kavita Ltd. and Savita Ltd. is to be valued at Rs. 8000 and Rs. 3000 Respectively.

b) All the assets and liabilities of Kavita Ltd. are to be taken over at their book values except motor vehicle which is valued at Rs. 3000

c) All the assets of Savita Ltd. are taken over at their book values except Debtors and cash but no the liabilities.

d) The Debentures of Savita Ltd. are to be discharged at a premium of 5% by issued them 9% Debentures of Godawari Ltd. as Part Payment of Purchase consideration.

e) The balance of Purchase Price to savita Ltd. and entire Purchase Price to Kavita Ltd is paid in Rs. 10 Fully paid Equity Shares of Godawari Ltd.

You are required to prepare.

i) Realisation Account, Shareholders Account and Godawari Ltd. Account in the books of Kavita Ltd.

ii) Opening Journal Entries and Balance Sheet of Godawari Ltd. as on 31-3-2014

(March 2013 - PUP)

Solution :

Statement of Purchase Consideration

Discharge of Purchase Consideration	Kavita (Rs.)	Savita (Rs.)	Particulars	Kavita (Rs.)	Savita (Rs.)
3500 Eq. Shares of Rs. 10 each	35,000		Net Assets taken : Building	10,500	6,000
			Machinery	2,500	1,500
			Motar Vehicles	3,000	-
9% Debenture	-	6,300	Stock	6,000	7,800
To Debenture			Debtors	8,200	-
Holder			Cash	4,300	-
6000 + 300 Premium			Good will	8,000	3,000
100 Equity Shares of	-	12,000		42,500	18,300
Godawari Ltd at Fully paid			Less - Liabilities taken taken creditors Purchase Consideration	7,500	-
	35,000	18300		35,000	18300

Realisation A/c

Particulars	Rs	Particulars	Rs.
To Sundry Assets :			
Building	10,500	**By Sundry Liabilities :**	
Machinery	2,500	Creditors	7,500
Motar Vehicles	1,000	By Godawari Ltd	35,000
Stock	6,000	(P.C)	
Debtors	8,200		
Cash	4,300		
To Equity Shareholder (Profit)	10,000		
	42,500		42,500

Godawari Ltd. A/c

Particulars	Rs.	Particular	Rs.
To Realisation A/c	35,000	By Eq. Shares in	35,000
		Godawari Ltd. A/c	
	35,000		35,000

Equity Shareholder A/c

Particulars	Rs.	Particulars	Rs.
To Eq. Shares in	35,000	By Eq. Share Capital A/c	15,000
Godawari Ltd. A/c		By General Reserve	8,000
(3500 × 100)		By P & L A/c	2,000
		By Realization A/c	10,000
		(Profit)	
	35,000		35,000

Opening Entries in the Book of Godawari Ltd.

Date	Particulars		L.F.	Dr. Rs.	Cr. Rs.
1)	Business Purchase A/c	Dr.		53,300	
	To Liquidator of Kavita Ltd.				35,000
	To Liquidator of Savita Ltd.				18,300
2)	Building A/c	Dr.		16,5000	
	Machinery A/c	Dr.		4,000	
	Motar Vehicles A/c	Dr.		3,000	
	Stock A/c	Dr.		13,800	
	Sundry Debtors A/c	Dr.		8,200	
	Cash A/c	Dr.		4,300	
	Goodwill A/c	Dr.		11,000	
	To Creditors A/c				7,500
	To Business Purchase A/c				53,300
3)	Liquidator of Kavita Ltd A/c			35,000	
	Liquidator of Savita Ltd A/c			18,300	
	To Eq Share Capital A/c				47,000
	(4700 × 10)				
	To 9% Debenture A/c				6,300

In the Books of Godawari A/c
Balance sheet As on 31.3.2014

Liabilities	Rs.	Assets	Rs.
Share Capital :		**Fixed Assets :**	
4700 Fully Paid Eq.			
Shares of Rs. 10 each	47,000	Good will	11,000
		Building	16,500
Secured Loans :		Machinery	4,000
9% Debenture	6,300	Motor vehicles	3,000
Current Liabilities :		**Current Assets :**	
Creditors	7,500	Stock	13,800
		Sundry Debtors	8,200
		Cash	4,300
	60,800		60,800

5.6 Problems on Absorption

Problem No. 11 : The following is the Balance Sheet of Black Ltd. as on 31ˢᵗ March, 2014.

Liabilities	Rs.	Assets	Rs.
Capital-		Goodwill	40,000
30,000 Equity shares		Plant & Machinery	3,00,000
of Rs. 10 each.	3,00,000	Stocks	1,60,000
20,000, 6% Cumulative		Sundry Debtors	2,40,000
Preference Shares		Cash at Bank	17,800
of Rs. 10 each	2,00,000	Profit & Loss A/c	80,200
1000, 5% Debentures		Preliminary Expenses	10,000
of Rs. 100 each	1,00,000	Commission and Brokerage	
Bank Overdraft	20,000	on shares	8,000
Employees' profit			
Sharing Account	28,000		
Sundry Creditors	1,83,000		
Interest Accrued on			
Debentures	5,000		
Depreciation Reserve	20,000		
Contingent liability			
Arrears of Cum. Pref.			
Dividend Rs. 24,000			
	8,56,000		8,56,000

With the view to avoid competition, Black Ltd. was taken over by White Ltd. as from 1ˢᵗ April 2014 on the following terms :

1) Take over all tangible assets with the exception of cash.
2) Pay the debentureholders at a premium of 10% by issue of its 6% cumulative preference shares of the face value of Rs. 10 each.
3) Issue one equity share of Rs. 10 each and make a payment of Rs. 4 in cash in exchange of every two equity shares in Black Ltd.
4) Sundry creditors to receive 90% of the sums due to then in fully paid equity shares of Rs. 10 each in White Ltd. in full settlement of all their claims.
5) Preference shareholders to be issued 5% Debentures in White Ltd. The preference shares of Black Ltd. are preferential as to capital and dividend in the event of winding up.
6) The Winding up expenses Rs. 2,000 are paid by White Ltd. separately.
7) The directors of white Ltd. subscribed 5,000 equity shares of Rs. 10 each and paid for the same in full.

Close the books of Black Ltd. by the way of passing journal entries and also the opening entries in the books of White Ltd. Prepare also purchase consideration statement in the books of White Ltd.

Solution :

Purchase Consideration (Payment Method)

Whom Payable	What Payable	How Payable	Rs.
1) Debentureholders of Black Ltd.	6% Cum, Pref. shares in white Ltd.	1,00,000 + 10% + for Accrued Int.	1,10,000 + 5,000
			1,15,000
2) Equity Share holders of Black Ltd.	Equity shares in White Ltd. and Cash	2 : 1 :: 30,000 : 15000 (15,000 × 10) For 2 shares Rs. 4 (15,000 × 4)	1,50,000 60,000
3) Sundry Creditors of Black Ltd.	Equity Shares in White Ltd.	1,83,000 - 10%	1,64,700
4) Preference Share holders of Black Ltd.	5% Debentures in White Ltd.	2,00,000 + 24,000 (for dividend)	2,24,000
		Total Rs.	7,13,700

Journal Entries in the Books of Black Ltd.
(Vendor Company)

Particulars	L.F.	Dr. Rs.	Cr. Rs.
1) Realisation A/c Dr.		7,40,000	
To Goodwill A/c			40,000
To Plant & Machinery A/c			3,00,000
To Stock A/c			1,60,000
To Sundry Debtors A/c			2,40,000
(Being Assets taken over transferred.)			
2) Equity shareholders' A/c Dr.		98,200	
To Profit & Loss A/c Dr.			80,200
To Preliminary ExpensesA/c			10,000
To Commission & Brokerage			8,000
(Being Balance Sheet losses transferred)			
3) Equity Share Capital A/c Dr.		3,00,000	
To Equity shareholders' A/c			3,00,000
(Being Equity share capital transferred)			

4) 6% Cum. Pref. Share Capital A/c
     To preference shareholders A/c
   (Being preference share capital transferred)
	Dr.	2,00,000	2,00,000

5) 5% Debentures A/c
 Debenture Accrued Interest A/c
     To Debentureholders' A/c
   (Being Debentures and accrued interest transferred)
	Dr.
	 Dr.
		1,00,000
		 5,000
			1,05,000

6) Bank Overdraft A/c
 Employees' profit Sharing A/c
     To Realisation A/c
   (Being remaining liabilities transferred to
 Realisation A/c)
	Dr.
	 Dr.
		20,000
		 28,000
			48,000

7) Depreciation Reserve A/c
     To Realisation A/c
   (Being Depreciation reserve on plant
 & Machinery transferred)
	Dr.	20,000	20,000

8) White Ltd. A/c
     To Realisation A/c
   (Being purchase consideration due from white Ltd.)
	Dr.	7,13,700	7,13,700

9) 6% Cum. pref. Shares in White Ltd. A/c
 Equity Shares in White Ltd. A/c
 5% Debenture in White Ltd. A/c
 Bank A/c
     To White Ltd. A/c
   (Being purchase consideration received from
 White Ltd.)
	Dr.
	 Dr.
	 Dr.
	 Dr.
		1,15,000
		 3,14,700
		 2,24,000
		 60,000
			7,13,700

10) Debentureholders' A/c
     To 6% Cum. Pref. Shares in White Ltd. A/c
   (Being preference shares allotted to Debentureholders)
	Dr.	1,15,000	1,15,000

11) Realisation A/c
     To Debentureholders A/c
   (Being loss on payment of debentures transferred)
	Dr.	10,000	10,000

12) Equity shareholders' A/c
     To Equity shares in White Ltd. A/c
   (Being equity shares allotted to equity shareholders)
	Dr.	1,50,000	1,50,000

Particulars		Dr.	Cr.
13) Sundry creditors A/c	Dr.	1,83,000	
To Equity shares in White Ltd. A/c			1,64,700
To Realisation A/c			18,300
(Being creditors allotted the equity shares and profit thereon transferred)			
14) Preference shareholders A/c	Dr.	2,24,000	
To 5% Debentures in White Ltd. A/c			2,24,000
(Being debentures allotted to preference shareholders)			
15) Realisation A/c	Dr.	24,000	
To Preference shareholders A/c			24,000
(Being loss on payment of preference shares transferred)			
16) Realisation A/c	Dr.	48,000	
To Bank A/c			48,000
(Being Bank overdraft and Employees' profit sharing A/c paid)			
17) Equity shareholders' A/c	Dr.	22,000	
To Realisation A/c			22,000
(Being realisation loss transferred)			
18) Equity shareholders' A/c	Dr.	29,800	
To Bank A/c			29,800
(Being final balance paid)			

Working Notes :

1) Bank overdraft and employees' profit sharing account are the outside liabilities. These are not taken over by White Ltd. Hence, paid by Black Ltd.
2) Arrears of pref. dividends are payable on liquidation of Black Ltd. These are paid by White Ltd. in form of 5% Debentures.
3) Depreciation reserve is not a liability.

Journal Entries in the Books of White Ltd.
(Purchasing Company)

Particulars	L.F.	Dr. Rs.	Cr. Rs.
1) Business purchase A/c Dr.		7,13,000	
To liquidator of Black Ltd. A/c			7,13,700
(Being business of Black Ltd. acquired)			

Particulars		L.F.	Dr. Rs.	Cr. Rs.
2) Goodwill A/c	Dr.		13,700	
Plant & Machinery A/c	Dr.		3,00,000	
Stocks A/c	Dr.		1,60,000	
Sundry Debtors A/c	Dr.		2,40,000	
To Business purchase A/c				7,13,700
(Being assets taken Over)				
3) Liquidator of Black Ltd. A/c	Dr.		7,13,700	
To Bank A/c				60,000
To 6% cum. pref. share capital A/c				1,15,000
To Equity share capital A/c				3,14,700
To 5% Debentures A/c				2,24,000
(Being purchase consideration paid)				
4) a) Liquidation expenses A/c	Dr.		2,000	
To Bank A/c				2,000
(Being liquidation expenses paid)				
b) Goodwill A/c	Dr.		2,000	
To liquidation Expenses				2,000
(Being expenses transferred)				
5) Bank A/c	Dr.		50,000	
To Equity share capital A/c				50,000
(Being 5,000 shares subscribed by directors)				

Problem No. 12 : The summarised Balance Sheets as on 31st March 2014 of Nitin Ltd. and Moti Ltd. were as under.

Nitin Ltd.

Liabilities	Rs.	Assets	Rs.
Share capital :		Buildings	6,00,000
15,000 Equity shares		Plant & Machinery	5,50,000
of Rs. 100 each.	15,00,000	Furniture	10,000
General Reserve	2,00,000	Stocks	3,80,000
Profit & Loss A/c	1,20,000	Sundry Debtors	2,30,000
Sundry Creditors	2,40,000	Cash & Bank balance	2,90,000
	20,60,000		20,60,000

Moti Ltd.

Liabilities	Rs.	Assets	Rs.
Share capital		Goodwill	1,00,000
5,000 Equity shares		Plant & Machinery	4,20,000
of Rs. 100 each.	5,00,000	Furniture	5,000
Capital Reserve	50,000	Stocks	1,80,000
Revenue Reserve	25,000	Sundry Debtors	1,80,000
Profit & Loss A/c	35,000	Expenses on new project	75,000
6% Debentures	3,00,000	Cash & Bank balances	45,000
Sundry Creditors	95,000		
	10,05,000		10,05,000

Moti Ltd. was absorbed by Nitin Ltd. on 1st April 2014 on the following terms :

a) Fixed assets other than goodwill to be valued at Rs. 5,00,000 including Rs. 6,000 for furniture.

b) Stock to be reduced by Rs. 20,000 in respect of obsolete items and sundry debtors by 5 per cent.

c) Nitin Ltd. to assume liabilities and pay cash to Moti Ltd. to enable it to discharge the debentures at 6% premium.

d) The new project was to be valued at Rs. 95,000.

e) The shareholders in Moti Ltd. to receive cash payment of Rs. 30 per share plus four equity shares in Nitin Ltd. for every five shares held.

f) Both the companies to declare and pay dividend of 6% prior to the merger.

g) Expenses of liquidation of Moti Ltd. were to be reimbursed by Nitin Ltd. to the extent of Rs. 5,000. The actual expenses amounted to Rs. 6,000.

Draft journal entries recording the scheme in the books of Moti Ltd. and prepare the Balance Sheet of Nitin Ltd. after absorption assuming that Nitin Ltd.'s authorised capital has been increased to Rs. 20,00,000.

Solution :

Calculation of Purchase consideration (Net Payment method)

For	Mode of Payment	Rs.
(i) Rs. 3,00,000 Debentures payment of cash at 6% premium	Cash	3,18,000
(ii) Liquidation Expenses	Cash	5,000
(iii) Shareholders, cash at Rs. 30 per share for 5,000 share	Cash	1,50,000
Total Cash		4,73,000
(iv) Shares in Nitin Ltd. @ four shares for every 5 shares in Moti Ltd. i.e. 4,000 shares @ Rs. 100 per share	Shares	4,00,000
Purchase Price Rs.		8,73,000

Journal Entries in the Books of Moti Ltd.

Date	Particulars	L.F.	Dr. Rs.	Cr. Rs.
	Realisation A/c Dr.		9,75,000	
	To Goodwill A/c			1,00,000
	To Plant & Machinery A/c			4,20,000
	To Furniture A/c			5,000
	To Stock A/c			1,80,000
	To Sundry Debtors A/c			1,80,000
	To New Project A/c			75,000
	To Cash & Bank A/c			15,000
	(Being transfer of assets to realisation)			
	Sundry Creditors A/c Dr.		95,000	
	To Realisation A/c			95,000
	(Being transfer of liabilities to Realisation)			
	Nitin Ltd. A/c Dr.		8,73,000	
	To Realisation A/c			8,73,000
	(Being Purchase price to be received from Nitin Ltd.)			
	Realisation A/c Dr.		6,000	
	To Bank A/c			6,000
	(Being Payment of Realisation Expenses.)			

Date	Particulars	L.F.	Dr. Rs.	Cr. Rs.
	Realisation A/c Dr.		18,000	
	To Debentureholders A/c			18,000
	(Being premium payable to debentureholders on Redemption of debentures.)			
	Equity Shareholders A/c Dr.		31,000	
	To Realisation A/c			31,000
	(Being loss on realisation is transferred to shareholders.)			
	Dividend A/c	Dr.	30,000	
	To Bank A/c			30,000
	(Being payment of Dividend @ 6% on Rs. 5,00,000.)			
	Bank A/c Dr.		4,73,000	
	Equity shares in Nitin Ltd. A/c Dr.		4,00,000	
	To Nitin Ltd.'s A/c			8,73,000
	(Being Receipt of 4,000 shares of Rs. 100 each as fully paid and cash Rs. 4,73,000 in settlement of purchase price from Nitin Ltd.)			
	6% Debenture A/c	Dr.	3,00,000	
	To Debentureholders A/c			3,00,000
	(Being transfer of balance on debentures to Debentureholders.)			
	Debentureholders A/c Dr.		3,18,000	
	To Bank A/c			3,18,000
	(Being Repayment of amount due to Debentureholders.)			
	Equity Share capital A/c Dr.		5,00,000	
	Capital Reserve A/c Dr.		50,000	
	Revenue Reserve A/c Dr.		25,000	
	Profit & Loss A/c Dr.		35,000	
	To Equity Shareholders A/c			6,10,000
	(Being balance on Share Capital, Reserves and Profit and Loss Account transferred to Equity Shareholders.)			

Date	Particulars	L.F.	Dr. Rs.	Cr. Rs.
	Equity Shareholders A/c Dr.		5,49,000	
	To Equity Shares in Nitin Ltd. A/c			4,00,000
	To Bank A/c			1,49,000
	(Being 4,000 shares issued of Rs. 100 each in Nitin Ltd. and paid cash to equity shareholders in satisfaction of their claim.)			

Working Notes :

1. After deduction of Realisation loss of Rs. 31,000 and Dividend A/c balance of Rs. 30,000, from Rs. 6,10,000. The final Net amount payable to shareholders is Rs. 5,49,000.

2. Out of original Bank balance of Rs. 45,000, Rs. 30,000 is paid as dividend and the balance of Rs. 15,000 is taken over by Nitin Ltd.

3. Out of Rs. 4,73,000 received from Nitin Ltd. Rs. 6,000 is paid towards expenses and Rs. 3,18,000 to debentureholders. Thus, the balance available to shareholders is Rs. 1,49,000 (i.e. 4,73,000 - 3,24,000)).

In the Books of Nitin Ltd.
Balance Sheet as on 1ˢᵗ April 2014

Liabilities	Rs.	Assets		Rs.
Share Capital :		Goodwill		27,000
Authorised :		Buildings		6,00,000
20,000 Equity shares of		Plant & Machinery		10,44,000
Rs. 100 each	20,00,000	Furniture		16,000
Issued & Paid-up :		New project		95,000
19,000 shares of Rs. 100 each		Stocks		5,40,000
of which 4,000 shares issued		Sundry Debtors	4,10,000	
to vendors as fully paid		Less : Provision	9,000	4,01,000
without receiving cash	19,00,000			
General Reserve	2,00,000			
Profit & Loss A/c	30,000			
Bank overdraft	2,58,000			
Sundry Creditors	3,35,000			
	27,23,000			27,23,000

Notes :

1. Goodwill

Agreed value of asset taken	9,41,000
Less : liabilities taken	95,000
Value of Net assets taken	8,46,000

Purchase price Rs. 8,73,000   Less : 8,46,000 = Rs. 27,000 Goodwill

2. Bank Overdraft -

Bank Balance taken over from Moti Ltd.		15,000
Original Bank Balance of Nitin Ltd.		2,90,000
Cash available		3,05,000
Cash paid to Moti Ltd.	4,73,000	
Dividend paid to shareholders of Nitin Ltd. @ 6%	90,000	5,63,000

As Rs. 5,63,000 cash required less Rs. 3,05,000 available = Overdraft Rs. 2,58,000

Problem No. 13 : Following is the Balance Sheet of Minal Ltd. as on 31st March 2014

Balance Sheet of Minal Ltd.
as on 31.3.2014

Liabilities	Rs.	Assets	Rs.
Share Capital		Land & Building	2,10,000
6,000 Share of		Plant & Machinery	1,60,000
Rs. 100 each	6,00,000	Vehicles	1,00,000
6% Debenture	20,000	Stock	80,000
Creditors	60,000	Debtors	60,000
Outstanding Expenses	4,000	Cash	64,000
		Underwriting Commission	10,000
	6,84,000		6,84,000

Nikita Ltd. absorbed Minal Ltd. on the following terms :

1. Nikita Ltd. acquired only the assets of Minal Ltd. except cash balance.

2. The purchase consideration was fixed as 5 equity shares of Rs. 100 each, at Rs. 140 per share for 7 equity shares of Minal Ltd. and 700, 6% preference shares of Rs. 100 each.

3. Realisation expenses amounted to Rs. 12,000 and were paid by Minal Ltd.

4. The Liquidator of Minal Ltd. transferred the preference shares, to creditors in full satisfication of their claims.

5. Debentures were paid at a premium of 10%.

6. Outstanding expenses were paid in full and in addition Minal Ltd. had to pay Rs. 4,200 as compensation to the worker.

7. Nikita Ltd. valued Land & Building, Plant & Machinery at 10% appreciation, Vehicles at 10% depreciation, stock was reduced to its market value which was Rs. 64,000. Debtors were taken subject to 5% Reserve for Doubtful Debts.

    Prepare the necessary ledger accounts in the books of Minal Ltd. Pass the opening entries in the books of Nikita Ltd.

Solution :

Statement showing Purchase consideration (Net Payment method)

Discharge	Rs.	Net Assets taken over	Rs.
Equity shares		Land & Building	2,31,000
Issued 5 shares		Plant & Machinery	1,76,000
for every 7 shares, the number		Vehicles	90,000
of shares to be issued		Stock	64,000
for 6000 shares will be		Debtors 60,000	
$\dfrac{6,000 \times 5}{7} = 4285\dfrac{5}{7}$ shares		- R.D.D. 3000	57,000
So 4285 full shares		Net Worth	6,18,000
of Rs. 140 each	5,99,900	PC- Net Worth	
Fraction share paid in		= Goodwill	
cash at market price		hence balancing	
(Paid in cash)		figure is	
$\dfrac{5}{7} \times 140 =$	100	Goodwill	52,000
700 preference shares at Rs.			
100 each	70,000		
Purchase Consideration	6,70,000		6,70,000

In the Books of Minal Ltd.

Realisation A/c

Dr.   Cr.

Particulars	Rs.	Particulars	Rs.
To Land & Building A/c	2,10,000	By outstanding expenses A/c	4,000
To Plant & Machinery A/c	1,60,000	By Nikita Ltd. A/c	6,70,000
To Vehicle A/c	1,00,000		
To Stock A/c	80,000		
To Debtors A/c	60,000		
To Debentures (premium) A/c	2,000		
To Creditors (premium) A/c	10,000		
To Cash A/c :			
Outstanding Commission 4,000			
Realisation Expenses 12,000			
Compensation to Worker 4,200	20,200		
To Equity Shareholders (profit) A/c	31,800		
	6,74,000		6,74,000

Nikita Ltd.'s A/c

Dr.   Cr.

Particulars	Rs.	Particulars	Rs.
To Realisation A/c	6,70,000	By Equity shares A/c	5,99,900
		By Cash A/c	100
		By 6% preference shares A/c	70,000
	6,70,000		6,70,000

Sundry Creditors A/c

Dr.   Cr.

Particulars	Rs.	Particulars	Rs.
To 7% pref. shares in Nikita Ltd.' A/c	70,000	By Balance b/d	60,000
		By Realisation A/c	10,000
	70,000		70,000

6% Debentures A/c

Dr.   Cr.

Particulars	Rs.	Particulars	Rs.
To Cash A/c	22,000	By Balance c/d	20,000
		By Realisation A/c	2,000
	22,000		22,000

Dr.   **7% Preference Shares in Nikita Ltd.'s A/c**   Cr.

Particulars	Rs.	Particulars	Rs.
To Nikita Ltd.'s A/c	70,000	By Sundry Creditors A/c	70,000
	70,000		70,000

Dr.   **Equity Shares in Nikita Ltd.' A/c**   Cr.

Particulars	Rs.	Particulars	Rs.
To Nikita Ltd.'s A/c	5,99,900	By Equity Shareholders A/c	5,99,900
	5,99,900		5,99,900

Dr.   **Cash A/c**   Cr.

Particulars	Rs.	Particulars	Rs.
To Balance	64,000	By Realisation A/c	20,200
To Nikita Ltd.'s A/c	100	By Debentures A/c	22,000
		By Equity shareholders A/c	21,900
	64,100		64,100

Dr.   **Equity Shareholders A/c**   Cr.

Particulars	Rs.	Particulars	Rs.
To Underwriting commission A/c	10,000	By Equity Share Capital A/c	6,00,000
To Equity Shares		By Realisation A/c	31,800
in Nikita Ltd.'s A/c	5,99,900		
To Cash A/c	21,900		
	6,31,800		6,31,800

In the Books of Nikita Ltd.
Journal Entries

Date	Particulars	L.F.	Dr. Rs.	Cr. Rs.
	Business Purchase A/c Dr.		6,70,000	
	To Liquidators of Minal Ltd.'s A/c			6,70,000
	(Being purchase of business from Minal Ltd. &			
	price payable to the liquidator)			

Date	Particulars		L.F.	Dr. Rs.	Cr. Rs.
	Land & Buildings A/c	Dr.		2,31,000	
	Plant & Machinery A/c	Dr.		1,76.000	
	Vehicle A/c	Dr.		90,000	
	Stock A/c	Dr.		64,000	
	Debtors A/c	Dr.		60,000	
	Goodwill A/c	Dr.		52,000	
	To Reserve for Doubtful Debts. A/c				3,000
	To Business Purchase A/c				6,70,000
	(Being purchase of Assets from Minal Ltd. at the values stated above.)				
	Liquidator of Minal Ltd. A/c	Dr.		6,70,000	
	To Equity Share Capital A/c				4,28,500
	To 7% Preference Share Capital A/c				70,000
	To Equity Share Premium A/c				1,71.400
	To Cash A/c				100
	(Being issued 4,285 Equity share of Rs. 100 each at Rs. 140 per share, 700, 7% preference shares of Rs. 100 each and paid cash Rs. 100 in settlement of purchase consideration.)				

Problem No. 14 : Long Ltd. has agreed to acquire goodwill and assets (except investments) of Short Ltd. as at 31st March 2014. The Balance Sheet of Short Ltd. as on that date was as follows :

Liabilities	Rs.	Assets	Rs.
Share Capital (Rs. 10)	1,60,000	Goodwill	20,000
General Reserve	25,000	Land and Buildings	80,000
Profit & Loss A/c	18,000	Plant	80,000
8% Debentures	60,000	Investments	30,000
Creditors	37,000	Stock	40,000
Provision for Taxation	20,000	Debtors	50,000
		Bank	20,000
	3,20,000		3,20,000

Long Ltd. Will :

1. Discharge the Debentures @ 8% premium by issue of 7% Debentures in Long Ltd. at 10% Discount.
2. Issue 3 shares of Long Ltd. at market price of Rs. 11 for 2 shares of Short Ltd.;
3. Pay Rupees 2 in cash for each share of Short Ltd.; and
4. Pay absorption expenses Rs. 3,000.

Short Ltd. sells the investments for Rs. 32,000, one-third of the shares received from Long Ltd. are sold @ 10.50 each. Tax liability is determined at Rs. 24,000. Before transfer Short Ltd. declares and pays 10% provision.

Long Ltd. values Land and Buildings at Rs. 1,00,000. Plant at 10% below book value. Stock at Rs. 35,000 and Debtors subject to 5% provision.

Show :   1. Ledger Accounts in the books of Short Ltd.

2. Journal entries and Balance Sheet in the books of Long Ltd.

Solution :

Purchase Consideration
(Net Payment Method)

Whom Payable	What Payable	How Payable	Rs.
1) 8% Debentures in Long Ltd.	7% Debentures	60,000 + 8% premium i.e. 4,800	64,800
2) Equity shares Long Ltd.	Equity shares in Long Ltd.	2 : 3 i.e. 16,000 : 24,000 24,000 shares in long Ltd. at Rs. 11 per share	2,64,000
3) Equity Shares	Cash	Rs. 2 × 16,000	32,000
4) Short Ltd.	Cash (Absorption Expenses)	3,000	3,000
		Purchase Consideration	3,63,800

Calculation of Goodwill

Purchase consideration		3,63,800
Less Net Worth/Assets		
L & B	1,00,000	
Plant	72,000	
Debtors	47,500	
Stock	35,000	
Cash	4,000	2,58,500
Goodwill		1,05,300

In the Books of Short Ltd.

Realisation A/c

Dr. | | | | Cr.

Particulars	Rs.	Particulars	Rs.
To Goodwill A/c	20,000	By Bank A/c (Sale of	
To Land & Buildings A/c	80,000	investments)	32,000
To Plant A/c	80,000	By Long Ltd.'s A/c (Purchase	
To Investments A/c	30,000	Price)	3,63,800
To Stock A/c	40,000		
To Debtors A/c	50,000		
To Bank A/c (Transfer)	4,000		
To Bank A/c (Expenses)	3,000		
To Income tax A/c	4,000		
To 8% Debentures A/c (premium)	4,800		
To Shares in Long Ltd.'s A/c			
(Loss on sale)	4,000		
To Shareholders A/c (profit)	76,000		
	3,95,800		3,95,800

Long Ltd.'s A/c

Dr. | | | | Cr.

Particulars	Rs.	Particulars	Rs.
To Realisation A/c	3,63,800	By Shares A/c	2,64,000
		By 7% Debentures A/c	64,800
		By Bank A/c	35,000
	3,63,800		3,63,800

8% Debentures A/c

Dr. | | | | Cr.

Particulars	Rs.	Particulars	Rs.
To 7% Debentures in		By Balance b/d	60,000
Long Ltd.'s A/c	64,800	By Realisation A/c	4,800
	64,800		64,800

Dr.		Shares in Long Ltd. A/c		Cr.
Particulars	**Rs.**	**Particulars**		**Rs.**
To Long Ltd.'s A/c	2,64,000	By Bank A/c (Sale of 8,000 Shares at Rs. 10.50)		84,000
		By Realisation A/c (Loss on sale)		4,000
		By Shareholders A/c		1,76,000
	2,64,000			2,64,000

Dr.		Shareholders A/c		Cr.
Particulars	**Rs.**	**Particulars**		**Rs.**
To Shares in Long Ltd.'s A/c	1,76,000	By Share Capital A/c		1,60,000
To Bank A/c	87,000	By General Reserve A/c		25,000
		By Profit & Loss A/c		2,000
		By Realisation A/c (Profit)		76,000
	2,63,000			2,63,000

Dr.		Provision for Taxation A/c		Cr.
Particulars	**Rs.**	**Particulars**		**Rs.**
To Income Tax A/c	24,000	By Balance		20,000
		By Realisation A/c (Excess over Provision)		4,000
	24,000			24,000

Dr.		Bank A/c		Cr.
Particulars	**Rs.**	**Particulars**		**Rs.**
To Balance	20,000	By Dividend (@ 10%) A/c		16,000
To Long Ltd.'s A/c	35,000	By Realisation A/c (Transfer)		4,000
To Realisation A/c (sale of Investments)	32,000	By Realisation A/c (Expenses)		3,000
		By Sundry Creditors A/c		37,000
To Shares in Long Ltd.'s A/c	84,000	By Provision for taxation A/c		24,000
		By Shareholders A/c		87,000
	1,71,000			1,71,000

Notes : 1. As 10% Dividend is paid before transfer to new company. Bank Balance and Profit & Loss A/c are reduced by the amount of Dividend i.e. Rs. 16,000.

In the Books of Long Ltd.
Journal Entries.

Date	Particulare	L.F.	Dr. Rs.	Cr. Rs.
	Business purchase A/c Dr.		3,63,800	
	To Liquidator of Short Ltd. A/c			3,63,800
	(Being business Purchased)			
	Land & Buildings A/c Dr.		100,000	
	Plant A/c Dr.		72,000	
	Debtors A/c Dr.		50,000	
	Stock A/c		35,000	
	Bank A/c Dr.		4,000	
	Goodwill A/c Dr.		1,05,300	
	(Balancing figure)			
	To Provision for			
	Bad debts A/c			2,500
	To Business Purchase A/c			3,63,800
	(Being Assets taken over)			
	Liquidator of short Ltd. A/c Dr.		3,63,800	
	Dis. on issue of Debentures A/c Dr.		7,200	
	To Share Capital A/c			2,40,000
	To Share Premium A/c			24,000
	To 7% Debentures A/c			72,000
	To Bank A/c			35,000
	(Being purchase consideration paid.)			

(**Note :** Debentures are issued at 10% discount. Therefore, to pay off Rs. 64,800 of the Debentureholders of Short Ltd. 7% Debentures of Rs. 72,000 must be issued i.e. face value of Rs. 72,000 less 10% discount Rs. 7,200 = 64,800.)

Balance Sheet of Long Ltd. (After Absorption) as on 1st April 2014

Liabilities	Rs.	Assets	Rs.
Share Capital :		Goodwill	1,05,300
24,000 shares of		Land & Building	1,00,000
Rs. 10 each	2,40,000	Plant	72,000
Share Premium	24,000	Stock	35,000
7% Debenture	72,000	Debtors 50,000	
Bank Overdraft	31,000	Provision for Bad Debts. 2500	47,500
		Discount on Issue of 7%	
		Debenture	7,200
	3,67,000		3,67,000

Problem No. 15 : Following is the Balance Sheet of Govind Ltd. as on 31st March, 2014.

Liabilities	Rs.	Assets	Rs.
Share Capital :		Goodwill	4,00,000
20,000 Equity Shares of		Land & Building	15,60,000
Rs. 100 each fully paid	20,00,000	Plant & Machinery	14,00,000
Reserve Fund	5,00,000	Patent Rights	3,50,000
Sinking Fund	1,00,000	Stocks	2,00,000
Workmen's accident Comp-		Sundry Debtors	4,00,000
ensation Fund (Estimated		Investment against	
Liabilities Rs. 9,000)	50,000	Sinking Fund	1,00,000
Employees Profit Sharing Fund	1,00,000	Cash at Bank	30,000
Staff provident Fund	1,50,000		
Sundry Creditors	1,40,000		
'A' Debentures	4,00,000		
'B' Debentures	10,00,000		
	44,40,000		44,40,000

Ramkrishna Ltd. absorbed Govind Ltd. on the date of its above Balance Sheet, the consideration being :

1. The Taking over of the liabilities.

2. The payment of cost of absorption (as part of purchase consideration) not exceeding Rs. 8,000.

3. The repayment of the 'B' Debentures at a premium 5% in cash.

4. The discharge of 'A' Debentures at a premium of 10% by the issue of 6% Debentures in Ramkrishna Ltd. at par.

5. A payment of Rs. 15 per share in cash.

6. Allotment of one 7% preference share of Rs. 100 each fully paid and five equity shares of Rs. 100 each fully paid for every four equity shares in Govind Ltd. The actual cost of absorption came to Rs. 10,000. Stock of Govind Ltd. includes goods valued at Rs. 56,000 purchased from Ramkrishna Ltd. which company invoices goods at cost plus $16\frac{2}{3}\%$. The creditors include Rs. 80,000 due by Govind Ltd. to Ramkrishna Ltd. The directors of Ramkrishna Ltd. decided to create a provision of 5% on sundry debtors against doubtful debts.

You are required to : (a) Prepare the following ledger accounts in the books of

Govind Ltd. (1) Realisation Account, (2) Ramkrishna Ltd. Account, (3) Sundry Shareholders Account.

(b) Pass Journal Entries in the books of Ramkrishna Ltd. and

(c) Show the working of purchase consideration.

Solution :

Calculation of Purchase Consideration

For whom	Mode of Payment	Rs.
1. Realisation Expenses	Cash	8,000
2. B Debentureholders @ 5% premium	Cash	10,50,000
3. A Debentureholders @ Rs. 10% premium	Debentures	4,40,000
4. Equity Shareholders @ Rs. 15 per share for 20,000 shares	Cash	3,00,000
7% Preference Shares @ 1 share for 4 shares i.e. 5,000 Pref. Shares of Rs. 100 each	Pref. shares	5,00,000
5. Eq. Shares for every 4 Shares i.e. 25,000 Shares of Rs. 100 each	Eq. shares	25,00,000
Total Purchase Price		47,98,000

Notes :

1. Since stock of Govind Ltd. includes Rs. 56,000 stock on which Ramkrishna Ltd. had made a profit $16\frac{2}{3}$ % on cost, the profit Rs. 8,000 included in this stock is cancelled while recording the stock in Ramkrishna Ltd.

2. Creditors of Govind Ltd. included Rs. 80,000 due to Ramkrishna Ltd. Hence, internal indebtedness is also cancelled.

In the Books of Govind Ltd.

Dr.   **Realisation A/c**   Cr.

Particulars	Rs.	Particulars	Rs.
To Sundry Assets A/c	44,40,000	By Creditors A/c	1,40,000
To Bank (Expenses) A/c	10,000	By Staff Provident Fund A/c	1,50,000
To A Debentureholders A/c	40,000	By Employees Profit	
To B Debentureholders A/c	50,000	Sharing Fund A/c	1,00,000
To Equity Shareholders A/c	6,57,000	By Workmen's Accdt.	
(Profit)		Comp. Fund A/c	9,000
		By Ramkrishna Ltd.'s A/c	47,98,000
	51,97,000		51,97,000

Dr.   **Ramkrishna Ltd.'s A/c**   Cr.

Particulars	Rs.	Particulars	Rs.
To Realisation A/c	47,98,000	By Equity Shares A/c	25,00,000
		By 7% Pref. Shares A/c	5,00,000
		By 6% Debentures A/c	4,40,000
		By Bank A/c	13,58,000
	47,98,000		47,98,000

Dr.   **Shareholders A/c**   Cr.

Particulars	Rs.	Particulars	Rs.
To Equity shares in Ramkrishna Ltd.'s A/c	25,00,000	By Share Capital A/c	20,00,000
		By Res. Fund A/c	5,00,000
To 7% pref. Shares in		By Sinking Fund A/c	1,00,000
Ramkrishna Ltd.'s A/c	5,00,000	By Workmen's Comp. Fund A/c	41,000
To Bank A/c	2,98,000	By Realisation A/c	6,57,000
	32,98,000		32,98,000

Journal Entries in the books of Ramkrishna Ltd.

Date	Particulars		L.F.	Dr. Rs.	Cr. Rs.
1	Business Purchase A/c	Dr.		47,98,000	
	To Liquidator of Govind Ltd. A/c				47,98,000
	(Being purchase of business of Govind Ltd.)				
2	Land & Buildings A/c	Dr.		15,60,000	
	Plant & Machinery A/c	Dr.		14,00,000	
	Patent Rights A/c	Dr.		3,50,000	
	Stock A/c	Dr.		1,92,000	
	Sundry Debtors A/c	Dr.		4,00,000	
	Investments A/c	Dr.		1,00,000	
	Bank A/c	Dr.		30,000	
	Goodwill A/c	Dr.		11,85,000	
	To Provision for D/Debts A/c				20,000
	To Sundry Creditors A/c				1,40,000
	To Staff Provident Fund A/c				1,50,000
	To Employees Profit Sharing Fund A/c				1,00,000

Date	Particulars	L.F.	Dr. Rs.	Cr. Rs.
	To Workmen's comp. Fund A/c			9,000
	To Business Purchase A/c			47,98,000
	(Being Assets & Liabilities taken over from Govind Ltd.)			
3	Sundry Creditors A/c Dr.		80,000	
	To sundry Debtors A/c			80,000
	(Being cancellation of internal indebtedness)			
4	Liquidator of Govind A/c Dr.		47,98,000	
	To Equity Share Capital A/c			25,00,000
	To 7% pref. Share Capital A/c			5,00,000
	To 6% Debentures A/c			4,40,000
	To Bank A/c			13,58,000
	(Being settlement of purchase price.)			

Problem No. 16 : The Balance Sheet of Venus Co. Ltd. and Apollo Co. Ltd. as on 31st March, 2014.

Venus Ltd.

Liabilities	Rs.	Assets	Rs.
Share Capital :		Sundry Assets	3,37,000
900 shares of Rs. 270 each	2,43,000	Cash	700
General Reserve	80,700		
Profit & Loss A/c	3,000		
Sundry Creditors	11,000		
	3,37,700		3,37,700

Apollo Ltd.

Liabilities	Rs.	Assets	Rs.
Share Capital :		Sundry Assets	8,71,500
4,000 shares of Rs.150 each	6,00,000	Cash	5,500
General Reserve	2,57,000		
Profit & Loss A/c	7,000		
Sundry Creditors	13,000		
	8,77,000		8,77,000

It was proposed that Venus Ltd. be absorbed by Apollo Ltd. and the following arrangement was accepted by them.

The holder of every three shares in Venus Ltd. was to receive five shares in Apollo Ltd. plus as much cash as is necessary to adjust the right of shareholders of both the companies in accordance with the intrinsic value of the shares as per their Balance Sheets.

Show the working of purchase consideration and give journal entries and Balance Sheet of Apollo Ltd.

Solution :

$$\text{Intrinsic Value} = \frac{\text{Value of Net Assets}}{\text{No. of shares issued and subscribed}}$$

Accordingly, intrinsic value of each share of Venus Ltd. and Apollo Ltd. is arrived at as under :

	Venus Ltd.	Apollo Ltd.
Value of Assets	3,37,700	8,77,000
Less : Value of liabilities i.e. Creditors	11,000	13,000
Value of Net Assets	3,26,700	8,64,000
	3,26,700	8,64,000
Therefore, Intrinsic Value =	900	4,000
	Rs. 363	Rs. 216
	per share	per share

Purchase Consideration :

Venus Ltd. to receive five shares for its every three shares and balance in cash :

	Rs.
The Intrinsic value of 3 shares is =	1,089
(363 × 3)	
Less : Intrinsic Value of 5 shares =	1,080
(216 × 5)	
Difference to be received in cash =	9

This means Venus Ltd. is to receive cash at the rate of Rs. 9 per 3 shares. Hence, the total purchase price =

(i) For every 3 shares in Venus Ltd.
   5 Shares in Apollo Ltd.

   i.e. $\dfrac{900}{3} \times 5 = 1500$ Shares at Rs. 150 each = 2,25,000

(ii) Cash $= \dfrac{900 \times 9}{3}$ 2,700

Purchase Consideration   2,27,700

Journal Entries in the books of Apollo Ltd.

Date	Particulars		L.F.	Dr. Rs.	Cr. Rs.
1	Business Purchases A/c	Dr.		2,27,700	
	To Liquidator of Venus Ltd. A/c				2,27,700
	(Being Business of Venus Ltd. Acquired)				
2	Sundry Assets A/c	Dr.		3,37,000	
	Cash A/c	Dr.		700	
	To Sundry Creditors A/c				11,000
	To Capital Reserve A/c				99,000
	To Liquidator of Venus Ltd.'s A/c				2,27,700
	(Being Assets & Liabilities taken over form and purchase consideration payable to Venus Ltd.)				
3	Liquidator of Venus Ltd.'s A/c	Dr.		2,27,700	
	To Share Capital A/c				2,25,000
	To Cash A/c				2700
	(Being payment of purchase Price in cash and by issue of 1500 shares of Rs. 150 each as fully paid)				

Note :

1) Calculation of Capital Reserve

	Rs.
Net Assets	
3,37,000 + 700 - 11000 =	3,26,700
Less Purchase consideration	2,27,700
Capital Reserve	99,000

In the Books of Apollo Ltd.
Balance Sheet as on 1-4-2014 (After Absorption)

Liabilities	Rs.	Assets	Rs.
Share Capital :		Sundry Assets	12,08,500
5,500 shares of Rs.150		Cash	3,500
each of which 1,500 issued to			
vendors without receiving cash	8,25,000		
Capital Reserve	99,000		
General Reserve	2,57,000		
Profit & Loss A/c	7,000		
Sundry Creditors	24,000		
	12,12,000		12,12,000

Problem No. 17 : Uptodate Ltd. has agreed to acquire the goodwill and assets (except stock) of Slowdown Ltd. as on 31st March, 2014 on which date the Balance Sheet of Slowdown Ltd. was as under :

Balance Sheet
as on 31-3-2014

Liabilities	Rs.	Assets	Rs.
Share Capital :		Fixed Assets	:
16,000 shares of Rs.100 each	1,60,000	Goodwill	20,000
Reserves	43,000	Freehold Property	80,000
9% Debentures	60,000	Machinery	80,000
Current liabilities & Provision	57,000	Current Assets :	
		Stocks	30,000
		Investments	40,000
		Sundry Debtors	50,000
		Bank Balance	20,000
	3,20,000		3,20,000

The consideration of acquisition agreed was as under :
  (a) Discharge of 9% debentures @ 10% premium by issue of 12% debentures in Uptodate Ltd.
  (b) Issue of 3 shares of Rs. 10 each in Uptodate Ltd. at market price of Rs. 12/- for every 2 shares of Slowdown Ltd.

(c) Payment of Rs. 2.50 in cash for each share in Slowdown Ltd.

(d) Acquisition expenses of Rs. 3,000/- to be met by Uptodate Ltd.

Slowdown Ltd. sold its stock (which was not taken over) at Rs. 32,000 and one third of the shares received from Uptodate Ltd; @ Rs. 12.50 each. Current Liabilities and Provisions (which were also not taken over) were settled at Rs. 55,000. Before the final liquidation it also declared a dividend of 12.50%.

Uptodate Ltd. valued freehold property at Rs. 1,20,000; machinery at Rs. 75,000; Investment at 10% increase and sundry debtors at 10% less. You are required to give -

(i) Ledger Accounts to close the books of Slowdown Ltd.

(ii) Opening Journal entries in the books of Uptodate Ltd.

Solution :

Calculation of Purchase Consideration

Purchase Consideration	Mode of Payment	Rs.
(i) Rs. 60,000 Debentures at 10% Premium	12% Debentures	66,000
(ii) For 16,000 shares, 24,000 shares at the rate of 3 shares for every 2 shares. Price of each share is Rs. 12 i.e. 24,000 × 12	Shares	2,88,000
(iii) Rs. 2.50 per share in cash i.e. 16,000 × 2.50	Cash	40,000
(iv) Acquisition Expenses	Cash	3,000
Purchase Consideration		3,97,000

Dr.		**Realisation A/c**		Cr.

Particulars	Rs.	Particulars	Rs.
To Goodwill A/c	20,000	By Uptodate Co. Ltd. A/c	3,97,000
To Freehold Property A/c	80,000	(Purchase Price)	
To Machinery A/c	80,000	By Cash A/c	32,000
To Investments A/c	40,000	(Sale of Stock)	
To Sundry Debtors A/c	50,000	By Current Liabilities A/c	2,000
To Bank A/c	20,000	(Discount)	
To Stock A/c	30,000		
To 9% Debentureholders A/c (Premium)	6,000		
To Cash (Expenses) A/c	3,000		
To Shareholders (Profit) A/c	1,02,000		
	4,31,000		4,31,000

Dr.	Uptodate Ltd. A/c			Cr.
Particulars	**Rs.**	**Particulars**		**Rs.**
To Realisation A/c (Purchase Price)	3,97,000	By Equity shares A/c		2,88,000
		By 12% Debentures A/c		66,000
		By Cash		43,000
	3,97,000			3,97,000

Dr.	9% Debentureholders A/c		Cr.
Particulars	**Rs.**	**Particulars**	**Rs.**
To 12% Debentures in Uptodate Ltd.'s A/c	66,000	By 9% Debentures A/c	60,000
		By Realisation (Premium) A/c	6,000
	66,000		66,000

Dr.	Current Liabilities & Provisions		Cr.
Particulars	**Rs.**	**Particulars**	**Rs.**
To Cash A/c	55,000	By Balance b/d	57,000
To Realisation (Discount) A/c	2,000		
	57,000		57,000

Dr.	Equity Shares in Uptodate Ltd.		Cr.
Particulars	**Rs.**	**Particulars**	**Rs.**
To Uptodate Co. Ltd.'s A/c	2,88,000	By Cash A/c (sale of 8,000 shares @ Rs. 12.50 each)	1,00,000
To Equity shareholders A/c (Profit on sale of shares)	4,000	By Equity Shareholders A/c	1,92,000
	2,92,000		2,92,000

Dr.	Cash A/c		Cr.
Particulars	**Rs.**	**Particulars**	**Rs.**
To Uptodate Co. Ltd.'s A/c	43,000	By Realisation A/c (Expenses)	3,000
To Shares in Uptodate Ltd.'s A/c (Sale)	1,00,000	By Current Liabilities & Provisions A/c	55,000
To Realisation A/c (Sale of Stock)	32,000	By Dividend A/c	20,000
		By Equity shareholders A/c	97,000
	1,75,000		1,75,000

Dr.   **Equity shareholders A/c**   Cr.

Particulars	Rs.	Particulars	Rs.
To Dividend A/c	20,000	By Equity share capital A/c	1,60,000
To Equity shares in		By Realisation (Profit) A/c	1,02,000
Uptodate Ltd. A/c	1,92,000	By Reserves A/c	43,000
To Cash A/c	97,000	By Profit on sale of shares	
		in Uptodate Ltd.'s A/c	4,000
	3,09,000		3,09,000

(**Note :** It is presumed that the dividend declared is paid out of cash subsequently received and the original Bank Balance is taken over by Uptodate Ltd. along with other assets)

Journal Entries in the books of Uptodate Ltd.

Date	Particulars		L.F.	Dr. Rs.	Cr. Rs.
1	Business Purchase A/c	Dr.		3,97,000	
	To liquidator of Slowdown Ltd.'s A/c				3,97,000
	(Being Business of Slowdown purchased)				
2	Freehold Property A/c	Dr.		1,20,000	
	Machinery A/c	Dr.		75,000	
	Investment A/c	Dr.		44,000	
	Sundry Debtors A/c	Dr.		50,000	
	Bank A/c	Dr.		20,000	
	Goodwill A/c	Dr.		93,000	
	To Provision for Doubtful Debt. A/c				5,000
	To Business Purchase A/c				3,97,000
	(Being Assets taken over)				
3	Liquidators of Slowdown Ltd. A/c	Dr.		3,97,000	
	To 12% Debentures A/c				66,000
	To Equity share capital A/c				2,40,000
	To Equity share premium A/c				48,000
	To Bank A/c				43,000
	(Being Purchase Consideration paid.)				

Balance Sheet of Uptodate Ltd.
as on 1-4-2014

Liabilities	Rs.	Assets		Rs.
Share Capital :		Freehold property		1,20,000
Equity Share Capital	2,40,000	Machinery		75,000
Share premium	48,000	Investment		44,000
12% Debenture	66,000	Sundry Debtors	50,000	
Bank Overdraft	23,000	- R.D.D.	5000	45,000
		Goodwill		93,000
	3,77,000			3,77,000

Problem No. 18 : The following is the Balance Sheet of Roopa Ltd. as on 31st March, 2014.

Balance Sheet

Liabilities	Rs.	Assets	Rs.
Share capital -		Land & Building	1,05,000
3,000 Shares of		Plant & Machinery	80,000
Rs. 100 each	3,00,000	Vehicles	50,000
6% Debentures	10,000	Stock	40,000
Creditors	30,000	Debtors	30,000
Outstanding Expenses	2,000	Cash	32,000
		Underwriting Commission	5,000
Total Rs.	3,42,000	Total Rs.	3,42,000

Sona Ltd. absorbed Roopa Ltd. on the following terms :

1) Sona Ltd. acquired only the assets of Roopa Ltd. except cash balance.

2) The purchase consideration was fixed as five equity shares of Rs. 100 each at Rs. 120 each for six equity shares of Roopa Ltd. and 350, 6% preference shares of Rs. 100 each.

3) Realisation expenses amounted to Rs. 6,000 and were paid by Roopa Ltd.

4) The liquidator of Roopa Ltd. transferred the preference shares to creditors in full satisfaction of their claims.

5) Debentures were paid at a premium of 10%.

6) Outstanding expenses were paid in full and in addition, Roopa Ltd. had to pay Rs. 2100 as compensation to the workers.

7) Sona Ltd. valued Land and Building and Plant and Machinery at 10% depreciation,

Stock was reduced to market value which was Rs. 32,000 and Debtors were taken subject to 5% Reserve for Doubtful Debts.

Prepare Realisation Account, Shareholders' Account and Cash Account in the books of Roopa Ltd. and Balance Sheet of Sona Ltd.

Solution :

Calculation of Purchase Consideration (Payment Method)

Particulars	Rs.
Equity share in Sona Ltd.	
6 : 5 :: 3000 : 2500 × 120 =	3,00,000
6% preference Shares = 350 × 100 =	35,000
Total Rs.	3,35,000

In the Books of Roopa Ltd.

Realisation A/c

Dr.   Cr.

Particulars	Rs.	Particulars	Rs.
To Land & Building A/c	1,05,000	By Sona Ltd.'s A/c	3,35,000
To Plant & Machinery A/c	80,000		
To Vehicles A/c	50,000		
To Stock A/c	40,000		
To Debtors A/c	30,000		
To Creditors A/c (Loss)	5,000		
To Bank A/c (Realisation Exp.)	6,000		
To Debentureholders A/c	1,000		
To Bank A/c (Compensation)	2,100		
To Equity Shareholders (Profit)	15,900		
	3,35,000		3,35,000

Creditors' A/c

Dr.   Cr.

Particulars	Rs.	Particulars	Rs.
To 6% Preference Shares in Sona Ltd.'s A/c	35,000	By Balance b/d	30,000
		By Realisation A/c	5,000
	35,000		35,000

Dr.   **Outstanding Expenses A/c**   Cr.

Particulars	Rs.	Particulars	Rs.
To Bank A/c	2,000	By Balance b/d	2,000
	2,000		2,000

Dr.   **Debentureholders' A/c**   Cr.

Particulars	Rs.	Particulars	Rs.
To Bank A/c	11,000	By Balance b/d	10,000
		By Realisation A/c	1,000
	11,000		11,000

Dr.   **Equity Shareholders' A/c**   Cr.

Particulars	Rs.	Particulars	Rs.
To Underwriting Com. A/c	5,000	By Equity Share Capital A/c	3,00,000
To Equity Shares in Sona Ltd.' A/c	3,00,000	By Realisation A/c	15,900
To Bank A/c	10,900		
	3,15,900		3,15,900

Dr.   **Sona Ltd. A/c**   Cr.

Particulars	Rs.	Particulars	Rs.
To Realisation A/c	3,35,000	By Equity shares in Sona Ltd.'s A/c	3,00,000
		By 6% Preference shares in Sona Ltd.'s A/c	35,000
	3,35,000		3,35,000

Dr.   **Bank / Cash A/c**   Cr.

Particulars	Rs.	Particulars	Rs.
To Balance b/d	32,000	By Realisation A/c	6,000
		By Debenture holders A/c	11,000
		By Realisation A/c	2,100
		By Outstanding Exp. A/c	2,000
		By Equity Shareholders A/c	10,900
	32,000		32,000

Note : Compensation paid Rs. 6,000 is shown on the debit side of Realisation A/c and credit side of cash A/c.

In the Books of Sona Ltd.
Balance Sheet (After Absorption) as on 1st April 2014

Liabilities	Rs.	Assets	Rs.
2500 Equity share of Rs. 100 each	2,50,000	Goodwill	26,000
		Land & Building	1,15,500
350, 6% preference		Plant & Machinery	88,000
Shares of Rs. 100 each	35,000	Vehicles	45,000
Share premium	50,000	Debtors 30000	
		- R.D.D. 1500	28,500
		Stock	32,000
	3,35,000		3,35,000

Note :-

Calculation of Goodwill		Rs.
Purchase consideration		3,35,000
Less Assets taken over		
Land & Building	1,15,500	
Plant & Machinery	88,000	
Vehicles	45,000	
Stock	32,000	
Debtors	28,500	3,09,000
Goodwill		26,000

Problem No. 19 : Following was the Balance Sheet of Apple Ltd. as on 31st March 2014

Balance Sheet as on 31-3-2014

Liabilities	Rs.	Assets	Rs.
Share Capital :		Land & Building	1,40,000
2,000 shares of Rs.100 each	2,00,000	Plant & Machinery	1,10,000
General Reserves	64,000	Stock	98,000
Profit & Loss A/c	60,000	Debtors	42,000
Bills Payable	42,000	Cash in Hand	14,000
Creditors	70,000	Advertising Suspenses A/c	32,000
	4,36,000		4,36,000

Apple Ltd. was absorbed by Banana Ltd. on the following terms :

1. Apple Ltd. agreed to write-off advertising suspense A/c against its own reserves.
2. Banana Ltd. revalued the assets of apple Ltd. as under :
   Land and Building Rs. 1,50,000, Plant & Machinery Rs. 1,04,000, Stock Rs. 1,20,000 and Debtors at Book value.
3. Banana Ltd. took over the assets and liabilities of Apple Ltd. and agreed to discharge the purchase consideration into 2,600 shares of Rs. 100 each at Rs. 110 per share and balance in cash.
4. Apple Ltd. paid its liquidation expenses of Rs. 4,000.
   Prepare Realisation A/c, Banana Ltd. A/c, Cash A/c and Shareholders A/c in the books of Apple Ltd. and opening Journal entries in the books of Banana Ltd.

Solution :

Calculation of Purchase Consideration

Particulars	Rs.	Rs.
Agreed Value of Assets taken		
Land & Building		1,50,000
Plant & Machinery		1,04,000
Stock		1,20,000
Debtors		42,000
Cash		14,400
Total		4,30,400
Less : Liabilities taken		
Creditors	70,000	
Bills Payable	42,000	1,12,400
Purchase Consideration		3,18,000

General Reserve Transferred to Shareholders' A/c as under

Particulars	Rs.
Balance as given	64,000
Less : Advertising Suspense A/c	32,000
Balance Transferred to Shareholders	32,000

In the Books of Apple Ltd.

Dr.   **Realisation A/c**   **Cr.**

Particulars	Rs.	Particulars	Rs.
To Land & Building A/c	1,40,000	By Creditors A/c	70,000
To Plant & Machinery A/c	1,10,000	By Bills Payable A/c	42,400
To Stock A/c	98,000	By Banana Ltd.'s A/c	3,18,000
To Debtors A/c	42,000	(Purchase Price)	
To Cash A/c	14,400		
To Cash A/c (Expenses)	4,000		
To Equity Shareholders A/c (profit)	22,000		
	4,30,400		4,30,400

Dr.   **Banana Ltd. A/c**   **Cr.**

Particulars	Rs.	Particulars	Rs.
To Realisation A/c	3,18,000	By Equity shares A/c	2,86,000
		By Cash A/c	32,000
	3,18,000		3,18,000

Dr.   **Cash A/c**   **Cr.**

Particulars	Rs.	Particulars	Rs.
To Balance b/d	14,400	By Realisation A/c (Transfer)	14,400
To Banana Ltd. A/c	32,000	By Realisation A/c (Expenses)	4,000
		By Equity Shareholders A/c	28,000
	46,400		46,400

Dr.   **Equity Shareholders A/c**   **Cr.**

Particulars	Rs.	Particulars	Rs.
To Equity Shares	2,86,000	By Share Capital A/c	2,00,000
To Cash	28,000	By General Reserve A/c	32,000
		By Profit & Loss A/c	60,000
		By Realisation A/c (Profit)	22,000
	3,14,000		3,14,000

In the Books of Banana Ltd. Journal Entries

Date	Particulars		L.F.	Dr. Rs.	Cr. Rs.
1	Business Purchase A/c	Dr,		3,18,000	
	To Apple Ltd. A/c				3,18,000
	(Purchase Price payable to Apple Ltd. for purchase of its business.)				
2	Land & Buildings A/c	Dr.		1,50,000	
	Plant & Machinery A/c	Dr.		1,04,000	
	Stock A/c	Dr.		1,20,000	
	Debtors A/c	Dr.		42,000	
	Cash A/c	Dr.		14,400	
	To Creditors A/c				70,000
	To Bills Payable A/c				42,400
	To Business Purchase A/c				3,18,000
	(Assets and Liabilities taken over from Apple Ltd. at the values stated above.)				
3	Apple Ltd.'s A/c	Dr.		3,18,000	
	To Equity Share capital A/c				2,60,000
	To Equity Share premium A/c				26,000
	To Cash A/c				32,000
	(Issued 2,600 Equity shares of Rs. 100 each at Rs. 110 per share as fully paid and paid cash in settlement of Purchase Price.)				

Problem No. 20 :

The following is the Balance sheet of Rupa Ltd. As on 31 st March, 2014

Liabilities	Rs.	Assets	Rs.
Share Capital :		Building	1,70,000
4000 Equity Shares of		Plant & Machinery	4,00,000
Rs. 100 each	4,00,000	Investment	50,600
General Reserve	50,000	Debtors	1,40,500
Profit & Loss A/c	5,600	Stock	80,700
5% Debentures	2,50,000	Cash at Bank	16,500
Creditors	1,28,700		
Dividend Equalisation Fund	24,000		
	8,58,300		8,58,300

Rupa Ltd. was absorbed by Dipa Ltd. on the above date, on the following terms and conditions, Dipa Ltd. to :

1) Assume all liabilities and to acquire all assets except investments which were sold by Rupa Ltd. For Rs. 45,500

2) Discharge the debentures at a discount of 5% by issue of 7% Debentures in Dipa Ltd.

3) Issue two shares of Rs. 60 each in Dipa Ltd. at Rs. 65 Per share and also pay Rs. 2 in cash to the shareholders of Rupa Ltd. in exchange for one share in Rupa Ltd.

4) Pay the cost of absorption for Rs. 1,500

With the consent of the shareholders, the Liquidator of Rupa Ltd. Sold off in open Market one fifth of the shares received from Dipa Ltd. at the average rate of Rs. 63 per share.

You are required to prepare.

   i) Statement of Purchase Consideration

  ii) Realisation A/c

 iii) Shareholder A/c

 iv) Bank A/c

  v) 5% Debentureholder A/c

 vi) Opening Journal Entries in the books of Dipa Ltd.   **(March 2011 - PUP)**

Solution :

Statement of Purchase Consideration.

For	Amount (Rs.)	Form
5% Debentureholders (2,50,000-12,500)	2,37,500	7% Debentures
Shareholders		
i) (8000 × 65)	5,20,000	Equity Shares
ii) Cash (4000 × 2)	8000	Cash
Cost of Absorption	1500	Cash
Purchase Consideration	7,67,000	

In the book of Rupa Ltd.
Realisation A/c

Particular	Rs	Particular	Rs
To Sundry Asset	8,58,300	By S. Liabilities	1,28,700
To Cash	1500	By Cash sale of Investment	45,500
To Equity Shareholder	93,900	By Dipa Ltd.	7,67,000
		By Debentureholders	12,500
	9,53,700		9,53,700

Equity Shareholders A/c

Particular	Rs	Particular	Rs
To shares in Dipa Ltd	4000	By Share Capital	4,00,000
To shares in Dipa Ltd	3,90,000	By General Reserve	50,000
To Bank	1,79,500	By Profit & Loss A/c	5,600
		By Dividend Equalisation Fund	24,000
		By Realisation	93,900
	5,73,500		5,73,500

Cash Bank A/c

Particular	Rs	Particular	Rs
To Dipa Ltd.	9,500	By Realisation	1,500
To Shares in Dipa Ltd	1,26,000	By Equity Shareholders	1,79,500
To Realisation	45,500		
	1,81,000		1,81,000

5% Debenturesholder A/c

Particular	Rs	Particular	Rs
To 7% Debentures in Dipa Ltd.	2,37,500	By 5% Debentures	2,50,000
To Realisation A/c	12,500		
	2,50,000		2,50,000

Opening Journal Entries in the books of Dipa Ltd

Date	Particulars		L.F.	Dr. Rs.	Cr. Rs.
1)	Business Purchase A/c	Dr.		17,67,000	
	To Liquidator of Rupa Ltd				17,67,000
2)	Building A/c	Dr.		1,70,000	
	Plant & Machinery A/c	Dr.		4,00,000	
	Debtors A/c	Dr.		1,40,500	
	Stock A/c	Dr.		80,700	
	Bank A/c	Dr.		16,500	
	Good will A/c	Dr.		88,000	
	To Creditors A/c				1,28,700
	To Business Purchase A/c				7,67,000
3)	Liquidator of Rupa Ltd A/c	Dr		7,67,000	
	To Equity Share Capital A/c (8000 × 60)				4,80,000
	To Share Premium A/c (8000 × 5)				40,000
	To 7% Debentures A/c				2,37,500
	To Cash A/c				9,500

Problem No. 21 : The Following are the Balance sheets of Express Limited and Super Fast Limited as on 31st March 2014

Balance sheet of Express Limited as on 31.3.2014

Liabilities	Rs.	Assets	Rs
Share Capital		Good will	1,00,000
10,000 Equity Shares of		Fixed Assets	7,50,000
Rs. 100 each	10,00,000	Stock	2,60,000
5% Debentures (Rs. 100 each)	2,50,000	Debtors	2,00,000
Creditors	3,60,000	Profit & Loss A/c	3,00,000
	16,10,000		16,10,000

Balance Sheet of Super Fast Ltd. as on 31-3-2014

Liabilities	Rs.	Assets	Rs.
Authorised Capital		Good will	1,50,000
20,000 Equity Shares of		Fixed Assets	12,00,000
Rs. 100 each	20,00,000	Stock	2,50,000
Issued Capital		Debtors	2,00,000
15,000 Equity Shares of		Cash and Bank	2,00,000
Rs. 100 each	15,00,000		
Profit & Loss A/c	2,00,000		
Creditors	3,00,000		
	20,00,000		20,00,000

Super Fast Limited agreed to absorb Express Limited upon the following terms

1) Payment of cash of Rs. 15 for every share in Express Limited.
2) The shareholders of Express Limited to receive one share in Super Fast Limited for every two shares held by them.
3) Payment in cash at Rs. 110 for every debentureholder in full discharge of debentures.
4) Expenses of liquidation amounted to Rs. 10,000 Which were paid by Super fast Ltd. (not included in purchase consideration)

You are required to :

a) Prepare Realisation A/c, Super Fast Ltd A/c, Equity Shares in Super Fast Ltd A/c, Cash A/c, Equity Shareholders A/c, 5% Debentureholders A/c in the books of Express Limited.
b) Pass Opening entries in the books of Super Fast Limited and prepare Balance Sheet of Super Fast Limited after absorption. **(Oct. 2012 - PUP)**

Solution :

Statement of Purchase Consideration

Particulars	Rs.
1) Cash Payment to Shareholders (15 × 10,000)	1,50,000
2) Issue of Shares in Superfast Ltd. to Share holder. (5000 × 100)	5,00,000
3) Cash Payment to Debenture holders	2,75,000
Purchase Considration	9,25,000

In the Books of Express Ltd.
Realisation A/c

To Good will	1,00,000	By Creditors	3,60,000
To Fix Assets	7,50,000	By Super Fast Ltd	9,25,000
To stock	2,60,000		
To Debtors	2,00,000	By Eq. Shareholder A/c	50,000
To 5% Debentureholders A/c	25,000		
	13,35,000		13,35,000

Super Fast Ltd A/c

To Realisation A/c	9,25,000	By Share in Super Fast Ltd A/c	5,00,000
		By Cash A/c	4,25,000
	9,25,000		9,25,000

Equity Shares in Super Fast Ltd A/c

To Super Fast Ltd	5,00,000	By Equity Shareholder A/c	5,00,000
	5,00,000		5,00,000

Cash A/c

To Super Fast Ltd	4,25,000	By Eq. Shareholder A/c	1,50,000
		By Debentureholder	2,75,000
	4,25,000		4,25,000

5% Debenture A/c

To Cash A/c	2,75,000	By 5% Debenture A/c	2,50,000
		By Realisation A/c	25,000
	2,75,00		2,75,000

Eq. Share Holder A/c

To P & L A/c	3,00,000	By Eq. Share Capital A/c	10,00,000
To Share in Super fast Ltd A/c	5,00,000		
To Cash A/c	1,50,000		
To Realisation A/c	50,000		
	10,00,000		10,00,000

Opening Enteries in the Books of Superfast Ltd.

Date	Particulas		L.F.	Debit Rs.	Credit Rs.
1)	Business Purchase A/c			9,25,000	
	To Liquidator of Express Ltd A/c				9,25,000
2)	Fixed Assets A/c	Dr.		7,50,000	
	Stock A/c	Dr.		2,60,000	
	Debtors A/c	Dr.		2,00,000	
	Good will A/c	Dr.		75,000	
	To Business Purchase A/c				9,25,000
	To Creditors A/c				3,60,000
3)	Liquidator of Express Ltd A/c	Dr.		9,25,000	
	To Share Capital A/c				5,00,000
	To Bank A/c				4,25,000
4)	Good will A/c	Dr.		10,000	
	To Bank A/c				10,000

Balance Sheet of Super Fast Ltd A/c

Liabilities	Rs	Assets	Rs
Share Capital		Good will	2,35,000
Authorised Capital		Fixed Assets	19,50,000
20,000 Shares of	20,00,000	Debtors	4,00,000
Rs. 100 each		Stock	5,10,000
Issued and Subscribed			
20,000 Shares of Rs. 100 each	20,00,000		
Profit and loss A/c	2,00,000		
Bank Over draft	2,35,000		
(2,00,000 + 35,000)			
Crditors	6,60,000		
	30,95,000		30,95,000

Problem No. 22 : Uma Ltd. has agreed to acquire the goodwill and assets except stock of Seema Ltd. As on 31st March 2013 on which date the Balance Sheet of Seema Ltd. Was as under.

Balance Sheet as on 31st March 2013

Liabilities	Rs	Assets	Rs
Share Capital		**Fixed Assets**	
16,000 Shares of Rs. 10 each	1,60,000	Good will	20,000
		Freehold Property	80,000
General Reserve	43,000	Machinery	80,000
9% Debentures	60,000	Investment	40,000
Current liabilities And		Current Assets :	
Provisions	57,000	Stock	30,000
		Sundry Debtors	50,000
		Bank Balance	20,000
	3,20,000		3,20,000

The consideration of acquisition agreed was as under.

1) Discharge of 9% debentures @ 10% Premium by issue of 12% Debentures in Uma Ltd.

2) Issue of 3 Shares of Rs. 10 each in Uma Ltd. at Market Price of Rs. 12 for every 2 Shares of Seema Ltd.

3) Payment of Rs. 2.50 in cash for each share in Seema Ltd.

4) Acquisition expenses of Rs. 3,000 to be met by Uma Ltd. as a part of purchase consideration

   Seema Ltd. Sold its stock (Which was not taken over) at Rs. 32,000 Current Liabilities and Provisions (Which were also not taken over were settled at Rs. 55,000

   Uma Ltd. Valued Freehold Property at Rs. 1,20,000, Machinery at Rs. 75,000, Investment at 10% increase and Sundry debtors at 10% less.

You are required to give :

1) Realisation A/c, Uma Ltd. A/c, Equity Shares in Uma Ltd. A/c, Cash A/c, 9% Debentureholder A/c and Equity Shareholders A/c in the books of Seema Ltd.

2) Opening Journal Entries in the books of Uma Ltd. and Balance Sheet After absorption.

(Oct. 2013 - PUP)

Calculation Parchase Consideration

Particulars	Amt (Rs.)	Payment	Rs.
1) 9% Debentureholders	66,000	1) 24000 Equity sheres at	2,88,000
2) Equity Shareholders	2,88,000	Rs. 12 each	
3) Equity Shareholders	40,000	2) 12% Debentures in Uma Ltd.	66,000
4) Liquidation Exp.	3,000	Cash	43,000
Parchase Consideration	3,97,000	Total	3,97,000

In the books of Seema Ltd
Realisation A/c

	Rs.		Rs.
To sundry Assets			
Good will	20,000	By Uma Ltd (P.C.)	3,97,000
Freehold Property	80,000	By Cash A/c (Sale of stock)	32,000
Machinery	80,000	By Current Liabilities &	2,000
Investments	40,000	Provisions (Discount)	
Stock	30,000		
Sundry Debtors	50,000		
Bank	20,000		
To 9% Debentureholders	6,000		
(Permium)			
To Cash A/c (Exp)	3,000		
To Equity Shareholders			
A/c (Profit)	1,02,000		
	4,31,000		4,31,000

Uma Ltd A/c

	Rs.		Rs.
To Realisation A/c (PC)	3,97,000	By Equity Shares in Uma Ltd A/c	2,88,000
		By 12% Debenture in Uma Ltd A/c	66,000
		By Cash A/c	43,000
	3,97,000		3,97,000

Equity Shares in Uma Ltd A/c

To Uma Ltd A/c	2,88,000	By Equity Shareholders A/c	2,88,000
	2,88,000		2,88,000

Cash Account

To Uma Ltd A/c	43,000	By Realisation A/c (Expenses)	3,000
To Realisation A/c	32,000	By Current Liab & Provisions	55,000
(Sale of Stock)		By Equity Shareholders	17,000
	75,000		75,000

9% Debentureholders A/c

To 12% Debentures in	66,000	By Debentures A/c	60,000
Uma Ltd A/c		By Realsiation A/c	6,000
		(Premium)	
	66,000		66,000

Equity Shareholders A/c

To Equity Shares in Uma Ltd.	2,88,000	By Equity Share Capital	1,60,000
To Cash A/c	17,000	By General Reserve	43,000
		By Realisation Profit	1,02,000
	305000		305000

Journal Entries in the books Uma Ltd

Date	Particulars		L.F.	Debit Rs.	Credit Rs.
1)	Business Purchase A/c	Dr.		3,97,000	
	To Liquidator of seema Ltd.				3,97,000
2)	Freehold Property A/c	Dr.		1,20,000	
	Machinery A/c	Dr.		75,000	
	Investment A/c	Dr.		44,000	
	Sundry Debtors A/c	Dr.		50,000	
	Bank A/c	Dr.		20,000	
	Good will A/c (Bal. Figure)			93,000	
	To R.D.D.				5,000
	To Business Purchase A/c				3,97,000
3)	Liquidator of Seema Ltd. A/c	Dr.		3,97,000	
	To 12% Debentures A/c				66,000
	To Equity share capital				2,40,000
	To Share Premium A/c				48,000
	To Cash A/c				43,000

Balance sheet of Uma Ltd as on 1.4.2013

Share Capital	Rs.	Fixed Assets		Rs.
24,000 Shares of Rs. 10 each	2,40,000	Good will		93,000
Reserve & Surplus :		Freehold Property		1,20,000
Share Premium A/c	48,000	Machinery		75,000
Secured Loans : 12% Debentures	66,000	Investment		44,000
Unsecured Loans :		**Current Assets**		
Bank Overdraft	23,000	Sundry Debtors	50,000	
		Less : R.D.D.	5,000	
				45,000
Current Liab & Provision	-	Cash in hand	-	
	3,77,000			3,77,000

Allocation of Marks

1) Pc   = 2 marks

2) Realisation A/c   = 3 marks

3) Equity Shareholders A/c   = 2 marks

4) Uma Ltd, Equity Share in Uma Ltd,

    Cash A/c, and Debenture holders A/c

    - one each 4 × 1   = 4 Marks

5) Entry No. 1   = 1 marks

6) Entry No. 2 & 3 = 2each 2 × 2   = 4 Marks

7) Balance Sheet   = 4 Marks

Problem No. 23 : Yash Ltd. Agreed to acquire the business of Jay Ltd. as on 31st March 2014 The Balance Sheet of Jay Ltd. as on that date was as follow.

Balance Sheet as on 31st March, 2014

Liabilities	Rs.	Assets	Rs.
Share Capital		**Fixed Assets**	
Authorised Capital		Good will	1,00,000
60,000 Equity Shares of		Land and Buildings	3,00,000
Rs. 10 each	6,00,000	Plant and Machinery	3,40,000
Issued, Subscribed		**Current Assets, Loans**	
and Paid up		**and Advances**	
60,000 Equity Shares	6,00,000	Stock	1,68,000
of Rs. 10 Each		Sundry Debtors	36,000
Reserve and Surplus :		Cash in hand	6,000
General Reserve	1,70,000	Cash at Bank	50,000
Profit and Loss	1,10,000		
Secured Loan :			
6% Debentures	1,00,000		
Current Liabilities			
and Provisions :			
Sundry Creditors	20,000		
	10,00,000		10,00,000

The Consideration payable by Yash Ltd. was agreed as follows.

i) A cash Payment of Rs. 2.50 per share in Jay Ltd.

ii) The issue of 90,000 Equity Shares of Rs. 10 Each in Yash Ltd. having an agreed value of Rs. 15 per share to equity Shareholders of Jay Ltd.

ii) The issue of such an amount of fully paid 8% debentures of Yash Ltd. at 96% as is sufficient to discharge the 6% debentures of Jay Ltd. at Premium of 20%

While computing the agreed consideration, the directors of Yash Ltd. Valued Land & Building at Rs. 6,00,000, Plant and Machinery at Rs. 6,00,000, Stock at Rs. 1,42,000 and Debtors at their face value subject to a reserve of 5% to cover doubtful debts. The cost of liquidation of Jay Ltd. Came to Rs. 5000

You are required to prepare.

i) Statement of Purchase Consideration

ii) Realisation Account, Equity Shareholders A/c, Yash Ltd A/c, 6% Debentureholders A/c, Equity Shares in Yash Ltd A/c, in the Books of Jay Ltd.

iii) Opening Journal Entries and Balance Sheet in the books of Yash Ltd.

(April 2014-PUP)

Calculation of Purchase Consideration

		Rs.
i)	Cash payment of × 2.50 Pershare	1,50,000
ii)	Issue of Equity Shares (90,000 × 15)	13,50,000
iii)	8% Debentures	1,20,000
	Purchase Consideration	16,20,000

In the books of Jay Ltd
Realisation A/c

	Rs.		Rs.
To Sundry Assets :		**By Sundry Liabilities :**	
Goodwill	1,00,000	Sundry Creditors	20,000
Land & Building	3,00,000	By Yash Ltd	16,20,000
Plant & Machinery	3,40,000		
Stock	1,68,000		
Sundry Debtors	36,000		
Cash in hand	6000		
Cash at Bank	50,000		
To 6% Debentureholders	20,000		
To Bank (Exp.)	5000		
To Equity Shareholders (Profit)	6,15,000		
	16,40,000		16,40,000

Yash Ltd A/c

	Rs.		Rs.
To Realisation A/c	16,20,000	By Equity Shares in Yash Ltd	13,50,000
		By Bank	1,50,000
		By 8% Debentures in Yash Ltd	1,20,000
	16,20,000		16,20,000

Equity Shares in Yash Ltd

	Rs.		Rs.
To Yash Ltd	13,50,000	By Equity Shareholders A/c	13,50,000
	13,50,000		13,50,000

Equity Shareholders A/c

To Equity Shares in Yash Ltd	13,50,000	By Equity Shares Capital	6,00,000
To Bank	1,45,000	By General Reserve	1,70,000
		By P & L A/c	1,10,000
		By Realisation A/c (Profit)	6,15,000
	14,95,000		14,95,000

6% Debentureholders A/c

To Debentures in Yash Ltd	1,20,000	By 6% Debentures	1,00,000
		By Realisation A/c	20,000
	1,20,000		1,20,000

Journal Entries in the books of Yash Ltd

Date	Particulars		L.F.	Debit Rs.	Credit Rs.
1)	Business Purchase A/c	Dr.		16,20,000	
	To Liquidator of Jay Ltd				16,20,000
2)	Land & Building			6,00,000	
	Plant & Machinery A/c	Dr.		6,00,000	
	Stock A/c	Dr.		1,42,000	
	Debtors A/c	Dr.		36,000	
	Cash in hand A/c	Dr.		6,000	
	Cash at Bank A/c	Dr.		50,000	
	Good will A/c (Bal. figure)	Dr.		2,07,800	
	To Sundry Creditors A/c				20,000
	To R.D.D.				1800
	To Business Purchase A/c				16,20,000
3)	Liquidators Jay Ltd	Dr.		16,20,000	
	Discount on Issue of Deb. A/c	Dr.		5,000	
	To Equity Share Capital A/c				9,00,000
	To Share Premium A/c				4,50,000
	To 8% Debentures A/c				1,25,000
	To Bank A/c				1,50,000

Balance Sheet of Yash Ltd as on 31-3-2014

	Rs.		Rs.
Equity Share Capital :		Good will	2,07,800
Shares of Rs. 10 each	9,00,000	Land & Building	6,00,000
Share Premium	4,50,000	Plant & Machinery	6,00,000
8% Debentures	1,25,000	Stock	1,42,000
Bank Overdraft	94,000	Debtors 36,000	
		Less : R.D.D. 1,800	
Sundry Creditors	20,000		34,200
		Discount on Issue of	5000
		Debentures	
	15,89,000		15,89,000

Problems on External Reconstruction

Problem No. 24 :

Trial Balance of A Co. Ltd.

Particulars	Dr. Rs.	Cr. Rs.
Share capital :		
5,000 shares of Rs. 10 each fully paid		50,000
Creditors		26,500
Patent Rights	48,000	
Debtors	4,500	
Stock	10,000	
Preliminary Expenses	1,800	
Profit & Loss A/c	12,050	
Cash	150	
	76,500	76,500

Efforts to secure sufficient new capital to pay off the liabilities and place the concern on a sound basis have proved unsuccessful, it was decided to reconstruct and the following scheme was submitted to and approved by the shareholders and creditors.

1. The company to go into voluntary liquidation and a new company B Ltd. having a normal capital of Rs. 1,00,000 to be formed to take over the assets and liabilities of the old company.
2. The assets to be taken over at book values with the exception of the patent rights, which were to be subjected to adjustment.
3. The creditors to be discharged by the new company on the following basis :

		Rs.
(a)	Preferential to be paid in full	500
(b)	Unsecured to be discharged by cash Composition of 50 paise in a rupee	13,400
(c)	Unsecured to be discharged by issue of 6% Debentures fully paid at bonus of 10%	12,600
		26,500

4. 5,000 Shares of Rs. 10 each, Rs. 5 paid up to be issued to the shareholders in the old company, payable Rs. 2.50 on application and Rs. 2.50 on allotment.
5. The cost of liquidation Rs. 250 to be paid by the new company as part of the purchase consideration.

Pass journal entries to close the books of A Co. Ltd. and also pass opening entries and Balance Sheet in the books of B Ltd.

Assume that all the shares and debentures have been allotted and all cash in respect of shares has been received.

Solution :

Calculation of Purchase Consideration

For	Mode of Payment	Rs.
1. For Creditors - (a) Preferential Creditors	in Cash	500
(b) Unsecured creditors for Rs. 13,400 @ 50 paise per rupee	in Cash	6,700
(c) Unsecured Creditors for Rs. 12,600 at 10% Bonus	6% Debentures	13,860
2. For Shareholders - 5000 shares of Rs. 10 each Rs. 5 paid-up	Shares	25,000
3. Cost of Liquidation	in Cash	250
Purchase Consideration		46,310

Payment of Purchase Price

Shares	25,000
6% Debentures	13,860
Cash	7,450
Purchase Price	46,310

Journal Entries in the Books of A Co. Ltd.

Date	Particulars	L.F.	Dr. Rs.	Cr. Rs.
	Realisation A/c Dr.		62,650	
	To Patent Rights A/c			48,000
	To Debtors A/c			4,500
	To Stock A/c			10,000
	To Cash A/c			150
	(Being transfer of assets to Realisation.)			
	B Ltd. A/c Dr.		46,310	
	To Realisation A/c			46,310
	(Being purchase price to be received from B Ltd.)			
	Sundry Creditors A/c Dr.		6,700	
	To Realisation A/c			6,700
	(Being Discount received from unsecured creditors for Rs. 13,400.)			
	Realisation A/c Dr.		250	
	To Cash A/c			250
	(Being Payment of Liquidation Expenses.)			
	Realisation A/c Dr.		1,260	
	To Sundry Creditors A/c			1,260
	(Being 10% Bonus payable to creditors for Rs. 12,600 who accept 6% debentures in B Ltd.)			
	Shareholders A/c Dr.		25,000	
	To Realisation A/c			11,150
	To Profit & Loss A/c			12,050
	To preliminary Expenses A/c			1,800
	(Being Loss on Realisation & Balances on profit & Loss A/c and preliminary expenses A/c transferred to Shareholders.)			

Date	Particulars		L.F.	Dr. Rs.	Cr. Rs.
	Cash A/c	Dr.		7,450	
	6% Debentures in B Ltd. A/c	Dr.		13,860	
	Shares in B Ltd. A/c	Dr.		25,000	
	To B Ltd. A/c				46,310
	(Being Received cash 6% Debentures and 5,000 shares of Rs. 10 each, Rs. 5 per share paid-up in settlement of purchase price.)				
	Sundry Creditors A/c	Dr.		21,060	
	To Cash A/c				7,200
	To 6% debentures in B Ltd. A/c				13,860
	(Being paid cash and issued debentures in B Ltd. to creditors as agreed.)				
	Share Capital A/c	Dr.		50,000	
	To Shareholders A/c				50,000
	(Being Balance on share capital transferred to shareholders.)				
	Shareholders A/c	Dr.		25,000	
	To Shares in B Ltd. A/c				25,000
	(Being Issued shares in B Ltd. to shareholders in satisfaction of their dues.)				

Journal Entries in the Books of B Co. Ltd.

Date	Particulars		L.F.	Dr. Rs.	Cr. Rs.
	Debtors A/c	Dr.		4,500	
	Stock A/c	Dr.		10,000	
	Cash A/c	Dr.		150	
	Patent Rights A/c (Balancing figure)	Dr.		31,660	
	To A Co. Ltd.				46,310
	(Being Assets taken over from and purchase price payable to A co. Ltd.)				
	Cash A/c	Dr.		12,500	
	To Share Application A/c				12,500
	(Being received application money on 5,000 shares @ Rs. 2.50 per Share)				

Date	Particulars	L.F.	Dr. Rs.	Cr. Rs.
	Share Application A/c Dr. To Share Capital A/c (Being application money is transferred to share capital.)		12,500	12,500
	Share Allotment A/c Dr. To Share capital A/c (Being allotment money due on 5,000 shares @ Rs. 2.50 per share.)		12,500	12,500
	Cash A/c Dr. To Share Allotment A/c (Being received on account of allotment.)		12,500	12,500

	A Co. Ltd. A/c Dr.
	   To Cash A/c
	   To 6% Debentures A/c
	   To Share Capital A/c
	(Issued 5,000 shares of Rs. 10 each Rs.5 paid-up 6% debentures of Rs. 13,860 and paid cash, Rs. 7,450 in payment of purchase price to A Ltd.)
			46,310	7,450
				13,860
				25,000

In the Books of 'B' Ltd.
Balance Sheet (After Reconstruction)
as on....

Liabilities	Rs.	Assets	Rs.
Share Capital **Authorised Capital** 10,000 Equity Shares of Rs. 10 each	 1,00,000	Cash in Hand (150 + 12,500 + 12,500- 7450) Patents Right Debtors	 17,700 31,660 4,500
Paid up Capital 10,000 Equity Shares of Rs. 10 each, Rs. 5 Paid.	 50,000	Stock	10,000
6% debentures	13,860		
	63,860		63,860

Problem No. 25 : The Shareholders and creditors of Small Co. Ltd. decided to reconstruct the company on account of its heavy losses. The financial position of the company as on 31st December 2014 was as under :

Liabilities	Rs.	Assets	Rs.
Share Capital		Land & Building	2,00,000
6,000 Equity Shares of	6,00,000	Plant & Machinery	1,00,000
Rs. 100 each		Stock in Trade	72,000
Sundry Creditors	52,000	Furniture	35,000
Bank Loan	20,000	Sundry Debtors	97,000
		Cash at Bank	28,000
		Profit & Loss Account	1,40,000
	6,72,000		6,72,000

The Scheme of reconstruction includes the following terms :
   a) The new company called Big Ltd. was to be formed with a capital of Rs. 10,00,000 divided into 10,000 shares of Rs. 100 each.
   b) The new company will take over only the assets of the old company.
   c) The new company will issue 8,000 shares of Rs. 100 each credited at Rs. 50 paid up and pay Rs. 75,000 in cash.
   d) Cost of liquidation amounted to Rs. 3,000 to be paid by the old company.
   e) The new company decided to write off Profit & Loss A/c completely and plant and Machinery by Rs. 10,000 and Land & Building as required.
   f) The new company made a call of Rs. 25 per share on the partly paid shares and it was received in full.

   You are required to prepare necessary ledger accounts in the books of Small Co. Ltd. and Journal Entries in the books of Big Co. Ltd. and Balance Sheet. (P.U.)

Solution :

Statement of Purchase Consideration

For	Mode of Payment	Rs.
1. Equity Shareholders	i) Equity Shares (8,000 shares at Rs. 50 each)	4,00,000
2. Expenses	ii) Cash	75,000
Purchase Consideration		4,75,000

In the Books of Small Co. Ltd.

Dr.　　　**Realisation A/c**　　　Cr.

Particulars		Rs.	Particulars		Rs.
To Sundry Assets A/c (Book Value)			By Sundry Liabilities A/c (Book Value)		
Land & Building	2,00,000		Sundry Creditors	52,000	
Plant & Machinery	1,00,000		Bank Loan	20,000	72,000
Stock	72,000		By Big. Co. Ltd. (P.C.) A/c		4,75,000
Furniture	35,000		By Equity Shareholder A/c		60,000
Debtors	97,000		(Loss)		
Cash	28,000	5,32,000			
To Cash A/c		75,000			
(Creditor loan and liquidation exp. paid)		-	-		
		6,07,000			6,07,000

Dr.　　　**Big Co. Ltd. A/c**　　　Cr.

Particulars	Rs.	Particulars	Rs.
To Realisation A/c	4,75,000	By Equity shares in Big Ltd.	4,00,000
		By Cash A/c	75,000
	4,75,000		4,75,000

Dr.　　　**Equity Shares in Big Co. Ltd. A/c**　　　Cr.

Particulars	Rs.	Particulars	Rs.
To Big Co. Ltd. A/c	4,00,000	By Equity Shareholders A/c	4,00,000
	4,00,000		4,00,000

Dr.　　　**Cash A/c**　　　Cr.

Particulars	Rs.	Particulars	Rs.
To Big Co. Ltd. A/c	75,000	By Realisation A/c	75.000
	75,000		75,000

Dr.		Equity Shareholders A/c		Cr.
Particulars	**Rs.**	**Particulars**		**Rs.**
To Profit & Loss A/c	1,40,000	By Equity Share capital A/c		6,00,000
To Equity Shares in				
Big Ltd. A/c	4,00,000			
To Realisation A/c (loss)	60,000			
	6,00,000			6,00,000

In the Books of Big Co. Ltd.
Journal Entries

Date	Particulare		L.F.	Dr. Rs.	Cr. Rs.
1.	Business Purchase A/c	Dr.		4,75,000	
	To Small Co. Ltd. A/c				4,75,000
	(Being business purchased)				
2.	Plant & Machinery A/c	Dr.		90,000	
	Land & Machinery A/c	Dr.		1,53,000	
	Stock A/c	Dr.		72,000	
	Furniture A/c	Dr.		35,000	
	Debtors A/c	Dr.		97,000	
	Cash at Bank A/c	Dr.		28,000	
	To Business Purchase A/c				4,75,000
	(Being assets taken over at agreed values)				
3.	Small Co Ltd. A/c	Dr.		4,75,000	
	To Equity Share capital A/c				4,00,000
	To Cash A/c				75,000
	(Being Purchase price paid off)				
4.	Equity share call A/c	Dr.		2,00,000	
	To Equity share capital A/c				2,00,000
	(Being first call money due on 8,000 shares at Rs. 25 per share)				
5.	Cash A/c	Dr.		2,00,000	
	To Equity share first call A/c				2,00,000
	(Being first call money received)				

In the books of Big Ltd.
Balance Sheet (After Reconstruction)
as on 1-1-2015.

Liabilities	Rs.	Assets	Rs.
Share Capital :		Cash at Bank	1,53,000
Authorised Capital :		Land & Building	1,53,000
10,000 Equity shares		Plant & Machinery	90,000
of Rs. 100 each.	10,00,000	Stock	72,000
Paid up Capital :		Furniture	35,000
8000 Equity shares		Debtors	97,000
of Rs. 100 each, 75 paid.	6,00,000		
	6,00,000		6,00,000

Note : Cash at Bank		
Original Balance	28,000	
+ First call Money	2,00,000	
	2,28,000	
Paid to Equity		
Share holders	75,000	
Balance of Cash	1,53,000	

Problem No. 26 : The following was the Balance Sheet of Unlucky Ltd. as on 31-3-2014.

Liabilities	Rs.	Assets	Rs.
Share Capital :		Goodwill	30,000
5,000 Equity shares of		Building	40,000
Rs. 20 each fully paid	1,00,000	Machinery	65,000
3,000 6% cumulative		Stock	25,000
preference shares of		Debtors	15,000
Rs. 20 each fully paid	60,000	Cash	5,000
Debentures	40,000	Preliminary Expenses	3,000
Creditors	10,000	Profit & Loss A/c	27,000
	2,10,000		2,10,000

(Note : Arrears of Cumulative preference share dividend of Rs. 6,000.)

The Scheme of reconstruction as agreed upon by all the parties was as follows :

1. A new company to be formed called 'Lucky Ltd.' with an authorised capital of Rs. 3,00,000 all in equity shares of Rs. 10 each.

2. Two equity shares as to Rs. 5 paid up in the new company to be issued for every one equity share in the old company.

3. Four equity shares, as to Rs. 5 paid up in the new company to be issued for every preference share in the old company.

4. Debentureholders to be allotted 4,000 equity shares as fully paid up in the new company.

5. Arrears of preference dividend to be cancelled.

6. Creditors to be taken over by the new company.

7. The remaining equity shares to be issued to the public and duly collected in full.

8. The assets of the old company to be taken over subject to writing down the value of machinery by 5000.

Show the necessary accounts in the books of old company and the opening entries in the books of new company.

Statement of purchase consideration.

For	Mode of Payment	Rs.
1) Equity shareholders	1) Equity shares. at 2 shares for 1 share held i.e. 10000 shares at Rs. 5 each	50,000
2) Preference shareholders.	2) Equity Shares at 4 Equity shares for 1 Preference Share held i.e. 12,000 shares at Rs. 5 each	60,000
3) Debentureholder	Equity Shares 4000 Equity shares of Rs. 10 each	40,000
	Purchase Consideration	1,50,000

Calculation of Goodwill

Assets taken over	1,75,000
Less Liabilities taken over (Creditors)	10,000
Total	1,65,000
Less :	
Purchase Price paid	1,50,000
Goodwill	15,000

In the Books of Unlucky Ltd.

Dr.   ### Realisation A/c   **Cr.**

Particulars	Rs.	Particulars	Rs.
To Sundry Assets A/c	1,80,000	By Creditors A/c	10,000
		By Lucky Ltd. A/c	1,50,000
		By Equity Shareholders A/c	
		(Net loss)	20,000
	1,80,000		1,80,000

Dr.   ### Lucky A/c   **Cr.**

Particulars	Rs.	Particulars	Rs.
To Realisation A/c	1,50,000	By Equity Shares A/c	1,50,000
	1,50,000		1,50,000

Dr.   ### Preference Shareholders A/c   **Cr.**

Particulars	Rs.	Particulars	Rs.
To Equity shares in Lucky Ltd. A/c	60,000	By Pref. Share Capital A/c	60,000
	60,000		60,000

Dr.   ### Debentureholders A/c   **Cr.**

Particulars	Rs.	Particulars	Rs.
To Equity Shares in Lucky Ltd. A/c	40,000	By Debentures A/c	40,000
	40,000		40,000

Dr.   ### Equity Shareholders A/c   **Cr.**

Particulars	Rs.	Particulars	Rs.
To Preliminary Expenses A/c	3,000	By Equity Share Capital A/c	1,00,000
To Profit & Loss A/c	27,000		
To Realisation (Loss) A/c	20,000		
To Equity Shares in Lucky Ltd. A/c	50,000		
	1,00,000		1,00,000

Journal Entries in the Books of Lucky Ltd.

Date	Particulars		L.F.	Dr. Rs.	Cr. Rs.
	Building A/c	Dr.		40,000	
	Machinery A/c	Dr.		60,000	
	Stock A/c	Dr.		25,000	
	Debtors A/c	Dr.		15,000	
	Cash A/c	Dr.		5,000	
	Goodwill A/c (Balancing Figure)	Dr.		15,000	
	To Creditors A/c				10,000
	To Liquidators of Unlucky Ltd.'s A/c				1,50,000
	(Being Assets & Liabilities taken over from and price payable to Unlucky Ltd.)				
	Liquidators of Unlucky Ltd. A/c	Dr.		1,50,000	
	To Equity Share Capital A/c				1,50,000
	(Being Issued 22,000 equity shares of Rs. 10 each as to Rs. 5 per share paid up and 4,000 equity Shares of Rs. 10 each as fully paid in settlement of purchase price.)				
	Bank A/c	Dr.		40,000	
	To Equity share Application & Allotment & Final Call A/c				40,000
	(Being received application & allotment money @ Rs. 10 per share on 4,000 shares.)				
	Equity Share application & allotment final call A/c	Dr.		40,000	
	To Equity Share Capital A/c				40,000
	(Being Transfer of application, allotment and final call money to share capital A/c)				

(Note :

    Arrears of Preference Share Dividend : It is a contingent liability and as such it is not recorded in the ledger. Therefore, if contingent liability is to be cancelled, no entry is to be passed in the books of any company for its cancellation.)

In the Books of Lucky Ltd.
Balance Sheet (After Reconstruction)
as on 1-4-2014

Liabilities	Rs.	Assets	Rs.
Share Capital :		Cash at Bank	45,000
Authorised Capital		Goodwill	15,000
30,000 Equity shares		Building	40,000
of Rs. 10 each	300,000	Machinery	60,000
Paid up Capital		Stock	25,000
8000 Equity shares		Debtors	15,000
of Rs. 10 each fully paid.	80,000		
22000 Equity share			
of Rs. 10 each, Rs. 5 paid.	1,10,000		
Creditors	10,000		
	2,00,000		2,00,000

Problem No. 27 : On 31st March, 2014, The Balance Sheet of Shruti Ltd. was as under :

Liabilities	Rs.	Assets	Rs.
Authorised & Issued Capital		Goodwill	40,000
5,000 5% cumulative		Patents	15,000
preference shares of		Sundry Assets	1,64,500
Rs. 10 each fully paid.	50,000	Cash	500
15,000 Equity share of		Profit & Loss A/c	28,000
Rs. 10 each fully paid	1,50,000	Preliminary Expenses	2,000
Debentures	30,000		
Creditors	20,000		
	2,50,000		2,50,000

Note : Preference dividend in arrears for four years.

A scheme of reconstruction was agreed upon as follows :

1. A new company to be formed called Kartiki Ltd. with an authorised capital of Rs. 3,25,000 all in ordinary shares of Rs. 10 each.
2. One ordinary share Rs. 5 paid, in the new company to be issued for each ordinary share in the old company.
3. Two ordinary shares Rs. 5 paid in the new company to be issued for each preference share in the old company.

4. Arrears to be cancelled.
5. Debentureholders to receive 3,000 ordinary shares in the new company credited as fully paid.
6. Creditors to be taken over by the new company.
7. The remaining unissued shares to be taken up and paid for in full by the directors.
8. The new company to take over the old company's assets except patents subject to writing sundry assets by Rs. 35,000.
9. Patents are realised by shruti Ltd. for Rs. 1,000.

Close the books of Shruti Ltd. and Balance Sheet of Kartiki Ltd. Expenses of Kartiki Ltd. come to Rs. 1,000.   (P.U.)

Solution :

Statement of Purchase consideration

For	Mode of payment	Rs
1) Equity shareholders	1) Ordinary Shares (15,000 shares at Rs.10 each at Rs. 5 per share)	75,000
2) Preference shareholders	2) Ordinary Shares (10,000 shares of Rs. 10 each at Rs. 5 per Share)	50,000
3) Debentureholder	i) Ordinary Shares (3,000 shares of Rs. 10 each at Rs. 10 per share)	30,000
	Purchase Consideration	1,55,000

In the Books of Shruti Ltd.

Dr.   **Realisation A/c**   Cr.

Particulars	Rs.		Particulars	Rs.
To Sundry Assets A/c (Book Value)			By Sundry Liab. A/c (Book Value)	
Goodwill 40,000			(Sundry Creditors)	20,000
Patents 15,000			By Kartiki Ltd. A/c (P.C.)	1,55,000
Sundry Assets 1,64,500			By Cash A/c (Patents Realised)	1,000
Cash 500	2,20,000		By Equity Shareholders A/c	44,000
	—		(Loss)	
	2,20,000			2,20,000

Dr.   **Kartiki A/c**   Cr.

Particulars	Rs.	Particulars	Rs.
To Realisation A/c	1,55,000	By Ordinary shares in Kartiki Ltd.A/c	1,55,000
	1,55,000		1,55,000

Dr.   **Ordinary Shares in Kartiki Ltd. A/c**   **Cr.**

Particulars	Rs.	Particulars	Rs.
To Kartiki Ltd. A/c	1,55,000	By Equity Shareholder A/c	75,000
		By Preference Shareholder A/c	50,000
		By Debentureholder A/c	30,000
	1,55,000		1,55,000

Dr.   **Debetureholders A/c**   **Cr.**

Particulars	Rs.	Particulars	Rs.
To Ordinary Shares in Kartiki Ltd. A/c	30,000 –	By Debentures A/c	30,000 –
	30,000		30,000

Dr.   **Preference Shareholders A/c**   **Cr.**

Particulars	Rs.	Particulars	Rs.
To Ordinary Shares in Kartiki Ltd. A/c	50,000	By 6% Preference Share Capital A/c	50,000 -
	50,000		50,000

Dr.   **Equity Shareholders A/c**   **Cr.**

Particulars	Rs.	Particulars	Rs.
To Profit & Loss A/c	28,000	By Equity Share capital A/c	1,50,000
To Preliminary Expenses A/c	2,000		
To Ordinary Shares in Kartiki Ltd. A/c	75,000		
To Cash A/c	1,000		
To Realisation A/c	44,000		
	1,50,000		1,50,000

Dr.   **Cash A/c**   **Cr.**

Particulars	Rs.	Particulars	Rs.
To Realisation A/c (Patents Realised)	1,000 –	By Equity Shareholders A/c (Bal. Fig.)	1,000 –
	1,000		1,000

Balance Sheet of Kartiki Ltd.
As at 1st April 2014

Liabilities		Rs.	Assets	Rs.
Authorised Share Capital			Cash	44,500
28,000 Ordinary Shares of			Goodwill	45,000
Rs. 10 each		2,80,000	Sundry Assets	1,29,500
Issued & Subscribed			Preliminary Expenses	1,000
25,000 shares Rs.	1,25,000			
3,000 Shares of	30,000	1,55,000		
Rs. 10 each				
(Issued to vendors)				
4,500 shares of Rs. 10 each				
fully paid		45,000		
(Issued to public for cash)				
Creditors		20,000		
		2,20,000		2,20,000

Problem No. 28 : X Limited, Pune, having proved unsuccessful, resolves by special Resolution to wind up for the purpose of Reconstruction and sale to the Y Ltd; newly formed company for the purpose. The Balance Sheet of the X Ltd. at the date of the confirmatory resolution was as follows :

Balance Sheet

Liabilities	Rs.	Assets		Rs.
Share Capital :		Land & Building		4,50,000
1,00,000 Equity Shares of		Plant & Machinery		2,40,000
Rs. 10 each, fully paid	10,00,000	Sundry Debtors	1,05,000	
Sundry Creditors	30,000	Less : R.D.D.	5,000	1,00,000
Bills payable	20,000	Stock		50,000
Contingent Liability :		Cash at Bank		10,000
Workmen's Compensation		Profit & Loss A/c		2,00,000
Claim Rs. 4,000	–			–
	10,50,000			10,50,000

The Scheme of Reconstruction assented to by all the parties was as follows :

   i) The new company to take over all the assets of old company but not the liabilities.

   ii) The new company was to purchase the Goodwill of the business and assets of the old company for the sum of Rs. 8,00,000 payable as to Rs. 7,00,000 by the issue of

1,40,000 Equity shares of Rs. 10 each with Rs. 5 per share credited as paid up and as to Rs. 1,00,000 in cash.

iii) The members of the new company were to pay in cash the balance of Rs. 5 per share due upon the shares issued to them.

iv) The expenses of Reconstruction amounted to Rs. 3,000. Workmen's compensation claims was settled at Rs. 2,000.

No Further shares were issued beyond those forming part of the purchase consideration as stated above.

a) Pass Journal Entries to close the books of the X Limited. Also give necessary ledger accounts, and

b) Pass opening entries and give an opening Balance Sheet in the books of Y Ltd. (P.U.)

Solution :

Statement of Purchase Consideration

For	Mode of payment	Rs
i) Equity Shares	1,40,000 shares of 10 each Rs. 5 per share paid up	7,00,000
ii) Cash		1,00,000
	Purchase Consideration	8,00,000

Journal Entries in the Books of X Ltd.

Date	Particulars		L.F.	Dr. Rs.	Cr. Rs.
1.	Realisation A/c	Dr.		8,55,000	
	To Land & Buildings A/c				4,50,000
	To Machinery & Plant A/c				2,40,000
	To Sundry Debtors A/c				1,05,000
	To Stock A/c				50,000
	To Bank A/c				10,000
	(Being transfer of balances on various assets accounts to Realisation A/c)				
2.	Reserve for doubtful debts A/c	Dr.		5,000	
	To Realisation A/c				5,000
	(Being transfer of R.D.D. to Realisation A/c)				
3.	Y Ltd. A/c	Dr.		8,00,000	
	To Realisation A/c				8,00,000
	(Being Purchase Consideration to be received from Y Ltd.)				

Date	Particulars		L.F.	Dr. Rs.	Cr. Rs.
4.	Realisation A/c To Bank A/c (Being Payment of Reconstruction expenses & Compensation Claim)	Dr.		5,000	5,000
5.	Shareholders A/c To Realisation A/c (Being loss on Realisation A/c transferred to Equity Shareholders A/c)	Dr.		55,000	55,000
6.	Share in Y Ltd. A/c Bank A/c To Y Ltd. A/c (Being received 1,40,000 shares of Rs. 10 each, Rs. 5 per share paid & cash Rs. 1,00,000 in settlement of purchase price)	Dr. Dr.		7,00,000 1,00,000	8,00,000
7.	Sundry Creditors A/c Bills Payable A/c To Bank A/c (Being Repayment of liabilities)	Dr. Dr.		30,000 20,000	50,000
8.	Equity share capital A/c To Shareholders A/c (Being balance on share capital A/c transferred to shareholders A/c)	Dr.		10,00,000	10,00,000
9.	Shareholders A/c To Profit & Loss A/c (Being debit balance on profit & Loss A/c transferred to shareholders)	Dr.		2,00,000	2,00,000

10.	Shareholders A/c
	    To Shares in Y Ltd. A/c
	    To Bank A/c
	(Being shares received from the Y Ltd.
	 issued and cash paid to shareholders
	in settlement of their claim)
		Dr.		7,45,000	7,00,000
					45,000

Dr. **Realisation A/c** Cr.

Particulars	Rs.	Particulars	Rs.
To Sundry Assets A/c (Book Value)		By Sundry Liab. A/c	
Land & Buildings	4,50,000	(Book value) (R.D.D.)	5,000
Machinery & Plant	2,40,000	By Y Ltd.'s A/c	8,00,000
Sundry Debtors	1,05,000	By Shareholders A/c	55,000
Stock	50,000	(Loss)	
Bank	10,000		
To Bank A/c	5,000		
(Expenses 3,000			
compensation claim 2,000)	–		–
	8,60,000		8,60,000

Dr. **Y Ltd. A/c** Cr.

Particulars	Rs.	Particulars	Rs.
To Realisation A/c	8,00,000	By Shares in Y Ltd. A/c	7,00,000
	–	By Bank A/c	1,00,000
	8,00,000		8,00,000

Dr. **Shares in Y Ltd. A/c** Cr.

Particulars	Rs.	Particulars	Rs.
To Y Ltd. A/c	7,00,000	By Shareholders A/c	7,00,000
	–		–
	7,00,000		7,00,000

Dr. **Sundry Creditors A/c** Cr.

Particulars	Rs.	Particulars	Rs.
To Bank A/c	30,000	By Balance b/d	30,000
	–		–
	30,000		30,000

Dr. **Bills Payable A/c** Cr.

Particulars	Rs.	Particulars	Rs.
To Bank A/c	20,000	By Balance b/d	20,000
	–		–
	20,000		20,000

Dr.   **Shareholders A/c**   Cr.

Particulars	Rs.	Particulars	Rs.
To Realisation A/c	55,000	By Share capital	10,00,000
To Profit & Loss A/c	2,00,000		
To Shares in Y Ltd. A/c	7,00,000		
To Bank A/c	45,000		
	10,00,000		10,00,000

Dr.   **Bank A/c**   Cr.

Particulars	Rs.	Particulars	Rs.
To Balance b/d	10,000	By Realisation (transfer) A/c	10,000
To Y Ltd. A/c	1,00,000	By Sundry Creditors A/c	30,000
		By Bills payable A/c	20,000
		By Realisation A/c	5,000
		By Shareholders A/c	45,000
	1,10,000		1,10,000

Note :

1. If it is not stated clearly as to which company is to bear the expenses it is always to be presumed that the purchased company has to bear the expenses.
2. Note the treatment of contingent liability. Actual amount paid is recorded and not the original amount.

Journal Entries in the books of Y Ltd.

Date	Particulars		L.F.	Dr. Rs.	Cr. Rs.
1.	Business Purchase A/c	Dr.		8,00,000	
	To X Ltd.				8,00,000
	(Being purchase price payable for purchase of business of X Ltd.)				
2.	Land & Buildings A/c	Dr.		4,50,000	
	Machinery & Plant A/c	Dr.		2,40,000	
	Sundry Debtors A/c	Dr.		1,05,000	
	Stock A/c	Dr.		50,000	
	Bank A/c	Dr.		10,000	
	To Reserve for doubtful debts A/c				5,000
	To Business Purchase A/c				8,00,000
	To Capital Reserve A/c				50,000
	(Being Assets taken over from X Ltd.)				

Date	Particulare		L.F.	Dr. Rs.	Cr. Rs.
3.	X Ltd. A/c	Dr.		8,00,000	
	To Equity Share capital A/c				7,00,000
	To Bank A/c				1,00,000
	(Being Issued 1,40,000 Equity shares of Rs.10 each, Rs. 5 per share paid and paid cash Rs. 1,00,000 to vendors in settlement of purchase price)				
4.	Equity share final call A/c Dr.			7,00,000	
	To Equity Share Capital A/c				7,00,000
	(Being made a final call of Rs. 5 per share on 1,40,000 shares issued as partly paid shares to the vendors)				
5.	To Bank A/c	Dr.		7,00,000	
	To Equity Share Final Call A/c				7,00,000
	(Being received cash for Final Call)				

Y Ltd.
Balance Sheet as on

Liabilities	Rs.		Assets		Rs.
Share Capital :			Bank		6,10,000
Authorised Issued and			Land & Buildings		4,50,000
Subscribed 1,40,000 shares of			Machinery & Plant		2,40,000
Rs. 10 each, issued to vendors			Stock		50,000
as partly paid and balance			Debtors	1,05,000	
received in cash	14,00,000		Less : R.D.D.	5,000	1,00,000
Capital Reserve	50,000				
	14,50,000				14,50,000

Notes :   **Rs.**

1. Total of assets taken Rs. 8,50,000

    Less Purchase price Rs. 8,00,000 = Capital Reserve   50,000

2. Bank Balance :

    Balance taken over from vendors   10,000

    Cash received on Final Call   7,00,000

                                        7,10,000

    Less cash paid to Vendors   1,00,000

    Balance as per B/s   6,10,000

Problem No. 29 : Following was the Balance Sheet of Short Ltd. as on 31st March, 2014.

Liabilities	Rs.	Assets	Rs.
Share Capital :		Fixed Assets	
10,000 Equity shares of		Land & Building	2,60,000
Rs. 50 each	5,00,000	Plant & Machinery	1,70,000
Profit prior to		Furniture	10,000
Incorporation	2,000	Patterns	40,000
Loans	1,33,000	Stock	60,000
Creditors	80,000	Debtors	48,000
		Cash	7,000
		Profit & Loss A/c	1,20,000
	7,15,000		7,15,000

The Short Ltd. adopted a scheme of reconstruction as working capital was badly needed. New company Long Ltd., was formed to take over the business of Short Ltd. on the following terms :

1. Out of the creditors Rs. 2,000 were preferential creditors and they were paid fully by the new company. The remaining creditors were given the following option.

(a) Either 50% of their claims will be paid in cash immediately as full settlement of their claims or (b) 5% Debentures in the new company will be issued to them equivalent to their claims in the old company. Half of the creditors opted for cash payment.

2. One equity share of Rs. 100 each, Rs. 75 paid up will be issued for every four shares of the old company.

3. Long Ltd. made a final call of Rs. 25 on Equity shares which was fully received.

4. The amount made available under the reconstruction scheme was utilised to write off stock by 25%, furniture by 50% and Plant & Machinery by 10%. The new company writes off Patterns completely. Debtors were valued at Rs. 40,000 keeping Rs. 8,000 as a reserve for doubtful debts. The value of Land & Building was adjusted to the extent possible.

5. Formation expenses of the new company were Rs. 25,000.

Show Realisation Account, Equity Shareholders Account, Creditors Account and Long Ltd. Account in the books of Short Ltd. and Opening Entries and Balance Sheet in the books of Long Ltd.

Solution :

Statement of Purchase Consideration

For	Mode of payment	Rs
1. Preferential Creditors	i) Cash	2,000
2. Other Creditors	i) Cash	19,500
	ii) 5% Debentures	39,000
3. Equity Shareholders	iv) Equity shares	
	(2,500 shares of Rs. 100 each at Rs. 75 paid)	1,87,500
	Purchase Consideration	2,48,000

Payment of Purchase Price	Rs.
i) Cash	21,500
ii) 5% Debentures	39,000
iii) Equity Shares	1,87,500
Total	2,48,000

In the Books of Short Ltd.
Realisation A/c

Dr.   Cr.

Particulars	Rs.	Particulars	Rs.
To Sundry Assets A/c (Book Value)	5,95,000	By Sundry Liab. A/c (Book Value)	1,33,000
Land & Building 2,60,000		By Creditors A/c	19,500
Plant & Machinery 1,70,000		By Long Ltd. A/c	2,48,000
Furniture 10,000		By Equity Shareholders A/c	1,94,500
Patents 40,000		(Loss)	
Stock 60,000			
Debtors 48,000			
Cash 7,000	–		–
	5,95,000		5,95,000

Long Ltd. A/c

Dr.   Cr.

Particulars	Rs.	Particulars	Rs.
To Realisation A/c	2,48,000	By Shares in Long Ltd. A/c	1,87,500
		By 5% Debentures in	
		Long Ltd. A/c	39,000
	–	By Cash A/c	21,500
	2,48,000		2,48,000

Dr.   **Equity Shares in Long Ltd. A/c**   Cr.

Particulars	Rs.	Particulars	Rs.
To Long Ltd. A/c	1,87,500	By Equity shareholder A/c	1,87,500
	—		—
	1,87,500		1,87,500

Dr.   **5% Debentures in Long Ltd. A/c**   Cr.

Particulars	Rs.	Particulars	Rs.
To Long Ltd. A/c	39,000	By Creditors A/c	39,000
	—		—
	39,000		39,000

Dr.   **Cash A/c**   Cr.

Particulars	Rs.	Particulars	Rs.
To Long Ltd. A/c	21,500	By Creditors A/c	21,500
	—		—
	21,500		21,500

Dr.   **Equity Shareholders A/c**   Cr.

Particulars	Rs.	Particulars	Rs.
To Shares in Long Ltd. A/c	1,87,500	By Share Capital A/c	5,00,000
To Profit & Loss A/c	1,20,000	By Profit prior to	2,000
To Realisation A/c (Loss)	1,94,500	Incorporation A/c	—
	5,02,000		5,02,000

Dr.   **Creditors A/c**   Cr.

Particulars	Rs.	Particulars	Rs.
To Cash A/c	21,500	By Balance b/d	80,000
To 5% Debentures in			
Long Ltd. A/c	39,000		
To Realisation A/c	19,500		—
	80,000		80,000

Opening Entries in the books of Long Ltd.

Date	Particulare		L.F.	Dr. Rs.	Cr. Rs.
1.	Business Purchase A/c	Dr		2,48,000	
	To Liquidator of Short Ltd.'s A/c				2,48,000
	(Being Purchase consideration payable)				
2.	Stock A/c	Dr.		45,000	
	Furniture A/c	Dr.		5,000	
	Plant & Machinery A/c	Dr.		1,53,000	
	Debtors A/c	Dr.		40,000	
	Land & Building A/c	Dr.		5,000	
	(Adjusted Value)				
	To Business Purchase A/c				2,48,000
	(Being Assets taken over)				
3.	Liquidators of Short Ltd. A/c Dr.			2,48,000	
	To Equity Share capital A/c				1,87,500
	To 5% Debentures A/c				39,000
	To Cash A/c				21,500
	(Being Payment of Purchase Consideration)				
4.	Bank A/c	Dr.		62,500	
	To Share Appli. & Allot. A/c				62,500
	(Being Appli & Allot. Money Received)				
5.	Share Appli. & Allot. A/c	Dr.		62,500	
	To Equity Share Capital A/c				62,500
	(Being Amount transferred to Share Capital)				
6.	Goodwill A/c	Dr.		25,000	
	To Bank A/c				25,000
	(Being Liquidation expenses paid)				

Balance Sheet (After Reconstruction)
as on 1-1-2014

Liabilities	Rs.	Assets	Rs.
Share Capital		Cash at Bank	16,000
2500 Equity shares of Rs.		(62500 - 25000 - 21500)	
100 each fully paid	2,50,000	Goodwill	25,000
5% Debentures	39,000	Stock	45,000
		Furniture	5,000
		Plant & Machinery	1,53,000
		Debtors	40,000
		Land & Building	5,000
	2,89,000		2,89,000

Problem No. 30 : Green Ltd. went into voluntary liquidation for its reconstruction on 31st March 2014 when its Balance Sheet was as follow :

Balance Sheet
As at 31st March 2014

Liabilities	Rs.	Assets		Rs.
Share Capital :		Freehold Property		4,15,000
3,000 6% preference		Plant & Machinery		2,15,000
Shares of Rs. 100 each	3,00,000	Vehicles		40,000
7,000 Equity shares of	7,00,000	Stock		1,75,000
Rs. 100 each		Debtors	50,000	
Share premium A/c	10,000	Less : R.D.D.	5,000	45,000
Unsecured Loans	50,000	Bills Receivable		10,000
Bills Payable	30,000	Cash		4,000
Creditors	70,000	Profit & Loss A/c		2,56,000
	11,60,000			11,60,000

New company. White Ltd. was formed to take over the following assets and liabilities of the Green Ltd.

Freehold Property at Rs. 3,60,000, plant and machinery at Rs 2,00,000, Vehicles at Rs.45,000, stock at Rs. 1,50,000. White Ltd. also took over unsecured loans and creditors at the book value.

The purchase consideration was satisfied in 2350, 7% Preference Shares of Rs.100 each and 10,000 Equity Shares of Rs.100 each, Rs. 40 paid up. There was a contingent liability for a Repair Bill amounting to Rs. 1,700 for which White Ltd. issued 11 Equity Shares of Rs.100 each fully paid in full satisfaction of the claim.

The preference shareholders of Green Ltd. accepted Preference Shares of White Ltd. in full satisfaction of their claims and Partly Paid Equity Shares of White Ltd. were allotted to the Equity Shareholders of Green Ltd.

The Debtors and Bills receivable of Green Ltd. realised Rs. 48,000 and Rs. 8,000 respectively. Bills payable were fully paid. The winding up expenses were Rs.4,500.

White Ltd. immediately made a call of Rs.60 on partly paid Equity Shares to pay the unsecured loans and creditors. The call money was fully received out of which liabilities were paid.

Preliminary expenses of White Ltd. amounted to Rs. 10,000 which were paid immediately.

Close the books of Green Ltd. by preparing the necessary Ledger Accounts and pass the journal entries in the books of White Ltd.   (P.U.)

Solution

Statement of purchase consideration

For	Mode of Payment	Rs.
1. 6% Preference shareholders	i) 7% Preference shares (2,350 shares of Rs. 100 each)	2,35,000
2. Equity Shareholders	i) Equity shares (Partly paid) (10,000 shares at Rs. 100 each at Rs. 40 paid)	4,00,000
3. Repair Bill	i) Equity Shares (Fully paid) (11 shares at Rs. 100 each)	1,100
		-
	Purchase Consideration	6,36,100

Payment of Purchase Consideration	Rs.
i) 7% Preference Shares	2,35,000
ii) Partly Paid Equity Shares	4,00,000
iii) Fully Paid Equity Shares	1,100
Total	6,36,100

In the Books of Green Ltd.

Dr.   **Realisation A/c**   Cr.

Particulars	Rs.	Particulars	Rs.
To Sundry Assets A/c (Book Value)		By R.D.D. A/c	5,000
Freehold Property	4,15,000	By Unsecured Loans A/c	50,000
Plant & machinery	2,15,000	By Creditors A/c	70,000
Vehicles	40,000	By White Ltd.'s A/c	6,36,100
Stock	1,75,000	(Purchase Consideration)	
Debtors	50,000	By Cash A/c	56,000
Bills Receivable	10,000	(Debtors & B/R)	
To Fully paid Equity Shares of White Ltd. A/c (Repairs Bill)	1,100	By Equity Shareholder's A/c (Net Loss)	93,500
To Cash A/c	4,500		
(Winding up expenses)	-	-	
	9,10,600		9,10,600

Dr. **Bills Payable A/c** Cr.

Particulars	Rs.	Particulars	Rs.
To Cash A/c	30,000	By Balance b/d	30,000
	30,000		30,000

Dr. **White Ltd. A/c** Cr.

Particulars	Rs.	Particulars	Rs.
To Realisation A/c	6,36,100	By 7% Preference shares in White Ltd. A/c	2,35,000
		By Partly paid equity shares in White Ltd. A/c	4,00,000
		By Fully paid equity shares in White Ltd. A/c	1,100
	-		-
	6,36,100		6,36,100

Dr. **7% Preference Shares in White Ltd. A/c** Cr.

Particulars	Rs.	Particulars	Rs.
To White Ltd. A/c	2,35,000	By 6% Preference shareholders A/c	2,35,000
	-		-
	2,35,000		2,35,000

Dr. **Partly paid Equity Shares in White Ltd. A/c** Cr.

Particulars	Rs.	Particulars	Rs.
To White Ltd. A/c	4,00,000	By Equity Shareholders A/c	4,00,000
	4,00,000		4,00,000

Dr. **Fully paid Equity Shares in White Ltd. A/c** Cr.

Particulars	Rs.	Particulars	Rs.
To White Ltd. A/c	1,100	By Realisation A/c	1,100
	1,100		1,100

Dr.   **Cash A/c**   Cr.

Particulars	Rs.	Particulars	Rs.
To Balance b/d	4,000	By Bills Payable A/c	30,000
To Realisation A/c	56,000	By Realisation A/c	4,500
(Debtors & B/R)		By Equity Shareholder's A/c	25,500
		(Bal. Fig.)	-
	60,000		60,000

Dr.   **6% Preference Shareholders A/c**   Cr.

Particulars	Rs.	Particulars	Rs.
To Preference shares in White Ltd. A/c	2,35,000	By Preference Shares Capital A/c	3,00,000
To Equity Shareholders A/c	65,000	-	
	3,00,000		3,00,000

Dr.   **Equity Shareholders A/c**   Cr.

Particulars	Rs.	Particulars	Rs.
To Profit & Loss A/c	2,56,000	By Equity Share Capital A/c	7,00,000
To Realisation A/c	93,500	By Share Premium A/c	10,000
To Partly paid Equity Shares in White Ltd.	4,00,000	By Preference Shareholders A/c (Profit)	65,000
To Cash A/c	25,500	-	
	7,75,000		7,75,000

Journal Entries in the Books of White Ltd.

Date	Particulars		L.F.	Dr. Rs.	Cr. Rs.
1.	Business Purchase A/c	Dr.		6,36,100	
	To Liquidator of Green Ltd. A/c				6,36,100
	(Being acquired the business of Green Ltd. as per the agreement)				

Date	Particulars		L.F.	Dr. Rs.	Cr. Rs.
2.	Goodwill A/c	Dr.		1,100	
	Freehold Property A/c	Dr.		3,60,000	
	Plant & Machinery A/c	Dr.		2,00,000	
	Vehicles A/c	Dr.		45,000	
	Stock A/c	Dr.		1,50,000	
	To Creditors A/c				70,000
	To Unsecured Loans A/c				50,000
	To Business Purchase A/c				6,36,100
	(Being acquired the various Assets & Liabilities of Green Ltd. as per the values stated above)				
3.	Liquidator of Green Ltd. A/c	Dr.		6,36,100	
	To Preference Share Capital A/c				2,35,000
	To Partly paid Equity Share Capital A/c				4,00,000
	To Fully paid Equity Share Capital A/c				1,100
	(Being discharged the purchase consideration in 2,350 preference shares of Rs. 100 each, 10,000 equity shares of Rs. 100 each, Rs. 40 paid up and 11 equity shares of Rs. 100 each fully paid)				
4.	Equity Share Final Call A/c	Dr.		6,00,000	
	To Equity Share Capital A/c				6,00,000
	(Being final Call made on 10,000 equity Shares at Rs. 60 per share)				
5.	Cash A/c	Dr.		6,00,000	
	To Equity Share Final call A/c				6,00,000
	(Being received equity share final call money on 10,000 equity shares at Rs. 60 per share)				
6.	Unsecured Loans A/c	Dr.		50,000	
	Creditors A/c	Dr.		70,000	
	To Cash A/c				1,20,000
	(Being Unsecured Loans & Creditors paid)				
7.	Preliminary Expenses A/c	Dr.		10,000	
	To Cash A/c				10,000
	(Being Preliminary Expenses paid)				

In the Books of White Ltd.
Balance Sheet (After Reconstruction)
as on 1-4-2014

Liabilities	Rs.	Assets	Rs.
Share Capital		Cash at Bank	4,70,000
2350, 7% Preference shares of		Goodwill	1,100
Rs. 100 each fully paid	2,35,000	Plant & Machinery	2,00,000
10,011 Equity Shares of		Freehold Property	3,60,000
Rs. 100 each fully paid	10,01,100	Vehicles	45,000
		Stock	1,50,000
		Preliminary Expenses	10,000
	12,36,100		12,36,100

Problem No. 31 : On 31st March 2014 the Balance Sheet of Dull Ltd. was as follows :

Liabilities	Rs.	Assets		Rs.
Authorised Capital :		Freehold Land &		
10,000 Equity Shares		Building		1,00,000
of Rs.10 each	1,00,000	Plant & Machinery		
1,000 6% Cumulative		at cost	80,000	
preference Shares of		Less : Depreciation	30,000	50,000
Rs. 100 each	1,00,000	Tools and Patterns		10,000
Issued Capital		Stocks in Trade		70,000
6,000 Equity Shares of		Trade Debtors		30,000
Rs. 10 each fully paid	60,000	Cash in Hand		1,000
600 6% cumulative		Profit & Loss		80,000
preference shares of				
Rs. 100 each fully paid	60,000			
8% Debentures	30,000			
Trade Creditors	1,30,000			
Bank Overdraft	61,000			
	3,41,000			3,41,000

It was decided to reconstruct the company and for this purpose, Bright Ltd. was registered with a capital of Rs. 2,00,000 divided into 8,000 equity shares of Rs. 10 each and 1,200 7% preference shares of Rs. 100 each to take over the assets and liabilities of the old company.

The debenture holders of Dull Ltd. agreed to accept 7% preference shares in the new company in exchange for their debentures.

The preference shareholders were to receive one preference share in the new company for every three preference shares held by them in the old company and the equity shareholders were to be allotted one equity share Rs. 8 paid in the new company for every four shares held by them in the old company.

Bright Ltd. issued 3,500 equity shares of Rs. 10 each at par and called up the balance of Rs. 2 on the shares issued to the old shareholders in Dull Ltd.

The cost of liquidation of Dulls Ltd. Rs. 250 was paid by the new company. The preliminary expenses of Bright Ltd. Which have been paid were Rs. 240.

You are required to prepare :

(a) Realisation A/c and Equity Shareholders A/c in the books of Dull Ltd. and

(b) Balance Sheet of Bright Ltd.

Solution :

Calculation of Purchase Consideration

For	Mode of Payment	Rs.
(i) Debentures of Rs. 30,000	7% Preference Shares	30,000
(ii) Preference Shares : one pref. share for 3 pref. shares held. Hence, for 600 shares held 200 pref. shares of Rs. 100 each	7% Pref. Shares	20,000
(iii) Equity Shares : One Equity share of Rs. 10 Rs. 8 paid for every 4 equity shares held. Hence, for 6,000 shares 1,500 shares at Rs. 8 per share	Equity Shares	12,000
(iv) Cost of Liquidation	Cash	250
Purchase Consideration		62,250

Payment of Purchase Consideration

Particulars	Rs.
Equity Shares	12,000
Preference Shares	50,000
Cash	250
Purchase Price	62,250

In the Books of Dull Ltd.

Realisation A/c

Dr.   Cr.

Particulars	Rs.	Particulars	Rs.
To Sundry Assets A/c	2,61,000	By Creditors A/c	1,30,000
To Cash (Expenses) A/c	250	By Bank Overdraft A/c	61,000
To Equity Shareholders A/c (Profit)	32,000	By Bright Ltd. A/c (Purchase price)	62,250
		By Preference Shareholders A/c (Discount)	40,000
	2,93,250		2,93,250

Equity Shareholders A/c

Dr.   Cr.

Particulars	Rs.	Particulars	Rs.
To Profit & Loss A/c	80,000	By Equity Share Capital A/c	60,000
To Equity Shares in Bright Ltd. A/c	12,000	By Realisation A/c (profit)	32,000
	92,000		92,000

In the Books of Bright Ltd.

Balance Sheet (After Reconstruction) as on 1st April 2014

Liabilities	Rs.	Assets	Rs.
Share Capital :		Freehold Land & Buildings	1,00,000
(i) Authorised Capital 8,000 Equity Shares of Rs. 10 each	80,000	Plant &s Machinery	50,000
		Tools & Patterns	10,000
1200 7% preferencce shares of Rs. 100 each	1,20,000	Stock-in Trade	70,000
		Trade Debtors	30,000
	2,00,000	Cash at Bank	38,510
(ii) Issued & paid-up capital 5,000 Equity shares of Rs.10 each, of which 1500 shares are issued to vendors	50,000	Preliminarys Expenses	240
500 7% preference Shares of Rs. 100 each issued to vendors	50,000		
Capital Reserve	7,750		
Trade Creditors	1,30,000		
Bank Overdraft	61,000		
	2,98,750		2,98,750

Working Notes.

1. Capital Reserve :

	Rs.
Agreed value of assets taken	2,61,000
Less : Trade Creditors and Bank Overdraft taken over	1,91,000
Value of Net Assets taken :	70,000
Less : Purchase Price	62,250
Capital Reserve	7,750

2. Bank Balance

		Rs.
Cash taken over		1,000
Cash received @ Rs. 2 per share on 1,500 shares		3,000
Cash received on 3,500 shares issued to Public		35,000
		39,000
Less : Cash Paid for		
Liquidation Cost	250	
Preliminary Exp.	240	490
Balance shown in B/S		38,510

Problem No. 32 : The Following Was the Balance Sheet of Poonam Ltd as on 31st March 2014

Balance Sheet as on 31-3-2014

Liabilities	Rs	Assets	Rs.
Share Capital		**Good will**	60,000
10,000 Equity Shares		Buildings	80,000
of Rs. 20 each	2,00,000	Machinery	1,30,000
6000, 8% Cumulative			
Preference shares of			
Rs. 20 each fully paid	1,20,000	Cash	10,000
		Stock	50,000
		Sundry Debtors	30,000
Debentures	80,000	Preliminary Expenses	6000
Sundry Creditors	20,000	Profit and Loss	54,000
	4,20,000		4,20,000

The Scheme of reconstruction was agreed as follows.

a) A new company to be formed "Sonam Ltd" with an authorised capital of Rs. 6,00,000 all in equity Shares of Rs. 10 each.

b) Two equity Shares of Rs. 5 Paid up in the new company issued for every one equity share in the old company.

c) Four equity Shares of Rs. 5 Paid up in the new Company to be issued for every Preference Share in the old company.

d) Debentureholders to be allotted 800 equity Shares as fully paid up in the new Company.

e) Sundry Creditors to be taken over by new Company.

f) The remaining equity Shares tobe issued to the public and duly collected in full.

g) The Assets of the old Company to be taken over subject to writing down the value of machinery by Rs. 10,000

Show the necessary Ledger accounts in the books of the old company and the opening journal entries and Balance sheet in the books of new Company.

(March - 2012 PUP)

Solution :

Statement of Purchase Consideration

Discharge of Purchase Price	Rs.	Particulars	Rs.
		Net Assets taken over	
To Eq. Share holder		Building	80,000
2 Shares of Rs. 10 each Rs. 5		Machinery	1,20,000
Paid For every one in old co.	100.000	Stock	50,000
20.000 × 6			
To Preference Shareholder		Debtors	30,000
4 equity shares of Rs. 10		Cash	10,000
each Rs. 5 Paid up			
24000 × 5	1,20,000		2,90,000
To Debenture holder		Less - Libilities taken over (creditors)	20,000
8000 Share at Rs. 10 each	80,000	Net Value	2,70,000
		Good will	30,000
P.C.	3,00,000		3,00,000

In the books of Poonam Ltd. Relisation A/c

Particulars	Rs	Particulars	Rs
To Sundry Assets		**By Sundry Liabilities**	
Goodwill	60,000	Creditors	20,000
Building	80,000	By Sonam Ltd (Pc)	3,00,000
Machinery	1,30,000	By Eq. Share holder	40,000
Stock	50,000	(Loss)	
Debtors	30,000		
Cash	10,000		
	3,60,000		3,60,000

Sonam Ltd A/c

Particulars	Rs	Particulars	Rs
To Realisation A/c	3,00,000	By Eq. Share in Sonam Ltd	
		44,000 × 5	2,20,000
		8000 × 10	80,000
		fully paid	
	3,00,000		3,00,000

8% Cumulative Preference Share Capital A/c

Particulars	Rs	Particulars	Rs
To Eq. Shere in Sonam Ltd A/c	1,20,000	8% Cum. preference Share Capital A/c	1,20,000
	1,20,000		1,20,000

Debenture Holder A/c

Particulars	Rs	Particulars	Rs
To Eq. Shares	80,000	By Debenture	80,000
in Sonam Ltd A/c	80,000		80,000

Eq. Share Holder A/c

Particulars	Rs	Particulars	Rs
To Preliminary exp.	6000	By Eq. Share Capital	2,00,000
To P & L	54,000		
To Realisation (loss)	40,000		
To Eq. Share in Sonam Ltd.	1,00,000		
	2,00,000		2,00,000

Opening Entries in the books of Sonam Ltd

Date	Particulars		L.F.	Debti Rs.	Credit Rs.
1)	Bus. Purchase A/c	Dr.		3,00,000	
	To Liquidator of Poonam Ltd				3,00,000
2)	Buiding A/c	Dr.		80,000	
	Machinery A/c	Dr.		1,20,000	
	Stock A/c	Dr.		50,000	
	S. Debtors A/c	Dr.		30,000	
	Cash A/c	Dr.		10,000	
	Good will	Dr.		30,000	
	To Bus. Purchase A/c				3,00,000
	To Sundry Creditors				20,000
3)	Liquidator of Poonam Ltd A/c			3,00,000	
	To Eq. Share Capital A/c				2,20,000
	To Eq. Share Capital A/c				80,000
4)	Bank A/c	Dr.		80,000	
	To Eq. Share Capital A/c				80,000

Balance Sheet as Sonam Ltd As on 1st April 2014

Liabilities		Rs	Assets		Rs
Share Capital :			Good will		30,000
Eq. Share of Rs. 5 each (44000 × 5)	2,20,000		Building		80,000
			Machinery		1,20,000
8000 eq. Share Rs. 10 = 80,000			Stock		50,000
New issue Eq.			Sundry Debtors A/c		30,000
Share capital			**Cash**		
(8000 × 10)	80,000	1,60,000	Old Co. 10,000		
Creditors		20,000	New issue 80,000		90,000
		4,00,000			4,00,00

5 : 8 AS 14 and Amalgamation

Note : Already discussed in Chapter No 3. Students are advised to see Chapter No. 3.

5.9 EXERCISES

Objective Type Questions.

(a) Fill in the gaps.

1) Taking over the business of two or more companies is called...

2) Absorption means... Liquidation and one...

3) The amount payable by purchasing company to vendor company is called...

4) Liabilities which are incurred on account of purchasing and selling are called as...

5) Assets less liabilities taken over by purchasing company is called...

Ans :- (1) Amalgamation, (2) one, formation, (3) Purchase consideration, (4) Trade Liabilities, (5) Net assets.

(b) State Whether the following statement are true or false.

1) Purchasing company is also knows as vendee company.

2) Outsiders liabilities are transferred to shareholders account.

3) A new company need not to be formed in case of amalgamation.

4) The term trade liabilities includes debentures and outstanding salaries.

5) Liabilities not taken over by the new company are not transferred to Realisation Account.

6) Accumulated losses and profits are transferred to realisation account in case of amalgamation of a company with another company.

7) A new company is formed in case of absorption.

Ans : 1 - True, 2 - False, 3 - False, 4 - False, 5 - True, 6 - False, 7 - False.

c) Select the most appropriate answer.

1) Accumulated profit includes :

(a) Provision for doubtful debts.

(b) Insurance Fund,

(c) Employee's provident Fund.

2) Preliminary expenses are transferred by the vendor company at the time of absorption to :

   (a) Purchasing Company's account,

   (b) Realisation Account,

   (c) Equity Shareholders account.

3) The Share capital to the extent already held by purchasing company is closed by vendor company by crediting it to :

   (a) Investment account,

   (b) Purchasing Company's Account,

   (c) Share Capital Account.

4) Two Companies X Ltd. and Y Ltd. go into liquidation to form a new company, Z Ltd, it is a case of :

   (a) Absorption,

   (b) External Reconstruction,

   (c) Amalgamation.

Ans : 1 - (b), 2 - (c), 3 - (b), 4 - (c)

A) Problems on Amalgamation

1) The Balance Sheets of Pune and Indapur Ltd. as on 31-3-2014 were as follows :

Balance Sheet of Pune Ltd. as on 31-3-2014

Liabilities	Rs.	Assets		Rs.
Share Capital :		Goodwill		22,500
675 Equity Shares		Land & Building		32,500
of Rs. 10 each	67,500	Plant & Machinery		12,500
General Reserve	3,000	Stock		20,000
Dividend Equalisation		Debtors	10,500	
Reserve	2,500	Less : R.D.D.	500	10,000
Profit and Loss A/c	4,500	Cash in hand		2,500
Creditors	20,000	Cash at Bank		10,000
Outstanding Exp.	1,250			
Provision for Taxation	11,250			
	1,10,000			1,10,000

Balance Sheet of Indapur Ltd.
as on 31-3-2014

Liabilities	Rs.	Assets		Rs.
Share Capital :		Land & Building		20,000
500 Equity Shares of		Plant & machinery		20,000
Rs. 100 each	50,000	Furniture and Fittings		3,750
Bank Overdraft	5,000	Vehicles		11,250
Creditors	17,500	Stock		12,500
		Debtors	3,500	
		Less : R.D.D.	1,000	2,500
		Cash-in-Hand		1,250
		Profit and Loss A/c		1,250
	72,500			72,500

The companies amalgamated as on date of above Balance Sheet and new Company Satara Ltd. was formed to carry on the business of Pune Ltd. and Indapur Ltd. on the following terms :

1. Satara Ltd. took all Assets of Pune Ltd.except debtors, cash and bank balance at 10% Depreciation and agreed to pay Rs. 25,000 for goodwill. It also took over creditors and outstanding expenses.
2. Tax liability for 2014 was realised at Rs.9,500.
3. Satara Ltd. took all assets of Indapur Ltd. except Cash and Debtors. Land and Building and Stock were taken at 20% appreciation and other assets were taken at book value. Satara Ltd. also agreed to take over the creditors of Indapur Ltd.
4. Indapur Ltd. paid bank overdraft in full.
5. The purchase consideration was satisfied as follows :
   Cash of Rs. 5,000 to Pune Ltd. and Rs.3,750 to Indapur Ltd. The Balance of purchase consideration was paid in the Equity Shares of Satara Ltd. of Rs. 100 each.
6. Debtors of Pune Ltd. and Indapur Ltd. realised Rs. 9,500 and Rs. 3,000 respectively.
   You are Required to prepare :
   Realisation Account, Cash Accout, Satara Ltd. Account and Equity Shareholders Account in the books of Pune Ltd. and Indapur Ltd.

Ans :- Pune Ltd. - P. C. = Rs. 62,250

    Realisation Loss Rs. 4,500

    Indapur Ltd. P.C. = Rs. 56,500

    Realisations Profit Rs. 7,000.

2) The following are the Balance Sheets of two companies, Sneha Ltd. and Prabha Ltd. as on 31st March 2014.

Liabilities	Sneha Ltd. Rs.	Prabha Ltd. Rs.	Assets	Sneha Ltd. Rs.	Prabha Ltd. Rs.
Share Capital	15,00,000	3,90,000	Goodwill	1,00,000	1,00,000
Share Premium A/c	1,500	-	Property	4,50,000	1,30,000
General Reserve	1,00,000	-	Machinery	3,50,000	1,10,000
P & L. A/c	1,68,650	-	Stock	6,82,760	1,52,000
10% Debentures	-	70,000	Sundry Debtors	2,58,500	95,000
8% Debentures	3,50,000	-	Bank Balance	3,36,740	-
Sundry Creditors	57,850	2,57,000	Profit & Loss A/c	-	1,36,000
Bank Overdraft	-	6,000			
	21,78,000	7,23,000		21,78,000	7,23,000

The two companies decided to amalgamate as on 31st March 2014 and a new company called "Sneha Prabha Ltd." was formed with an authorised capital of Rs. 25,00,000 in shares of Rs. 10 each.

The following terms were agreed upon :

Sneha Ltd.

1) The consideration was 6 shares of Rs. 10 each fully paid in the new company in exchange for every 5 shares in Sneha Ltd. and Rs. 10,000 in cash.

2) The debenture holders were to be alloted such debentures in the new company bearing interest at 7% as would bring them the same amount of interest.

3) The new company to take over all the assets and liabilities at their book values.

Prabha Ltd.

1) The consideration was one share of Rs. 10 each fully paid in the new company in exchange for every three shares in Prabha Ltd. and Rs. 5,000 in cash.

2) The debentureholders were to be allotted such debentures in the new company bearing interest at 7% as would bring them the same amount of interest.

3) The new company was to take over all the assets and liabilities at their book values. You are requested to calculate purchase consideration in case of each company and prepare the Balance Share of Sneha Prabha Ltd. after amalgamation.   (P.U.)

Ans : P.C. Sneha Ltd. Rs. 22,10,000

Prabha Ltd. Rs. 2,35,000

3) Fort Ltd. and Dadar Ltd. carry on business of a similar nature and it is agreed that they should amalgamate and form a new company Bombay Ltd. The position of the two companies was :

Fort Ltd.

Liabilities	Rs.	Assets	Rs.
Paid-up Capital :		Goodwill	14,000
600 Equity Shares of		Stock	40,000
Rs. 100 each	60,000	Debtors	36,000
Profit & Loss A/c	10,000		
Sundry Creditors	20,000		
	90,000		90,000

Dadar Ltd.

Liabilities	Rs.	Assets	Rs.
Paid-up Capital :		Stock	44,000
4,000 Equity Shares of		Debtors	16,000
Rs. 10 each	40,000		
Profit & Loss A/c	8,400		
Sundry Creditors	11,600		
	60,000		60,000

The average profits of the Fort Ltd. and the Dadar Ltd. have been Rs. 18,000 and Rs. 6,000 respectively. Mumbai Ltd. agrees with Fort Ltd. and Dadar Ltd. to take over both concerns for the sum of Rs. 1,20,000 and in addition to discharge all liabilities. Mumbai Ltd. agreed to issue shares at face value in discharge of purchase consideration.

It is agreed that the stock of Fort Ltd. and Dadar Ltd. before being taken over by Mumbai Ltd. will be written off to the extent of 10% of their respective book figures.

The profit on the conversion is to be divided between the shareholders of Fort Ltd. and Dadar Ltd. in the same proportion as the profit previously earned by them.

Show Realisation A/c and Shareholders A/c in the books of Fort Ltd. and Journal entries in the books of Mumbai Ltd.

Ans : Fort Ltd. - P. C. = Rs. 73,500

Realisation Profit Rs. 7,500

4) The following are the Balance Sheet of two companies A Ltd. and B Ltd. on 31st March, 2014.

A Ltd.

Liabilities	Rs.	Assets		Rs.
Equity Share of Rs. 1		Goodwill		10,000
each fully paid	1,50,000	Building		45,000
Forfeited shares A/c	150	Machinery at cost		
Reserve Fund	10,000	Less : Depreciation		35,000
4% Debentures	35,000	Sundry Debtors		25,850
Sundry Creditors	5,785	Stock		68,276
Profit & Loss A/c	16,865	Cash at Bank		33,674
	2,17,800			2,17,800

B Ltd.

Liabilities	Rs.	Assets		Rs.
Equity Shares of Rs. 1		Goodwill		10,000
each fully paid	39,000	Building		13,000
5% Debentures	7,000	Machinery		11,000
Sundry Creditors	25,700	Sundry Debtors	10,000	
Bank Overdraft	600	Less : R.D.D.	500	9,500
		Stock		15,200
		Profit & Loss A/c		13,600
	72,300			72,300

The two companies decided to amalgamate as on 31-3-2014 and a new company called XY Ltd. was formed with an authorised capital of Rs. 2,50,000 in shares of Re. 1 each. The following terms were agreed.

The Consideration was :

1. 6 shares of Re. 1 each at Rs. 1.10 fully paid in the new company in exchange for every five shares in A Ltd. and Rs. 1,000 in cash. One share of Re. 1 each at Rs. 1.10 fully paid in the new company in exchange for every 3 shares in B Ltd. and Rs. 500 in cash.

2. The debentureholders were to be allotted such debentures in the new company bearing interest at $3\frac{1}{2}$ % as would bring them the same amount of interest.

3. A Ltd. to pay its own cost of winding up which amounted to Rs. 300 and the cost of winding up of B Ltd. is to be paid by XY Ltd. (not included in purchase price) which amounted to Rs. 200.

4. The new company to take over all the assets and the liabilities at book values.

You are requested to draw up necessary ledger accounts in the books of A Ltd. and B Ltd. and give journal entries and a Balance Sheet in the books of XY Ltd.

Ans : A Ltd. = P.C. Rs. 2,39,000

Realisation profit Rs. 21,685

B Ltd. = P.C. Rs. 24,800

Realisation Loss Rs. 10,600

5) Given below are the balance Sheets as on 31st March, 2014 of Alpha Ltd. and Beta Ltd. which are amalgamated to form a new company Gamma Ltd.

Liabilities	Alpha Rs.	Beta Rs.	Assets	Alpha Rs.	Beta Rs.
Share Capital in Shares of Rs.100 each fully paid	1,00,000	2,00,000	Fixed Assets Goodwill Building	- - 30,000	40,000 25,000
Reserves & Surplus			Plant	60,000	80,000
Capital Reserve	50,000	10,000	Furniture	5,000	10,000
Profit & Loss A/c	40,000	-	Current Assets		
General Reserve	10,000	-	Stock	1,14,000	1,50,000
Loans	80,000	60,000	Debtors	90,000	3,000
Other Liabilities	20,000	80,000	Cash at Bank	1,000	2,000
	-	-	Profit & Loss A/c	-	40,000
	3,00,000	3,50,000		3,00,000	3,50,000

The shareholders in the amalgamated companies are to be allotted fully paid equity shares in Gamma Ltd. for the amount of purchase consideration for which purpose all assets and liabilities are to be taken at book values except goodwill of Beta Ltd. which is considered worthless.

Give Journal Entries to close the books of Beta Ltd. and show the opening Balance Sheet of Gamma Ltd. (P.U.)

Ans : Purchase Consideration

Alpha Ltd.   Rs. 2,00,000

Beta Ltd.   Rs. 1,30,000

B/S Total   5,70,000

B) Problems on Absorption

6) The Engineers Ltd. agreed to acquire the goodwill and assets, other than cash of Stainless Ltd. as on 31st March, 2014. A summary of the Balance Sheet of Stainless Ltd. as on 31st March, 2014 was as follows :

Liabilities	Rs.	Assets	Rs.
Share capital in Rs. 10/-		Goodwill	50,000
Equity share fully paid	5,00,000	Land, Building & Plant	6,70,000
General Reserve	1,80,000	Stock	1,04,000
Profit & Loss A/c	90,000	Debtors	38,000
8% Debentures	1,00,000	Cash	28,000
Creditors	20,000		
	8,90,000		8,90,000

The consideration payable by Engineers Ltd. was agreed as follows :

1. A cash payment equivalent to Rs. 5/- for every Rs. 10/- Equity Shares in Stainless Ltd.
2. The issue of 80,000 Rs. 10/- Equity Shares fully paid in Engineers Ltd. having an agreed value of Rs. 12.50 per share.
3. The issue of such an amount of fully paid 6% Debentures of Engineers Ltd. at Rs. 96/- as is sufficient to discharge the 8% Debentures of Stainless Ltd. at Rs. 120. The liabilities of Stainless Ltd. other than Debentures were discharged by that company.

When computing the agreed consideration, the directors of Engineers Ltd. valued the Land, Building and Plant at Rs. 11,50,000. The stock at Rs. 90,000 and the debtors at the amount stated on the Balance Sheet of Stainless Ltd. subject to allowance of 5% to cover doubtful debts. On the sales of its assets stainless Ltd. went into liquidation, the Equity Shareholders receiving cash and Equity Shares in Engineers Ltd. as repayments of their capital in Stainless Ltd.

You are required to draft the Journal entries, (a) To record the acquisition in the books of Engineers Ltd., (b) To close the books of Stainless Ltd.

Ans : - Purchase Consideration   Rs. 13,70,000

Realisations   Rs. 4,88,000

7) The summarised Balance Sheets of the Thick Ltd. and Thin Ltd. on 31st March, 2014 were as follows :

Liabilities	Thick Ltd. Rs.	Thin Ltd. Rs.	Assets	Thick Ltd. Rs.	Thin Ltd. Rs.
Shares of Rs. 10 each fully paid	2,00,000	1,50,000	Goodwill	-	30,000
			Fixed Assets	1,60,000	50,000
Trade Liabilities	25,000	60,000	Floating Assets	95,000	80,000
Profit & Loss A/c	30,000	-	Profit & Loss A/c	-	50,000
	2,55,000	2,10,000		2,55,000	2,10,000

The management of Thick Ltd. resolved to take over the business of Thin Ltd. with effects from April, 1st 2014. The shareholders of the company agreed to accept shares in the former company on the basis that the shares of Thick Ltd. were worth Rs. 12.50 each and that the shares of Thin Ltd. were worth Rs. 5 each. The purchasing company took over the fixed assets of Thin Ltd. together with the floating assets and the liabilities.

Assuming the necessary formalities were carried out, make journal entries necessary for these transactions in the books of Thick Ltd. and draw up its Balance Sheet immediately after the merger.

Ans :- Purchase Consideration Rs. 75,000

B/S Total Rs. 3,85,000

8) Long Ltd. has agreed to acquire goodwill and assets (except investments) of Short Ltd. as at 31st March 2014. The Balance Sheet of Short Ltd. as on that date was as follows :

Liabilities	Rs.	Assets	Rs.
Share Capital	1,60,000	Goodwill	20,000
16,000 Equity shares of		Land and Buildings	80,000
Rs. 10 each		Plant	80,000
General Reserve	25,000	Investments	30,000
Profit & Loss A/c	18,000	Stock	40,000
8% Debentures	60,000	Debtors	50,000
Creditors	37,000	Bank	20,000
Provision for Taxation	20,000		
	3,20,000		3,20,000

Long Ltd. will :

1. Discharge the Debentures @ 8% premium by issue of 7% Debentures in Long Ltd. at 10% discount.

2. Issue 3 shares of Long Ltd. at market price of Rs. 11 for 2 shares of Short Ltd.

3. Pay Rupee 2 in cash for each share of Short Ltd.

4. Pay absorption expenses Rs. 3,000.

Short Ltd. sells the investments for Rs. 32,000, one-third of the shares received from Long Ltd. are sold @ Rs. 10.50 each. Tax liability is determined at Rs.24,000. Before transfer Short Ltd., declares and pays 10% Dividend.

Long Ltd. values Land & Buildings at Rs. 1,00,000. Plant at 10% below book value, stock at Rs. 35,000 and Debtors subject to 5% Provision.

Show 1. Ledger Accounts in the books of Short Ltd.

2. Journal Entries in the books of Long Ltd.

Ans : - 1) Purchase consideration Rs. 3,63,800

Realisation profit Rs. 76,000.

9) The Assets of Rukmini Company Limited are purchased by the Shrikrishna Company Limited. The purchase consideration was agreed upon as under :

(a) A cash payment of Rs. 90/- per share for shares held by the members in the vendor company.

(b) Settlement of Debentures in the Rukmini Company Limited by repayments at Rs. 550/- per Debenture held.

(c) To exchange four shares of Shrikrishna Company Limited of Rs. 75/- each, quoted in the market at Rs. 140/- each for one share held by the members in the vendor company.

(d) Payments of Realisation expenses Rs. 12,000.

The Balance Sheet of Rukmini Company Limited as on 31st March, 2014 was as follows :

Capital & Liabilities	Rs.	Property & Assets		Rs.
Share Capital :		Land & Buildings		10,00,000
6,000 Equity Shares of		Plant & Machinery		16,00,000
Rs. 500 each fully paid	30,00,000	Furniture & Fixtures		3,10,000
Insurance Fund	65,000	Vehicles		2,40,000
General Reserve	2,75,000	Stock on Hand		8,10,000
Profit & Loss A/c	60,000	Bills Receivable		1,90,000
1,300 7%s Debenture of		Sundry Debtors	3,00,000	
Rs. 500 each	6,50,000	Less : Provision		
Sundry Creditors	1,10,000	For Doubtful Debts	35,000	2,65,000
Bills Payable	1,40,000	Cash in Hand		85,000
Bank Overdraft	2,00,000			
	45,00,000			45,00,000

You are required to prepare in the books of accounts of Rukmini Company Limited : (a) Realisation Account, (b) Equity Shareholders Account and (c) Cash Account and Journal Entries in the Books of the Purchasing Company including entries for cash.

Ans:- Purchase Consideration Rs. 30,67,000

Realisation Loss Rs. 15,10,000.

10) The following is the Balance Sheet of Pandurang Ltd. as on 31st March 2014.

Liabilities	Rs.	Assets	Rs.
Share Capital-		Goodwill	35,000
2,000 Shares of Rs. 100		Land & Building	85,000
each	2,00,000	Plant & ,Machinery	1,60,000
Reserve Fund	20,000	Stock	55,000
5% Debentures	1,00,000	Sundry Debtors	65,000
Loan from A (a director)	40,000	Cash & Bank	34,000
Sundry Creditors	80,000	Discount on Debentures	6,000
Total Rs.	4,40,000	Total Rs.	4,40,000

The business of the company is taken over by Eshwar company Ltd. as on that date on the following terms :

a) Eshwar Co. to take over all assets except cash, to value the assets at book values less 10% except Goodwill which is to be valued at 4 years' purchase of the excess of average (5 years) profits over 8% of the combined amount of share capital and reserves.

b) Eshwar Co. to take over trade liabilities which was subject to a discount of 5%.

c) The purchase consideration was to be discharged in cash to the extent of Rs. 1,50,000, and the balance in fully paid equity shares of Rs. 10 each valued at Rs. 12.50 per share. The average of the five years' profit was Rs. 30,100/-. The expenses of absorption Rs. 4,000 were paid by Pandurang Co. Ltd; but afterwards reimbursed by Eshwar Co. Ltd.

Show the necessary ledger accounts in the books of Pandurang Co. Ltd. and the working of Purchase consideration.

Ans :- Purchase Consideration   3,02,500

Realisation Loss A/c   17,500

11) The following is the Balance Sheet of Small Ltd. as on 31st March 2014.

Liabilities	Rs.	Assets	Rs.
4,000 Equity shares of	4,00,000	Buildings	1,70,000
Rs. 100 each		Plant & Machinery	4,00,000
General Reserve	50,000	Investments	50,600
Profit & Loss A/c	5,600	Debtors	1,40,500
5% Debentures	2,50,000	Stock	80,700
Creditors	1,28,700	Cash At Bank	16,500
Dividend Equilisation Ltd.	24,000		
	8,58,300		8,58,300

Small Ltd. was absorbed by Big Ltd. on the above on the following terms and conditions. Big Ltd. to

a) Assume all liabilities and to acquire all assets excepts investments which were sold by small Ltd. for Rs. 45,500/-

b) Discharge the debenture debt at a discount of 5% by issue of 7%s Debentures in Big Ltd.

c) Issue two shares of Rs. 60 each in Big Ltd. at Rs. 65 per share and also pay Rs. 2 in cash to the shareholders of Small Ltd. in exchange for one share in small Ltd.

d) Pay the cost of absorption Rs. 1,500.

With the consents of the shareholders, the liquidator of Small Ltd. sold off in open market, one-fourth of the shares received from Big Ltd. at the average rate of Rs. 63 per share.

Prepare :

i) Statement of purchase consideration.

ii) Realisation A/c.

iii) Shareholders' A/c.

iv) Bank A/c.

in the books of Small Ltd.

(P.U.)

Ans :   1) Purchase consideration Rs. 7,67,000

       2) Realisation Profit Rs. 93,900.

12) Abhay Ltd. is absorbed by Bharat Ltd. as 31st March 2014, when the Balance Sheet of Abhay Ltd. was as follows :

Liabilities	Rs.	Assets	Rs.
Share Capital -		Land & Building	17,50,000
20,000 Equity Shares		Plant & Machinery	18,00,000
of Rs. 100 each fully paid	20,00,000	Stock	2,00,000
Sinking Fund	3,00,000	Debtors	3,60,000
Share Premium	1,50,000	Sinking Fund investment	3,00,000
Provident Fund	1,50,000	Cash at Bank	30,000
Employees' Saving	3,00,000		
Sundry Creditors	1,40,000		
8% Debentures	4,00,000		
6% Debentures	10,00,000		
Total Rs.	44,40,000	Total Rs.	44,40,000

The purchase consideration for absorption was agreed as under :
a) Taking over of all liabilities.
b) Payment of cost of absorption not exceeding Rs. 8,000/-
c) Repayment of 6% Debentures at 5% premium.
d) Discharge of 8% Debentures at 10% premium by issue of 5% Debentures in Bharat Ltd.
e) A payment of Rs. 15 per share in cash and an allotment of one 7% preference share of Rs. 100 each and 5 equity shares of Rs. 100 each in Bharat Ltd. for every four shares in Abhay Ltd.

Actual cost of absorption was Rs. 10,000/- you are required to present necessary accounts in the books of Abhay Ltd. and opening entries in the books of Bharat Ltd.

(P.U.)

Ans : Purchase Consideration Rs. 47,98,000
Realisation profit Rs. 8,48,000.

C) Problems on External Reconstruction

13) The Balance Sheet as on March, 31st 2014 of the Delta Co. Ltd. was as follows :

Liabilities	Rs.	Assets	Rs.
Share capital :		Land & Building	65,000
1,000 shares of Rs. 100		Machinery	22,000
each fully paid	1,00,000	Furniture	3,000
8% Debentures	40,000	Stock	25,000
Creditors	6,000	Debtors	15,000
		Cash	4,000
		Profit & Loss A/c	12,000
	1,46,000		1,46,000

It was decided to reconstruct the company and for this purpose a new company called the Omega Co. Ltd. was formed with nominal capital of Rs. 1,00,000 divided into 500 9% preference shares of Rs. 100 each and 500 equity shares of Rs. 100 each to take over the assets and liabilities of the Delta Co. Ltd. on the following basis :
(a) The debentureholders in Delta Co. Ltd. are to accept 400 preference shares.
(b) The Shareholders of Delta Co. Ltd. are to receive one equity share in Omega Co. Ltd. for every two shares held by them.
(c) The cost of liquidation Rs. 600 is paid by the new company itself (i.e. not include in purchase price)
The balance of preference shares has been issued and taken up by the public.

Give important ledger accounts in the books of Delta Co. Ltd. and journal entries in the books of Omega Ltd.

(**Ans :** Purchase consideration Rs. 90,000; Loss on Realisation Rs. 38,000)

14) On the 31st March, 2014 the Balance Sheet of H Ltd. was :

Liabilities	Rs.	Assets	Rs.
Authorised & Issued :		Goodwill	55,000
Share Capital :		Sundry Assets	1,64,500
50,000 6% cum. pref.		Cash	500
shares of Re. 1 each	50,000	Profit & Loss A/c	30,000
1,50,000 ordinary shares			
of Re. 1 each	1,50,000		
5% Debentures	30,000		
Creditors (Pref. dividend	20,000		
are in arrears for 4 years)			
	2,50,000		2,50,000

A. Scheme of reconstruction was agreed upon as follows :

1. A new company to be formed called J Ltd. with Authorised Capital of Rs. 3,25,000 all in ordinary shares of Re. 1 each.

2. One ordinary share, 50 paise, paid, in the new company, to be issued for each ordinary share in the old company.

3. Two ordinary shares, 50 paise paid, in the new company to be issued for each preference share in the old company.

4. Arrears of dividend to be cancelled.

5. Debentureholders to receive 30,000 ordinary shares in the new company credited fully paid.

6. Creditors to be taken over by the new company.

7. The remaining unissued shares to be taken up and paid for in full by the directors.

8. The new company to take over the old company's assets, subject to : (a) Writing down sundry assets by Rs. 35,000, (b) Adjusting Goodwill as required.

Show : (i) Realisation Account of H Ltd., (ii) Opening entries of J Ltd. (iii) Balance sheet of J Ltd. Ignore Costs.

(**Ans :** Purchase price Rs. 1,55,000; Realisation Loss 45,000; B/S of J Ltd. Rs. 2,20,000)

15) On 31st March 2014 the Balance Sheet of Blank Co. Ltd. was as follows :

Liabilities	Rs.	Assets	Rs.
Share Capital		Patents	1,20,000
12,000 Equity Shares		Plant & Machinery	40,000
of Rs. 10 each	1,20,000	Stock	30,000
Sundry Creditors	1,40,000	Book Debts	50,000
		Cash	1,250
		Preliminary Expenses	7,250
		Profit & Loss A/c	11,500
	2,60,000		2,60,000

The company being unable to raise further capital and the patents standing in the books at a figure largely in excess of their value, the following scheme of reconstruction was submitted to the shareholders and creditors :

(a) The Company to go into voluntary liquidation and a new company called "The Blank Co. Ltd." to be formed with an authorised capital of Rs. 2,00,000 in Rs. 10 shares to take over the assets and liabilities.

(b) Liabilities to be discharged by the new company as follows :
Preferential creditors for Rs. 2,000 to be paid in full and the other creditors to be paid 25 Ps. in the rupee in cash and 50 ps. in the rupee in 6% debentures of the new company.

(c) 12,000 shares, Rs. 5 per share paid, to be issued to the shareholders of the old company, the balance of Rs. 5 being payable on allotment.

(d) The costs of liquidation amounting to Rs. 1,750 to be paid by the new company as part of the purchase consideration.

Assuming that the scheme has been approved and sanctioned, you are required :

(i) To prepare the Realisation Account in the books of the Blank Co. Ltd.

(ii) To pass journal entries in the books of the new company and give its initial Balance Sheet.

(**Ans :** Purchase Price Rs. 1,67,250; Realisation Loss Rs. 4,21,250.)

16) Bharat Ltd. decided to reconstruct and consequently went into voluntary liquidation. The Balance Sheet was -

Liabilities	Rs.	Assets		Rs.
Share Capital :		Land & Building		31,800
Authorised & Issued :		Plant & machinery		16,500
40,000 7% preference shares		Stock in Hand		8,970
of Re. 1 each fully paid	40,000	Trade Debtors	13,400	
60,000 Equity Shares		Less : Provision	300	13,100
of Re. 1 each fully paid	60,000	Cash in Hand		40
Profit prior to Incorporation	1,210	Profit & Loss A/c		41,270
Loans	500			
Trade Creditors	8,610			
Bills Payable	420			
Bank Overdraft	940			
	1,11,680			1,11,680

There is a contingent liability in respect of claim for Rs. 1,450 for royalties.

It was arranged that a new company. New Bharat Ltd. should be formed to acquire the under mentioned assets at the value stated; Land and Buildings Rs. 20,000; Plant & Machinery Rs. 12,000; Stock Rs. 8,000. The total of Rs. 40,000 payable was satisfied by the allotment of 20,000 6% preference shares of Re. 1 each, fully paid and 2,000 Equity Shares of Rs. 15 each, credited with Rs. 10 paid up. The new company also satisfied the contingent liability in respect of the claim by allotting to the claimant 40 Equity Shares, fully paid.

The preference shareholders in the old company accepted the preference shares in the new company in full satisfaction and the Equity shareholders took the partly paid Equity Shares.

The book debts realised Rs. 12,725 and the amount of trade creditors proved to be Rs. 8,314. The liabilities were discharged and the costs of winding up were Rs. 1,071.

Preliminary expenses were Rs. 2,000 payable by the new company.

(a) Close the books of the old company, showing the necessary cash book entries and ledger accounts.

(b) Give the journal entries recording the transactions of the new company.

Ans : Purchase Consideration Rs. 40,000

Realisation Profit Rs. 1,760.

17) The Balance Sheet of the cautious Ltd. before reconstruction was as follows :

Liabilities	Rs.	Assets	Rs.
Share Capital :		Fixed Assets :	
Authorised & Issued :		Land & Buildings	63,600
800 7% pref. shares of		Plant & Machinery	33,000
Rs. 100 each fully paid	80,000	Furniture	1,240
12,000 equity shares		**Current Assets :**	
of Rs. 10 each fully paid	1,20,000	Stock-in-trade	16,700
Reserves & Surplus		Sundry Debtors	26,200
Capital Reserve	2,420	Cash in Hand	80
Unsecured Loans		Profit & Loss A/c	82,540
From Bank	1,880		
From Others	1,000		
Current Liabilities & Provisions :			
Sundry Creditors	18,060		
	2,23,360		2,23,360

A new company Wise Ltd. was formed to acquire the following assets at the values stated - Land & Buildings Rs. 40,000; Plant & Machinery Rs. 24,000; Furniture Rs. 800; Stock in Trade Rs. 15,200.

The total purchase consideration was satisfied by the allotment of 6% preference shares of Rs. 100 each fully paid and 8,000 Equity shares of Rs. 10 each Rs. 5 paid.

The preference shareholders in the old company accepted the preference shares in the new company in full satisfaction and the equity shareholders took the partly paid equity shares. The sundry debtors realised Rs. 25,450 and the amount of sundry creditors proved to be Rs. 18,508. The liabilities were discharged. The liquidation expenses were Rs. 1,071.

Give Journal entries to close the books of the old company and to record the transactions in the books of the new company.

Ans. : Purchase Price Rs. 80,000; Realisation Profit Rs. 3,191.

18) The Balance Sheet of Dhanvardhini Ltd. as on 31st March, 2014 was :

Liabilities	Rs.	Assets	Rs.
Share Capital :		Land & Building	3,20,000
40,000 Shares of Rs. 10		Plant & Machinery	1,20,000
each fully paid	4,00,000	Stock	80,000
Sundry Creditors	3,00,000	Trade Debtors	1,20,000
		Cash	500
		Preliminary Expenses	10,000
		Profit & Loss A/c	49,500
	7,00,000		7,00,000

The following scheme of reconstruction was sactioned. The company to go into voluntary liquidation and a new company with an authorised capital of Rs. 8,00,000 to be formed to take over the assets & liabilities on the following terms :

(a) Preferential creditors for Rs. 10,000 to be paid in full.

(b) Half of the remaining creditors were to receive cash of 50 paise in a rupee in full settlement of their claims and the rest were to receive 6% Debentures of the new company at par.

(c) The shareholders of the old company to receive one share in the new company of Rs. 10 each Rs. 5 paid up for every share in the old company.

(d) The new company to pay the cost of liquidation amounting to Rs. 6,000.

(e) The shares issued to vendors were fully called and paid.

Prepare the Balance Sheet of the new company assuming that the Plant & Machinery, Stock and Trade debtors were taken over at book values.

Ans : B/S Rs. 5,45,000; Purchase Price Rs. 4,33,500.)

19) The Balance Sheet of Planners Ltd. on 31st March, 2014 is as follows :

Balance Sheet as on 31-3-2014

Liabilities	Rs.	Assets		Rs.
Share Capital :		Goodwill		20,000
1,20,000 ordinary shares of		Fixed Assets		1,00,000
Re. 1 each	1,20,000	**Current Assets :**		
50,000 6% Cumulative Prefe-		Stock	22,000	
rence shares of Re. 1 each	50,000	Work-in-progress	5,500	
Secured Loans		Debtors	34,000	
6% Debentures Rs. 10 each	50,000	Bank	17,500	79,000
Current Liabilities :		Miscellaneous Expenses		
Creditors	20,000	Formation Expenses	1,000	
		Profit & Loss A/c	40,000	41,000
	2,40,000			2,40,000

The dividend on the preference shares Rs. 5,400 was in arrears. A scheme of reconstruction was accepted by all parties and was completed on 1-4-2014.

A new company was formed, Budgets Ltd. with an Authorised capital of Rs. 2,00,000 consisting of 2,00,000 ordinary shares of Re. 1 each. This company took over all the assets (except Goodwill) of planners Ltd. The purchase consideration was satisfied partly in cash and partly by the issue at par of shares and the debentures by the new company in accordance with the following arrangements.

1. The creditors of the old company received, in settlement of Rs. 10 due to them, Rs. 7 in cash and three fully paid ordinary shares in the new company.

2. The holders of preference shares in the old company received seven fully paid ordinary shares in the new company to every eight preference shares in the old company and in addition they received 5,400 ordinary shares in the new company for arrears of dividend.

3. The ordinary shareholders in the old company received one fully paid share in the new company for every five ordinary shares in the old company.

4. The holders of 6% Debentures in the old company received Rs. 40 cash and 6% Debentures issued at par for every Rs. 100 debentures held in the old company.

5. The balance of the authorised capital of the new company was issued at par for cash & was fully paid on 1st April, 2014.

6. The stock was valued at Rs. 20,000 and the other current Assets were brought into the new company's books at the amounts at which they appeared in the old company's Balance Sheet. The balance of the purchase consideration represented the agreed value of the fixed assets.

You are requested to show :

(a) Realisation Account, Sundry Shareholders Account in the books of planners Ltd.

(b) Your calculation of the purchase consideration.

(c) The Summarised Balance Sheet of Budgets Ltd. as on 1st April, 2014.

Ans : P.C. Rs. 1,63,150; Realisation Loss Rs. 55,000.

6.1 Meaning of Reconstruction

The term 'reconstruction' means reorganising the capital structure of a company including the reduction of the claims of both shareholders and creditors against the company. Such a reconstruction generally becomes necessary on account of bad financial position of a company. The reconstruction may be of following two types :-
i) External Reconstruction
ii) Internal Reconstruction

i) External Reconstruction :

In case of external reconstruction, a new company is formed to take over the business of the existing company, which is in a bad financial condition. The vendor company then is liquidated and a new company is formed for the reconstruction.

ii) Internal Reconstruction :

In case of internal reconstruction, neither the old company is liquidated nor a new company is formed. To facilitate this process of internal reconstruction, the existing capital structure of the company is re-organised to infuse new life into it. The claims of various parties, viz. creditors, debentureholders, shareholders are suitably adjusted to write off accumulated losses, fictitious assets etc. In short, the existing company reconstitutes its capital structure and continues to carry on its business. The internal reconstruction is simpler than external reconstruction. The main objective of internal reconstruction is to write off miscellaneous expenses like preliminary expenses, Discount on issue of shares and debentures and underwriting commission etc. These assets are treated as 'lost capital' and hence capital reduction is required. Another objective of internal reconstruction is to write off fictitious assets like goodwill, patents etc. The reconstructed company may be in a position to carry forward its losses for income tax purposes against future profits. This will considerably reduce the income tax liability of the company in periods when good profits are made by it.

Internal reduction may require :
1) Alteration of Share Capital.
2) Reduction in Share Capital.

6.2 Alteration of Share Capital :

The Companies Act has used the word "Alteration Proper" for alteration of share capital. Alteration of share capital can be done under the provisions of Sections 94 to 97 of the Companies Act. The term alteration proper includes the following : –
1) Increase in share capital by issue of new shares.
2) Consolidation or sub-division of existing shares into shares of larger or smaller denomination.
3) Conversion of fully-paid shares into stocks and vice versa.
4) Cancellation of un-issued shares.

Alteration in share capital can be made by passing ordinary resolution, only if it is authorised by Articles of Association to do so. This change of alteration of capital must be communicated to the Registrar within 30 days of the date of passing the ordinary resolution.

Accounting Entries for Alteration of Share Capital :

1) Increase in share capital : This is similar to making a fresh issue of share capital and usual entries are to be passed for the increase in share capital.

2) Consolidation and conversion of shares into stock : In case of consolidation of shares, shares of smaller denominations are to be converted into shares of larger denomination. In such a case, the paid-up capital remains the same but the number of shares is reduced. For example : if the equity share capital Rs.1,00,000 of Rs.10 each, are to be consolidated into shares of Rs. 100 each, the entry will be as under :-

Equity share capital (Rs.10) Dr.   1,00,000
   To Equity share capital (Rs.100)   1,00,000
(Being conversion of 10,000 equity shares of
Rs.10 each into 1,000 shares of Rs.100 each)

3) Sub-division of shares : In case of sub-division of shares, larger denominations are converted into shares of smaller denominations. The journal entry in respect of such a conversion would be on the same pattern as explained in the case of consolidation of shares except that the number of shares would increase. For example : A company having equity share capital of Rs.1,00,000 divided into shares of Rs.100 each decides to convert it into shares of Rs.10 each, the journal entry will be as under :-

     Equity Share Capital A/c (Rs. 100) ..... Dr.   1,00,000
       To Equity Share Capital A/c (Rs.10)   1,00,000
     (Being conversion of 1,000 shares of Rs.100
     each into 10,000 equity shares of Rs.10 each)

4) Conversion of shares into stock : A Company may convert its fully paid-up shares into stock or vice versa. In case, shares are converted into stock, the entry will be as under :-

     Share Capital A/c .....Dr.
       To Capital Stock A/c
     (Being conversion of shares into stock)

5) Cancellation of un-issued shares : As the un-issued shares are not recorded in the books of accounts, no entry is required to cancel them. Only the unauthorised capital is to be reduced to the extent of shares cancelled.

6.3 Reduction of Share Capital i.e. Internal Reconstruction

A Company can reduce its share capital as per provision of Sections 100 to 105 of the Companies Act. In order to effect share capital reduction, the following formalities must be completed :-

1) The Company must be authorised by its Articles of Association to reduce share capital. If there is no provision in the articles in this respect, it must pass a special resolution to alter its Articles of Association.

2) The Company must pass a special resolution to reduce share capital.

3) The Company must file a petition in the Court for seeking an order as regards confirming the reduction. If the Court is satisfied that the creditor's interest have been secured, it may confirm the reduction. However, it may impose the terms and conditions including a direction that the word "And Reduced" should be added after the name of the company for a certain period of time and that the company should publish the reasons for such reduction thereto. If the company fails to add the words **"And Reduced"**, a penalty of Rs.500 is payable.

4) The Company has to deliver to the Registrar, a certified copy of the Court's order and minutes approved by the Court showing the details of the shares for registration.

5) The Registrar will then register the order and the minutes.

6) After registration of these, the resolution to reduce capital shall take effect.

7) Notice of the registration shall be published in such a manner as the court may direct.

Causes for Internal Reconstruction

Following are the causes of capital reduction or internal reconstruction :-

1) Heavy accumulated losses

2) Over-valuation of assets

3) Declining turnover or profitability
4) Fall in the value of assets.
5) Increase in fictitious assets.
6) Future financial needs.

Forms of Capital Reduction

The reduction of share capital may take any of the following forms :-
a) Writing-off lost capital.
b) Refunding surplus of paid-up capital.
c) Reducing liability of members for uncalled capital.

6.4 Accounting Entries

a) Writing off lost capital

Internal reconstruction means the reduction of share capital to cancel any paid share capital which is lost i.e. not represented by the real value of assets. For example : The following is the balance sheet of a company.

Balance Sheet

Liabilities	Rs.	Assets	Rs.
7,000 shares of Rs.10 each	70,000	Fixed Assets	40,000
Creditors	30,000	Current Assets	30,000
		Profit & Loss A/c	10,000
		Goodwill	20,000
	1,00,000		1,00,000

The above balance sheet shows that the company has lost Rs. 30,000 (i.e. P & L A/C Rs. 10,000 + Goodwill Rs. 20,000) of its paid-up share capital. This will be written off by the help of following journal entry :-

       Share Capital A/c .... Dr   30,000
          To Capital Reduction A/c   30,000
       (Being loss of capital)

The share capital now stands reduced to Rs. 40,000. However, this reduction of share capital can be effected in two ways : One alternative could be only to reduce the paid-up value of the existing shares from Rs. 10 to Rs. 4 each without reducing the nominal value of the shares. This means the shareholders can be asked in future to pay Rs. 6 more, if the company requires additional capital. The journal entry in such a case will be the same as explained above.

Generally, the shareholders will be unwilling for the above alternative, since it puts an additional burden on them. Other alternative, can therefore be, to reduce both nominal as well as paid up value of shares to Rs. 4/- each. In such a case, the journal entry will be as under :

Share Capital A/c (Rs. 10) ...... Dr.	70,000	
To Share Capital A/c (Rs. 4)		40000
To Capital Reduction A/c		30,000

(Being value of share reduced to Rs. 4 each)

b) Refunding Surplus paid-up capital

If a company has more funds than what it can profitably use, then it may decide to refund the surplus capital to shareholders. For example : A Company has a share capital of Rs. 1,00,000 divided into shares of Rs. 10 each and it decides to repay to its members Rs. 2 per share and make share as of Rs. 8 each fully paid. The journal entry will be as under :-

Share Capital A/c (Rs. 10) ... Dr	1,00,000	
To Share Capital A/c (Rs. 8)		80,000
To Bank A/c		20,000

(Being value of each share reduced to Rs. 8)

c) Uncalled capital to be cancelled

In case the liability of members in respect of uncalled share capital is reduced, the paid-up value of the share capital will remain unchanged. However, the members will stand to gain since they will not have to pay money to the company to the extent of uncalled capital cancelled. For example : A company has a share capital of Rs. 1,00,000, divided into shares of Rs. 10 each called-up and paid-up Rs. 5 each. The company decides to cancel the liability of members to the extent of Rs. 5 per share thus making Rs. 5 paid-up. For this, following journal entry will be passed -

Share Capital A/c (Rs. 10) Dr	50,000	
To Share Capital A/c (Rs. 5)		50,000

(Being uncalled capital cancelled)

Note : In this case, no amount of capital is reduced and transferred to Capital Reduction Account

d) Surrender of Shares

In a reconstruction scheme, the shareholder may be required to surrender a part of their holding. Such a surrender can either be for immediate cancellation of the share capital or for issue of shares surrendered to some of the creditors of the company in satisfaction of their claims. The following accounting entries are to be passed in case of surrender of shares.

  a) On Surrender of Shares

    Share Capital A/c   ..... Dr

      To Shares Surrendered A/c

  b) On re-issue of Surrendered Shares

    Shares Surrendered A/c   ..... Dr

      To Share Capital A/c

  c) On Cancellation of Surrendered Shares

    Shares Surrendered A/c   ..... Dr

      To Capital Reduction A/c

If a creditor or any other claimant reduces his claim, and in consideration, some of the shares surrendered are issued to him, the Capital Reduction Account is to be credited by the amount of claim waived by the creditor, irrespective of the consideration of shares surrendered issued to him. For e.g. If a creditor for Rs. 60,000 reduces his claim to Rs. 40,000 and in consideration, he is given shares surrendered amounting to Rs. 14,000, the Capital Reduction Account is to be credited with Rs. 20,000 (i.e. 60,000 less 40,000 reduction in his claim) and not by 6,000. It means the issue of shares surrendered Rs. 14,000 is not taken into account. Further, if a creditor agrees to accept additional shares surrendered of Rs. 10,000 in part payment of Rs. 40,000, this amount of Rs. 10,000 is also credited to Capital Reduction Account and the claim for creditors will be shown at Rs. 30,000 in the Balance Sheet. The entry for this will be as under :–

```
Creditors A/c                        .... Dr.        30,000
    To Capital Reduction A/c                                 30,000
(Being reduction of the claims of creditors from Rs. 60,000 to Rs. 30,000)
```

Journal Entries

1) On reduction of paid-up capital

```
Share Capital (old face value) A/c                          ....Dr
    To Share Capital (new face value) A/c
    To Capital Reduction (with difference) A/c
(Being face value changed and paid-up value of shares reduced)
```

2) For reduction in shares without change in face value of shares.

```
Share Capital A/c                                           ....Dr
    To Capital Reduction A/c (with the amount of reduction)
(Being capital reduced without change in the face value)
```

3) If any sacrifice has been made by creditor i.e. reduction in the amount of credit.

```
Creditors A/c                                              ..... Dr
    To Capital Reduction A/c
(Being liability on creditors reduced)
```

4) For reduction in the amount of debentures or sacrifice made by debentureholders

```
Debentures A/c (with sacrifice)                            .....Dr.
Outstanding Interest on Debentures A/c (if any)            .....Dr
    To Capital Reduction A/c
(Being liability of debentures reduced)
```

5) For the appreciation in the value of Asset

```
Asset A/c (with appreciation)                              .....Dr
    To Capital Reduction A/c
(Being appreciation in the value of asset)
```

6) When the amount of capital reduction is utilised for writing off fictitious assets, past losses and excess value of other assets

Capital Reduction A/c   .....Dr
    To Profit & Loss A/c
    To Goodwill A/c
    To Preliminary Expenses A/c
    To Discount on issue of Shares or Debentures A/c
    To Patents and Trademarks A/c
    To Plant and Machinery A/c
    To Land & Building A/c
    To Stock A/c
    To Debtors A/c
    To Other Assets A/c
    To Capital Reserve A/c (It any balance is left)
(Being the balance of capital reduced utilised for uniting off assets and losses)

7) For transfer of Reserves & Surplus, Share premium to Capital Reduction A/c

General Reserve or Reserve A/c   .... Dr
Profit & Loss A/c (credit balance) A/c   .... Dr
Share Premium A/c   .... Dr
    To Capital Reserve A/c
(Being reserves and surplus and share premium account transferred)

8) For Sale of an asset

i) Sale of asset **at profit**

Bank A/c   .... Dr
    To Asset A/c
    To Capital Reduction A/c (Profit on Asset)
(Being asset sold on profit)

or

ii) Sale of an asset **at a loss**

Bank A/c   .... Dr
Capital Reduction A/c   .... Dr (with loss)
    To Asset A/c
(Being asset sold at a loss)

9) Contingent liability paid

a) Contingent Liability A/c   .... Dr
    To Bank A/c
(Being contingent liability paid)

b) Capital Reduction A/c   ..... Dr
    To Contingent Liability A/c
(Being loss on payment of contingent liability transferred.)

10) For payment of recorded liability
Liability A/c ...... Dr
    To Bank A/c
(Being liability paid)

11) For payment of unrecorded liability
 i) Unrecorded liability A/c ....Dr
    To Bank A/c
(Being payment of unrecorded liability)
 ii) Capital Reduction A/c ...... Dr.
    To Unrecorded Liability
(Being balance of unrecorded liability transferred to capital reduction account)

12) For selling of unrecorded asset
 i) Bank A/c .... Dr
    To Unrecorded Assets A/c
 ii) Unrecorded Asset A/c ...... Dr
    To Capital Reduction A/c
(Being balance of unrecorded asset transferred to capital reduction account)

13) For payment of Reconstruction Expenses
Capital Reduction A/c ..... Dr
    To Bank A/c

14) For provision for taxation utilised for capital reduction
Provision for Taxation A/c .... Dr
    To Capital A/c
(Being balances utilised for capital reduction)

15) For exchange of new debentures for old debentures
Debentures (old) A/c .... Dr
    To Debenture (New) A/c
(Being debentures exchanged)

16) For Issue of new shares for cash
Bank A/c .... Dr
    To Share Capital A/c
(Being fresh shares issued)

17) For assets given to loan creditors
Loan Creditors A/c .... Dr
    To Asset A/c
(Being asset given to loan creditors.)

18) For changing the rate of dividend on preference shares
Preference Share Capital (old rate) A/c ..... Dr
    To Preference Share Capital (New rate) A/c.
    (Being rate fo dividend on preference Share changed)

19) For arrears of preference share dividend cancelled -
* No Entry

20) For arrears of preference dividend are settled by issue of shares or cash -
Capital Reduction A/c   .... Dr
     To Cash A/c
     To Shares A/c
(Being arrears of dividend settled)

21) For penalty paid
Capital Reduction A/c   ..... Dr
     To Bank A/c
(Being penalty paid)

22) For fees refunded by directors
Bank A/c   ..... Dr
     To Capital Reduction A/c
(Being fees refunded by directors)

23) For taking over assets / shares by debentureholders
Debentureholders A/c   ... Dr
     To Asset A/c
     To Share Capital A/c
(Being assets / share taken by debentureholders)

24) For exchange of preference shares to equity share capital or debentures -
Preference Share Capital A/c   .... Dr
     To Equity Share Capital
     To Debentures A/c
(Being exchange of shares for debentures)

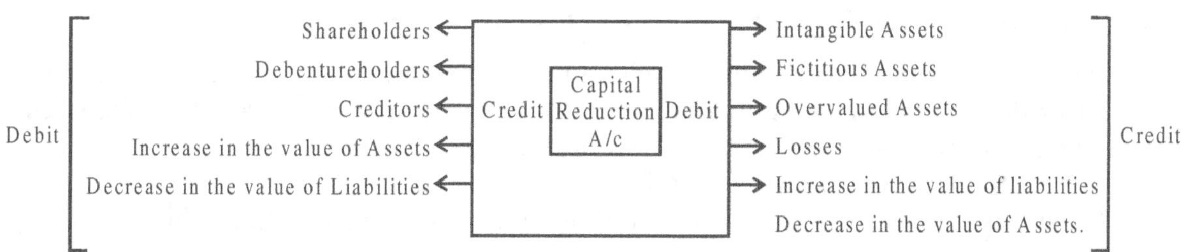

6.5 Capital Reduction Account

Capital reduction account is opened at the time of internal reconstruction of a company. The capital reduction account represents the sacrifice made by the different parties, i.e. shareholders, debentureholders and creditors. This sacrifice is used for writing off accumulated losses, intangible assets, over-valuation of assets etc. Similarly, any appreciation in the value of asset, capital profits etc are credited to this account. The balance of this account is transferred to capital reserve. If this account has no balance, it automatically tallies.

Proforma of Capital Reduction Account

Capital Reduction Account

Dr   Cr.

Particulars	Rs.	Particulars	Rs.
To P & L A/c (Loss written off) To Goodwill A/c (Written off) To Preliminary Expenses A/c (Written off) To Discount on issue of Shares or Debentures (Written off) To Asset A/c (Decrease in value) To Bank A/c (Payment of unrecorded liability / reconstruction exp.) To Bank A/c (Refund of Directors' fees) To Capital Reserves A/c (Balancing figure)		By Share Capital A/c (Reduction in capital) By Debentures A/c (Reduction in debentures) By Creditors (Sacrifice of creditors) By Asset A/c (Increase in the value) By Bank A/c (Sale of unrecorded asset)	

6.6 Preparation of Balance Sheet after Internal Reconstruction

After implementation of Capital Reduction Scheme, the balance sheet is prepared by considering the changes in the assets and liabilities. There must be the word **"And Reduced"** after the name of the balance sheet of ..... Co Ltd. as on .....

For example : Balance Sheet (and Reduced) as on.....

Generally, the following points should be taken into consideration while preparing the balance sheet :-

1) The capital reduced is shown at reduced paid-up value.
2) The liabilities reduced are shown at reduced value. If some liabilities are paid, they will not be shown in the Balance Sheet.
3) All fictitious assets are not shown.
4) Intangible assets written off are not shown.
5) Past losses / accumulated losses are not shown.
6) Tangible assets are shown at reduced figures.
7) The assets and liabilities which are not affected by capital reduction scheme are intact

and they are shown by their original values.

8) Change in authorised capital is shown in the Balance Sheet. Of course, no entry is passed for change in the authorised capital.

9) The balance of Capital Reserve is shown on the liability side of Balance Sheet.

10) If any call made, it increases the cash at bank as well as paid value of capital.

Important Note :

Under the capital reduction scheme, the words "To" and "By" play a very important role. They should not be misinterpreted. The word "To" implies the reduction as required to that amount. For example : If a share of Rs. 10 is reduced to Rs. 3, it means there is a reduction (10-3) of Rs. 7 per share and the paid-up capital will be Rs. 3 per share. The word "By" implies that there is a reduction by the amount given. For example : If a share of Rs. 10 is reduced by Rs. 7 per share, it means there is a reduction of Rs. 7 per share and the paid-up value will be Rs. 3 per share.

6.7 Problems on Internal Reconstruction

Problem No. 1 : The Balance Sheet of "S". Co. Ltd. as on 31st March 2014 was as follows :

Liabilities	Rs.	Assets	Rs.
Share Capital		Goodwill	15,000
2,000 Preference Shares of		Freehold Properties	2,00,000
Rs. 100 each	2,00,000	Plant and Machinery	3,00,000
4,000 Equity Shares of		Stock-in-trade	50,000
Rs. 100 each	4,00,000	Debtors	40,000
5% Mortgage Debentures	1,00,000	Profit and Loss A/c	2,45,000
Bank Overdraft	50,000		
Creditors	1,00,000		
	8,50,000		8,50,000

The company got the following scheme of capital reduction approved by the Court :

1. The Preference Shares to be reduced to Rs. 75 per share; fully paid-up and the Equity Shares to Rs. 37.50.

2. The debentureholders took over the stock-in-trade and the book debts in full satisfaction of the amount due to them.

3. The Goodwill Account to be eliminated.

4. The freehold properties to be depreciated by 50%

5. The value of the Plant and Machinery to be increased by Rs. 50,000

Pass the journal entries required to record the effect of the order of the Court and to draw up an amended Balance Sheet and Capital Reduction Account. **(P.U.)**

Solution

In the Books of "S" Co. Ltd.
Journal Entries

Date	Particulars	L.F.	Dr. Rs.	Cr. Rs.
2014 Mar.31	Preference Share Capital A/c Dr.		50,000	
	To capital Reduction A/c			50,000
	(Being the reduction of 2,000 preference shares of Rs. 100 to an equal number of shares of Rs. 75 each)			
Mar. 31	Equity Share Capital A/c Dr.		2,50,000	
	To Capital Reduction A/c			2,50,000
	(Being the reduction of 4,000 equity shares of Rs. 100 each to an equal number of shares of Rs. 37.50 each)			
Mar. 31	Debenture A/c Dr.		1,00,000	
	To Stock-in-trade A/c			50,000
	To Debtors A/c			40,000
	To Capital Reduction A/c			10,000
	(Being stock and debtor taken over by debentureholders in full satisfaction of their claims)			
Mar. 31	Plant and Machinery A/c Dr.		50,000	
	To Capital Reduction A/c			50,000
	(Being the appreciation in the value of plant and machinery)			
Mar. 31	Capital Reduction A/c Dr.		3,60,000	
	To Goodwill A/c			15,000
	To Freehold Properties A/c			1,00,000
	To Profit and Loss A/c			2,45,000
	(Being the assets and losses written off out of capital reduction account)			

In the books of "S" Ltd.

Capital Reduction A/c

Dr.   Cr.

Particulars	Rs.	Particulars	Rs.
To Goodwill A/c	15,000	By Preference Share Capital A/c	50,000
To Freehold Properties A/c	1,00,000	By Equity Share Capital A/c	2,50,000
To Profit & Loss A/c	2,45,000	By Debentures A/c	10,000
		By Plant & Machinery A/c	50,000
	3,60,000		3,60,000

In the books of "S" Co. Ltd.

Balance Sheet (And Reduced) As at 31st March 2014

Liabilities	Rs.	Assets	Rs.
		Fixed Assets	
Share Capital		Freehold Properties	1,00,000
2,000 Preference		Plant and Machinery	3,50,000
Shares of Rs. 75 each	1,50,000		
4,000 Equity Shares of			
Rs. 37.50 each	1,50,000		
Current Liabilities :			
Bank Overdraft	50,000		
Creditors	1,00,000		
	4,50,000		4,50,000

Problem No. 2 : Uptodate Company Ltd. presents you with the following Balance Sheet as on 31st March 2014.

Liabilities	Rs.	Assets	Rs.
Share Capital :		Goodwill	30,000
Equity Share of Rs. 100		Land & Building	75,000
each, fully paid	2,00,000	Plant & Machinery	1,50,000
7% Preferences Shares		Patents	15,000
of Rs. 100 each	1,50,000	Stock	1,10,000
Profit prior to Incorporation	5,000	Sundry Debtors	75,000
6% Debentures	1,50,000	Cash	2,500
Sundry Creditors	1,00,000	Preliminary Expenses	12,500
		Profit & Loss A/c	1,35,000
	6,05,000		6,05,000

The following scheme of reconstruction was duly approved :

1. 7% Preference Shares be converted into 9% Preference Shares, the amount being reduced by 30%
2. Equity shares be reduced to fully paid shares of Rs. 50 each.
3. Land and Building be appreciated by 20%
4. Debentures be reduced by 20%
5. All intangible assets and fictitious amounts including Patents be written off. Utilise profit prior to incorporation, if necessary.
6. Equity Shareholders to subscribe equity shares of Rs. 50,000. The amount to be utilised for acquiring new Plant and Machinery.

Assuming the whole scheme to have been put through, give journal entries resulting from it and prepare the resultant Balance Sheet. **(P.U)**

Solution **Inter Book of Uptodate Co. Ltd.**

Journal Entries

Date	Particulars		L.F.	Dr. Rs.	Cr. Rs.
31.3.2014	7% Preference Share Capital A/c	Dr.		1,50,000	
	To 9% Preference Share Capital				1,05,000
	To Capital Reduction A/c				45,000
	(Being 7% preference shares of Rs. 100 each converted into 9% preference shares and reduced to Rs. 70 each.)				
31.3.2014	Equity Share Capital A/c	Dr.		1,00,000	
	To Capital Reduction A/c				1,00,000
	(Being equity shares of Rs. 100 each fully paid reduced to Rs. 50 each fully paid)				
31.3.2014	Land & Buildings A/c	Dr.		15,000	
	Debentures A/c	Dr.		30,000	
	To Capital Reduction A/c				45,000
	(Being land and building appreciated by 20% and debentures reduced to Rs. 1,20,000)				
31.3.2014	Capital Reduction A/c	Dr.		1,90,000	
	Profit prior to Incorporation A/c	Dr.		2,500	
	To Goodwill A/c				30,000
	To Patents A/c				15,000
	To Preliminary Expenses A/c				12,500
	To Profit & Loss A/c				1,35,000
	(Being intangible and fictitious assets written off)				

Date	Particulars	L.F.	Dr. Rs.	Cr. Rs.
31.3.2014	Bank A/c Dr.		50,000	
	To Equity Shares Application			
	& Allotment money A/c			50,000
	(Being application and allotment money received)			
31.3.2014	Equity Share Application and Allotment A/c Dr.		50,000	
	To Equity Shares Capital A/c			50,000
	(Being application and allotment money			
	transferred to share capital account)			

Balance Sheet of Uptodate Ltd.
as on 1st April 2014 (And Reduced)

Liabilities	Rs.	Assets	Rs.
		Fixed Assets :	
Share Capital :		Land & Building	90,000
Equity Shares of Rs. 50 each	1,50,000	Plant & Machinery	1,50,000
9% Preference Shares		Stock	1,10,000
of Rs. 70 each	1,05,000	Sundry Debtors	75,000
Profit prior to Incorporation	2,500	Cash at Bank	52,500
6% Debentures	1,20,000		
Sundry Creditors	1,00,000		
	4,77,500		4,77,500

Problem No. 3 : Following is the Balance Sheet of Krinti Ltd.

Balance Sheet as at 31.3.2014

Liabilities	Rs.	Assets	Rs.
Share Capital :		Goodwill	50,000
1,500 6% Preference Shares		Debtors	30,200
of Rs. 100 each	1,50,000	Leasehold Property (at cost)	80,000
2,000 Equity Shares of		Plant and Machinery (at cost)	2,10,000
Rs. 100 each	2,00,000	Stock-in-trade	79,175
Capital Reserve	36,000	Profit and Loss A/c	1,10,375
Creditors	42,500	Preliminary Expenses	7,250
Bank Overdraft	51,000		

Liabilities	Rs.	Assets	Rs.
Depreciation Provision :			
Leasehold Property	30,000		
Plant and Machinery	57,500		
	5,67,000		5,67,000

The approval of the Court was obtained for the following scheme for reduction of capital -

  i) The Preference Shares to be reduced to Rs. 50 per share.

  ii) The Equity shares to be reduced to Rs. 12.50 per share.

  iii) The balance in Capital Reserve Account should not be utilised.

  iv) Plant and Machinery to be written down to Rs. 75,000.

  v) The Profit and Loss Account balance and all intangible assets including preliminary expenses to be written off.

Pass the necessary journal entries in the books of Krinti Ltd. Also prepare Capital Reduction A/c and Balance Sheet. **(P.U.)**

Solution

Journal Entries in the books of Krinti Ltd.

Date	Particulars	L.F.	Dr. Rs.	Cr. Rs.
2014 Mar. 31	6% Preference Share Capital A/c Dr.		75,000	
	To Capital Reduction A/c			75,000
	(Being reduction of 1,500 preference shares of Rs. 100 each to Rs. 50 each.)			
Mar.31	Equity Share Capital A/c Dr.		1,75,000	
	To Capital Reduction A/c			1,75,000
	(Being reduction of 2,000 equity shares of Rs. 100 each to Rs. 12.50 each)			
Mar. 31	Capital Reduction A/c Dr.		2,50,000	
	To Goodwill A/c			50,000
	To Profit and Loss A/c			1,10,375
	To Preliminary Expenses A/c			7,250
	To Plant and Machinery A/c			77,500
	To Capital Reserve A/c			4,875
	(Being utllisation of capital reduction account to write off the fictitious and intangible assets)			

Working Note :

		Rs.
1)	Valuation of Plant and Machinery	
	Cost price of Plant and Machinery	2,10,000
	- Depreciation	57,500
		1,52,500
	- Written down	75,000
	Plant and Machinery written off	77,500

In the books of Krinti Ltd.
Capital Reduction A/c

Dr.   Cr.

Particulars	Rs.	Particulars	Rs.
To Goodwill A/c	50,000	By 6% Pref. Share Capital A/c	75,000
To Profit & Loss A/c	1,10,375	By Equity Share Capital A/c	1,75,000
To Preliminary Expenses A/c	7,250		
To Plant & Machinery A/c	77,500		
To Capital Reserve A/c	4,875		
(Balancing Figure)			
	2,50,000		2,50,000

Balance Sheet (And Reduced)
as on 1-4-2014

Liabilities	Rs.	Assets	Rs.
1,500, 6% Preference		Leasehold Property (at cost)	80,000
Shares at Rs. 50 each	75,000	Debtor	30,200
2,000 Equity Shares	25,000	Stock-in-trade	79,175
at Rs. 12.50 each		Plant & Machinery	75,000
Creditors	42,500		
Bank Overdraft	51,000		
Depreciation provision on			
Leasehold Property	30,000		
Capital Reserve	40,875		
	2,64,375		2,64,375

Problem No. 4 : The following is the summarised Balance Sheet of RMS Ltd. as on 31st March, 2014

Liabilities	Rs.	Assets	Rs.
Authorised & Issued Capital :		Goodwill	1,20,000
30,000 6% Preference Shares		Land & Building	2,67,000
of Rs. 10 each	3,00,000	Plant	2,55,000
6,00,000 Equity Shares		Shares in Subsidiary Ltd. (at Cost)	75,000
of Re. 1 each	6,00,000	Stock	2,25,000
8% Debentures (Secured		Debtors	2,70,000
on Land & Building) 1,20,000		Profit & Loss A/c	2,64,000
Accrued Interest 6,000	1,26,000		
Bank Overdraft		**Deferred Expenditure :**	
(Secured on Stock)	1,65,000	Advertisement	60,000
Directors' Loans	75,000		
Creditors	2,70,000		
	15,36,000		15,36,000

(**Note :** There is a contingent liability for damages of Rs. 30,000)

    Preference Shares are cumulative and dividends are in arrears for three years.

    A Capital Reduction Scheme setting the following terms was duly approved –

i) The preference shares to be reduced to Rs. 8 per share and the equity shares to 25 paise each and to be consolidated as shares of Rs. 10 each and Re. 1 each fully paid, respectively. The preference shareholders waive two-thirds of the dividend arrears and receive equity shares for the balance. The authorised capital to be restored to : 30,000 preference shares of Rs. 10 each and 6,00,000 equity shares of Re. 1 each.

ii) The shares in Subsidiary Ltd. are sold to an outside interest for Rs. 1,50,000

iii) All intangible assets are to be eliminated and bad debts of Rs. 21,000 and obsolete stock of Rs. 30,000 to be written off.

iv) The debentureholders to take over one of the company's properties (book value Rs. 54,000) at a price Rs. 60,000 in part satisfaction of the debentures and to provide further cash Rs. 45,000 on a floating charge. The arrears of interest are paid.

v) Directors refund Rs. 10,000 of the fees previously received by them.

vi) The contingent liability materialised in the sum stated but the company recovered Rs. 15,000 of these damages in action against one of its directors. This was debited to his Loan A/c of Rs. 24,000, the balance of which was paid in cash on his resignation.

vii) The remaining Directors agreed to take equity shares in satisfaction of their loans.

    You are required to : (i) give the necessary journal entries, including cash transactions, and (ii) set out the revised Balance Sheet.

Solution

Journal Entries in the books of RMS Ltd.

Date	Particulars		L.F.	Dr. Rs.	Cr. Rs.
2014 Mar. 31	6% Preference Share Capital A/c	Dr.		60,000	
	Equity Share Capital A/c	Dr.		4,50,000	
	To Capital Reduction A/c				5,10,000
	(Being share capital reduced)				
Mar. 31	Capital Reduction A/c	Dr.		18,000	
	To Equity Share Capital A/c				18,000
	(Being equity shares issued against 1/3rd arrears of preference share dividends.)				
Mar. 31	Bank A/c	Dr.		1,50,000	
	To Shares in Subsidiary Co. A/c				75,000
	To Capital Reduction A/c				75,000
	(Being investment sold and profits credited to capital reduction account)				
Mar. 31	8% Debentures A/c	Dr.		60,000	
	To Land & Building A/c				54,000
	To Capital Reduction A/c				6,000
	(Being cancellation of debentures by transfer of land building at profit)				
Mar. 31	Bank A/c	Dr.		10,000	
	To Capital Reduction A/c				10,000
	(Being refund of fees by Directors)				
Mar. 31	Accrued Interest A/c	Dr.		6,000	
	Outstanding Claim A/c	Dr.		30,000	
	To Bank A/c				36,000
	(Being interest paid accrued on debentures and contingent liability materialised)				
Mar. 31	Bank A/c	Dr.		45,000	
	To 6% Debentures A/c				45,000
	(Being debentures issued against loan from Debentureholders)				

Date	Particulars	L.F.	Dr. Rs.	Cr. Rs.
Mar. 31	Director's Loan A/c Dr.		24,000	
	To Outstanding Claim A/c			15,000
	To Bank A/c			9,000
	(Being contingent liability charged to director and balance of his loan paid in cash.)			
Mar. 31	Director's Loan A/c Dr.		51,000	
	To Equity Share Capital A/c			51,000
	(Being issued shares to directors in payment of their loan.)			
Mar. 31	Capital Reduction A/c Dr.		5,83,000	
	To Goodwill A/c			1,20,000
	To Stock A/c			30,000
	To Bad Debts A/c			21,000
	To Advertisement A/c			60,000
	To Outstanding Claim A/c			15,000
	To Profit & Loss A/c			2,64,000
	To Capital Reserve A/c			73,000
	(Being utilisation of capital reduction account to write off the various accounts as stated above and transfer of excess to capital reserve)			

Balance Sheet of RMS Ltd. (And Reduced)
as on 1st April, 2014

Liabilities	Rs.	Assets	Rs.
Authorised Capital :		**Fixed Assets :**	
30,000, 6% Preference Shares		Land & Building	2,13,000
of Rs. 10 each	3,00,000	Plant	2,55,000
6,00,000 Equity Shares		**Current Assets :**	
of Re. 1 each	6,00,000	Stock	1,95,000
Issued & Paid-up :		Debtors	2,49,000
24,000, 6% Preference Shares		Bank	1,60,000
of Rs. 10 each	2,40,000		
2,19,000 Equity Shares of			
Re. 1 each	2,19,000		
Reserves and Surplus :			
Capital Reserve	73,000		

Liabilities	Rs.	Assets	Rs.
Secured Loans :			
6% Debentures			
(Old) 60,000			
(New) 45,000	1,05,000		
Bank Overdraft	1,65,000		
Current Liabilities :			
Creditors	2,70,000		
	10,72,000		10,72,000

(Note : (1) Bank Overdraft is presumed to have been paid off)

Problem No. 5 : The following was the Balance Sheet of Hopeful Ltd. as on 31-3-2014

Liabilities	Rs.	Assets	Rs.
Share Capital :		Freehold	23,75,000
15,000 7% Cumulative		Plant and Machinery	8,00,000
Preference Shares of		Goodwill	3,00,000
Rs. 100 each	15,00,000	Stock	3,50,000
2,75,000 Equity Shares		Debtors	2,25,000
of Rs. 10 each	27,50,000	Preliminary	2,50,000
Share Premium A/c	4,00,000	Profit and Loss A/c	7,50,000
Sundry Creditors	4,00,000		
	50,50,000		50,50,000

Dividend on preference shares was in arrears as from 1st January, 2012. The following scheme of reconstruction was approved and duly sanctioned.

a) Preference shares to be reduced to Rs. 80 per share.

b) Equity Shares to be reduced to Rs. 5 per share.

c) Write off all intangible assets and premium account.

d) One equity share of Rs. 5 each to be issued for Rs. 10 of gross preference dividend in arrears.

e) Freehold to be written down to Rs. 18,50,000.

Give necessary journal entries and prepare a revised balance sheet.   **(P.U.)**

Solution : **Journal Entries in the books of Hopeful Ltd**

Date	Particulars	L.F.	Dr. Rs.	Cr. Rs.
2014 Mar. 31	7% Preference Share Capital A/c Dr.		3,00,000	
	Equity Share Capital A/c Dr.		13,75,000	
	To Capital Reduction A/c			16,75,000
	(Being 15,000, 7% preference shares of Rs. 100 each reduced to Rs. 80 each and 2,75,000 equity shares of Rs. 10 each reduced to Rs. 5 each)			
Mar. 31	Preference Shares Dividend A/c Dr.		1,57,500	
	To Equity Share Capital A/c			1,57,500
	(Being issued 31,500 equity shares of Rs. 5 each in full payment of arrears of dividend for last 3 years)			
Mar. 31	Capital Reduction A/c Dr.		16,75,000	
	Share Premium A/c Dr.		4,00,000	
	To Goodwill A/c			3,00,000
	To Preliminary Expenses A/c			2,50,000
	To Preference Share Dividend A/c			1,57,500
	To Profit and Loss A/c			7,50,000
	To Freehold A/c			5,25,000
	To Capital Reserve A/c			92,500
	(Being intangible assets written off and value of freehold reduced)			

Balance Sheet of Hopeful Ltd., (And Reduced) as on 1st April, 2014

Liabilities	Rs.	Assets	Rs.
Share Capital :		**Fixed Assets :**	
15,000 7% Preference		Freehold	18,50,000
Shares of Rs. 80 each	12,00,000	Plant and Machinery	8,00,000
3,06,500 Equity Shares		**Current Assets :**	
of Rs. 5 each	15,32,500	Debtors	2,25,000
Reserves and Surplus :		Stock	3,50,000
Capital Reserve	92,500		
Current Liabilities :			
Sundry Creditors	4,00,000		
	32,25,000		32,25,000

Problem No. 6 : The following is the Balance Sheet of Uma Ltd., as on 31st March 2014

Liabilities	Rs.	Assets	Rs.
Share Capital :		Goodwill	70,000
4,000 Equity Shares		Land and Building	1,50,000
of Rs. 100 each	4,00,000	Plant and Machinery	3,50,000
3000 - 8% Preference		Patents	20,000
Shares of Rs. 100 each	3,00,000	Stock	2,20,000
Profit prior to Incorporation	10,000	Sundry Debtors	1,00,000
4% Debentures	3,00,000	Cash at Bank	5,000
Sundry Creditors	2,00,000	Preliminary Expenses	21,000
		Profit and Loss A/c	2,74,000
	12,10,000		12,10,000

The following scheme of reconstruction was approved :

1. 8% preference shares be converted into 9% preference shares, the amount being reduced by 30%.
2. Equity share be reduced to fully-paid shares of Rs. 50 each.
3. Land and Buildings be appreciated by 20%.
4. The debentureholders are agreeable to have their claims reduced by 20%.
5. All intangible assets and fictitious amounts including patents written off. Utilise profit prior to incorporation, if necessary.
6. The Company issued 2,000 equity shares of Rs. 50 each to the public and all were subscribed, the amount to be utilised for acquiring new plant and machinery.

Pass the journal entries in the books of the Company and draw a balance sheet. (P.U.)

Solution :

Journal Entries in the books of Uma Ltd.

Date	Particulars	L.F.	Dr. Rs.	Cr. Rs.
31.3.2014				
	8% Preference Share Capital A/c Dr.		3,00,000	
	To 9% Preference Share Capital A/c			3,00,000
	(Being the convertion of 8% preference shares			
	into 9% preference shares)			

Date	Particulars		L.F.	Dr. Rs.	Cr. Rs.
31.3.2014	9% Preference Share Capital A/c	Dr.		90,000	
	To Share Capital Reduction A/c				90,000
	(Being the reduction of 3,000 9% preference shares of Rs. 100 each to equal number of shares of Rs. 70 each)				
31.3.2014	Equity Share Capital A/c	Dr.		2,00,000	
	To Share Capital Reduction A/c				2,00,000
	(Being the reduction of 4,000 equity shares of Rs. 100 each to an equal number of shares of Rs. 50 each)				
31.3.2014	Land and Building A/c	Dr.		30,000	
	To Share Capital Reduction A/c				30,000
	(Being the appreciation in the value of land and building)				
31.3.2014	4% Debentures A/c	Dr.		60,000	
	To Share Capital Reduction A/c				60,000
	(Being the sacrifice by debentureholders)				
31.3.2014	Bank A/c	Dr.		1,00,000	
	To Equity Share Capital A/c				1,00,000
	(Being the issue of 2,000 equity shares of Rs. 50 each to the public)				
31.3.2014	Share Capital Reduction A/c	Dr.		3,80,000	
	Profit prior to Incorporation A/c	Dr.		10,000	
	To Goodwill A/c				70,000
	To Patents A/c				20,000
	To Preliminary Expenses A/c				21,000
	To Capital Reserve A/c				5,000
	To Profit & Loss A/c				2,74,000
	(Being the assets and losses written off out of capital reduction account)				

In the books of Uma Ltd.,
Balance Sheet (And Reduced)
As on 1st April 2014

Liabilities	Rs.	Assets	Rs.
Share Capital :		**Fixed Assets :**	
6,000 Equity Shares of		Land and Buildings	1,80,000
Rs.50 each	3,00,000	Plant and Machinery	3,50,000
3000 - 9% Preference Shares		**Current Assets :**	
of Rs.70 each	2,10,000	Stock	2,20,000
Reserves and Surplus :		Sundry Debtors	1,00,000
Capital Reserve	5,000	Cash at Bank	1,05,000
Secured Loans :			
4% Debentures	2,40,000		
Current Liabilities :			
Creditors	2,00,000		
	9,55,000		9,55,000

Problem No. 7 : Given below is the Balance Sheet of Amrut Ltd. as on 31st March 2014.

Liabilities	Rs.	Assets	Rs.
2,000 Preference Shares of		Land and Building	80,000
Rs.100 each	2,00,000	Fixtures	70,000
3,000 Equity Shares		Machinery	1,20,000
of Rs.100 each	3,00,000	Investments	90,000
Workmen Compensation		(Market Value Rs.65,000)	
Fund	10,000	Stock	78,000
Loans	75,000	Sundry Debtors	58,000
Secured Creditors		Cash	1,000
against Machinery	12,000	Profit and Loss A/c	1,88,000
Sundry Creditors	88,000		
	6,85,000		6,85,000

The scheme of reconstruction is prepared and approved as under :

1) Land and Building should be brought upto the present market value of Rs.1,50,000.
2) Equity shares to be reduced to Rs.20 per share paid-up cancelling Rs.80 per share and preference shares to be reduced to Rs.60 each cancelling Rs. 40 per share. The face value of these shares remain the same.

3) The equity shareholders to pay the call money of Rs. 40 per share and preference shareholders to pay the call money of Rs.20 per share immediately.

4) Unsecured creditors are paid 10% of their dues and they accept a reduction of 30% of their claims.

5) Loans are paid off completely.

6) Liabilities to the workmen's compensation materialised to Rs.15,000.

7) Out of the funds available, the assets are to be written off as under :

    a)   Profit and Loss A/c and fixtures totally.

    b)   Machinery to the extent of Rs.80,000.

    c)   Investments to its market value.

    d)   Stock to its cost price of Rs.50,000.

    e)   Creating a reserve for doubtful debts at 10% of the sundry debtors.

Pass the necessary journal entries in the books of Amrut Ltd., and give its balance sheet after reconstruction. **(P.U.)**

Solution :

Journal Entries
In the books of Amrut Ltd.

Date	Particulars		L.F.	Dr. Rs.	Cr. Rs.
31.3.2014	Land and Building A/c	Dr.		70,000	
	To Capital Reduction A/c				70,000
	(Being the appreciation in the value of land and building)				
31.3.2014	Equity Share Capital A/c	Dr.		2,40,000	
	Preference Share Capital A/c	Dr.		80,000	
	To Capital Reduction A/c				3,20,000
	(Being Rs. 80 per share on 3,000 equity shares at Rs.40 per share and on 200 preference shares at Rs.20 per share)				
31.3.2014	Bank A/c	Dr.		1,60,000	
	To Equity Share Capital A/c				1,20,000
	To Preference Share Capital A/c				40,000
	(Being call money received on 3,000 equity shares at Rs.40 per share and on 2,000 preference shares at Rs.20 per share)				

Date	Particulars		L.F.	Dr. Rs.	Cr. Rs.
31.3.2014	Loan A/c	Dr.		75,000	
	To Bank A/c				75,000
	(Being loans paid off)				
31.3.2014	Creditors A/c	Dr.		35,200	
	To Bank A/c				8,800
	To Capital Reduction A/c				26,400
	(Being 10% unsecured creditors are paid and 30% unsecured creditors are reduced)				
31.3.2014	Workmen's Compensation Fund A/c	Dr.		10,000	
	Capital Reduction A/c	Dr.		5,000	
	To Bank A/c				15,000
	(Being workmen's compensation paid)				
31.3.2014	Capital Reduction A/c	Dr.		4,11,400	
	To Profit and Loss A/c				1,88,000
	To Fixtures A/c				70,000
	To Machinery A/c				80,000
	To Investment A/c				25,000
	To Stock A/c				28,000
	To R.D.D A/c				5,800
	To Capital Reserve A/c				14,600
	(Being various assets and losses written off)				

Balance Sheet of Amrut Ltd. (And Reduced)
as on 1st April 2014

Liabilities	Rs.	Assets		Rs.
Share Capital :		**Fixed Assets :**		
2,000 Preference Shares of		Land and Building		1,50,000
Rs.100 each,	1,60,000	Machinery		40,000
Rs.80 paid up		Investment (Market Price)		65,000
3,000 Equity Shares of Rs.100		**Current Assets :**		
each, Rs.60 paid up	1,80,000	Stock (Cost Price)		50,000
Reserves and Surplus :		Debtors	58,000	
Capital Reserve	14,600	**Less :** R.D.D.	5,800	52,200
Current Liabilities :		Cash		62,200
Creditors (including Rs.12,000	64,800			
fully secured against machinery)				
	4,19,400			4,19,400

Problem No. 8 : A special resolution was passed by Sneha Ltd. and was sanctioned by the Court to the following effects :

1) 10,000, 6% preference shares of Rs.10 each, Rs.8/- paid-up to be reduced to 10,000, 6% preference shares of Rs.10 each, Rs.6/- paid up.

2) 30,000 equity shares of Rs.10 each fully paid to be reduced to Rs.2 each, fully paid.

3) 600, 7% debentures of Rs.100 each fully paid to be reduced to 600, 6% debentures of Rs. 80/- each, fully paid.

4) The debentureholders agreed to forgo the outstanding interest due to them.

5) Sundry creditors agreed to forgo 20% of their claims in exchange for fully paid equity shares for the balance.

6) The sum available will be applied :

    a)   To write off preliminary expenses and profit and loss account balance.

    b)   To reduce the value of plant by 25% and buildings by 40%.

    The Balance Sheet of Sneha Ltd., as on 31st March 2014, was as follows :

Balance Sheet

Liabilities	Rs.	Assets	Rs.
Authorised Capital		Plant	2,00,000
50,000 Equity Shares	5,00,000	Buildings	1,00,000
30,000 Preference Shares	3,00,000	Stock	45,000
Issued Capital			
30,000 Equity Shares of		Debtors	35,000
Rs.10 each	3,00,000	Bills Receivable	12,000
10,000 6% Preference Shares		Cash at Bank	7,000
of Rs,10 each, Rs.8/-		Profit and Loss A/c	99,000
paid-up	80,000	Preliminary Expenses	1,200
600, 7% Debentures			
of Rs.100 each	60,000		
Interest outstanding on			
Debentures	4,200		
Creditors	50,000		
Bills Payable	5,000		
	4,99,200		4,99,200

You are required to prepare Capital Reduction Account in the books of the Company and its balance sheet immediately after the implementation of the scheme and also pass the Journal Entries.

(P.U.)

Solution :

Journal Entries
In the books of Sneha Ltd.

Date	Particulars	L.F.	Dr. Rs.	Cr. Rs.
31.3.2014	6% Preference Share Capital A/c Dr.		20,000	
	To Share Capital Reduction A/c			20,000
	(Being the reduction of 10,000 6% preference shares of Rs. 10 each, Rs. 8 paid up to an equal number of shares of Rs. 10 each, Rs. 6 paid-up)			
31.3.2014	Equity Share Capital A/c Dr.		2,40,000	
	To Share Capital Reduction A/c			2,40,000
	(Being the reduction of 30,000 equity shares of Rs.10 each to an equal number of shares of Rs.2 each fully paid)			
31.3.2014	7% Debentures A/c (Rs.100) Dr.		60,000	
	To 6% Debentures A/c (Rs.80)			48,000
	To Share Capital Reduction A/c			12,000
	(Being the reduction of debentures)			
31.3.2014	Interest Outstanding on Debentures A/c Dr.		4,200	
	To Share Capital Reduction A/c			4,200
	(Being interest outstanding on debentures has been sacrificed by debentureholders)			
31.3.2014	Sundry Creditors A/c Dr.		50,000	
	To Equity Share Capital A/c			40,000
	To Share Capital Reduction A/c			10,000
	(Being the equity shares accepted by sundry creditors)			
31.3.2014	Share Capital Reduction A/c Dr.		2,86,200	
	To Preliminary Expenses			1,200
	To Profit and Loss A/c			99,000
	To Plant A/c			50,000
	To Building A/c			40,000
	To Capital Reserve A/c			96,000
	(Being the assets and losses written off out of capital reduction account)			

Capital Reduction A/c

Dr.   Cr.

To Preliminary Expenses	1,200	By Preference Share	
To Profit and Loss A/c	99,000	Capital A/c	20,000
To Plant A/c	50,000	By Equity Share	
To Building A/c	40,000	Capital A/c	2,40,000
To Capital Reserve A/c		By Debentures A/c	12,000
(Transfer)	96,000	By Interest Outstanding	
		on Debentures A/c	4,200
		By Creditors A/c	10,000
	2,86,200		2,86,200

Inter Books of M/s. Sneha Ltd.,
Balance Sheet (And Reduced)
as at 1st April 2014

Liabilities	Rs.	Assets	Rs.
Share Capital :		**Fixed Assets :**	
10,000, 6% Preference Shares		Plant	1,50,000
of Rs. 10 each, Rs. 6 paid-up	60,000	Building	60,000
50,000 Equity Shares of		**Current Assets :**	
Rs. 2 each	1,00,000	Stock	45,000
Reserves and Surplus :		Debtors	35,000
Capital Reserve	96,000	Bills Receivable	12,000
Secured Loans :		Cash at Bank	7,000
6% Debentures	48,000		
Current Liabilities :			
Bills Payable	5,000		
	3,09,000		3,09,000

Problem No. 9 : Swati Ltd., has been suffering heavy losses in the past. It is now considered that the worst is over and a sound re-organisation will enable its business to run successfully in the future. The Balance Sheet of the company immediately before the reconstruction is as follows :

Balance Sheet as on 31st March 2014

Liabilities	Rs.	Assets	Rs.
Share Capital :		Goodwill	3,00,000
Authorised Capital :		Fixed Assets	15,85,000
20,000 Equity Shares		Stock-in-trade	95,000
of Rs. 100 each	20,00,000	Sundry Debtors	50,000
5,000, 6% Preference Shares of		Investment	20,000
Rs. 100 each.	5,00,000	Cash at Bank	12,000
Issued Capital :		Preliminary Expenses	
10,000 Equity Shares of		(not written off)	5,000
Rs. 100 each	10,00,000	Discount on issue of Shares	3,000
2,000, 6% Preference Shares		Profit & Loss A/c	12,90,000
of Rs. 100 each	2,00,000		
(dividend in arrears for 5 years)			
5% Debentures of Rs. 100 each	16,60,000		
Sundry Creditors	4,80,000		
Liabilities for			
Income Tax	20,000		
	33,60,000		33,60,000

The following scheme of reconstruction was agreed upon and duly confirmed by the Court :

i) The equity shares shall be reduced to the shares of Rs. 10 each, Rs. 5 per share being paid-up.

ii) The preference shareholders shall forgo 90% of their claims in shares and the remaining shares shall be converted to 7% preference shares of Rs. 10 each, while their claim for arrears of dividend shall be reduced to one year's dividend and the same shall be discharged by the issue of fully paid equity shares.

iii) The debentureholders agreed to have 60% of their claims, which shall be discharged by the issue of 7½% debentures of Rs. 100 each.

iv) The sundry creditors are required to forgo 60% of their claims.

v) The assets to be revalued as follows : Fixed Assets Rs. 12,00,000, Stock-in-trade Rs. 70,000, Sundry Debtors Rs. 40,000, Investment Rs. 10,000.

vi) In order to provide sufficient working capital, the equity shareholders are to pay the balance amount due against each share.

Show the journal entries in the books of the company and also the balance sheet after implementation of the scheme.

Solution : **Journal Entries**

Date	Particulars	L.F.	Dr. Rs.	Cr. Rs.
31.3.2014	Equity Shares Capital A/c Dr. To Capital Reduction A/c (Being 10,000 equity shares of Rs. 100 each fully paid are reduced to Rs. 10 each, Rs. 5 paid-up as per special resolution and court sanction.)		9,50,000	9,50,000

31.3.2014	6% Preference Share Capital A/c Dr.
	     To 7% Preference Share Capital A/c
	     To Capital Reduction A/c
	 (Being 6% preference shares of Rs. 100 each are reduced to 7% preference shares of Rs. 10 each, cancelling 90% of the original capital as per special resolution and court sanction.)
			2,00,000	20,000
				 1,80,000

31.3.2014	Preference Share Dividend A/c Dr. To Equity Share Capital A/c (Being issued 1,200 equity shares of Rs. 10 each fully paid in satisfaction of preference dividend in arrears.)		12,000	12,000

31.3.2014	5% Debentures A/c Dr.
	     To 7½% Debentures A/c
	     To Capital Reduction A/c
	 (Being issued 7½% debentures of 9,96,000 in full satisfaction of Rs. 16,60,000 due to 5% debentureholders.)
			16,60,000	9,96,000
				 6,64,000

31.3.2014	Sundry Creditors A/c Dr. To Capital Reduction A/c (Being sundry creditors forgo 60% of their claim.)		2,88,000	2,88,000

31.3.2014	Capital Reduction A/c Dr.
	     To Profit & Loss A/c
	     To Discount on Issue of Shares A/c
	     To Preliminary Expenses A/c
	     To Goodwill A/c
	     To Fixed Assets A/c
	     To Stock-in-trade A/c
	     To Sundry Debtors A/c
			20,82,000	12,90,000
				 3,000
				 5,000
				 3,00,000
				 3,85,000
				 25,000
				 10,000

Date	Particulars	L.F.	Dr. Rs.	Cr. Rs.
	To Investments A/c			12,000
	To Dividend on Preference Share A/c			42,000
	To Capital Reserve A/c			10,000
	(Being use of capital reduction account to write off losses and to reduce values of assets as stated above, balance being transferred to capital.)			
31.3.2014	Equity Share Final Call A/c Dr.		50,000	
	To Equity Share Capital A/c			50,000
	(Being final call made of Rs. 5 per share on 10,000 equity shares.)			
31.3.2014	Bank A/c Dr.		50,000	
	To Equity Share Final Call A/c			50,000
	(Being received on account of final call.)			

Balance Sheet of Swati Ltd., as on 1st April 2014 (And Reduced)

Liabilities	Rs.	Assets	Rs.
Share Capital :		**Fixed Assets :**	12,00,000
Authorised :		Investments	10,000
20,000 Equity Shares of		Stock-in-trade	70,000
Rs 10 each	2,00,000	Sundry Debtors	40,000
5,000, 7% Preference Shares of		Cash at Bank	62,000
Rs. 10 each	50,000		
Issued, Subscribed & Paid-up :			
11,200 Equity Shares of Rs. 10			
each fully paid, of which			
1,200 issued in satisfaction of			
Dividend-in-Arrears	1,12,000		
2,000, 7% Preference Shares of			
Rs. 10 each	20,000		
Reserves and Surplus :			
Capital Reserve	42,000		
Secured Loan :			
7½% Debentures	9,96,000		
Current Liabilities :			
Sundry Creditors	1,92,000		
Income Tax Liability	20,000		
	13,82,000		13,82,000

(**Note** - It is presumed creditors and income tax are not yet paid.)

Problem No. 10 : The following is the Balance Sheet of Kamini Ltd. as on 31 March 2014

Liabilities	Rs.	Assets	Rs.
Share Capital :		Goodwill	15,000
5%, 2,000 Cumulative Preference		Freehold Property	2,00,000
Shares of Rs. 100 each	2,00,000	Plant and Machinery	3,00,000
4,000 Equity Shares of		Stock-in-trade	50,000
Rs. 100 each	4,00,000	Debtors	40,000
6% Mortgage Debenture	1,00,000	Profit and Loss A/c	2,40,000
Bank Overdraft	50,000	Cash	5,000
Creditors	1,00,000		
	8,50,000		8,50,000

The Company got the following scheme of capital reduction approved by the court.
1) The Preference Shares to be reduced to Rs. 75 per share fully paid up and Equity Shares to Rs. 40 fully paid-up.
2) The Debentureholders took over the stock-in-trade and the book debts in full satisfaction of the amount due to them.
3) The Goodwill Account is to eliminated.
4) The Freehold Properties to be increased by 30%.
5) The value of Plant and Machinery to be depreciated by $33\frac{1}{3}\%$.
6) The expenses of reconstruction amounted to Rs. 3,000.

Give the journal entries for the above and prepare the revised Balance Sheet and also prepare Capital Reduction Account. **(P.U.)**

Journal Entries in the books of Kamini Ltd.

Date	Particulars	L.F.	Dr. Rs.	Cr. Rs.
2014 Mar. 31	Cumulative Preference Share Capital A/c Dr. To Capital Reduction A/c (Being the reduction of 2,000 preference shares at Rs. 75 each)		50,000	50,000
Mar. 31	Equity Share Capital A/c Dr. To Capital Reduction A/c (Being the reduction of 4,000 equity shares at Rs. 40 each)		2,40,000	2,40,000

Date	Particulars		L.F.	Dr. Rs.	Cr. Rs.
Mar. 31	6% Mortgage Debenture A/c	Dr.		1,00,000	
	To Stock in trade A/c				50,000
	To Debtors A/c				40,000
	To Capital Reduction A/c				10,000
	(Being stock and debtors taken over by debentureholders in full satisfaction of their claim)				
Mar. 31	Freehold property A/c	Dr.		60,000	
	To Capital Reduction A/c				60,000
	(Being the appreciation in the value of property)				
Mar. 31	Re-construction Expenses A/c	Dr.		3,000	
	To Cash A/c				3,000
	(Being reconstruction expenses paid)				
Mar. 31	Capital Reduction A/c	Dr.		3,60,000	
	To Goodwill A/c				15,000
	To Plant and Machinery A/c				1,00,000
	To Profit and Loss A/c				2,40,000
	To Reconstruction Expenses A/c				3,000
	To Capital Reserve A/c				2,000
	(Being assets and losses written off out of capital reduction account)				

Capital Reduction Account

Dr.   Cr.

Particulars	Rs.	Particulars	Rs.
To Goodwill A/c	15,000	By Cumulative Preference shares A/c	50,000
To Plant & Machinery A/c	1,00,000	By Equity Share Capital A/c	2,40,000
To Profit & Loss A/c	2,40,000	By Freehold Property A/c	60,000
To Reconstruction Expenses A/c	3,000	By 6% Mortgage Debentures A/c	10,000
To Capital Reserve A/c	2,000		
	3,60,000		3,60,000

In the books of Kamini Ltd.
Balance Sheet As on 1st April, 2014 (And Reduced)

Liabilities	Rs.	Assets	Rs.
Share Capital :		**Fixed Assets :**	
5%, 2,000 Cumulative Preference		Freehold Property	2,60,000
Shares of Rs. 75 each	1,50,000	Plant and Machinery	2,00,000
4,000 Equity Shares of		**Current Assets :**	
Rs. 40 each	1,60,000	Cash	2,000
Reserves and Surplus :			
Capital Reserve	2,000		
Current Liabilities :			
Bank Overdraft	50,000		
Creditors	1,00,000		
	4,62,000		4,62,000

Problem No. 11 : The Balance Sheet of Great Ltd., as on 31st March 2014 is as follows :-

Liabilities	Rs.		Assets	Rs.
Share Capital			**Fixed Assets :**	
Authorised and Issued			Land, Building and Machinery	14,30,000
8,000 Shares of Rs. 100			Stock-in-trade	80,000
each, fully paid		8,00,000	Sundry Debtors	30,000
Debentures	13,50,000		Investments	17,000
Interest Accrued	50,000	14,00,000	Cash	33,000
Sundry Creditors :			Profit & Loss A/c	10,70,000
Income Tax	10,000			
Trade and General	4,50,000	4,60,000		
		26,60,000		26,60,000

The fixed assets are heavily overvalued. The debentureholders have a floating charge on the assets of the company. They are prepared to accept a modification of their claims in consideration of substantial interest in share capital. A scheme of reorganisation is prepared accordingly as follows :-

1) Each share shall be sub-divided into twenty fully paid equity shares of Rs. 5 each.

2) After sub-division, each shareholder shall surrender to the Company 95% of his holdings, for the purpose of re-issue to debentureholders and creditors, so far as

required and otherwise for cancellation.

3) Of those surrendered, 46,000 shares of Rs. 5 each shall be converted into 8% participating preference shares of Rs. 5 each, fully paid.

4) The debentureholders total claims shall be reduced to Rs. 2,30,000, and in consideration of this, they were allotted 46,000 participating preference shares of Rs. 5 each fully paid.

5) The liability for income Tax is to be satisfied in full.

6) The claims of unsecured creditors shall be reduced by 4/5th of the amount and the balance shall be satisfied by allotting them Equity Shares of Rs. 5 each from the shares surrendered.

7) Shares surrendered and not re-issued shall be cancelled.

Journalise the above transactions and show the Balance Sheet after the Reconstruction Scheme has been carried out. **(P.U.)**

Solution

Journal Entries in the books of Great Ltd.

Date	Particulars	L.F.	Dr. Rs.	Cr. Rs.
31.3.2014	Share Capital A/c (Rs. 100) Dr.		8,00,000	
	To Share Capital A/c (Rs. 5)			8,00,000
	(Being the sub-division of 8,000 shares of Rs. 100 each into 1,60,000 shares of Rs. 5 each)			
31.3.2014	Share Capital A/c Dr.		7,60,000	
	To Share Surrendered A/c			7,60,000
	(Being the surrender of 95% shares for conversion or cancellation as per reconstruction scheme)			
31.3.2014	Shares Surrendered A/c Dr.		2,30,000	
	To 8% Participating Preference Share Capital A/c			2,30,000
	(Being issue of preference shares to debenture holders out of shares surrender account)			
31.3.2014	Shares Surrendered A/c Dr.		90,000	
	To Share Capital A/c			90,000
	(Being the shares issued to sundry creditors out of share surrender account)			

Date	Particulars		L.F.	Dr. Rs.	Cr. Rs.
31.3.2014	Shares Surrender A/c	Dr.		4,40,000	
	Debentures A/c	Dr.		13,50,000	
	Interest Accrued A/c	Dr.		50,000	
	Sundry Creditors A/c	Dr.		4,50,000	
	To Reorganisation A/c				22,90,000
	(Being the transfer to re-organisation account)				
31.3.2014	Re-organisation A/c	Dr.		22,90,000	
	To Profit and Loss A/c				10,70,000
	To Fixed Assets A/c				12,20,000
	(Being fixed assets and losses written off out of re-organisation account)				

Balance Sheet of Great Ltd., (And Reduced) as on 1st April 2014

Liabilities	Rs.	Assets	Rs.
Share Capital :		**Fixed Assets**	2,10,000
26,000 Shares of Rs. 5 each	1,30,000	Investments	17,000
8% Participating		**Current Assets**	
Preference Shares of		Stock-in-trade	80,000
Rs. 5/- each	2,30,000	Sundry Debtors	30,000
Current Liabilities		Cash	33,000
Provision for Income Tax	10,000		
	3,70,000		3,70,000

Problem No. 12 : The following is the Balance Sheet of "X" Ltd. as on 31st March, 2014.

Balance Sheet

Liabilities	Rs.	Assets	Rs.
Share Capital :		Goodwill	1,20,000
8,000 Shares of		Land & Building	4,30,000
Rs. 100 each	8,00,000	Plant & Machinery	3,70,000
6% Debentures	3,00,000	Patents	50,000
Sundry Creditors	80,000	Stock	80,000
		Sundry Debtors	45,000
		Cash in Hand	1,000
		Profit & Loss A/c	84,000
	11,80,000		11,80,000

The Company is not getting well due to heavy losses and the following scheme of reconstruction was accepted by all.

1) Each Equity Share shall be sub-divided into Equity Shares of Rs. 10 each.
2) After sub-division, each equity shareholder will surrender 50% of his shareholdings.
3) Debentureholders' total claim be reduced to Rs. 1,80,000 and this would be satisfied by issuing them the shares surrendered.
4) The claim of the sundry creditors shall be reduced by 20%,
5) Out of the balance available, the company decided to write off Goodwill, Profit and Loss Account, Patents completely and Plant and Machinery by Rs. 2,25,000
6) Shares surrendered and not re-issued shall be cancelled.

Pass necessary journal entries and prepare balance sheet after reconstruction of a company.

(P.U.)

Solution :   **Journal Entries in the books of "X" Ltd.**

Date	Particulars		L.F.	Dr. Rs.	Cr. Rs.
2014 Mar. 31	(Rs. 100) Equity Share Capital A/c	Dr.		8,00,000	
	To (Rs. 10) Equity Share Capital A/c				8,00,000
	(Being sub-division of 8,000 equity shares of Rs. 100 each into 80,000 equity shares of Rs. 10 each as per special resolution and court sanction.)				
Mar. 31	Equity Share Capital A/c	Dr.		4,00,000	
	To Shares Surrendered A/c				4,00,000
	(Being surrender of 50% of the shares according to the scheme.)				
Mar. 31	Shares Surrendered A/c	Dr.		1,80,000	
	To Equity Share Capital				1,80,000
	(Being debentureholders reduced their claim to Rs. 1,80,000, shares surrendered are issued.)				
Mar. 31	Sundry creditors A/c	Dr.		16,000	
	To capital Reduction Account				16,000
	(Being sundry creditors reduced their claim by 20%)				
Mar. 31	Shares Surrendered A/c	Dr.		2,20,000	
	Capital Reduction A/c	Dr.		16,000	
	6% Debentures A/c	Dr.		3,00,000	
	To Goodwill A/c				1,20,000
	To Profit & Loss A/C				84,000
	To Patents A/c				50,000
	To Plant and Machinery A/c				2,25,000

Date	Particulars	L.F.	Dr. Rs.	Cr. Rs.
	To Capital Reserve A/c			57,000
	(Being cancellation of fictitious and intangible assets and reduction in the value of plant and machinery.)			

Balance Sheet of X Ltd.(After Reduced) as on 1-4-2014

Liabilities	Rs.	Assets	Rs.
		Fixed Assets :	
Share Capital :		Land & Building	4,30,000
58,000, Equity Shares		Plant & Machinery	1,45,000
of Rs. 10 each	5,80,000	Stock	80,000
Sundry Creditors	64,000	Debtors	45,000
Capital Reserve	57,000	Cash in Hand	1000
	7,01,000		7,01,000

Problem No. 13 : Onida Ltd. Presents You With the following Balance Sheet as on 31st March 2014

Liabilities	Rs	Assets	Rs
Share Capital :		Good will	30,000
Equity Shares of Rs. 100		Land & Building	75,000
each fully Paid	2,00,000	Plant & Machinery	1,50,000
7% Preference Shares of		Patents	15,000
Rs. 100 each	1,50,000	Stock	1,10,000
Profit Prior to Incorporation	5000	Sundry Debtors	75,000
6% Debentures	1,50,000	Cash	2,500
Sundry Creditors	1,00,000	Preliminary Expenses	12,500
		Profit & Loss A/c	1,35,000
	6,05,000		6,05,000

The following Scheme of reconstruction was duly approved.

1) 7% Preference Shares be converted into 9% Preference Shares, the amount being reduced by 30%

2) Equity Shares be reduced to fully paid shares of Rs. 50 each.

3) Land and Building be appreciated by 20%

4) Debentures be reduced by 20%

5) All intangible Assets and fictitious Assets including patents be written off. Utilise Profit Prior to incorporation if necessary.

6) Equity Shareholders to subscribe Equity Shares of Rs. 50,000 The amount to be utilised for acquiring new plant and Machinery.

Give necessary journal entries in the books of Onida Ltd. and prepare the resultant Balance Sheet.   **(March - 2011 PUP)**

Solution :   **Journal Entries in the books of Onida Ltd.**

S.N.	Particulars		L.F.	Debit (Rs.)	Credit (Rs.)
31.3.2014	7% Pref Share Capital A/c	Dr.		1,50,000	
	To 9% Prof. Share Capital A/c				1,05,000
	To Capital Reduction A/c				45,000
31.3.2014	Equity Share Capital A/c	Dr.		1,00,000	
	To Capital Reduction A/c				1,00,000
31.3.2014	Land & Building A/c	Dr.		15,000	
	To Capital Reduction A/c				15,000
31.3.2014	6% Debenture A/c	Dr.		30,000	
	To Capital Reduction A/c				30,000
31.3.2014	Capital Reduction A/c	Dr.		1,90,000	
	Profit Prior to Incorporation A/c	Dr.		2500	
	To Profit & Loss A/c				1,35,000
	To Preliminary Expenses A/c				12,500
	To Goodwill				30,000
	To Patents				15,000
31.3.2014	Bank A/c	Dr.		50,000	
	To Equity Share Capital A/c				50,000
31.3.2014	Machinery A/c	Dr.		50,000	
	To Bank				50,000

Balance Sheet of Onida Ltd as on 1st April 2014

Liabilities	Rs	Assets		Rs
Share Capital : Equity	1,50,000	Land & Building	75000	
9% Pref. Share Capital	1,05,000	Add : Increase	15,000	90,000
6% Debentures	1,20,000	Plant & Machinery	1,50,000	
S.Creditors	1,00,000	New	50,000	2,00,000
Profit Prior to Income	2500	Stock		1,10,000
		Debtors		75,000
		Cash		2500
	4,77,500			4,77,500

Problem No. 14 : The Following is the Balance Sheet of Ajantha Ltd. As on 31-3-2014

Balance Sheet as on 31-3-2014

Liabilities	Rs	Assets	Rs
Share Capital :		Good will	50,000
1,500 6% Preference Shares		Leasehold Property (at cost)	80,000
of Rs. 100 each	1,50,000	Plant & Machinery (at (cost)	2,10,000
2000 Equity Shares of Rs. 100		Debtors	30,200
each	2,00,000	Stock in Trade	79,175
Capital Reserve	36,000	Preliminary Expenses	7,250
Creditors	42,500	Profit & Loss A/c	1,10,375
Bank Overdraft	51,000		
Depreciation Provision :			
Leasehold Property	30,000		
Plant & Machinery	57,500		
	5,67,000		5,67,000

The approval of the court was obtained for the following scheme of reduction of Capital.

1) The Preference Shares to the reduced to Rs. 50 Per share.
2) The Equity Shares to be reduced to Rs. 12.50 Per Share.
3) The Balance in Capital Reserve A/c Should not be utilised.
4) Plant and Machinery to be written down to Rs. 75,000
5) The profit and Loss A/c Balance and all intangible assets including preliminary expenses to be written off.

Pass Journal entries in the books of Ajantha Ltd. and give its Balance Sheet after reconstruction.   **(Oct - 2011 PUP)**

Solution :   **Journal of Ajantha Ltd**

Date	Particulars		L.F.	Debit Rs	Credit Rs.
2014 Mar. 31	6% Preference Share Capital A/c	Dr.		75,000	
	To Capital Reduction A/c				75,000
Mar. 31	Equity Share Capital A/c	Dr.		1,75,000	
	To Capital Reduction A/c				1,75,000
Mar. 31	Capital Reduction A/c	Dr.		2,50,000	
	To Good will A/c				50,000
	To Profit and Loss A/c				1,10,375
	To Preliminary Exps. A/c				7,250
	To Plant & Machinery A/c				77,500
	To Capital Reserve A/c				4,875

Balance Sheet of Ajantha Ltd. on 31-3-2014 and Reduced)

Liabilities	Rs.	Assets	Rs.
1500 6% Pref. Shares of Rs. 50 Each	75,000	Leasehold Property	50,000
		Plant & Machinery	75,000
2000 Equity Shares of Rs. 12.50 each	25,000	Debtors	30,200
		Stock in Trade	79,175
Capital Reserve (36000 + 4875)	40,875		
Creditors	42,500		
Bank Overdraft	51,000		
	2,34,375		2,34,375

Problem No. 15 : The Following was the Balance Sheet of Navin Ltd as on 31-3-2014

Balance Sheet as on 31-3-2014

Liabilities	Rs	Assets	Rs
Share Capital :		Freehold Property	23,75,000
15,000 7% Cumulative		Plant and Machinery	8,00,000
Preference Shares of		**Goodwill**	3,00,000
Rs. 100 each	15,00,000	Stock	3,50,000
2,75,000 Equity Shares		Debtors	2,25,000
of Rs. 10 each	27,50,000	Preliminary Exp.	2,50,000
Share Premium A/c	4,00,000	Profit and Loss A/c	7,50,000
Sundry Creditors	4,00,000		
	50,50,000		50,50,000

The following Scheme of reconstruction was approved and duly sanctined.
a) Preference Shares to be reduced to Rs. 80 Per Share.
b) Equity Shares to be reduced to Rs. 5 Per share.
c) Write off all intangible assets and share premium account.
d) Freehold property to be written down to Rs. 18,50,000

Give necessary journal entries to record the above transactions in the books of Navin Ltd. Also Prepare a Revised Balance Sheet after the scheme of reconstruction as on 31-3-2014.   **(Mrach 2012 - PUP)**

Solution :

In the books of Navin Ltd.

Date	Particulars		L.F.	Debit (Rs.)	Credit (Rs.)
31.3.2014	7% Pref. Share Capital A/c	Dr.		3,00,000	
	To Capital Reduction A/c				3,00,000
31.3.2014	Eq. Share Capital A/c	Dr.		13,75,000	
	To Capital Redcution A/c				13,75,000
31.3.2014	Share Primium A/c	Dr.		4,00,000	
	To Capital Reduction A/c				4,00,000

31.3.2014	Capital Reduction A/c	Dr.		20,75,000	
	To Good will A/c				3,00,000
	To Preiliminary exp. A/c				2,50,000
	To Profit & Loss A/c				7,50,000
	To freehold Property A/c				5,25,000
	To Capital Reserve				2,50,000

Balance Sheet of Navin Ltd. as on 31.3.2014

Liabilities	Rs	Assets	Rs
Share Capital		Freehold Property	18,50,000
15000 7% Pref. Shares	12,00,000	Plant & Machinery	8,00,000
of Rs. 80 each			
2,75,000 Eq. Shares	13,75,000	Debtors	2,25,000
of Rs. 5 each.		Stock	3,50,000
Reserve & Surplus			
Capital Reserve	2,50,000		
Sundry Creditors	4,00,000		
	32,25,000		32,25,000

Problem No. 16 : The Balance Sheet of Chemical Industries Ltd. at 31 st March, 2014 was as under.

Balance Sheet as on 31 st March 2014

Liabilities	Rs	Assets	Rs
Share Capital :		Good will	15,000
2000 Preference Shares		Freehold Properties	2,00,000
of Rs. 100 each	2,00,000	Plant & Machinery	3,00,000
4,000 Equity Shares		Stock in Trade	50,000
of Rs. 100 each	4,00,000	Debtors	40,000
5% Debentures	1,00,000	Profit & Loss A/c	2,45,000
Bank Overdraft	50,000		
Creditors	1,00,000		
	8,50,000		8,50,000

The Company gets the following scheme of capital reduction approved by the court.

a) The preference Shares to be reduced to Rs. 75 Per Share, fully paid up and equity Shares to Rs. 37.50

b) The debentureholders took over stock in trade and book debts in full settlement of the amount due to them.

c) The goodwill account to be eliminated.

d) The freehold properties to be depreciated by 50%

e) The value of Plant and Machinery to be increased by Rs. 50,000

Pass journal entries in the books of Chemical Industries Ltd. and prepare its revised Balance Sheet. **(Oct 2012 - PUP)**

Solution :

In the books of Chemical Industries Ltd
Journal Entries

Date	Particulars		Debit Rs.	Credit Rs.
31.3.2014	Preference Share Capital A/c	Dr.	2,00,000	
	To Preference Share Capital			1,50,000
	To Capital Reduction Account			50,000
31.3.2014	Equity Share Capital A/c	Dr.	4,00,000	
	To Equity Share Capital A/c			1,50,000
	To Capital Reduction A/c			2,50,000
31.3.2014	5% Pref. Shares A/c	Dr.	1,00,000	
	To Debentureholders A/c			1,00,000
31.3.2014	Debentureholder A/c	Dr.	1,00,000	
	To Stock A/c			50,000
	To Book Debts A/c			40,000
	To Capital Reduction A/c			10,000
31.3.2014	Plant and Machinery A/c	Dr.	50,000	
	To Capital Reduction A/c			50,000
31.3.2014	Capital Reduction A/c	Dr.	3,60,000	
	To Good will A/c			15,000
	To Depreciation on Freehold A/c		1,00,000	
	To Profit and Loss A/c			2,45,000

Balance Sheet of Chemic & Industries Ltd. as on 31st March 2014

Liabilities	Rs	Assets		Rs
2000 preference Shares of Rs. 75, each	1,50,000	Freehold Property Less : Depreciation	2,00,000 1,00,000	1,00,000
4,000 Equity Shares of Rs. 37.50 each	1,50,000	Plant & Machinery	3,00,000	
Bank overdraft	50,000	Add : 50,000	50,000	3,50,000
Creditors	1,00,000	Increase		
	4,50,000			4,50,000

Problem No. 17 : The Following is the balance sheet of Sai Ltd. as on 31st March 2014

Balance Sheet As on 31st March 2014

Liabilities	Rs	Assets	Rs
Share Capital		Good will	70,000
4000, Equity Shares of Rs. 100 each	4,00,000	Land and Building	1,50,000
		Plant and Machinery	3,50,000
3,000, 8% Preference Shares of Rs. 100 each	3,00,000	Patents	20,000
		Stock	2,20,000
Profit Prior to Incorporation	10,000	Sundry Debtors	1,00,000
		Cash at Bank	5000
4% Debentures	3,00,000	Preliminary Expenses	21,000
Sundry Creditors	2,00,000	Profit and Loss A/c	2,74,000
	12,10,000		12,10,000

The Following Scheme of reconstruction was duly approved.

i) 8% Preference shares be converted into 9% preference Shares, the amount being reduced by 30%

ii) Equity Shares be reduced to fully paid Shares of Rs. 50 each.

iii) Land and Buildings be appreciated by 20%

iv) The debentureholders are agreeable to have their claims reduced by 20%

v) All intangible Assets and fictitious assets including patents written off, utilise Profit prior to incorporation if necessary.

Pass the Journal Entries in the books of Sai Ltd. and draw a Balance Sheet.

(March 2013 - PUP)

Solution :

In the books of Sai Ltd. Journal Entries

Date	Particulars		Debit Rs.	Credit Rs.
31.3.2014	8% Preference Share Capital A/c	Dr.	3,00,000	
	To 9% Preference Share Capital A/c			2,10,000
	To Capital Reduction A/c			90,000
31.3.2014	9% Preference Share Capital A/c	Dr.	90,000	
	To Share Capital Reduction A/c			90,000
31.3.2014	Equity Share Capital A/c	Dr.	2,00,000	
	To Capital Reduction A/c			2,00,000
31.3.2014	Land and Building A/c	Dr.	30,000	
	To Capital Reduction A/c			30,000
31.3.2014	4% Debentures A/c	Dr.	60,000	
	To Capital Reduction A/c			60,000
31.3.2014	Capital Reducation A/c	Dr.	3,80,000	
	Profit Prior to Incorporation	Dr.	10,000	
	To Good will			70,000
	To Patents			20,000
	To Preliminiary Expenses			21,000
	To Capital Reserve A/c			5000
	To Profit And Loss A/c			2,74,000

In the Books of Sai Ltd.

Balance Sheet As on 1st April 2014

Liabilities	Rs	Assets	Rs
Share Capital :		Land and buildings	1,80,000
4000 Equity Shares of 50 each	2,00,000	Plant and Machinery	3,50,000
3000 9% Preference Shares	2,10,000	Stock	2,20,000
of Rs. 70 each			
Capital Reserve	5,000	Sundry Debtors	1,00,000
4% Debentures	2,40,000	Cash at band	5,000
Creditors	2,00,000		
Total	8,55,000	Total	8,55,000

Problem No. 18 : The Balance Sheet of Bhandari Ltd. as as 31 st March 2013 was as follows.

Balance Sheet as on 31-3-2013

Liabilities	Rs	Assets	Rs
Authorised Capital :		Plant	2,00,000
50,000 Equity Shares	5,00,000	Buildings	1,00,000
30,000 Preference		Stock	45,000
Shares	3,00,000	Debtors	35,000
Issued Capital :		Bills Receivable	12,000
30,000 Equity Shares		Cash at Bank	7000
of Rs. 10 each	3,00,000	Preliminary Expenses	1,200
10,000 6% Preference		Profit & Loss A/c	99,000
Shares of Rs. 10 each			
Rs. 8 Paid up	80,000		
600, 7% Debentures			
of Rs. 100 each	60,000		
Interest outstanding			
on debentures	4,200		
Creditors	50,000		
Bills payable	5000		
	4,99,200		4,99,200

The special resolution was passed by the Bhandari Ltd. and was sanctioned by the court to the following effects.

1) 10,000 6% preference shares of Rs. 10 each, Rs. 8 Paid up to be reduced to 10,000 6% preference Shares of Rs. 10 each Rs. 6 paid up.

2) 30,000 Equity Shares of Rs. 10 each fully paid to be reduced to Rs. 2 each fully paid.

3) 600, 7% Debentures of Rs. 100 each fully paid to be reduced to 600, 7% Debentures of Rs. 80 each fully paid.

4) The Debentureholders agreed to forego the outstanding interest due to them.

5) Sundry Creditors agreed to forego 20% of their Claims in exchange for fully paid equity Shares for the balance.

6) Write off Preliminary Expenses and Profit and loss Account Balance.

7) Reduce the value of Plant by 25% and Buildings by 40% Pass the Journal Entries in the books of Bhandari Ltd. and Prepare a Balance Sheet after Reconstruction.

(Oct 2013 - PUP)

Solution :

In the books of Bhandari Ltd

Date	Particulars		L.F.	Debit (Rs.)	Credit (Rs.)
31.3.2014	6% Prof. Share Capital A/c	Dr.		20,000	
	To Share Capital Reduction A/c				20,000
31.3.2014	Equity Share Capital A/c	Dr.		2,40,000	
	To Capital Reduction A/c				2,40,000
31.3.2014	7% Debentures A/c	Dr.		60,000	
	To 7% Debentures A/c				48,000
	To Capital Reduction A/c				12,000
31.3.2014	Interest O/s on Debentures A/c	Dr		4,200	
	To Capital Reductions A/c				4,200
31.3.2014	Sundry Creditors A/c	Dr.		50,000	
	To Equity Share Capital A/c				40,000
	To Capital Reduction A/c				10,000
31.3.2014	Capital Reduction A/c	Dr.		2,86,200	
	To Preliminary Exp.				1,200
	To P & L A/c				99,000
	To Building A/c				40,000
	To Plant A/c				50,000
	To Capital Reserve				96,000

Balance Sheet of Bhandari Ltd. as on 31-3-2013

Liabilities	Rs	Assets	Rs
Share Capital :		Plant	1,50,000
10,000 6% Prof. Shares		Building	60,000
of ₹ 10 each ₹ 6 Paid up	60,000	Stock	45,000
50,000 Equity shares			
of ₹ 2 each Fully Paid up	1,00,000	Debtors	35,000
Capital Reserve	96,000	Bill Receivable	12,000
7% Debentures	48,000	Cash at Bank	7000
Bills Payable	5000		
	3,09,000		3,09,000

Problem No. 19 : Balance Sheet of Akshay Ltd. As on 31st March, 2014 Was as follows.

Balance sheet as on 31st March 2014

Liabilities	Rs	Assets	Rs
Issued Capital :		Good will	10,000
16,000 Equity Shares		Plant and Machinery	1,10,000
of Rs. 10 each	1,60,000	Patent and Trademark	21,000
10,000, 6% Cumulative		Debtors	15,000
Preference Shares of		Freehold Property	56,000
Rs. 10 each	1,00,000	Stock	24,000
Share Premium	30,000	Profit and Loss Account	55,000
Creditors	26,000	Preliminary Expenses	25,000
	3,16,000		3,16,000

A Special Resoultion was passed by Akshay Ltd. For Reduction of Capital and was sanctioned by the court to the following effects.

i) 6% Preference Shares of Rs. 10 each to be reduced to Rs. 9 Per Share.

ii) Equity Shares of Rs. 10 each Fully Paid to be reduced to Rs. 1.25 Per Share.

iii) The Share Premium Account and intangible assets to be written of.

iv) Plant and Machinery to be revalued at Rs. 90,000

v) On equity Share of Rs. 1.25 to be issued for each Rs. 10 gross Preference dividend Arrears, which is in arrears for 4 years.

Pass Journal entries in the books of Akshay Ltd. and prepare the revised Balance Sheet.

(April 2014 - PUP)

Solution :

Journal Entries in the books of Akshay Ltd

Date	Particulars		L.F.	Debit (Rs.)	Credit (Rs.)
31.3.2014	6% Pref. Share Capital A/c	Dr.		10,000	
	To Capital Reduction A/c				10,000
31.3.2014	Equity Share Capital A/c	Dr.		1,40,000	
	To Capital Reduction A/c				1,40,000
31.3.2014	Capital Reduction A/c	Dr.		1,50,000	
	Share Premium A/c	Dr.		30,000	
	To Preliminary Exp. A/c				25,000
	To Profit & Loss A/c				55,000
	To Plant & Machinery A/c				20,000
	To Goodwill A/c				10,000
	To Patents & Trademark				21,000
	To Prof. Share dividend A/c				24,000
	To Capital Reserve A/c				25,000
31.3.2014	Arrears of Pref Share Dividend A/c	Dr.		24,000	
	To Equity Share Capital				24,000

Balance Sheet of Akshay Ltd.
as on 31.3.2014

Liabilities	Rs	Assets	Rs
Share Capital		Plant & Machinery	90,000
1000 Prof. Shares of		Freehold Property	56,000
₹ 10 each ₹ 9 Paid up	90,000		
35,200 Equity Shares of		Stock	24,000
₹ 1.25 Paid up	44,000	Debtors	15,000
Capital Reserve	25,000		
Creditors	26,000		
	1,85,000		1,85,000

6.8 EXERCISES :

Objective type questions :

a) State whether each of the following statements is True or False

1) Permission of the Court is not required for the increase of share capital.

2) The term "Alteration Proper" and reduction of capital are synonymous.

3) Refunding surplus capital do not amount to reduction of share capital.

4) Reconstruction necessarily involves liquidation of the Company concerned.

5) The balance in the share premium account can be transfered to capital reduction account.

6) The Company can carry forward accumulated losses for taxation purposes in case of internal reconstruction.

Ans. 1) True   2) False   3) False   4) False   5) True   6) True

b) Fill in the gaps

1) The main purpose of internal reconstruction is to ..... capital of a Company.

2) The sacrifice made by different parties are shown in ..... account.

3) The balance of capital reduction account is transferred to .... account.

4) Expenses on reconstruction account are transferred to ..... account.

5) A share of Rs. 10 is reduced to Rs. 2, it means there is a reduction of ..... in the value of share.

Ans : 1) reduce   2) Capital Reduction Account   3) Capital Reserve Account   4) Capital Reduction Account   5) Rs. 8

c) Select the most appropriate answer :

i) The accumulated losses under the scheme of internal reconstruction are written off against :

(a)   Share Capital Account

(b)   Capital Reduction Account

(c)   None of the above.

ii) A Contingent Liability not provided for, if not materialised is credited to :

(a)   Capital Reduction Account

(b)   Profit and Loss Account

(c)   None of the two.

iii) The balance of Capital Reduction Account after writing off accumulated losses is transferred to :

    (a) General Reserve   (b) Share Capital   (c) Capital

iv) Reduction in Share Capital requires the permission of :

    (a) The Central Government   (b) Court

    (c) Controller of Capital Issues.

Ans : i) (b)   ii) (c)   iii) (c)   iv) (b)

Practical Problems

1) The Unsuccessful Company Ltd., prepared a scheme for reconstruction, which was duly approved by the Court. The terms of reconstruction were as under :

1. The shareholders to receive in lieu of their present holding (viz. 50,000 shares of Rs. 10 each) the following :

    a)   Fully-paid Equity Share equal to 2/5th of their holding.

    b)   5% Preference Shares, fully paid, to the extent of 1/5th of the above new Equity.

    c)   Rs. 60,000 in 6% second Debentures.

2. An issue of Rs. 5,00,000 5% Debentures was made and allotted, payment for the same have been received in cash.

3. The Goodwill which stood at Rs. 3,00,000 was written down to Rs. 1,50,000; the Plant and Machinery standing at Rs. 1,00,000 was written down to Rs. 75,000; Freehold and Leasehold Premises standing at Rs. 1,50,000 were written down to Rs. 1,25,000

    Pass journal entries to give effect to the above scheme.

Ans : Capital Reduction Account total Rs. 2,00,000

2) Following is the Balance Sheet of Kiran Ltd.

Balance Sheet as on 31-3-2014

Liabilities	Rs.	Assets	Rs.
Share Capital :		Goodwill	50,000
1,500, 6% Preference Shares		Debtors	30,200
of Rs. 100 each	1,50,000	Leasehold Property	
2,000 Equity Shares of		(at cost)	80,000
Rs. 100 each	2,00,000	Plant & Machinery	

Liabilities	Rs.	Assets	Rs.
Capital Reserve	36,000	(at cost)	2,10,000
Creditors	42,500	Stock-in-trade	79,175
Bank Overdraft	51,000	Profit & Loss A/c	1,10,375
Depreciation Provision :		Preliminary Exp.	7,250
Leasehold Property	30,000		
Plant & Machinery	57,500		
	5,67,000		5,67,000

The approval of the Court was obtained for the following scheme for reduction of capital –

i) The Preference Shares to be reduced to Rs. 50 per share.

ii) The Equity Shares to be reduced to Rs. 12.50 per share.

iii) The balance on Capital Reserve Account should not be utilised.

iv) Plant and Machinery to be written down to Rs. 75,000.

v) The Profit and Loss Account balance and all Intangible Assets including preliminary expenses to be written off.

Pass the journal entries in the books of Kiran Ltd.

Ans. : Capital Reserve Rs. 4,875

3) The Following was the Balance Sheet of "AB" Ltd. as on 31-3-2014

Liabilities	Rs.	Assets	Rs.
Share Capital :		Freehold	23,75,000
15,000, 7% Cumulative		Plant & Machinery	8,00,000
Preference Shares of		Goodwill	3,00,000
Rs. 100 each	15,00,000	Stock	3,50,000
2,75,000 Equity Shares of		Debtors	2,25,000
Rs. 10 each	27,50,000	Preliminary Expenses	2,50,000
Share Premium A/c	4,00,000	Profit & Loss A/c	7,50,000
Sundry Creditors	4,00,000		
	50,50,000		50,50,000

Dividend on Preference Shares was in arrears as from 1st April, 2008. The following scheme of reconstruction was approved and duly sanctioned.

a) Preference Shares to be reduced to Rs. 80 per share.

b) Equity Shares to be reduced to Rs. 5 per share.

c) Write off all intangible assets and premium account.

d) One Equity Share of Rs. 5 each to be issued for Rs. 10 of gross Preference Dividend in arrears.

e) Freehold to be written down to Rs. 18,50,000.

Give necessary journal entries and prepare revised Balance Sheet. **(P.U.)**

Ans : Capital Reserve Rs. 92,500

4) On 31st March 2014, the following balances appeared in the books of Kartiki Co. Ltd.

Particulars	Debit (Rs.)	Credit (Rs.)
Share Capital - Authorised and Issued		
6000 - 7% Cumulative Preference Shares of		
Rs. 100 each		6,00,000
1,10,000 Ordinary Shares of Rs. 10 each		11,00,000
Share Premium A/c		1,60,000
Freehold Premises at cost	12,00,000	
Plant and Machinery at cost	4,00,000	
Depreciation Account		
Freehold Premises		2,50,000
Plant and Machinery		80,000
Goodwill	1,20,000	
Stock on Hand as on 31.3.2014	1,40,000	
Sundry Debtors	90,000	
Preliminary Expenses	1,00,000	
Profit and Loss A/c	3,00,000	
Creditors		1,60,000
	23,50,000	23,50,000

Dividends on Preference Shares are in arrears as from 1st April 2012

The following terms were settled under a duly approved scheme –

a) Preference Shares to be reduced to Rs.80 each and the Ordinary Shares to Rs. 5 each.

b) One Rs. 5 Ordinary Share to be issued for each Rs. 10 of gross Preference Share Dividend arrears.

c) All intangible assets and the Share Premium Account to be written off.

d) Freehold premises to be written down upto Rs. 7,40,000.

You are required to give : a) necessary journal entries; and b) Balance Sheet after reconstruction. **(P.U.)**

Ans. Capital Reserve Rs. 37,000

5) Abhishek Company Ltd., has been suffering heavy losses in the past. It is now considered that the worst is over and a sound re-organisation will enable its business successfully in the future. The Balance Sheet of the company immediately before the reconstruction is as folllows :-

Balance Sheet as on 31st March 2014

Liabilities	Rs.	Assets	Rs.
Share Capital		Goodwill	3,00,000
Authorised Capital		Fixed Assets	15,85,000
20,000 Equity Shares of		Stock-in-trade	95,000
Rs. 100 each	20,00,000	Sundry Debtors	50,000
5,000, 6% Preference Shares		Investment	20,000
of Rs. 100 each	5,00,000	Cash at Bank	12,000
Issued Capital		Preliminary Expenses	
10,000 Equity Shares of		(not written off)	5,000
Rs. 100 each	10,00,000	Discount on issue of Shares	3,000
2,000, 6% Preference Shares		Profit and Loss A/c	12,90,000
of Rs. 100 each	2,00,000		
(dividend in arrears for			
5 years)			
5% Debentures of Rs. 100 each	16,60,000		
Sundry Creditors	4,80,000		
Liabilities for Income Tax	20,000		
	33,60,000		33,60,000

The following scheme of reconstruction was agreed upon and duly confirmed by the Court –

  i) The Equity Shares shall be reduced to the shares of Rs. 10 each, Rs. 5 per share being paid-up.

 ii) The Preference shareholders shall forgo 90% of their claims in shares and the remaining shares shall be converted to 7% Preference Shares of Rs. 10 each, while their claim for arrears of dividend shall be reduced to one year's dividend and the same shall be discharged by the issue of fully paid Equity Shares.

iii) The debentureholders agreed to have 60% of their claims which shall be discharged by the issue of 7½% debentures of Rs. 100 each.

 iv) The sundry creditors are required to forgo 60% of their claims.

  v) The assets to be revalued as follows.

     Fixed Assets Rs. 12,00,000, Stock-in-trade Rs. 70,000, Sundry Debtors Rs. 40,000, Investment Rs. 10,000.

 vi) In order to provide sufficient working capital, the equity shareholders are to pay the balance amount due against each share.

     Show the journal entries in the books of the company and also the Balance sheet after implementation of the scheme.   **(P.U.)**

Ans. : Capital Reserve Rs. 42,000

6) On 31-3-2014, the following balances appeared in the books of a limited company.

Particulars	Dr. Rs.	Cr. Rs.
Share Capital :		
6,000, 7% Cumulative Pref. Shares of Rs. 100 each		6,00,000
1,10,000 Equity Shares of Rs. 10 each		11,00,000
Share Premium Account		1,60,000
Freehold Premises	12,00,000	
Plant and Machinery	4,00,000	
Depreciation Fund : Freehold Premises		2,50,000
Plant and Machinery		80,000
Goodwill	1,20,000	
Stock	1,40,000	
Sundry Debtors	90,000	
Preliminary Expenses	1,00,000	
Profit and Loss A/c	3,00,000	
Creditors		1,60,000
	23,50,000	23,50,000

Dividend on the Preference Shares are in arrears as from 1st April, 2011. The following terms were settled under a duly approved Capital Reduction Scheme –

a) The Preference Shares to be reduced to Rs. 80 each and the Equity Shares to Rs. 5 each.

b) One Rs. 5 Equity Share to be issued for each Rs. 10 of gross Preference Share dividend in arrears.

c) All intangible assets and the Share Premium Account to be written off.

d) Freehold Premises to be written down to Rs. 7,40,000.

Pass journal entries to implement the above scheme.

Ans. : Capital Reserve Rs. 37,000

7) **Balance Sheet of Air Ltd. as on 31 st March 2014**

Liabilities	Rs.	Assets		Rs.
Share Capital :		Goodwill		30,000
25,000 Equity Shares of		Land and Building		1,30,000
Rs. 10 each, fully paid	2,50,000	Plant and Machinery		1,05,000
25,000, 7% Cumulative		Patents		75,000
Pref. Shares of Rs. 10 each,		Stock		1,10,000
fully paid	2,50,000	Debtors		1,40,000
6% Debentures (giving a		Bank		2,500
floating charge on assets)	1,50,000	Profit & Loss A/c		
Interest on Debentures	18,000	(Dr.) Balance	1,65,000	
Bank Overdraft	30,000	Less Profit	45,000	1,20,000
Creditors	14,500			
	7,12,500			7,12,500

The Preference dividends are in arrears for one year. The working of the Company for the year 2012-2013 having shown considerable improvement. Directors decided upon a scheme of reconstruction. With a view to assist the Scheme, the debentureholders have agreed to accept fully paid Equity Shares of Re. 1 each for half the amount of interest due to them and to forgo the balance and to accept further Debentures for Rs. 60,000 of cash to help repayment of Bank Overdraft and to provide working capital, Preference shareholders are also agreeable to forgo half the amount of their accumulated dividend, accept fully paid Equity Shares of Re. 1 each for the remaining half and reduce the future rate of dividend to 6%. The Equity Shares are to be reduced to shares of Re. 1 each. The amount thus available is to be utilised. a) to write off Goodwill; b) to write off accumulated losses; c) to depreciate Plant and Machinery by 10%; d) to write off Patents by Rs. 45,000; e) to provide 5% for doubtful debts; and f) To depreciate Stock by 10%.

Prepare Balance Sheet of the Company after reconstruction.

Ans. : Capital Reduction Rs. 2,34,000; Capital Reserve Rs. 1,750, Balance Sheet Total Rs. 5,19,000, Bank Balance Rs. 32,500)

(Debentureholders to take stock)

8) The Balance Sheet of Kolhapur Industries Ltd., as on 31st March 2014 was as follows :-

Liabilities	Rs.	Assets	Rs.
Share Capital :		Goodwill	15,000
2,000, 11.5% Preference		Freehold Properties	2,00,000
Shares of Rs. 100 each	2,00,000	Plant and Machinery	3,00,000
4,000 Equity Shares of		Stock-in-trade	50,000
Rs. 100 each	4,00,000	Debtors	40,000
16% Mortgage Debentures	1,00,000	Profit and Loss A/c	2,45,000
Bank Overdraft	75,000		
Creditors	75,000		
	8,50,000		8,50,000

The Company got the following scheme of capital reduction approved by the Court –

a) The Preference Shares to be reduced to Rs. 75 per share, fully paid-up and the Equity Shares to Rs. 37.50.

b) The debentureholders took over the Stock-in-trade and the book debts in full satisfaction of the amount due to them.

c) The Goodwill Account to be eliminated.

d) The Freehold Properties to be depreciated by 50%.

e) The value of the Plant and Machinery to be increased by Rs. 50,000.

    Give journal entries for the above and prepare the revised Balance Sheet.

Ans. : Balance Sheet Total Rs. 4,50,000

9) The following is the Balance Sheet of Shreyas Ltd., as on 31st March, 2014.

Balance Sheet

Liabilities	Rs.	Assets	Rs.
Share Capital :		Goodwill	1,20,000
8,000 Shares of Rs. 100 each	8,00,000	Land and Building	4,30,000
6% Debentures	3,00,000	Plant and Machinery	3,70,000
Sundry Creditors	80,000	Patents	50,000
		Stock	80,000
		Sundry Debtors	45,000
		Cash in Hand	1,000
		Profit and Loss A/c	84,000
	11,80,000		11,80,000

The Company is not getting well due to heavy losses and the following Scheme of Reconstruction was accepted by all –

1) Each Equity Share shall be sub-divided into Equity Shares of Rs. 10 each.

2) After sub-division, each Equity Shareholder will surrender 50% of his shareholdings.

3) Debentureholders total claim be reduced to Rs. 1,80,000 and this would be satisfied by issuing them the shares surrendered.

4) The claim of the sundry creditors shall be reduced by 20%.

5) Out of the balance available, the Company decided to write off Goodwill, Profit and Loss A/c and Patents completely and Plant and Machinery by Rs. 2,25,000.

6) Shares surrendered and not re-issued shall be cancelled. Pass necessary journal entries.

(P.U.)

Ans. : Capital Reserve Rs. 57,000.

10)   **Balance Sheet of "AB" Ltd. as on 31-3-2014**

Liabilities		Rs.	Assets	Rs.
Authorised & Issued Capital :			Land & Building	8,30,000
8,000 Shares of			Machinery	6,90,000
Rs. 100 each		8,00,000	Investment	17,000
Debentures		14,00,000	Stock-in-trade	60,000
Interest Accrued		70,000	Debtors	50,000
Sundry Creditors :			Cash	13,000
Income Tax	10,000		Profit & Loss A/c	10,70,000
Trade & General	4,50,000	4,60,000		
		27,30,000		27,30,000

The fixed assets (including a floating charge in favour of the debentureholders) are much over-valued. The debentureholders are prepared to accept a modification of their claims in consideration of a substantial interest in share capital. A scheme of reorganisation is accordingly prepared and confirmed by the Court. The main terms of the scheme are –

1) Each share shall be sub-divided into twenty fully paid Equity Shares of Rs. 5 each.

2) After sub-division, each shareholder shall surrender to the Company 95% of his holding. For the purpose of re-issue to debentureholders and creditors so far as required, and otherwise for cancellation.

3) Of those surrendered, 46,000 shares of Rs. 5 each shall be converted into 8% Participating Preference Shares of Rs. 5 each, fully paid.

4) The debentureholders total claim shall be reduced to Rs. 2,30,000. This will be satisfied by the issue to them of 46,000 Participating Preference Shares of Rs. 5 each, fully paid.

5) The liability for Income Tax is to be satisfied in full.

6) The claims of unsecured creditors shall be reduced by 4/5th and the balance shall be satisfied by allotting them Equity Shares of Rs. 5 each, fully paid, from the shares surrendered.

7) Shares surrendered and not re-issued shall be cancelled.

Journalise the above transactions assuming that the liability for Income Tax has not been discharged. Also give the Balance Sheet.

Ans. : - Total of Capital Reduction Account – 23,60,000

CHAPTER 7

Holding Company's Balance Sheet

7.1 Definition of Holding Company
7.2 Final Accounts
7.3 Preparation of Consolidated Balance Sheet
7.4 Treatment to important items in Balance Sheet
7.5 Problems on Consolidated Balance Sheet
7.6 Exercises

Introduction :

A holding company is the one that holds either the whole of the share capital or a majority of the shares in one or more companies. A holding company acquires majority of the shares of another company or having direct or indirect power to appoint majority of the directors of another company. Thus, a company acquires majority shares or acquires a power to appoint a majority of directors, is called a Holding Company. The other company which is controlled by a holding company is called a subsidiary a company. The object of holding company is to promote combination movement so that competition may be eliminated, advantages of monopoly or near monopoly may be enjoyed and economies in production and management may be secured. Such advantages can be enjoyed by amalgamation or absorbing two or more companies into one, but in such a case, the companies which are being amalgamated or absorbed have to liquidate themselves and lose their identity. But a holding company is one of the pattern of combination, so under this pattern a Holding Company and its subsidiaries continue to have their independent existence and thereby their trade names, reputation, goodwill etc. are retained with them. The holding may be wholly-owned subsidiary or partly-owned subsidiary company.

a) Wholly-owned Subsidiary :

When a holding company acquires all the shares of the subsidiary, such a subsidiary is called as wholly-owned subsidiary.

b) Partly-owned Subsidiary :

When a holding company acquires not all but major portion (generally more than 51%) of the shares of a subsidiary, such-subsidiary is known as "partly-owned subsidiary." The remaining shares of such company are held by outsiders, who are known as minority shareholders and their interest is called minority interest.

7.1 Definition of Holding Company :

A holding company is better defined in the context of the definitions of a subsidiary company. Section 4 of the Companies Act, 1956, defines a subsidiary company. According to this Section (1), a company shall be deemed to be a subsidiary company of another if, and only, if :–

    a) that other company controls the composition of its board of directors; or b) that other -

  i) When the first mentioned company is an existing company in respect of which the holders of preference shares issued before the commencement of this Act have the same voting rights in all respects as the shareholders of equity shares, exercises or controls more than half of the total voting power of such a company;

  ii) when the first mentioned company is another comapny, holds more than half in nominal value of its equity share capital : or

  c) the company is the subsidiary of any company which is that other company's subsidiary."

For example :

  a) "S" Ltd., is having a share capital of Rs. 1,00,000 divided into shares of Rs. 100 each. So the number of shares come to 1,000. If H Ltd. acquires 700 shares in "S" Ltd., then "H" Ltd. will be called as a holding company and "S" Ltd., will be the subsidiary of "H" Ltd.

  b) If "H" Ltd., purchases only 400 shares or less than 50% of the shares, then "H" Ltd., will not be treated as a Holding Company.

7.2 Final Accounts

Financial year of holding and subsidiary companies :

It seems to be the intention of the Companies Act that the financial year of a holding company and subsidiary company should end on the same date. Section 213(1) of the Companies Act, therefore, provides that the Central Government, may, if considered desirable, issue the necessary direction to the holding or subsidiary company to extend its financial year, if necessary.

According to Section 219(2) (c), the time gap between the close of the financial year of the holding company and that of its subsidiary company should not be more than 6 months. If it is more than 6 months, the Central Government is bound to give the necessary directions to reduce the time gap to not more than 6 months on the application of the directors of the Holding Company or its subsidiary.

Consolidated Final Accounts

In India, it is not compulsory for the holding company to make consolidated balance sheet and consolidated profit and loss account incorporating its own operations as well as operations of the subsidiary companies. However, according to Section 212 of the Companies Act, the holding company has to attach the following documents with its Balance Sheet in respect of each of its subsidiaries –

  i) a copy of the balance sheet of the subsidiary,

  ii) a copy of its profit and loss account,

  iii) a copy of the report of its board of directors,

  iv) a copy of the report of its auditor and

  v) a statement showing : (i) The extent of holding companies interest in the subsidiary at the end of financial year (ii) The profits (after deduction of losses of the subsidiary) separately for the current financial year and for the previous financial year and separately so far as they concern the holding company for profits already dealt with i.e. profit earned by the subsidiary after the date of acquisition of shares by a holding company.

However, it is preferred to prepare a consolidated balance sheet and a consolidated profit and loss account in order to make it necessary to understand by the members of the holding company, in addition to holding company's separate final accounts.

7.3 Preparation of Consolidated Balance Sheet

In India, although a Holding Company is not required by law to prepare a consolidated Balance Sheet and consolidated Profit and Loss Account, preparation of consolidated Balance Sheet and consolidated Profit and Loss Account is of much help to the holding company to show the clear picture, so in addition to the "legal" Balance Sheet as prescribed in Schedule VI, the holding company may also publish the Balance Sheet in which the assets and liabilities of all subsidiaries are given alongwith its own assets and liabilities as the Balance Sheet of head office incorporates the assets and liabilites of its branches.

Shareholders of the holding company are interested in knowing the affairs of the subsidiary company as part of their money given to the holding company is invested in the subsidiary company. So, it becomes safe for the directors of the holding company to disclose to the shareholders of the holding company, the extent to which they are entitled to the net assets of the subsidiary company.

In the preparation of Consolidated Balance Sheet, many important problems are involved. They are as follows :–

  1) Elimination of investment in shares of subsidiaries account.

  2) Minority Interest

  3) Cost of control

  4) Capital Profits and Revenue profits

  5) Inter-Company transactions.

  6) Contingent Liabilities.

  7) Unrealised Profits.

  8) Revaluation of Assets and Liabilities

  9) Preference Shares in Subsidiaries.

  10) Bonus shares

  11) Dividends

12) Share Premium, Capital Reserve etc.
13) Preliminary Expenses.

7.4 Treatement to important items in Consolidated Balance Sheet

1) Elimination of Investment in shares of subsidiaries Account or Cancellation of Investment and Share Capital –

Consolidated Balance Sheet can be prepared by combining all the assets and liabilities of the holding company and its subsidiaries. It will certainly balance, but it is not the consolidated Balance Sheet. This is because the inter-company balances have first to be eliminated. The "Investment in Subsidiary company" by holding company should cancel out the share capital of the subsidiary company. It will be clear from the following example:-

Balance Sheets

Liabilities	Holding Co.	Subsidiary Co.	Assets	Holding Co.	Subsidiary Co.
Equity Shares of Rs. 10 each	2,00,000	1,00,000	Fixed Assets	2,50,000	1,20,000
Liabilities	1,50,000	20,000	Investment in subsidiary company – 10,000 shares	1,00,000	-
	3,50,000	1,20,000		3,50,000	1,20,000

All the shares of subsidiary company have been purchased by the holding company. So, all the assets and liabilities of subsidiary company belong to the holding company.

In this case, the subsidiary company is wholly-owned subsidiary company of the holding company. The consolidated Balance Sheet will be prepared as follows :

Consolidated Balance Sheet

Liabilities	Rs.	Assets	Rs.
20,000 Equity Shares of Rs. 10 each	2,00,000	Fixed Assets 2,50,000 + 1,20,000	3,70,000
Liabilities (1,50,000 + 20,000)	1,70,000	Investment in 10,000 shares of Rs 10 each of the subsidiary company (All the shares held)	–
	3,70,000		3,70,000

From the above example, it follows that while preparing the consolidated balance sheet, investment of the holding company in the subsidiary company should be replaced by the assets and liabilities of the subsidiary company if all the shares of the subsidiary company have been purchased by the holding company.

2) Minority Interest :

A holding company may not hold the entire share capital of the subsidiary company : Generally, a majority portion of Share Capital is purchased by the holding company and remaining shares are purchased by outsiders. These outsiders have less than 50% of the shares of the subsidiary company and hence they are called minority shareholders. The interest of minority shareholders is known as Minority Interest and it must be shown on the liability side of the consolidated balance sheet. For example : If a holding company holds only $3/4^{th}$ of the equity share capital of the subsidiary company, it will be entitled to only $3/4^{th}$ of the net assets of the subsidiary company, while other $1/4^{th}$ of net assets belong to outsiders or minority shareholders. It is a usual practice to incorporate all assets and liabilities of the subsidiary company in the consolidated balance sheet and show the interest of minority in the subsidiary company as a separate liability under the heading "Minority Interest."

The minority interest is calculated as follows :

	Particulars	Rs.
	Paid-up value of Equity and Preference Shares held by outsiders.	×××
Add :	1) Proportionate share in all undistributed profit or General Reserve / Capital Profit of subsidiary comapny	×××
	2) Proportionate share in Revenue Profit of subsidiary company.	×××
	3) Proportionate increase in the value of assets of subsidiary company.	×××
	Total	×××
Less :	1) Proportionate share of losses of the subsidiary company.	×××
	2) Proportionate decrease in the value of assets of the subsidiary company	×××
	Minority Interest	×××

If the preference shares are held by outsiders, the paid-up value of such shares together with dividend thereon (if there are profits) is also added to the value of minority interest or shown separately. Proportionate share of the subsidiary company's profits and reserves belonging to the outsiders is calculated, keeping in view the value of equity shares held by them and the value of preference shares held is not considered because profits and reserves belong to equity shareholders and not to preference shareholders.

3) Cost of Control (Goodwill or Capital Reserve)

In case the subsidiary company has accumulated profits or accumulated losses, the holding company may acquire the shares of subsidiary company at a premium or at a discount, as the case may be. In other words, the price paid by the holding company for the shares of the subsidiary company is also affected by the accumulated profits or accumulated losses in the subsidiary company's balance sheet on the date such of acquisition. Such excess or less payment of net worth of assets represent cost of control. So such losses or profits should be taken into consideration while preparing the consolidated balance sheet.

If a holding company pays higher price then the net worth of assets of the subsidiary company, then is called **Goodwill**. If the price paid is less than its net worth of the assets, it is a profit which is earned prior to acquisition of shares and hence treated as **Capital Reserve.**

Calculation of Goodwill

Particulars	Rs.
Market price of shares acquired in subsidiary company (Investment in subsidiary company)	× × ×
Add : Holding company's share in capital losses	× × ×
Total	× × ×
Less : 1) Face value of shares acquired by holding company	× × ×
2) Holding company's share in capital profit	× × ×
3) Dividend received by holding company from the capital profit of subsidiary company	× × ×
Goodwill / Cost of Capital	× × ×

If there is a goodwill, in the balance sheets of both companies, it will be added to this Goodwill.

Note : If the balance is negative, it will be considered as Capital Reserve.

4) Capital Profits and Revenue Profits :

The holding company may acquire the shares in the subsidiary company either on the balance sheet date or any date earlier than the balance sheet date. If the holding company acquires shares in the subsidiary company on the balance sheet date, all profits earned by the subsidiary company have been taken as capital profits for the holding company. In case the holding company acquires the shares on the date other than balance sheet date of the subsidiary company, the profits of the subsidiary company will have to be apportioned between capital profits and revenue profits from the point of view of the holding company. The profit earned by the subsidiary company before holding company acquires its shares or control is known as capital profit or pre-acquisition profit. Undrawn pre-acquisition profit is taken into consideration for the calculation of goodwill or capital reserve.

The profit earned by the subsidiary company after the holding company acquires the shares or its control is known as Revenue Profits or Post-acquisition Profits of the subsidiary company and do not form part of goodwill or Capital Reserve calculation. In other words, while preparing the consolidated balance sheet, capital profits or losses should be adjusted with the cost of control and revenue profits should be merged with the balance in profit and loss account of the holding company.

Minority shareholders are not concerned whether the profits are pre-acquisition or post-acquisition. Post-acquisition profit is apportioned between the holding company and minority shareholders. The share of the holding company is added with its profit, while the share of minority shareholders form a part of the calculation of minority interest.

5) Inter-company Transactions :

While preparing a consolidated Balance Sheet, common transactions appearing in both the balance sheets of holding company and the subsidiary company should be eliminated. Such transactions may be –

1) **Goods sold on credit** by the holding company to subsidiary company or vice-versa will appear as debtors in the balance sheet of the company selling goods and as creditors in the balance sheet of the company purchasing goods.

2) **Bills drawn** by one company and accepted by the other company are eliminated while preparing consolidated balance sheet but bill discounted will continue to appear as liability, because the company which has accepted bills, will have to make the payment to an outsider i.e. bank on the due date.

3) **Loans advanced** by the holding company to the subsidiary company or vice versa appears as an asset in the balance sheet of the Company which gives such loans and as a liability in the balance sheet of the Company that takes these loans.

4) **Debentures issued** by one Company and held by the other Company.

6) Contingent Liability :

Contingent liability is a liability which may or may not arise or happen. It is customary to show contingent liabilities as a footnote to the balance sheet. Contingent Liability may be of two types :

a) External Contingent Liability

b) Internal Contingent Liability

External contingent liability is on account of a transaction between the Company and the third party while internal contingent liability is on account of a transaction between the companies of the same group. While preparing a consolidated balance sheet, the external contingent liabilities are shown as a footnote to the balance sheet, while internal contingent liabilities are eliminated from the footnote, since they appear as actual liabilities in the consolidated balance sheet.

7) Unrealised profit

When the goods are sold by the holding company to subsidiary company or vice-versa and if the goods remain unsold at the end of financial year, such goods are included in stock and appear as an asset in the balance sheet of the purchasing company. The profits earned by the selling company cannot be considered as a real profit. So, while preparing the consolidated balance sheet such unrealised profits on inter-company sales should be deducted from the profit of the selling company and also by deducting it from stock of the buying company. It is recorded as under :–

i) Ascertain the total amount of unrealised profit included in the stock lying with purchasing company. For example, if the goods costing Rs.10,000 were sold by "H" Ltd., to "S" Ltd., for the sum of Rs.12,000 and 40% of the goods are still in stock with "S" Ltd., the amount of unrealised profit will be as follows :–

Selling price - cost price = profit.

Rs.12,000 - Rs.10,000 = Rs.2,000

40% goods are still in stock, so, $\dfrac{2,000 \times 40}{100}$ = Rs.800

Unrealised profit is Rs. 800

ii) Reduce the amount of unrealised profit to the extent of the interest of the holding, company. For example, if in the above case, "H" Ltd., holds $\frac{3}{4}^{th}$ of the share capital of "S" Ltd., it will be advisable to reduce the unrealised profit to $\frac{3}{4}^{th}$ of Rs.800 i.e. Rs.600

It has become a common practice these days to consider the total profit on stock as unrealised without taking note of minority interest. For example, in the above case, the unrealised profit can also be taken as Rs.800. However, the former course is preferable.

iii) Finally deduct the unrealised profit from the profit of the company selling the goods and from the stock of the company purchasing the goods.

8) Revaluation of Assets and Liabilities :

If the assets and liabilities of the subsidiary company are revalued at the time of acquisition of shares in the subsidiary company, profit or loss on account of such revaluation is treated as capital profit or capital loss and is divided among minority shareholders and the holding company, according to the proportion of equity shares held by them. The holding company's share of such capital profit is transferred to capital reserve or deducted from cost of control or Goodwill and vice-versa, if there is a loss on revaluation. Share of profit of minority shareholders is added to the minority interest and a deduction is made from the minority interest, if there is a loss on revaluation.

9) Preference Shares in Subsidiaries :

(i) When preferenee shares are held by the holding company : If the holding company holds preference share in the subsidiary company, the difference between the price paid for these shares and their paid-up value is adjusted against Goodwill or Capital Reserve as the case may be, as is done in case of equity shares.

For example : If the holding company purchases 100 preference shares of Rs.100 each fully paid for a sum of Rs. 13,000 the excess of Rs. 3,000 of the cost of shares over paid-up value will be charged to Goodwill. However, if the cost of acquiring preference shares in the above case is only Rs. 8,000, the sum of Rs. 2,000, excess paid-up value over the cost of shares will be shown as Capital Reserve in the consolidated Balance Sheet.

ii) When shares are held by outsiders : In case the preference shares are held by outsiders, the paid-up value of such shares will be included in minority interest.

iii) Arrears of preference Dividend : In case the preference dividend are in arrears and the profits of the subsidiary company are adequate for making provision for such dividend, the amount of arrears should be provided out of the profits. The share of holding company in such arrears should be taken to its profit and loss account, if they have been provided out of post-acquisition profits. However, if such arrears or dividend have been provided out of pre-acquisition profits, they should be taken to cost of control. The shares of minority should be added to minority interest. In case the profits are not adequate to provide for all the arrears of dividend, there is no necessity of providing for the arrears of preference dividend.

10) Bonus Shares :

If the subsidiary company issues bonus shares to the existing shareholders, the holding company as well as minority shareholders will be receiving additional shares without making any Payment. The bonus shares may be issued out of pre-acquisition profits and reserves or post-acquisition profits and reserves.

Treatment to Bonus Shares :

a) Issue of Bonus Shares out of pre-acquisition profit - If the subsidiary company has issued bonus shares out of pre-acquisition profit or reserve, it will have no effect on the consolidated balance sheet. It is so because the holding company's share in pre-acquisition profits is reduced as bonus shares are issued out of it. But on the other hand, the paid-up value and number of shares held by the holding company will increase. The cost of control i.e. Goodwill or Capital Reserve will ultimately remain the same as it was before the issue of bonus shares.

b) Issue of Bonus Shares out of post-acquisition profits : If the bonus shares are issued by the subsidiary company out of post-acquisition profits, the balance of post-acquisition profits will be reduced to the extent of bonus shares issued. The remaining balance of post-acquisition profits will be divided between the holding company and minority shareholders.

11) Dividends :

The holding company owns majority of the shares of its subsidiary. When a dividend is paid out of profits of the subsidiary company, the holding company is likely to receive majority portion of it as a shareholder. It should be noted that, such a dividend may be paid out of the pre-acquisition profits or post-acquisition profits. The accounting treatment in the books of the holding company may vary accordingly.

a) Dividend paid out of pre-acquisition profits of a subsidiary company : If the subsidiary company has paid the dividend out of pre-acquisition profits, the holding company's share therein is required to be credited to Investment Account (shares in subsidiary company) reducing the cost of shares of subsidiary company in the holding company. Thus, dividend received by the holding company from subsidiary company out of pre-acquisition profits is added to Capital Reserve, which in turn, reduces the value of Goodwill. Since such a dividend is not available for distribution to the shareholders of the holding company, it is not credited to its profit and loss account.

b) Dividend paid out of post-acquisition profits by subsidiary company : Dividend received by the holding company from a subsidiary out of post-acquisition profits is treated as investment income and credited to profit and losss account of the holding company.

It should be noted that any Interim Dividend paid by subsidiary company is also treated in the books of holding company in the same manner as discussed above.

c) Unclaimed Dividend : Out of the total amount, the proportion belonging to the inter-company is cancelled in the consolidated Balance Sheet, being the mutual indebtedness and the amount payable to outsiders only is shown as a liability.

d) Proposed Dividend : When the dividend is proposed by the holding company, it will be deducted from the post-acquisition profits of the holding company (if it is not appearing in B/S of holding company) and will be shown in the consolidated Balance Sheet as a current liability.

The holding company's share of such proposed dividend is added with the profit and loss account of the holding company. Minority's share of proposed dividend can be added with the minority interest or it can be shown as a current liability in the consolidated balance sheet alongwith the proposed dividend of holding company, if any.

12) Share Premium, Capital Reserve etc.

In consolidated Balance Sheet, generally only the Share Premium Account of the holding company appears. However, it will be appropriate to adjust any share premium charged by the holding company, in respect of issue of its own shares in exchange for the shares of subsidiary company, against cost of control in the consolidated balance sheet.

The share premiun or any capital reserve appearing in the books of the subsidiary company on the date of acquisition of shares should be taken as a pre-acquisition profit and may be adjusted against cost of control. However, any share premium or capital reserve arising in the books of subsidiary company after acquisition, should not be taken as pre-acquisition profit. The holding company's share in such profits should be merged with the share premium or capital reserve. The proportionate share of minority should be included in the minority interest.

13) Provision for Taxation :

Any provision for taxation in the books of the subsidiary company should be taken to the consolidated balance sheet and be shown on the liability side.

14) Preliminary Expenses :

The preliminary expenses of the subsidiary company may be taken as an item of capital loss and treated accordingly. Alternatively, the amount may be added with the amount of preliminary expenses of the holding company.

7.5 Problems on Consolidated Balance Sheet

Problem No. 1 : Following are the balance sheets of 'H' Ltd., and 'S' Ltd., as on 31st, March, 2009

Balance Sheets

Liabilities	'H' Ltd. Rs.	'S' Ltd. Rs.	Assets	'H' Ltd. Rs.	'S' Ltd. Rs.
Share Capital			**Fixed Assets**	3,00,000	1,00,000
Share of Rs. 10 each	5,00,000	2,00,000	Plant & Machinery	1,00,000	1,00,000
General Reserve	1,00,000	50,000	60% Shares in 'S' Ltd.	1,62,400	—
P. & L. A/c	60,000	35,000	Debtors	52,600	39,000
Creditors	80,000	80,000	Bills Receivables	—	20,000
Bills payable	40,000	-	Current Assets	1,65,000	1,00,000
			Preliminary Expenses	-	6,000
	7,80,000	3,65,000		7,80,000	3,65,000

'H' Ltd., acquires shares on 1st April, 2008 on which date the General Reserve and profit and loss Account showed balances of Rs. 40,000 and Rs. 8,000 respectirely. No part of the preliminary expenses was written off during the year ending 31st March, 2009. The fixed assets are undervalued by Rs. 20,000 The Plant and Machinery was overvalued by Rs. 10,000. Debtors of 'S' Ltd. include Rs. 9,000 due from 'H' Ltd., in respect of goods supplied. Bills Receivable held by 'S' Ltd., accepted by 'H' Ltd.

Prepare a consolidated Balance sheet.   **(P.U.)**

Solution :

    Working Notes

  1) **Calculation of Shareholding Ratio**

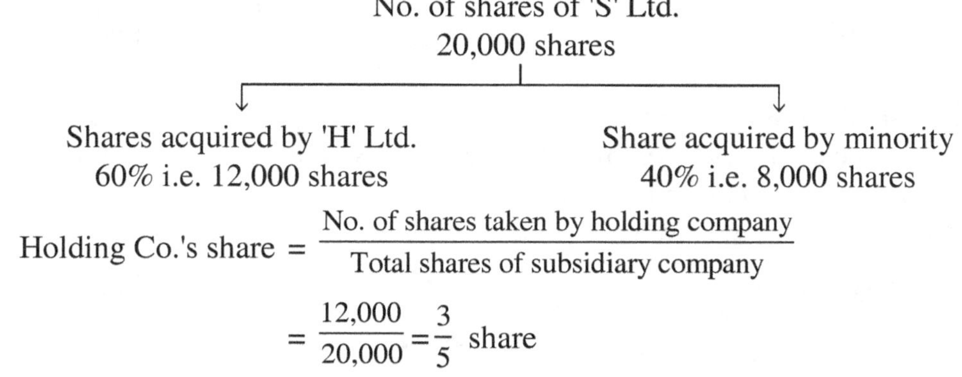

$$\text{Holding Co.'s share} = \frac{\text{No. of shares taken by holding company}}{\text{Total shares of subsidiary company}}$$

$$= \frac{12,000}{20,000} = \frac{3}{5} \text{ share}$$

Subsidiary Company's share (i.e. minority) : $1 - \dfrac{3}{5} = \dfrac{2}{5}$ share

2) Calculation of Capital Profit

i)	General Reserve (1-4-2008)	40,000
ii)	Profit & Loss A/c (cr. bal) 1-4-2008)	8,000
iii)	Increase in fixed Assets	20,000
	(i.e. under-valuation)	68,000

Less

i)	Decrease in Plant & Machinery (i.e. over-valuation)	10,000	
ii)	Preliminary Expenses (written off)	6,000	16,000
	Capital Profit		52,200

Holding co's share in capital profit

$52,000 \times \dfrac{3}{5} =$ 31,200

Minority's share in capital profit

$52,000 \times \dfrac{2}{5} =$ 20,800

3) Calculation of Revenue Profit

		Rs.
1)	General Reserve (50,000 - 40,000) =	10,000
2)	Profit & Loss A/c (35,000 - 8,000) =	27,000
	Revenue Profit	37,000

Holding Company's share in Revenue Profit

$\left(37,000 \times \dfrac{3}{5}\right) =$ 22,200

Minority's Shares in Revenue Profit

$\left(37,000 \times \dfrac{2}{5}\right) =$ 14,800

4) Calculation of Minority Interest

		Rs.
1)	Face value of shares taken by Subsidiary Co. (8,000 × 10)	80,000
2)	Minority's Share in Capital Profit	20,800
3)	Minority's Share in Revenue Profit	14,800
	Minority Interest	1,15,600

5) Calculation of cost of control i.e. Goodwill

i) Market value of shares taken by holding Company i.e. Investments		1,62,400
Less :		
i) Face value shares taken by holding company	1,20,000	
ii) Holding Co's share in Capital Profit	31,200	1,51,200
Goodwill		11,200

Consalidated Balance Sheet as on 31-3-2009

Liabilities		Rs.	Assets		Rs.
Share capital			**Fixed Assets.**		
Shares of Rs. 10 each.		5,00,000	'H' Ltd.	3,00,000	
General Reserve		1,00,000	'S' Ltd.	1,00,000	
Profit & Loss A/C	60,000			4,00,000	
+ Holding Co's share	22,200		+ Interest	20,000	4,20,000
in Revenue Profit		82,200	Plant & Machinery		
Minority Interest		1,15,600	'H' Ltd.	1,00,000	
Creditors 'H' Ltd.	80,000		'S' Ltd.	1,00,000	
'S' Ltd	80,000		Less	2,00,000	
	1,60,000		Decrease	10,000	1,90,000
Less Mutual owing	9,000	1,51,000	**Debtors**		
			'H' Ltd.	52,600	
Bills Payable	40,000	20,000	'S' Ltd.	39,000	
– B. R.	20,000		Less	91,600	
			Mutual owing	9,000	82,600
			Current Asset.		
			'H' Ltd.	1,65,000	
			'S' Ltd.	1,00,000	2,65,000
			Goodwill		11,200
		9,68,800			9,68,800

Problem No. 2 : From the following balance sheets of 'H' Ltd. and 'S' Ltd. as on 31st March, 2009 and the additional information thereon, prepare a consolidated Balance Sheet.

Liabilities	'H' Ltd. Rs.	'S' Ltd. Rs.	Assets	'H' Ltd. Rs.	'S' Ltd. Rs.
Share Capital					
Shares of Rs. 10 each			Fixed Assets	11,62,000	1,80,000
Fully paid	10,00,000	2,00,000	70% Shares of S Ltd.		
General Reserve	3,10,000	-	at cost	1,42,000	-
Prolit & Loss Account	1,50,000	40,000	Current Assets	3,86,000	1,24,000
Creditors	2,30,000	69,000	Preliminary Expenses	-	5,000
	16,90,000	3,09,000		16,90,000	3,09,000

'H' Ltd., acquired the shares on 31st Dec., 2008. On 1st April, 2008, profit and loss account showed a debit balance of Rs. 8,000. On 31st March, 2009, 'S' Ltd., decided to revalue its fixed assets at Rs. 2,00,000. **(P.U.)**

Solution :

Working Notes :

1) Calculation of Shareholdings

i) Holding Co's Share $= \dfrac{\text{Shares held by Holding Company}}{\text{Total shares of Sub. Company}}$

$= \dfrac{14,000\,\text{shares}}{20,000\,\text{shares}}$

ii) Minority's Share $= 1 - \dfrac{7}{10} = \dfrac{3}{10}$

2) Calculation of profit earned during the year.

Profit & Loss Appro. A/c

Particulars	Rs.	Particulars	Rs.
To Opening balance (Loss)	8,000	By Profit earned during the year	48,000
To Closing balance of profit	40,000		
	48,000		48,000

Alternalively : Profit on 31 st March, 2009 is Rs. 40,000. It is calculated after adjusting the loss. Hence, total profit may be Rs. 48,000. After deduction of loss, the profit is i.e. 48,000 - 8,000 = Rs. 40,000

Thus, total profit earned during the year is Rs. 48,000.

Date of acquisition of business is 31st Dec., 2008

Pre-acquisition period	**Post-acquisition period**
31st March, 2008 to 31st Dec., 2008	31st Dec., 2008 to 31st March, 2009
i.e. 9 months	i.e. 3 months

The profit earned during the pre-acquisition period is Capital Profit and profit earned during post-acquisition period is Revenue Profit. Such profits are calculated as under :–

$$48,000 \times \frac{9}{12} = \text{Rs. } 36,000 \text{ Capital Profit}$$

$$48,000 \times \frac{3}{12} = \text{Rs. } 12,000 \text{ Revenue Profit}$$

i) Calculation of total Capital Profit

	Rs.
Capital profit before acquisition	36,000
+ Appreciation in the value of fixed assets	
(Rs. 2,00,000 - Rs. 11,80,000)	20,000
	56,000
Less	
i) Loss on 1st April, 2008 Rs.8,000	
ii) Preliminary Expenses 5,000	13,000
Total Capital Profit	43,000

a) Holding Co's share in capital profit

$$\text{Rs. } 43,000 \times \frac{7}{10} = \text{Rs. } 30,100$$

b) Minority's share in capital profit

$$\text{Rs. } 43,000 \times \frac{3}{10} = \text{Rs. } 12,900$$

ii) Distribution of Revenue Profit

a) Holding Co's share = $\text{Rs. } 12,000 \times \dfrac{7}{10} = \text{Rs. } 8,400$

b) Minority share = $\text{Rs. } 12,000 \times \dfrac{3}{10} = \text{Rs. } 3,600$

3) Calculation of Minority Interest

	Rs.
1) Face value of shares taken by subsidiary company (6,000 × 10)	60,000
2) Minority'share in capital profit	12,900
3) Minority's share in Revenue profit	3,600
Minority Interest	76,500

4) Calculation of Capital Reserve | | **Rs.**

	Rs.
Face value of shares taken by holding company 14,000 shares × 10	1,40,000
+ Holding Co's share in capital profit	30,100
	1,70,100
Less	
Cost value of shares taken by holding company	
i.e. investments	1,42,000
Capital Reserve	28,100

Consolidated Balance Sheet
as on 31-3-2009

Liabilities		Rs.	Assets			Rs.
Share Capital			**Fixed Assets**			
Shares of Rs. 10 each		10,00,000	'H' Ltd.	11,62,000		
			'S' Ltd.	+ 1,80,000		
General Reserve		3,10,000		13,42,000		
P & L. A/c	1,50,000		Add. Income	20,000	13,62,000	
+ Holding Co's Share in			Current Assets			
Revenue Profits	8,400	1,58,400	'H' Ltd.	3,86,000		
Creditors			'S' Ltd.	+ 1,24,000	5,10,000	
'H' Ltd.	2,30,000					
'S' Ltd.	+ 69,000	2,99,000				
Capital Reserve		28,100				
Minority Interest		76,500				
		18,72,000				18,72,000

Problem No. 3 : The following are the summarised Balance Sheets of 'H' Ltd., and 'S' Ltd., on 31-3-2009

Liabilities	'H' Ltd. Rs.	'S' Ltd. Rs.	Assets	'H' Ltd. Rs.	'S' Ltd. Rs.
Share Capital :			Sundry Assets	1,90,000	80,000
Shares of Rs. 10 each	1,80,000	1,00,000	Debtors	50,000	25,000
Profit & Loss A/c	35,000	–	Investments, Shares in		
Creditors	80,000	30,000	'S' Ltd. (8,000 shares)	55,000	–
			Profit & Loss A/c	–	25,000
	2,95,000	1,30,000		2,95,000	1,30,000

'H' Ltd., acquired the shares in 'S' Ltd., on 1st August, 2008. The Balance Sheet of 'S' Ltd., as on 31st March, 2008, showed a Debit Balance on Profits & Loss A/c Rs. 40,000.

The debtors of 'H' Ltd., include Rs. 10,000 due from S Ltd, whereas the creditors of 'S' Ltd., include Rs. 5,000 due to 'H' Ltd. As a cheque of Rs. 5,000 remitted by 'S' Ltd., to 'H' Ltd., being in transit.

Prepare a consolidated Balance Sheet. **(P.U.)**

Solution :

Working Notes

1) Pre and Post Acquisition period

Holding company acquires shares on 1st Aug., 2008 of 'S' Ltd.
i)   Pre-acquisition period – 1-4-2008 to 31-7-2008 = 4 months.
ii) Post acquisition period – 1-8-2008 to 31-3-2009 = 8 months.

2) Shareholding Ratio

No. of shares of 'S' Ltd.
10,000 Shares
↓

Shares acquired by 'H' Ltd.	Shares acquired by minority
8,000 shares	2,000 Shares

'H' Ltd.'s share = $\dfrac{8,000}{10,000} = \dfrac{4}{5}$

'S' Ltd.'s share = $1 - \dfrac{4}{5} = \dfrac{1}{5}$

3) Calculation of Capital Loss

	'H' Ltd.	'S' Ltd.	
	4	1	
Loss on 1-4-2008			40,000
Loss profit upto 1-8-2008 $\dfrac{1}{3}$ of 15,000			5,000

(Loss of Rs. 40,000 is reduced to Rs. 25,000 at the end of the year.   35,000
It means during the year, Company earned profit of Rs. 15,000)
Division of capital loss between   35,000   28,000   7,000
'H' Ltd., and 'S' Ltd., in the ratio of 4:1

4) Revenue Profit

Profit from 1-8-2008 to 31-3-2009

$15,000 \times \dfrac{2}{3}$ 10,000

Division of Revenue profit between 'H' Ltd., & 'S' Ltd., in   10,000   8,000   2,000
the ratio of 4 : 1

5) Goodwill

Market price of shares held by 'H' Ltd. (Investment)	55,000
Add : 'H' Co's share in capital loss	28,000
	83,000
Less : Face value of shares	
held by holding company (8,000 × 10)	80,000
Goodwill	**3,000**

6) Minority Interest

Face value of shares	
taken by minority (2,000 × 10)	20,000
Subsidiary's (minority) Share Revenue	2,000
Profit	22,000
Less : Subsidiary Co's (minority) shares in capital loss	7,000
Minority Interest	**15,000**

Consolidated Balance Sheet
of 'H' Ltd., and its subsidiary 'S' Ltd., as on 31st March, 2009

Liabilities		Rs.	Assets		Rs.
Share Capital :			Goodwill		3,000
18,000 Shares of Rs. 10 each		1,80,000	Sundry Assets		
Profit & Loss A/c			'H' Ltd.	1,90,000	
'H' Ltd.	35,000		'S' Ltd.	80,000	2,70,000
Add : 'H' Ltd's Share in			Debtors		
Revenue Profits of Ltd. Co.	8,000	43,000	'H' Ltd.	50,000	
Creditors			Less : Due from		
'H' Ltd.		80,000	'S' Ltd.	10,000	
'S' Ltd.	30,000			40,000	
Less : Due to			'S' Ltd.	25,000	65,000
'H' Ltd.	5,000	25,000	Cash in Transit		5,000
Minority Interest		15,000			
		3,43,000			3,43,000

Problem No. 4 : 'H' Ltd., acquired shares in 'S' Ltd., on 1-4-2008. Their Balance Sheet as on 31-3-2009 were :

Balance Sheets as on 31-3-2009

Liabilities	'H' Ltd. Rs.	'S' Ltd. Rs.	Assets	'H' Ltd. Rs.	'S' Ltd. Rs.
Share Capital :			Land & Building	1,00,000	20,000
Shares of Rs. 100			Plant & Machinery	1,50,000	30,000
each, fully paid	2,50,000	50,000	Investment :		
General Reserve	50,000	20,000	400 shares in		
(as on 1-4-2008)			'S' Ltd. (at cost)	50,000	–
Profit & Loss A/c	70,000	25,000	Stock	40,000	25,000
Creditors	30,000	5,000	Debtors	30,000	15,000
			Cash	30,000	10,000
	4,00,000	1,00,000		4,00,000	1,00,000

Additional Information :

1. Sundry Debtors of 'H' Ltd. include Rs. 5,000 due from 'S' Ltd.
2. Stock of 'S' Ltd., includes goods purchased from 'H' Ltd., for Rs. 20,000 on which 'H' Ltd., made a profit of 25% on sale
3. On 1-4-2008, Profit & Loss A/c of 'S' Ltd., showed a credit balance of Rs. 5,000
   Prepare a consolidated Balance Sheet of 'H' Ltd., and it's subsidiary 'S' Ltd.   **(P.U.)**

Solution :

Working Notes

1) Shareholding Ratio :

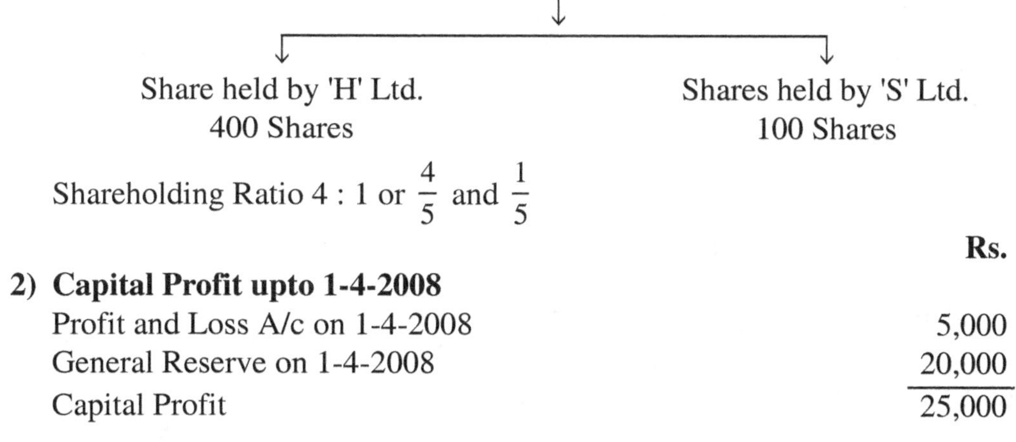

Shareholding Ratio 4 : 1 or $\dfrac{4}{5}$ and $\dfrac{1}{5}$

                       Rs.

2) Capital Profit upto 1-4-2008

	Rs.
Profit and Loss A/c on 1-4-2008	5,000
General Reserve on 1-4-2008	20,000
Capital Profit	25,000

i) Holding Co's share in Capital Profit

$$25,000 \times \frac{4}{5} = \text{Rs. } 20,000$$

ii) Minority's share in Capital Profit

$$25,000 \times \frac{1}{5} = \text{Rs. } 5,000$$

3) Revenue Profit

	Rs.
Profit & Loss A/c on 31-3-2009	25,000
Less : Profit & Loss on 1-4-2008	5,000
Revenue profit	20,000

i) Holding Co's share in Revenue Profit

$$20,000 \times \frac{4}{5} = \text{Rs. } 16,000$$

ii) Minority's share in Revenue Profit

$$20,000 \times \frac{1}{5} = \text{Rs. } 4,000$$

4) Minority Interest

	Rs.
Face value of shareholding by Minority (100 × 100)	10,000
Add : Capital Profit of Minority	5,000
Revenue Profit of Minority	4,000
Minority Interest	19,000

5) Capital Reserve

	Rs.
Face value of shares held by minority ('S' Ltd.)	40,000
Add : Capital Profit of 'H' Ltd.	20,000
	60,000
Less : Market value of shares of 'S' Ltd.	50,000
Capital Reserve	10,000

6) Unrealised Profit

25% Profit on selling price

cost + profit = selling price

100 + 25 = 125

Selling Price = Rs. 125 and Profit = Rs. 25

$$20,000 \text{ selling price } \frac{20,000 \times 25}{125} = \text{Rs. } 5,000$$

$$\text{Holding Co's share Rs. } 5,000 \times \frac{4}{5} = \text{Rs. } 4,000$$

Consolidated Balance sheet
as on 31-3-2009

Liabilities	Rs.		Assets	Rs.	
Share Capital			**Fixed Assets**		
2500 Equity Shares			Land & Building		
of Rs. 100 each	2,50,000		'H' Ltd.	1,00,000	
			'S' Ltd.	20,000	1,20,000
Reserve & Surplus					
General Reserve	50,000		Plant & Machinery		
Capital Reserve	10,000		'H' Ltd.	1,50,000	
Profit & Loss A/c	70,000		'S' Ltd.	30,000	1,80,000
Add : Revenue					
Profit of 'H' Ltd.	16,000		**Current Assets**		
	86,000		Stock		
Less : unrealised profit	4,000	82,000	'H' Ltd.	40,000	
			'S' Ltd.	25,000	
				65,000	
Current Liabilities			Less : Unrealised profit	4,000	61,000
Sundry Creditors			Sundry Debtors		
'H' Ltd.	30,000		'H' Ltd.	30,000	
'S' Ltd.	5,000		'S' Ltd.	15,000	
	35,000			45,000	
Less Internal owing	5,000	30,000	Less : Internal owing	5,000	40,000
Minority Interest		19,000	Cash		
			'H' Ltd.	30,000	
			'S' Ltd.	10,000	40,000
	4,41,000				4,41,000

Problem No. 5 : The following are the Balance Sheets of two companies as at 31st December, 2008

Liabilities	'AB' Ltd. Rs.	'CD' Ltd. Rs.	Assets	'AB' Ltd. Rs.	'CD' Ltd. Rs.
Equity Share Capital			Land and Building	2,00,000	1,50,000
Shares of Rs. 10 each	10,00,000	5,00,000	Machinery	3,00,000	3,00,000
General Reserve			Stock	75,000	50,000
on 1.1.2008	1,00,000	1,00,000	Sundry Debtors	50,000	60,000

Liabilities	'AB' Ltd. Rs.	'CD' Ltd. Rs.	Assets	'AB' Ltd. Rs.	'CD' Ltd. Rs.
Profit & Loss A/c on 1.1.2008	50,000	30,000	Investment at cost Shares in 'CD' Ltd.	5,00,000	
Profit for the year 2008	60,000	40,000	Bills Receivable	10,000	5,000
Sundry Creditors	70,000	50,000	Cash at Bank	1,55,000	1,60,000
Bills Payable	10,000	5,000			
	12,90,000	7,25,000		12,90,000	7,25,000

1) 'AB' Ltd., acquired 40,000 equity shares of 'CD' Ltd., on 1.1.2008
2) Bills Receivable of 'AB' Ltd., includes Rs. 3,000 accepted by 'CD' Ltd.
3) Sundry Debtors of 'AB' Ltd., includes Rs. 10,000 due from 'CD' Ltd.
4) Stock of 'CD' Ltd., includes goods purchased from 'AB' Ltd., for Rs. 30,000 which were invoiced by 'AB' Ltd., at a profit of 25% on invoice price.

Prepare a consolidated Balance Sheet of 'AB' Ltd., and its subsidiary 'CD' Ltd., as at 31.12.2008, giving the necessary workings. **(P.U.)**

Solution :

Working Notes :

1) Shares Acquisition Ratio : 4 : 1

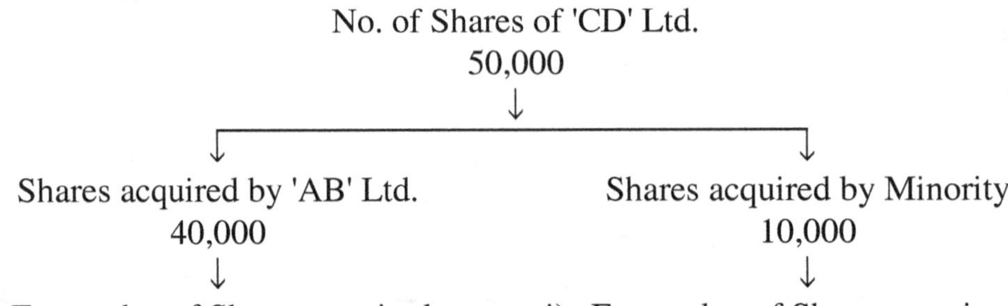

Shareholding Ratio = 'AB' Ltd. $\dfrac{4}{5}$ and 'CD' Ltd. $\dfrac{1}{5}$

2) Capital Profit (upto 1.1.2008)   Rs.

Profit and Loss A/c on 1.1.2008   30,000

General Reserve on 1.1.2008   1,00,000

Capital Profit   1,30,000

i) Holding Co's share in Capital Profit = $1,30,000 \times \dfrac{4}{5}$ = Rs. 1,04,000

ii) Subsidiary Co's share in Capital Profit = $1,30,000 \times \dfrac{1}{5}$ = Rs. 26,000

3) Revenue Profit (1.1.2008 to 31.12.2008)   **Rs.**

Profit & Loss Account   40,000

Revenue Profit   40,000

i) Holding Co's share in Revenue Profit

$$4,00,000 \times \dfrac{4}{5} = \text{Rs. } 32,000$$

ii) Subsidiary Co's (minority) share in Revenue Profit

$$40,000 \times \dfrac{1}{5} = \text{Rs. } 8,000$$

4) Minority Interest :   **Rs.**

Face value of shares acquired by Minority		1,00,000
Add : i) Capital Profit of Minority		26,000
ii) Revenue Profit of Minority		8,000
Minority Interest		1,34,000

5) Goodwill Capital Reserve :   **Rs.**

Market Price of shares acquired by 'AB' Ltd.	5,00,000
Less : Face value of shares acquired by 'AB' Ltd.	4,00,000
	1,00,000
Less : Capital Profit of 'AB' Ltd.	1,04,000
Capital Reserve	4,000

6) Unrealised Profit

Stock of 'CD' Ltd., includes Rs. 30,000 worth goods purchased from 'AB' Ltd., on which 'AB' Ltd., charged profit @ 25% on invoice price.

$$\text{Hence, Profit on invoice price} = 30,000 \times \dfrac{25}{100}$$

$$= 7,500$$

Holding Co's Shares 4/5th of 7,500; i.e. Rs. 6,000.

Consolidated Balance Sheet of 'AB' Ltd., together with its Subsidiary 'CD' Ltd., as on 31-12-2008

Liabilities		Rs.	Assets		Rs.
Share Capital			**Fixed Assets**		
1,00,000 equity shares of			Land and Building		
Rs. 10 each		10,00,000	'AB' Ltd.	2,00,000	
Reserves and Surplus :			'CD' Ltd.	1,50,000	3,50,000
General Reserve		1,00,000	Machinery		
Profit and Loss A/c			'AB' Ltd.	3,00,000	
(1.1.2008)	50,000		'CD' Ltd.	3,00,000	6,00,000
Add : i) Profit during			**Current Assets**		
2008	60,000		**Loans and Advances :**		
ii) Revenue Profit			Stock		
('AB' Ltd.)	32,000		'AB' Ltd.	75,000	
	1,42,000		'CD' Ltd.	50,000	
Less : Unrealised Profit	6,000	1,36,000		1,25,000	
Capital Reserve		4,000	Less : Unrealised Profit	6,000	1,19,000
Current Liabilities & Provisions :			Debtors		
Sundry Creditors			'AB' Ltd.	50,000	
'AB' Ltd.	70,000		'CD' Ltd.	60,000	
'CD' Ltd.	50,000			1,10,000	
	1,20,000		Less : Inter co. owing	10,000	1,00,000
Less : Inter-Co. owing	10,000	1,10,000	Bills Receivable		
Bills payable			'AB' Ltd.	10,000	
'AB' Ltd.	10,000		'CD' Ltd.	5,000	
'CD' Ltd.	5,000			15,000	
	15,000		Less : Inter-Co. owing	3,000	12,000
Less : Inter-Co. owing	3,000	12,000	Cash at Bank		
Minority Interest		1,34,000	'AB' Ltd.	1,55,000	
			'CD' Ltd.	1,60,000	3,15,000
		14,96,000			14,96,000

Problem No. 6 : From the following Balance Sheet of 'H' Ltd., and its subsidiary 'S' Ltd., drawn on 31st December 2008, prepare a consolidated Balance Sheet as on that date.

Liabilities	'H' Ltd. Rs.	'S' Ltd. Rs.	Assets	'H' Ltd. Rs.	'S' Ltd. Rs.
Share Capital :			**Fixed Assets :**	3,50,000	1,50,000
in Shares of			Stock	90,000	40,000
Rs. 100 each	5,00,000	2,00,000	Debtors	60,000	30,000
General Reserve	1,00,000	–	9% Debentures		
Profit & Loss A/c	80,000	–	in 'S' Ltd. at par	60,000	–
9% Debentures	–	1,00,000	1,500 shares of 'S' Ltd.		
Trade Creditors	75,000	45,000	@ Rs. 80 each	1,20,000	–
			Bank	75,000	25,000
			Profit and Loss A/c	–	1,00,000
	7,55,000	3,45,000		7,55,000	3,45,000

'H' Ltd., acquired the shares on 1st May, 2008. The Profit and Loss Account of 'S' Ltd., showed a debit balance of Rs. 1,50,000 on 1st January, 2008. During March, 2008, goods costing Rs. 6,000 were destroyed against which the insurers paid Rs. 2,000. Trade Creditors of 'S' Ltd., include Rs. 20,000 for goods supplied by 'H' Ltd., on which H. Ltd. made a profit Rs. 2,000. Half of the goods were still in stock on 31st December, 2008.

(CS Inter, and P.U)

Solution :

Working Notes :

1) Pre and Post Acquisition Period Ratio : 1 : 2

   Holding Co. 'H' Ltd. acquired shares of 'S' Ltd. on 1.5.2008

   i) Pre acquisition period is 1.1.2008 to 1.5.2008 i.e. 4 months

   ii) Post acquisition is 1.5.2008 to 31.12.2008 i.e. 8 months

2) Share Acquisition Ratio : 3 :1 (1500 : 500)

No. of Shares of 'S' Ltd.

2,000

↓

Shares acquired by 'H' Ltd. 1,500	Shares acquired by Minority 500
i) Face value of shares acquired by H Ltd. = Rs. 1,50,000	i) Face value of shares acquired by Minority = Rs. 50,000
ii) Market price of shares acquired by H Ltd. = Rs. 1,20,000	

Note :

	Rs.
Profit Prior and after purchase of shares	
Profit and Loss A/c on 1.1.2008 (Loss)	1,50,000
Less : Profit and Loss A/c on 31.12.2008 (Loss)	1,00,000
Profit during the year	50,000

But, it is after deducting loss of goods Rs. 4,000. It means the profit before loss was Rs. 54,000. The period ratio is 1 : 2. Hence, division of profit is Rs. 18,000 and Rs. 36,000. The Loss of Rs. 4,000 is before the purchase of shares. Hence, Profit from 1.1.2008 to 1.5. 2008 = 18,000 - 4,000 = Rs. 14,000

3) Capital Loss upto 1-5-2008

	Rs.
Profit & Loss A/c (Loss on 1-1-2008)	1,50,000
Less - P and L A/c (Profit) 1-1-08 to 1-5-08	14,000
Capital Loss	1,36,000

Division of Capital Loss between 'H' Ltd. & 'S' Ltd.

i)	Holding Co's shares in capital loss $(1,36,000 \times \frac{3}{4})$	1,02,000
ii)	Minority's share in capital loss $(1,36,000 \times \frac{1}{4})$	34,000

4) Revenue Profit (1-5-2008 t0 31-12-2008)

Profit & Loss A/c (see note)	36,000

Division of Revenue Profit between 'H' Ltd. & 'S' Ltd.

i)	Holding Co's share in Revenue Profit $(36,000 \times \frac{3}{4})$	27,000
ii)	Minority share in Revenue Profit $(36000 \times \frac{1}{4})$	9,000

5) Minority Interest

	Rs.
Face value of shares held by Minority	50,000
Add - Revenue Profit of Minority	9,000
	59,000
Less - Capital Loss of Minority	34,000
Minority Interest	25,000

6) Goodwill

	Rs.
Cost price of shares held by 'H' Ltd.	1,20,000
Add - Capital Loss of 'H' Ltd.	1,02,000
	2,22,000
Less - Face value of shares held by 'H' Ltd.	1,50,000
Goodwill	72,000

7) Unrealised Profit

Stock of 'S' Ltd., includes Rs. 10,000, goods purchased from 'H' Ltd., on which 'H' Ltd., charged profit is Rs. 1,000.

Hence, Holding Companies shares 3/4th of 1,000 i.e. Rs. 750.

Consolidated Balance Sheet of 'H' Ltd., with its subsidiary 'S' Ltd. as on 31-12-2008

Liabilities		Rs.	Assets		Rs.
Share Capital			Good will		72,000
5,000 equity shares of			Fixed Assets		
Rs. 100 each		5,00,000	'H' Ltd.	3,50,000	
Reserves and Surplus			'S' Ltd.	1,50,000	5,00,000
General Reserve		1,00,000			
Profit and Loss A/c	80,000		**Current Assets and**		
Add - Revenue Profit	27,000		**Loans and Advances**		
	1,07,000		Stock		
Less - Unrealised			'H' Ltd.	90,000	
Profit	750	1,06,250	'S' Ltd.	40,000	
Creditors				1,30,000	
'H' Ltd.	75,000		Less - Unrealised		
'S' Ltd.	45,000		Profit	750	1,29,250
	1,20,000		Debtors		
Less - Inter-Co. owing	20,000	1,00,000	'H' Ltd.	60,000	
Secured Loans :			'S' Ltd.	30,000	
6% Debenture	1,00,000			90,000	
Less - held by 'H' Ltd.	60,000	40,000	Less Inter-Co. owing	20,000	70,000
Minority Interest		25,000	Cash at Bank		1,00,000
		8,71,250			8,71,250

Problem No. 7 : Prepare a Consolidated Balance Sheet with necessary workings from the Balance Sheet of 'H' Ltd. and 'S' Ltd. and additional information given below :–

Balance Sheet as on 31-12-2008

Liabilities	'H' Ltd. Rs.	'S' Ltd. Rs.	Assets	'H' Ltd. Rs.	'S' Ltd. Rs.
Share Capital :			Land & Buildings	2,00,000	1,00,000
Share of Rs. 100			Plant & Machinery	1,50,000	2,00,000
each	5,00,000	3,00,000	Investment in		
General Reserve	40,000	10,000	2,700 shares of		
Profit & Loss A/c	70,000	5,000	'S' Ltd.	2,97,000	
Bills Payable	50,000	25,000	Stock	40,000	30,000
Creditors	1,40,000	60,000	Debtors	50,000	60,000
			Bills Receivable	63,000	10,000
	8,00,000	4,00,000		8,00,000	4,00,000

Additional Information :

1) On the date of purchase of shares there was no balance in General Reserve and Profit and Loss A/c showed a debit balance of Rs. 10,000 in the books of 'S' Ltd.
2) Sundry Debtors of 'S' Ltd., include Rs. 40,000 due from 'H' Ltd.
3) Bills Payable of 'S' Ltd., include Rs. 18,000/- in favour of 'H' Ltd., which has discount of Rs. 3,000/- of them.
4) Stock of 'S' Ltd., includes Rs. 4,000 being purchased from 'H' Ltd., on which the later company made a profit of $33\frac{1}{3}$ on Cost.   **(P.U.)**

Solution :

Working Notes : -

1) Shares Acquisition Ratio - 9 : 1

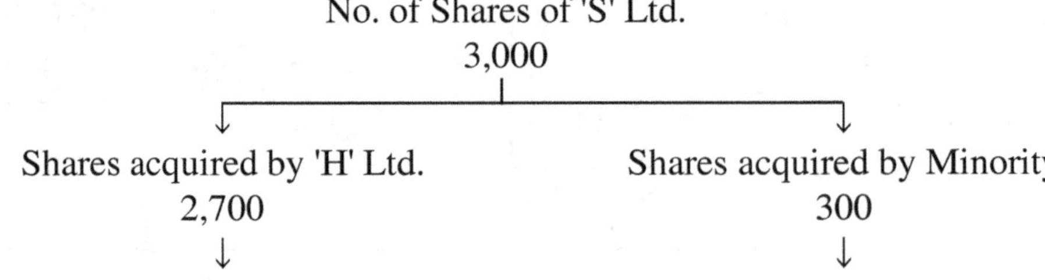

2) Capital Loss -

	Rs.
Profit and Loss A/c (loss)	10,000
Capital Loss =	10,000

i) Holding Co's shares in Capital Loss

$$10,000 \times \frac{9}{10} = \text{Rs. } 9,000$$

ii) Minority's shares in Revenue Profit

$$10,000 \times \frac{1}{10} = \text{Rs. } 1,000$$

3) Revenue Profit

Profit and loss A/c (loss)	10,000
Add : Profit and Loss A/c (Profit) 31-12-2008	5,000
	15,000
Add : General Reserve on 31-12-2008	10,000
Revenue Profit	25,000

i) Holding Co's shares in Revenue Profit.

$$25,000 \times \frac{9}{10} = \text{Rs. } 22,500$$

ii) Minority's shares in Revenue Profit

$$25,000 \times \frac{1}{10} = \text{Rs. } 2,500$$

4) Minority Interest

Face value of shares acquired by Minority	30,000
Add : Revenue Profit of Minority	2,500
	32,500
Less : Capital Loss of Minority	1,000
Minority Interest	31,500

5) Goodwill

	Rs.
Market price of shares acquired by 'H' Ltd.	2,97,000
Add : Capital Loss of 'H' Ltd.	9,000
	3,06,000
Less : Face value of shares acquired by 'H' Ltd.	2,70,000
Goodwill	36,000

6) Unrealised Profit

Stock of 'S' Ltd., includes Rs. 4,000 worth goods purchased from 'H' Ltd., on which

'H' Ltd., charged profit @ $33\frac{1}{3}\%$ on cost.

Hence, Cost price + Profit = Selling price

$$100 \quad + \quad 33\frac{1}{3} \quad = 133\frac{1}{3}$$

$$\therefore \text{ Profit on selling price} = \frac{33\frac{1}{3}}{133\frac{1}{3}} = \frac{1}{4}$$

$\therefore$ Profit in Rs. 4,000 is $\frac{1}{4}$ th of 4,000; i.e. Rs. 1,000.

Holding Co's Shares $\frac{9}{10}$ th of 1,000; i.e. Rs. 900.

Consolidated Balance Sheet
of 'H' Ltd., together with its Subsidiary 'S' Ltd.
as on 31-12-2008

Liabilities		Rs.	Assets		Rs.
Share Capital			**Fixed Assets**		
5,000 Equity Shares of			Goodwill		36,000
Rs. 100 each		5,00,000	Land and Building		
Reserves and Surplus			'H' Ltd.	2,00,000	
General Reserve		40,000	'S' Ltd.	1,00,000	3,00,000
Profit and Loss A/c	70,000		Plant and Machinery		
Add - Revenue profit	22,500		'H' Ltd	1,50,000	
	92,500		'S' Ltd	2,00,000	3,50,000
Less - Unrealised			**Current Assets Loans**		
Profit	900	91,600	**and Advances**		
Current Liabilities			Stock		
and Provisions			'H' Ltd.	40,000	
Bills Payable			'S' Ltd.	30,000	
'H' Ltd.	50,000			70,000	
'S' Ltd.	25,000		Less - Unrealised		
	75,000		Profit	900	69,100

Liabilities		Rs.	Assets		Rs.
Less - Inter-Co.			Debtors		
Owing	15,000	60,000	'H' Ltd.	50,000	
Sundry Creditors			'S' Ltd.	60,000	
'H' Ltd.	1,40,000			1,10,000	
'S' Ltd.	60,000		Less - Inter-Co.		
	2,00,000		Owing	40,000	70,000
Less - Inter-Co.			Bills Receivable		
Owing	40,000	1,60,000	'H' Ltd.	63,000	
Minority Interest		31,500	'S' Ltd.	10,000	
				73,000	
			Less - Inter-Co.		
			Owing	15,000	58,000
		8,83,100			8,83,100

Problem No. 8 : From the following information, prepare the consolidated Balance Sheet of 'H' Ltd., and its subsidiary 'S' Ltd., as at 31st December, 2008, giving detailed workings.

Balance Sheet as at 31st December, 2008

Liabilities	'H' Ltd. Rs.	'S' Ltd. Rs.	Assets	'H' Ltd. Rs.	'S' Ltd. Rs.
Share Capital			Goodwill	1,00,000	—
Equity Shares of			Fixed Assets	2,00,000	2,50,000
Rs. 10 each	4,00,000	2,00,000	Investments		
General Reserve	2,00,000	60,000	16,000 Shares of		
Profit and Loss A/c	1,00,000	40,000	Rs. 10 each in 'S'		
6% Debentures	—	1,00,000	Ltd. (at Cost)	2,00,000	
Loan from 'H' Ltd.	—	10,000	6% Debentures of		
Sundry Creditors	1,00,000	40,000	'S' Ltd. (Face Value		
Bills Payable	50,000	30,000	Rs. 60,000)	60,000	—
			Govt. Securities		50,000
			Stock	1,00,000	40,000
			Sundry Debtors	80,000	40,000
			Bills Receivable	40,000	—
			Bank Balance	60,000	1,00,000
			Loan to 'S' Ltd.	10,000	—
	8,50,000	4,80,000		8,50,000	4,80,000

1) Sundry Creditors of 'H' Ltd., include Rs. 20,000 due to 'S' Ltd.

2) The Closing Stock of 'H' Ltd., includes stock worth Rs. 30,000 supplied by 'S' Ltd., which was invoiced at cost plus 20% profit on cost.

3) Bills payable of 'S' Ltd., include Rs. 24,000 issued in favour of 'H' Ltd., which was discounted but not yet matured Rs. 4,000 of them.

4) 'H' Ltd., acquired 16,000 equity shares in 'S' Ltd., on 1st January, 2008 on which date the Balance Sheet of 'S' Ltd., showed General Reserve at Rs. 20,000 and Profit and Loss A/c Credit balance of Rs. 10,000.

5) 'H' Ltd., revalued Fixed Assets of 'S' Ltd., as on 1st January, 2008, at Rs. 2,60,000.

(P.U.)

Solution :

Working Notes

1) Shares Acquisition Ratio = 4 : 1

No. of shares of 'S' Ltd.
20,000

Shares acquired by 'H' Ltd. 16,000	Shares acquired by Minority 4,000
↓	↓
i) Face value of shares held by 'H' Ltd. = Rs. 1,60,000 ii) Market price of shares held by 'H' Ltd. = Rs. 2,00,000	i) Face value of shares held by Minority = Rs. 40,000

2) Capital Profit (upto 1-1-2008)

General Reserve on 1-1-2008	20,000
Profit and Loss A/c on 1-1-2008	10,000
Appreciation of Fixed Assets	10,000
Capital Profit	**40,000**

i) Holding Co's Share in Capital Profit

$$40,000 \times \frac{4}{5} = \text{Rs. } 32,000$$

ii) Minority's share in Capital Profit'

$$40,000 \times \frac{1}{5} = \text{Rs. } 8,000$$

3) Revenue Profit (1-1-2008 to 31-12-2008)

i)	General Reserve on 31-12-2008	60,000	
	Less - General Reserve on 1-1-2008	20,000	40,000
ii)	Profit and Loss A/c on 31-12-2008	40,000	
	Less = Profit and Loss A/c 1-1-2008	10,000	30,000
	Revenue Profit		70,000

i) Holding Co's share in Revenue Profit

$$70,000 \times \frac{4}{5} = 56,000$$

ii) Minority share in Revenue Profit

$$70,000 \times \frac{1}{5} = Rs.\ 14,000$$

4) Minority Interest

	Face value of shares held by Minority	40,000
Add -	i) Capital Profit of Minority	8,000
	ii) Revenue Profit of Minority	14,000
	Minority Interest	62,000

5) Goodwill

	Rs.
Market price of Shares held by 'H' Ltd.	
Face value of Shares held by 'H' Ltd.	2,00,000
Less - Face value of Bonus Shares held by 'H' Ltd.	1,60,000
	40,000
Less - Capital Profit of 'H' Ltd.	32,000
Goodwill	8,000

6) Unrealised Profit

Unsold stock with 'H' Ltd.	
(of goods purchased from 'S' Ltd.)	30,000
Unrealised Profit included in this stock cost plus 20%	
i.e. 1/6 on Sale	5,000

'H' Ltd's share in Unrealised Profit $\frac{4}{5}$ th of 5,000 = 4,000

Consolidated Balance sheet of 'H' Ltd., with its Subsidiary 'S' Ltd., as on 31-12-2008

Liabilities		Rs.	Assets		Rs.
Share Capital			**Fixed Assets**		
40,000 equity shares of			Goodwill		1,08,000
Rs. 10 each		4,00,000	Fixed Assets		
Reserves and Surplus			'H' Ltd.	2,00,000	
General Reserve		2,00,000	'S' Ltd.	2,50,000	
Profit and Loss A/c	1,00,000		**Add :** Appreciation	10,000	4,60,000
Add - Revenue profit	56,000		**Investments**		
	1,56,000		Govt. Securities		50,000
Less - Unrealised Profit	4,000	1,52,000	**Currents Assets**		
Secured Loans			**Loans and Advances**		
6% Debentures	1,00,000		'H' Ltd.	1,00,000	
Less - internal	60,000	40,000	'S' Ltd.	40,000	
Current Liabilities and				1,40,000	
Provisions			**Less -** Unrealised		
Sundry Creditors			Profit	4,000	1,36,000
'H' Ltd.	1,00,000		Sundry Debtors		
'S' Ltd.	40,000		'H' Ltd.	80,000	
	1,40,000		'S' Ltd.	40,000	
Less - Inter-Co.				1,20,000	
Owing	20,000	1,20,000	Less - Inter-Co.		
Bills Payable			Owing	20,000	1,00,000
'H' Ltd.	50,000		Bills Receivable	40,000	
'S' Ltd.	30,000		Less - Inter-Co.		
	80,000		Owing	20,000	20,000
Less - Inter-Co.					
Owing	20,000	60,000	Bank Balance		
Minority Interest		62,000	'H' Ltd.	60,000	
			'S' Ltd.	1,00,000	1,60,000
		10,34,000			10,34,000

Problem No. 9 : The following are the Balance Sheets of Satara Ltd., and Pune Ltd., as on 31st March, 2009.

Balance Sheets

Liabilities	Satara Ltd. Rs.	Pune Ltd. Rs.	Assets	Satara Ltd. Rs.	Pune Ltd. Rs.
Share Capital			Goodwill	60,000	20,000
Shares of Rs.10 each	10,00,000	4,00,000	Machinery	7,32,000	2,72,000
General Reserve	1,50,000	—	Stock	1,80,000	90,000
Profit & Loss A/c	1,42,000	60,000	Debtors	2,95,000	1,23,000
Creditors	1,82,000	87,000	Cash	35,000	27,000
Bills Payable	20,000	—	Investment (24,000 shares of Pune Ltd. at Cost)	1,92,000	—
			Bills Receivable	—	15,000
	14,94,000	5,47,000		14,94,000	5,47,000

Other Information -

a) Satara Ltd., acquired the shares in Pune Ltd., on 1st Oct., 2008

b) The Profit & Loss Account of Pune Ltd., showed a debit balance of Rs. 20,000 on 1st April, 2008

c) Included in the Stock of Pune Ltd., are goods of Rs. 20,000 which were supplied by Satara Ltd., as cost plus 25%.

d) The Bills payable in Satara Ltd., represented Rs. 15,000 issued in favour of Pune Ltd. Prepare a consolidated Balance Sheet with full working. **(P.U.)**

Solution

Working Notes :

1) Calculation of Shareholding Ratio.

i) Holding Co's share $= \dfrac{\text{Shares held by Holding Company}}{\text{Total shares of Subsidiary Company}}$

$$= \frac{24,000 \text{ Shares}}{40,000 \text{ Shares}} = \frac{3}{5} \text{ Share}$$

ii) Minority's share $= 1 - \dfrac{3}{5} = \dfrac{2}{5}$ Share.

Shareholding Ratio $= 3 : 2$

2) Pre and post acquisition period

i) Pre-acquisition period - 1st April, 2008 to 1st Oct., 2008 = 6 months.

ii) Post-acquisition period - 1st Oct., 2008 to 31-3-2009 = 6 months.

3) Capital Profit

	Rs.
Profit & Loss Account 1-4-2008 to 1-10-2008	
(Rs. 60,000 + 20,000 ÷ 2)	40,000
Less Profit and Loss A/c (Loss on 1-4-2008)	20,000
Capital Profit	20,000

i) Holding Co's share in Capital Profit

$$20,000 \times \frac{3}{5} = Rs.\ 12,000$$

ii) Minority's share in Capital Profit

$$20.000 \times \frac{2}{5} = Rs.\ 8,000$$

4) Revenue Profit

Profit & Loss Account	
(1-10-2008 to 31-3-2009)	40,000

i) Holding Co's share in Revenue Profit.

$$40,000 \times \frac{3}{5} = Rs.\ 24,000$$

ii) Minority's share in Revenue Profit

$$40,000 \times \frac{2}{5} = Rs.\ 16,000$$

5) Minority Interest

Face value of shares held by Minority	1,60,000
Add - i) Capital Profit of Minority	8,000
ii) Revenue Profit of Minority	16,000
Minority Interest	1,84,000

6) Goodwill

Balance of Goodwill		
Satara Ltd., 60,000 + Poona Ltd., 20,000		80,000
Add : Market price of shares held.		
(Investment) by Satara Ltd.		1,92,000
		2,72,000
Less : i) Face value of shares held by Satara Ltd.	2,40,000	
ii) Capital Profit of Satara Ltd.	12,000	
		2,52,000
Goodwill		20,000

7) Unrealised Profit

Stock of Poona Ltd., includes Rs. 20,000 worth goods purchased from Satara Ltd., on which Satara Ltd., charged profit at cost plus 25%.

Hence,   cost   +   profit   = selling price

Rs. 100 +   Rs. 25   = Rs.125

$\therefore$ Selling price is Rs.125 and profit Rs. 25

$$20,000 \text{ selling price} = \frac{20,000 \times 25}{125} = \text{Rs. } 4,000$$

$$\text{Holding Co's share} = 4,000 \times \frac{3}{5} = \text{Rs. } 2,400$$

Consolidated Balance Sheet
as on 31-3-2009

Liabilities		Rs.	Assets		Rs.
Share Capital			**Fixed Assets**		
1,00,000 Equity shares		10,00,000	Goodwill		20,000
of Rs. 10 each			Machinery		
Reserves & Surplus		1,50,000	'S' Ltd.	7,32,000	
General Reserve			'P' Ltd.	2,72,000	10,04,000
P & L A/c	1,42,000		**Current Assets**		
Add. Revenue profit	24,000		Stock		
	1,66,000		'S' Ltd.	1,80,000	
Less			'P' Ltd.	90,000	
Unrealised profit	2,400	1,63,600	Less	2,70,000	
Current Liabilities			Unrealised Profit	2,400	2,67,600
Creditors			Cash – 'S' Ltd.	35,000	
'S' Ltd.	1,82,000		'P' Ltd.	27,000	62,000
'P' Ltd.	87,000	2,69,000	Debtors		
Bills payable			'S' Ltd.	2,95,000	
'S' Ltd	20,000		'P' Ltd.	1,23,000	4,18,000
Less Internal owing	15,000	5,000	Bills Receivable		
Minority Interest		1,84,000	Poona Ltd.	15,000	
			Less Internal owing	15,000	
		17,71,600			17,71,600

Problem No. 10 : 'A' Ltd., acquired 2,000 Equity Shares of Rs. 100 each in 'B' Ltd., on 1st January, 2008.

The summarised Balance Sheets of the two companies as on 31st December, 2008 were as follows :

Liabilities	'A' Ltd. Rs.	'B' Ltd. Rs.	Assets	'A' Ltd. Rs.	'B' Ltd. Rs.
Share Capital			Fixed Assets	7,00,000	2,50,000
Equity Shares of			Current Assets	4,00,000	2,00,000
Rs. 100 each	8,00,000	2,50,000	2,000 Shares		
Reserves	3,00,000	50,000	in 'B' Ltd., at cost	3,00,000	
Profit & Loss A/c	1,00,000	1,00,000			
Creditors	2,00,000	50,000			
	14,00,000	4,50,000		14,00,000	4,50,000

'B' Ltd., had a credit balance of Rs. 50,000 in the Reserves and Rs. 20,000 in the Profit and Loss Account when 'A' Ltd., acquired shares in 'B' Ltd.

'B' Ltd., issued bonus shares in the ratio of one for every five shares held out of the profit earned during 2008. This is not shown in the above Balance Sheet of 'B' Ltd.

Prepare a consolidated Balance Sheet of 'A' Ltd., and its subsidiary, as on 31st December, 2008, giving all necessary workings. **(P.U.)**

Solution :

Working Notes :

   1. Shares Acquisition Ratio : 4:1

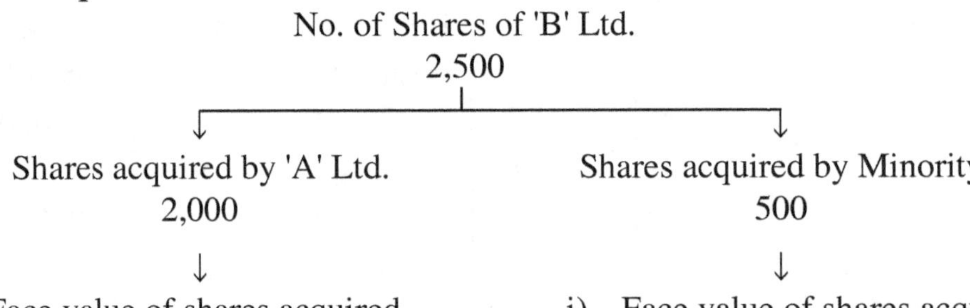

  i)   Face value of shares acquired by 'A' Ltd. = Rs. 2,00,000

  ii) Market price of shares acquired by 'A' Ltd. = Rs. 3,00,000

  i)   Face value of shares acquired by Minority = Rs. 50,000

2. Capital Profit (upto 1-1-2008)   Rs.

Reserve on 1-1-2008   50,000

Profit and Loss A/c on 1-1-2008   20,000

Capital Profit   70,000

i) Holding Co's share in Capital Profit

$$20,000 \times \frac{4}{5} = 56,000$$

ii) Minority Share in Capital Profit

$$70,000 \times \frac{1}{5} = 14,000$$

3. Revenue Profit (1-1-2008 to 31-12-2008)   Rs.

Profit & Loss A/c on 31-12-2008   1,00,000

Less : Profit and Loss A/c on. 1-1-2008   20,000

                                                                          80,000

Less : Issue of Bonus Shares   50,000

Revenue Profit   30,000

Division of Revenue Profit   Division of Bonus Shares.

i) Holding Co's share in Revenue   i)   Holding Co's share in Bonus shares

$$30,000 \times \frac{4}{5} = Rs.\ 24,000 \qquad 50,000 \times \frac{4}{5} = Rs.\ 40,000$$

ii) Minority's share in Revenue Profit   ii)   Minority's Bonus Shares

$$30,000 \times \frac{1}{5} = Rs.\ 6,000 \qquad 50,000 \times \frac{1}{5} = Rs.\ 10,000$$

4. Minority Interest :   Rs.

Face value of shares acquired by Minority   50,000

Add : i)   Bonus Shares   10,000

    ii) Capital Profit of Minority   14,000

    iii) Revenue Profit of Minority   6,000

Minority Interest   80,000

Goodwill

Market price of shares held by 'A' Ltd.   3,00,000

Less : i)   Face Value of Shares

    held by 'A' Ltd.   2,00,000

    ii) Face value of Bonus shares

    held by 'A' Ltd.   40,000   2,40,000

                                                                          60,000

Less : Capital Profit of 'A' Ltd.   56,000

Goodwill   4,000

Consolidated Balance Sheet of 'A' Ltd., with its Subsidiary 'B' Ltd., as on 31-12-2008

Liabilities		Rs.	Assets			Rs.
Share Capital :			**Fixed Assets :**			
8,000 equity Shares of			Goodwill			4,000
Rs. 100 each		8,00,000	Fixed Assets			
Reserves and Surplus :			'A' Ltd.		7,00,000	
Reserve		3,00,000	'B' Ltd.		2,50,000	9,50,000
Profit and Loss A/c	1,00,000		**Current Assets**			
Add : Revenue Profit	24,000	1,24,000	'A' Ltd.		4,00,000	
Current Liabilities			'B' Ltd.		2,00,000	6,00,000
and Provisions :						
Creditors						
'A' Ltd.	2,00,000					
'B' Ltd.	50,000	2,50,000				
Minority Interest		80,000				
		15,54,000				15,54,000

Problem No. 11 : 'H' Ltd., acquired 12,000 Shares of 'S' Ltd., for Rs.1,70,000 on 1st April, 2008, on which date 'S' Ltd's Profit and Loss Account showed a credit balance of Rs. 50,000. In August, 2008 'S' Ltd., declared a dividend at 10% for the year ended 31st March, 2008. This dividend was credited by 'H' Ltd., to its Profit and Loss Account. On 31st March, 2008, the Balance Sheets were as under :–

Balance Sheets

Liabilities	'H' Ltd. Rs.	'S' Ltd. Rs.	Assets	'H' ltd. Rs.	'S' Ltd. Rs.
Share Capital			Goodwill	30,000	20,000
Equity Shares			Machinery	2,50,000	—
of Rs. 10	5,00,000	2,00,000	Furniture	85000	50,000
each, fully paid			12,000 Shares		
General Reserve	1,30,000	55,000	in 'S' Ltd.	1,70,000	—
(31-3-2008)					
P & L A/c	1,60,000	65,000	Stock	2,10,000	2,30,000
Sundry Creditors	1,00,000	75,000	Debtors	65,000	58,000
			Bank	80,000	37,000
	8,90,000	3,95,000		8,90,000	3,95,000

You are required to prepare the consolidated balance sheet of 'H' Ltd., and S Ltd.

(P.U.)

Solution :

Working Notes :

1) Shareholding Ratio 3:2

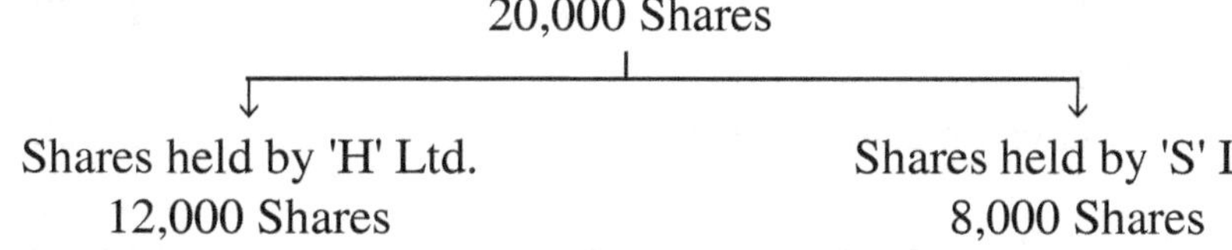

Shareholding Ratio 12,000 : 8,000 = 3:2 or 3/5 & 2/5

2) Capital Profit		Rs.
General Reserve 31-3-2008		55,000
Profit & Loss Account		Rs.
1-4-2008	50,000	
Less Dividend (10% on 200,000)	20,000	30,000
Capital Profit		85,000

i) Holding Co's share in Capital Profit

$$85,000 \times \frac{3}{5} = 51,000$$

ii) Minority's shares in Capital Profit

$$85,000 \times \frac{2}{5} = 34,000$$

3) Revenue Profit	Rs.
Profit on 31-3-2009	65,000
(P & L A/c)	
Add : Dividend paid on 31-9-2008	20,000
	85,000
Less : Profit & Loss A/c (31-3-2008)	50,000
Revenue profit	35,000

i) Holding Co's share in Capital Profit

$$35,000 \times \frac{3}{5} = Rs.\ 21,000$$

ii) Minority's share in Capital Profit

$$35,000 \times \frac{2}{5} = Rs.\ 14,000$$

4) Minority Interest

	Rs.
Shares held by Minority (8,000 shares × 10)	80,000
Add : Minority's Share in Capital Profit	34,000
Add : Minority's Share in Revenue Profit	14,000
Minority Interest	1,28,000

5) Capital Reserve

Face value of Shares held by Minority (12,000 × 10)	1,20,000
Add : Holding Co's share in Capital Profit	51,000
Holding Co's share in dividend $(20000 \times \frac{3}{5})$	12,000
	1,83,000
Less : Market value of Investment i.e. shares held by minority.	1,70,000
Capital Reserve	13,000

Consolidated Balance Sheet of 'H' Ltd., & S Ltd., as on 31-3-2009

Liabilities	Rs.	Assets		Rs.
Share Capital		**Fixed Assets**		
50,000 Equity Shares of		Machinery		2,50,000
Rs. 10 each	5,00,000	Furniture		
Reserve & Surplus		'H' Ltd.	85,000	
General Reserve		'S' Ltd.	50,000	1,35,000
P & L A/c 1,60,000	1,30,000	Goodwill		
Add : Share in Revenue 21,000		'H' Ltd.	30,000	
Profit 1,81,000		'S' Ltd.	20,000	
			50,000	
Less : 3/5 Dividend 12,000	1,69,000	Less : Capital Reserve 13,000		37,000
Current Liabilities		**Current Assets**		
Sundry Creditors		Stock 'H' Ltd.	2,10,000	
'H' Ltd 1,00,000		'S' Ltd.	2,30,000	4,40,000
'S' Ltd 75,000	1,75,000	Debtors.		
Minority Interest	1,28,000	'H' Ltd.	65,000	
		'S' Ltd.	58,000	1,23,000
		Bank		
		'H' Ltd	80,000	
		'S' Ltd	37,000	1,17,000
	11,02,000			11,02,000

Problem No. 12 : XYZ Ltd., acquired 75% of both classes of shares of ABC Ltd., as on 1-1-2008 at a total cost of Rs. 5,00,000. The Balance Sheets at 31-12-2008 were as follows :-

XYZ Ltd.

Liabilities	Rs.	Assets	Rs.
Share Capital in Shares of		Cash at Bank	1,30,000
Rs. 100 each	7,50,000	Investments	5,00,000
Sundry Creditors (A)	70,000	Stock (B)	1,70,000
General Reserve	3,80,000	Sundry Debtors	1,20,000
Profit and Loss A/c (C)	4,00,000	Plant and Machinery	3,80,000
		Land and Building	3,00,000
	16,00,000		16,00,000

a) Includes Rs. 20,000 for purchases from ABC Ltd., on which the latter Company made a profit of Rs. 5,000/-.

b) Includes Rs. 10,000 Stock at cost purchased from ABC Ltd., as a part of Rs. 20,000 purchases.

c) Includes dividend at 16% per annum from ABC Ltd., for the year 2007.

ABC Ltd.

Liabilities	Rs.	Assets	Rs.
Share Capital		Cash at Bank	60,000
1,000, 6% Preference Shares		Land and Building	90,000
of Rs. 100 each	1,00,000	Plant and Machinery	1,80,000
20,000 Equity Shares of		Stock	1,10,000
Rs. 10 each	2,00,000	Sundry Debtors	90,000
Sundry Creditors	70,000		
General Reserve as on			
1st January, 2008	10,000		
Profit and Loss A/c	1,50,000		
	5,30,000		5,30,000

The Balance of Profit and Loss A/c on 1st January, 2008, was Rs. 60,000, out of which a dividend of 16% was paid on equity shares for the year 2007. Prepare a consolidated Balance Sheet as at 31-12-2008. **(P.U.)**

Solution :

Working Notes :

1. Share Acquistion Ratio : 3:1 (Holding company held 75% of shares of subsidiary Co.)

i)

No. of Preference Shares of ABC Ltd.

1,000

Shares acquired by XYZ Ltd.	Shares acquired by Minority
750	250
Face value of shares acquired	Face value of Shares acquired
by XYZ = Rs. 75,000	by Minority = 25,000

ii)

No. of Equity Shares of ABC Ltd.

20,000

Shares acquired by XYZ Ltd.	Shares acquired by Minority
15,000	5,000
Face value of shares acquired	Face value of Shares acquired
by XYZ = Rs. 1,50,000	by Minority = 50,000

iii) Market price of both shares acquired by XYZ = Rs. 5,00,000.

2. Capital Profit (upto 1-1-2008)   **Rs.**

	Rs.
Profit and Loss A/c on 1-1-2008	60,000
Less : Equity Dividend (2007)	32,000
Profit as on 1-1-2008	28,000
Add : General Reserve on 1-1-2008	10,000
Capital Profit	38,000

	XYZ Ltd. (3/4)	ABC Ltd. (Minority 1/4)
Capital Profit	28,500	9,500
Add : Equity Dividend (2007)	24,000	-
	52,500	9,500

3. Revenue Profit (1-1-2008 to 31-12-2008)   **Rs.**

	Rs.
Profit and Loss A/c as on 31-12-2008	1,50,000
Less : Profit as on 1-1-2008	28,000
Profit during the year 2008	1,22,000

Less : Preference Dividend payable (2008)	6,000	
Revenue Profit	1,16,000	

	XYZ Ltd. (3/4)	ABC Ltd. (Minority (1/4)
Revenue Profit	87,000	29,000
Add : Preference Dividend (2008)	4,500	1,500
	91,500	30,500

4. Minority Interest :

		Rs.
Face value of Shares acquired by Minority		
i) Preference Shares	25,000	
ii) Equity Shares	50,000	75,000
Add : i) Capital Profit of Minority		9,500
ii) Revenue Profit of Minority		30,500
Minority Interest		1,15,000

5. Goodwill :

		Rs.
Market price of Shares held by XYZ Ltd.		5,00,000
Less : Face value of Shares held by XYZ Ltd.		
i) Preference Shares	75,000	
ii) Equity Shares	1,50,000	2,25,000
		2,75,000
Less : Capital Profit of XYZ		52,500
Goodwill		2,22,500

6. Unrealised Profit :

Stock of XYZ Ltd., includes Rs. 10,000 goods purchased from ABC Ltd., on which ABC Ltd., charged profit is Rs. 2,500. (50% of Rs. 5,000)

Hence, Holding Company's shares 3/4 of 2,500 i.e. Rs. 1,875.

Consolidated Balance Sheet of XYZ Ltd., with its Subsidiary ABC Ltd., as on 31-12-2008

Liabilities	Rs.	Assets		Rs.
Share Capital		**Fixed Assets**		
7,500 Shares of Rs. 100 each	7,50,000	Goodwill		2,22,500
Reserves and Surplus :		Land & Building :		
General Reserve	3,80,000	XYZ Ltd.	3,00,000	
Profit & Loss A/c 4,00,000		ABC Ltd.	90,000	3,90,000

Liabilities		Rs.	Assets		Rs.
Less : Equity			Plant & Machinery		
Dividend (2007)	24,000		XYZ Ltd.	3,80,000	
	3,76,000		ABC Ltd.	1,80,000	5,60,000
Add : Revenue Profit	91,500		**Current Assets, Loans**		
	4,67,500		**and Advances :**		
Less : Unrealised			Stock		
Profit	1,875	4,65,625	XYZ Ltd.	1,70,000	
Current Liabilities			ABC Ltd.	1,10,000	–
and Provisions :				2,80,000	
Sundry Creditors			Less : Unrealised Profit 1,875		2,78,125
XYZ Ltd.	70,000		**Debtors**		
ABC Ltd.	70,000		XYZ Ltd.	1,20,000	
	1,40,000		ABC Ltd.	90,000	
Less : Internal Owing	20,000	1,20,000		2,10,000	
Minority Interest		1,15,000	Less : Internal Owing 20,000		1,90,000
			Cash at Bank		
			XYZ Ltd.	1,30,000	
			ABC Ltd.	60,000	1,90,000
		18,30,625			18,30,625

Problem No. 13 : From the following, information, prepare a Consolidated Balance Sheet of 'H' Ltd. and its Subsidiary 'S' Ltd. as at 31.3.2009 giving detailed workings.

Balance Sheets (as on 31-3-2009)

Liabilities	'H' Ltd Rs.	'S' Ltd Rs.	Assets	'H' Ltd Rs.	'S' Ltd Rs.
Share Capital :			Good will	1,00,000	-
Equity shares of			Fixed Assets	2,00,000	2,50,000
Rs. 10 each	4,00,000	2,00,000	Investments.		
General Reserve	2,00,000	60,000	i) 16,000 Shares		
Profit & Loss A/c	1,00,000	40,000	Of Rs. 10 each		
6% Debentures	-	1,00,000	in S Ltd		
Loan From Hawai			at Cost	2,00,000	-
Ltd.	-	10,000	ii) 6% Debentures		
Sundary Creditors	1,00,000	40,000	Of S Ltd.		
Bills Payable	50,000	30,000	(Face Value)		
			Rs. 60,000)	60,000	-

Liabilities	'H' Ltd Rs.	'S' Ltd Rs.	Assets	'H' Ltd Rs.	'S' Ltd Rs.
			iii)Governement Securities	-	50,000
			Stock	1,00,000	40,000
			Sundry Debtors	80,000	40,000
			Bill Receivable	40,000	-
			Bank Balance	60,000	1,00,000
			Loan to Ltd.	10,000	-
		8,50,000	4,80,000	8,50,000	4,80,000

Additional Information :

i) Sundry Creditors of Ltd. includes Rs. 20,000 due to S. Ltd.

ii) The Closing Stock of H. Ltd. includes stock worth Rs. 30,000 Supplied by S. Ltd. which had invoiced at cost plus 20% Profit on cost.

iii) Bills Payable of S. Ltd. include Rs. 24,000 issued in favour of H. Ltd. Which was discounted but not yet matured Rs. 4000 of them.

iv) H. Ltd. acquired 16,000 equity Shares in S. Ltd. on 1-4-2008 on which date the Balance Sheet of S. Ltd. Showed General Reserve at Rs. 20,000 and Profit & Loss A/c Credit Balance of Rs. 10,000

v) H. Ltd. revalued Fixed Assets of S. Ltd. as on 1-4-2008 at Rs. 2,60,000

(March 2010 - PUP)

Solution :

Workings

1) **Ratio -**

	Holding	Minority
	16000	4000
	4 :	1

2) **Capital Profit**

General Reserve (1-4-2008)	20,000
Profit & Loss A/c (1-4-2008) (cr. Balance)	10,000
Increase in value of Fixed Assets	10,000
	40,000
4/5 Share of Holding co.	32,000
1/5 Share of Minority	8,000

3) Revenue Profit

(60,000-20,000)

General Reserve	40,000
Profit & Loss (cr.)	30,000
(40,000 - 10,000 = 30,000	70,000
4/5 th share of H. Ltd	56,000
1/5 Share of of Minority	14,000

4) Minority Interest

Face Value of 4000 Shares	40,000
Add : Capital Profit	8000
Add : Revenue Profit	14,000
62,000	62,000

5) Cost of Control / Goodwill

Cost of Shares acquired by H. Ltd.	2,00,000
Less : Face value of 16000 Shares × Rs 10	1,60,000
	40,000
Less : 4/5 th Share in Capital Profit	32,000
Good will	8000
Add : **Good will** as per B/s	1,00,000
Good will	1,08,000

6) Unrealised

Closing Stock	30,000
H. Ltd	
total Profit 30,000 × 1/6	5000
4/5 the share of H. Ltd	
5000 × 4/5	4000
Unrealised Profit	4000

Consolidated Balance Sheet of H. Ltd. And it Subsidary S. Ltd.
as on 31-3-2009

Liabilities		Rs	Assets			Rs
Share Capital :			**Good Will**			**1,08,000**
Equity Shares of		4,00,000	**Fixed Assets :**			
Rs. 10 each						
General Reserve		2,00,000	H. Ltd.	2,00,000		
Profit & loss A/c	1,00,000		S. Ltd	2,60,000	4,60,000	
Add : Share in 56,00			1) Government			
Revenue Profit	56,000		Securities		50,000	
	1,56,000		2) 6% Debenture	60,000		
Less : Unrealised Profit 4000		1,52,000	Less : held by Hawai Ltd 60,000		Nil	
6% Debentures			Stock :			
S. Ltd	1,00,000		H. Ltd	1,00,000		
Less : held by	60,000	40,000	S. Ltd	40,000		
H. Ltd				1,40,000		
			Less : Unrealised Profit (-)4,000		1,36,000	
Loan From 'H'			**Sundry Debtors :**			
Ltd :	10,000		H. Ltd	80,000		
Less : Inter Company	10,000	Nil	S. Ltd	40,000		
owings				1,20,000		
			Less : inter co-owings	20,000	1,00,000	
Sundry Creditors :						
H. Ltd	1,00,000		Bills Receivable :			
S. Ltd	40,000		H. Ltd.		40,000	
	1,40,000		Less : inter co-owings	20,000	20,000	
Less : Inter co. owings 20,000		1,20,000	**Bank Balance :**			
Bills Payable :			H. Ltd	60,000		
H. Ltd	50,000		S. Ltd	1,00,000	1,60,000	
S. Ltd	30,000		Loan to S. Ltd	10,000		
	80,000	60,000	Less : inter co-owings	10,000	Nil	
Less : Inter Co-owings 20,000						
Contingent Liability :						
Bills discounted Rs. 4000						
Minority Interest		62,000				
		10,34,000				10,34,000

Problem No. 14 : The following are the summarised Balance Sheets of Sujata Ltd. and Vanita Ltd. As on 31st March 2011

Liabilities	Sujata Ltd Rs.	Vanita Ltd Rs.	Assets	Sujata Ltd Rs.	Vanita Ltd Rs.
Share Capital			Freehold Premises	3,00,000	1,00,000
(Rs. 20 each)	7,00,000	4,00,000	Machinery	4,80,000	2,20,000
Profit & Loss A/c	1,60,000	-	Shares in Vanita Ltd		
Sundry Creditors	3,60,000	1,40,000	(16,000 Shares)	2,20,000	-
Bills Payable	20,000	-	Sundry Debtors	2,40,000	1,00,000
			Bills Receivable	-	20,000
			Profit & Loss A/c	-	1,00,000
	12,40,000	5,40,000		12,40,000	5,40,000

Additinal Information :

1) The Debtors of Sujata Ltd. included Rs. 40,000 due from Vanita Ltd.

2) Sujata Ltd. acquired the Shares of Vanita Ltd. On 1st April 2010 when Vanita Ltd had a debit balance in Profit & Loss A/c of Rs. 1,60,000

3) Bill Payable of Sujata Ltd. are all issued in favour of Vanita Ltd.

Prepare a Consolidated Balance Sheet With detail Working.

(March 2011 - PUP)

Solution :

Working Notes

1) **Ratio :** 4/5 : 1/5

2) **Capital Loss**

Profit & Loss A/c Debit Bal.	1,60,000	Holding Rs. 1,28,000
Capital Loss	1,60,000	Minority Rs. 1,32,000

3) **Revenue Profit**

P & L A/c Debit Bal (Op)	1,60,000	Holding Rs. 48,000
Less : P & L A/c Debit Bal (Cl)	1,00,000	
Revenue Profit	60,000	Minority Rs. 12,000

4) Minority Interest

Face Value of Shares held by minority	80,000
Add : Revenue Profit	12,000
	92,000
Less : Capital loss of	32,000
Minority Interest	60,000

5) Cost of Control / Goodwill

Amount paid	2,20,000
Add : Capital loss of Holding Co.	1,28,000
	3,48,000
Less : Face Value	3,20,000
Good will	28,000

Consolidated Balance Sheet of Holding Co. & Subsidiary Co.

Liabilities		Rs.	Assets		Rs
Share Capital		7,00,000	Good will		28,000
Profit & Loss A/c	1,60,000		Freehold Premises		4,00,000
(+) Revenue Profit			(3,00,000 + 1,00,000)		
from Vanita Ltd.	48,000	2,08,000	Machinery		7,00,000
			(4,80,000 + 2,20,000)		
S. Creditors			S. Debtors		
(3,60,000 + 1,40,000)	5,00,000		(2,40,000 + 1,00,000)	3,40,000	
Less : Mutual Holding	40,000	4,60,000	Less : Mutual Holding	40,000	3,00,000
Bills Payable	20,000		Bills Receivable	20,000	
Less : Mutual Holding	20,000	–	Less : Mutual Holding	20,000	–
Minority Interest		60,000			
		14,28,000			14,28,000

Problem No. 15 : From The following Balance Sheets and other information given below, Prepare a consolidated Balance Sheet of Jivan Limited and its subsidiary Jyoti Limited as at 31st March 2011 Show your workings in detail.

Balance Sheet as on 31st March 2011

Liabilities	Jivan Ltd Rs.	Jyoti Ltd Rs.	Assets	Jivan Ltd Rs.	Jyoti Ltd. Rs.
Share Capital :			**Fixed Assets :**		
Authorised & Issued :			**Good will :**	48,000	36,000
Equity Shares of			Land & Buildings	1,50,000	1,20,000
Rs 100 each	6,00,000	2,40,000	Plant & Machinery	2,40,000	1,32,000
Reserve & Surplus :					
General Reserve as			Furniture & Fixtures	42,000	12,000
On 1-4-2010	1,20,000	72,000	**Investments :**		
Profit & Loss A/c			1800 Equity Shares		
on 1-4-2010	60,000	24,000	in Jyoti Ltd	2,88,000	-
Profit For the year	1,08,000	84,000	**Curent Assets :**		
Current Liabilities			Stock in Trade	1,20,000	1,08,000
& Provisions :			Debtors	24,000	90,000
Bills Payable	-	48,000	Cash at Bank	72,000	30,000
Creditors	96,000	60,000			
	9,84,000	5,28,000		9,84,000	5,28,000

Other informations :

1) Jivan Ltd. acquired the shares in Jyoti Ltd. on 1st October 2010

2) The Bills Payable of Jyoti Ltd. Were all issued in favour of Jivan Ltd. which the company got discounted.

3) The Creditors of Jyoti Ltd. included Rs. 24,000 Payable to Jivan Ltd. for goods supplied by that Company.

4) The stock of Jyoti Ltd. included goods of the value Rs. 9,600 which were supplied by Jivan Ltd. at a profit of $33\frac{1}{3}\%$ on cost.

(Oct 2011 PUP)

Solution :
Working Notes :

1) Ratio 3 : 1

Total Shares	2400
Acquired By	1800
Holding co.	
Held by Minority 600	
1800 : 600	
3:1	

2) Revenue Profit.

Profit & Loss A/c	42,000
3/4th Share of Holding	31,500
1/4th Share of Minority	10,500

3) Capital Profit

General Reserve On 1-4-2010	72,000
Profit & Loss A/c on 1-4-2010	24,000
Profit & Loss A/c (1-4-2010 to 1-10-10)	42,000
	138,000
3/4th share of Holding co.	1,03,500
1/4th share of Minority	34,500

4) Cost of Control

Cost of 1800 Shares	2,88,000
Less : Face Value (1800 × 100)	1,80,000
	1,08,000
Less : Capital Profit	1,03,500
Good will	4500
Add : Good will as per B/s	84,000
	88,500

5) Minority Interest

Nominal Value of 600 Shares	60,000
Add : 1/4th Share in Revenue Profit	10,500
	70,500
Add : 1/4th Share in Capital Profit	34,500
	1,05,000

6) Unrealised Profit

Total Profit 9600 × 1/4	2400
Share of Holding co. 2400 × 3/4	1800

Consolidated Balance Sheet of Jivan Ltd. and Its Subsidiary Jyoti Ltd as at 21-3-2011

Liabilities	Rs	Rs	Assets	Rs	Rs
Share Capital			**Fixed Assets**		
Equity Shares of			Good will		88,500
Rs. 100 Each		6,00,000	**Land & Buildings :**		
Reserve & Surplus :			Jivan Ltd	1,50,000	2,70,00
General Reserve		1,20,000	Jyoti Ltd	1,20,000	
Profit & Loss A/c	1,68,000		Plant & Machinery		
Add : Share in Jyoti	31,500		Jivan Ltd	2,40,000	3,72,000
Ltd	1,99,5000		Jyoti Ltd	1,32,0000	
Less : Unrealised	1800	1,97,700	Furniture & fitting		
Profit			Jivan Ltd	42,000	54,000
			Jyoti Ltd	12,000	
Current Liabilities			**Current Assets**		
& Provisions					
Bills Payable		48,000	**Stock in Trade :**		
Creditors			Jivan Ltd	1,20,000	
Jivan Ltd	96,000		Jyoti Ltd	1,08,000	
Jyoti Ltd	60,000			2,28,000	
	1,56,000		Less : Unrealised Profit	1800	2,26,200
Less : Inter co-owing	24,000	1,32,000	**Sundry Debtors :**		
Contingent Liab.			Jivan Ltd.	24,000	
For bills Discounted	48,000		Jyoti Ltd	90,000	
				1,14,000	
			Less : Inter co-owings	24,000	90,000
Minority Interest		1,05,000	Cash at Bank		
			Jivan Ltd	72,000	
			jyoti Ltd	30,000	1,02,000
		12,02,700			12,02,700

Problem No. 16 : Amit Ltd. acquired equity Shares in Sumit Ltd on 1-4-2010 Their Balance sheet as on 31-3-2011 were as follows.

Balance Sheet as on 31-3-2011

Liabilities	Amit Ltd (Rs)	Sumit Ltd (Rs)
Share Capital :		
Shares of Rs. 100 each	5,00,000	3,00,000
General Reserve	40,000	10,000
Profit and Loss A/c	70,000	5,000
Bills Payable	50,000	25,000
Creditors	1,40,000	60,000
	8,00,000	4,00,000
Assets	**Amit Ltd (Rs)**	**Sumit Ltd (Rs)**
Land and Building	2,00,000	1,00,000
Plant and Machinery	1,50,000	2,00,000
Investments 2700 Shares in Sumit Ltd	2,97,000	-
Stock	40,000	30,000
Debtors	50,000	60,000
Bills Receivable	63,000	10,000
	8,00,000	4,00,000

Additional Information :

i) On the date of Purchase of shares there was no balance in General Reserve and Profit and loss showed a debit balance of Rs. 10,000 in the books of Sumit Ltd.

ii) Sundry Debtors of Sumit Ltd include Rs. 40,000 due from Amit Ltd.

iii) Bills Payable of Sumit Ltd include Rs. 18,000 in favour of Amit Ltd. Which has discounted Rs. 3000 of Them.

iv) Stock of Sumit Ltd includes Rs. 4000 being Purchased from Amit Ltd. on which the company made a profit of $33\frac{1}{3}\%$ on cost.

Prepare Consolidated Balance Sheet with necessary workings from the balance sheet of Amit Ltd. And Sumit Ltd.

(March 2012 - PUP)

Solution :

Holding Company

1) Ratio -

1)	Holding Cos. Share	$\dfrac{2700}{3000} = \dfrac{9}{10}$
2)	Minority's Company Share	$\dfrac{300}{3000} = \dfrac{1}{10}$

2) Capital Loss :   **Rs.**

G/R as on 1-4-2010	Nil
Profit & Loss On 1-4-2010 (Dr.)	10,000 loss
Capital Loss	10000
$\dfrac{9}{10}$ Holding Company Share	9000
$\dfrac{1}{10}$ Minority Share	1000

3) Revenue Profit   **Rs.**

Profit earned from 1-4-2010 to 31-3-2011	
General Reserve (Date of Purch)	10,000
Profit & Loss = Profit	+ 15,000
(B/s = 5000 + 10,000 Dr. = 15,000) Revenue Profit	25,000
$\dfrac{9}{10}$ Holding Company Share	22,500
$\dfrac{1}{10}$ Minority Share	2500

4) Statement of Good will :

Cost of Shares Purchase by Holding Company	2,97,000
Less : Face Value of Shares Purchased (2700 × 100)	- 2,70,000
Add : Holding Company's Share in Capital Loss	+ 9000
Good will	36,000

5) Minority Interest

Face value of Shares held by minority (3000 × 100)	30,000
Less : Share in Capital Loss	- 1000
Add : Revenue Profit	2500
Minority Interest	31,500

6) Unrealised Profit :

$$Sp = Cp + P$$

$$133\frac{1}{3} = 100 + 33\frac{1}{3}$$

$$\frac{P}{SP} = \frac{33\frac{1}{3}}{133\frac{1}{3}} = \frac{1}{4} \times 4000 = \qquad 1000$$

$$\text{Holding Company's Share} = 1000 \times \frac{9}{10} = \qquad 900$$

Consolidated Balance Sheet of Amit with is Subsiday Sumit as on 31-3-2011

Liabilities		Rs	Assets		Rs
Share Capital :		5,00,000	**Good Will**		36,000
G/R		40,000	**L & B :** Amit	2,00,000	
			Sumit	1,00,000	3,00,000
Profit & Loss A/c		91,600			
(70,000 + 22,500 - 900)			**P & M :** Amit	1,50,000	
Bills Payable Amit Ltd.	50,000		Sumit	2,00,000	3,50,000
Sumit Ltd.	25,000		**B/R :** Amit	63,000	
	75,000		Sumit	10,000	
				73,000	
Less : Inter Co-owings	15,000	60,000	Less : Inter Co-owings	15,000	58,000
Minority Interest		31,500			
Creditors : Amit	1,40,000		**Debtors :** Amit	50,000	
Sumit	60,000		Sumit	60,000	
	2,00,000			1,10,000	
Less : Inter Co-owing	40,000	1,60,000	Less : Inter Co-owings	40,000	70,000
Contingent Liability	3000		Stock (40,000 + 30,000)	70,000	
			Unrealised Profit	900	69,100
		8,83,100			8,83,100

Problem No. 18 : From the following information, prepare a Consolidated Balance Sheet of Sagar Ltd. and its Subsidiary Sarita Ltd as at 31-3-2011 giving Detailed workings.

Balance Sheet as on 31-3-2011

Liabilities	Sagar Ltd (Rs)	Sarita Ltd (Rs)
Share Capital :		
Equity Shares of Rs. 10 each	6,00,000	3,00,000
General Reserve	3,00,000	90,000
Profit & Loss A/c	1,50,000	60,000
6% Debentures	-	1,50,000
Loan From Sagar Ltd	-	15,000
Sundry Creditors	1,50,000	60,000
Bills Payable	75,000	45,000
Total	12,75,000	7,20,000

Assets	Sagar Ltd (Rs)	Sarita Ltd (Rs.)
Good will	1,50,000	-
Fixed Assets	3,00,000	3,75,000
Investments :		
i) 24,000 Shares of Rs. 10 each in Sarita Ltd at cost	3,00,000	-
ii) 6% Debentures of Sarita Ltd (Face value Rs. 90,000)	90,000	-
iii) Government Securities	-	75,000
Stock	1,50,000	60,000
Sundry Debtors	1,20,000	60,000
Bills Receivable	60,000	-
Bank Balance	90,000	1,50,000
Loan to Sarita Ltd	15,000	-
Total	12,75,000	7,20,000

Additional Information :

1) Sundry Creditors of Sagar Ltd. include Rs. 30,000 due to Sarita Ltd.

2) The Closing Stock of Sagar Ltd. includes Stock Worth Rs. 45,000 supplied by Sarita Ltd Which had invoiced at cost Plus 20% profit on cost.

3) Bills Payable of Sarita Ltd Include Rs. 36,000 issued in favour of Sagar Ltd. Which was discounted but not yet matured Rs. 6000 of them.

4) Sagar Ltd acquired 24,000 Equity Shares in Sarita Ltd on 1-4-2010 on Which date the balance Sheet of Sarita Ltd. Showed General Reserve at Rs. 30,000 and Profit & Loss A/c Credit Balance of Rs. 15,000

5) Sagar Ltd. revalued Fixed Assets of Sarita Ltd. as on 1-4-2010 at Rs. 3,90,000

(Oct. 2012 - PUP)

Solution :

1) Ratio Of Holding

Total number of Shares of Sarita Ltd	30,000
Shares held by Sagar Ltd (Holding co)	24,000
Shares held by minority Shareholders	6000

24000 : 6000 = 4 : 1

2) Revenue Profit

General Reserve	60,000
Profit & Loss A/c	45,000
	1,05,000
4/5th share of Sagar Ltd	84,000
1/5th Share of minority Share holders	21,000

3) Capital Profit

General Reserve (1-4-2010)	30,000
Profit & Loss A/c	15,000
Increase in value of Fixed Assets	15,000
	60,000
4/5th Share of Sagar Ltd	48,000
1/5th Share of Minority Share holders	12,000

4) Cost of Control

Cost of acquisition of 24000 Shares		3,00,000
Less :		
i) F.V. of 24000 shares		
24,000 × 10	2,40,000	
ii) Share in Capital	48,000	
Profit		2,88,000
Goodwill		12,000
Add : Good will as per		1,50,000
Balance sheet		1,62,000

5) Minority Interest

F.v. of 6000 Shares	60,000
Add : Share in Revenue Profit	21,000
Add : Share in Capital Profit	12,000
	93,000

6) Unrealised Profit on stock

$$\text{Total Profit} = 45,000 \times \frac{1}{6} = \qquad 7,500$$

$$\text{Share of Sagar LTd} = 75,000 \times \frac{4}{5} = \qquad 6000$$

Consolidated Balance Sheet of Sagar Ltd and its Subsidiary Sarita Ltd
as on 1-4-2011

Liabilities		Rs	Assets		Rs
Share Capital - Equity			Good will		1,62,000
Shares of Rs 10 Each		6,00,000	Fixed Assets	3,00,000	
General Reserve		3,00,000		3,90,000	6,90,000
Profit & Loss A/c	1,50,000				
Add : Share in	8,4000		6% Debentures	90,000	
Revenue Profit			Less : Inter co-owings	90,000	-
	2,34,000				
Less : Unrealised	6,000	2,28,000	Government Securities		75,000
Profit					
6% Debentures	1,50,000		Stock	1,50,000	
Less : Inter co-owings	90,000	60,000		60,000	
				2,10,000	
Loan From Sagar Ltd	15,000		Less:Unrealised Profit	6,000	2,04,000
Less : Inter co-owings	15,000		Sundry Debtors	1,20,000	
Sundry Creditors	1,50,000			60,000	
	60,000			1,80,000	

Liabilities		Rs	Assets		Rs
	2,10,000		Less inter co-owings	30,000	1,50,000
Less : Inter co-owings	30,000	1,80,000	Bills Receivable	60,000	
Bills Payables	75,000		Inter co-owings	30,000	30,000
	45,000		Bank Balance		
	120,000		(90,000 + 1,50,000)		2,40,000
Less : Inter co-owing	30,000	90,000	Loan	15,000	
Minority Interest		93,000		15,000	-
Contingent Liability	6,000		Less Inter co-owings		
		15,51,000			15,51000

Problem No. 18 : The Following are the Balance Sheets of two companies as on 31st March 2011

Balance Sheets As on 31st March 2011

Liabilities	AB Ltd Rs.	CD Ltd Rs.
Equity Share Capital :		
Shares of Rs. 10 each	10,00,000	5,00,000
General Reserve on 1-4-2010	1,00,000	1,00,000
Profit and loss A/c on 1-4-2010	50,000	30,000
Profit for the year 2010-11	60,000	40,000
Sundry Creditors	70,000	50,000
Bills Payable	10,000	5,000
Total	12,90,000	7,25,000

Assets	AB Ltd Rs.	CD Ltd Rs.
Land and Building	2,00,000	1,50,000
Machinery	3,00,000	3,00,000
Stock	75,000	50,000
Sundry Debtors	50,000	60,000
Investment at Cost Shares		
in CD Ltd	5,00,000	-
Bills Receivable	10,000	5000
Cash at Bank	1,55,000	1,60,000
Total	12,90,000	7,25,000

1) AB Ltd acquired 40,000 equity Shares of CD Ltd on 1st April, 2010

2) Bills Receivable of AB Ltd includes Rs. 3000 accepted by CD Ltd.

3) Sundry Debtors of AB Ltd includes Rs. 10,000 due from CD Ltd.

4) Stock of CD Ltd includes goods Purchased from AB Ltd for Rs. 30,000. Which were invoiced by AB Ltd. at Profit of 25% on the invoice Price.

Prepare a consolidated Balance Sheet of AB Ltd and its subsidiary CD Ltd as on 31st March 2011 giving the necessary workings. **(March 2013 - PUP)**

Solution :

1) Holding Ratio : 4 :1

Holding	Minority
40,000	10,000

2) Capital Profit : Rs.

Profit & Loss as on date of Purchase	30,000
G/R as on Date of Purchase	1,00,000
Capital Profit	1,30,000
$\frac{4}{5}$ Holding Co. Share	1,04,000
$\frac{1}{5}$ Minority Share	26,000

3) Revenue Profit

Profit & Loss A/c After the date of Purchase	40,000
	40,000
$\frac{4}{5}$ Holdings Share	32,000
$\frac{1}{5}$ Minority Share	8,000

4) Minority Interest

Face Value of Shares held by minority	1,00,000
+ Share in Capital Profit	+ 26,000
Share in Revenue Profit	+ 8,000
M.I.	1,34,000

5) Calculation of Good will

Cost Price of Shares	5,00,000
Purchase by holding co.	
Less : Face Value of Shares	4,00,000
Purchase by holding co.	1,00,000
Less : $\frac{4}{5}$ Share in Capital Profit	1,04,000
Capital Reserve	(-) 4000

6) Unrealised Profit :

Profit on invoice Price $30,000 \times \dfrac{25}{100}$ 7500

$\dfrac{4}{5}$ Holding Company Share $= 7500 \times \dfrac{4}{5}$ 6000

Consolidated Balance Sheet of AB Ltd. with is Subsidiary CD Ltd. as on 31.3.2011

Liabilities		Rs	Assets			Rs
Share Capital :			**Fix Assets**			
1,00,000 equity Shares		10,00,000	**L & B-AB**	2,00,000		
of Rs. 10 each			CD	1,50,000	3,50,000	
Reserve & Surplus :			**Machinery**			
G/R		1,00,000	AB	3,00,000		
P & L A/c	50,000		CD	3,00,000	6,00,000	
Add : Revenue Profit	+ 32,000		**Current Assets**			
Add : Profit during	+ 60,000		Stock AB	75,000		
the year			CD	50,000		
	1,42,000			1,25,000		
Less : Unrealised Profit	6000	1,36,000	Less : Unrealised Profit	6000	1,19,000	
Capital Reserve		4000	**Debtors**			
			AB	50,000		
			CD	60,000		
				1,10,000		

Liabilities		Rs	Assets		Rs	
Current Liabilities :						
Creditors AB	70,000		Less : Inter		10,000	1,00,000
CD	50,000		Co. owing			
	120,000					
Less : Inter co-owing	10,000	1,10,000				
Bills Payable :			**Bills Receivable**			
AB	10,000		AB		10,000	
CD	5000		CD		5000	
	15,000				15,000	
Less : Inter Co owing	3000	12,000	Less : Inter Co. Owing		3000	12,000
Minority Interst		1,34,000	**Cash at Bank :**			
			AB		1,55,000	
			CD		1,60,000	3,15,000
		14,96,000				14,96,000

Problem No. 19 : The Balance Sheets of Suresh Ltd and Harish Ltd as on 31st March 2013 is as follows.

Balance Sheets as on 31-3-2013

Liabilities	Suresh Ltd (Rs)	Harish Ltd (Rs)
Share Capital :		
Shares of Rs. 10 each	10,00,000	4,00,000
General Reserve	1,50,000	-
Profit and Loss A/c	1,42,000	60,000
Creditors	1,82,000	87,000
Bills Payable	20,000	-
	14,94,000	5,47,000

Assets	Suresh Ltd (Rs)	Harish Ltd (Rs)
Good will	60,000	20,000
Machinery	7,32,000	2,72,000
Stock	1,80,000	90,000
Debtors	2,95,000	1,23,000
Cash	35,000	27,000
Investment :		
24,000 Shares of Harish Ltd at cost	1,92,000	-
Bills Receivable	-	15,000
	14,94,000	5,47,000

Other Information :

1) Suresh Ltd Acquired the shares in Harish Ltd. On 1-10-2012
2) The Profit and Loss A/c of Harish Ltd. Showed a debit balance of Rs. 20,000 on 1-4-2012
3) Included in the stock of Harish Ltd are goods of Rs. 20,000 Which were Supplied by Suresh Ltd at cost Plus 25%
4) The Bills Payable in Suresh Ltd represented Rs. 15,000 issued in favour of Harish Ltd. Prepare Consolidated Balance Sheet as on 31-3-2013   **(Oct 2013 - PUP)**

Solution :

Working Notes

1) Share Holding Ratio $= \dfrac{3}{5} : \dfrac{2}{5}$ 24,000 / 16,000

2) Capital Profit

1)	Profit & Loss (Dr) on 1-4-2012 (-)	20,000
2)	Profit earned 1-4-2012 to 1-10-12 (+)	40,000
	(B/S - P & L Ac/ 60,000 + 20,000 Dr. Bal = 80,000)	
	Holding ₹ 12,000 80,000 T.R = 1:1	20,000
	Minority ₹ 8000	

3) Revenue Profit

Profit earned 1-10-2012 to 31-3-13	40,000
(B/s P & L the 60,000 + 20,000 Dr. bal 80,000)	40,000
Holding ₹ 24,000 TR 1 : 1)	
Minority ₹ 16,000	

4) Good will / Cost of Control

Cost of acquisition of 24,000 Shares	1,92,000
(-) Face Value of 24,000 Shares	(-) 2,40,000
(-) Capital Profit of Holding	(-) 12,000
	(-) 60,000
Add : Good will as per B/s	(+) 80,000
Good will	20,000

5) Minority Interest

Face value of shares	1,60,000
held by minority	8000
Add : capital Profit	16000
Add - Revenue Profit	184,000

6) Unrealised Profit

Total unrealised profit $20,000 \times \dfrac{1}{5} =$	4000
Holding co. share $4000 \times \dfrac{3}{5} =$	2400

Consolidated Balance Sheet of Suresh Ltd and its Subsidiary Harish Ltd As on 31-3-2013

Liabilities		₹	Assets		₹
Share Capital			Good will		20,000
Shares of ₹ 10 each		10,00,000	**Machinery :**		
General Reserve		1,50,000	Suresh Ltd	7,32,000	
Profit & Loss A/c	1,42,000		Harish Ltd	2,72,000	10,04,000
Add : Revenue	24,000		**Debtors :**		
	1,66,000		Suresh Ltd	2,95,000	
Less Unrealised Profit	2400	163600	Harish Ltd	12,3,000	4,18,000
Creditors			Bills Receivable	15,000	Nil
Suresh Ltd	1,82,000		Less : Inter Co. owings	15,000	
Harish Ltd	87,000	2,69,000	**Stock**		
Bills Pay able	20,000		Suresh Ltd	1,80,000	
Less : Inter Co. owings	15,000	5000	Harish Ltd	90,000	
			(-) Unrealised Profit	2,70,000	2,67,600
				2,400	
Minority Interest		1,84,000	**Cash**		
			Suresh Ltd	35,000	
			Harish Ltd	27,000	62,000
Total		17,71,600			17,71,600

Problem No. 20 : From the following Balance Sheets and Particulars given below, Prepare a Consolidated Balance Sheet of Ashoka Ltd. and its Subsidiary Radhika Ltd. As at 31st March 2014

Balance Sheet as on 31st March, 2014

Liabilities	Ashoka Ltd (Rs)	Radhika Ltd (Rs)
Share Capital		
Authorised & Issued Equity		
Shares of Rs. 10 each Fully Paid	1,00,000	40,000
Reserve & Surplus		
General Reserve	20,000	12,000
Profit & Loss A/c	28,000	18,000
Current Liabilities and Provisions :		
Bills Payable	-	8000
Creditors	16,000	10,000
	1,64,000	88,000
Assets	**Ashoka Ltd (Rs)**	**Radhika Ltd (Rs)**
Fixed Assets :		
Good will	8,000	6,000
Land & Building	25,000	20,000
Plant & Machinery	40,000	22,000
Furniture & Fittings	7,000	2,000
Investment		
3,000 Equity Shares in		
Radhika Ltd. at cost	48,000	-
Current Assets :		
Stock in Trade	20,000	18,000
Debtors	4,000	15,000
Cash at Bank	12,000	5,000
	1,64,000	88,000

Additional Information :

i) Ashoka Ltd acquired the shares in Radhika LTd. on 1st October 2013

ii) The bills Payable of Radhika Ltd were all issued in favour of Ashoka Ltd Which Company got the bills discounted.

iii) The creditors of Radhika Ltd included Rs. 4,000 Payable to Ashoka Ltd for goods supplied by that Company.

iv) The stock of Radhika Ltd included goods of the value of 1,600 which were supplied by the Ashoka Ltd. at a profit of $33\frac{1}{3}\%$ on cost.

v) The credit balance on Profit and Loss Account of the Radhika Ltd. on 1st April, 2013 was Rs. 4,000 and on General Reserve Rs. 10,000. **(April 2014 - PUP)**

Solution :

1) **Holding Company -** Share Ratio i.e. 3 : 1
   Holding co. 3000 Shares, Minority 100 Shares

2) **Capital Profit**   **Rs.**

   General Reserve Bal on 1-4-12   10,000

   Bal 2000 × 6 Month up to 1-10-2013   1,000

   Profit & Loss A/c Bal on 1-4-13   4000

   Bal 14,000 ÷ 6 Month up to 1-10-2013   7000   Holding   16,500

                                             22,000   Minority   5,500

3) **Revenue Profit -**

   General Reserve 1-10-13 to 31-3-14   1000

   Profit & Loss A/c 1-10-13 To 31-3-14   7000   Holding co. 6000

                                            8000   Minority   2000

4) **Good will**

   Cost of Share acquired by Holding Co.   48,000

   Less : Face of Value of Shares (+)   30,000

   Less : Capital Profit of Holding co. (-)   16,500

   Good will as per B/s   1500

                                             14,000

                                             15,500

5) **Minority Interest**

   Face Value of Shares of Minority   10,000

   Add : Capital Profit   5,500

   Add : Revenue Profit   2,000

                                             17,500

6) **Unrealised Profit**

   $$\text{Stock } ₹\,1600 = \text{Profit } 33\frac{1}{3} \text{ on cost i.e. } \frac{33\frac{1}{3}}{133\frac{1}{3}} = \frac{1}{4} \times 1600 = 400$$

   $$400 \times \frac{3}{4} = 300$$

Consolidated Balance Sheet

Liabilities		Rs	Assets		Rs
Share Capital :			Good will		15,500
Authorised Capital issued			**Land & Building :**		
1000 Shares of ₹ 100 each		1,00,000	Ashoka Ltd	25,000	
General Reserve		20,000	Radhika Ltd	20,000	45,000
Profit & Loss A/c	28,000		**Plant & Machinery :**		
Add : Revenue Profit	6000		Ashoka Ltd	40,000	
Less : Unrealised Rent (-)	300	33,700	Radhika Ltd	22,000	62,000
Sundry Creditors :			**Furniture & Fittings :**		
Ashoka Ltd	16,000		Ashoka Ltd	7,000	
Radhika Ltd	10,000		Radhika Ltd	2,000	9,000
	26,000				

Liabilities		Rs	Assets			Rs
Less : Inter Co. owing	4,000	22,000	**Stock in Trade :**			
Bills Payable :			Ashoka Ltd	20,000		
Ashoka Ltd		8,000	Radhika Ltd	18,000		
				38,000		
Minority Interest		17,500	Less : Unrealised Profit	300	37,700	
			Sundry Debtors :			
			Ashoka Ltd	4,000		
			Radhika Ltd	15,000		
				19,000		
			Less :Inter Co- owings	4,000	15,000	
			Cash at Bank :			
			Ashoka Ltd	12,000		
			Radhika Ltd	5,000	17,000	
		2,01,200				2,01,200

7.6 EXCERCISES

1) From the following Balance Sheets and particulars given below prepare a consolidated Balance Sheet of 'S' Ltd., and 'T' Ltd., as on 31-3-2009

Balance Sheets as on 31-3-2009

Liabilities	'S' Ltd. Rs.	'T' Ltd. Rs.	Assets	'S' Ltd. Rs.	'T' Ltd. Rs.
Share Capital			Goodwill	12,000	9,000
Equity Shares of			Land & Building	37,500	30,000
Rs.100 each, fully paid	1,50,000	60,000	Plant & Machinery	60,000	33,000
General Reserve	30,000	18,000	Furniture	10,500	3,000
Profit & Loss A/c	42,000	27,000	Investment :		
Bills Payable	–	12,000	450 Equity Shares		
Creditors	27,000	21,000	in 'T' Ltd.	72,000	–
			Stock	30,000	27,000
			Debtors	9,000	28,500
			Cash at Bank	18,000	7,500
	2,49,000	1,38,000		2,49,000	1,38,000

Additional Information :

a) 'S' Ltd., acquired the shares in 'T' Ltd., on 1st July, 2008

b) The balance on Profit & Loss A/c of 'T' Ltd., as on 1st April, 2008, was Rs. 6,000 (credit) and on General Reserve Rs. 15,000

c) The Bills Payable of 'T' Ltd., were all issued in favour of 'S' Ltd., of which company got bills discounted.

d) The Stock of 'T' Ltd., included goods worth Rs. 2,400 which were supplied by 'S' Ltd., at a profit of 25% on cost. **(P.U.)**

Ans. : B/S Total Rs. 3,21,290

2) 'H' Ltd., acquired 4,000 shares of 'S' Ltd., on 1st July, 2008. Their Balance Sheets as on 31st December, 2008, stood as follows :

Balance Sheet as on 31-12-2008

Liabilities	'H' Ltd. Rs.	'S' Ltd. Rs.	Assets	'H' Ltd. Rs.	'S' Ltd. Rs.
Share Capital :			**Assets :**		
Equity shares of			Fixed Assets	6,00,000	5,00,000
Rs. 100 each	10,00,000	5,00,000	Investments		
General Reserve	2,50,000	1,50,000	4,000 Equity Shares		
Profit & Loss A/c	1,00,000	50,000	(at Rs. 120 each)	4,80,000	—
Creditors	1,50,000	50,000	**Current Assets :**		
			Sundry Debtors	2,50,000	1,50,000
			Stock	1,50,000	50,000
			Cash at Bank	20,000	50,000
	15,00,000	7,50,000		15,00,000	7,50,000

On 1-1-2008, the Profit and Loss A/c and the General Reserve of 'S' Ltd., showed the Credit Balance of Rs. 30,000 and Rs. 1,00,000 respectively. Debtors of 'H' Ltd., include Rs. 15,000 due from 'S' Ltd.

Stock of 'H' Ltd., includes Rs. 20,000 purchased from 'S' Ltd., which made 20% profit on selling price.

Prepare a consolidated Balance Sheet of 'H' Ltd., and it's Subsidiary 'S' Ltd., as on that date. **(P.U.)**

Ans. B/S Total 17,51,800

3) From the following Balance Sheets and particulars given below, prepare a consolidated Balance Sheet of 'H' Ltd., and 'S' Ltd., as on 31-3-2009

Balance Sheets as on 31-3-2009

Liabilities	'H' Ltd. Rs.	'S' Ltd. Rs.	Assets	'H' Ltd. Rs.	'S' Ltd. Rs.
Share Capital :			Goodwill	8,000	6,000
Equity Shares of			Land & Building	25,000	20,000
Rs. 100 each,			Plant & Machinery	40,000	22,000
fully paid	1,00,000	40,000	Furniture	7,000	2,000
General Reserve	20,000	12,000	300 Equity		
Profit & Loss A/c	28,000	18,000	Shares in 'S'		
Bills Payable		8,000	Ltd., at cost	48,000	—
Creditors	18,000	14,000	Stock	20,000	18,000
			Debtors	6,000	19,000
			Cash at Bank	12,000	5,000
	1,66,000	92,000		1,66,000	92,000

a) 'H' Ltd., acquired the shares in 'S' Ltd., on 1-10-2008

b) The balance on Profit and Loss Account of 'S' Ltd., as on 1-4-2008 was Rs. 4,000 (credit) and on General Reserve Rs. 10,000

c) The Bills Payable of 'S' Ltd., were all issued in favour of 'H' Ltd., of which company got bills discounted.

d) The stock of 'S' Ltd., included goods worth Rs. 1,600 which were supplied by 'H' Ltd., as a profit of 25% on cost. **(P.U.)**

Ans. B/S Total 2,11,260

4) Following are the Balance Sheets of 'P' Ltd., and 'R' Ltd., as at December, 2008 :

Liabilities	'P' Ltd. Rs.	'R' Ltd. Rs.	Assets	'P' Ltd. Rs.	'R' Ltd. Rs.
Share Capital :			Goodwill	20,000	10,000
(Rs. 10 each)	2,50,000	1,00,000	Fixed Assets	2,00,000	1,20,000
General Reserve	75,000	30,000	Stock	80,000	30,000
P & L A/c	70,000	60,000	Debtors	60,000	50,000
Creditors	50,000	20,000	Investments 6,000		
Bills Payable	5,000	2,000	Shares of 'R' Ltd.	85,000	—
			Cash	5,000	2,000
	4,50,000	2,12,000		4,50,000	2,12,000

Additional Information :

1) Shares in 'R' Ltd., were acquired by 'P' Ltd., on 1st July 2008.

2) 'R' Ltd., had on 1-1-2008 Rs. 18,000 in General Reserve and Rs. 14,000 in Profit and Loss Account.

3) Included in the Creditors of 'R' Ltd., is Rs. 12,000 for goods supplied by 'P' Ltd.

4) Included in stock of 'R' Ltd., are the goods to the value of Rs. 6,000, Which were supplied by 'P' Ltd., at the profit of 25% on cost.

   Prepare consolidated Balance Sheet as at 31-12-2008 Showing necessary working.

   (P.U.)

Ans. B/S Total Rs. 5,64,280.

5) The following are the Balance Sheets of 'H' Ltd., and 'S' Ltd., as at 31st March, 2009

Liabilities	'H' Ltd. Rs.	'S' Ltd. Rs.	Assets	'H' Ltd. Rs.	'S' Ltd. Rs.
Equity Shares of Rs. 10 each	6,00,000	2,00,000	Machinery	3,90,000	1,35,000
			Furniture	80,000	40,000
General Reserve	3,40,000	80,000	80% shares		
P & L A/c	1,00,000	60,000	in 'S' Ltd., at cost	3,40,000	—
Creditors	70,000	35,000	Stock	1,80,000	1,20,000
			Debtors	50,000	30,000
			Cash at Balance	70,000	50,000
	11,10,000	3,75,000		11,10,000	3,75,000

The following additional information is provided to you.

1) Profit and Loss Account of 'S' Ltd., stood at Rs. 30,000 on 1-4-2008, whereas General Reserve has remained unchanged since that date.

2) 'H' Ltd., acquired 80% shares in 'S' Ltd., on 1-10-2008 for Rs. 3,40,000 as mentioned above.

3) Included in debtors of 'S' Ltd., is a sum of Rs. 10,000 due from 'H' Ltd., for goods sold at a profit of 25% on cost price. Till 31-3-2009, only one-half of the goods had been sold while the remaining goods were lying in the godown of 'H' Ltd., as on that date.

You are required to prepare a consolidated Balance sheet as at 31st March, 2009. Show all calculations.

(P.U.)

Ans. B/S Total Rs. 12,14,200.

6) The following are the Balance Sheets of 'X' Ltd., its subsidiary 'Y' Ltd., as at 31st Dec., 2008.

Liabilities	'X' Ltd. Rs.	'Y' Ltd. Rs.	Assets	'X' Ltd. Rs.	'Y' Ltd. Rs.
Share Capital			Land & Building	50,000	30,000
Equity shares of Rs. 10			Plant & Machinery	40,000	—
each, fully paid	1,00,000	50,000	Furniture & Fixtures	20,000	15,000
General Reserve	50,000	25,000	Stock-in-trade	20,000	30,000
P & L. A/c	–	25,000	Sundry Debtors	5,000	10,000
6% Debentures			Cash in Hand	5,000	5,000
of Rs. 100 each	20,000	–	Cash at Bank	40,000	20,000
Sundry Creditors	60,000	10,000	Investment		
			4,000 Equity Shares		
			in 'P' Ltd.	50,000	—
	2,30,000	1,10,000		2,30,000	1,10,000

The following information is supplied :–

1) 'X' Ltd., acquire is shares in 'Y' Ltd., on 1st Jan., 2008, when 'Y' Ltd., had Rs. 25,000 in General Reserve and Rs. 20,000 in Profit & Loss A/c (credit balance)
2) Stock-in-trade of 'Y' Ltd., include the goods of the value of Rs 20,000 purchased from 'X' Ltd., on which 'X' Ltd., charged cost plus 25%.
3) Debtors of 'Y' Ltd., includes Rs. 2,000 due from 'X' Ltd.
4) The proper value of Land & Building which stood at Rs. 30,000 in the books of 'Y' Ltd., as at the date of acquisition was Rs.50,000. **(P.U.)**

Ans : B/S Total 3,04,800

7) Following are the Balance Sheets of Poona Ltd., and Mumbai Ltd., as on 31st Dec., 2008.

Liabilities	Pune Ltd. Rs.	Mumbai Ltd Rs.	Assets	Pune Ltd. Rs.	Mumbai Ltd Rs.
Share Capital			Land & building	3,00,000	1,06,000
Equity Shares			Plant & Machinery	1,50,000	1,80,000
of Rs.100 each	6,00,000	3,00,000			
General Reserve	40,000	10,000	Investments		
P & L A/c	70,000	5,000	(2,700 shares in		
Bills Payable	25,000	31,000	Mumbai Ltd., at cost)	2,97,000	—
Sundry Creditors	1,42,000	60,000	Stock	40,000	50,000
Bank Overdraft	25,000	—	Sundry Debtors	52,000	60,000
			Bills Receivables	63,000	10,000
	9,02,000	4,06,000		9,02,000	4,06,000

Additional Information :

1) Poona Ltd., acquires shares in Mumbai Ltd., on 1st January, 2008, on which date the Profit and Loss A/c showed a debit balance Rs.10,000 in the books of Mumbai Ltd., and there was no balance in General Reserve.

2) Sundry debtors of Mumbai Ltd., included Rs.40,000 due from Poona Ltd.

3) Bills Payable of Mumbai Ltd., include Rs.18,000 issued in favour of Poona Ltd., which was discounted at Rs. 3,000 by them.

Prepare a consolidated Balance Sheet. **(P.U.)**

Ans : B/S Total Rs.10,28,000

8) Hard Ltd., acquired 80% shares of Soft Ltd., on 1st January, 2008, at the total cost of Rs.3,25,000. The Balance Sheets of the two Companies on 31st Dec. 2008 were as follows :

Liabilities	'H' Ltd. Rs.	'S' Ltd. Rs.	Assets	'H' Ltd. Rs.	'S' Ltd. Rs.
Equity shares			Land and Building	4,50,000	1,50,000
of Rs.10 each	6,00,000	2,00,000	Plant and Machinery	3,50,000	1,00,000
Preference Shares			Stock	1,50,000	70,000
of Rs.100 each	2,00,000	—	Investment	3,25,000	
General Reserve	2,50,000	30,000	Debtors	1,20,000	60,000
P & L A/c	3,00,000	1,50,000	Bank Balance	5,000	20,000
Creditors	50,000	20,000			
	14,00,000	4,00,000		14,00,000	4,00,000

The following further information is relevant –

1) Creditors of Hard Ltd., include Rs.20,000 for goods purchased from Soft Ltd., on which Soft Ltd., made a profit of Rs.5,000.

2) Half of the goods sold as above were still included in the stock of Hard Ltd.

3) The General Reserve of Soft Ltd., represents balance as on 1st Jan., 2008.

4) Profit and Loss A/c balance as on 1st Jan., 2008 was Rs.60,000, out of which dividend at 15% was paid for the year 2007.

Prepare a consolidated Balance Sheet.

Ans : B/S Total 15,46,000

KEY TERMS

Isuue, Forfeiture and Their Re - Issue :

1) **Company :** A Company is a particular kind of association. It is a voluntary and autonomous association formed to carry out a particular purpose in comnon. A company is an artificial person created by law having a common seal and perpetual succession.

2) **Share Capital :** The Capital collected by the Company through the issue of shares is called as "Share Capital".

3) **Share :** The Capital of a Company is divided into small parts called as "Shares".

4) **Authorised Capital :** It is the maximum amount of share capital which the Company is authorised to raise by way of public subscription.

5) **Issued Capital :** It is represented by the number of shares that have been issued to the public for Cash and to the vendors as fully or partly paid against purchase consideration.

6) **Subscribed Capital :** It is that part of issued capital for which applications are received from the public.

7) **Called-up Capital :** The amount on the shares which is actually demanded by the Company to be paid is called "Called-up Capital".

8) **Paid-up Capital :** It is that part of called-up capital which is actually paid by the shareholders.

9) **Equity Shares :** It is those shares, the holders of which are entitled to profits after all prior charges have been paid.

10) **Preference Shares :** It is those shares, the holders of which enjoy the preferential rights as to dividend and repayment of capital in the event of winding up of the company.

11) **Calls-in-arrears :** It is that part of called-up capital which has not been paid by the shareholders fully or partially.

12) **Calls-in-advance :** The amount received before making the calls is called as "calls-in-advance"

13) **Cumulative Preference Shares :** It is those shares on which the arrears of dividend are carried forward and accumulated and are payable in future when the company earns the profit.

14) **Non - Cumulative Preference Shares :** It is those shares on which arrears of dividend cannot be accumulated.

15) **Redeemable Preference Shares :** It is thore shares, which are to be redeemed after expiry of certain term as per agreement.

16) **Irredeemable Preference Shares :** It is those shares the amount of which are not to be redeemed during the lifetime of the company.

17) **Participative Preference Shares :** It is those shares which carry the right of sharing profits left after paying preference and equity dividends at a fixed rate.

18) **Non-Participating Preference Shares :** It is those shares which do not carry the right of sharing in the surplus left after paying equity dividend.

19) **Convertible Preference Shares :** It is those shares which can be converted into equity shares.

20) **Non-convertible Preference Shares :** It is those shares which cannot be converted into equity shares.

21) **Issue of Shares at Par :** When a shareholder is required to pay the face value of the shares of the company, it is called "issue of shares at par".

22) **Issue of Shares at Premium :** When a shareholder is required to pay more than the face value of the shares of the company, it is called "issue of shares at premium".

23) **Issue of Shares at a Discount :** When a shareholder is required to pay less amount than the face value of shares, it is called "issue of shares at discount."

24) **Right Issue :** When in further issue, the shares are given only to the existing shareholders in proportion of their holdings is called as "right issue".

25) **Prospectus :** It is a document in which the Company invites the public for subscription of shares or debentures of the Company.

26) **Share Allotment :** It is an act of distributing shares to the applicants.

27) **Pro-rata Allotment :** In case of over-subscription, when the Company reduces the, demand of each

applicant proportionately on the basis of their total demand and number of shares issued it is called as "pro-rata allotment".

28) **Forfeiture of Shares :** When a shareholder fails to pay the calls made on him, his shares may be taken away as cancelled as a penalty. It is called "forfeiture of shares".

29) **Re-issue of Forfeited Shares :** When forfeited shares are issued to others by a Company it is called as "re-issue of forfeited shares'.

30) **Debentures :** It is a document issued by a Company acknowledging the debt under its common seal.

31) **Secured Debentures :** Those debentures which are secured by a charge on the assets of the Company.

32) **Unsecured Debentures :** Those debentures which are not secured by charge or pledge on the assets of the Company.

33) **Redeemable Debentures :** The debentures which are to be redeemed after the expiry of certain term as per agreement.

34) **Registed Debentures :** Those debentures which are registered in the Register of Company.

35) **Bearer Debentures :** Those debentures which are not registered with the Company, and hence Rare payable to the bearer of debentures.

36) **Sinking Fund :** It is a specific fund created by a Company against the profits

37) **Profit prior to Incorporation :** Profits earned from the date of purchase of running business till the date of incorporation is called as Capital Profit.

38) **Post-incorporation Profit :** Profits earned from the date of incorporation to the date of closing the accounts is known as revenue profit.

39) **Loss prior to Incorporation :** The loss incurred from the date of purchase of running business till the date of incorporation is treated as capital loss.

40) **Post-incorporation loss :** The loss incurred from the date of incorporation to the date of closing the Accounts is treated as capital loss.

41) **Profit and Loss Account :** The account which shows a true and fair view of the profit or loss of the company at the end of accounting year.

42) **Profit and loss Appropriation Account :** The account which shows the disposal of profits.

43) **Divisible Profit :** Profits available for dividend to shareholders is known as "Divisible Profit".

44) **Balance Sheet :** A Balance Sheet is a statement of Assets & Liabilities on a particular date.

45) **Dividend :** The share in the profits payable to sharehoders is known as Dividend.

46) **Interim Dividend :** An interim Dividend is a dividend paid by the directors at any time between two Annual General Meetings.

47) **Proposed Dividend :** A dividend recommended or proposed by Board of Directors at certain rate on paid-up capital is known an "proposed dividend".

48) **Unclaimed Dividend :** Dividend declared but not claimed is known as "unclaimed dividend".

49) **Contingent Liabilities :** Contingent liabilities are those liabilities which are not the actual liabilities on the date of balance sheet. They may or may not turn into liabilities depending upon the happening of the certain events in the future.

50) **Current Liabilities :** Current liabilities are those which are to be paid out within a span of short period.

51) **Provisions :** Provision means any amount written off or retained by way of providing for depreciation renewal etc., or for any known liability.

52) **Fixed Assets :** Fixed assets are those which are of the permanent nature and which are acquired by the business for its own use and which are not for resale.

53) **Redemption :** Redemption means repayment.

54) **Preliminary Expenses :** Those expenses which are incurred on the formation of the company.

55) **Accounting Standards :** Accounting Standards are the authoritative bases for preparation and presentation of financial statements of the enterprises.

56) **Liquidation :** Liquidation is one of the processes by which, dissolution of Company is brought about.

57) **Compulsory winding up :** Winding up of a Company by Court is called compulsory winding up.

58) **Voluntary winding up :** Winding up of a Company by the members or creditors without any intervention

of the Court is called voluntary winding up.

59) Liquidator : The commencement of winding up of a Company does not put an end to the existence of the Company. Its assets are to be realised and distributed among the creditors, debentureholders and shareholders. For this purpose, somebody has to act as an agent of the company. Such an agent is called liquidator.

60) Liquidator's Final Statement of Account : The liquidator is required to prepare an account of winding up of a Company and such account is called Liquidator's Final Statement of Account.

61) Liquidator's Remuneration : The Liquidator normally gets the commission for winding up of a company. Such commission is called liquidator's remuneration.

62) Fully Secured Creditors : The creditors who are given security for the full payment of their loan, are called fully secured creditors.

63) Unsecured Creditors : The creditors who are not given any security for the payment of loan, are called unsecured creditors.

64) Preferential Creditors : The creditors who get preference or proirity in respect of returning the amount, over other creditors are called preferential creditors.

65) Amalgamation : Amalgamation refers to the merger of two or more existing companies into a single new Company.

66) Absorption : The term absorption means taking over of the business of one or more companies by the Company already in existence.

67) Reconstruction : When a Company has accumulated huge losses or in financial difficulties or is over-capitalised, then it is reconstructed. This is called reconstruction of a company.

68) Internal Reconstruction : Internal reconstruction means reduction of capital of a Company which is to be reconstructed.

69) External Reconstruction : External reconstruction takes place when a new Company of similar name is formed to take over the business of the existing Company.

70) Purchase Consideration : Purchase consideration is the amount which is paid by the purchasing Company for the purchase of the business of the vendor Company.

71) Net worth of business : Assets taken over - Liabilities taken over.

72) Holding Company : A Company which holds more than 51% of shares of another Company is called a holding company.

73) Subsidiary Company : A Company whose shares have been acquired by a holding company is called Subsidiary Company.

74) Minority Interest : The interest of minority shareholders are called as minority interest.

75) Goodwill on consolidation : When the value of "investment in Subsidiary" in the holding Company's Balance Sheet is more than the book value of the net assets acquired, the difference represents Goodwill on consolidation.

76) Capital Reserve on Consolidation : If the value of investment in Subsidiary is less than book value of net assets acquired, the difference represents capital reserve on consolidation.

77) Capital Profit : The profit earned by a subsidiary company before the holding company acquires its control is known as capital profit or pre-acquisition profit.

78) Revenue Profit : The profit earned by a subsidiary company after the holding company acquires its control is known as revenue or post-acquisition profit.

79) Unrealised Profit : If the goods are sold by the subsidiary company to the holding company or vice-versa, remain unsold at the close of financial year, the profit charged by the Company on unsold goods remains unrealised. This is called unrealised profit.

80) Inter - company Debts and Acceptance : It is very common that member companies have business dealing not only with outsiders but also with each other. Inter-company transactions may lead to inter-company debts and acceptances. These transactions are to be the cancelled in consolidated balance sheet.

CHAPTER 8

Valuation of Shares

8.1 Valuation of Shares
8.2 Need for Valuation
8.3 Methods of Valuation
    8.3.1 Net Asset Banking Method
    8.3.2 Yield Method
8.4 Exercises

8.1 Valuation of shares:

By the term 'value of shares', we mean either its face value or the market value. The face value of a share is the value assigned to it by the promoters of a joint stock company in the capital clause of the Memorandum of Association. This value is supposed to be more or less permanently fixed during the lifetime of a company, unless the company otherwise alters it, subjects to the provisions of the companies Act.

The market value of a share, on the other hand, is the value established by the market forces of demand and supply. The shares of a public joint stock company, quoted on the stock exchange, have a value different from the face value. Although this value, determined by market forces, is not the same as the face value, neither of these values can be taken as the proper value of a share.

A company, having been in existence for many years, will have its financial position as reflected by its balance sheet quite different from what it was in the year of its formation. In the same way, the market value affected by a number of factors cannot also be taken to be the proper value of its shares. It is still more difficult to ascertain the proper value of the shares of a public company whose shares are not quoted on the stock exchange. Besides, in the case of private companies, because of the restriction on the transferability of shares, their shares have no market value at all.

8.2 Need for Valuation

The need for valuation of shares arises' in one or more of the following circumstances:
(i) Assessments under estate duty, wealth tax, gift tax, etc.
(ii) Purchase of a block of shares generally involving acquisition of controlling interest in the company.

(iii) Formulations of schemes of amalgamation, absorption, etc.
(iv) Acquisition of interest of dissenting shareholders under reconstruction scheme,
 (v) Conversion of preference shares into equity shares,
(vi) Advancing Joans on the security of shares.
(vii) Compensating shareholders on the acquisition of their shares, by the government under a scheme of nationalisation.

Valuation and Stock Exchange Prices

In case of shares quoted on a recognised stock exchange, stock exchange prices are generally taken as the basis for the valuation of those shares. However, the stock exchange quotations are not generally acceptable when a large block of company's shares is involved. This is because stock exchange price is basically determined on the interactions of demand and supply and business cycles. They cannot form a fair and equitable or rational basis for compensation.

The Council of the London Stock Exchange has also expressed the same opinion in the following words:

"The stock exchange may be likened to a scientific recording instrument which registers, not its own actions and opinions but the actions and opinions of private institutional investors all over the country and indeed the world. These actions and opinions are the result of fear, guess work, intelligent or otherwise, good or bad investment policy and many other considerations. The quotations that result definitely do not represent valuation of a company by reference to its assets and its earning potential."

On account of the above reasons, accountants are frequently required to place a proper value on the shares in a company. The methods adopted by them are being explained in the following pages.

8.3 Methods of Valuation

The methods of valuation of share may be broadly classified as follows:
1. Net Assets Backing Method, 2. Yield Method.
Both the above methods are generally used for valuation of equity shares. However, they can also be used to some extent in case of preference shares, as explained later.

8.3.1 Net Assets Backing Method :

This is also termed as balance sheet method or asset backing method or intrinsic or break-up value method. In case of this method, the net assets of the company (including goodwill and non-trading assets) are divided by the number of issued shares to arrive at the asset backing for each share. For instance, if the assets total Rs 50,000, liabilities Rs 10,000 and the number of shares 20,000, the value of each share according to the method would be Rs 2 (i.e. Rs 40,000/20,000). The following points should be kept in mind while valuing shares according to this method:

  (i) A proper value should be placed on the goodwill of the business,

 (ii) Fictitious assets, such as preliminary expenses, debit balance in the profit and loss account etc. should be excluded.

(iii) All other assets, (including non-grading assets, such as investments) should be taken at their market values. In the absence of information in the question about the market values of the different assets, book values may rightly be taken as the market values of the different assets. Liabilities payable to third parties and preference share capital should be deducted from the total assets. It should be noted that items constituting part of the equity shareholders' funds (*e.g.* general reserve, profit and loss account credit balance, debentures redemption fund, dividends equivalisation reserve, contingency reserve etc.) should not be deducted.

(iv) The net assets so arrived at should be divided by the number of equity shares to arrive at value of the share. However, this has to be done only when all shares are equally paid-up. In case the company's equity shares are of different paid-up values, the total net assets should allocated to the different paid-up value groups. Each such allocation should then be divided by the number of shares in each of such groups.

Thus, the value of an equity share, according to this method, can be found out as shown in the following statement:

Particulars	Rs.	Rs.
Goodwill as valued		......
Investments at market value		......
Other assets at market value		......
Less: Debentures	......	
Accounts payable	......	
Other liabilities	......	
Preference capital	......	......
Net assets available for equity shareholders (i)		......
Number of equity shares (ii)		......
Value of an equity share (i)/(ii)		......

This method of valuation is generally not recommended for going concerns since in their case yield is the predominant factor. However, in case of companies like, investment companies, such a basis of valuation may be acceptable since yield, in their case primarily depends upon the assets position. Similarly in case of companies having highly uneven past results, this method of valuation may be the only choice since no reliable information is available about the expected earnings of the company. The method is also suitable for a company which has been showing consistent losses with no apparent prospect of recovery.

PROBLEMS :

Problems No. 1 : The following particulars relate to a company:

	Rs.
Total assets	18,50,000
External liabilities	2,50,000
Share capital:	
14% Preference shares of Rs 10 each, fully paid	5,00,000
40,000 Equity shares of Rs 10 each, fully paid	4,00,000
60,000 Equity shares of Rs 10 each, Rs 7.50 paid	4,50,000

Calculate the value of each category of equity shares of the company based on a deemed liquidation.

Solution :

Asset-Basis Value of an Equity Share

Particular	Rs.
Total assets	18,50,000
Less : Liabilities	2,50,000
Net worth	1 6,00,000
Less : Preference shares	5,00,000
Net worth applicable to equity	11,00,000
Add: Notional call on 60000 equity shares	1,50,000
@ Rs 2.5 per share	
Adjusted net worth	12,50,000
No. of equity shares	1,00,000
Value per share {fully paid)	Rs 12.50
Value of equity share on which Rs 7.50 paid	Rs.12.50-Rs. 2.50 = Rs.10

Problems No. 2 : Below is given the Balance sheet of Prosperous Ltd. as at 31 March, 2014:

Liabilities	Rs.	Assets	Rs.
Share capital		Land and building	2,70,000
Authorised and issued:		Plant and machinery	1,00,000
6,000 Shares of Rs 100 each fully		Stock	3,60,000
paid-up	6,00,000	Sundry debtors	1,60,000
Profit and loss account	40,000		
Bank overdraft	10,000		
Creditors	80,000		
Provision for taxation	1,00,000		
Proposed dividend	60,000		
	8,90,000		8,90,000

The net profits of the company, after deducting usual working expenses but before providing for taxation, were as under:

Year	Rs
2009-10	1,70,000
2010-11	2,10,000
2011-12	1,80,000
2012-13	2,20,000
2013-14	2,00,000

On 31 March 2014, Land Buildings, were valued at Rs. 2,80,000 and Plant Machinery at Rs. 1,20,000. Sundry Debtors, on the same date, included Rs. 4,000 as irrecoverable.

Keeping in mind the nature of the business, a 10 per cent return, on net tangible capital invested, is considered reasonable.

You are required to value the company's shares ex-dividend. Your own valuation of goodwill may be based on five years' purchase of the annual super profits (The tax rate is to be assumed at 50%).

Solution :

Statement Showing Valuation of Shares

Particulars	Rs.	Rs.
Goodwill (see working note ii)		1,44,500
Land and buildings		2,80,000
Plant and machinery		1,20,000
Sundry debtors		1,56,000
Stock		3,60,000
Total		10,60,500
Less: Liabilities:		
Bank overdraft	10,000	
Creditors	80,000	
Provision for taxation	1,00,000	
Proposed dividend	60,000	2,50,000
		8,10,500

Value per share : 8,10,500 ÷ 6,000 = Rs. 135.08.

Working Notes:

Particulars	Rs.	Rs.
(i) Net Tangible Capital Employed:		
Assets at their present values:		
Land and building		2,80,000
Plant and machinery		1,20,000
Stocks		3,60,000
Sundry debtors		1,56,000
Total :		9,16,000
Less: Liabilities:		
Bank overdraft	10,000	
Creditors	80,000	
Provision for taxation	1,00,000	1,90,000
Net Tangible capital		7,26,000
Less: ½ of the profits (after tax)		50,000
Average Tangible capital employed		6,76,000

(ii)   Goodwill

Particulars		Rs.	Rs.
	Total profit (as given) for 5 years		9,80,000
Less :	Bad debts		4,000
			9,76,000
	Average profits		1,95,200
Less :	Adjustment for depreciation on change in value of assets (rates assumed):		
	Land and building @ 2% on Rs 10,000	200	
	Plant and machinery @ 10% on Rs 20,000	2,000	2,200
			1,93,000
	Taxation @ 50%		96,500
	Average annual profits aftertax (assumed maintainable in future)		96,500
Less :	10% return on average tangible capital employed		67,600
	Average annual super profits		28,900
	Goodwill at 5 years purchase of super profits (28900 × 5)		1 ,44,500

Problems No. 3 : The following is the Balance Sheet (as on 31st December, 2013) of Sun Ltd.:

Liabilities	Rs.	Assets	Rs.
Share Capital:		**Fixed Assets:**	
80,000 Equity shares of Rs 10 each fully paid up	8,00,000	Goodwill	1,00,000
50,000 Equity shares of Rs 10 each Rs 8 paid up	4,00,000	Plant and Machinery	8,00,000
36,000 Equity shares of Rs 5 each fully paid up	1,80,000	Land and Building	1,00,000
30,000 Equity shares of Rs 5 each Rs 4 paid up	1,20,000	Furniture and Fixtures	1,00,000
3,000 10% Preference shares of Rs 100 each fully paid up	3,00,000	Vehicles	2,00,000
		Investments	3,00,000
Reserve and Surplus:		**Current Assets:**	
General reserve	1,40,000	Stock	2,10,000
Profit and Loss account	2,10,000	Debtors	1,95,000

Liabilities	Rs.	Assets	Rs.
Secured Loan: 12% Debenture	2,00,000	Prepaid Expenses	40,000
Unsecured Loan: 15% Term loan	1,50,000	Advances	45,000
Deposits	1,00,000	Cash and Bank Balance	2,00,000
Current Liabilities:		Preliminary Expenses	10,000
Bank Loan	50,000		
Creditors	1,50,000		
Outstanding Expenses	20,000		
Provision for Tax	2,00,000		
Proposed Dividend:			
Equity	1,50,000		
Preference	30,000		
	32,00,000		32,00,000

Additional Information:

(1) In 2011 a new machinery costing Rs 50,000 was purchased, but wrongly charged to revenue (no rectification has yet been made for the same).

(2) Stock is overvalued by Rs 10,000 in 2012. Debtors are to be reduced by Rs 5,000 in 2013, some old furniture (Book value Rs 10,000) was disposed of for Rs 6,000.

(3) Fixed assets are worth 5 per cent more than their actual book value. Depreciation on appreciated value of Fixed assets except machinery is not to be considered for valuation of goodwill.

(4) Of the investment 20 per cent is trading and the balance is non-trading. All trade investments are to be valued at 20 per cent below cost. Trade investment were purchased on 1 st January, 2013.50 per cent of the non-trade investments were acquired on 1 st January, 2012 and the rest on 1 st January, 2011. A uniform rate of dividend of 10 per cent is earned on all investments.

(5) Expected increase in expenditure without commensurate increase in selling price is Rs 20,000.

(6) Research and Development expenses anticipated in future Rs 30,000 per annum.

(7) In a similar business a normal return on capital employed is 10%.

(8) Profit (after tax) are as follows:

In 2011 - Rs 2,10,000, in 2012 - Rs 1,90,000 and in 2013—Rs 2,00,000.

(9) Current income tax rate is 50%, expected income tax rate will be 40%.

From the above, ascertain the ex-dividend and cum-dividend intrinsic value for different categories of equity shares. For this purpose goodwill may be taken as 3 years purchase of super profits. Depreciation is charged on machinery @ 10% on reducing system.

(CA Final, May 2007)

Solution :

Computation of Intrinsic Value of Shares:

(1) Computation of Net Assets for Equity Shares:

Particulars	Rs.	Rs.
Value of Net Assets (as computed for Goodwill)		21,02,073
Value of Goodwill [W.N. 3]		11,406
Non-trade investments		2,40,000
		23,53,479
Less: i) Preference Share Capital	3,00,000	
ii) Proposed Dividend of Preference Shares	30,000	
iii) Proposed Dividend of Equity Shares	1,50,000	4,80,000
Net Assets available for Equity Shareholders		18,73,479

(2) Computation of Number of Equivalent Equity Shares:

Particulars	No. *of Equivalent shares*
i) 80,000 shares + 50,000 shares = 1,30,000 shares of Rs 10 each = $1,30,000 \times \dfrac{10}{10}$	1,30,000
ii) 36,000 shares + 30,000 shares = 66,000 shares of Rs 5 each = $66,000 \times \dfrac{5}{10}$	33,000
Total Equivalent Equily Shares of Rs. 10 each	1,63,000

(3) Net Assets Available to Deemed Fully Paid-up Equity Shareholders:

= Net Assets as computed above + Notional Cash from partly paid-up shares

= Rs 18,73,479 + (50,000 × 2 + 30,000 × 1)

= Rs 18,73,479 + 1,00,000 + 30,000 = Rs 20,03,479

(4) Computation of Ex-Dividend Value per Equity Share:

(i) Value of Rs 10 fully paid Equity Share $= \dfrac{20,03,479}{1,63,000}$

= Rs 12.29 per share (approx.)

(ii) Value of Rs 8 paid-up Equity Share = 12.29 - 2

= Rs 10.29 per share (approx.)

(iii) Value of Rs 5 fully paid-up Equity Share $= 12.29 \times \dfrac{5}{10}$

= Rs 6.15 per share (approx.)

(iv) Value of Rs 4 paid-up Equity Share = 6.15-1

= Rs 5.15 per share (approx.)

(5) Value of Net Assets:

Value of Net Assets (including proposed dividend on equity shares)

= Rs 18,73,479 + 1,50,000

= Rs 20,23,479

Net assets (including dividend) available to deemed fully paid-up Equity Shareholders

= Net Assets as computed above + Notional cash from partly paid-up shares

= Rs 20,23,479 + (50,000 × 2 + 30,000 × 1)

= Rs 20,23,479 + 1,00,000 + 30,000 = Rs 21,53,479.

(6) Computation of Earning-Dividend Value per Share:

(i)   Value of Rs 10 fully paid Equity Share

$$= \dfrac{21,53,479}{1,63,000} = \text{Rs } 13.21 \text{ per share (approx.)}$$

(ii)   Value of Rs 8 paid-up Equity Share

= 1 3.21 - 2   = Rs 11.21 per share (approx.)

(iii)   Value of Rs 5 fully paid-up Equity Share

$= 13.21 \times \dfrac{5}{10}$ = Rs 6.605 per share (approx.)

(iv)   Value of the 4 Paid-up equtity Share

= 6.605 - 1   = Rs 5.605 per share (approx.)

Working Notes :

1. Computation of Average Capital Employed:

Particulars	Rs.	Rs.
Fixed Assets:		
i) Plant and Machinery (including Rs 36,450 for a Machine charged in 2011)		8,36,450
ii) Land and Building		10,00,000
iii) Furniture & Fixtures (1,00,000-4,000)		96,000
iv) Vehicles		2,00,000
		21,32,450

Particulars	Rs.	Rs.
Add : Appreciation @ 5%		1,06,623
		22,39,073
Trade investment $\left(3,00,000 \times \dfrac{20}{100} \times \dfrac{80}{100}\right)$		48,000
Current Assets :		
Stock		2,10,000
Debtors (1,95,000 - 5,000)		1,90,000
Prepaid Expenses		40,000
Advances		45,000
Cash and Bank Balance		2,00,000
		29,72,073
Less: Outside Liabilities:		
12% Debentures	2,00,000	
15% Term Loan	1,50,000	
Deposits	1,00,000	
Bank Loan	50,000	
Creditors	1,50,000	
Outstanding Expenses	20,000	
Provision for Tax	2,00,000	8,70,000
Capital employed at the end of the year i.e. Net Assets		21,02,073
Less: ½ of the current year's Accounting Profit after Tax:		
Profit before Tax	3,80,950	
Less: Tax 40%* of Rs 3,80,950	1,52,380	
	2,28,570	
50% of Rs 2,28,570		1,14,285
Average capital employed		19,87,788

* Future tax rate has been considered.

2. Future Maintainable Profits Statement of Average Profit

Particulars	Rs	Rs	Rs
	2011	**2012**	**2013**
Profit after Tax	2,10,000	1,90,000	2,00,000
Profit before Tax $\left(\text{PAT}\times\dfrac{1}{0.50}\right)$	4,20,000	3,80,000	4,00,000
Add: Capital expenditure charged to revenue	50,000	—	—
Less: Depreciation of the Machinery	(5,000)	(4,500)	(4,050)
Dividend on Non-Trade Investments	(12,000)	(24,000)	(24,000)
Over-valuation of closing stock	—	(10,000)	—
Add: Overvaluation of opening stock	—	—	10,000
Add: Loss on sale of furniture	—	—	—
(presumed to be extraordinary items)	—	_	4,000
Less: Provision for debtors	—	—	(5,000)
	4,53,000	3,41,500	3,80,950
Total Profit for the three years			11,75,450
Average Profit $=\dfrac{\text{Rs.}11,75,450}{3}$			
Less: Depreciation @ 10% on increase in the value of machinery			
$8,36,450\times\dfrac{5}{100}\times\dfrac{10}{100}=\text{Rs. }41,823\times\dfrac{10}{100}$ i.e.,		4,182	
Expected increase in expenditure		20,000	
Annual R & D Expenses anticipated in future		30,000	54,182
Future Maintainable profit before tax			3,37,635
Less: Tax @ 40% of Rs 3,37,635			1,35,054
Future Maintainable Profit After Tax			2,02,281

3. Computation of Goodwill

	Rs.
Future Maintainable Profit After Tax	2,02,581
Less: Normal Profit (10% of Rs 19,87,788)	1,98,779
Super Profit	3,802
Value of Goodwill = Super Profit × No. of years purchase	
= Rs 3,802 × 3	11,406

8.3.2 Yield Method :

The yield basis of valuation may take any of the following two forms:

(i) Valuation based on rate of return.

(ii) Valuation based on productivity factor.

(i) **Valuation based on rate of return.** The term "rate of return" refers to the return which a shareholder earns on his investment. It may further be classified as *(a)* rate of dividend and *(b)* rate of earning.

    (a) Valuation based on rate of dividend : This method of valuation is particularly suitable for valuing small block of shares. The value of a share according to this method can be found out by applying the following formula:

    Paid-up value of share × Possible rate of dividend ÷ Normal rate of dividend.

    For example, if the paid-up value of a share is Rs 80, the normal rate of return 1 0 per cent and the past results show that the company will pay a dividend of 12 per cent in future, the value of a share, according to this method will be arrived at as follows:

    $80 \times 12 \div 10 = Rs. 96$

    (b) Valuation based on rate of Earning : This method of valuation is particularly suitable for valuing a large block of the company's shares. A big investor is more interested in what the company earns and not simply in what the company distributes. This is because the rate of earning of the company explains the effective utilisation of the company's assets. In case the company does not distribute 100 per cent of its earning among its shareholders, it, as a matter of fact, strengthens the financial position of the company. The value of a share according to this method can be calculated by the following formula:

    Paid-up value × Possible earning rate ÷ Normal earning rate.

For example, if the paid-up value of a share is Rs 80, normal earning rate 16 per cent and the company's past performance shows that it is expected to earn at 20 per cent in future, the value of a share, according to this method, will be calculated as follows:

    $80 \times 20 \div 16 = Rs. 100$

The valuation of shares on yield basis requires determination of normal rate of return (dividend or earnings as the case may be). Such normal rate is determined in the same way as in case of goodwill. However, following additional factors must also be kept in mind.

- *Restrictions on transfer of shares.* If the restrictions are more it will increase the normal rate while less restrictions will decrease the normal rate.

- *Disabilities attached to shares.* For example, shares may be partly *paid-up* or they may be subject to a right of lien by the company etc. More disabilities will increase the normal rate.
- *Dividend performance.* Stability in dividend will decrease the normal rate. Net asset backing. The poor net asset backing will increase the normal rate since the investors will consider themselves more unsafe.
- *Financial prudence.* Financial prudence on the part of the company's management also affects the normal rate of return. In case of companies whose management follow sound financial policies, an investor is prepared to accept a lower rate of return. Contrary is the case, in case of companies which do not follow such policies.

PROBLEMS

Problem No. 4 : On 31 st March, 2012, the balance sheet of Raghuvans Ltd. disclosed the following position:

Liabilities	Rs
Subscribed share capital in shares of Rs 10 each, fully paid	4,00,000
General reserve	1,90,000
Profit and loss account	1,20,000
14% Debentures	1,00,000
Current liabilities	1,30,000
	9,40,000
Assets:	
Goodwill	40,000
Fixed assets (tangible)	5,00,000
Current assets	4,00,000
	9,40,000

On the above-mentioned date, the tangible fixed assets were independently valued at Rs. 3,50,000 and goodwill at Rs 50,000. The net profits for the three years were – 2009-10 Rs 1,03,200; 2010-11: Rs 1,04,000; and 2011-12: Rs 1,03,300 of which 20% was placed to general reserve, this proportion being considered reasonable in the industry in which the company is engaged and where a fair return on investment may be taken at 18%.

Compute the value of the company's share by - (*/*) the net assets method; and (*//*) the yield method. Ignore taxation.

Solution :

Computation of value of an equity share

(i) *Net Assets Method :*

Particulars	Rs.	Rs.
Goodwill as revalued		50,000
Tangible Fixed Assets (revalued)		3,50,000
Current Assets (as per balance sheet)		4,00,000
		8,00,000
Less: 14% Debentures	1,00,000	
Current liabilities	1,30,000	2.30,000
Net Assets		5,70,000

Value per share   = Net assets/No, of shares
               = Rs 5,70,000/40,000
               = Rs 14.25		

(ii) *Yield Method :*

Particulars	Rs.
Average Profits for last 3 years	1,03,500
Less: Transfer to general reserve @ 20%	20,700
	82,800
Expected return on equity $= \dfrac{\text{Rs.}82,000}{\text{Rs.}4,00,00} \times 100 = 20.7\%$ Value per share $= \dfrac{20.7}{18} \times 10 = $ Rs. 11.50	

Problems No. 5 :

Particulars	Rs.
The capital structure of a company is as follows :	
12% Preference shares of Rs 10 each	5,00,000
Equity shares of Rs 10 each	8,00,000
Reserves and surplus	4,00,000
10% Debentures	6,00,000
11% Term loan	7,00,000
Total	30,00,000

The average annual profit before payment of tax and interest is Rs 6,00,000. The income-tax rate is 45%.

You are required to state what valuation should be put upon the equity shares of the company if the applicable price-earnings ratio is 9.   *(CS Inter, Dec. 2003, adapted)*

Solution :

Computation of Earning Per Share

Particulars		Rs.	Rs.
PBIT			6,00,000
Less: Interest			
10% Debentures		60,000	
11% Loan		77,000	1,37,000
PBT			4,63,000
Less: Tax (45%)			2,08,350
PAT			2,54,650
Less: Preference dividend			60,000
Profit available to equity shareholders	(1)		19,46,650
No. of equity shares	(2)		80,000
Earnings per share (EPS)	(1) ÷ (2)		Rs. 2.43

Computation of value of equity share:

$$\text{PER} = \frac{\text{Market price per share}}{\text{Earnings per share}}$$

$$9 = \frac{x}{\text{Rs. } 2.43} \; ; \text{ so } x = \text{Rs. } 21.87$$

Problem No. 6 : The capital structure of a company, on 31st March, 2013 was as under:

Particulars	Rs.
Equity share captial	5,00,000
11% Preference captial	3,00,000
12% Secured debentures	4,00,000
Reserves	3,00,000

The company, on an average, earns a profit of Rs 4 lakhs annually before deduction of interest on debentures and income tax, which works out to 45%.

The normal return on equity shares of companies similarly placed is 1 5%, provided:
(a) The profit after tax covers the fixed interest and fixed dividends at least four times;
(b) Equity capital and reserves are 150% of debentures and preference capital;
(c) Yield on shares is calculated at 60% of profits 'distributed and 5% on undistributed profits;

The company has been paying regularly an equity dividend at 18%.

Ascertain the value of each equity shares of the company.

Solution :

Basic Calculations :

(i) Computation of profit for interest and fixed dividend coverage:

Particulars	Rs.
Average profit of the company (before interest and taxation)	4,00,000
Less: Debenture interest (12% on Rs 4,00,000)	48,000
	3,52,000
Less: Tax @ 45%	1,58,400
Profit after interest and Tax	1 ,93,600
Add: Debenture interest	48,000
Profit before interest but after tax	2,41 ,600

(ii) Computation of interest and fixed dividend coverage:

Debenture interest (1 2% on Rs 4,00,000)	48,000	
Preference dividends (1 1 % on Rs 3,00,000)	33,000	81,000

$$\text{Fixed interest and dividend coverage} = \frac{\text{Rs. } 2,41,000}{\text{Rs. } 81,000} = 2.98 \text{ times}$$

Interest and dividend coverage is 2.98 times. It is less than the prescribed 4 times cover.

(iii) Computation of percentage of equity share capital and reserve to debentures and preference share capital:

Equity share capital + Reserves = Rs. 5,00,000 + Rs. 3,00,000 = Rs. 8,00,000

Preference share capital + Debentures = Rs. 3,00,000 + Rs. 4,00,000 = Rs. 7,00,000

$$\text{Ratio } \frac{8,00,000}{7,00,000} \times 100 = 114\%$$

The ratio of 114% of equity share captial and reserves to debentures and preference share capital is less than the prescribed ratio of 150%.

(iv) Computation of yield on equity shares:

Particulars	Rs.	Rs.
Average profit after interest and tax (see (i) above)		1,93,600
Less: Dividends : Preference	33,000	
Equity 18% on Rs 5,00,000	90,000	1,23,000
Undistributed profit		70,600
60% of Distributed profit (60% of Rs 90,000)		54,000
5% of Undistributed profit (5% of Rs70,600)		3,530
		57,530

$$\text{Yield on equity shares} = \frac{\text{Rs.}57,530}{\text{Rs.}5,00,000} \times 100 = 11.51\%$$

(v) Expected yield of equity shares:

Normal Return   15.00%

Add: For low coverage of fixed interest and dividends (see (ii) above)   0.50 (say)*

For low ratio of equity share capital and reserves (see (iii) above)   0.50 (say)*

     16.00

*The students may take any other reasonable presumption.

$$\text{Value of an equity share (yield basis)} = \frac{\text{Paid-up value} \times \text{Possible yield rate}}{\text{Expected yield rate}}$$

$$= \frac{100 \times 11.51}{16} = \text{Rs } 71.94$$

Note :

It has been assumed that each equity share is of Rs 100 each fully paid.

Valuation based on price earning ratio : This method is particularly suitable for ascertaining the market value of shares which are quoted on a recognised stock exchange. According to this method, the value of share is ascertained as: Earning per share x Price earning ratio. The earning per share and price earning ratio are ascertained as follows:

$$\text{Earning per share} = \frac{\text{Profit available for equity shareholders}}{\text{Number of equity shares}}$$

$$\text{Price earning ratio} = \frac{\text{Market value of a share}}{\text{Earnings per share}}$$

For example, if the persent 'earning per share' is Rs. 10 and the market value of a share is Rs 40, the 'price earning ratio' comes to 4. In case the earning per share is expected to be 12 per share, the probable market value of the share will be Rs 48 (*i.e.* 4 × 12).

Capitalisation factor : The value of a share, according to yield basis can also be found out by finding out the capitalisation factor or the multiplier. For example, if the yield expected in the market is 8 per cent, the capitalisation factor would be 100/8 or 12.5. In case the company earns a profit of Rs 4 lacs, the total value of the business would be Rs 50 lakhs (*i.e* Rs. 4 lakhs × 12.5). The value of an equity share can be ascertained by dividing the total value of the business by the number of equity shares.

Problem No. 7 : From the following particulars calculate the value of share of Z Ltd. on yield basis:

Z Ltd.
BALANCE SHEET as *on 31st December, 2013*

Liabilities	Rs	Assets	Rs
8,000 Equity shares of Rs 100 each	8,00,000	Land & buildings	5,00,000
4,00,000 9% Preference shares of		Plant & machinery	6,00,000
Rs. 1 00 each	4,00,000	Patents	2,00,000
6% Debentures	2,00,000	Sundry debtors	3,00,000
Reserves	4,00,000	Work-in-progress and stock	5,00,000
Sundry creditors	4,00,000	Cash at bank	1,00,000
	22,00,000		22,00,000

Land and building to be valued at Rs 9,00,000. The company's earnings were as follows:

Year	Profit (loss) before tax (RS)	Tax (Rs)
2009	3,00,000	80,000
2010	4,00,000	1,60,000
2011	(1,00,000)	40,000 (Strike)
2012	5,00,000	2,30,000
2013	5,50,000	3,00,000

The company paid managerial remuneration of Rs 60,000 per annum but it will become Rs 1,00,000 in future. There has been no change in capital empolyed. The company paid dividend of Rs 9 per share and it will maintain the same in future . The company proposes to build up a plant rehabilitation reserve. Dividend rate in this type of company is fluctuating and the asset backing of an equity share is about 1½ times. The equity shares with an average dividend of 8% sell at par.

Solution :

(i) **Computation of average maintainable profits:**

Year	Profit Rs.	Weight	Product Rs
2009	3,00,000	1	3,00,000
2010	4,00,000	2	8,00,000
2011	—	—	—
2012	5,00,000	3	15,00,000
2013	5,50,000	4	22,00,000
		10	48,00,000

Weighted average profits : Rs. 48,00,000 ÷ 10 = Rs 4,80,000

Notes : (a) Since the profits are showing a definite trend, weights have been given.

(b) The loss of the year 2011 has not been considered since it is .an abnormal year.

(ii) **Computation of profits available for dividend:**

Particulars	Rs.	Rs.
Weighted average profits		4,80,000
Less: Increase in managerial remuneration		40,000
		4,40,000
Less: Tax (50% assumed)		2,20,000
Profit available for distribution		2,20,000
Less: Rehabilitation reserve (15% assumed)		33,000
		1,87,000
Loss: Dividend on preference shares		36,000
Profit available for distribution to equity shareholders		1,51,000

(iii) **Asset backing per equity share:**

Particulars	Rs.	Rs.
Total Assets as per Balance Sheet		22,00,000
Add: Increase in value of land & building		4,00,000
		26,00,000
Less: Sundry creditors	4,00,000	
6% Debentures	2,00,000	
9% Pref. capital	4,00,000	10,00,000
Net Asset available for equity Shareholders		16,00,000
Equity Share Capital		8,00,000
Asset backing		2 Times

(iv) **Dividend rate:**

Normal dividend rate	8.0%
Less: For higher dividend rate (9%) and stability (say)	0.5%
Less: For higher asset backing {2 times as compared to 1.5) (say)	0.5%
	7.0%

(v) **Capitalisation factor :**

$100 \div 7 = 14.286$

(vi) **Value of an equity share:**

$$\frac{\text{Profit available for equity shareholders} \times \text{Capitalisation factor}}{\text{No. of equity shares}}$$

$$= \frac{1,51,000 \times 14.286}{8,000} = \text{Rs. } 269.64 \text{ or say Rs } 270.$$

Valuation based on productivity factor. Productivity factor represents the earning power of the company in relation to the value of the assets employed for such earning. The factor is applied to the net worth of the company on the valuation date to arrive at the projected earnings of the company. The projected earnings after necessary adjustments (as discussed later) are multiplied by the appropriate capitalisation factor to arrive at the value of the company's business. The total value is divided by the number of equity shares to ascertain the value of each share.

The productivity factor based valuation is merely a method for ascertaining a reliable figure of future profits. The steps involved in such a method of valuation are as follows:

(a) Average net worth of the business is ascertained by taking those number of years whose results are relevant to the future. It will be appropriate to determine the average net worth of each year on the basis of net worth of the business at the commencement and at close of each of the accounting years under consideration. The average net worth of the business for the period under study would be calculated on the basis of the average net worth calculated as above for each of the accounting years.

(b) Net worth of the business on the valuation date is ascertained.

(c) Average profit earned for the period under consideration is ascertained on the basis of the profit earned by the business during the period by simple or weighted average method as may be considered appropriate.

(d) The productivity factor is found out as : $\dfrac{\text{Average profit}}{\text{Average net worth}} \times 100$

(e) The productivity factor calculated as above is applied to the net worth of the business on the valuation date to ascertain the projected income of the business in future.

(f) The projected income so calculated is adjusted further by making appropriations for replacement, tax, rehabilitation of plant and equipments, under-utilisation of productive capacity, effects of restrictions on monopoly and dividend on preference shares. Thus, the profits available for the equity shareholders are ascertained.

(g) The normal rate of return for the company is ascertained keeping in view nature and size of the undertaking.

(h) Appropriate capitalisation factor or multiplier based on normal rate of return is ascertained, as explained earlier.

(i) The capitalisation factor obtained as above is applied to adjusted projected profits available for the equity shareholders to ascertain the capitalised value of the undertaking.

(j) The capitalised value of the undertaking as ascertained above is divided by the number of equity shares to arrive at the value per share.

Problems No. 8 : The following figures relate to a company which has Rs 1 0,00,000 in equity shares and Rs 3,00,000 in 9 per cent preference shares, all of Rs 1 00 each:

Year	Average net worth (excluding investment) Rs	Adjustment taxed profit Rs
2011	18,60,000	1,90,000
2012	21,50,000	2,10,000
2013	21,90,000	2,50,000

The company has investment worth Rs 2,80,000 (at Market value) on the valuation date, the yield in respect of which has been excluded, in arriving at the adjusted tax profit figures. It is customary for similar types of companies to set aside 25 per cent of the taxed profit for rehabilitation and replacement purposes. On the valuation date, the net worth (excluding investments) amount to Rs 22,50,000. The normal rate of return expected is 9 per cent. The company has paid dividends consistently within a range of 8 per cent to 1 0 per cent on equity shares over the previous seven years and it expects to maintain the same.

You are required to ascertain the value of each equity share on the basis of productivity, applying suitable weighted averaging.

Solution :

Computation of Productivity Factor

Year	Average net worth Rs	Adjusted taxed profit Rs	Weight	Weighted net worth Rs	Weighted adjusted taxed profits Rs
2011	18,60,000	1,90,000	1	18,60,000	1,90,000
2012	21,50,000	2,10,000	2	43,00,000	4,20,000
2013	21,90,000	2,50,000	3	65,70,000	7,50,000
				1,27,30,000	13,60,000
				21 ,21,667	2,26,667

Average net worth and Adjusted taxed profits

Productivity Factor* : $\dfrac{2,26,667}{21,21,667} \times 100 = 10.68$ per cent

* ('Profit as a percentage of Capital employed)

Valuation of Equity Shares

Particulars	Rs
Maintainable profit: 10.68 per cent on Rs 22,50,000	2,40,300
Less; Rehabilitation and Replacement Reserve @ 25% of maintainable profits	60,075
	1,80,225
Less: Preference dividends	27,000
Profits available for equity shareholders	1,53,225
Capitalised value of profit for equity shareholders Rs 1 ,53,225 at 9 per cent	17,02,500
Add: Value of investments	2,80,000
Value of total assets	19,82,500
Value of an equity share 19,82,500 ÷ 10,000 = 198.25	

    Fair value of a share : The fair value of a share is the average of the value obtained by the net asset method and the yield method. This is of course, no valuation but a compromise formula for bringing the parties to an agreement. However, it is recognised in government circles for valuing shares of investment companies for wealth tax purposes.

Problems No. 9 :

Diamond Ltd.
BALANCE SHEET
as on 30. 6.2013

Liabilities	Rs	Assets	Rs
Share Capital:		Land and buildings	1,10,000
2,000 shares of Rs 100 each	2,00,000	Plant and machinery	1,30,000
General reserve	40,000	Patents and trade marks	20,000
Profit and loss account	32,000	Stock	48,000
Sundry creditors	1,28,000	Debtors	88,000
Income-tax	60,000	Bank balance	52,000
		Preliminary expenses	12,000
	4,60,000		4,60,000

The expert valuer valued the land and buildings at Rs 2,40,000; goodwill at Rs 1,60,000; and plant and machinery at Rs 1,20,000. Out of the total debtors, it is found that debtors of Rs 8,000 are bad. The profits of the company have been as follows:

Year	Rs
2011	80,000
2012	90,000
2013	1,06,000

The company follows the practice of transferring 25% of profits to general reserve. Similar type of companies earn at 10% of the value of their shares. Ascertain the value of the company's shares under: (i) intrinsic value method; *(ii)* yield value method; and (iii) fair value method. Ignore taxation.

Solution :

Valuation of Shares of Diamond Ltd.

(i) Intrinsic Value Method:

Particulars	Rs
Assets:	
Land & buildings	2,40,000
Goodwill	1,60,000
Plant & machinery	1,20,000
Patents and trade marks	20,000
Stock	48,000
Debtors *less* bad debts	80,000
Bank balance	52,000
	7,20,000
Less: Liabilities:	
Sundry creditors	1,28,000
Net assets	5,92,000

$$\text{Intrinsic value of shares (each share)} = \frac{\text{Net Assets}}{\text{No. of shares}} = \frac{\text{Rs.}5,92,000}{2,000} = \text{Rs } 296$$

(ii) Yield Value Method :

Particulars	Rs
Total profit of last three years	2,76,000
Less: Bad debts	8,000
	2,68,000
Average profit = 2,68,000 + 3	89,333
Add: Decrease in depreciation on plant & mach.	
(say @ 15% on Rs 10,000)	1,500
	90,833
Less: Increase in depreciation on Land & Bldg.	
(say @ 10% on Rs 1,30,000)	13,000
Average profit	77,833
Less: Transfer to reserve (@ 25% of Rs 77,833)	19,458
Profit available for Dividend	58,375

$$\text{Rate of Dividend} = \text{Rs } \frac{58,375}{2,00,000} \times 100 = 29.187\%$$

Yield Value of each share

$$= \frac{\text{Possible rate of dividend}}{\text{Normal rate of return}} \times \text{Paid up value of a share} = \frac{29.187}{10} \times 100 = \text{Rs } 291.87$$

(iii) Fair Value Method:

$$\text{Fair Value of a share} = \frac{\text{Intrinsic value} + \text{Yield value}}{2} = \frac{296 + 291.87}{2} = \text{Rs } 293.93$$

Problems No. 10 : Yogesh Ltd. showed the following performance over 5 years ended 31 st March, 2013:

Ended 31st March	Net Profit before Tax* (in Rs)	Prior period Adjustment (in Rs)	Remarks
2009	4,00,000 (-)	1,00,000	Relating to 2007-08
2010	3,50,000 (-)	2,50,000	Relating equally to 2007-08 and 2008-09
2011	6,50,000 (+)	1,50,000	Relating to 2009-10
2012	5,50,000 (-)	1,75,000	Relating to 2010-11
2013	6,00,000 (-)	1,00,000	Relating to 2010-11
	(+)	25,000	Relating to 2011-12

* Net profit before tax is after debiting or crediting the figures of loss (-) or gains (+) mentioned under the columns for prior period adjustments.

The net worth of the business as per the balance sheet of 31 st March, 2008 is Rs 6,00,000 backed by 10,000 fully paid equity shares of Rs 10 each. Reserve and surplus constitute the balance net worth. Yogesh Ltd. has not declared any dividend till date. You are asked to value equity shares on :

(a) Yield basis as on 31.3.2013, assuming:

(i) 40% rate of tax (ii) anticipated after tax yield of 20% (iii) differentia! weightage of 1 to 5 being given for the six years starting on 1.4.2008 for the actual profits of the respective years.

(b) Net asset basis as per corrected balance sheets for each of the six years ended 31.3.2013. Looking at the performance of the company over the 5-year period, would you invest in the company?

Solution :

(a)

Valuation of Shares on Yield Basis
as on 31 March, 2013

Ended 31st March	Profits as given	Adjustments Increase	Adjustments Decrease	Revised profits	Tax provisions	After Tax Profit	We- ights	Weighted Profit
2009	4,00,000	1,00,0000	1,25,000	3,75,000	1,50,000	2,25,000	1	2,25,000
2010	3,50,000	2,50,0001⌐ 1,50,000⌋	1,00,000⌐ 1,75,000⌋	4,75,000	1,90,000	2,85,000	2	5,70,000
2011	6,50,000	Nil	1,50,000	5,00,000	2,00,000	3,00,000	3	9,00,000
2012	5,50,000	1,75,0001⌐ 25,000⌋	Nil	7,50,000	3,00,000	4,50,000	4	18,00,000
2013	6,00,000	1,00,000	25,000	6,75,000	2,70,000	4,05,000	5	20,25,000
							15	55,20,000

$$\text{Weighted average profit (after tax)} = \frac{\text{Rs.}55,20,000}{15} = \text{Rs } 3,68,000$$

$$\text{Value of business} = \frac{3,68,000}{20\%} = \text{Rs } 18,40,000$$

$$\text{Value of an equity share} = \frac{\text{Value of business}}{\text{No. of equity shares}} = \frac{18,40,000}{10,000} = \text{Rs}184$$

(b)

Valuation of Shares on Net Asset Basis

Particulars	Rs.	Rs.
(i) Revised net worth as on 31st March, 2008		6,00,000
Net worth as given		
Less: Adjustments since made during		
2008-09	1,00,000	
2009-10	1,25,000	
	2,25,000	
Less: Relief from Tax @ 40%	90,000	1,35,000
		4,65,000

(ii) Net asset value

As on	(No. of Shares = 10,000)	
31st March	*Rs*	*Rs*
2008 : Revised net worth (See (i) above)	4,65,000	
Value per share (4,65,000 ÷ 10,000)		46.50
2009 : Revised net worth as on 31.3.2008	4,65,000	
Add: after tax revised profits of 2008-2009	2,25,000	
Net worth as on 31.3.2009	6,90,000	
Value per share (6,90,000 ÷ 10,000)		69.00
2010 : Revised net worth, as on 31.3.2009	6,90,000	
Add: After tax revised profits of 2009-10	2,85,000	
Net worth as on 31 .3.2010	9,75,000	
Value per share (9,75,000 ÷ 10,000)		97.50
2011 : Revised net worth as on 31.3.2010	9,75,000	
Add: after tax revised profits of 2004-05	3,00,000	
Net worth as on 31.3.2011	12,75,000	
Value per share (12,75,000 ÷ 10,000)		127.50
2012 : Revised net worth as on 31.3.2011	12,75,000	
Add: after tax revised profit of 2011-12	4,50,000	
Net worth as on 31.3.2012	17,25,000	
Value per share (17,25,000 ÷ 10,000)		172.50
2013 : Revised net worth as on 31.3.2012	17,25,000	
Add: after tax revised profits of 2012-13	4,05,000	
Net worth as on 31.3.2013	21,30,000	
Value per share (21,30,000 ÷ 10,000)		213.00

Statement of Performance Appraisal
as on 31 of March, 2008

Revised net worth as on 31st March	Rs	Profit after Tax during the year ended 31st March	Rs	Return on Net Worth %
2008	4,65,000	2009	2,25,000	48.39
2009	6,90,000	2010	2,85,000	41.30
2010	9,75,000	2011	3,00,000	30.77
2011	12,75,000	2012	4,50,000	35.29
2012	17,25,000	2013	4,05,000	23.48

The company's return has come down from 48.39% as on 31st March 2008 to 23.48% as on 31st March, 2012. This may perhaps be due to the fact that the company has been ploughing back its profits without having adequate reinvestment opportunities. Hence, in the absence of profitable investment opportunities, it may not be advisable to invest in the company.

Note :

Return on Net worth may also be calculated on the basis of average net worth during the relevant accounting year.

Valuation of Preference Shares

In India, preference shares have priority as to payment of dividend and repayment of capital over equity shares in the event of company's winding up. They are taken as cumulative but non-participating unless otherwise stated. Their valuation is generally on "Dividend Basis" according to the formula: Paid up value × Average maintainable dividend rate ÷ Normal rate of return.

For example, if the paid up value of a preference share is Rs 80, average dividend rate 12%, normal rate of return 10%, the value of a preference share would be Rs 96 (*i.e..* Rs 80 × 12 ÷ 10).

In case the dividend on cumulative preference shares is in arrears, the present value of such arrears of dividend (if there is a possibility of their payment) should be added to the value of a preference share calculated as above.

The dividend basis for valuation of preference shares is useful only in those cases where th preference share capital has adequate assets backing and the company is a going concern. In case th preference share capital does not have adequate assets backing or the company is going into liquidation it will be appropriate to value preference shares according to the net assets method.

In case of participating preference shares of companies in liquidation, their share in the surplus, assets remaining after payment to the equity shareholders is taken into account.

Problems No. 11 : A company has net assets of Rs 1 lakh before payment to the shareholders. The share capital consists of 5,000 equity shares of Rs 10 each and 2,000 preference shares of Rs 10 each The preference shareholders are entitled to share 25 per cent of the surplus assets remaining after payment to the equity shareholders. Calculate the value of a preference share.

Solution :

Computation of Value of a Preference Share

Particulars	Rs.
Net assets before payment to shareholders	1,00,000
Less: Preference share capital	20,000
	80,000
Less: Equity share capital	50,000
Surplus	30,000
Share of preference shareholders in the surplus	7,500
Total net assets available for preference shareholders (20,000 + 7,500)	27,500
Number of preference shares	2,000
Value of preference share (27,500 ÷ 2,000)	13.75

Problems No. 12 : The following figures are extracted from the Books of M/s. Prosperous Limited.

Particulars	Rs.
Share Capital	
9 per cent Preference shares of Rs 100 each	3,00,000
1,000 Equity shares of Rs 100 each, Rs 50 called up	50,000
1,000 Equity shares of Rs 100 each, Rs 25 called up	25,000
1,000 Equity shares of Rs 100 each, fully called up	1,00,000
	4,75,000
Reserves and Surplus:	
General Reserve	2,00,000
Profit and Loss Account	50,000
	7,25,000

On a fair valuation of all the assets of the Company, it is found that they have an appreciation of Rs 75,000.

The articles of association provided that, in case of liquidation, the preference shareholders will have a further claim to the extent of 10 per cent of the surplus assets. Ascertain the value of each preference and equity share, assuming a liquidation. Ignore expenses of winding up.

Solution :

Valuation of Preference and Equity Shares of M/s Prosperous Ltd.

	Paid-up value Rs	Share of surplus Rs	Total Rs	Per share Rs
3,000 9% Preference shares	3,00,000	32,500	3,32,000	110.83
1,000 Equity shares:				
Rs 50 called up	50,000	97,500	1,47,500	147.50
Rs 25 called up	25,000	97,500	1,22,500	122.50
Rs 100 called up	1,00,000	97,500	1,97,500	197.50

Working Note:

Computation of Surplus

Particulars	Rs.
As per books	2,50,000
Appreciation in value of assets	75,000
	3,25,000
10 per cent thereof to preference shareholders	32,500
Surplus for equity shareholders	2,92,500

Note:

It is to be noted that values in the question are to be determined assuming a liquidation. In such a case the surplus is to be distributed among the equity shareholders according to the nominal value of the shares held by them (equal in this case). Uncalled capital is an asset of the company and, if one presumes that uncalled money has been called up the truth of the statement made above will be self-evident. It will be incorrect to distribute the surplus in the ratio of the paid-up amounts.

Problems No. 13 : Following is the summarised Balance sheet of X & Co. as at 31 Dec. 2013:

Particulars	Rs (in lakhs)	Rs.
Share capital		512,00
Reserves and surplus		1,031,50
Shareholder's funds		1,543,50
Loans:		
Secured	1,048,73	
Unsecured	382,77	1,431,50
Total		2,975,00
		1,701,63
Fixed assets		
Current assets	1,657,60	
Loans and Advances	719,50	
	2,377,10	
Less: Current liabilities and provisions	1,103,73	1,273,37
Total		2,975,00

The company has been granted an Industrial licence for manufacturing a new prodcut, the capital cost of which is expected to be around Rs 9 crores. The company desires to finance the new project to the extent of Rs 4 crores partly from the internal resources and partly by accepting public deposits, the balance of Rs 5 crores by issue of fresh capital, *i.e.,* 20,00,000 equity shares of Rs 100 each at a premium of Rs 150 per share.

You are required to make a report to the directors of the company, stating your reasons whether or not the premium amount of Rs 150 per share is, in your opinion, justified. In order to enable you to issue the report, which is to be forwarded to the *SEBIfor* its perusal, you are furnished the following additional information:

Rs

(i) Issued, subscribed and paid-up capital as on 31 December 2011.

	Rs
5,00,000 Equity shares of 100 each, fully paid	5,00,00,000
12,000 9 per cent Cumulative preference shares of	12,00.000
Rs 100 each fully paid	5,12,00,000

(ii) Rate of dividend on equity shares for the last five years:

2009	18 per cent	2012	22 per cent
2010	20 per cent	2013	22 per cent
2011	20 per cent		

(iii) Normal earning capacity (net of tax) of the business may be presumed at 8 per cent.

(iv) Annual turnover for the last 3 years:

| 2011 | Rs 50 crores | 2013 | Rs 57 crores |
| 2012 | Rs 55 crores | | |

(v) Expected annual turnover of the new project for the next three years would be Rs 10 crores.

(vi) The net profit before tax had remained around 10% of the sales during the last three years. It is expected to go up to 12% in the future on account of the internal savings and the product sales.

(vii) The rate of tax may be presumed at 65 per cent.

(viii) The trend of market price of the equity shares of X &. Co. Ltd., as per stock exchange quotations, was as follows:

	High	Low
2011	525	400
2012	535	420
2013	550	450

Solution :

The Board of Directors,

X & Co. Ltd.

Dear Sirs,

Sub: **Proposed issue of 2 lacs equity shares of Rs 100 each**

at a premium of Rs 150 per share

As desired by you, we have carefully examined the question of the value that may be placed on the shares of your company. This, we have particularly studied keeping in mind the desirability or otherwise of charging a premium of Rs 150 per share. Our report is as follows:

(i) The market value of a share over a period of time depends particularly on two factors:

    (a) the profit likely to be earned by the company in the future or earnings per share, and

    (b) the yield that well-informed investors expect on the investment in the shares.

(ii) The present earning per share (EPS) is as follows: (Rs in lakhs)

10 percent profit on Rs 57 crores	570.00
Income-tax at 65 per cent	370.50
Net profit after tax	199.50
Preference dividend	1.08
Profit available for the equity shareholders	198.42
Number of equity shares 5 lakhs	
Earning per share (198.42 ÷ 5 lacs)	39.68

(iii) The amount of profit after the new project becomes operational is estimated.

                                             Rs

Turnover in 2013	57.00	crores
Additional turnover resulting from the project	10.00	crores
Total likely turnover in future	67.00	crores
Profit @ 12 per cent on sales as estimated by the directors	804.00	lakhs
Income-tax at 65 per cent	522.60	lakhs
Profit after tax	281.40	lakhs

(iv) Estimated earnings per share:

Profit as calculated above	281.40	lakhs
Preference dividend	1.08	lakhs
Profit available for equity shareholders	280.32	lakhs
Number of equity shares 7 lakhs		
Earning per share (280.32 lakhs ÷ 7 lakhs)	40.05	

(v) The price earning ratio works out at 12.60 in 2005 as calculated below:

Average price of a share in 2013	500.00
Earning per share	39.68
Price earning ratio (500 ÷ 39.68)	12.60

       The price earning ratio is likely to be maintained if not improved since the company's dividend record has shown consistent improvement. It was 18 per cent in 2009 and has gone up to 22 per cent in 2005.

(vi) On the basis of the estimated earning per share it can be said that the value of the company's share after the project become operational will be Rs 504.63 (i.e. Rs 40.05 ×12.60). The present book value of the share is Rs 306.30. The stock exchange quotations show that the market price of the company's share has been consistently going up. It is expected to further go up because of higher profitability. The valuation of the share at Rs 504.63 as calculated above seems to be quite safe. However this valuation is based on the following assumptions:

(a) The company will be in a position to make an additional sale of Rs 10 crores on account of the new project-

(b) The company will be in a position to maintain the present sales..

(c) The profit margin is likely to go upto 12%.

In case any of these assumptions go wrong, the market price of the share will be seriously affected. In any case the issue price of Rs 250 per share appears to be quite safe even if the new project does not prove to be very profitable.

(vii) At this stage, one more point needs careful consideration the company. It is clear that the proposed financing pattern is not going to improve the earning per share much, which will increase only marginally from Rs 39.68 to Rs 40.50. Thus, the present shareholders are not going to gain much from the new project unless they agree to take the new shares. In case the new shares are offered to the outsiders, they will gain about Rs 250, per share since they will get a share worth Rs 500 only for Rs 250. The company should, therefore, reconsider the entire scheme of financing. Moreover, the company is in a very high income-tax bracket of 65% with sufficient debt capacity. It will be therefore be appropriate to borrow money through debentures or long terms loans rather than raise them through issue of equity shares. In case Rs 5 crores are raised by debentures carrying 11 % interest the price of a share is likely to be Rs 657.85 as calculated below:

	Rs (in lacs)
Profit at 12 per cent on a turnover of Rs 67 crores (6700 lacs)	804.00
Interest at 11 per cent on Rs 5 crores	55.00
Profit after interest	749.00
Income-tax at 65 per cent	486.85
Profit after tax	262.15
Preference dividend	1.08
Profit available for equity shareholders	261.07
Earning per share (261.07 lacs/5 lacs)	52.21
Value of a share with 12.60 as price earning ratio	657.85

We, therefore, feel strongly that the company should reconsider its financial plan. We shall be happy to provide any further information or clarification that you may require.

Yours faithfully,

....

New Delhi, 5 April 2014   Chartered Accountant

Problem No. 14 : The Balance Sheet of *RNR* Limited as on 31 -12-2013 is as follows:

Liabilities	Rs (in lakhs)	Assets	Rs (in lakhs)
1,00,000 equity shares of		Goodwill	5
Rs 10 each full paid	10	Fixed Assets	15
1 ,00,000 equity shares of		Other Tangible Assets	5
Rs 6 each, paid up fully	6	Intangible Assets (marked value)	3
Reserves and Surplus	4	Miscellaneous Expenditure	
Liabilities	10	to the extent not written off	2
	30		30

Fixed assets are worth Rs 24 lakhs. Other tangible assets are revalued at Rs 3 lakhs. The company is expected to settle the disputed bonus claim of Rs 1 lakh not provided for in the accounts. Goodwill appearing in the Balance Sheet is purchased goodwill. It is considered reasonable to increase the value of goodwill by an amount equal to average of the book value and a valuation made at 3 years' purchase of average super-profit for the last 4 years.

After tax profits and dividend rates were as follows:

Year	PAT (Rs in lakhs)	Dividend %
2010	3.0	11%
2011	3.5	12%
2012	4.0	13%
2013	4.1	14%

Normal expectation in the industry to which the company belongs is 10%.

Akbar holds 20,000 equity shares of Rs 10 each fully paid and 10,000 equity shares of Rs 6 each fully paid up. He wants to sell away his holdings.

(i) Determine the break-up value and market value of both kinds of shares.

(ii) What should be the fair value of shares, if controlling interest is being sold?

Solution :

Basic Workings

(1) Computation of Average Capital employed

Particulars	Rs. (in lakhs)	Rs. (in lakhs)
Fixed Assets		24.00
Other Tangible Assets		3.00
Intangible Assets		3.00
		30.00
Less: Liabilities	10	
Bonus claim	1	11.00
		19.00
Less: ½ of Profits earned during 2013 [½ (4.1 -Bonus 1.0)}]		1.55
Average Capital employed		17.45

(2) Computation of Super Profit

$$\text{Average Profit} = \frac{1}{4}\,(3 + 3.5 + 4 + 4.1 - \text{Bonus } 1.0)$$

$$= \frac{1}{4} \times 13.6 \qquad\qquad 3,400$$

Less: Normal Profit = 10% of Rs 17.45 lakhs $\qquad$ 1.745

Super Profit $\qquad$ 1.655

(3) Computation of Goodwill

3 years' purchase of average super profit = 3×1.655 = Rs 4.965 lakhs

$$\text{Increase in Value of Goodwill} = \frac{1}{2}\,(\text{book value} + 3 \text{ years' super profit})$$

$$= \frac{1}{2}\,(5 + 4.965)$$

$$= \text{Rs } 4.9825 \text{ lakhs}$$

Net Assets as revalued including book value of goodwill (19 + 5) $\qquad$ 24.00

Add: Increase in goodwill (rounded off) $\qquad$ 4.98

Net Assets available for shareholders $\qquad$ 28.98

(i) Computation of Value of Shares

(a) Break-up value of Re 1 of share capital $= \dfrac{\text{Rs. 28.98 lakhs}}{\text{Rs. 16.00 lakhs}}$

$= \text{Rs}1.81$

Break-upvalue of Rs 10 paid-up share $= 1.81 \times 10 = \text{Rs } 18.10$

Break-up value of Rs 6 paid-up share $= 1.81 \times 6 = \text{Rs } 10.86$

(b) Market value of shares:

Average Dividend $= \dfrac{11\%+12\%+13\%+14\%}{4} = 12.5\%$

Market value of Rs 10 paid-up share $= \dfrac{12.5\%}{10\%} \times 10 = \text{Rs } 12.50$

Market value of Rs. 6 paid-up share $= \dfrac{12.5\%}{10\%} \times 6 = \text{Rs } 7.50$

(ii) The break-up value of a share will remain same as before even if the controlling interest is being sold. However, the market value of shares will be different since the controlling interest would enable the declaration of dividend up to the limit of disposable profit.

$$\dfrac{\text{Average Profit}^{1}}{\text{Paid up Value of Shares}} \times 100 = \dfrac{\text{Rs. 3.4 lakhs}}{\text{Rs. 16 lakhs}} \times 100 = \text{Rs. } 21.25$$

Market value of shares:

For Rs 10 paid-up share $= \dfrac{21.25\%}{10\%} \times 10 = \text{Rs}21.25$

For Rs 6 paid-up share $= \dfrac{21.25\%}{10\%} \times 6 = \text{Rs}12.75$

Fair value of a share $= \dfrac{\text{Break-upvalue + Market value}}{2}$

Fair value of Rs 10 paid-up share $= \dfrac{18.10+21.25}{2} = \text{Rs } 19.68$

Fair value of Rs 6 paid-up share $= \dfrac{18.86+12.75}{2} = \text{Rs } 15.81$

Note: While solving the problem, tax effect of disputed bonus and corporate dividend tax have been ignored.

---

[1] Transfer to reserves has been ignored.

Problems No. 15 : Following are the information of two companies for the year ended 31 st March, 2013 :

Particulars	Company A	Company B
Equity Shares of Rs 10 each	8,00,000	10,00,000
10% Preference Shares of Rs 10 each	6,00,000	4,00,000
Profit aftertax	3,00,000	3,00,000

Assume the market expectation is 18% and 80% of the profits are distributed.

(i) What is the rate you would pay to the Equity Shares of each Company?

   (a) If you are buying a small lot.

   (b) If you are buying controlling interest shares.

(ii) If you plan to invest only in preference shares which company's preference shares would you prefer?

(iii) Would your rates be different for buying small lot, if the company 'A' retains 30% and company B 10% of the profits? (CA Final, Nov. 2002)

Solution :

(i) (a) *Buying a small lot of equity shares.* In case the purpose of valuation is to provide data base to assist in deciding to buy a small (non-controlling) position of the equity of the companies, dividend capitalisation method is most appropriate Under this method, value of equity share is computed as under:

$$\frac{\text{Dividend per share}}{\text{Market capitalisation rate}} \times 100$$

$$\text{Company A: Rs } \frac{2.4}{18} \times 100 = \text{Rs } 13.33$$

$$\text{Company B: Rs } \frac{2.08}{18} \times 100 = \text{Rs } 11.56$$

   (b) *Buying controlling interest equity shares.* In case the purpose of valuation is to provide information to decide to buy controlling interest in the company, EPS capitalisation method is most appropriate. Under this method, value of equity is given by:

$$\frac{\text{Earning per share (EPS)}}{\text{Market capitalisation rate}} \times 100$$

Company A: Rs $\dfrac{3}{18} \times 100$ = Rs 16.67

Company B: Rs $\dfrac{2.6}{18} \times 100$ = Rs 14.44

(ii) Investment in preference shares. Preference dividend coverage ratios of both company to be compared to make such a decision. Preference dividend coverage ratio can be computed as under:

$$\frac{\text{Profit after Tax}}{\text{Preference Dividend}}$$

Company A : $\dfrac{\text{Rs.}3,00,000}{\text{Rs.}60,000}$ = 5 times

Company B : $\dfrac{\text{Rs.}3,00,000}{\text{Rs.}40,000}$ = 7.5 times

In case one is planning to invest only in preference shares, he would prefer shares of B Company as there is more coverage for preference dividend.

(iii) Buying small lot. Yes, the rates will be different for buying a small lot of equity shares, if the company 'A' retains 30% and company 'B' 10% of profits. The new rates will be computed as under:

Company A Rs $\dfrac{2.1}{18} \times 100$ = Rs11.67

Company S: Rs $\dfrac{2.34}{18} \times 100$ = 13.00

Working Notes:

1. Computation of Earning Per Share and Dividend Per Share

(Companies distribute 80% of profits)

			Company A	Company B
Profit before Tax (Rs)			3,00,000	3,00,000
Less: Preference Dividend (Rs)			60,000	40,000
Earnings available to Equity Shareholders	(A)	(Rs)	2,40,000	2,60,000
Number of Equity Shares	(B)		80,000	1,00,000
Earning per Share	(A/B)	(Rs)	3.0	2.60
Retained Earnings 20%			48,000	52,000
Dividend Declared 80%	(C)	(Rs)	1,92,000	2,08,000
Dividend per Share	(C/B)	(Rs)	2.40	2.80

2. Computation of Dividend Per Share

(Company A retains 30% and Company B 10% of profits)

	Company A	Company B
Earnings available for Equity Shareholders (Rs)	2,40,000	2,60,000
Number of Equity Shares (Rs)	80,000	1,00,000
Retained Earnings (Rs)	72,000	26,000
Dividend Distribution (Rs)	1,68,000	2,34,000
Dividend per share (Rs)	2.10	2.34

8.4 EXERCISES

1. Explain the Yield Method of Valuation of Shares.

2. What is intrinsic value of Shares? How is it determined?

Balance Sheet

1. Followinf is the Balance Sheet of lyer & Co. Private Ltd. as at 31 st March, 2014

Liabilities	Rs.	Assets	Rs.
20,000 Shares of	2,00,000	Land & Building	75,000
Rs. 10 each		Market Value 1,50,000)	
General Reserve	50,000	Plant & Machinery	80,000
Creditors	50,000	(Market Value 1,00,000)	
Workmen's Savings A/c	50,000	Trade Marks	10,000
P & L A/c	25,000	(Market Value 8,000)	
		Stock	1,00,000
		Debtors	54,000
		Investments	20,000
		Cash at Bank	20,000
		Preliminary Expenses	16,000
	3,75,000		3,75,000

Find out intrinsic value after taking into account :	**Rs.**
Interest Payable to Creditors	1,000
Bad Debts amount to	2,000
Investments are worth	16,000

(**Ans.** I. V. = Rs. 1,725)

2. From the following Balance Sheet of General Engineering Co. Limited as on 31-3-2014 Find out the intrinsic value of Shares after taking into account the information given below.

Balance Sheet

Liabilities	Rs.	Assets	Rs.
Shares Capital		Land & Buildings	3,00,000
20,000 Ordinary Shares		Plant & Machinery	4,00,000
of Rs. 10/-	2,00,000	Stock in Trade, Book	
6% Mortgage Debentures	5,00,000	Debtors & Bills Receivable	4,00,000
5% Bank Loan	2,00,000	Investments	1,00,000
Sundry Liabilities	4,00,000	Bank & Cash Balance	2,00,000
Profit & Loss A/c	2,00,000	Preliminary Expenses	1,00,000
	15,00,000		15,00,000

The Following additional informations are given.

1) Against the Net Profit of Rs. 2,00,000 the following adjustments Were not provided.
   a) Interest on 6% Mortgage Debentures of the half year ending 1994
   b) Interest on Bank Loan for the quarter ending 31-3-1994
   c) Bad Debts 20,000 and Dishonour of Bills Rs. 10,000

2) The Market values of the assets are as under.
   a) Land & Building Rs. 4,00,000
   b) Plant & Machinery Rs. 6,00,000
   c) Stock in trade values at Cost is less by Rs. 50,000 compared to Market Value on that date.
   d) Market value of Investment is Rs. 1,17,500

(Ans. I. V. = Rs. 1,725)

3.

Ultra Chemicals Limited
Balance Sheet
as on 31 st March 2012

Liabilities		Rs.	Assets		Rs.
Authorised Capital			Buildings : At cost		80,000
10,000 Equity Shares			Furniture : at cost		3,000
of Rs. 100 each		10,00,000	Stock in Trade at Market		
Issued and Paid up			value		4,50,000
Capital			Investments : at cost		3,80,000
5,000 Equity Shares			Sundry Debtors		
of Rs. 100 each fully			considered good		3,00,000
Paid up		5,00,000	Cash & Bank Balances		
Reserve Fund		1,50,000	Bank of India	50,500	
Depreciation Fund			Cash on hand	19,500	70,000
Building	10,000				
Investment	45,000	55,000			
Bad Debts Reserve		20,000			
Profit & Loss A/c					
Balance Profit For					
1990-91	80,000				
Net profit For					
1991-92	4,30,000	5,10,000			
Creditors		48,000			
		12,83,000			12,83,000

You are Further informated that

1. The Company's Prospects in the near future are equally good.
2. The buildings are now worth Rs. 3,50,000
3. Chemical companies doing similar type of Business show, on an average, profit earning capacity of 15% on the market value of their Shares.
4. The Market Value of the investments is Rs. 3,35,000
5. Profits earned by the company during the past three years show a reasonable increase from the year to year.

   Find out fair value of the share

4. The following is the Balance sheet of Cosmos Steel Ltd, Kolhapur as on 30th june 2013

Balance Sheet

Liabilities	Rs.	Assets	Rs.
Share Capital		Buildings	55,000
Subscribed 2000 6%		Machinery (Less Depr)	65,000
Preference Shares of Rs.	20,000	Patents	10,000
10 each 8000 Eq. Shares		Stock	28,000
Rs. 10 each fully paid	80,000	Sundry Debtors	40,000
	1,00,000	Cash at Bank	26,000
Reserve Fund	50,000	Preliminary Expenses	6000
Profit & Loss A/c	16,000		
Worker's Saving's A/c	15,000		
Sundry Creditors	49,000		
	2,30,000		2,30,000

1. It was discovered that Machinery was underdepreciated by Rs. 5000 2. Independent Valuation of Building had been worked out to Rs. 1,30,00
3. Out of Debtors, Rs. 6000 Worth Debts are bad
4. The preference Shares have Priority for Capital Repayament.
5. Value of Good will is Rs. 20,000

   Find out the intrinsic Values of both the types of Shares.

(Ans : I. V. Eq. Share - Rs. 28 Pref. Share Rs. 10)

5. Swakarm Prakalp Private Ltd. has provided in its articles of association that on the death of a shareholder his shares are to be purchased by the remaining shareholders in proportion of their holdings in the Prakalp at a pirce equal to the intrinsic value of shares. The Good will is to be valued on the basis of three years purchase of the average annual profits for the last five years Following is the Balance Sheet of Swakarm Prakalp Pvt. Ltd. on 30th june 2013 on which date Shriyans prasad, a member holding 10,000 shares died.

Profits for the four years were Rs. 20,000 Rs. 25,000 Rs. 30,000 Rs. 20,000 and Loss for one year was Rs. 15,000

Fixed assets were valued at Rs. 3,72,000

Balance Sheet as on 30-6-2013

Liabilities	Rs.	Assets	Rs.
50,000 Equity Shares of		Good Will	1,20,000
Rs. 20 each	10,00,000	Fixed Assets	3,70,000
Reserve Fund	1,50,000	Current Assets	14,30,000
Debenture Redemption		Misc. Expenses & Losses	5000
Fund	1,00,000		
Debentures	2,50,000		
Premium of Redemption			
of debentures	25,000		
Sundry Creditors	3,25,000		
Profit & Loss A/c	75,000		
	19,25,000		19,25,000

Find out the amount payable by Rajendra Prasad, a member of Prakalp, who held 4000 Shares in the Prakalp.

(**Ans.** Intrinsic Value Rs. 25, Amount Payable Rs. 25,000)

6. The Summarised Balance Sheet of Prashant Ltd as at 31 st March 2013 is as follows.

Balance Sheet

Liabilities	Rs.	Assets	Rs.
10,000 6% Pref Shares of Rs. 10 each	1,00,000	Sundry Assets	5,10,000
30,000 Ordinary		Investment in Shares	10,000
Share of Rs. 10 each	3,00,000	Preliminary Expenses	90,000
General Reserve	20,000		
Depreciation Fund	10,000		
Deb. Redemption Fund	30,000		
7% Debentures	50,000		
Sundry Creditors	1,00,000		
Contingent Liability			
Rs 650 in respect of Compensation			
Payable to worker			
	6,10,000		6,10,000

The Preference Shares are Preferential as to capital and arrears of preference dividend are not payable on liquidation.

Assets in the Balance Sheet are worth their effective book values. There is in existence an asset worth Rs. 1,500 not recorded in the books. Assume that the dividend on the Preference Shares in two years in arrears.

Show the intrinsic Value of Shares.

7. Balance Sheet of Assam Timber (P) Ltd As on 31-12-2008

Liabilities	Rs.	Assets	Rs.
Equity Share Capital	5,00,000	Good will	10,000
6% Preference Share		Shed	60,000
Capital Consisting of Share		Machinery	3,50,000
of Rs. 1000 each	1,00,000	Stock	1,20,000
Reserve	50,000	Debtors	1,60,000
Profit & Loss A/c	20,000	Cash at Bank	10,000
Sundry Creditors	40,000	Preliminary Expenses	10,000
Other Liabilities	10,000		
	7,20,000		7,20,000

Good will is valued at Rs. 31,000 and Shed at Rs. 50,000 Machinery is to be depreciated by Rs. 25,000 Stock is worth Rs. 1,40,000 Debtors are expected to realised 90% of Book Value.

Find out the value of different types of Equity Shares if.

	Rs
Equity Share Capital represents 30,000 Shares of Rs. 10 each	
Fully Paid up	3,00,000
40,000 Shares of Rs. 10 Rs. 5 Paid up	2,00,000

(Ans : Rs. 11 and Rs. 5.50 Pre Share Respectively)

8. You are asked to value Shares as on 31st March 2014 of a private Company engaged in engineering business, With a view to floating it as a Public Company. The followin information is extracted from the audited accounts.

Year ending 31st March	Net Profit before Taxation Rs.	Salary of Managing Director rs.
1988	2,34,000	72,000
1989	3,24,000	72,000
1990	5,400 (Loss)	36,000
1991	72,000	54,000
1992	3,42,000	1,08,000
1993	4,50,000	1,08,000
1994	2,52,000	1,08,000

The audited Balance Sheet as at 31st March 2014 showed the following position.

Liabilities	Rs.	Rs.	Assets	Rs.	Rs.
Shareholder's Funds			Fixed Assets (at cost		
Capital			Less Depreciation)		
Equity Shares of			Freehold Land and		
Rs. 10 each	3,60,000		Building	6,48,000	
Reserves	3,06,000		Plant & Mach.	5,40,000	
Surplus in			Factory and		
P & L A/c	2,34,000	9,00,000	Office Fittings	1,80,000	13,68,000
Current liabilities and			Current Assets,		
Provisions		12,60,000	Loans and Advances		7,92,000
		21,60,000			21,60,000

The various assets were value by independent values as on 31-3-2014 as under

Freehold Land and Building Rs. 7,92,000 Plant and Machinery Rs. 7,20,000 Factory and Officer Fittings Rs. 1,80,000

In lieu of Salary to Managing Director, the Public Company would include directors fees of Rs. 18,000 Per annum. Assume Income Tax at 60% Normal rate of Profit 12* and 20% of the Average Maintainable Profit transfer to Reserve You are required to calculate the value of Shares on (i) net assets basis; ii) earnings and dividends, and (iii) the basis of capitalisation of Profits. Which value will you prefer for purchase of a small or large number of shares? Take preceding three years profits for average Maintainable profit and rate of depreciation is 1% on Building and 1% on Plant and Machinery.

(**Ans :** (i) Rs. 34, (ii) 26.67, (iii) Rs. 33.33 For a Small Purchase of Shares value as per (ii) is relevant but for a large purchase of Shares and a long term investments, value as per (iii) will be more appropriate.)

9. The Balance Sheet of Swaraj & Co. Private Ltd, is closed the following financial Position as at 31st March 2005

Liabilities	Rs.	Assets	Rs.
Share Capital		Good will (at cost)	1,00,000
2,000 Equity Shares		Land and Buildings	80,000
Rs. 10 each	2,00,000	Plant and Machinery	60,000
General Reserve	50,000	Stock in Trade	2,40,000
Profit & Loss Account	80,000	Sundry Creditors	1,64,000
Debentures	1,00,000	Cash at Bank	98,000
Sundry Creditors	3,12,000		
	7,42,000		7,42,000

You are asked to value the shares of the company for which purpose the following information is supplied.

a) The above Balance Sheet does not provide the unassessed income tax which is estimated at Rs. 37,000

b) The net profits, taxes paid, and Payable (including the provision for taxation of Rs. 37,000 Stated above) and dividends paid during the last five years ended 31st March 2005 were as follows.

Year ended 31st March	Net Profits Rs.	Taxes Rs.	Net Amount available Fro Dividend
2001	62,000	30,000	32,000
2002	68,000	32,000	36,000
2003	73,000	35,000	38,000
2004	75,000	36,000	39,000
2005	80,000	37,000	43,000

c) The Companys Shares are not quoted at the stock exchange.

d) It is fund that shares of Similar concerns are quoted at the Stock Exchange at such price as to earn 10 per cent by way of dividend on their Market value.

e) It may be assumed that the company will be able to maintain its profit for the next five years.

f) The valuation should be on the basis of the mean of the intrinsic value calculated by accepting the value of the good will as per Balance Sheet and calculating such good will on the basis of the present value of an annuity of the average expected profits for the Coming five years. Assuming interest at 10 per cent per annum given, that the present value of one rupee per annum for five years at 10 per cent interest is Rs. 3,78

(Ans. Rs. 15,70)

10. The summarised Balance Sheet of Jai Private Ltd. As on 20-6-2010 follows.

Balance Sheet
as on 30-6-2010

Liabilities		Rs.	Assets		Rs.
Share Capital			Fixed Assets		
(in shares of Rs. 10 each)			Good will	1,50,000	
1,500 6% Pref. Shares			Freehold property	3,75,000	
	1,50,000		Plant & Machinery	1,50,000	
4,500 Eq. Shares	4,50,000	6,00,000	(Less : Depreciation)		6,75,000
Profit & Loss Account		7,50,000	Quoted Investments		3,00,000
5% Debentures		3,00,000	Current Assets		
Sundry Creditors		2,39,250	Stock	2,70,000	
			Debtors (Net)	2,99,250	
			Bank Balance	2,45,000	9,14,250
		18,89,250			18,89,250

Profit (after tax) for the three years after charging debenture interest but before providing for preference dividend were Rs. 2,20,500 Rs 3,22,500 and Rs. 2,40,000 Respectively.

It is decided to sell the business. You are required to compute the purchase price of equity shares after taking into consideration the following relevat facts.

a) Preference Shares are payable at par on liquidation.

b) The purchaser wants to acquire all the 4,500 equity shares.

c) The Price for equity shares is to be based on the following assumptions.

    i)   The normal return of 10% on net assets (at revised valuation) Attributable equity shares.

    ii)   The good will to be calculated at three times the adjusted average super profit of the three years referred to above.

    iii)   Debentures will be redeemed at a discount of 25% prior to the sale of the business.

    iv)   The value of freehold property is agreed to be ascertained on the basis of 8% return. The current rental value is Rs. 50,400

    v)   A claim of Rs. 8,250 was omitted to be provided in the year.

    vi)   Market value of quoted investments was Rs. 3,75,000 and were sold to redeem debentures.

    vii)   Non recurring profits are to be eliminated 10% of the profits referred to above arose from a transaction of a non recurring nature.

    viii)   A provision of 5% on Sundry Debtors Was made which is no longer required. Assume tax rate to be 50% and income 26% gross on book value of quoted investment.

(**Ans :** Purchase Price of equity Shares Rs. 17,46,750 Value of on share Rs. 388.17)

11. Balance Sheet of Sound Ltd, as at 31st March 2014 is given below.

Liabilities	Rs.	Assets	Rs.
Share Capital :		Fixed Assets :	
6000 Equity Shares of		Building	1,50,000
Rs. 100 each fully paid up	6,00,000	Machineries	2,20,000
Reserve & Surplus		Current Assets, Loans	
Profit and Loss A/c	50,000	and Advances	
Current Liabilities and		Stock	3,00,000
Provisions		Sundry Debtors	1,60,000
Bank Overdraft	10,000	Bank	60,000
Creditors	60,000		
Provision Fro Taxation	1,10,000		
Proposed Dividend	60,000		
	8,90,000		8,90,000

The net Profits of the company, after deducting usual working expenses but before providing for taxation were as under.

2011-12 Rs. 2,00,000 2012-13 Rs. 2,40,000 2013-14 Rs. 2,20,000

On 31st March 2014 Building was revalued at Rs. 2,00,000 and Machineries Rs. 2,50,000 Sundry Debtors on the same date, included Rs. 10,000 as irrecoverable having regard to nature of the business, a 10% return on net tangible capital invested is considered reasonable

You are required to value the campany's share ex dividend Valuation of good will may be based on three year's Purchase of annual super profits. Depreciation on Building 2% Machineries 10% The income tax is to be assumed at 50% All working should form part to your answer.

(**Ans.** Average Capital Employed Rs. 7,80,000 Super Profit Rs. 28,334 Value of Good will rs. 85,000 Value per Share Rs. 134.17)

12. Mr. X who desired to invest Rs. 33,00 in equity Shares in a public limited company, seeks you advice as to the fair value of the shares. The following information is made available

Issued and Paid up Capital	**Rs**
6% Preference Shares of Rs. 100 each	5,50,000
Equity Shares of Rs. 10 each	3,50,000
	9,00,000

Average net profit of the business is Rs. 75,000 Expected normal yield is 8 per cent in case of Such equity Shares. It is observed that the net assets on revaluation are worth Rs. 70,000 More than the amounts at which they are stated in the books. Good will is the be calculated at 5 year's purchase of the super profits, if any (Ignor income Tax)

Give you working of the fair value of equity Shares and determine the number of Shares which Mr. X Should purchase (Use Average of intrinsic value basis and yield basis)

(C.A.)

(**Ans :** Good will Rs. 42,000 Intrinsic Value Rs. 13.20; Value on yield (EPS) basis Rs. 15 No. of shares to be purchased 2,340)

13. The Balance Sheets of two companies A Ltd. And B Ltd, as at 31 st March 2009 are

Balance Sheet

Liabilities	(Rs. in Lakhs)	
	A Ltd	**B. Ltd**
Equity Capital	3.00	4.00
Reserves	3.00	...
5% Debentures	....	2.00
Sundry Creditors	2.00	2.50
	8.00	8.50

Assets	A Ltd	B Ltd
Fixed Assets	5.00	4.00
Stocks	1.25	1.30
Debtors	1.70	1.10
Cash and Bank	0.05	0.10
Profit & Loss A/c	......	2.00
	8.00	8.50

A Ltd, Proposes to take over B Ltd For this Purpose the assets were revalued as under :

Fixed Assets Rs. 6.15 Lakhs, Stocks Rs. 1.00 Lakh, Debtors Rs. 1.05 Lakhs.

The Additional factor to be considered is that B Ltd, is an industry which is not licensed under current policy of the government Hence, there is an advantage as an existing unit. For this premium of Rs. 5 Lakhs is assessed.

Calculate and suggest Share Valuation of B Ltd, for the take over and suggest a fair exchange ratio or Shares.

(**Ans.** Exchange Ratio according to Break up 11.10)

14. Given below is the Balance Sheet of Devta Ltd. as at 31st Dec. 2011

Liabilities		Rs.	Assets	Rs.
Share Capital			Fixed Assets	
Equity Shares of			Good will	20,000
Rs. 10 each	2,00,000		Machinery	1,10,000
Less : Calls in arrear			Land and Building	1,20,000
(Rs. 2 for final Call)	5000	1,95,000	Furniture & Fixture	60,000
6% Preference Shares			Vehicles	80,000
of Rs 10 each	1,00,000		Investments	80,000
Less : Calls in arrear			Current Assets	
(Rs. 2 for Final Call)	1,000	99,000	Stock in Trade	55,000
Reserves and Surplus			Sundry Debtors	90,000
General Reserve		80,000	Cash at Bank	10,000
Profit & Loss A/c		16,000	Preliminary Expenses	10,000
Current Liabilities				
Bank Loan				
Sundry Creditors		1,55,000		
Bills Payable		30,000		
		6,35,000		6,35,000

1. For the Purpose of valuation of Shares, Good will is to be considered on the basis of 2 year's Purchase of the super profits based on the average profit of last 4 years. Profits are as follows.

   2008 Rs. 80,000, 2009-Rs. 90,000, 2010-Rs. 1,05,000, 2011-Rs. 1,10,000

2. In a similar business normal return on capital employed is 15%

3. Fixed assets are worth 30% above their actual book value. Stock is over valued by Rs. 5,000 Debtors are to be reduced by Rs. 1000 All trade All trade in investments are to be valued at 10% below cost.

4. Of the investments 10% is trade and the balance non trade. Trade investments were purchased on 1st January 2011 50% of the non trade investments were acquired on 1st January 2010 and the rest on 1st january, 2009 A uniform rate of dividend of 10% is earned on all investments

   i) In 2009 a new Machinery Costing Rs. 10,000 was purchased but wrongly charged to revenue (No rectification has yet been made for above.)

   ii) In 2010 some old furniture (Book value Rs. 5000) was disposed of for Rs. 3000 You are required to value each fully paid and partly paid equity Share.

   (Depreciation is charged on Machinery @ 10 per cent on reducing system. Ignore Taxation and Dividend)

(Ans. Value of an Equity Share Fully paid Rs. 21.86
Partly Paid Rs. 19.86 Good will Rs. 57.604)

   (**Hint :** Value of Good will at 2 year's Purchase of average annual super Profits Rs. 57,604)

15. Following is the Balance Sheet of Star & Co Ltd, as at 31st December 2005

Balance Sheet

Liabilities	Rs.	Assets	Rs.
Share Capital		Fixed Assets	
Equity Shares of		Good will	1,00,000
Rs. 100 each	10,00,000	Machinery	5,00,000
Less : Calls in Arrears		Factory Shed	5,50,000
(Rs. 20 for final Call)	1,00,000	Vehicles	1,50,000
	9,00,000	Furniture	50,000
10% Preference Shares of		Investment	2,00,000
Rs. 10 each fully paid	4,00,000	Current Assets	

Liabilities	Rs.	Assets	Rs.
Reserves and Surplus		Stock in trade	4,00,000
General Reserve	4,00,000	Sundry Debtors	7,00,000
Profit & Loss A/c	3,00,000	Cash at Bank	1,00,000
Current Liabilities		Miscellaneous	
Bank Loan	2,00,000	Eqpenditure :	
Sundry Creditors	6,00,000	Preliminary Expenses	50,000
	28,00,000		28,00,000

Additional Information :

1. Fixed Assets are worth 20% above their value. Depreciation on appreciated value of fixed assets not to be considered for valuation of good will.
2. Of the investment, 60% is non trading and the balance is trading. All trade investments are to be valued at 25% above the cost. A uniform rate of dividend @ 15% is earned on all investments.
3. For the purpose of Valuation of Shares, Good will is to be considered on the basis of 4 year's purchase of the super profits based on average profits (after tax) of the last 3 years.

   Profits (after tax) are as follows. 2003-Rs 4,00,00 2004 - Rs. 4,30 2005 Rs. 4,50,00

In a similar business, return on capital employed is 15% (after tax)

4. In 2003 new machinery costing Rs. 20,000 was purchased but wrongly charged to revenue (no effect has yet been given for rectifying the same)

   Depreciation charged on machinery is @ 10% on reducing balance Method. Find out the value of each fully paid and partly paid equity Share on net assets.

   (Ans : **Value of a share**   **Proposition I**   **Proposition II**
   Fully Paid   Rs. 230.74   Rs. 238.74
   Partly paid   Rs. 210.74   Rs. 218.74
   Good will   Rs. 4,69,892   Rs. 5,49,892)

<u>REFERENCES</u>

1. Dr. S. N. Maheshwari & S.K. Maheshwari - Corporate Accounting

2. D. S. Rawat - Corporate Accounting Standard

3. Institute of Chartered Accountants of India - Accounting Standards

4. K. N. Jagtap, Dr. S. D. Zagade, Dr. H. M. Jare - Corporate Accounting (Diamond Publications)

5. M.C. Shukla & S.P. Grewal - Advanced Accounts (S.Chand & Co. Ltd.)

6. Mukharji & Hanif - Corporate Accounting

7. Paul Sr. - Advanced Accounts

8. R.L.Gupta & M. Radhaswamy - Advanced Accountancy (Sultan Chand & Sons)

9. S.P. Jain & K.N. Narang - Advanced Accountancy (Kalyani Publishers)

10. S.P. Jain & K.L. Narang - Company Accounts

<u>REFERENCES</u>

1. M.C. Shukla & S.P. Grewal - Advanced Accounts (S.Chand & Co. Ltd.)

2. S.P. Jain & K.N. Narang - Advanced Accountancy (Kalyani Publishers)

3. R.L.Gupta & M. Radhaswamy - Advanced Accountancy (Sultan Chand & Sons)

4. S.P. Jain & K.L. Narang - Company Accounts

5. Paul Sr. - Advanced Accounts

6. Dr. S. N. Maheshwari & S.K. Maheshwari - Corporate Accounting

7. Mukharji & Hanif - Corporate Accounting

8. K. N. Jagtap, Dr. S. D. Zagade, Dr. H. M. Jare - Corporate Accounting (Diamond Publications)

9. D. S. Rawat - Corporate Accounting Standard

10. Institute of Chartered Accountants of India - Accounting Standards